THE GOOD NEW
STUFF

THE GOOD NEW STUFF

ADVENTURE SF
IN THE GRAND TRADITION

EDITED BY
GARDNER DOZOIS

ST. MARTIN'S GRIFFIN

NEW YORK

For Isabella Marie Amelio Casper—
the good new stuff.

Library of Congress Cataloging-in-Publication Data

Dozois, Gardner R.
    The good new stuff : adventure SF in the grand tradition / edited by
Gardner Dozois. — 1st St. Martin's Griffin ed.
        p.   cm.
    ISBN 0-312-19890-6
    1. Science fiction, American.   2. Adventure stories, American.
PS648.S3G65   1999
813'.0876208—dc21   98-42824
                                                                CIP

First St. Martin's Griffin Edition: February 1999

10 9 8 7 6 5 4 3 2 1

Contents

Preface

"They don't write 'em like that anymore," you often hear people say, talking about fast-paced, no-holds-barred, flat-out *adventure* stories, stories drenched with color, wonder, and action, stories that take us to far worlds for adventures of a sort that could not be encountered on our familiar, present-day Earth, stories that bring us face-to-face with strange dangers and even stranger wonders—but, actually, they *do* still write stories like that!

Yes, they really do. Don't listen to the voices that say you can't find anything like that anymore—they're the voices of people so lost in nostalgia for the stories of their youth that they can't look around them and see what's happening right in front of their own eyes. If they did look around, they'd find that the space adventure story is not only alive and well here at the end of the nineties, it's flourishing.

As I hope to demonstrate in this anthology, you can still find science fiction adventure stories today every bit as wild and woolly and mind-blowing as anything from the old pulp days, stories as full of swashbuckling action, dash, and élan as any of the Planetary Romances from the old *Planet Stories* and *Thrilling Wonder Stories*, stories just as full of cosmic sweep and scale and grandeur and the immense, sun-shattering, planet-busting clash of titanic forces in conflict as anything from the old "Superscience" days of the thirties when Edmond Hamilton was earning his nickname of "World-Wrecker Hamilton" (except with much more accurate, up-to-date, cutting-edge science!).

Adventure writing is not the only sort of science fiction there is, of course, or the only thing science fiction does well, and never has been. Science fiction can be serious-minded and substantial and profound; it can be a window on worlds we'd never otherwise see and people and creatures we'd never otherwise know; it can provide us with insights into the inner workings of our society that are difficult to gain in any other way, grant us perspectives into social mores and human nature itself mostly otherwise unreachable; it can be an invaluable tool with which to take preconceived notions and received wisdom to pieces and reassemble them into something new; it can prepare us for the inevitable and sometimes dismaying changes ahead of us, helping to buffer us against the winds of Future Shock—but sometimes it's just *fun*. Sometimes it's "just" pure entertainment (with any more serious implications or troubling social issues—and they do get raised, even in the most seemingly insubstantial of stories—largely left to be dealt with in the subtext), adventure writing as vivid and entertaining as any that has ever been written in any genre anywhere.

Although adventure writing is often looked down on by critics (it's hard even to think of the phrase *adventure writing* without automatically adding the prefix *mere*, since that's the way it's almost always referred to) or ignored completely, it's no more but certainly no less valid and valuable than any other kind of science fiction. It's something that's always been part of the palette of the science fiction genre as well, ever since the days of Hugo Gernsback's *Amazing Stories* in the late twenties, when the specific *science fiction* adventure story began to precipitate out from the larger and older tradition of the generalized pulp adventure story—often Lost World/Lost Race tales—that goes all the way back into the middle of the nineteenth century. (Although the SF adventure story has always had—and still has—other branches as well, the Space Adventure story or the Space Opera, of one subvariety or another, remains to this day probably the most characteristic sort of SF adventure tale, the form that slowly emerged as being most specific to science fiction, and that's the kind of story I've primarily stuck with for this anthology.)

The previous anthology in this series, *The Good Old Stuff*, published in 1998, traced the development of the genre space adventure tale, from its beginnings in the Gernsback magazines through the "Superscience" era of the thirties and early forties (the First Great Age of the Space Opera, when writers such as E. E. "Doc" Smith, Ray Cummings, Raymond Z. Gallun, Edmond Hamilton, John W. Campbell Jr., Jack Williamson, Clifford D. Simak, and others developed and refined a form of adventure tale specific to science fiction), and on through the years from the mid-forties to the mid-sixties, the Second Great Age of the Space Opera, when writers such as A. E. van Vogt, L. Sprague de Camp, James H. Schmitz, Murray Leinster, Leigh Brackett, Jack Vance, Poul Anderson, Gordon R. Dickson, and H. Beam Piper would add an increased social-political sophistication and an increase in line-by-line writing craft to the form, a trend taken to new heights of complexity, flamboyance, and vividness by writers such as Cordwainer Smith, Alfred Bester, Frank Herbert, Robert A. Heinlein, Brian W. Aldiss, Larry Niven, Ursula K. Le Guin, Roger Zelazny, Samuel R. Delany, James Tiptree, Jr., and many others.

By the late sixties and early seventies, however, perhaps because of the prominence of the "New Wave" revolution in SF, which concentrated both on introspective, stylistically "experimental" work and work with more immediate sociological and political "relevance" to the tempestuous social scene of the day, perhaps because of scientific proof that the other planets of the solar system were not likely abodes for life (and so, it seemed, not interesting settings for adventure stories), perhaps because the now more widely understood limitations of Einsteinian relativity had come to make the idea of far-flung interstellar empires seem improbable at best, science fiction as a genre was tending to turn away from the Space Adventure tale. Although it would never disappear completely, it had become widely regarded as outmoded and déclassé; the radical new writers of the generation just about to rise to prominence would collectively produce less adventure SF, particularly Space Opera, than any other comparable generational group of authors, and there would be less Space Adventure stuff written in the following ten years or so than in any other comparable period in SF history. By far the majority of work published during this period would be set on Earth, often in the near future—even the solar system had been largely deserted as a setting for stories, let alone the distant stars. Although stalwarts such as Poul Anderson and Jack Vance and Larry Niven continued to soldier on throughout those years, it was a common—and frequently expressed—opinion that Space Opera was dead.

But by the late seventies and early eighties, new writers such as John Varley, George R.R. Martin, Bruce Sterling, Michael Swanwick, Vernor Vinge, and others would begin to become interested in the Space Adventure again, reinvented to better fit the aesthetic style and tastes of the day. And by the nineties, a whole new boom in Baroque Space Opera would be underway, on both sides of the Atlantic (there are some slight but perceptible differences in flavor between the New British Space Opera and the New American Space Opera, although they clearly are responses to the same evolutionary impetus—and, as was also true of the New Wave, which also manifested itself in slightly different forms on either side of the ocean, the similarities are far more significant than the differences are), fueled by authors such as Iain M. Banks, Dan Simmons, Orson Scott Card, C. J. Cherryh, Gregory Benford, Greg Bear, Colin Greenland, Paul J. McAuley, Alexander Jablokov, Stephen Baxter, Walter Jon Williams, Stephen R. Donaldson, John Barnes, Lois McMaster Bujold, Charles Sheffield, Eleanor Arnason, Peter F. Hamilton, and a dozen others, ushering in the Third Great Age of Space Opera.

Which brings us into the territory of the book you hold in your hands, *The Good New Stuff.*

Even having decided on the territory that I would cover in this volume, though (the mid-seventies to the present day), I found, as is usually the case with these retrospective anthologies, that there were many more stories that I would have liked to use than I had room to use. Some arbitrary decisions clearly needed to be made to winnow the mass of potential stories down to a usable number, and, arbitrarily, I made them.

Most of these judgment calls are subjective, again as always. While there's often plenty of action in a William Gibson story, for instance, action alone is not the only criterion, and somehow Cyberpunk doesn't *feel* like adventure writing to me—too intense, too noir-ish, too gloomy (plus the fact that almost all cyberpunk writing, or the bulk of it, anyway, takes place on Earth in the relatively near future). So, arbitrarily, I decided to omit Cyberpunk stories from consideration, although it cost me first-rate authors from Gibson to Pat Cadigan to Lewis Shiner (Bruce Sterling gets in, but for his earlier, more Space Opera-ish work, not his later cyberpunk and post-cyberpunk stuff). Similarly, Military SF, although concerned largely with the exploits of Space Mercenaries and usually chockablock with battle scenes, doesn't feel right to me either—too narrowly specialized, and too often easily recognized as only Horatio Hornblower stories "translated" into science fiction terms, or thinly disguised recastings of Vietnam War or World War II scenarios. Lucius Shepard's stuff always has strong action elements, but it's usually on the borderland of horror fiction as well, or at least partakes of that aesthetic tone, and again that was not the "flavor" I was subjectively groping for (and again, the vast majority of Shepard's stories take place on Earth, or in interconnecting fantasy realms). So all of that was out as well.

The last major judgment call I made was even more subjective. Parallel with the new boom in Space Opera has been a boom in the "Hard Science" story, also reinvented to fit the styles and prejudices of the times better, and although there are many similarities between the two forms, and the reader who likes one is at least fairly likely to like the other, and although the situation is complicated by the fact that many authors have a foot in both camps, sometimes producing one kind of thing and sometimes another, I still thought that I could discern enough differences between the two styles to assign writers, arbitrarily, to one camp or the other. Stephen Baxter, Greg Egan, Greg Benford, Brian Stableford, and Paul J. McAuley, for instance, all write some of the hardest SF around, but somehow *some* of what Baxter and Benford and McAuley are doing strikes me as being legitimately classifiable as Space Opera, while what Egan and Stableford are doing does not. So no Egan or Stableford, even though they're excellent writers, and Egan in particular may be one of the best new writers of the nineties. (It's hard to articulate exactly what I'm instinctively basing this decision on, except perhaps a vague feeling that Space Opera or Space Adventure needs a quality of flamboyance, exaggeration, scope, swagger, outrageousness, overheatedness, perhaps even lurid excess—an over-the-top quality that the cool, mannered, cerebral, tightly controlled work of Egan and Stableford doesn't have.)

Some other decisions made themselves for me. Some of the major players in the current subgenre of the New Space Opera, such as Iain M. Banks and Colin Greenland, for instance, write almost no short fiction at all, and while others, such as Orson Scott Card, Dan Simmons, Stephen Donaldson, and C. J. Cherryh, do occasionally write short fiction, almost none of it is in the Space Adventure mode (almost all of Cherryh's short work is fantasy, for instance, as is the bulk of Donaldson's, while most of Simmons's is horror, and so on). And the practical difficulties involved in the assembling of an anthology necessitated the omission of still other stories, those, say, which had recently appeared in a competing anthology, or those for which the reprint rights were either encumbered or priced too high for me to be able to afford them on the limited budget I had to work with.

Even with all of those winnowing screens in place, I was still left with a mass of material too large to use. The constraints of a technically feasible book length dictated the omission of other stories, but I could easily have produced an anthology twice the length of this one, with little or no discernable letdown in quality, and I would have if I could have.

There are a *lot* of good new stories of this sort out there, and if you like this book, I urge you to go and seek them out on your own. They're not hard to find, believe me, in spite of what "they" say. All you have to do is open your eyes and look around you.

So, then, this is the Good New Stuff. Enjoy!

John Varley

GOODBYE, ROBINSON CRUSOE

John Varley appeared on the SF scene in 1974, and by the end of 1976—in what was a meteoric rise to prominence even for a field known for meteoric rises—he was already being recognized as one of the hottest new writers of the seventies. His first story, "Picnic on Nearside," appeared in 1974 in *The Magazine of Fantasy & Science Fiction,* and was followed by as concentrated an outpouring of first-rate stories as the genre has ever seen, stories such as "Retrograde Summer," "In the Bowl," "Gotta Sing, Gotta Dance," "In the Hall of the Mountain King," "Equinoctial," "The Black Hole Passes," "Overdrawn at the Memory Bank," "The Phantom of Kansas," and many others: smart, bright, fresh, brash, audacious, effortlessly imaginative stories that seemed to suddenly shake the field out of its uneasy slumber like a wake-up call from a brand-new trumpet. It's hard to think of a group of short stories that has had a greater, more concentrated impact on the field, with the exception of Robert Heinlein's early work for John W. Campbell's *Astounding,* or perhaps Roger Zelazny's early stories in the mid-sixties (maybe a better example anyway, since, although Heinlein has always been one of Varley's major influences, his early Eight Worlds stuff in some ways had more in common with Zelazny, if only in that quality of good-natured effrontery and easy ostentation, and the almost insolent you-ain't-seen-*nothing*-yet ease and fecundity of his invention). By 1978, largely because of Varley's work, it would be possible for Algis Budrys to say (in the introduction to Varley's first collection, appropriately enough), "There is beginning to be, in other words, yet another new SF: vigorous, relevant, richer than ever"—a statement that would have been inconceivable a few years before, in the dull gray doldrums that had been left behind after the ferocious tempest of the New Wave Era had blown itself out and died away to stillness.

Varley was one of the first new writers to become interested in the solar system again, after several years in which it had been largely abandoned as a setting for stories because the space probes of the late sixties and early seventies had "proved" that it was nothing but an "uninteresting" collection of balls of rock and ice, with no available abodes for life—dull as a supermarket parking lot. Instead, Varley seemed to find the solar system lushly romantic *just as it was,* lifeless balls of rock and all (and this was even before the later Pioneer probes to the Jupiter and Saturn systems had proved the solar system to be a lot more surprising than people thought that it was). He makes this obvious in "In the Bowl," where he specifically invokes the richly romantic Venus of the *Planet Stories* days (and of Heinlein's *Between Planets,* which is even more specifically referenced), describing the human settlements of Venus as places of "steamy swamps and sleazy hotels" where you can "hunt the prehistoric monsters that wallow in the field marshes that are just a swamp-buggy ride out of town," or rub shoulders in the teeming streets with the "eight-legged dragons with eyestalks" who go lumbering by . . . and then, when the tourists go home, they *shut all that off,* all the *Planet Stories* dreams that are just there to amuse the rubes, and then "the place reverts to an ordinary cluster of silvery domes sitting in darkness and eight-hundred-degree temperature." The remarkable thing here, the revolutionary thing, is that Varley finds Venus *more* romantic once the pulp *Planet Stories* dreams are switched off and you're left with the uncompromising reality of Venus to deal with instead—finds it more romantic *because* it's an airless hellhole of eight-hundred-degree temperature and deadly crushing pressure, completely and totally unlike the Earth, instead of the ersatz copy of Earth in the dinosaur age that had been the dream of earlier writers. This is an aesthetic shift in perception that will go ringing on down through the eighties and nineties in the work of writers such as G. David Nordley, Stephen Baxter, and a dozen others.

This perceptual shift was common to all his early stories, which share a common setting in which humankind has been forcibly exiled from the Earth and forced to live instead on the other planets of the solar system—but where the children of those outcasts have adapted so well that they've made a virtue of necessity, and actually *enjoy* living in hostile environments such as Venus or Mercury or the Moon, something that's made clear and explicit in stories such as "Retrograde Summer," among others. They've become new people, different in values from their parents, just as Varley himself was different in values even from his biggest role model (although there are echoes in his work of Zelazny, James Tiptree, Jr., Samuel R. Delany, and Larry Niven as well), Robert A. Heinlein. I always felt that Varley had made this explicit in his very first story, "Picnic on Nearside," when the young Varley Individuals (children by today's standards, although fully mature and sexually active) find what I take to be the last Heinlein Individual living as a hermit on the other side of the Moon, a crusty, competent, self-sufficient, ferociously independent, politically and sexually conservative, somewhat paranoid individual whom the children regard with affection and a certain degree of respect, but who also seems to them outmoded and out of touch and faintly pathetic, and whose problems and ultimate demise are caused by his own stubbornness and inability to compromise, and by the obsolete social attitudes that he is unable to change or even suspect that he should change. This always struck me as a highly significant moment in genre history. The Varley Individuals had won, not by fighting, not by Campbell-esque political Dirty Tricks, but simply because they *were* new people, with new attitudes that made the old ones obsolete. From now on the future would belong to them and *their* children, not to the Heinlein Individual, who had owned it for more than thirty years.

Varley often uses children as protagonists of his Eight Worlds stories, in fact. As in the one that follows, one of the best but also one of the lesser-known of those stories, in which he demonstrates that when you become a man, it's time to put away childish things—but that sometimes doing that can be very hard indeed.

Varley somehow never had as great an impact with his novels as he did with his short fiction, with the possible exception of his first novel, *Ophiuchi Hotline.*

His other novels include the somewhat disappointing "Gaean" trilogy, consisting of *Titan, Wizard,* and *Demon,* and a novelization of one of his own short stories that was also made into a movie, *Millennium;* he has also published four collections, *The Persistence of Vision, The Barbie Murders, Picnic on Nearside,* and *Blue Champagne.*

In the eighties, Varley moved away from the print world to produce a number of screenplays for Hollywood producers, most of which were never produced. He produced one last significant story, 1984's "Press Enter■," which won him both the Hugo and the Nebula Award (he also won a Hugo in 1982 for his story "The Pusher," and a Hugo and a Nebula in 1979 for his novella "The Persistence of Vision.") After "Press Enter■," little was heard from Varley in the genre until the publication of a major new novel, *Steel Beach,* in 1992, which was successful commercially, but received a lukewarm reception from many critics. Since then he has been largely silent, but that may be about to change; a new novel, *The Golden Globe,* has just been published, and another book, *Irontown Blues,* has already been announced.

It was summer, and Piri was in his second childhood. First, second; who counted? His body was young. He had not felt more alive since his original childhood back in the spring, when the sun drew closer and the air began to melt.

He was spending his time at Rarotonga Reef, in the Pacifica disneyland. Pacifica was still under construction, but Rarotonga had been used by the ecologists as a testing ground for the more ambitious barrier-type reef they were building in the south, just off the "Australian" coast. As a result, it was more firmly established than the other biomes. It was open to visitors, but so far only Piri was there. The "sky" disconcerted everyone else.

Piri didn't mind it. He was equipped with a brand-new toy: a fully operational imagination, a selective sense of wonder that allowed him to blank out those parts of his surroundings that failed to fit with his current fantasy.

He awoke with the tropical sun blinking in his face through the palm fronds. He had built a rude shelter from flotsam and detritus on the beach. It was not to protect him from the elements. The disneyland management had the weather well in hand; he might as well have slept in the open. But castaways *always* build some sort of shelter.

He bounced up with the quick alertness that comes from being young and living close to the center of things, brushed sand from his naked body, and ran for the line of breakers at the bottom of the narrow strip of beach.

His gait was awkward. His feet were twice as long as they should have been, with flexible toes that were webbed into flippers. Dry sand showered around his legs as he ran. He was brown as coffee and cream, and hairless.

Piri dived flat to the water, sliced neatly under a wave, and paddled out to waist-height. He paused there. He held his nose and worked his arms up and down, blowing air through his mouth and swallowing at the same time. What looked like long, hairline scars between his lower ribs came open. Red-orange fringes became visible inside them, and gradually lowered. He was no longer an air-breather.

He dived again, mouth open, and this time he did not come up. His esophagus and trachea closed and a new valve came into operation. It would pass water in only one direction, so his diaphragm now functioned as a pump pulling water through his mouth and forcing it out through the gill-slits. The water flowing through this lower chest area caused his gills to engorge with blood, turning them purplish-red and forcing his lungs to collapse upward into his chest cavity. Bubbles of air trickled out his sides, then stopped. His transition was complete.

The water seemed to grow warmer around him. It had been pleasantly cool; now it seemed no temperature at all. It was the result of his body temperature lowering in response to hormones released by an artificial gland in his cranium. He could not afford to burn energy at the rate he had done in the air; the water was too efficient a coolant for that. All through his body arteries and capillaries were constricting as parts of him stabilized at a lower rate of function.

No naturally evolved mammal had ever made the switch from air to water breathing, and the project had taxed the resources of bio-engineering to its limits. But everything in Piri's body was a living part of him. It had taken two full days to install it all.

He knew nothing of the chemical complexities that kept him alive where he should have died quickly from heat loss or oxygen starvation. He knew only the joy of arrowing along the white sandy bottom. The water was clear, blue-green in the distance.

The bottom kept dropping away from him, until suddenly it reached for the waves. He angled up the wall of the reef until his head broke the surface, climbed up the knobs and ledges until he was standing in the sunlight. He took a deep breath and became an air-breather again.

The change cost him some discomfort. He waited until the dizziness and fit of coughing had passed, shivering a little as his body rapidly underwent a reversal to a warm-blooded economy.

It was time for breakfast.

He spent the morning foraging among the tidepools. There were dozens of plants and animals that he had learned to eat raw. He ate a great deal, storing up energy for the afternoon's expedition on the outer reef.

Piri avoided looking at the sky. He wasn't alarmed by it; it did not disconcert him as it did the others. But he had to preserve the illusion that he was actually on a tropical reef in the Pacific Ocean, a castaway, and not a vacationer in an environment bubble below the surface of Pluto.

Soon he became a fish again, and dived off the sea side of the reef.

The water around the reef was oxygen-rich from the constant wave action. Even here, though, he had to remain in motion to keep enough water flowing past his external gill fringes. But he could move more slowly as he wound his way down into the darker reaches of the sheer reef face. The reds and yellows of his world were swallowed by the blues and greens and purples. It was quiet. There were sounds to hear, but his ears were not adapted to them. He moved slowly through shafts of blue light, keeping up the bare minimum of water flow.

He hesitated at the ten-meter level. He had thought he was going to his Atlantis Grotto to check out his crab farm. Then he wondered if he ought to hunt up Ocho the Octopus instead. For a panicky moment he was afflicted with the bane of childhood: an inability to decide what to do with himself. Or maybe it was worse, he thought. Maybe it was a sign of growing up. The crab farm bored him, or at least it did today.

He waffled back and forth for several minutes, idly chasing the tiny red fish that flirted with the anemones. He never caught one. This was no good at all. Surely there was an adventure in this silent fairyland. He had to find one.

An adventure found him, instead. Piri saw something swimming out in the open water, almost at the limits of his vision. It was long and pale, an attenuated missile of raw death. His heart squeezed in panic, and he scuttled for a hollow in the reef.

Piri called him the Ghost. He had seen him many times in the open sea. He was eight meters of mouth, belly and tail: hunger personified. There were those who said the great white shark was the most ferocious carnivore that ever lived. Piri believed it.

It didn't matter that the Ghost was completely harmless to him. The Pacifica management did not like having its guests eaten alive. An adult could elect to go into the water with no protection, providing the necessary waivers were on file. Children had to be implanted with an equalizer. Piri had one, somewhere just below the skin of his left wrist. It was a sonic generator, set to emit a sound that would mean terror to any predator in the water.

The Ghost, like all the sharks, barracudas, morays, and other predators in Pacifica, was not like his cousins who swam the seas of Earth. He had been cloned from cells stored in the Biological Library on Luna. The library had been created two hundred years before as an insurance policy against the extinction of a species. Originally, only endangered species were filed, but for years before the Invasion the directors had been trying to get a sample of everything. Then the Invaders had come, and Lunarians were too busy surviving without help from Occupied Earth to worry about the library. But when the time came to build the disneylands, the library had been ready.

By then, biological engineering had advanced to the point where many modifications could be made in genetic structure. Mostly, the disneyland biologists had left nature alone. But they had changed the predators. In the Ghost, the change was a mutated organ attached to the brain that responded with a flood of fear when a supersonic note was sounded.

So why was the Ghost still out there? Piri blinked his nictating membranes, trying to clear his vision. It helped a little. The shape looked a bit different.

Instead of moving back and forth, the tail seemed to be going up and down, perhaps in a scissoring motion. Only one animal swims like that. He gulped down his fear and pushed away from the reef.

But he had waited too long. His fear of the Ghost went beyond simple danger, of which there was none. It was something more basic, an unreasoning reflex that prickled his neck when he saw that long white shape. He couldn't fight it, and didn't want to. But the fear had kept him against the reef, hidden, while the person swam out of reach. He thrashed to catch up, but soon lost track of the moving feet in the gloom.

He had seen gills trailing from the sides of the figure, muted down to a deep blue-black by the depths. He had the impression that it was a woman.

Tongatown was the only human habitation on the island. It housed a crew of maintenance people and their children, about fifty in all, in grass huts patterned after those of South Sea natives. A few of the buildings concealed elevators that went to the underground rooms that would house the tourists when the project was completed. The shacks would then go at a premium rate, and the beaches would be crowded.

Piri walked into the circle of firelight and greeted his friends. Nighttime was party time in Tongatown. With the day's work over, everybody gathered around the fire and roasted a vat-grown goat or lamb. But the real culinary treats were the fresh vegetable dishes. The ecologists were still working out the kinks in the systems, controlling blooms, planting more of failing species. They often produced huge excesses of edibles that would have cost a fortune on the outside. The workers took some of the excess for themselves. It was understood to be a fringe benefit of the job. It was hard enough to find people who could stand to stay under the Pacifica sky.

"Hi, Piri," said a girl. "You meet any pirates today?" It was Harra, who used to be one of Piri's best friends but had seemed increasingly remote over the last year. She was wearing a hand-made grass skirt and a lot of flowers, tied into strings that looped around her body. She was fifteen now, and Piri was . . . but who cared? There were no seasons here, only days. Why keep track of time?

Piri didn't know what to say. The two of them had once played together out on the reef. It might be Lost Atlantis, or Submariner, or Reef Pirates; a new plot line and cast of heroes and villains every day. But her question had held such thinly veiled contempt. Didn't she care about the Pirates anymore? What was the matter with her?

She relented when she saw Piri's helpless bewilderment.

"Here, come on and sit down. I saved you a rib." She held out a large chunk of mutton.

Piri took it and sat beside her. He was famished, having had nothing all day since his large breakfast.

"I thought I saw the Ghost today," he said, casually.

Harra shuddered. She wiped her hands on her thighs and looked at him closely.

"Thought? You thought you saw him?" Harra did not care for the Ghost. She had cowered with Piri more than once as they watched him prowl.

"Yep. But I don't think it was really him."

"Where was this?"

"On the sea side, down about, oh, ten meters. I think it was a woman."

"I don't see how it could be. There's just you and—and Midge and Darvin with—did this woman have an air tank?"

"Nope. Gills. I saw that."

"But there's only you and four others here with gills. And I know where they all were today."

"You used to have gills," he said, with a hint of accusation.

She sighed. "Are we going through that again? I *told* you, I got tired of the flippers. I wanted to move around the *land* some more."

"I can move around the land," he said, darkly.

"All right, all right. You think I deserted you. Did you ever think that you sort of deserted *me?*"

Piri was puzzled by that, but Harra had stood up and walked quickly away. He could follow her, or he could finish his meal. She was right about the flippers. He was no great shakes at chasing anybody.

Piri never worried about anything for too long. He ate, and ate some more, long past the time when everyone else had joined together for the dancing and singing. He usually hung back, anyway. He could sing, but dancing was out of his league.

Just as he was leaning back in the sand, wondering if there were any more corners he could fill up—perhaps another bowl of that shrimp teriyaki?—Harra was back. She sat beside him.

"I talked to my mother about what you said. She said a tourist showed up today. It looks like you were right. It was a woman, and she was amphibious."

Piri felt a vague unease. One tourist was certainly not an invasion, but she could be a harbinger. And amphibious. So far, no one had gone to that expense except for those who planned to live here for a long time. Was his tropical hideout in danger of being discovered?"

"What—what's she doing here?" He absently ate another spoonful of crab cocktail.

"She's looking for *you,*" Harra laughed, and elbowed him in the ribs. Then she pounced on him, tickling his ribs until he was howling in helpless glee. He fought back, almost to the point of having the upper hand, but she was bigger and a little more determined. She got him pinned, showering flower petals on him as they struggled. One of the red flowers from her hair was in her eye, and she brushed it away, breathing hard.

"You want to go for a walk on the beach?" she asked.

Harra was fun, but the last few times he'd gone with her she had tried to kiss him. He wasn't ready for that. He was only a kid. He thought she probably had something like that in mind now.

"I'm too full," he said, and it was almost the literal truth. He had stuffed himself disgracefully, and only wanted to curl up in his shack and go to sleep.

Harra said nothing, just sat there getting her breathing under control. At last she nodded, a little jerkily, and got to her feet. Piri wished he could see her face to face. He knew something was wrong. She turned from him and walked away.

Robinson Crusoe was feeling depressed when he got back to his hut. The walk down the beach away from the laughter and singing had been a lonely one. Why had he rejected Harra's offer of companionship? Was it really so bad that she wanted to play new kinds of games?

But no, damn it. She wouldn't play his games, why should he play hers?

After a few minutes of sitting on the beach under the crescent moon, he got into character. Oh, the agony of being a lone castaway, far from the company of fellow creatures, with nothing but faith in God to sustain oneself. Tomorrow he would read from the scriptures, do some more exploring along the rocky north coast, tan some goat hides, maybe get in a little fishing.

With his plans for the morrow laid before him, Piri could go to sleep, wiping away a last tear for distant England.

The ghost woman came to him during the night. She knelt beside him in the sand. She brushed his sandy hair from his eyes and he stirred in his sleep. His feet thrashed.

He was churning through the abyssal deeps, heart hammering, blind to everything but internal terror. Behind him, jaws yawned, almost touching his toes. They closed with a snap.

He sat up woozily. He saw rows of serrated teeth in the line of breakers in front of him. And a tall, white shape in the moonlight dived into a curling breaker and was gone.

"Hello."

Piri sat up with a start. The worst thing about being a child living alone on an island—which, when he thought about it, was the sort of thing every child dreamed of—was not having a warm mother's breast to cry on when you had nightmares. It hadn't affected him much, but when it did, it was pretty bad.

He squinted up into the brightness. She was standing with her head blocking out the sun. He winced, and looked away, down to her feet. They were webbed, with long toes. He looked a little higher. She was nude, and quite beautiful.

"Who . . . ?"

"Are you awake now?" She squatted down beside him. Why had he expected sharp, triangular teeth? His dreams blurred and ran like watercolors in the rain, and he felt much better. She had a nice face. She was smiling at him.

He yawned, and sat up. He was groggy, stiff, and his eyes were coated with sand that didn't come from the beach. It had been an awful night.

"I think so."

"Good. How about some breakfast?" She stood, and went to a basket on the sand.

"I usually—" but his mouth watered when he saw the guavas, melons, kippered herring, and the long brown loaf of bread. She had butter, and some orange marmalade. "Well, maybe just a—" and he had bitten into a succulent slice of melon. But before he could finish it, he was seized by an even stronger urge. He got to his feet and scuttled around the palm tree with the waist-high dark stain and urinated against it.

"Don't tell anybody, huh?" he said, anxiously.

She looked up. "About the tree? Don't worry."

He sat back down and resumed eating the melon. "I could get in a lot of trouble. They gave me a thing and told me to use it."

"It's all right with me," she said, buttering a slice of bread and handing it to him. "Robinson Crusoe never had a portable EcoSan, right?"

"Right," he said, not showing his surprise. How did she know *that?*

Piri didn't know quite what to say. Here she was, sharing his morning, as much a fact of life as the beach or the water.

"What's your name?" It was as good a place to start as any.

"Leandra. You can call me Lee."

"I'm—"

"Piri. I heard about you from the people at the party last night. I hope you don't mind me barging in on you like this."

He shrugged, and tried to indicate all the food with the gesture. "Anytime," he said, and laughed. He felt good. It was nice to have someone friendly around after last night. He looked at her again, from a mellower viewpoint.

She was large; quite a bit taller than he was. Her physical age was around thirty, unusually old for a woman. He thought she might be closer to sixty or seventy, but he had nothing to base it on. Piri himself was in his nineties, and who could have known that? She had the slanting eyes that were caused by the addition of transparent eyelids beneath the natural ones. Her hair grew in a narrow band, cropped short, starting between her eyebrows and going over her head to the nape of her neck. Her ears were pinned efficiently against her head, giving her a lean, streamlined look.

"What brings you to Pacifica?" Piri asked.

She reclined on the sand with her hands behind her head, looking very relaxed.

"Claustrophobia." She winked at him. "Not really. I wouldn't survive long in Pluto with *that.*" Piri wasn't even sure what it was, but he smiled as if he knew. "Tired of the crowds. I heard that people couldn't enjoy themselves here, what with the sky, but I didn't have any trouble when I visited. So I bought flippers and gills and decided to spend a few weeks skin-diving by myself."

Piri looked at the sky. It was a staggering sight. He'd grown used to it, but knew that it helped not to look up more than he had to.

It was an incomplete illusion, all the more appalling because the half of the sky that had been painted was so very convincing. It looked like it really was the sheer blue of infinity, so when the eye slid over to the unpainted overhanging canopy of rock, scarred from blasting, painted with gigantic numbers that were barely visible from twenty kilometers below—one could almost imagine God looking down through the blue opening. It loomed, suspended by nothing, gigatons of rock hanging up there.

Visitors to Pacifica often complained of headaches, usually right on the crown of the head. They were cringing, waiting to get conked.

"Sometimes I wonder how *I* live with it," Piri said.

She laughed. "It's nothing for me. I was a space pilot once."

"Really?" This was catnip to Piri. There's nothing more romantic than a space pilot. He had to hear stories.

The morning hours dwindled as she captured his imagination with a series of tall tales he was sure were mostly fabrication. But who cared? Had he come to the South Seas to hear of the mundane? He felt he had met a kindred spirit, and gradually, fearful of being laughed at, he began to tell her stories of the Reef Pirates, first as wishful wouldn't-it-be-fun-if's, then more and more seriously as she listened intently. He forgot her age as he began to spin the best of the yarns he and Harra had concocted.

It was a tacit conspiracy between them to be serious about the stories, but that was the whole point. That was the only way it would work, as it had worked with Harra. Somehow, this adult woman was interested in playing the same games he was.

Lying in his bed that night, Piri felt better than he had for months, since before Harra had become so distant. Now that he had a companion, he realized that maintaining a satisfying fantasy world by yourself is hard work. Eventually you need someone to tell the stories to, and to share in the making of them.

They spent the day out on the reef. He showed her his crab farm, and introduced her to Ocho the Octopus, who was his usual shy self. Piri suspected the damn thing only loved him for the treats he brought.

She entered into his games easily and with no trace of adult condescension. He wondered why, and got up the courage to ask her. He was afraid he'd ruin the whole thing, but he had to know. It just wasn't normal.

They were perched on a coral outcropping above the high tide level, catching the last rays of the sun.

"I'm not sure," she said. "I guess you think I'm silly, huh?"

"No, not exactly that. It's just that most adults seem to, well, have more 'important' things on their minds." He put all the contempt he could into the word.

"Maybe I feel the same way you do about it. I'm here to have fun. I sort of feel like I've been reborn into a new element. It's *terrific* down there, you know that. I just didn't feel like I wanted to go into that world alone. I was out there yesterday . . ."

"I thought I saw you."

"Maybe you did. Anyway, I needed a companion, and I heard about you. It seemed like the polite thing to, well, not to ask you to be my guide, but sort of fit myself into your world. As it were." She frowned, as if she felt she had said too much. "Let's not push it, all right?"

"Oh, sure. It's none of my business."

"I like you, Piri."

"And I like you. I haven't had a friend for . . . too long."

That night at the luau, Lee disappeared. Piri looked for her briefly, but was not really worried. What she did with her nights was her business. He wanted her during the days.

As he was leaving for his home, Harra came up behind him and took his hand. She walked with him for a moment, then could no longer hold it in.

"A word to the wise, old pal," she said. "You'd better stay away from her. She's not going to do you any good."

"What are you talking about? You don't even know her."

"Maybe I do."

"Well, do you or don't you?"

She didn't say anything, then sighed deeply.

"Piri, if you do the smart thing you'll get on that raft of yours and sail to Bikini. Haven't you had any . . . feelings about her? Any premonitions or anything?"

"I don't know what you're talking about," he said, thinking of sharp teeth and white death.

"I think you do. You have to, but you won't face it. That's all I'm saying. It's not my business to meddle in your affairs."

"I'll say it's not. So why did you come out here and put this stuff in my ear?" He stopped, and something tickled at his mind from his past life, some earlier bit of knowledge, carefully suppressed. He was used to it. He knew he was not really a child, and that he had a long life and many experiences stretching out behind him. But he didn't think about it. He hated it when part of his old self started to intrude on him.

"I think you're jealous of her," he said, and knew it was his old, cynical self talking. "She's an adult, Harra. She's no threat to you. And, hell, I know what you've been hinting at these last months. I'm not ready for it, so leave me alone. I'm just a kid."

Her chin came up, and the moonlight flashed in her eyes.

"You idiot. Have you looked at yourself lately? You're not Peter Pan, you know. You're growing up. You're damn near a man."

"That's not true." There was panic in Piri's voice. "I'm only . . . well, I haven't exactly been counting, but I can't be more than nine, ten years—"

"Shit. You're as old as I am, and I've had breasts for two years. But I'm not out to cop you. I can cop with any of seven boys in the village younger than you are, but not you." She threw her hands up in exasperation and stepped back from him. Then, in a sudden fury, she hit him on the chest with the heel of her fist. He fell back, stunned at her violence.

"She *is* an adult," Harra whispered through her teeth. "That's what I came here to warn you against. *I'm* your friend, but you don't know it. Ah, what's the use? I'm fighting against that scared old man in your head, and he won't listen to me. Go ahead, go with her. But she's got some surprises for you."

"What? What surprises?" Piri was shaking, not wanting to listen to her. It was a relief when she spat at his feet, whirled, and ran down the beach.

"Find out for yourself," she yelled back over her shoulder. It sounded like she was crying.

That night, Piri dreamed of white teeth, inches behind him, snapping.

But morning brought Lee, and another fine breakfast in her bulging bag. After a lazy interlude drinking coconut milk, they went to the reef again. The pirates gave them a rough time of it, but they managed to come back alive in time for the nightly gathering.

Harra was there. She was dressed as he had never seen her, in the blue tunic and shorts of the reef maintenance crew. He knew she had taken a job with the disneyland and had been working days with her mother at Bikini, but had not seen her dressed up before. He had just begun to get used to the grass skirt. Not long ago, she had been always nude like him and the other children.

She looked older somehow, and bigger. Maybe it was just the uniform. She still looked like a girl next to Lee. Piri was confused by it, and his thoughts veered protectively away.

Harra did not avoid him, but she was remote in a more important way. It was like she had put on a mask, or possibly taken one off. She carried herself with a dignity that Piri thought was beyond her years.

Lee disappeared just before he was ready to leave. He walked home alone, half hoping Harra would show up so he could apologize for the way he'd talked to her the night before. But she didn't.

He felt the bow-shock of a pressure wave behind him, sensed by some mechanism he was unfamiliar with, like the lateral line of a fish, sensitive to slight changes in the water around him. He knew there was something behind him, closing the gap a little with every wild kick of his flippers.

It was dark. It was always dark when the thing chased him. It was not the wispy, insubstantial thing that darkness was when it settled on the night air, but the primal, eternal night of the depths. He tried to scream with his mouth full of water, but it was a dying gurgle before it passed his lips. The water around him was warm with his blood.

He turned to face it before it was upon him, and saw Harra's face corpse-pale and glowing sickly in the night. But no, it wasn't Harra, it was Lee, and her mouth was far down her body, rimmed with razors, a gaping crescent hole in her chest. He screamed again—

And sat up.

"What? Where are you?"

"I'm right here, it's going to be all right." She held his head as he brought his sobbing under control. She was whispering something but he couldn't understand it, and perhaps wasn't meant to. It was enough. He calmed down quickly, as he always did when he woke from nightmares. If they hung around to haunt him, he never would have stayed by himself for so long.

There was just the moonlit paleness of her breast before his eyes and the smell of skin and sea water. Her nipple was wet. Was it from his tears? No, his lips were tingling and the nipple was hard when it brushed against him. He realized what he had been doing in his sleep.

"You were calling for your mother," she whispered, as though she'd read his mind. "I've heard you shouldn't wake someone from a nightmare. It seemed to calm you down."

"Thanks," he said quietly. "Thanks for being here, I mean."

She took his cheek in her hand, turned his head slightly, and kissed him. It was not a motherly kiss, and he realized they were not playing the same game. She had changed the rules on him.

"Lee . . ."

"Hush. It's time you learned."

She eased him onto his back, and he was overpowered with *deja vu*. Her mouth worked downward on his body and it set off chains of associations from his past life. He was familiar with the sensation. It had happened to him often in his second childhood. Something would happen that had happened to him in much the same way before and he would remember a bit of it. He had been seduced by an older woman the first time he was young. She had taught him well, and he remembered it all but didn't want to remember. He was an experienced lover and a child at the same time.

"I'm not old enough," he protested, but she was holding in her hand the evidence that he was old enough, had been old enough for several years. *I'm fourteen years old*, he thought. How could he have kidded himself into thinking he was ten?

"You're a strong young man," she whispered in his ear. "And I'm going to be very disappointed if you keep saying that. You're not a child anymore, Piri. Face it."

"I . . . I guess I'm not."

"Do you know what to do?"

"I think so."

She reclined beside him, drew her legs up. Her body was huge and ghostly and full of limber strength. She would swallow him up, like a shark. The gill slits under her arms opened and shut quickly with her breathing, smelling of salt, iodine, and sweat.

He got on his hands and knees and moved over her.

• • •

He woke before she did. The sun was up: another warm, cloudless morning. There would be two thousand more before the first scheduled typhoon.

Piri was a giddy mixture of elation and sadness. It was sad, and he knew it already, that his days of frolicking on the reef were over. He would still go out there, but it would never be the same.

Fourteen years old! Where had the years gone? He was nearly an adult. He moved away from the thought until he found a more acceptable one. He was an adolescent, and a very fortunate one to have been initiated into the mysteries of sex by this strange woman.

He held her as she slept, spooned cozily back to front with his arms around her waist. She had already been playmate, mother, and lover to him. What else did she have in store?

But he didn't care. He was not worried about anything. He already scorned his yesterdays. He was not a boy, but a youth, and he remembered from his other youth what that meant and was excited by it. It was a time of sex, of internal exploration and the exploration of others. He would pursue these new frontiers with the same single-mindedness he had shown on the reef.

He moved against her, slowly, not disturbing her sleep. But she woke as he entered her and turned to give him a sleepy kiss.

They spent the morning involved in each other, until they were content to lie in the sun and soak up heat like glossy reptiles.

"I can hardly believe it," she said. "You've been here for . . . how long? With all these girls and women. And I know at least one of them was interested."

He didn't want to go into it. It was important to him that she not find out he was not really a child. He felt it would change things, and it was not fair. Not fair at all, because it *had* been the first time. In a way he could never have explained to her, last night had been not a rediscovery but an entirely new thing. He had been with many women and it wasn't as if he couldn't remember it. It was all there, and what's more, it showed up in his lovemaking. He had not been the bumbling teenager, had not needed to be told what to do.

But it was *new*. That old man inside had been a spectator and an invaluable coach, but his hardened viewpoint had not intruded to make last night just another bout. It had been a first time, and the first time is special.

When she persisted in her questions he silenced her in the only way he knew, with a kiss. He could see he had to rethink his relationship to her. She had not asked him questions as a playmate, or a mother. In the one role, she had been seemingly as self-centered as he, interested only in the needs of the moment and her personal needs above all. As a mother, she had offered only wordless comfort in a tight spot.

Now she was his lover. What did lovers do when they weren't making love?

• • •

They went for walks on the beach, and on the reef. They swam together, but it was different. They talked a lot.

She soon saw that he didn't want to talk about himself. Except for the odd question here and there that would momentarily confuse him, throw him back to stages of his life he didn't wish to remember, she left his past alone.

They stayed away from the village except to load up on supplies. It was mostly his unspoken wish that kept them away. He had made it clear to everyone in the village many years ago that he was not really a child. It had been necessary to convince them that he could take care of himself on his own, to keep them from being overprotective. They would not spill his secret knowingly, but neither would they lie for him.

So he grew increasingly nervous about his relationship with Lee, founded as it was on a lie. If not a lie, then at least a withholding of the facts. He saw that he must tell her soon, and dreaded it. Part of him was convinced that her attraction to him was based mostly on age difference.

Then she learned he had a raft, and wanted to go on a sailing trip to the edge of the world.

Piri did have a raft, though an old one. They dragged it from the bushes that had grown around it since his last trip and began putting it into shape. Piri was delighted. It was something to do, and it was hard work. They didn't have much time for talking.

It was a simple construction of logs lashed together with rope. Only an insane sailor would put the thing to sea in the Pacific Ocean, but it was safe enough for them. They knew what the weather would be, and the reports were absolutely reliable. And if it came apart, they could swim back.

All the ropes had rotted so badly that even gentle wave action would have quickly pulled it apart. They had to be replaced, a new mast erected, and a new sailcloth installed. Neither of them knew anything about sailing, but Piri knew that the winds blew toward the edge at night and away from it during the day. It was a simple matter of putting up the sail and letting the wind do the navigating.

He checked the schedule to be sure they got there at low tide. It was a moonless night, and he chuckled to himself when he thought of her reaction to the edge of the world. They would sneak up on it in the dark, and the impact would be all the more powerful at sunrise.

But he knew as soon as they were an hour out of Rarotonga that he had made a mistake. There was not much to do there in the night but talk.

"Piri, I've sensed that you don't want to talk about certain things."

"Who? Me?"

She laughed into the empty night. He could barely see her face. The stars were shining brightly, but there were only about a hundred of them installed so far, and all in one part of the sky.

"Yeah, you. You won't talk about yourself. It's like you grew here, sprang up from the ground like a palm tree. And you've got no mother in evidence. You're old enough to have divorced her, but you'd have a guardian somewhere. Someone would be looking after your moral upbringing. The only conclusion is that you don't need an education in moral principles. So you've got a co-pilot."

"Um." She had seen through him. Of course she would have. Why hadn't he realized it?

"So you're a clone. You've had your memories transplanted into a new body, grown from one of your own cells. How old are you? Do you mind my asking?"

"I guess not. Uh . . . what's the date?"

She told him.

"And the year?"

She laughed, but told him that, too.

"Damn. I missed my one-hundredth birthday. Well, so what? It's not important. Lee, does this change anything?"

"Of course not. Listen, I could tell the first time, that first night together. You had that puppy-dog eagerness, all right, but you knew how to handle yourself. Tell me: what's it like?"

"The second childhood, you mean?" He reclined on the gently rocking raft and looked at the little clot of stars. "It's pretty damn great. It's like living in a dream. What kid hasn't wanted to live alone on a tropic isle? I can, because there's an adult in me who'll keep me out of trouble. But for the last seven years I've been a kid. It's you that finally made me grow up a little, maybe sort of late, at that."

"I'm sorry. But it felt like the right time."

"It was. I was afraid of it at first. Listen, I *know* that I'm really a hundred years old, see? I know that all the memories are ready for me when I get to adulthood again. If I think about it, I can remember it all as plain as anything. But I haven't wanted to, and in a way, I still don't want to. The memories are suppressed when you opt for a second childhood instead of being transplanted into another full-grown body."

"I know."

"Do you? Oh, yeah. Intellectually. So did I, but I didn't understand what it meant. It's a nine- or ten-year holiday, not only from your work, but from yourself. When you get into your nineties, you might find that you need it."

She was quiet for a while, lying beside him without touching.

"What about the reintegration? Is that started?"

"I don't know. I've heard it's a little rough. I've been having dreams about something chasing me. That's probably my former self, right?"

"Could be. What did your older self do?"

He had to think for a moment, but there it was. He'd not thought of it for eight years.

"I was an economic strategist."

Before he knew it, he found himself launching into an explanation of offensive economic policy.

"Did you know that Pluto is in danger of being gutted by currency transfers from the Inner Planets? And you know why? The speed of light, that's why. Time lag. It's killing us. Since the time of the Invasion of Earth it's been humanity's idea—and a good one, I think—that we should stand together. Our whole cultural thrust in that time has been toward a total economic community. But it won't work at Pluto. Independence is in the cards."

She listened as he tried to explain things that only moments before he would have had trouble understanding himself. But it poured out of him like a breached dam, things like inflation multipliers, futures buying on the oxygen and hydrogen exchanges, phantom dollars and their manipulation by central banking interests, and the invisible drain.

"Invisible drain? What's that?"

"It's hard to explain, but it's tied up in the speed of light. It's an economic drain on Pluto that has nothing to do with real goods and services, or labor, or any of the other traditional forces. It has to do with the fact that any information we get from the Inner Planets is already at least nine hours old. In an economy with a stable currency—pegged to gold, for instance, like the classical economies on Earth—it wouldn't matter much, but it would still have an effect. Nine hours can make a difference in prices, in futures, in outlook on the markets. With a floating exchange medium, one where you need the hourly updates on your credit meter to know what your labor input will give you in terms of material output—your personal financial equation, in other words—and the inflation multiplier is something you simply *must* have if the equation is going to balance and you're not going to be wiped out, then time is really of the essence. We operate at a perpetual disadvantage on Pluto in relation to the Inner Planet money markets. For a long time it ran on the order of point three percent leakage due to outdated information. But the inflation multiplier has been accelerating over the years. Some of it's been absorbed by the fact that we've been moving closer to the I.P.; the time lag has been getting shorter as we move into summer. But it can't last. We'll reach the inner point of our orbit and the effects will really start to accelerate. Then it's war."

"War?" She seemed horrified, as well she might be.

"War, in the economic sense. It's a hostile act to renounce a trade agreement, even if it's bleeding you white. It hits every citizen of the Inner Planets in the pocketbook, and we can expect retaliation. We'd be introducing instability by pulling out of the Common Market."

"How bad will it be? Shooting?"

"Not likely. But devastating enough. A depression's no fun. And they'll be planning one for us."

"Isn't there any other course?"

"Someone suggested moving our entire government and all our corporate headquarters to the Inner Planets. It could happen, I guess. But who'd feel like it was ours? We'd be a colony, and that's a worse answer than independence, in the long run."

She was silent for a time, chewing it over. She nodded her head once; he could barely see the movement in the darkness.

"How long until the war?"

He shrugged. "I've been out of touch. I don't know how things have been going. But we can probably take it for another ten years or so. Then we'll have to get out. I'd stock up on real wealth if I were you. Canned goods, air, water, so forth. I don't think it'll get so bad that you'll need those things to stay alive by consuming them. But we may get to a semibarter situation where they'll be the only valuable things. Your credit meter'll laugh at you when you punch a purchase order, no matter how much work you've put into it."

The raft bumped. They had arrived at the edge of the world.

They moored the raft to one of the rocks on the wall that rose from the open ocean. They were five kilometers out of Rarotonga. They waited for some light as the sun began to rise, then started up the rock face.

It was rough: blasted out with explosives on this face of the dam. It went up at a thirty-degree angle for fifty meters, then was suddenly level and smooth as glass. The top of the dam at the edge of the world had been smoothed by cutting lasers into a vast table top, three hundred kilometers long and four kilometers wide. They left wet footprints on it as they began the long walk to the edge.

They soon lost any meaningful perspective on the thing. They lost sight of the sea-edge, and couldn't see the dropoff until they began to near it. By then, it was full light. Timed just right, they would reach the edge when the sun came up and they'd really have something to see.

A hundred meters from the edge when she could see over it a little, Lee began to unconsciously hang back. Piri didn't prod her. It was not something he could force someone to see. He'd reached this point with others, and had to turn back. Already, the fear of falling was building up. But she came on, to stand beside him at the very lip of the canyon.

Pacifica was being built and filled in three sections. Two were complete, but the third was still being hollowed out and was not yet filled with water except in the deepest trenches. The water was kept out of this section by the dam they were standing on. When it was completed, when all the underwater trenches and mountain ranges and guyots and slopes had been built to specifications, the bottom would be covered with sludge and ooze and the whole wedge-shaped section flooded. The water came from liquid hydrogen and oxygen on the surface, combined with the limitless electricity of fusion powerplants.

"We're doing what the Dutch did on Old Earth, but in reverse," Piri pointed out, but he got no reaction from Lee. She was staring, spellbound, down the sheer face of the dam to the apparently bottomless trench below. It was shrouded in mist, but seemed to fall off forever.

"It's eight kilometers deep," Piri told her. "It's not going to be a regular trench when it's finished. It's there to be filled up with the remains of this dam after the place has been flooded." He looked at her face, and didn't bother with more statistics. He let her experience it in her own way.

The only comparable vista on a human-inhabited planet was the Great Rift Valley on Mars. Neither of them had seen it, but it suffered in comparison to this because not all of it could be seen at once. Here, one could see from one side to the other, and from sea level to a distance equivalent to the deepest oceanic trenches on Earth. It simply fell away beneath them and went straight down to nothing. There was a rainbow beneath their feet. Off to the left was a huge waterfall that arced away from the wall in a solid stream. Tons of overflow water went through the wall, to twist, fragment, vaporize and blow away long before it reached the bottom of the trench.

Straight ahead of them and about ten kilometers away was the mountain that would become the Okinawa biome when the pit was filled. Only the tiny, blackened tip of the mountain would show above the water.

Lee stayed and looked at it as long as she could. It became easier the longer one stood there, and yet something about it drove her away. The scale was too big, there was no room for humans in that shattered world. Long before noon, they turned and started the long walk back to the raft.

She was silent as they boarded, and set sail for the return trip. The winds were blowing fitfully, barely billowing the sail. It would be another hour before they blew very strongly. They were still in sight of the dam wall.

They sat on the raft, not looking at each other.

"Piri, thanks for bringing me here."

"You're welcome. You don't have to talk about it."

"All right. But there's something else I have to talk about. I . . . I don't know where to begin, really."

Piri stirred uneasily. The earlier discussion about economics had disturbed him. It was part of his past life, a part that he had not been ready to return to. He was full of confusion. Thoughts that had no place out here in the concrete world of wind and water were roiling through his brain. Someone was calling to him, someone he knew but didn't want to see right then.

"Yeah? What is it you want to talk about?"

"It's about—" she stopped, seemed to think it over. "Never mind. It's not time yet." She moved close and touched him. But he was not interested. He made it known in a few minutes, and she moved to the other side of the raft.

He lay back, essentially alone with his troubled thoughts. The wind gusted, then settled down. He saw a flying fish leap, almost passing over the raft. There was a piece of the sky falling through the air. It twisted and turned like a feather, a tiny speck of sky that was blue on one side and brown on the other. He could see the hole in the sky where it had been knocked loose.

It must be two or three kilometers away. No, wait, that wasn't right. The top of the sky was twenty kilometers up, and it looked like it was falling from the center. How far away were they from the center of Pacifica? A hundred kilometers?

A piece of the sky?

He got to his feet, nearly capsizing the raft.

"What's the matter?"

It was *big*. It looked large even from this far away. It was the dreamy tumbling motion that had deceived him.

"The sky is . . ." he choked on it, and almost laughed. But this was no time to feel silly about it. "The sky is falling, Lee." How long? He watched it, his mind full of numbers. Terminal velocity from that high up, assuming it was heavy enough to punch right through the atmosphere . . . over six hundred meters per second. Time to fall, seventy seconds. Thirty of those must already have gone by.

Lee was shading her eyes as she followed his gaze. She still thought it was a joke. The chunk of sky began to glow red as the atmosphere got thicker.

"Hey, it really is falling," she said. "Look at that."

"It's big. Maybe one or two kilometers across. It's going to make quite a splash, I'll bet."

They watched it descend. Soon it disappeared over the horizon, picking up speed. They waited, but the show seemed to be over. Why was he still uneasy?

"How many tons in a two-kilometer chunk of rock, I wonder?" Lee mused. She didn't look too happy, either. But they sat back down on the raft, still looking in the direction where the thing had sunk into the sea.

Then they were surrounded by flying fish, and the water looked crazy. The fish were panicked. As soon as they hit they leaped from the water again. Piri felt rather than saw something pass beneath them. And then, very gradually, a roar built up, a deep bass rumble that soon threatened to turn his bones to powder. It picked him up and shook him, and left him limp on his knees. He was stunned, unable to think clearly. His eyes were still fixed on the horizon, and he saw a white fan rising in the distance in silent majesty. It was the spray from the impact, and it was still going up.

"Look up there," Lee said, when she got her voice back. She seemed as confused as he. He looked where she pointed and saw a twisted line crawling across the blue sky. At first he thought it was the end of his life, because it appeared that the whole overhanging dome was fractured and about to fall in on them. But then he saw it was one of the tracks that the sun ran on, pulled free by the rock that had fallen, twisted into a snake of tortured metal.

"The dam!" he yelled. "The dam! We're too close to the dam!"

"What?"

"The bottom rises this close to the dam. The water here isn't that deep. There'll be a wave coming, Lee, a big wave. It'll pile up here."

"Piri, the shadows are moving."

"Huh?"

Surprise was piling on surprise too fast for him to cope with it. But she was right. The shadows were moving. But *why*?

Then he saw it. The sun was setting, but not by following the tracks that led to the concealed opening in the west. It was falling through the air, having been shaken loose by the rock.

Lee had figured it out, too.

"What is that thing?" she asked. "I mean, how big is it?"

"Not too big, I heard. Big enough, but not nearly the size of that chunk that fell. It's some kind of fusion generator. I don't know what'll happen when it hits the water."

They were paralyzed. They knew there was something they should do, but too many things were happening. There was not time to think it out.

"Dive!" Lee yelled. "Dive into the water!"

"What?"

"We have to dive and swim away from the dam, and down as far as we can go. The wave will pass over us, won't it?"

"I don't know."

"It's all we can do."

So they dived. Piri felt his gills come into action, then he was swimming down at an angle toward the dark-shrouded bottom. Lee was off to his left, swimming as hard as she could. And with no sunset, no warning, it got black as pitch. The sun had hit the water.

He had no idea how long he had been swimming when he suddenly felt himself pulled upward. Floating in the water, weightless, he was not well equipped to feel accelerations. But he did feel it, like a rapidly rising elevator. It was accompanied by pressure waves that threatened to burst his eardrums. He kicked and clawed his way downward, not even knowing if he was headed in the right direction. Then he was falling again.

He kept swimming, all alone in the dark. Another wave passed, lifted him, let him down again. A few minutes later, another one, seeming to come from the other direction. He was hopelessly confused. He suddenly felt he was swimming the wrong way. He stopped, not knowing what to do. Was he pointed in the right direction? He had no way to tell.

He stopped paddling and tried to orient himself. It was useless. He felt surges, and was sure he was being tumbled and buffeted.

Then his skin was tingling with the sensation of a million bubbles crawling over him. It gave him a handle on the situation. The bubbles would be going up, wouldn't they? And they were traveling over his body from belly to back. So down was that way.

But he didn't have time to make use of the information. He hit something hard with his hip, wrenched his back as his body tried to tumble over in the foam and water, then was sliding along a smooth surface. It felt like he was going very fast, and he knew where he was and where he was heading and there was nothing he could do about it. The tail of the wave had lifted him clear of the rocky slope of the dam and deposited him on the flat surface. It was now spending itself, sweeping him along to the edge of the world. He turned around, feeling the sliding surface beneath him with his hands, and tried to dig in. It was a nightmare; nothing he did had any effect. Then his head broke free into the air.

He was still sliding, but the huge hump of the wave had dissipated itself and was collapsing quietly into froth and puddles. It drained away with amazing speed. He was left there, alone, cheek pressed lovingly to the cold rock. The darkness was total.

He wasn't about to move. For all he knew, there was an eight-kilometer drop just behind his toes.

Maybe there would be another wave. If so, this one would crash down on him instead of lifting him like a cork in a tempest. It should kill him instantly. He refused to worry about that. All he cared about now was not slipping any further.

The stars had vanished. Power failure? Now they blinked on. He raised his head a little, in time to see a soft, diffused glow in the east. The moon was rising, and it was doing it at breakneck speed. He saw it rotate from a thin crescent configuration to bright fullness in under a minute. Someone was still in charge, and had decided to throw some light on the scene.

He stood, though his knees were weak. Tall fountains of spray far away to his right indicated where the sea was battering at the dam. He was about in the middle of the tabletop, far from either edge. The ocean was whipped up as if by thirty hurricanes, but he was safe from it at this distance unless there were another tsunami yet to come.

The moonlight turned the surface into a silver mirror, littered with flopping fish. He saw another figure get to her feet, and ran in that direction.

The helicopter located them by infrared detector. They had no way of telling how long it had been. The moon was hanging motionless in the center of the sky.

They got into the cabin, shivering.

The helicopter pilot was happy to have found them, but grieved over other lives lost. She said the toll stood at three dead, fifteen missing and presumed dead. Most of these had been working on the reefs. All the land surface of Pacifica had been scoured, but the loss of life had been minimal. Most had had time to get to an elevator and go below or to a helicopter and rise above the devastation.

From what they had been able to find out, heat expansion of the crust had moved farther down into the interior of the planet than had been expected. It was summer on the surface, something it was easy to forget down here. The engineers had been sure that the inner surface of the sky had been stabilized years ago, but a new fault had been opened by the slight temperature rise. She pointed up to where ships were hovering like fireflies next to the sky, playing searchlights on the site of the damage. No one knew yet if Pacifica would have to be abandoned for another twenty years while it stabilized.

She set them down on Rarotonga. The place was a mess. The wave had climbed the bottom rise and crested at the reef, and a churning hell of foam and debris had swept over the island. Little was left standing except the con-

crete blocks that housed the elevators, scoured of their decorative camouflage.

Piri saw a familiar figure coming toward him through the wreckage that
had been a picturesque village. She broke into a run, and nearly bowled him
over, laughing and kissing him.

"We were sure you were dead," Harra said, drawing back from him as if
to check for cuts and bruises.

"It was a fluke, I guess," he said, still incredulous that he had survived. It
had seemed bad enough out there in the open ocean; the extent of the disaster was much more evident on the island. He was badly shaken to see it.

"Lee suggested that we try to dive under the wave. That's what saved us.
It just lifted us up, then the last one swept us over the top of the dam and
drained away. It dropped us like leaves."

"Well, not quite so tenderly in my case," Lee pointed out. "It gave me
quite a jolt. I think I might have sprained my wrist."

A medic was available. While her wrist was being bandaged, she kept
looking at Piri. He didn't like the look.

"There's something I'd intended to talk to you about on the raft, or soon
after we got home. There's no point in your staying here any longer anyway, and I don't know where you'd go."

"No!" Harra burst out. "Not yet. Don't tell him anything yet. It's not fair.
Stay away from him." She was protecting Piri with her body, from no assault
that was apparent to him.

"I just wanted to—"

"No, no. Don't listen to her, Piri. Come with me." She pleaded with the
other woman. "Just give me a few hours alone with him; there's some things
I never got around to telling him."

Lee looked undecided, and Piri felt mounting rage and frustration. He
had known things were going on around him. It was mostly his own fault
that he had ignored them, but now he had to know. He pulled his hand free
from Harra and faced Lee.

"Tell me."

She looked down at her feet, then back to his eyes.

"I'm not what I seem, Piri. I've been leading you along, trying to make
this easier for you. But you still fight me. I don't think there's any way it's
going to be easy."

"No!" Harra shouted again.

"What are you?"

"I'm a psychiatrist. I specialize in retrieving people like you, people who
are in a mental vacation mode, what you call 'second childhood.' You're
aware of all this, on another level, but the child in you has fought it at every
stage. The result has been nightmares—probably with me as the focus,
whether you admitted it or not."

She grasped both his wrists, one of them awkwardly because of her injury.

"Now listen to me." She spoke in an intense whisper, trying to get it all out before the panic she saw in his face broke free and sent him running. "You came here for a vacation. You were going to stay ten years, growing up and taking it easy. That's all over. The situation that prevailed when you left is now out of date. Things have moved faster than you believed possible. You had expected a ten-year period after your return to get things in order for the coming battles. That time has evaporated. The Common Market of the Inner Planets has fired the first shot. They've instituted a new system of accounting and it's locked into their computers and running. It's aimed right at Pluto, and it's been working for a month now. We cannot continue as an economic partner to the C.M.I.P., because from now on every time we sell or buy or move money the inflationary multiplier is automatically juggled against us. It's all perfectly legal by all existing treaties, and it's necessary to their economy. But it ignores our time-lag disadvantage. We have to consider it as a hostile act, no matter what the intent. You have to come back and direct the war, Mister Finance Minister."

The words shattered what calm Piri had left. He wrenched free of her hands and turned wildly to look all around him. Then he sprinted down the beach. He tripped once over his splay feet, got up without ever slowing, and disappeared.

Harra and Lee stood silently and watched him go.

"You didn't have to be so rough with him," Harra said, but knew it wasn't so. She just hated to see him so confused.

"It's best done quickly when they resist. And he's all right. He'll have a fight with himself, but there's no real doubt of the outcome."

"So the Piri I know will be dead soon?"

Lee put her arm around the younger woman.

"Not at all. It's a reintegration, without a winner or a loser. You'll see." She looked at the tear-streaked face.

"Don't worry. You'll like the older Piri. It won't take him any time at all to realize that he loves you."

He had never been to the reef at night. It was a place of furtive fish, always one step ahead of him as they darted back into their places of concealment. He wondered how long it would be before they ventured out in the long night to come. The sun might not rise for years.

They might never come out. Not realizing the changes in their environment, night fish and day fish would never adjust. Feeding cycles would be disrupted, critical temperatures would go awry, the endless moon and lack of sun would frustrate the internal mechanisms, bred over billions of years, and fish would die. It had to happen.

The ecologists would have quite a job on their hands.

But there was one denizen of the outer reef that would survive for a long time. He would eat anything that moved and quite a few things that didn't, at any time of the day or night. He had no fear, he had no internal clocks dictating to him, no inner pressures to confuse him except the one overriding urge to attack. He would last as long as there was anything alive to eat.

But in what passed for a brain in the white-bottomed torpedo that was the Ghost, a splinter of doubt had lodged. He had no recollection of similar doubts, though there had been some. He was not equipped to remember, only to hunt. So this new thing that swam beside him, and drove his cold brain as near as it could come to the emotion of anger, was a mystery. He tried again and again to attack it, then something would seize him with an emotion he had not felt since he was half a meter long, and fear would drive him away.

Piri swam along beside the faint outline of the shark. There was just enough moonlight for him to see the fish, hovering at the ill-defined limit of his sonic signal. Occasionally, the shape would shudder from head to tail, turn toward him, and grow larger. At these times Piri could see nothing but a gaping jaw. Then it would turn quickly, transfix him with that bottomless pit of an eye, and sweep away.

Piri wished he could laugh at the poor, stupid brute. How could he have feared such a mindless eating machine?

Good-bye, pinbrain. He turned and stroked lazily toward the shore. He knew the shark would turn and follow him, nosing into the interdicted sphere of his transponder, but the thought did not impress him. He was without fear. How could he be afraid, when he had already been swallowed into the belly of his nightmare? The teeth had closed around him, he had awakened, and remembered. And that was the end of his fear.

Good-bye, tropical paradise. You were fun while you lasted. Now I'm a grownup, and must go off to war.

He didn't relish it. It was a wrench to leave his childhood, though the time had surely been right. Now the responsibilities had descended on him, and he must shoulder them. He thought of Harra.

"Piri," he told himself, "as a teenager, you were just too dumb to live."

Knowing it was the last time, he felt the coolness of the water flowing over his gills. They had served him well, but had no place in his work. There was no place for a fish, and no place for Robinson Crusoe.

Good-bye, gills.

He kicked harder for the shore and came to stand, dripping wet, on the beach. Harra and Lee were there, waiting for him.

George R.R. Martin

THE WAY OF CROSS AND DRAGON

Born in Bayonne, New Jersey, George R.R. Martin made his first sale in 1971, and soon established himself as one of the most popular SF writers of the seventies. He quickly became a mainstay of the Ben Bova *Analog* with stories such as "With Morning Comes Mistfall," "And Seven Times Never Kill Man," "The Second Kind of Loneliness," "The Storms of Windhaven" (in collaboration with Lisa Tuttle, and later expanded by them into the novel *Windhaven*), "Override," and others, although he also sold to *Amazing, Fantastic, Galaxy, Orbit,* and other markets. One of his *Analog* stories, the striking novella "A Song for Lya," won him his first Hugo Award in 1974.

By the end of the seventies, he had reached the height of his influence as a science fiction writer, and was producing his best work in that category with stories such as the famous "Sandkings," his best-known story, which won both the Nebula and the Hugo in 1980, "The Way of Cross and Dragon," which won a Hugo Award in the same year (making Martin the first author ever to receive two Hugo Awards for fiction in the same year), "Bitterblooms," "The Stone City," "Starlady," and others. These stories would be collected in *Sandkings,* one of the strongest collections of the period. By now he had mostly moved away from *Analog,* although he would have a long sequence of stories about the droll interstellar adventures of Haviland Tuf (later collected in *Tuf Voyaging*) running throughout the eighties in the Stanley Schmidt *Analog,* as well as a few strong individual pieces such as the novella "Nightflyers"—most of his major work of the late seventies and early eighties, though, would appear in *Omni.* The late seventies also saw the publication of his memorable novel *Dying of the Light,* his only solo SF novel.

By the early middle years of the eighties, though, Martin's career was turning in other directions, directions that would take him far from the kind of career path that might have been forecast for him in the seventies. Horror was starting to burgeon then as a separate publishing category, in the early and middle eighties, and that was the direction in which Martin moved at first, with what was until recently probably his best-known novel, 1982's *Fevre Dream,* an intelligent and suspenseful horror novel set in a vividly realized historical milieu, still one of the best of modern vampire novels. His next horror novel, though, the big, ambitious *Armageddon Rag,* a rock 'n' roll horror apocalypse, was a severe commercial disappointment, and would pretty much bring Martin's career as a horror writer to an end, although he'd later win the Bram Stoker Award for his horror story "The

Pear-Shaped Man" and the World Fantasy Award for his werewolf novella "The Skin Trade." Increasingly, though, he'd turn away from the print world altogether, and move into the world of television instead, becoming a story editor on the new *Twilight Zone* series in the mid eighties, and later becoming a producer on the fantasy series *Beauty and the Beast.*

Highly successful as a writer/story editor/producer in the television world, Martin had little contact with the print world throughout the mid-eighties (although he did win another Nebula in 1985 for his story "Portraits of His Children") and throughout most of the decade of the nineties, except as editor of the long-running *Wild Cards* shared-world anthologies, which reached nine volumes before the series faltered in the late nineties. By then, soured on the television business by the failure of his stillborn series *Doorways* to make it onto the air, Martin returned to the print world with the publication in 1996 of the immensely popular and successful fantasy novel *A Game of Thrones,* one of 1996's best-selling genre titles. A free-standing novella taken from that work, "Blood of the Dragon," won Martin another Hugo Award in 1997, the novel is on this year's Nebula final ballot as I type these words, and two further books in the *Thrones* series are planned. It's clear that Martin has returned to the print world with a bang, and I hope he stays here this time (in fact, what I'd like to see him write next is a new *science fiction* novel).

Martin has always been a richly romantic writer, clearly a direct descendant of the old *Planet Stories* tradition, probably influenced by Leigh Brackett in particular, although you can see strong traces of writers such as Jack Vance and Roger Zelazny in his work as well. In spite of long being a mainstay of *Analog*, science and technology play little real part in his work, where the emphasis is on color, adventure, exoticism, and lush romance, in a universe crowded and jostling both with alien races and human societies that have evolved toward strangeness in isolation, and where the drama is often generated by the inability of one of these cultures to understand clearly the psychology and values and motivations of another. As is evident in the story that follows, a powerful and exotic study of the future of religion, and of a very special kind of heresy.

George R.R. Martin's other books include the collections *A Song for Lya, Songs of Stars and Shadows, Songs the Dead Men Sing, Nightflyers,* and *Portraits of His Children.* In addition to the *Wild Cards* series, he's also the editor of the five-volume *New Voices* series, and of *The Science Fiction Weight-Loss Book,* edited with Isaac Asimov and Martin H. Greenberg. He lives in Santa Fe, New Mexico.

"Heresy," he told me. The brackish waters of his pool sloshed gently.

"Another one?" I said wearily. "There are so many these days."

My Lord Commander was displeased by that comment. He shifted position heavily, sending ripples up and down the pool. One broke over the side, and a sheet of water slid across the tiles of the receiving chamber. My boots were soaked yet again. I accepted that philosophically. I had worn my worst boots, well aware that wet feet are among the inescapable consequences of paying call on Torgathon Nine-Klariis Tûn, elder of the ka-Thane people, and also Archbishop of Vess, Most Holy Father of the Four Vows, Grand Inquisitor of the Order Militant of the Knights of Jesus Christ, and councillor to His Holiness, Pope Daryn XXI of New Rome.

"Be there as many heresies as stars in the sky, each single one is no less dangerous, Father," the Archbishop said solemnly. "As Knights of Christ, it is our ordained task to fight them one and all. And I must add that this new heresy is particularly foul."

"Yes, my Lord Commander," I replied. "I did not intend to make light of it. You have my apologies. The mission to Finnegan was most taxing. I had hoped to ask you for a leave of absence from my duties. I need rest, a time for thought and restoration."

"Rest?" The Archbishop moved again in his pool; only a slight shift of his immense bulk, but it was enough to send a fresh sheet of water across the floor. His black, pupilless eyes blinked at me. "No, Father, I am afraid that is out of the question. Your skills and your experience are vital to this new mission." His bass tones seemed then to soften somewhat. "I have not had time to go over your reports on Finnegan," he said. "How did your work go?"

"Badly," I told him, "though I think that ultimately we will prevail. The Church is strong on Finnegan. When our attempts at reconciliation were rebuffed, I put some standards into the right hands, and we were able to shut down the heretics' newspaper and broadcast facilities. Our friends also saw to it that their legal actions came to nothing."

"That is not *badly*," the Archbishop said. "You won a considerable victory for the Lord."

"There were riots, my Lord Commander," I said. "More than a hundred of the heretics were killed, and a dozen of our own people. I fear there will be more violence before the matter is finished. Our priests are attacked if they so much as enter the city where the heresy has taken root. Their leaders risk their lives if they leave that city. I had hoped to avoid such hatreds, such bloodshed."

"Commendable, but not realistic," said Archbishop Torgathon. He blinked at me again, and I remembered that among people of his race, that was a sign of impatience. "The blood of martyrs must sometimes be spilled, and the blood of heretics as well. What matters it if a being surrenders his life, so long as his soul is saved?"

"Indeed," I agreed. Despite his impatience, Torgathon would lecture me for another hour if given a chance. That prospect dismayed me. The receiving chamber was not designed for human comfort, and I did not wish to remain any longer than necessary. The walls were damp and moldy, the air hot and humid and thick with the rancid-butter smell characteristic of the ka-Thane. My collar was chafing my neck raw, I was sweating beneath my cassock, my feet were thoroughly soaked, and my stomach was beginning to churn. I pushed ahead to the business at hand. "You say this new heresy is unusually foul, my Lord Commander?"

"It is," he said.

"Where has it started?"

"On Arion, a world some three weeks distance from Vess. A human world entirely. I cannot understand why you humans are so easily corrupted. Once a ka-Thane has found the faith, he would scarcely abandon it."

"That is well known," I said politely. I did not mention that the number of ka-Thane to find the faith was vanishingly small. They were a slow, ponderous people, and most of their vast millions showed no interest in learning any ways other than their own, nor in following any creed but their own ancient religion. Torgathon Nine-Klariis Tûn was an anomaly. He had been among the first converts almost two centuries ago, when Pope Vidas L had ruled that non-humans might serve as clergy. Given his great lifespan and the iron certainty of his belief, it was no wonder that Torgathon had risen as far as he had, despite the fact that less than a thousand of his race had followed him into the Church. He had at least a century of life remaining to him. No doubt he would someday be Torgathon Cardinal Tûn, should he squelch enough heresies. The times are like that.

"We have little influence on Arion," the Archbishop was saying. His arms moved as he spoke, four ponderous clubs of mottled green-gray flesh churning the water, and the dirty white cilia around his breathing hole trembled with each word. "A few priests, a few churches, and some believers, but no power to speak of. The heretics already outnumber us on this world. I rely on your intellect, your shrewdness. Turn this calamity into an opportunity. This heresy is so spurious that you can easily disprove it. Perhaps some of the deluded will turn to the true way."

"Certainly," I said. "And the nature of this heresy? What must I disprove?" It is a sad indication of my own troubled faith to add that I did not really care. I have dealt with too many heresies. Their beliefs and their questionings echo in my head and trouble my dreams at night. How can I be sure of my own faith? The very edict that had admitted Torgathon into the clergy had caused a half-dozen worlds to repudiate the Bishop of New Rome, and those who had followed that path would find a particularly ugly heresy in the massive naked (save for a damp Roman collar) alien who floated before me, who wielded the authority of the Church in four great webbed hands. Christianity is the greatest single human religion, but that means little. The non-Christian outnumber us five-to-one, and there are well over seven hundred Christian sects, some almost as large as the One True Interstellar Catholic Church of Earth and the Thousand Worlds. Even Daryn XXI, powerful as he is, is only one of seven to claim the title of Pope. My own belief was once strong, but I have moved too long among heretics and non-believers. Now even my prayers do not make the doubts go away. So it was that I felt no horror—only a sudden intellectual interest—when the Archbishop told me the nature of the heresy on Arion.

"They have made a saint," he said, "out of Judas Iscariot."

As a senior in the Knights Inquisitor, I command my own starship, which it pleases me to call the *Truth of Christ*. Before the craft was assigned to me, it was named the *Saint Thomas*, after the apostle, but I did not consider a saint notorious for doubting to be an appropriate patron for a ship enlisted in the fight against heresy.

I have no duties aboard the *Truth*, which is crewed by six brothers and sisters of the Order of Saint Christopher the Far-Travelling, and captained by a young woman I hired away from a merchant trader. I was therefore able to devote the entire three-week voyage from Vess to Arion to a study of the heretical Bible, a copy of which had been given to me by the Archbishop's administrative assistant. It was a thick, heavy, handsome book, bound in dark leather, its pages tipped with gold leaf, with many splendid interior illustrations in full color with holographic enhancement. Remarkable work, clearly done by someone who loved the all-but-forgotten art of bookmaking. The paintings reproduced inside—the originals, I gathered, were to be found on the walls of the House of Saint Judas on Arion—were masterful, if blasphemous, as much high art as the Tammerwens and RoHallidays that adorn the Great Cathedral of Saint John on New Rome.

Inside, the book bore an imprimatur indicating that it had been approved by Lukyan Judasson, First Scholar of the Order of Saint Judas Iscariot.

It was called *The Way of Cross and Dragon*.

I read it as the *Truth of Christ* slid between the stars, at first taking copious notes to better understand the heresy I must fight, but later simply absorbed by the strange, convoluted, grotesque story it told. The words of text had passion and power and poetry.

Thus it was that I first encountered the striking figure of Saint Judas Iscariot, a complex, ambitious, contradictory, and altogether extraordinary human being.

He was born of a whore in the fabled ancient city-state of Babylon on the same day that the savior was born in Bethlehem, and he spent his childhood in the alleys and gutters, selling his own body when he had to, pimping when he was older. As a youth he began to experiment with the dark arts, and before the age of twenty he was a skilled necromancer. That was when he became Judas the Dragon-Tamer, the first and only man to bend to his will the most fearsome of God's creatures, the great winged fire-lizards of Old Earth. The book held a marvelous painting of Judas in some great dank cavern, his eyes aflame as he wields a glowing lash to keep a mountainous green-gold dragon at bay. Beneath his arm is a woven basket, its lid slightly ajar, and the tiny scaled heads of three dragon chicks are peering from within. A fourth infant dragon is crawling up his sleeve. That was in the first chapter of his life.

In the second, he was Judas the Conqueror, Judas the Dragon-King, Judas of Babylon, the Great Usurper. Astride the greatest of his dragons, with an iron crown on his head and a sword in his hand, he made Babylon the capital of the greatest empire Old Earth had ever known, a realm that stretched from Spain to India. He reigned from a dragon throne amid the Hanging Gardens he had caused to be constructed, and it was there he sat when he tried Jesus of Nazareth, the troublemaking prophet who had been dragged before him bound and bleeding. Judas was not a patient man, and he made Christ bleed still more before he was through was Him. And when Jesus would not answer his questions, Judas contemptuously had Him cast back out into the streets. But first, he ordered his guards to cut off Christ's legs. "Healer," he said, "heal thyself."

Then came the Repentance, the vision in the night, and Judas Iscariot gave up his crown, his dark arts, and his riches to follow the man he had crippled. Despised and taunted by those he had tyrannized, Judas became the Legs of the Lord, and for a year carried Jesus on his back to the far corners of the realm he once ruled. When Jesus did finally heal Himself, then Judas walked at his side, and from that time forth he was Jesus' trusted friend and counselor, the first and foremost of the Twelve. Finally, Jesus gave Judas the gift of tongues, recalled and sanctified the dragons that Judas had sent away, and sent his disciple forth on a solitary ministry across the oceans, "to spread My Word where I cannot go."

There came a day when the sun went dark at noon and the ground trembled, and Judas swung his dragon around on ponderous wings and flew back across the raging seas. But when he reached the city of Jerusalem, he found Christ dead on the cross.

In that moment his faith faltered, and for the next three days the Great Wrath of Judas was like a storm across the ancient world. His dragons razed the Temple in Jerusalem, drove the people forth from the city, and struck as well at the great seats of power in Rome and Babylon. And when he found the others of the Twelve and questioned them and learned of how the one named Simon-called-Peter had three times betrayed the Lord, he strangled Peter with his own hands and fed the corpse to his dragons. Then he sent those dragons forth to start fires throughout the world, funeral pyres for Jesus of Nazareth.

And Jesus rose on the third day, and Judas wept, but his tears could not turn Christ's anger, for in his wrath he had betrayed all of Christ's teachings.

So Jesus called back the dragons, and they came, and everywhere the fires went out. And from their bellies he called forth Peter and made him whole again, and gave him dominion over the Church.

Then the dragons died, and so too did all dragons everywhere, for they were the living sigil of the power and wisdom of Judas Iscariot, who had sinned greatly. And He took from Judas the gift of tongues and the power of healing He had given, and even his eyesight, for Judas had acted as a blind man (there was a fine painting of the blinded Judas weeping over the bodies of his dragons). And He told Judas that for long ages he would be remembered only as Betrayer, and people would curse his name, and all that he had been and done would be forgotten.

But then, because Judas had loved Him so, Christ gave him a boon: an extended life, during which he might travel and think on his sins and finally come to forgiveness. Only then might he die.

And that was the beginning of the last chapter in the life of Judas Iscariot. But it was a very long chapter indeed. Once dragon-king, once the friend of Christ, now he was only a blind traveler, outcast and friendless, wandering all the cold roads of the Earth, living still when all the cities and people and things he had known were dead. Peter, the first Pope and ever his enemy, spread far and wide the tale of how Judas had sold Christ for thirty pieces of silver, until Judas dared not even use his true name. For a time he called himself just Wandering Ju', and afterward many other names. He lived more than a thousand years and became a preacher, a healer, and a lover of animals, and was hunted and persecuted when the Church that Peter had founded became bloated and corrupt. But he had a great deal of time, and at last he found wisdom and a sense of peace, and finally, Jesus came to him on a long-postponed deathbed and they were reconciled, and Judas wept once again. Before he died, Christ promised that he would permit a few to remember who and what Judas had been, and that with the passage of centuries the news would spread, until finally Peter's Lie was displaced and forgotten.

Such was the life of St. Judas Iscariot, as related in *The Way of Cross and Dragon*. His teachings were there as well and the apocryphal books he had allegedly written.

When I had finished the volume, I lent it to Arla-k-Bau, the captain of the *Truth of Christ*. Arla was a gaunt, pragmatic woman of no particular faith, but I valued her opinion. The others of my crew, the good sisters and brothers of Saint Christopher, would only have echoed the Archbishop's religious horror.

"Interesting," Arla said when she returned the book to me.

I chuckled. "Is that all?"

She shrugged. "It makes a nice story. An easier read than your Bible, Damien, and more dramatic as well."

"True," I admitted. "But it's absurd. An unbelievable tangle of doctrine, apocrypha, mythology, and superstition. Entertaining, yes, certainly. Imaginative, even daring. But ridiculous, don't you think? How can you credit dragons? A legless Christ? Peter being pieced together after being devoured by four monsters?"

Arla's grin was taunting. "Is that any sillier than water changing into wine, or Christ walking on the waves, or a man living in the belly of a fish?" Arla-k-Bau liked to jab at me. It had been a scandal when I selected a nonbeliever as my captain, but she was very good at her job, and I liked her around to keep me sharp. She had a good mind, Arla did, and I valued that more than blind obedience. Perhaps that was a sin in me.

"There is a difference," I said.

"Is there?" she snapped back. Her eyes saw through my masks. "Ah, Damien, admit it. You rather liked this book."

I cleared my throat. "It piqued my interest," I acknowledged. I had to justify myself. "You know the kind of matter I deal with ordinarily. Dreary little doctrinal deviations; obscure quibblings on theology somehow blown all out of proportion; bald-faced political maneuverings designed to set some ambitious planetary bishop up as a new pope, or wrest some concession or other from New Rome or Vess. The war is endless, but the battles are dull and dirty. They exhaust me spiritually, emotionally, physically. Afterward I feel drained and guilty." I tapped the book's leather cover. "This is different. The heresy must be crushed, of course, but I admit that I am anxious to meet this Lukyan Judasson."

"The artwork is lovely as well," Arla said, flipping through the pages of *The Way of Cross and Dragon* and stopping to study one especially striking plate—Judas weeping over his dragons, I think. I smiled to see that it had affected her as much as me. Then I frowned.

That was the first inkling I had of the difficulties ahead.

So it was that the *Truth of Christ* came to the porcelain city Ammadon on the world of Arion, where the Order of Saint Judas Iscariot kept its House.

Arion was a pleasant, gentle world, inhabited for these past three centuries. Its population was under nine million; Ammadon, the only real city, was home to two of those millions. The technological level was medium high, but chiefly imported. Arion had little industry and was not an innovative world, except perhaps artistically. The arts were quite important here, flourishing and vital. Religious freedom was a basic tenet of the society, but Arion was not a religious world either, and the majority of the populace lived devoutly secular lives. The most popular religion was Aestheticism, which hardly counts as a religion at all. There were also Taoists, Erikaners, Old True Christers, and Children of the Dreamer, plus adherents of a dozen lesser sects.

And finally there were nine churches of the One True Interstellar Catholic faith. There had been twelve. The other three were now houses of Arion's fastest-growing faith, the Order of Saint Judas Iscariot, which also had a dozen newly built churches of its own.

The Bishop of Arion was a dark, severe man with close-cropped black hair who was not at all happy to see me. "Damien Har Veris!" he exclaimed with some wonderment when I called on him at his residence. "We have heard of you, of course, but I never thought to meet or host you. Our numbers here are small."

"And growing smaller," I said, "a matter of some concern to my Lord Commander, Archbishop Torgathon. Apparently you are less troubled, Excellency, since you did not see fit to report the activities of this sect of Judas worshippers."

He looked briefly angry at the rebuke, but quickly swallowed his temper. Even a bishop can fear a Knight Inquisitor. "We are concerned, of course," he said. "We do all we can to combat the heresy. If you have advice that will help us, I will be glad to listen."

"I am an Inquisitor of the Order Militant of the Knights of Jesus Christ," I said bluntly. "I do not give advice, Excellency. I take action. To that end I was sent to Arion, and that is what I shall do. Now, tell me what you know about this heresy, and this First Scholar, this Lukyan Judasson."

"Of course, Father Damien," the Bishop began. He signaled for a servant to bring us a tray of wine and cheese, and began to summarize the short but explosive history of the Judas cult. I listened, polishing my nails on the crimson lapel of my jacket until the black paint gleamed brilliantly, interrupting from time to time with a question. Before he had half finished, I was determined to visit Lukyan personally. It seemed the best course of action. And I had wanted to do so all along.

Appearances were important on Arion. I gathered, and I deemed it necessary to impress Lukyan with myself and my station. I wore my best boots—sleek, dark hand-made boots of Roman leather that had never seen the inside of Torgathon's receiving chamber—and a severe black suit with deep burgundy lapels and stiff collar. Around my neck was a splendid crucifix of pure gold; my collarpin was a matching golden sword, the sigil of the Knights Inquisitor. Brother Denis carefully painted my nails, all black as ebon, and darkened my eyes as well, and used a fine white powder on my face. When I glanced in the mirror, I frightened even myself. I smiled, but only briefly. It ruined the effect.

I walked to the House of Saint Judas Iscariot. The streets of Ammadon were wide and spacious and golden, lined by scarlet trees called whisperwinds whose long, drooping tendrils did indeed seem to whisper secrets to the gentle breeze. Sister Judith came with me. She is a small woman, slight of build even in the cowled coveralls of the Order of Saint Christopher. Her face is meek and kind, her eyes wide and youthful and innocent. I find her useful. Four times now she has killed those who attempted to assault me.

The House itself was newly built. Rambling and stately, it rose from amid gardens of small bright flowers and seas of golden grass; the gardens were surrounded by a high wall. Murals covered both the outer wall around the property and the exterior of the building itself. I recognized a few of them from *The Way of Cross and Dragon*, and stopped briefly to admire them before walking through the main gate. No one tried to stop us. There were no guards, not even a receptionist. Within the walls, men and women strolled languidly through the flowers, or sat on benches beneath silverwoods and whisperwinds.

Sister Judith and I paused, then made our way directly to the House itself.

We had just started up the steps when a man appeared from within, and stood waiting in the doorway. He was blond and fat, with a great wiry beard that framed a slow smile, and he wore a flimsy robe that fell to his sandaled feet. On the robe were dragons, dragons bearing the silhouette of a man holding a cross.

When I reached the top of the steps, he bowed to me. "Father Damien Har Veris of the Knights Inquisitor," he said. His smile widened. "I greet you in the name of Jesus, and in the name of Saint Judas. I am Lukyan."

I made a note to myself to find out which of the Bishop's staff was feeding information to the Judas cult, but my composure did not break. I have been a Knight Inquisitor for a long, long time. "Father Lukyan Mo," I said, taking his hand. "I have questions to ask of you." I did not smile.

He did. "I thought you might," he said.

Lukyan's office was large but spartan. Heretics often have a simplicity that the officers of the true Church seem to have lost. He did have one indulgence, however. Dominating the wall behind his desk console was the painting I had already fallen in love with: the blinded Judas weeping over his dragons.

Lukyan sat down heavily and motioned me to a second chair. We had left Sister Judith outside in the waiting chamber. "I prefer to stand, Father Lukyan," I said, knowing it gave me an advantage.

"Just Lukyan," he said. "Or Luke, if you prefer. We have little use for hierarchy here."

"You are Father Lukyan Mo, born here on Arion, educated in the seminary on Cathaday, a former priest of the One True Interstellar Catholic Church of Earth and the Thousand Worlds," I said. "I will address you as befits your station, Father. I expect you to reciprocate. Is that understood?"

"Oh, yes," he said amiably.

"I am empowered to strip you of your right to perform the sacraments, to order you shunned and excommunicated for this heresy you have formulated. On certain worlds I could even order your death."

"But not on Arion," Lukyan said quickly. "We're very tolerant here. Besides, we outnumber you." He smiled. "As for the rest, well, I don't perform those sacraments much anyway, you know. Not for years. I'm First Scholar now. A teacher, a thinker. I show others the way, help them find the faith. Excommunicate me if it will make you happy, Father Damien. Happiness is what all of us seek."

"You have given up the faith, then, Father Lukyan," I said. I deposited my copy of *The Way of Cross and Dragon* on his desk. "But I see you have found a new one." Now I did smile, but it was all ice, all menace, all mockery. "A more ridiculous creed I have yet to encounter. I suppose you will tell me that you have spoken to God, that he trusted you with this new revelation, so that you might clear the good name, such that it is, of Holy Judas?"

Now Lukyan's smile was very broad indeed. He picked up the book and beamed at me. "Oh, no," he said. "No, I made it all up."

That stopped me. "What?"

"I made it all up," he repeated. He hefted the book fondly. "I drew on many sources, of course, especially the Bible, but I do think of *Cross and Dragon* as mostly my own work. It's rather good, don't you agree? Of course, I could hardly put my name on it, proud as I am of it, but I did include my imprimatur. Did you notice that? It was the closest I dared come to a byline."

I was speechless only for a moment. Then I grimaced. "You startle me," I admitted. "I expected to find an inventive madman, some poor self-deluded fool, firm in his belief that he had spoken to God. I've dealt with such fanatics before. Instead I find a cheerful cynic who has invented a religion for his own profit. I think I prefer the fanatics. You are beneath contempt, Father Lukyan. You will burn in hell for eternity."

"I doubt it," Lukyan said, "but you do mistake me, Father Damien. I am no cynic, nor do I profit from my dear Saint Judas. Truthfully, I lived more comfortably as a priest of your own Church. I do this because it is my vocation."

I sat down. "You confuse me," I said. "Explain."

"Now I am going to tell you the truth," he said. He said it in an odd way, almost as a cant. "I am a Liar," he added.

"You want to confuse me with a child's paradoxes," I snapped.

"No, no," he smiled. "A *Liar*. With a capital. It is an organization, Father Damien. A religion, you might call it. A great and powerful faith. And I am the smallest part of it."

"I know of no such church," I said.

"Oh, no, you wouldn't. It's secret. It has to be. You can understand that, can't you? People don't like being lied to."

"I do not like being lied to," I said.

Lukyan looked wounded. "I told you this would be the truth, didn't I? When a Liar says that, you can believe him. How else could we trust each other?"

"There are many of you?" I asked. I was starting to think that Lukyan was a madman after all, as fanatical as any heretic, but in a more complex way. Here was a heresy within a heresy, but I recognized my duty: to find the truth of things, and set them right.

"Many of us," Lukyan said, smiling. "You would be surprised, Father Damien, really you would. But there are some things I dare not tell you."

"Tell me what you dare, then."

"Happily," said Lukyan Judasson. "We Liars, like those of all other religions, have several truths we take on faith. Faith is always required. There are some things that cannot be proven. We believe that life is worth living. That is an article of faith. The purpose of life is to live, to resist death, perhaps to defy entropy."

"Go on," I said, interested despite myself.

"We also believe that happiness is a good, something to be sought after."

"The Church does not oppose happiness," I said dryly.

"I wonder," Lukyan said. "But let us not quibble. Whatever the Church's position on happiness, it does preach belief in an afterlife, in a supreme being and a complex moral code."

"True."

"The Liars believe in no afterlife, no God. We see the universe as it *is*, Father Damien, and these naked truths are cruel ones. We who believe in life, and treasure it, will die. Afterward there will be nothing, eternal emptiness, blackness, nonexistence. In our living there has been no purpose, no poetry, no meaning. Nor do our deaths possess these qualities. When we are gone, the universe will not long remember us, and shortly it will be as if we had never lived at all. Our worlds and our universe will not long outlive us. Ultimately, entropy will consume all, and our puny efforts cannot stay that awful end. It will be gone. It has never been. It has never mattered. The universe itself is doomed, transient, uncaring."

I slid back in my chair, and a shiver went through me as I listened to poor Lukyan's dark words. I found myself fingering my crucifix. "A bleak philosophy," I said, "as well as a false one. I have had that fearful vision myself. I think all of us do, at some point. But it is not so, Father. My faith sustains me against such nihilism. It is a shield against despair."

"Oh, I know that, my friend, my Knight Inquisitor," Lukyan said. "I'm glad to see you understand so well. You are almost one of us already."

I frowned.

"You've touched the heart of it," Lukyan continued. "The truths, the great truths—and most of the lesser ones as well—they are unbearable for most men. We find our shield in faith. Your faith, my faith, any faith. It doesn't matter, so long as we *believe*, really and truly believe, in whatever lie we cling to." He fingered the ragged edges of his great blond beard. "Our psychs have always told us that believers are the happy ones, you know. They may believe in Christ or Buddha or Erika Stormjones, in reincarnation or immortality or nature, in the power of love or the platform of a political faction, but it all comes to the same thing. They believe. They are happy. It is the ones who have seen truth who despair, and kill themselves. The truths are so vast, the faiths so little, so poorly made, so riddled with error and contradiction that we see around them and through them, and then we feel the weight of darkness upon us, and can no longer be happy."

I am not a slow man. I knew, by then, where Lukyan Judasson was going. "Your Liars invent faiths."

He smiled. "Of all sorts. Not only religious. Think of it. We know truth for the cruel instrument it is. Beauty is infinitely preferable to truth. We invent beauty. Faiths, political movements, high ideals, belief in love and fellowship. All of them are lies. We tell those lies, among others, endless others. We improve on history and myth and religion, make each more beautiful, better, easier to believe in. Our lies are not perfect, of course. The truths are too big. But perhaps someday we will find one great lie that all humanity can use. Until then, a thousand small lies will do."

"I think I do not care for your Liars very much," I said with a cold, even fervor. "My whole life has been a quest for truth."

Lukyan was indulgent. "Father Damien Har Veris, Knight Inquisitor, I know you better than that. You are a Liar yourself. You do good work. You ship from world to world, and on each you destroy the foolish, the rebels, the questioners who would bring down the edifice of the vast lie that you serve."

"If my lie is so admirable," I said, "then why have you abandoned it?"

"A religion must fit its culture and society, work with them, not against them. If there is conflict, contradiction, then the lie breaks down, and the faith falters. Your Church is good for many worlds, Father, but not for Arion. Life is too kind here, and your faith is stern. Here we love beauty, and your faith offers too little. So we have improved it. We studied this world for a long time. We know its psychological profile. Saint Judas will thrive here. He offers drama, and color, and much beauty—the aesthetics are admirable. His is a tragedy with a happy ending, and Arion dotes on such stories. And the dragons are a nice touch. I think your own Church ought to find a way to work in dragons. They are marvelous creatures."

"Mythical," I said.

"Hardly," he replied. "Look it up." He grinned at me. "You see, really, it all comes back to faith. Can you really know what happened three thousand years ago? You have one Judas, I have another. Both of us have books. Is yours true? Can you really believe that? I have been admitted only to the first circle of the order of Liars, so I do not know all our secrets, but I know that we are very old. It would not surprise me to learn that the gospels were written by men very much like me. Perhaps there never was a Judas at all. Or a Jesus."

"I have faith that that is not so," I said.

"There are a hundred people in this building who have a deep and very real faith in Saint Judas, and the way of cross and dragon," Lukyan said. "Faith is a very good thing. Do you know that the suicide rate on Arion has decreased by almost a third since the Order of Saint Judas was founded?"

I remember rising slowly from my chair. "You are fanatical as any heretic I have ever met, Lukyan Judasson," I told him. "I pity you the loss of your faith."

Lukyan rose with me. "Pity yourself, Damien Har Veris," he said. "I have found a new faith and a new cause, and I am a happy man. You, my dear friend, are tortured and miserable."

"That is a lie!" I am afraid I screamed.

"Come with me," Lukyan said. He touched a panel on his wall, and the great painting of Judas weeping over his dragons slid up out of sight. There was a stairway leading down into the ground. "Follow me," he said.

In the cellar was a great glass vat full of pale green fluid, and in it a thing was floating, a thing very like an ancient embryo, aged and infantile at the same time, naked, with a huge head and a tiny atrophied body. Tubes ran from its arms and legs and genitals, connecting it to the machinery that kept it alive.

When Lukyan turned on the lights, it opened its eyes. They were large and dark and they looked into my soul.

"This is my colleague," Lukyan said, patting the side of the vat, "Jon Azure Cross, a Liar of the fourth circle."

"And a telepath," I said with a sick certainty. I had led pogroms against other telepaths, children mostly, on other worlds. The Church teaches that the psionic powers are one of Satan's traps. They are not mentioned in the Bible. I have never felt good about those killings.

"The moment you entered the compound, Jon read you and notified me," Lukyan said. "Only a few of us know that he is here. He helps us lie most efficiently. He knows when faith is true, and when it is feigned. I have an implant in my skull. Jon can talk to me at all times. It was he who initially recruited me into the Liars. He knew my faith was hollow. He felt the depth of my despair."

Then the thing in the tank spoke, its metallic voice coming from a speaker-grill in the base of the machine that nurtured it. *"And I feel yours, Damien Har Veris, empty priest. Inquisitor, you have asked too many questions. You are sick at heart, and tired, and you do not believe. Join us, Damien. You have been a Liar for a long, long time!"*

For a moment I hesitated, looking deep into myself, wondering what it was I *did* believe. I searched for my faith—the fire that had once sustained me, the certainty in the teachings of the Church, the presence of Christ within me. I found none of it, none. I was empty inside, burned out, full of questions and pain. But as I was about to answer Jon Azure Cross and the smiling Lukyan Judasson, I found something else, something I *did* believe in, had always believed in.

Truth.

I believed in truth, even when it hurt.

"He is lost to us," said the telepath with the mocking name of Cross.

Lukyan's smile faded. "Oh, really? I had hoped you would be one of us, Damien. You seemed ready."

I was suddenly afraid, and I considered sprinting up the stairs to Sister Judith. Lukyan had told me so very much, and now I had rejected them.

The telepath felt my fear. *"You cannot hurt us, Damien,"* it said. *"Go in peace. Lukyan has told you nothing."*

Lukyan was frowning. "I told him a good deal, Jon," he said.

"Yes. But can he trust the words of such a Liar as you?" The small misshapen mouth of the thing in the vat twitched in a smile, and its great eyes closed, and Lukyan Judasson sighed and led me up at the stairs.

It was not until some years later that I realized it was Jon Azure Cross who was lying, and the victim of his lie was Lukyan. I *could* hurt them. I did.

It was almost simple. The Bishop had friends in government and media. With some money in the right places, I made some friends of my own. Then I exposed Cross in his cellar, charging that he had used his psionic powers to tamper with the minds of Lukyan's followers. My friends were receptive to the charges. The guardians conducted a raid, took the telepath Cross into custody, and later tried him.

He was innocent, of course. My charge was nonsense; human telepaths can read minds in close proximity, but seldom anything more. But they are rare, and much feared, and Cross was hideous enough so that it was easy to make him a victim of superstition. In the end, he was acquitted, but he left the city Ammadon and perhaps Arion itself, bound for regions unknown.

But it had never been my intention to convict him. The charge was enough. The cracks began to show in the lie that he and Lukyan had built together. Faith is hard to come by, and easy to lose. The merest doubt can begin to erode even the strongest foundation of belief.

The Bishop and I labored together to sow further doubts. It was not as easy as I might have thought. The Liars had done their work well. Ammadon, like most civilized cities, had a great pool of knowledge, a computer system that linked the schools and universities and libraries together, and made their combined wisdom available to any who needed it.

But when I checked, I soon discovered that the histories of Rome and Babylon had been subtly reshaped, and there were three listings for Judas Iscariot—one for the betrayer, one for the saint, and one for the conqueror-king of Babylon. His name was also mentioned in connection with the Hanging Gardens, and there is an entry for a so-called "Codex Judas."

And according to the Ammadon library, dragons became extinct on Old Earth around the time of Christ.

We finally purged all those lies, wiped them from the memories of the computers, though we had to cite authorities on a half-dozen non-Christian worlds before the librarians and academics would credit that the differences were anything more than a question of religious preference. By then the Order of Saint Judas had withered in the glare of exposure. Lukyan Judasson had grown gaunt and angry, and at least half of his churches had closed.

The heresy never died completely, of course. There are always those who believe no matter what. And so to this day *The Way of Cross and Dragon* is read on Arion, in the porcelain city Ammadon, amid murmuring whisperwinds.

Arla-k-Bau and the *Truth of Christ* carried me back to Vess a year after my departure, and Archbishop Torgathon finally gave me the rest I had asked for, before sending me out to fight still other heresies. So I had my victory, and the Church continued on much as before, and the Order of Saint Judas Iscariot was crushed and diminished. The telepath Jon Azure Cross had been wrong, I thought then. He had sadly underestimated the power of a Knight Inquisitor.

Later, though, I remembered his words.

You cannot hurt us, Damien.

Us?

The Order of Saint Judas? Or the Liars?

He lied, I think, deliberately, knowing I would go forth and destroy the way of cross and dragon, knowing too that I could not touch the Liars, would not even dare mention them. How could I? Who would believe it? A grand star-spanning conspiracy as old as history? It reeks of paranoia, and I had no proof at all.

The telepath lied for Lukyan's benefit, so that he would let me go. I am certain of that now. Cross risked much to snare me. Failing, he was willing to sacrifice Lukyan Judasson and his lie, pawns in some greater game.

So I left, and carried within me the knowledge that I was empty of faith but for a blind faith in truth, a truth I could no longer find in my Church.

I grew certain of that in my year of rest, which I spent reading and studying on Vess and Cathaday and Celia's World. Finally I returned to the Archbishop's receiving room, and stood again before Torgathon Nine-Klariis Tûn in my very worst pair of boots. "My Lord Commander," I said to him, "I can accept no further assignments. I ask that I be retired from active service."

"For what cause?" Torgathon rumbled, splashing feebly.

"I have lost the faith," I said to him, simply.

He regarded me for a long time, his pupilless eyes blinking. At last he said, "Your faith is a matter between you and your confessor. I care only about your results. You have done good work, Damien. You may not retire, and we will not allow you to resign."

The truth will set us free.

But freedom is cold and empty and frightening, and lies can often be warm and beautiful.

Last year the Church finally granted me a new and better ship. I named this one *Dragon*.

Dubuque, Iowa.
December, 1978

SWARM

One of the most powerful and innovative new talents to enter SF in recent years, a man with a rigorously worked-out and aesthetically convincing vision of what the future may have in store for humanity, Bruce Sterling as yet may still be better known to the cognoscente than to the SF-reading population at large, in spite of a recent Hugo win. If you look behind the scenes, though, you will find him everywhere, and he had almost as much to do—as writer, critic, propagandist, aesthetic theorist, and tireless polemicist—with the shaping and evolution of SF in the eighties and nineties as Michael Moorcock did with the shaping of SF in the sixties; it is not for nothing that many of the other writers of the eighties and nineties refer to him, half ruefully, half admiringly, as "Chairman Bruce."

Sterling published his first story in 1976, in an obscure anthology of stories by Texas writers called *Lone Star Universe,* and followed it up in 1977 with his first novel, *Involution Ocean.* Neither story nor novel attracted much attention, nor would his second novel, *The Artificial Kid,* in 1980—indeed, both novels remain fundamentally unread even today, although, in retrospect, *The Artificial Kid* is interesting, if for nothing else because it is clearly an early cyberpunk work; at the time the few critics who mentioned it seemed to be puzzled by it, and dismissed it as a grotesque curiosity. Although Sterling would later produce much better work, both novels are still readable, and in some ways closer to the canons of traditional adventure fiction than some of his more mature later work. They're also interesting because some of Sterling's influences show up more clearly there than they do elsewhere. William Gibson has refered to *The Artificial Kid* as being like "a Jack Vance novel, but with a protagonist who seemed to be compounded of equal parts Bruce Lee, Iggy Pop, and Johnny Rotten," but both that novel and *Involution Ocean* demonstrate as well a heady stew of (sometimes only partially digested) influences from writers as diverse as Melville, Dickens, the J. G. Ballard of the "Vermilion Sands" stories, Harlan Ellison, and Jules Verne, as well as from a number of other pop culture sources, many of them not only outside the SF genre but outside the print genre altogether. Perhaps most noticeably, the strong influence of the early work of Samuel R. Delany can be seen—Sterling's Artificial Kid is clearly a variant of the Magic Kid character (to borrow Algis Budrys's useful critical phrase) who figures in most of Delany's early work, and it's easy to picture him strolling into Sterling's novel for a side gig after working a day job in *The Einstein Intersection* or *The Jewels of Aptor.*

Sterling's early work raised hardly a ripple in the gunmetal-placid surface of the SF world of the late seventies, though. Like many another new writer of the day, Sterling would have to wait for "steam engine time," for the revolutionary surge of new creative energy that would sweep into the field around 1982, before his work was suddenly accessible to, and ready to be appreciated by, the SF readership. And like many another new writer, he first caught on with his short fiction, attracting interest and acclaim with a series of stories he published in the middle eighties in places like *The Magazine of Fantasy & Science Fiction, Omni,* and *Universe.*

The first such story was the one that follows, "Swarm," published in 1982 in *F&SF.* It was clear at once that this was something new; although there were still recognizable influences on Sterling's new work—A. E. van Vogt, Charles Harness, Alfred Bester, Cordwainer Smith, Larry Niven, Olaf Stapledon, along with echoes of Delany and James Tiptree, Jr.—he had integrated those influences better, melded them successfully to produce a strong and individual new voice of his own. With his usual flair for the vivid phrase, Sterling himself has said of "Swarm" that "with that story, I finally gnawed my way through the insulation and got my teeth set into the buzzing copper wire."

"Swarm" was followed in the next three years by a string of other "Shaper/ Mechanist" stories such as "Cicada Queen," "Spider Rose," and "Sunken Gardens," all set against the backdrop of Sterling's exotic Shaper/Mechanist future, a complex and disturbing future where warring political factions struggle to control the shape of human destiny and the nature of humanity itself. Although there were only a few "Shaper/Mechanist" stories, they rank among the strongest work of the decade, and had a disproportionate impact on the SF scene of the day, being especially influential on other new writers and authors-in-the-egg.

The Shaper/Mechanist vision of the future would reach its purest expression in his landmark 1985 novel *Schismatrix,* a vivid, complex, chewy meditation on cultural evolution, Stapledonian and yet buzzing with paranoid energy and tension, something like what you might get if Alfred Bester and A. E. van Vogt had collaborated to write *Last and First Men.*

(Shaper/Mechanist stories were far from all that Sterling produced in the eighties, although much of his other work takes us far enough away from the adventure tradition to be outside the purview of this book. With only the partial exception of the Shaper/Mechanist series, though, no two stories by Sterling are ever much alike in tone or setting or style; there is so much difference between the Sterling of "Dinner in Audoghast" and the Sterling of "The Beautiful and the Sublime" and the Sterling of "Green Days in Brunei" and the Sterling of "Flowers of Edo" and the Sterling of "Dori Bangs" that they might as well all be different individual writers—which makes their influence on later work more difficult to spot.)

Sterling would spend the rest of the eighties up to his hips in blood as one of the chief antagonists in the newly launched Cyberpunk War in SF, editing the influential anthology *Mirrorshades: The Cyberpunk Anthology,* writing fierce manifestos and letters, and relentlessly hyping cyberpunk in his agitprop organ, *Cheap Truth,* almost certainly the most influential, admired, and loathed critical magazine of the decade, even though it was only a shoddy-looking photocopied fanzine sent out to a reader list—selected personally by Sterling—of only a few hundred people. What would be obscured by all the fierce polemics and bitter in-fighting was the fact that Sterling was undoubtedly the best new hard-science writer of the decade, rivaled for the title only by Greg Bear. Ironically, the traditional hard science audience, centered now around *Analog* and Jim Baen's *Far Frontiers,* would be put off by Sterling's political stance and by the punk flavor of his work, and would have nothing to do with him, while he would receive most of his support outside of his own core clique from the leftist literary intellectuals like John Kessel that *Cheap Truth* would devote a good deal of its energy to attacking.

Toward the end of the eighties and the beginning of the nineties, Sterling would publish two more novels, a somewhat overblown "steampunk" novel in collaboration with William Gibson, *The Difference Engine,* and a complex political future thriller, *Islands in the Net.* Perhaps because of backlash from the Cyberpunk Wars, *Islands in the Net* would be largely ignored, although it was more mature and thoughtful than his earlier work, with more fully rounded and more psychologically complex characters. After this, perhaps partially as a result, Sterling retreated into the "New Journalism" for a couple of years, making a major impact with his first (and, so far, only) nonfiction book, a study of First Amendment issues in the world of computer networking, *The Hacker Crackdown: Law and Disorder on the Electronic Frontier,* as well as with a series of articles for *Wired* magazine that made him one of that magazine's big guns (ironically, he may have a bigger reputation as a journalist, especially with the Internet crowd, than he does as a science fiction writer).

In the mid-nineties, after the dust settled and the Cyberpunk Wars had retreated into memory (to the point that critics are now beginning to speak about "post-cyberpunk" work), Sterling returned to the field with two of his best books, *Heavy Weather* and *Holy Fire* (with *Holy Fire* in particular providing as complex, detailed, and fully realized a vision of what the future might actually be like as any that science fiction as a genre has to offer), and a handful of new short stories such as "Sacred Cow" and "Deep Eddy," one of which, "Bicycle Repairman," finally earned him a long-overdue Hugo in 1997.

Sterling is still a young writer by any reasonable definition of the term, and—unless he gets hit by a truck or snuffed by one of the Russian mafia types and computer criminals he hangs out with in his capacity as a hip techno-journalist—will probably keep on growing and evolving well into the next century. Already, his influence has been profound. Although widely recognized as one of the two main "cyberpunk" works, *Schismatrix* was overshadowed at the time by William Gibson's first novel, *Neuromancer,* a more accessible book that would have a powerful and immediate impact on much subsequent SF. I've heard critics say that it was odd that *Schismatrix* didn't have a greater impact . . . but, in fact, its impact may ultimately turn out to be as large as that of *Neuromancer*—it's just taken longer to show up. If you want to know where all of *Schismatrix*'s influence went, all you have to do is look at some of the recent works of the New Baroque Space Opera, especially British Space Opera, being written by people such as Iain M. Banks, Colin Greenland, Stephen Baxter, Paul J. McAuley, Alastair Reynolds, and Peter F. Hamilton. In fact, on the British side of the Atlantic, at least, I'd have to say that *Schismatrix* has probably had more influence on the development of the New Space Opera than any other single book, with the exception of Samuel R. Delany's *Nova*. It would be very interesting to see Sterling himself return to the Baroque Space Opera somewhere down the road, and I hope he does.

Sterling's other books include the collections *Crystal Express* and *Globalhead*. His most recent book is the omnibus collection (it contains the novel *Schismatrix* as well as the rest of his Shaper/Mechanist stories) *Schismatrix Plus*. He lives with his family in Austin, Texas. His latest novel, *Distraction*, is due out soon.

"I will miss your conversation during the rest of the voyage," the alien said.

Captain-Doctor Simon Afriel folded his jeweled hands over his gold-embroidered waistcoat. "I regret it also, ensign," he said in the alien's own hissing language. "Our talks together have been very useful to me. I would have paid to learn so much, but you gave it freely."

"But that was only information," the alien said. He shrouded his bead-bright eyes behind thick nictitating membranes. "We Investors deal in energy, and precious metals. To prize and pursue mere knowledge is an immature racial trait." The alien lifted the long ribbed frill behind his pinhole-sized ears.

"No doubt you are right," Afriel said, despising him. "We humans are as children to other races, however; so a certain immaturity seems natural to us." Afriel pulled off his sunglasses to rub the bridge of his nose. The starship cabin was drenched in searing blue light, heavily ultraviolet. It was the light the Investors preferred, and they were not about to change it for one human passenger.

"You have not done badly," the alien said magnanimously. "You are the kind of race we like to do business with: young, eager, plastic, ready for a wide variety of goods and experiences. We would have contacted you much earlier, but your technology was still too feeble to afford us a profit."

"Things are different now," Afriel said. "We'll make you rich."

"Indeed," the Investor said. The frill behind his scaly head flickered rapidly, a sign of amusement. "Within two hundred years you will be wealthy enough to buy from us the secret of our starflight. Or perhaps your Mechanist faction will discover the secret through research."

Afriel was annoyed. As a member of the Reshaped faction, he did not appreciate the reference to the rival Mechanists. "Don't put too much stock in mere technical expertise," he said. "Consider the aptitude for languages we Shapers have. It makes our faction a much better trading partner. To a Mechanist, all Investors look alike."

The alien hesitated. Afriel smiled. He had appealed to the alien's personal ambition with his last statement, and the hint had been taken. That was where the Mechanists always erred. They tried to treat all Investors consistently, using the same programmed routines each time. They lacked imagination.

Something would have to be done about the Mechanists, Afriel thought. Something more permanent than the small but deadly confrontations between isolated ships in the Asteroid Belt and the ice-rich Rings of Saturn. Both factions maneuvered constantly, looking for a decisive stroke, bribing away each other's best talent, practicing ambush, assassination, and industrial espionage.

Captain-Doctor Simon Afriel was a past master of these pursuits. That was why the Reshaped faction had paid the millions of kilowatts necessary to buy his passage. Afriel held doctorates in biochemistry and alien linguistics, and a master's degree in magnetic weapons engineering. He was thirty-eight years old and had been Reshaped according to the state of the art at the time of his conception. His hormonal balance had been altered slightly to compensate for long periods spent in free-fall. He had no appendix. The structure of his heart had been redesigned for greater efficiency, and his large intestine had been altered to produce the vitamins normally made by intestinal bacteria. Genetic engineering and rigorous training in childhood had given him an intelligence quotient of one hundred and eighty. He was not the brightest of the agents of the Ring Council, but he was one of the most mentally stable and the best trusted.

"It seems a shame," the alien said, "that a human of your accomplishments should have to rot for two years in this miserable, profitless outpost."

"The years won't be wasted," Afriel said.

"But why have you chosen to study the Swarm? They can teach you nothing, since they cannot speak. They have no wish to trade, having no tools or technology. They are the only spacefaring race that is essentially without intelligence."

"That alone should make them worthy of study."

"Do you seek to imitate them, then? You would make monsters of yourselves." Again the ensign hesitated. "Perhaps you could do it. It would be bad for business, however."

There came a fluting burst of alien music over the ship's speakers, then a screeching fragment of Investor language. Most of it was too high-pitched for Afriel's ears to follow.

The alien stood, his jeweled skirt brushing the tips of his clawed birdlike feet. "The Swarm's symbiote has arrived," he said.

"Thank you," Afriel said. When the ensign opened the cabin door, Afriel could smell the Swarm's representative; the creature's warm yeasty scent had spread rapidly through the starship's recycled air.

Afriel quickly checked his appearance in a pocket mirror. He touched powder to his face and straightened the round velvet hat on his shoulder-length reddish-blond hair. His earlobes glittered with red impact-rubies, thick as his thumbs' ends, mined from the Asteroid Belt. His knee-length coat and waistcoat were of gold brocade; the shirt beneath was of dazzling fineness, woven with red-gold thread. He had dressed to impress the Investors, who expected and appreciated a prosperous look from their customers. How could he impress this new alien? Smell, perhaps. He freshened his perfume.

Beside the starship's secondary airlock, the Swarm's symbiote was chittering rapidly at the ship's commander. The commander was an old and sleepy Investor, twice the size of most of her crewmen. Her massive head was encrusted in a jeweled helmet. From within the helmet her clouded eyes glittered like cameras.

The symbiote lifted on its six posterior legs and gestured feebly with its four clawed forelimbs. The ship's artificial gravity, a third again as strong as Earth's, seemed to bother it. Its rudimentary eyes, dangling on stalks, were shut tight against the glare. It must be used to darkness, Afriel thought.

The commander answered the creature in its own language. Afriel grimaced, for he had hoped that the creature spoke Investor. Now he would have to learn another language, a language designed for a being without a tongue.

After another brief interchange the commander turned to Afriel. "The symbiote is not pleased with your arrival," she told Afriel in the Investor language. "There has apparently been some disturbance here involving humans, in the recent past. However, I have prevailed upon it to admit you to the Nest. The episode has been recorded. Payment for my diplomatic services will be arranged with your faction when I return to your native star system."

"I thank Your Authority," Afriel said. "Please convey to the symbiote my best personal wishes, and the harmlessness and humility of my intentions—" He broke off short as the symbiote lunged toward him, biting him savagely in the calf of his left leg. Afriel jerked free and leapt backward in the heavy artificial gravity, going into a defensive position. The symbiote had ripped away a long shred of his pants leg; it now crouched quietly, eating it.

"It will convey your scent and composition to its nest-mates," said the commander. "This is necessary. Otherwise you would be classed as an invader, and the Swarm's warrior caste would kill you at once."

Afriel relaxed quickly and pressed his hand against the puncture wound to stop the bleeding. He hoped that none of the Investors had noticed his reflexive action. It would not mesh well with his story of being a harmless researcher.

"We will reopen the airlock soon," the commander said phlegmatically, leaning back on her thick reptilian tail. The symbiote continued to munch the shred of cloth. Afriel studied the creature's neckless segmented head. It had a mouth and nostrils; it had bulbous atrophied eyes on stalks; there were hinged slats that might be radio receivers, and two parallel ridges of clumped wriggling antennae, sprouting among three chitinous plates. Their function was unknown to him.

The airlock door opened. A rush of dense, smoky aroma entered the departure cabin. It seemed to bother the half-dozen Investors, who left rapidly.

"We will return in six hundred and twelve of your days, as by our agreement," the commander said.

"I thank Your Authority," Afriel said.

"Good luck," the commander said in English. Afriel smiled.

The symbiote, with a sinuous wriggle of its segmented body, crept into the airlock. Afriel followed it. The airlock door shut behind them. The creature said nothing to him but continued munching loudly. The second door opened, and the symbiote sprang through it, into a wide, round stone tunnel. It disappeared at once into the gloom.

Afriel put his sunglasses into a pocket of his jacket and pulled out a pair of infrared goggles. He strapped them to his head and stepped out of the airlock. The artificial gravity vanished, replaced by the almost imperceptible gravity of the Swarm's asteroid nest. Afriel smiled, comfortable for the first time in weeks. Most of his adult life had been spent in free-fall, in the Shapers' colonies in the Rings of Saturn.

Squatting in a dark cavity in the side of the tunnel was a disk-headed furred animal the size of an elephant. It was clearly visible in the infrared of its own body heat. Afriel could hear it breathing. It waited patiently until Afriel had launched himself past it, deeper into the tunnel. Then it took its place in the end of the tunnel, puffing itself up with air until its swollen head securely plugged the exit into space. Its multiple legs sank firmly into sockets in the walls.

The Investors' ship had left. Afriel remained here, inside one of the millions of planetoids that circled the giant star Betelgeuse in a girdling ring with almost five times the mass of Jupiter. As a source of potential wealth it dwarfed the entire solar system, and it belonged, more or less, to the Swarm. At least, no other race had challenged them for it within the memory of the Investors.

Afriel peered up the corridor. It seemed deserted, and without other bodies to cast infrared heat, he could not see very far. Kicking against the wall, he floated hesitantly down the corridor.

He heard a human voice. "Dr. Afriel!"

"Dr. Mirny!" he called out. "This way!"

He first saw a pair of young symbiotes scuttling toward him, the tips of their clawed feet barely touching the walls. Behind them came a woman wearing goggles like his own. She was young, and attractive in the trim, anonymous way of the genetically reshaped.

She screeched something at the symbiotes in their own language, and they halted, waiting. She coasted forward, and Afriel caught her arm, expertly stopping their momentum.

"You didn't bring any luggage?" she said anxiously.

He shook his head. "We got your warning before I was sent out. I have only the clothes I'm wearing and a few items in my pockets."

She looked at him critically. "Is that what people are wearing in the Rings these days? Things have changed more than I thought."

Afriel glanced at his brocaded coat and laughed. "It's a matter of policy. The Investors are always readier to talk to a human who looks ready to do business on a large scale. All the Shapers' representatives dress like this these days. We've stolen a jump on the Mechanists; they still dress in those coveralls."

He hesitated, not wanting to offend her. Galina Mirny's intelligence was rated at almost two hundred. Men and women that bright were sometimes flighty and unstable, likely to retreat into private fantasy worlds or become enmeshed in strange and impenetrable webs of plotting and rationalization. High intelligence was the strategy the Shapers had chosen in the struggle for cultural dominance, and they were obliged to stick to it, despite its occasional disadvantages. They had tried breeding the Superbright—those with quotients over two hundred—but so many had defected from the Shapers' colonies that the faction had stopped producing them.

"You wonder about my own clothing," Mirny said.

"It certainly has the appeal of novelty," Afriel said with a smile.

"It was woven from the fibers of a pupa's cocoon," she said. "My original wardrobe was eaten by a scavenger symbiote during the troubles last year. I usually go nude, but I didn't want to offend you by too great a show of intimacy."

Afriel shrugged. "I often go nude myself, I never had much use for clothes except for pockets. I have a few tools on my person, but most are of little importance. We're Shapers, our tools are here." He tapped his head. "If you can show me a safe place to put my clothes . . ."

She shook her head. It was impossible to see her eyes for the goggles, which made her expression hard to read. "You've made your first mistake, Doctor. There are no places of our own here. It was the same mistake the Mechanist agents made, the same one that almost killed me as well. There is no concept of privacy or property here. This is the Nest. If you seize any part of it for yourself—to store equipment, to sleep in, whatever—then you become an intruder, an enemy. The two Mechanists—a man and a woman—tried to secure an empty chamber for their computer lab. Warriors broke down their door and devoured them. Scavengers ate their equipment, glass, metal, and all."

Afriel smiled coldly. "It must have cost them a fortune to ship all that material here."

Mirny shrugged. "They're wealthier than we are. Their machines, their mining. They meant to kill me, I think. Surreptitiously, so the warriors wouldn't be upset by a show of violence. They had a computer that was learning the language of the springtails faster than I could."

"But you survived," Afriel pointed out. "And your tapes and reports—especially the early ones, when you still had most of your equipment—were of tremendous interest. The Council is behind you all the way. You've become quite a celebrity in the Rings, during your absence."

"Yes, I expected as much," she said.

Afriel was nonplused. "If I found any deficiency in them," he said carefully, "it was in my own field, alien linguistics." He waved vaguely at the two symbiotes who accompanied her. "I assume you've made great progress in communicating with the symbiotes, since they seem to do all the talking for the Nest."

She looked at him with an unreadable expression and shrugged. "There are at least fifteen different kinds of symbiotes here. Those that accompany me are called the springtails, and they speak only for themselves. They are savages, Doctor, who received attention from the Investors only because they can still talk. They were a spacefaring race once, but they've forgotten it. They discovered the Nest and they were absorbed, they became parasites." She tapped one of them on the head. "I tamed these two because I learned to steal and beg food better than they can. They stay with me now and protect me from the larger ones. They are jealous, you know. They have only been with the Nest for perhaps ten thousand years and are still uncertain of their position. They still think, and wonder sometimes. After ten thousand years there is still a little of that left to them."

"Savages," Afriel said. "I can well believe that. One of them bit me while I was still aboard the starship. He left a lot to be desired as an ambassador."

"Yes, I warned him you were coming," said Mirny. "He didn't much like the idea, but I was able to bribe him with food. . . . I hope he didn't hurt you badly."

"A scratch," Afriel said. "I assume there's no chance of infection."

"I doubt it very much. Unless you brought your own bacteria with you."

"Hardly likely," Afriel said, offended. "I have no bacteria. And I wouldn't have brought microorganisms to an alien culture anyway."

Mirny looked away. "I thought you might have some of the special genetically altered ones. . . . I think we can go now. The springtail will have spread your scent by mouth-touching in the subsidiary chamber, ahead of us. It will be spread throughout the Nest in a few hours. Once it reaches the Queen, it will spread very quickly."

She jammed her feet against the hard shell of one of the young springtails and launched herself down the hall. Afriel followed her. The air was warm and he was beginning to sweat under his elaborate clothing, but his antiseptic sweat was odorless.

They exited into a vast chamber dug from the living rock. It was arched and oblong, eighty meters long and about twenty in diameter. It swarmed with members of the Nest.

There were hundreds of them. Most of them were workers, eighty-legged and furred, the size of Great Danes. Here and there were members of the warrior caste, horse-sized furry monsters with heavy fanged heads the size and shape of overstuffed chairs.

A few meters away, two workers were carrying a member of the sensor caste, a being whose immense flattened head was attached to an atrophied body that was mostly lungs. The sensor had great platelike eyes, and its furred chitin sprouted long coiled antennae that twitched feebly as the workers bore it along. The workers clung to the hollowed rock of the chamber walls with hooked and suckered feet.

A paddle-limbed monster with a hairless, faceless head came sculling past them, through the warm reeking air. The front of its head was a nightmare of sharp grinding jaws and blunt armored acid spouts. "A tunneler," Mirny said. "It can take us deeper into the Nest—come with me." She launched herself toward it and took a handhold on its furry, segmented back. Afriel followed her, joined by the two immature springtails, who clung to the thing's hide with their forelimbs. Afriel shuddered at the warm, greasy feel of its rank, damp fur. It continued to scull through the air, its eight fringed paddle feet catching the air like wings.

"There must be thousands of them," Afriel said.

"I said a hundred thousand in my last report, but that was before I had fully explored the Nest. Even now there are long stretches I haven't seen. They must number close to a quarter of a million. This asteroid is about the size of the Mechanists' biggest base—Ceres. It still has rich veins of carbonaceous material. It's far from mined out."

Afriel closed his eyes. If he was to lose his goggles, he would have to feel his way, blind, through these teeming, twitching, wriggling thousands. "The population's still expanding, then?"

"Definitely," she said. "In fact, the colony will launch a mating swarm soon. There are three dozen male and female alates in the chambers near the Queen. Once they're launched, they'll mate and start new Nests. I'll take you to see them presently." She hesitated. "We're entering one of the fungal gardens now."

One of the young springtails quietly shifted position. Grabbing the tunneler's fur with its forelimbs, it began to gnaw on the cuff of Afriel's pants. Afriel kicked it soundly, and it jerked back, retracting its eyestalks.

When he looked up again, he saw that they had entered a second chamber, much larger than the first. The walls around, overhead, and below were buried under an explosive profusion of fungus. The most common types were swollen barrellike domes, multibranched massed thickets, and spaghettilike tangled extrusions that moved very slightly in the faint and odorous breeze. Some of the barrels were surrounded by dim mists of exhaled spores.

"You see those caked-up piles beneath the fungus, its growth medium?" Mirny said.

"Yes."

"I'm not sure whether it is a plant form or just some kind of complex biochemical sludge," she said. "The point is that it grows in sunlight, on the outside of the asteroid. A food source that grows in naked space! Imagine what that would be worth, back in the Rings."

"There aren't words for its value," Afriel said.

"It's inedible by itself," she said. "I tried to eat a very small piece of it once. It was like trying to eat plastic."

"Have you eaten well, generally speaking?"

"Yes. Our biochemistry is quite similar to the Swarm's. The fungus itself is perfectly edible. The regurgitate is more nourishing, though. Internal fermentation in the worker hind-gut adds to its nutritional value."

Afriel stared. "You grow used to it," Mirny said. "Later I'll teach you how to solicit food from the workers. It's a simple matter of reflex tapping—it's not controlled by pheromones, like most of their behavior." She brushed a long lock of clumped and dirty hair from the side of her face. "I hope the pheromonal samples I sent back were worth the cost of transportation."

"Oh, yes," said Ariel. "The chemistry of them was fascinating. We managed to synthesize most of the compounds. I was part of the research team myself." He hesitated. How far did he dare trust her? She had not been told about the experiment he and his superiors had planned. As far as Mirny knew, he was a simple, peaceful researcher, like herself. The Shapers' scientific community was suspicious of the minority involved in military work and espionage.

As an investment in the future, the Shapers had sent researchers to each of the nineteen alien races described to them by the Investors. This had cost the Shaper economy many gigawatts of precious energy and tons of rare metals and isotopes. In most cases, only two or three researchers could be sent; in seven cases, only one. For the Swarm, Galina Mirny had been chosen. She had gone peacefully, trusting in her intelligence and her good intentions to keep her alive and sane. Those who had sent her had not known whether her findings would be of any use or importance. They had only known that it was imperative that she be sent, even alone, even ill-equipped, before some other faction sent their own people and possibly discovered some technique or fact of overwhelming importance. And Dr. Mirny had indeed discovered such a situation. It had made her mission into a matter of Ring security. That was why Afriel had come.

"You synthesized the compounds?" she said. "Why?"

Afriel smiled disarmingly. "Just to prove to ourselves that we could do it, perhaps."

She shook her head. "No mind-games, Dr. Afriel, please. I came this far partly to escape from such things. Tell me the truth."

Afriel stared at her, regretting that the goggles meant he could not meet her eyes. "Very well," he said. "You should know, then, that I have been ordered by the Ring Council to carry out an experiment that may endanger both our lives."

Mirny was silent for a moment. "You're from Security, then?"

"My rank is captain."

"I knew it. . . . I knew it when those two Mechanists arrived. They were so polite, and so suspicious—I think they would have killed me at once if they hadn't hoped to bribe or torture some secret out of me. They scared the life out of me, Captain Afriel. . . . You scare me, too."

"We live in a frightening world, Doctor. It's a matter of faction security."

"Everything's a matter of faction security with your lot," she said. "I shouldn't take you any farther, or show you anything more. This Nest, these creatures—they're not *intelligent*, Captain. They can't think, they can't learn. They're innocent, primordially innocent. They have no knowledge of good and evil. They have no knowledge of *anything*. The last thing they need is to become pawns in a power struggle within some other race, light-years away."

The tunneler had turned into an exit from the fungal chambers and was paddling slowly along in the warm darkness. A group of creatures like gray, flattened basketballs floated by from the opposite direction. One of them settled on Afriel's sleeve, clinging with frail whiplike tentacles. Afriel brushed it gently away, and it broke loose, emitting a stream of foul reddish droplets.

"Naturally I agree with you in principle, Doctor," Afriel said smoothly. "But consider these Mechanists. Some of their extreme factions are already more than half machine. Do you expect humanitarian motives from them? They're cold, Doctor—cold and soulless creatures who can cut a living man or woman to bits and never feel their pain. Most of the other factions hate us. They call us racist supermen. Would you rather that one of these cults do what we must do, and use the results against us?"

"This is double-talk." She looked away. All around them workers laden down with fungus, their jaws full and guts stuffed with it, were spreading out into the Nest, scuttling alongside them or disappearing into branch tunnels departing in every direction, including straight up and straight down. Afriel saw a creature much like a worker, but with only six legs, scuttle past in the opposite direction, overhead. It was a parasite mimic. How long, he wondered, did it take a creature to evolve to look like that?

"It's no wonder that we've had so many defectors, back in the Rings," she said sadly. "If humanity is so stupid as to work itself into a corner like you describe, then it's better to have nothing to do with them. Better to live alone. Better not to help the madness spread."

"That kind of talk will only get us killed," Afriel said. "We owe an allegiance to the faction that produced us."

"Tell me truly, Captain," she said. "Haven't you ever felt the urge to leave everything—everyone—all your duties and constraints, and just go somewhere to think it all out? Your whole world, and your part in it? We're trained so hard, from childhood, and so much is demanded from us. Don't you think it's made us lose sight of our goals, somehow?"

"We live in space," Afriel said flatly. "Space is an unnatural environment, and it takes an unnatural effort from unnatural people to prosper there. Our minds are our tools, and philosophy has to come second. Naturally I've felt those urges you mention. They're just another threat to guard against. I believe in an ordered society. Technology has unleashed tremendous forces that are ripping society apart. Some one faction must arise from the struggle and integrate things. We Shapers have the wisdom and restraint to do it humanely. That's why I do the work I do." He hesitated. "I don't expect to see our day of triumph. I expect to die in some brush-fire conflict, or through assassination. It's enough that I can foresee that day."

"But the arrogance of it, Captain!" she said suddenly. "The arrogance of your little life and its little sacrifice! Consider the Swarm, if you really want your humane and perfect order. Here it is! Where it's always warm and dark, and it smells good, and food is easy to get, and everything is endlessly and perfectly recycled. The only resources that are ever lost are the bodies of the mating swarms, and a little air. A Nest like this one could last unchanged for hundreds of thousands of years. Hundreds . . . of thousands . . . of years. Who, or what, will remember us and our stupid faction in even a thousand years?"

Afriel shook his head. "That's not a valid comparison. There is no such long view for us. In another thousand years we'll be machines, or gods." He felt the top of his head; his velvet cap was gone. No doubt something was eating it by now.

The tunneler took them deeper into the asteroid's honeycombed free-fall maze. They saw the pupal chambers, where pallid larvae twitched in swaddled silk; the main fungal gardens; the graveyard pits, where winged workers beat ceaselessly at the soupy air, feverishly hot from the heat of decomposition. Corrosive black fungus ate the bodies of the dead into coarse black powder, carried off by blackened workers themselves three-quarters dead.

Later they left the tunneler and floated on by themselves. The woman moved with the ease of long habit; Afriel followed her, colliding bruisingly with squeaking workers. There were thousands of them, clinging to ceiling, walls, and floor, clustering and scurrying at every conceivable angle.

Later still they visited the chamber of the winged princes and princesses, an echoing round vault where creatures forty meters long hung crooked-legged in midair. Their bodies were segmented and metallic, with organic rocket nozzles on their thoraxes, where wings might have been. Folded along their sleek backs were radar antennae on long sweeping booms. They looked more like interplanetary probes under construction than anything biological. Workers fed them ceaselessly. Their bulging spiracled abdomens were full of compressed oxygen.

Mirny begged a large chunk of fungus from a passing worker, deftly tapping its antennae and provoking a reflex action. She handed most of the fungus to the two springtails, which devoured it greedily and looked expectantly for more.

Afriel tucked his legs into a free-fall lotus position and began chewing with determination on the leathery fungus. It was tough, but tasted good, like smoked meat—a delicacy he had tasted only once. The smell of smoke meant disaster in a Shaper's colony.

Mirny maintained a stony silence. "Food's no problem," Afriel said. "Where do we sleep?"

She shrugged. "Anywhere . . . there are unused niches and tunnels here and there. I suppose you'll want to see the Queen's chamber next."

"By all means."

"I'll have to get more fungus. The warriors are on guard there and have to be bribed with food."

She gathered an armful of fungus from another worker in the endless stream, and they moved on. Afriel, already totally lost, was further confused in the maze of chambers and tunnels. At last they exited into an immense lightless cavern, bright with infrared heat from the Queen's monstrous body. It was the colony's central factory. The fact that it was made of warm and pulpy flesh did not conceal its essentially industrial nature. Tons of predigested fungal pap went into the slick blind jaws at one end. The rounded billows of soft flesh digested and processed it, squirming, sucking, and undulating, with loud machinelike churnings and gurglings. Out of the other end came an endless conveyorlike blobbed stream of eggs, each one packed in a thick hormonal paste of lubrication. The workers avidly licked the eggs clean and bore them off to nurseries. Each egg was the size of a man's torso.

The process went on and on. There was no day or night here in the lightless center of the asteroid. There was no remnant of a diurnal rhythm in the genes of these creatures. The flow of production was as constant and even as the working of an automated mine.

"This is why I'm here," Afriel murmured in awe. "Just look at this, Doctor. The Mechanists have cybernetic mining machinery that is generations ahead of ours. But here—in the bowels of this nameless little world, is a genetic technology that feeds itself, maintains itself, runs itself, efficiently, endlessly, mindlessly. It's the perfect organic tool. The faction that could use these tireless workers could make itself an industrial titan. And our knowledge of biochemistry is unsurpassed. We Shapers are just the ones to do it."

"How do you propose to do that?" Mirny asked with open skepticism. "You would have to ship a fertilized queen all the way to the solar system. We could scarcely afford that, even if the Investors would let us, which they wouldn't."

"I don't need an entire Nest," Afriel said patiently. "I only need the genetic information from one egg. Our laboratories back in the Rings could clone endless numbers of workers."

"But the workers are useless without the Nest's pheromones. They need chemical cues to trigger their behavior modes."

"Exactly," Afriel said. "As it so happens, I possess those pheromones, synthesized and concentrated. What I must do now is test them. I must prove that I can use them to make the workers do what I choose. Once I've proven it's possible, I'm authorized to smuggle the genetic information necessary back to the Rings. The Investors won't approve. There are, of course, moral questions involved, and the Investors are not genetically advanced. But we can win their approval back with the profits we make. Best of all, we can beat the Mechanists at their own game."

"You've carried the pheromones here?" Mirny said. "Didn't the Investors suspect something when they found them?"

"Now it's you who has made an error," Afriel said calmly. "You assume that the Investors are infallible. You are wrong. A race without curiosity will never explore every possibility, the way we Shapers did." Afriel pulled up his pants cuff and extended his right leg. "Consider this varicose vein along my shin. Circulatory problems of this sort are common among those who spend a lot of time in free-fall. This vein, however, has been blocked artificially and treated to reduce osmosis. Within the vein are ten separate colonies of genetically altered bacteria, each one specially bred to produce a different Swarm pheromone."

He smiled. "The Investors searched me very thoroughly, including X-rays. But the vein appears normal to X-rays, and the bacteria are trapped within compartments in the vein. They are indetectable. I have a small medical kit on my person. It includes a syringe. We can use it to extract the pheromones and test them. When the tests are finished—and I feel sure they will be successful, in fact I've staked my career on it—we can empty the vein and all its compartments. The bacteria will die on contact with air. We can refill the vein with the yolk from a developing embryo. The cells may survive during the trip back, but even if they die, they can't rot inside my body. They'll never come in contact with any agent of decay. Back in the Rings, we can learn to activate and suppress different genes to produce the different castes, just as is done in nature. We'll have millions of workers, armies of warriors if need be, perhaps even organic rocketships, grown from altered alates. If this works, who do you think will remember me then, eh? Me and my arrogant little life and little sacrifice?"

She stared at him; even the bulky goggles could not hide her new respect and even fear. "You really mean to do it, then."

"I made the sacrifice of my time and energy. I expect results, Doctor."

"But it's kidnapping. You're talking about breeding a slave race."

Afriel shrugged, with contempt. "You're juggling words, Doctor. I'll cause this colony no harm. I may steal some of its workers' labor while they obey my own chemical orders, but that tiny theft won't be missed. I admit to the murder of one egg, but that is no more a crime than a human abortion. Can the theft of one strand of genetic material be called 'kidnapping'? I think not. As for the scandalous idea of a slave race—I reject it out of hand. These creatures are genetic robots. They will no more be slaves than are laser drills or cargo tankers. At the very worst, they will be our domestic animals."

Mirny considered the issue. It did not take her long. "It's true. It's not as if a common worker will be staring at the stars, pining for its freedom. They're just brainless neuters."

"Exactly, Doctor."

"They simply work. Whether they work for us or the Swarm makes no difference to them."

"I see that you've seized on the beauty of the idea."

"And if it worked," Mirny said, "If it worked, our faction would profit astronomically."

Afriel smiled genuinely, unaware of the chilling sarcasm of his expression.

"And the personal profit, Doctor . . . the valuable expertise of the first to exploit the technique." He spoke gently, quietly. "Ever see a nitrogen snowfall on Titan? I think a habitat of one's own there—larger, much larger than anything possible before . . . A genuine city, Galina, a place where a man can scrap the rules and discipline that madden him . . ."

"Now it's you who are talking defection, Captain-Doctor."

Afriel was silent for a moment, then smiled with an effort. "Now you've ruined my perfect reverie," he said. "Besides, what I was describing was the well-earned retirement of a wealthy man, not some self-indulgent hermitage . . . there's a clear difference." He hesitated. "In any case, may I conclude that you're with me in this project?"

She laughed and touched his arm. There was something uncanny about the small sound of her laugh, drowned by a great organic rumble from the Queen's monstrous intestines. . . . "Do you expect me to resist your arguments for two long years? Better that I give in now and save us friction."

"Yes."

"After all, you won't do any harm to the Nest. They'll never know anything has happened. And if their genetic line is successfully reproduced back home, there'll never be any reason for humanity to bother them again."

"True enough," said Afriel, though in the back of his mind he instantly thought of the fabulous wealth of Betelgeuse's asteroid system. A day would come, inevitably, when humanity would move to the stars en masse, in earnest. It would be well to know the ins and outs of every race that might become a rival.

"I'll help you as best I can," she said. There was a moment's silence. "Have you seen enough of this area?"

"Yes." They left the Queen's chamber.

"I didn't think I'd like you at first," she said candidly. "I think I like you better now. You seem to have a sense of humor that most Security people lack."

"It's not a sense of humor," Afriel said sadly. "It's a sense of irony disguised as one."

There were no days in the unending stream of hours that followed. There were only ragged periods of sleep, apart at first, later together, as they held each other in free-fall. The sexual feel of skin and body became an anchor to their common humanity, a divided, frayed humanity so many light-years away that the concept no longer had any meaning. Life in the warm and swarming tunnels was the here and now; the two of them were like germs in a bloodstream, moving ceaselessly with the pulsing ebb and flow. Hours stretched into months, and time itself grew meaningless.

The pheromonal tests were complex, but not impossibly difficult. The first of the ten pheromones was a simple grouping stimulus, causing large numbers of workers to gather as the chemical was spread from palp to palp. The workers then waited for further instructions; if none were forthcoming, they dispersed. To work effectively, the pheromones had to be given in a mix, or series, like computer commands; number one, grouping, for instance, together with the third pheromone, a transferral order, which caused the workers to empty any given chamber and move its effects to another. The ninth pheromone had the best industrial possibilities; it was a building order, causing the workers to gather tunnelers and dredgers and set them to work. Others were annoying; the tenth pheromone provoked grooming behavior, and the workers' furry palps stripped off the remaining rags of Afiel's clothing. The eighth pheromone sent the workers off to harvest material on the asteroid's surface, and in their eagerness to observe its effects the two explorers were almost trapped and swept off into space.

The two of them no longer feared the warrior caste. They knew that a dose of the sixth pheromone would send them scurrying off to defend the eggs, just as it sent the workers to tend them. Mirny and Afriel took advantage of this and secured their own chambers, dug by chemically hijacked workers and defended by a hijacked airlock guardian. They had their own fungal gardens to refresh the air, stocked with the fungus they liked best, and digested by a worker they kept drugged for their own food use. From constant stuffing and lack of exercise the worker had swollen up into its replete form and hung from one wall like a monstrous grape.

Afriel was tired. He had been without sleep recently for a long time; how long, he didn't know. His body rhythm had not adjusted as well as Mirny's, and he was prone to fits of depression and irritability that he had to repress with an effort. "The Investors will be back sometime," he said. "Sometime soon."

Mirny was indifferent. "The Investors," she said, and followed the remark with something in the language of the springtails, which he didn't catch. Despite his linguistic training, Afriel had never caught up with her in her use of the springtails' grating jargon. His training was almost a liability; the springtail language had decayed so much that it was a pidgin tongue, without rules or regularity. He knew enough to give them simple orders, and with his partial control of the warriors he had the power to back it up. The springtails were afraid of him, and the two juveniles that Mirny had tamed had developed into fat, overgrown tyrants that freely terrorized their elders. Afriel had been too busy to seriously study the springtails or the other symbiotes. There were too many practical matters at hand.

"If they come too soon, I won't be able to finish my latest study," she said in English.

Afriel pulled off his infrared goggles and knotted them tightly around his neck. "There's a limit, Galina," he said, yawning. "You can only memorize so much data without equipment. We'll just have to wait quietly until we can get back. I hope the Investors aren't shocked when they see me. I lost a fortune with those clothes."

"It's been so dull since the mating swarm was launched. If it weren't for the new growth in the alates' chamber, I'd be bored to death." She pushed greasy hair from her face with both hands. "Are you going to sleep?"

"Yes, if I can."

"You won't come with me? I keep telling you that this new growth is important. I think it's a new caste. It's definitely not an alate. It has eyes like an alate, but it's clinging to the wall."

"It's probably not a Swarm member at all, then," he said tiredly, humoring her. "It's probably a parasite, an alate mimic. Go on and see it, if you want to. I'll be here waiting for you."

He heard her leave. Without his infrareds on, the darkness was still not quite total; there was a very faint luminosity from the steaming, growing fungus in the chamber beyond. The stuffed worker replete moved slightly on the wall, rustling and gurgling. He fell asleep.

When he awoke, Mirny had not yet returned. He was not alarmed. First, he visited the original airlock tunnel, where the Investors had first left him. It was irrational—the Investors always fulfilled their contracts—but he feared that they would arrive someday, become impatient, and leave without him. The Investors would have to wait, of course. Mirny could keep them occupied in the short time it would take him to hurry to the nursery and rob a developing egg of its living cells. It was best that the egg be as fresh as possible.

Later he ate. He was munching fungus in one of the anterior chambers when Mirny's two tamed springtails found him. "What do you want?" he asked in their language.

"Food-giver no good," the larger one screeched, waving its forelegs in brainless agitation. "Not work, not sleep."

"Not move," the second one said. It added hopefully, "Eat it now?"

Afriel gave them some of his food. They ate it, seemingly more out of habit than real appetite, which alarmed him. "Take me to her," he told them.

The two springtails scurried off; he followed them easily, adroitly dodging and weaving through the crowds of workers. They led him several miles through the network, to the alates' chamber. There they stopped, confused. "Gone," the large one said.

The chamber was empty. Afriel had never seen it empty before, and it was very unusual for the Swarm to waste so much space. He felt dread. "Follow the food-giver," he said. "Follow the smell."

The springtails snuffled without much enthusiasm along one wall; they knew he had no food and were reluctant to do anything without an immediate reward. At last one of them picked up the scent, or pretended to, and followed it up across the ceiling and into the mouth of a tunnel.

It was hard for Afriel to see much in the abandoned chamber; there was not enough infrared heat. He leapt upward after the springtail.

He heard the roar of a warrior and the springtail's choked-off screech. It came flying from the tunnel's mouth, a spray of clotted fluid bursting from its ruptured head. It tumbled end over end until it hit the far wall with a flaccid crunch. It was already dead.

The second springtail fled at once, screeching with grief and terror. Afriel landed on the lip of the tunnel, sinking into a crouch as his legs soaked up momentum. He could smell the acrid stench of the warrior's anger, a pheromone so thick that even a human could scent it. Dozens of other warriors would group here within minutes, or seconds. Behind the enraged warrior he could hear workers and tunnelers shifting and cementing rock.

He might be able to control one enraged warrior, but never two, or twenty. He launched himself from the chamber wall and out an exit.

He searched for the other springtail—he felt sure he could recognize it, since it was so much bigger than the others—but he could not find it. With its keen sense of smell, it could easily avoid him if it wanted to.

Mirny did not return. Uncountable hours passed. He slept again. He returned to the slates' chamber; there were warriors on guard there, warriors that were not interested in food and brandished their immense serrated fangs when he approached. They looked ready to rip him apart; the faint reek of aggressive pheromones hung about the place like a fog. He did not see any symbiotes of any kind on the warriors' bodies. There was one species, a thing like a huge tick, that clung only to warriors, but even the ticks were gone.

He returned to his chambers to wait and think. Mirny's body was not in the garbage pits. Of course, it was possible that something else might have eaten her. Should he extract the remaining pheromone from the spaces in his vein and try to break into the alates' chamber? He suspected that Mirny, or whatever was left of her, was somewhere in the tunnel where the springtail had been killed. He had never explored that tunnel himself. There were thousands of tunnels he had never explored.

He felt paralyzed by indecision and fear. If he was quiet, if he did nothing, the Investors might arrive at any moment. He could tell the Ring Council anything he wanted about Mirny's death; if he had the genetics with him, no one would quibble. He did not love her; he respected her, but not enough to give up his life, or his faction's investment. He had not thought of the Ring Council in a long time, and the thought sobered him. He would have to explain his decision. . . .

He was still in a brown study when he heard a whoosh of air as his living airlock deflated itself. Three warriors had come for him. There was no reek of anger about them. They moved slowly and carefully. He knew better than to try to resist. One of them seized him gently in its massive jaws and carried him off.

It took him to the slates' chamber and into the guarded tunnel. A new, large chamber had been excavated at the end of the tunnel. It was filled almost to bursting by a black-spattered white mass of flesh. In the center of the soft speckled mass were a mouth and two damp, shining eyes, on stalks. Long tendrils like conduits dangled, writhing, from a clumped ridge above the eyes. The tendrils ended in pink, fleshy plug-like clumps.

One of the tendrils had been thrust through Mirny's skull. Her body hung in midair, limp as wax. Her eyes were open, but blind.

Another tendril was plugged into the braincase of a mutated worker. The worker still had the pallid tinge of a larva; it was shrunken and deformed, and its mouth had the wrinkled look of a human mouth. There was a blob like a tongue in the mouth, and white ridges like human teeth. It had no eyes.

It spoke with Mirny's voice. "Captain-Doctor Afriel . . ."

"Galina . . ."

"I have no such name. You may address me as Swarm."

Afriel vomited. The central mass was an immense head. Its brain almost filled the room.

It waited politely until Afriel had finished.

"I find myself awakened again," Swarm said dreamily. "I am pleased to see that there is no major emergency to concern me. Instead it is a threat that has become almost routine." It hesitated delicately. Mirny's body moved slightly in midair; her breathing was inhumanly regular. The eyes opened and closed. "Another young race."

"What are you?"

"I am the Swarm. That is, I am one of its castes. I am a tool, an adaptation; my specialty is intelligence. I am not often needed. It is good to be needed again."

"Have you been here all along? Why didn't you greet us? We'd have dealt with you. We meant no harm."

The wet mouth on the end of the plug made laughing sounds. "Like yourself, I enjoy irony," it said. "It is a pretty trap you have found yourself in, Captain-Doctor. You meant to make the Swarm work for you and your race. You meant to breed us and study us and use us. It is an excellent plan, but one we hit upon long before your race evolved."

Stung by panic, Afriel's mind raced frantically. "You're an intelligent being," he said. "There's no reason to do us any harm. Let us talk together. We can help you."

"Yes," Swarm agreed. "You will be helpful. Your companion's memories tell me that this is one of those uncomfortable periods when galactic intelligence is rife. Intelligence is a great bother. It makes all kinds of trouble for us."

"What do you mean?"

"You are a young race and lay great stock by your own cleverness," Swarm said. "As usual, you fail to see that intelligence is not a survival trait."

Afriel wiped sweat from his face. "We've done well," he said. "We came to you, and peacefully. You didn't come to us."

"I refer to exactly that," Swarm said urbanely. "This urge to expand, to explore, to develop, is just what will make you extinct. You naively suppose that you can continue to feed your curiosity indefinitely. It is an old story, pursued by countless races before you. Within a thousand years—perhaps a little longer—your species will vanish."

"You intend to destroy us, then? I warn you it will not be an easy task—"

"Again you miss the point. Knowledge is power! Do you suppose that fragile little form of yours—your primitive legs, your ludicrous arms and hands, your tiny, scarcely wrinkled brain—can *contain* all that power? Certainly not! Already your race is flying to pieces under the impact of your own expertise. The original human form is becoming obsolete. Your own genes have been altered, and you, Captain-Doctor, are a crude experiment. In a hundred years you will be a relic. In a thousand years you will not even be a memory. Your race will go the same way as a thousand others."

"And what way is that?"

"I do not know." The thing on the end of the Swarm's arm made a chuckling sound. "They have passed beyond my ken. They have all discovered something, learned something, that has caused them to transcend my understanding. It may be that they even transcend *being*. At any rate, I cannot sense their presence anywhere. They seem to do nothing, they seem to interfere in nothing; for all intents and purposes, they seem to be dead. Vanished. They may have become gods, or ghosts. In either case, I have no wish to join them."

"So then—so then you have—"

"Intelligence is very much a two-edged sword, Captain-Doctor. It is useful only up to a point. It interferes with the business of living. Life, and intelligence, do not mix very well. They are not at all closely related, as you childishly assume."

"But you, then—you are a rational being—"

"I am a tool, as I said." The mutated device on the end of its arm made a sighing noise. "When you began your pheromonal experiments, the chemical imbalance became apparent to the Queen. It triggered certain genetic patterns within her body, and I was reborn. Chemical sabotage is a problem that can best be dealt with by intelligence. I am a brain replete, you see, specially designed to be far more intelligent than any young race. Within three days I was fully self-conscious. Within five days I had deciphered these markings on my body. They are the genetically encoded history of my race . . . within five days and two hours I recognized the problem at hand and knew what to do. I am now doing it. I am six days old."

"What is it you intend to do?"

"Your race is a very vigorous one. I expect it to be here, competing with us, within five hundred years. Perhaps much sooner. It will be necessary to make a thorough study of such a rival. I invite you to join our community on a permanent basis."

"What do you mean?"

"I invite you to become a symbiote. I have here a male and a female, whose genes are altered and therefore without defects. You make a perfect breeding pair. It will save me a great deal of trouble with cloning."

"You think I'll betray my race and deliver a slave species into your hands?"

"Your choice is simple, Captain-Doctor. Remain an intelligent, living being, or become a mindless puppet, like your partner. I have taken over all the functions of her nervous system; I can do the same to you."

"I can kill myself."

"That might be troublesome, because it would make me resort to developing a cloning technology. Technology, though I am capable of it, is painful to me. I am a genetic artifact; there are fail-safes within me that prevent me from taking over the Nest for my own uses. That would mean falling into the same trap of progress as other intelligent races. For similar reasons, my life span is limited. I will live for only a thousand years, until your race's brief flurry of energy is over and peace resumes once more."

"Only a thousand years?" Afriel laughed bitterly. "What then? You kill off my descendants, I assume, having no further use for them."

"No. We have not killed any of the fifteen other races we have taken for defensive study. It has not been necessary. Consider that small scavenger floating by your head, Captain-Doctor, that is feeding on your vomit. Five hundred million years ago its ancestors made the galaxy tremble. When they attacked us, we unleashed their own kind upon them. Of course, we altered our side, so that they were smarter, tougher, and, naturally, totally loyal to us. Our Nests were the only world they knew, and they fought with a valor and inventiveness we never could have matched. . . . Should your race arrive to exploit us, we will naturally do the same."

"We humans are different."

"Of course."

"A thousand years here won't change us. You will die and our descendants will take over this Nest. We'll be running things, despite you, in a few generations. The darkness won't make any difference."

"Certainly not. You don't need eyes here. You don't need anything."

"You'll allow me to stay alive? To teach them anything I want?"

"Certainly, Captain-Doctor. We are doing you a favor, in all truth. In a thousand years your descendants here will be the only remnants of the human race. We are generous with our immortality; we will take it upon ourselves to preserve you."

"You're wrong, Swarm. You're wrong about intelligence, and you're wrong about everything else. Maybe other races would crumble into parasitism, but we humans are different."

"Certainly. You'll do it, then?"

"Yes. I accept your challenge. And I will defeat you."

"Splendid. When the Investors return here, the springtails will say that they have killed you, and will tell them to never return. They will not return. The humans should be the next to arrive."

"If I don't defeat you, they will."

"Perhaps." Again it sighed. "I'm glad I don't have to absorb you. I would have missed your conversation."

THE BLIND MINOTAUR

One of the most popular and respected of all the new writers who entered the field in the eighties, Michael Swanwick made his debut in 1980 with two strong and compelling stories, "The Feast of St. Janis" and "Ginungagap," both of which were Nebula Award finalists that year, and which were both selected either for a Best of the Year anthology or for that year's annual Nebula Awards volume—as auspicious a debut as anyone has ever made.

He stayed in the public eye, and on major award ballots, throughout the rest of the eighties with intense and powerful stories such as "Mummer Kiss," "The Man Who Met Picasso," "Trojan Horse," "Dogfight" (written with William Gibson), "Covenant of Souls," "The Dragon Line," "Snow Angels," "A Midwinter's Tale," and many others—all of which earned him a reputation as one of the most powerful and consistently inventive short-story writers of his generation. Nor has his output of short fiction slackened noticeably in the nineties, in spite of a burgeoning career as a novelist, and recent years have seen the appearance of major Swanwick stories such as "The Edge of the World," "The Changeling's Tale," "Griffin's Egg," "Cold Iron," and "The Dead," which was on the final Hugo ballot in 1997 and is on the Nebula final ballot as I type these words in 1998; he remains one of SF's most prolific writers at short lengths, writing and selling seven or eight new stories in 1997 alone, for instance. By the end of the nineties, his short work had won him several *Asimov's* Reader's Awards, a Sturgeon Award, and the World Fantasy Award (for his bizarre and powerful after-death fantasy "Radio Waves").

At first, his reputation as a novelist lagged behind his reputation as a short-story writer, with his first novel, *In the Drift*—published in 1985 as part of Terry Carr's resurrected Ace Specials line, along with first novels by William Gibson, Kim Stanley Robinson, and Lucius Shepard—largely ignored by critics, and panned by some of them. His second novel, though, the critically acclaimed *Vacuum Flowers,* caused a stir, and his third and perhaps best-known novel, *Stations of the Tide,* established him firmly among the vanguard of the hot novelists of the nineties; *Stations of the Tide* won him a Nebula Award in 1991. His next novel, *The Iron Dragon's Daughter,* a finalist for both the World Fantasy Award *and* the Arthur C. Clarke Award (a unique distinction!), explored new literary territory on the ambiguous borderland of science fiction and fantasy, and has been hailed by some critics as the first example of an as yet still nascent subgenre called "Hard Fantasy" (sort of a mix between the Dickensian sensibilities of "steampunk," high-tech science fiction, and traditional Tolkienesque fantasy). His most recent novel, *Jack Faust,* a sly reworking of the Faust legend that explores the unexpected impact of technology on society, blurs genre boundaries even more, and has garnered rave reviews from nearly every source from *The Washington Post* to *Interzone*.

Swanwick is a chameleonic writer, difficult to pin down as belonging firmly to one aesthetic camp or another. He writes everything from hard-science to Tolkienesque fantasy, but puts his own unique spin on everything he writes. During the eighties, during the Cyberpunk Wars, most critics included him in the cyberpunk camp, although the cyberpunks themselves never really seemed to accept him as One of Them, in spite of his famous collaboration with Gibson on "Dogfight," and in spite of the fact that *Vacuum Flowers* is usually listed as part of the cyberpunk canon by outside critics who are not themselves cyberpunks— and indeed, whatever it was that he was doing that made him appear to some to be writing cyberpunk, he was doing it on his own in stories such as "Ginnungagap"—published in 1980—before the cyberpunks themselves were publishing much that looked like cyberpunk, certainly long before the publication of Gibson's *Neuromancer* in 1985. So it was a matter of convergent evolution rather than influence, I think, as far as Swanwick's relationship to cyberpunk is concerned. Similarly, Swanwick is now widely accepted as having written one of the two main "Post-Cyberpunk" works with *Stations of the Tide* (the other is Neal Stephenson's *Snow Crash*)—but if you go back and look at works such as "Ginnungagap," you can see that he was writing stuff that resembles "post-cyberpunk" *then,* before the Cyberpunk Revolution had even really gotten underway. So pinning him down to one of these categories is rather like trying to catch fog in a net.

This is not to say that there are no influences on his work. I think that recognizable traces of the influence of the work of writers such as Jack Vance, Cordwainer Smith, Brian W. Aldiss, Philip K. Dick, Howard Waldrop, Walter M. Miller, Jr., and Roger Zelazny can be seen in Swanwick's work, and perhaps even the influence of John Varley, although Varley started publishing only a few years before Swanwick himself did (influences turn over *fast* in the science fiction field!). Another big influence on Swanwick, as on Sterling, was clearly the early work of Samuel R. Delany; this is especially clear with the evocative story that follows, "The Blind Minotaur," which rings with strong echoes of Delany's work, particularly *The Einstein Intersection*—although, as always, Swanwick has changed the melody line and the orchestration and the fingering to make the material uniquely his own.

Although Swanwick's last few novels seem to be taking him away from science fiction (and perhaps even away from conventional genre fantasy toward that vaguely defined territory that might be described as "American Magic Realism," or perhaps "Postmodernism"), I don't think he will ever entirely abandon the field (at least some of his short fiction remains solidly centered here, and, in fact, falls under the heading of "hard science"), and it will be interesting to see what he produces the next time he returns to it at novel length. Like Sterling, Swanwick is also still a young writer by any reasonable definition, and I have a feeling he will be one of the factors shaping the evolution of SF well into the next century.

Swanwick's other books include the novella-length *Griffin's Egg*, one of the most brilliant and compelling of modern-day Moon-colony stories. His short fiction has been assembled in *Gravity's Angels* and in a collection of his collaborative short work with other writers, *Slow Dancing Through Time*. His most recent books are a collection of critical articles, *The Postmodern Archipelago,* and a new collection, *A Geography of Unknown Lands.* Swanwick lives in Philadelphia with his wife, Marianne Porter, and their son, Sean.

It was late afternoon when the blinded Minotaur was led through the waterfront. He cried openly, without shame, lost in his helplessness.

The sun cast shadows as crisp and black as an obsidian knife. Fisherfolk looked up from their nets or down from the masts of their boats, mild sympathy in their eyes. But not pity; memory of the Wars was too fresh for that. They were mortals and not subject to his tragedy.

Longshoremen stepped aside, fell silent at the passing of this shaggy bull-headed man. Offworld tourists stared down from their restaurant balconies at the serenely grave little girl who led him by the hand.

His sight stolen away, a new universe of sound, scent, and touch crashed about the Minotaur. It threatened to swallow him up, to drown him in its complexity.

There was the sea, always the sea, its endless crash and whisper on the beach, and quicker irregular slap at the docks. The sting of salt on his tongue. His callused feet fell clumsily on slick cobblestones, and one staggered briefly into a shallow puddle, muddy at its bottom, heated piss-warm by the sun.

He smelled creosoted pilings, exhaust fumes from the great shuttles bellowing skyward from the Starport, a horse sweating as it clipclopped by, pulling a groaning cart that reeked of the day's catch. From a nearby garage, there was the *snap* and ozone crackle of an arc-welding rig. Fishmongers' cries and the creaking of pitch-stained tackle overlaid rattling silverware from the terrace cafés, and fan-vented air rich with stews and squid and grease. And, of course, the flowers the little girl—was she really his daughter?—held crushed to her body with one arm. And the feel of her small hand in his, now going slightly slippery with sweat, but still cool, yes, and innocent.

This was not the replacement world spoken of and promised to the blind. It was chaotic and bewildering, rich and contradictory in detail. The universe had grown huge and infinitely complex with the dying of the light, and had made him small and helpless in the process.

The girl led him away from the sea, to the shabby buildings near the city's hot center. They passed through an alleyway between crumbling sheetbrick walls—he felt their roughness graze lightly against his flanks— and through a small yard ripe with fermenting garbage. The Minotaur stumbled down three wooden steps and into a room that smelled of sad, ancient paint. The floor was slightly gritty underfoot.

She walked him around the room. "This was built by expatriate Centaurimen," she explained. "So it's laid out around the kitchen in the center, *my* space to this side"—she let go of him briefly, rattled a vase, adding her

flowers to those he could smell as already present, took his hand again—
"and yours to this side."

He let himself be sat down on a pile of blankets, buried his head in his
arms while she puttered about, raising a wall, laying out a mat for him
under the window. "We'll get you some cleaner bedding in the morning,
okay?" she said. He did not answer. She touched a cheek with her tiny hand,
moved away.

"Wait," he said. She turned, he could hear her. "What—what is your
name?"

"Yarrow," she said.

He nodded, curled about himself.

By the time evening had taken the edge off the day, the Minotaur was
cried out. He stirred himself enough to strip off his loincloth and pull a
sheet over himself, and tried to sleep.

Through the open window the night city was coming to life. The Minotaur shifted as his sharp ears picked up drunken laughter, the calls of street-
walkers, the wail of jazz saxophone from a folk club, and music of a more
contemporary nature, hot and sinful.

His cock moved softly against one thigh, and he tossed and turned, kicking off the crisp sheet (it was linen, and it had to be white), agonized, remembering similar nights when he was whole.

The city called to him to come out and prowl, to seek out women who
were heavy and slatternly in the *tavernas*, cool and crisp in white, gazing out
from the balconies of their husbands' *casavillas*. But the power was gone
from him. He was no longer that creature that, strong and confident, had
quested into the night. He twisted and turned in the warm summer air.

One hand moved down his body, closed about his cock. The other joined
it. Squeezing tight his useless eyes, he conjured up women who had opened
to him, coral-pink and warm, as beautiful as orchids. Tears rolled down his
shaggy cheeks.

He came with great snorts and grunts.

Later he dreamed of being in a cool white *casavilla* by the sea, salt breeze
wafting in through open windowspaces. He knelt at the edge of a bed and
wonderingly lifted the sheet—it billowed slightly as he did—from his sleeping lover. Crouching before her naked body, his face was gentle as he mar-
veled at her beauty.

It was strange to wake to darkness. For a time he was not even certain he
was awake. And this was a problem, this unsureness, that would haunt him
for all his life. Today, though, it was comforting to think it all a dream, and
he wrapped the uncertainty around himself like a cloak.

The Minotaur found a crank recessed into the floor, and lowered the
wall. He groped his way to the kitchen, and sat by the cookfire.

"You jerked off three times last night," Yarrow said. "I could hear you."
He imagined that her small eyes were staring at him accusingly. But appar-

ently not, for she took something from the fire, set it before him, and innocently asked, "When are you going to get your eyes replaced?"

The Minotaur felt around for the platedough, and broke off a bit from the edge. "Immortals don't heal," he mumbled. He dipped the fragment into the paste she ladled onto the dough's center, stirred it about, let the bread drop. "New eyes would be rejected, didn't your mother tell you that?"

She chose not to answer. "While you were asleep, a newshawk came snooping around with that damned machine grafted to his shoulder. I told him he had the wrong place." Then, harshly, urgently, "Why won't they just leave you *alone?*"

"I'm an immortal," he said. "I'm not supposed to be left alone." Her mother really *should* have explained all this, if she was really what she claimed to be. Perhaps she wasn't; he would have sworn he had never bedded another of his kind, had in fact scrupulously avoided doing so. It was part of the plan of evasion that had served him well for so many years, and yet ended with his best friend dying in the sand at his feet.

Yarrow put some fragment of foodstuff in his hand, and he automatically placed it in his mouth. It was gummy and tasteless, and took forever to disappear. She was silent until he swallowed, and then asked, "Am I going to die?"

"What kind of question is that?" he asked angrily.

"Well, I just thought—my mother said that I was an immortal like her, and I thought . . . Isn't an immortal supposed to be someone who never dies?"

He opened his mouth to tell her that her mother should be hung up by her hair—and in that instant the day became inarguably, inalterably real. He wanted to cling to the possibility that it was all a dream for just a while longer, but it was gone. Wearily, he said, "Yarrow, I want you to go get me a robe. And a stick"—he raised a hand above his head—"so high. Got that?"

"Yes, but—"

"Go!"

A glimmering of his old presence must have still clung to him, for the child obeyed. The Minotaur leaned back, and—involuntarily—was flooded with memories.

He was young, less than a year released from the crèche by gracious permission of the ministries of the Lords. The Wars were less than a year away, but the Lords had no way of knowing that—the cabarets were full, and the starlanes swollen with the fruits of a thousand remarkable harvests. There had never been such a rich or peaceful time.

The Minotaur was drunk, and at the end of his nightly round of bars. He had wound up in a *taverna* where the patrons removed their shirts to dance and sweet-smelling sweat glistened on their chests. The music was fast and heavy and sensual. Women eyed him as he entered, but could not politely approach him, for he still wore his blouse.

He bellied up to the bar, and ordered a jarful of the local beer. The barkeep frowned when he did not volunteer money, but that was his right as an immortal.

Crouched on their ledge above the bar, the musicians were playing hot and furious. The Minotaur paid them no attention. Nor did he notice the Harlequin, limbs long and impossibly thin, among them, nor how the Harlequin's eyes followed his every move.

The Minotaur was entranced by the variety of women in the crowd, the differences in their movements. He had been told that one could judge how well a woman made love by how well she danced, but it seemed to him, watching, that there must be a thousand styles of making love, and he would be hard put to choose among them, were the choice his.

One woman with flashing brown feet stared at him, ignoring her partner. She wore a bright red skirt that flew up to her knees when she whirled around, and her nipples were hard and black. He smiled in friendly cognizance of her glance, and her answering grin was a razor-crisp flash of teeth that took his breath away, a predatory look that said: *You're* mine *tonight*.

Laughing, the Minotaur flung his shirt into the air. He plunged into the dancers and stooped at the woman's feet. In a rush he lifted her into the air, away from her partner, one hand closing about her ankles, the other supporting her by the small of her back. She gasped, and laughed, and balanced herself, so that he could remove one hand and lift her still higher, poised with one foot on the palm of his great hairy hand.

"I am strong!" he shouted. The crowd—even the woman's abandoned partner—cheered and stamped their feet. The Harlequin stepped up the band. The woman lifted her skirts and kicked her free leg high, so that one toe grazed the ceiling beams. She threw her head back and laughed.

The dancers swirled about them. For a single pure moment, life was bright and full and good. And then . . .

A touch of cool air passed through the crowd. A chance movement, a subtle shifting of colors, brought the Minotaur's eyes around to the door. A flash of artificial streetlight dazzled and was gone as the door swung shut.

The Woman entered.

She was masked in silver filigree, and her breasts were covered. Red silk washed from shoulder to ankle, now caressing a thigh, now releasing it. Her eyes were a drenched, saturated green. She walked with a sure and sensual authority, knowing the dancers would part for her. No one could mistake her for a mortal.

The Minotaur was stunned. Chemical and hormonal balances shifted in preparation for the bonding to come. Nerveless, his arms fell to his sides. With an angry squawk, the woman he had hoisted into the air leapt, arms waving, to avoid falling. The Minotaur did not notice. He stepped forward, eyes wide and helpless, toward the immortal.

The silver mask headed straight for him. Green eyes mocked, challenged, promised.

Behind him, unnoticed, the Harlequin slipped to the floor. He wrapped long fingers lovingly around a length of granite pipe, and brought it down, fast and surprisingly forcefully, into the back of the Minotaur's neck.

Bright shards of light flashed before the Minotaur's eyes. The dance floor washed out and faded to white. He fell.

At the Minotaur's direction, Yarrow led him out to the bluffs on the outskirts of the city. There was a plaza there, overlooking the ocean. He sent the child away.

Though his every bone protested, he slowly crouched, and then carefully spread out a small white cloth before him. He was a beggar now.

Salt breezes gusted up from the ocean, and he could feel the cobalt sky above, and the cool cumulus clouds that raced across the sun. There were few passersby, mostly dirt farmers who were not likely to be generous. Perhaps once an hour a small ceramic coin fell on his cloth.

But that was how he preferred it. He had no interest in money, was a beggar only because his being demanded a role to play. He had come to remember, and to prepare himself for death by saying farewell to the things of life.

Times had changed. There was a stone altar set in the center of this very plaza where children had been sacrificed. He had seen it himself, the young ones taken from their homes or schooling-places by random selection of the cruel Lords. They had shrieked like stuck pigs when the gold-masked priests raised their bronze knives to the noonday sun. The crowds were always large at these events. The Minotaur was never able to determine whether the parents were present or not.

This was only one of the means the Lords had of reminding their subjects that to be human was often painful or tragic.

"Let's not sleep the day away, eh? Time to start rehearsing."

The Minotaur awoke to find himself sprawled on the wooden floor of a small caravan. The Harlequin, sitting cross-legged beside him, thrust a jar of wine into his hand.

Groggily, the Minotaur focused his eyes on the Harlequin. He reached for the man's neck, only to find one hand taken up by the winejar. He squinted at it. The day was already hot, and his throat as dry as the Severna. His body trembled from the aftereffects of its raging hormonal storm. He lifted the wine to his lips.

Chemical imbalances shifted, found a new equilibrium.

"Bravo!" The Harlequin hauled the Minotaur to his feet, clapped him on the back. "We'll be famous friends, you and I. With luck, we may even keep each other alive, eh?"

It was a new idea to the Minotaur, and a disquieting, perhaps even blasphemous, one. But he grinned shyly, and dipped his head. He *liked* the little fellow. "Sure," he said.

The sun was setting. The Minotaur felt the coolness coming off of the sea, heard the people scurrying to their homes. He carefully tied the ceramics into his cloth, and knotted it onto his belt. He stood, leaning wearily on his staff. Yarrow had not yet come for him, and he was glad; he hoped she had gone off on her own, forgotten him, left him behind forever. But the city's rhythms demanded that he leave, though he had nowhere to go, and he obeyed.

He went down into the city, taking the turns by random whim. He could not be said to be lost, for one place was as good as another to him.

It was by mistake, though, that he found himself in a building whose doors were never shut, whose windows were not shuttered. He had entered, thinking the way yet another alley. No doors barred progress down halls or into rooms. Still, he felt closed in. The corridors smelled—there was the male stench and the female, and intermingled with them, almost overpowering, an insect smell, the odor of something large and larval.

He stopped. Things stirred about him. There was the pat of bare feet on stone, the slow breathing of many people, and—again—a sluggish movement of creatures larger than anything smelling thus should be. People were gathering; twelve, eighteen, more. They surrounded him. He could tell they were all naked, for there was not the whisper of cloth on cloth. Some walked as if they had almost forgotten how. In the distance, he thought he could hear someone crawling.

"Who are you?" Panic touched him lightly; sourceless, pure.

"Whrrarrwr," began one of the people. He stopped, swallowed, tried again. "Why are you in the Hive?" His voice sounded forced, as if he were unused to speech. "Why are you here? You are a creature of the old days, of the Lords. This is no place for you."

"I took a wrong turn," the Minotaur said simply. Then, when there was no reply, "Who are you people? Why do you cohabit with insects?"

Someone coughed and sputtered and made hacking noises. A second joined her, making the same sounds, and then others, and yet more. With a start, the Minotaur realized they were laughing at him. "Is it religious or political?" he demanded. "Are you seeking transcendence?"

"We are trying to become victims," the speaker said. "Does that help you understand?" He was growing angry. "How can we explain ourselves to you, Old Fossil? You never performed a free act in your life."

Some whim, then, of internal chemistry made him want these strangers, these creatures, to understand him. It was the same compulsion that had forced him to empty himself to the newshawks before Yarrow appeared to lead him out of the arena.

"I had a friend, another immortal," the Minotaur said. "Together, we cheated the patterning instinct by making our own pattern, a safe, strong one, we were like"—his short, powerful fingers joined, closing around the staff, intermeshing—"like *this*, you see. And it worked, it worked for years. It was only when our predators worked *within* the patterns we formed that we were destroyed." The words gushed out, and he trembled as the hormones that might give him the power to explain *almost* keyed in.

But the communards did not want to understand. They closed in on him, their laughter growing sharper, with more of a bark, more of a bite to it. Their feeble footsteps paltered closer, and behind them the chitinous whine grew louder, was joined by that of more insects, and more, until all the world seemed to buzz. The Minotaur flinched back.

And then they seemed to hesitate in confusion. They milled about uncertainly for a moment, then parted, and quick, small footsteps passed through them, ran to his side. A cool, smooth hand took his.

"Come home with me," Yarrow said. And he followed.

He dreamed of the arena that night, of the hot white sands underfoot that drank up his friend's blood. The Harlequin's body lay limp at his feet, and the bronze knife was as heavy as guilt in his hands.

It was as if his eyes had opened, as if he were seeing clearly for the first time. He stared around the encircling bleachers, and every detail burned into his brain.

The people were graceful and well-dressed; they might almost have been the old Lords, deposed these many years ago in violent public revulsion. The Woman sat ringside. Her silver mask rested lightly on the lip of the white limestone wall, beside a small bowl of orange ices. She held a spoon in her hand, cocked lightly upward.

The Minotaur stared into her blazing green eyes, and read in them a fierce triumph, an obscene gloating, a very specific and direct lust. She had hunted him out of hiding, stripped him of his protection, and chivvied him into the open. She had forced him to rise to his destiny. To enter the arena.

Try though he might, the Minotaur could not awaken. If he had not known all this to be a dream, he would have gone mad.

Waking, he found himself already dressed, the last bit of breakfast in his hand. He dropped it, unnerved by this transition. Yarrow was cleaning the kitchen walls, singing an almost tuneless made-up song under her breath.

"Why aren't you out being taught?" he demanded, trying to cover over his unease with words. She stopped singing. "Well? Answer me!"

"I'm learning from you," she said quietly.

"Learning what?" She did not answer. "Learning how to tend to a cripple? Or maybe how a beggar lives? Hey? What could you possibly learn from me?"

She flung a wet cloth to the floor. "You won't tell me anything," she cried. "I ask you and you won't tell me."

"Go home to your mother," he said.

"I can't." She was crying now. "She told me to take care of you. She said not to come back until my task was done."

The Minotaur bowed his head. Whatever else she might or might not be, the mother had the casual arrogance of an immortal. Even he could be surprised by it.

"Why won't you tell me anything?"

"Go and fetch me my stick."

. . .

Bleak plains dominated the southern continent, and the Minotaur came to know them well. The carnival worked the long route, the four-year circuit of small towns running up the coast and then inland to the fringes of the Severna Desert.

Creeping across the plains, the carnival was small, never more than eight hands of wagons and often fewer. But when the paper lanterns had been lit, the fairway laid out, the holographic-woven canvases blazing neon-bright, they created a fantasy city that stretched to the edge of forever.

The Minotaur grunted. Muscles glistening, he bent the metal bar across his chest. Portions of the audience were breathing heavily.

It was the last performance of the evening. Outside the hot, crowded tent, the fairgoers were thinning, growing quieter. The Minotaur was clad only in a stained white loincloth. He liked to have room to sweat.

Applause. He threw the bar to the stage and shouted: "My last stunt! I'll need five volunteers!" He chose the four heaviest, and the one who blushed most prettily. Her he helped up on the stage, and set in the middle of the lifting bench, a pair of hefty *bouergers* to either side.

The Minotaur slid his head under the bench. His face emerged between the young woman's legs, and she shrieked and drew them up on the bench. The audience howled. He rolled his eyes, flared his nostrils. And indeed, she did have a pleasant scent.

He dug into the stage with naked toes, placed his hands carefully. With a grunt, the Minotaur lifted the bench a handsbreath off the floor. It wobbled slightly, and he shifted his weight in compensation. A surge—he was crouching.

Sweat poured down the Minotaur's face, and ran in rivulets from his armpits. The tent was saturated with the sweet smell, redolent with his pheromones. He felt a light touch on his muzzle. The woman on the bench had reached down to caress his nose with quick, shy fingertips. The Minotaur quirked a half-grin on one side of his mouth.

By the tent flap, the Harlequin lounged on a wooden crate, cleaning his toenails with a knife. They had a date with a sculptor in town after the show.

The Minotaur awoke suddenly, reached out and touched the cloth laid out before him. There was nothing on it, though he distinctly remembered having heard ceramics fall earlier. He swept his hands in great arcs in the dust, finding nothing.

Snickers and derisive jeers sounded from the stone in the plaza's center. Small feet scurried away—children running to deliver the swag to their masters. "Little snots," the Minotaur grumbled. They were an ever-present nuisance, like sparrows. He fell back into his daydreaming.

The sculptor had had stone jugs of wine sent up. By orgy's end they were empty, and the women lay languid on the sheets of their couches. They all stared upward, watching the bright explosions in space, like slow-blossoming flowers. "What do they hope to accomplish, these rebels?" the Minotaur asked wonderingly. "I can see no pattern to their destruction."

"Why should a man like you—a *real* man—look any higher than his waist?" the sculptor asked coarsely. He laid a hand on the Minotaur's knee. His lady of the moment laughed throatily, reached back over her head to caress his beard.

"I'd just like to know."

The Harlequin had been perched on the wall. He leapt down now, and tossed the Minotaur his clothes. "Time we went home," he said.

The streets were dark and still, but there were people in the shadows, silently watching the skies. The sidestreet cabarets were uncharacteristically crowded. They stopped in several on their way back to the carnival.

The Minotaur was never sure at exactly what point they picked up the woman with skin the color of orange brick. She was from offworld, she said, and needed a place to hide. Her hands were callused and beautiful from work. The Minotaur liked her strong, simple dignity.

Back at the carnival, the Harlequin offered their wagon, and the woman refused. The Minotaur said that he would sleep on the ground, it didn't bother him, and she changed her mind.

Still, he was not surprised when, sometime later, she joined him under the wagon.

The sun hot on his forehead, the Minotaur again dreamed of the arena. He did not relive the murder—that memory had been driven from his mind, irretrievably burned away, even in dream. But he remembered the killing rage that drove the knife upward, the insane fury that propelled his hand. And afterward he stood staring into the Woman's eyes.

Her eyes were as green as oceans, and as complex, but easy to read for all that. The lusts and rages, and fears and evil, grasping desire that had brought them all to this point—they were all there, and they were . . . insignificant. For the true poisoned knowledge was that she was lost in her own chemical-hormonal storm, her body trembling almost imperceptibly, all-but-invisible flecks of foam on her lips. She had run not only him, but herself as well, to the blind end of a tangled and malignant fate. She was as much a puppet as he or the Harlequin.

There, on the burning sands, he tore out his eyes.

The newshawks vaulted the fence to get at him. His drama completed, he was fair game. They probed, scanned, recorded—prodded to find the least significant detail of a story that might be told over campfires a thousand years hence, in theatrical productions on worlds not yet discovered, in uninvented media, or possibly merely remembered in times of stress. Trying to get in on a story that might have meaning to the human race as it grew away from its homeworld, forgot its origins, expanded and evolved and changed in ways that could not be predicted or prepared for.

They questioned the Minotaur for hot grueling hours. The corpse of his friend began to rot, or perhaps that was only olfactory hallucination, a side effect of his mind telling his body that it had no further purpose. He felt dizzy and without hope, and he *could not* express his grief, *could not* cry, *could not* scream or rage or refuse their questions or even move away until they were done with him.

And then a cool hand slipped into his, and tugged him away. A small voice said, "Come home, Papa," and he went.

Yarrow was screaming. The Minotaur awoke suddenly, on his feet and slashing his stick before him, back and forth in pure undirected reaction. "Yarrow?" he cried.

"No!" the child shrieked in anger and panic. Someone slapped her face so hard she fell. The sound echoed from the building walls. "Fuckpigs!" she swore from the ground.

The Minotaur lurched toward her, and someone tripped him up, so that he crashed onto the road. He heard a rib crack. He felt a trickle of blood from one nostril. And he heard laughter, the laughter of madwomen. And under that he heard the creaking of leather harness, the whirring of tiny pumps, the metal snicks of complex machinery.

There was no name for them, these madwomen, though their vice was not rare. They pumped themselves full of the hormone drugs that had once been the exclusive tools of the Lords, but they used them randomly, to no purpose. Perhaps—the Minotaur could not imagine, did not care—they enjoyed the jolts of power and importance, of sheer godlike caprice.

He was on his feet. The insane ones—there were three, he could tell by their sick laughter—ignored him. "What are you doing?" he cried. "Why are you doing it?" They were dancing, arms linked, about the huddled child. She was breathing shallowly, like a hypnotized animal.

"Why?" asked the one. "Why do you ask why?" and convulsed in giggles.

"We are all frogs!" laughed the second.

Yarrow lay quietly now, intimidated not so much by the women's hyperadrenal strength as by the pattern of victim laid out for her. There were microtraces of hormones in the air, leaks from the chemical pumps.

"She has interesting glands," said the third. "We can put their secretions to good use."

The Minotaur roared and rushed forward. They yanked the stick from his hand and broke it over his head. He fell against the altar stone, hard, nearly stunning himself.

"We need to use that stone," said a madwoman. And when he did not move away, said, "Well, we'll wait."

But again the Minotaur forced himself to stand. He stepped atop the stone. Something profound was happening deep within him, something beyond his understanding. Chemical keys were locking into place, hormones shifting into balance. Out of nowhere his head was filled with eloquence.

"Citizens!" he cried. He could hear the people at their windows, in their doorways, watching and listening, though with no great interest. They had not interfered to save Yarrow. The Lords would have interfered, and human society was still in reaction to the rule of the Lords. "Awake! Your freedom is being stolen from you!"

A lizard, startled, ran over the Minotaur's foot, as quick and soft as a shiver. The words poured from him in a cold fever, and he could hear the householders straighten, lean forward, step hesitantly out onto the cobblestones. "No one is above you now," he shouted. "But I still see the dead hands of the Lords on your shoulders."

That got to them—he could smell their anger. His throat was dry, but he dared not spare the time to cough. His head was light, and a cool breeze stirred his curls. He spoke, but did not listen to the words.

Yarrow was lost, somewhere on the plaza. As he spoke, the Minotaur listened for her, sniffed the air, felt for vibrations through the stone—and could not find her. "Inaction is a greater tyrant than error ever was!" he cried, listening to heads nodding agreement with the old familiar homily. He could hear the frantic hopping motions the madwomen made, forward and back again, baffled and half-fascinated by the hormones he was generating, by the cadences and odd rhythms of his words.

The speech was a compulsion, and the Minotaur paid it no more mind than he did to the sliding of muscles under skin that went into his gestures, some wide and sweeping, others short and blunt. A whiff of girlish scent finally located Yarrow, not two arm's lengths away, but he could not go to her. The words would not release him, not until he had spoken them all.

And when, finally, he lowered his arms, the plaza was filled with people, and the madwomen's harnesses had been ripped from them, the drug pumps smashed underfoot, their necks snapped quickly and without malice.

He turned to Yarrow, offered his hand. "Come," he said. "It's time to go home."

The Minotaur lay belly-down on the earth under the wagon. He stared down his muzzle at a slice of early-morning sky framed by two wheel spokes. The clouds of energy were still slowly dissipating. "I'd love to go out there," he said. "To see other worlds."

The orange-skinned woman scratched him above the ears, at the base of his small ivory horns. Her hands were strong and sure. "They couldn't refuse you passage. What's stopping you?"

He nodded upward. "He gets sick—I'd have to go alone."

A triceratops beetle crept laboriously past his nose. He exhaled sharply, trying to turn it over, failed. "You two are inseparable, aren't you?" the woman asked.

The beetle was getting away. He snorted sharply again, twice. "I guess."

"Won't he be upset that I chose you over him?"

It took the Minotaur a moment to puzzle out her meaning. "Ah! You mean—I see. Good joke, very good joke!" He laughed without taking his eyes away from the beetle, watched it escape into the grass. "No, the Harlequin doesn't know that women are important."

• • •

It did not take long to gather belongings: the Minotaur had none and Yarrow few. "You can find your mother?" he asked her. They left the door open behind them, an old Centaurimen custom at final partings.

"I can always find my mother," Yarrow said.

"Good." Still, he did not let her go. He led her by the hand back along the waterfront. There, among the sounds and smells, the subliminal tastes and touches that had grown familiar to him, he leaned forward to kiss her tenderly on the cheeks and forehead.

"Good-bye," he said. "I am proud that you are my daughter."

Yarrow did not move away. There was a slight tremble in her voice when she spoke. "You still haven't *told* me anything."

"Ah," the Minotaur said. For a moment he was silent, mentally cataloging what she would need to know. The history of the Lords, to begin with. Their rise to power, how they had shaped and orchestrated the human psyche, and why they thought the human race had to be held back. She needed to know of the crèches, of their bioprogramming chemicals, and of those immortals released from them who had gone on to become legend. She needed to know everything about the immortals, in fact, for the race had been all but exterminated in the Wars. And how the Lords had endured as long as they had. How their enemies had turned their toys against them. All the history of the Wars. It would not be a short telling.

"Sit down," he commanded. There, in the center of the thoroughfare, he sat, and Yarrow followed.

The Minotaur opened his mouth to speak. At the sound of his words, resonant and deep, people would stop to listen for the briefest second . . . for just a moment longer . . . they would sit down in the road. The hormonal combinations that enforced strictest truth before the newshawks were to be in his voice, but combined with the strong eloquence of earlier in the day. He would speak plainly, with a fine parsimony of syllables. He would speak in strict accord with the ancient oratorical traditions. He would speak with tongues of fire.

The waterfront would fill and then overflow as people entered and did not leave, as they joined the widening circle of hushed listeners, as the fisherfolk came up from their boats and down from their masts, the boy prostitutes came out from the brothels, the offworld *tourista* joined with the kitchen help to lean over the edges of their terraces.

In future years this same telling, fined down and refined, elaborated and simplified, would become the epic that was to mark this age—his age—as great for its genesis. But what was to come in just a moment was only a first draft. A prototype. A seed. But it was to be beautiful and moving beyond all possible imagining of its listeners, for it was new, an absolutely new word, a clear new understanding. It was to sum up an age that most people did not realize was over.

"Listen," said the Minotaur.

He spoke.

THE BLABBER

Born in Waukesha, Wisconsin, Vernor Vinge now lives in San Diego, California, where he is an associate professor of math sciences at San Diego State University. He sold his first story, "Apartness," to *New Worlds* in 1965; it immediately attracted a good deal of attention, was picked up for Donald A. Wollheim and Terry Carr's collaborative *World's Best Science Fiction* anthology the following year, and still strikes me as one of the strongest stories of that entire period, holding up well even in comparison with more famous stories also reprinted in that same anthology, such as Clarke's "Sunjammer" or Ellison's " 'Repent, Harlequin!' Said the Ticktockman." Since this impressive debut, he has become a frequent contributor to *Analog;* he has also sold to *Orbit, Far Frontiers, If, Stellar,* and other markets. His novella "True Names" was a finalist for both the Nebula and Hugo awards in 1981, his novel *A Fire Upon the Deep,* one of the most epic and sweeping of modern Space Operas, won him a Hugo Award in 1993, and these days Vinge is regarded as one of the best of the new breed of American "hard science" writers, along with people such as Charles Sheffield and Greg Bear.

Vinge is not a prolific writer, although the few stories he does produce usually have a strong impact on the field. "True Names," for instance, is famous in Internet circles and among computer enthusiasts well outside of the usual limits of the genre, and is cited by some as having been the *real* progenitor of cyberpunk rather than William Gibson's "Burning Chrome" or *Neuromancer.* Certainly, at the very least, it can be said to have prefigured many of the tropes of "cyberspace" before Gibson got there, although it lacks the aesthetic/political "punk" flavor of Gibson's work, as well as the intensely romantic and attractive archetype of the Gibson Hero, an alienated hacker/cowboy who must go down the Mean Streets of the future all alone—both elements which helped to make Gibson's stuff the cult favorite that it became. "True Names" has an even better claim to being one of the first Virtual Reality stories and, as such, the progenitor of a host of "computer gaming/VR" stories that would follow in years to come.

Adventure elements have always been strong in Vinge's work, from "Apartness" through such stories as "The Barbarian Princess," "Gemstone," and "Grimm's World" (later expanded into the novel *Tatja Grimm's World*), on to novels such as *The Witling* and *A Fire Upon the Deep.* Seldom has he—or anybody else—put everything together better, though, than in the fast-paced, colorful, highly inventive novella that follows, "The Blabber." The influence of Robert A. Heinlein is strong and obvious here—in fact, the story is in part an undisguised homage to Heinlein's *The Star Beast,* which novel is specifically invoked in the text—although traces of the influence of Larry Niven, Poul Anderson, Charles

Harness, and perhaps Roger Zelazny (whose influence shows up even more clearly in "True Names," I think) can be discerned as well. Although consciously modeled on the plot of *The Star Beast,* Vinge does some exciting new things with this familiar story, as well as a lot of shrewd and radical new thinking about what interstellar societies would *really* be like, thinking that prefigures his well-known speculations about "The Singularity" (the point waiting ahead for us all where technological change speeds up to *such* a degree that society becomes incomprehensible even to the people living in it)—and thinking that would perhaps have as great an impact (although a largely unacknowledged one) on future Space Adventure stories as "True Names" had had on the Virtual Reality tale.

Vinge's other books include the well-received novels *The Peace War* and *Marooned in Realtime,* Hugo finalists, which have been released in an omnibus volume as *Across Realtime,* and two short-story collections, *True Names and Other Dangers,* and *Threats and Other Promises.* He has not published a new novel since *A Fire Upon the Deep,* but the current word is that a new novel entitled *A Deepness in the Sky* will be out soon. His fans wait eagerly for it—as do I.

Some dreams take a long time in dying. Some get a last-minute reprieve . . . and that can be even worse.

It was just over two klicks from the Elvis revival to the center of campus. Hamid Thompson took the long way, across the Barker's stubbly fields and through the Old Subdivision. Certainly the Blabber preferred that route. She raced this way and that across Ham's path, rooting at roach holes, and covertly watching the birds that swooped close on her seductive calls. As usual, her stalking was more for fun than food. When a bird came within striking distance, the Blab's head would flick up, touching the bird with her nose, blasting it with a peal of human laughter. The Blab hadn't taken this way in some time; all the birds in her regular haunts had wised up, and were no fun anymore.

When they reached the rock bluffs behind the subdivision, there weren't any more roach holes, and the birds had become cautious. Now the Blab walked companionably beside him, humming in her own way: scraps of Elvis overlaid with months-old news commentary. She went a minute or two in silence . . . listening? Contrary to what her detractors might say, she could be both awake and silent for hours at a time—but even then Hamid felt an occasional buzzing in his head, or a flash of pain. The Blab's tympana could emit across a two hundred kilohertz band, which meant that most of her mimicry was lost on human ears.

They were at the crest of the bluff. "Sit down, Blab. I want to catch my breath." *And look at the view . . . And decide what in heaven's name I should do with you and with me.*

The bluffs were the highest natural viewpoints in New Michigan province. The flatlands that spread around them were pocked with ponds, laced with creeks and rivers, the best farmland on the continent. From orbit, the original colonists could find no better. Water landings would have been easier, but they wanted the best odds on long-term survival. Thirty klicks away, half hidden by gray mist, Hamid could see the glassy streaks that marked the landing zone. The history books said it took three years to bring down the people and all the salvage from the greatship. Even now the glass was faintly radioactive, one cause for the migration across the isthmus to Westland.

Except for the forest around those landing strips, and the old university town just below the bluff, most everything in this direction was farmland, unending squares of brown and black and gray. The year was well into autumn and the last of the Earth trees had given up their colored leaves. The wind blowing across the plains was chill, leaving a crispness in his nose that promised snow someday soon. Halloween was next week. Halloween indeed. *I wonder if in Man's thirty thousand years, there has ever been a celebration of that holiday like we'll be seeing next week.* Hamid resisted the impulse to look back at Marquette. Ordinarily it was one of his favorite places: the planetary capital, population four hundred thousand, a real city. As a child, visiting Marquette had been like a trip to some far star system. But now reality had come, and the stars were so *close*. . . . Without turning, he knew the position of every one of the Tourist barges. They floated like colored balloons above the city, yet none massed less than a thousand tonnes. And those were their *shuttles*. After the Elvis revival, Halloween was the last big event on the Marquette leg of the Tour. Then they would be off to Westland, for more semi-fraudulent peeks at Americana.

Hamid crunched back in the dry moss that cushioned the rock. "Well, Blabber, what should I do? Should I sell you? We could both make it Out There if I did."

The Blabber's ears perked up. "Talk? Converse? Disgust?" She settled her forty kilo bulk next to him, and nuzzled her head against his chest. The purring from her foretympanum was like some transcendental cat. The sound was pink noise, buzzing through his chest and shaking the rock they sat on. There were few things she enjoyed more than a good talk with a peer. Hamid stroked her black and white pelt. "I said, should I sell you?"

The purring stopped, and for a moment the Blab seemed to give the matter thoughtful consideration. Her head turned this way and that, bobbing—a good imitation of a certain prof at the University. She rolled her big dark eyes at him, "Don't rush me! I'm thinking. I'm thinking." She licked daintily at the sleek fur at the base of her throat. And for all Hamid knew, she really seemed to try to understand . . . and sometimes she almost made sense. Finally she shut her mouth and began talking.

"Should I sell you? Should I sell you?" The intonation was still Hamid's but she wasn't imitating his voice. When they talked like this, she typically sounded like an adult human female (and a very attractive one, Hamid thought). It hadn't always been that way. When she had been a pup and he a little boy, she'd sounded to him like another little boy. The strategy was clear: she understood the type of voice he most likely wanted to hear. Animal cunning? "Well," she continued, "*I* know what *I* think. Buy, don't sell. And always get the best price you can."

She often came across like that: oracular. But he had known the Blab all his life. The longer her comment, the less she understood it. In this case . . . Ham remembered his finance class. That was before he got his present apartment, and the Blab had hidden under his desk part of the semester. (It had been an exciting semester for all concerned.) "Buy, don't sell." That was a quote, wasn't it, from some nineteenth-century tycoon?

She blabbered on, each sentence having less correlation with the question. After a moment, Hamid grabbed the beast around the neck, laughing and crying at the same time. They wrestled briefly across the rocky slope, Hamid fighting at less than full strength, and the Blab carefully keeping her talons retracted. Abruptly he was on his back and the Blab was standing on his chest. She held his nose between the tips of her long jaws. "Say Uncle! Say Uncle!" she shouted.

The Blabber's teeth stopped a couple of centimeters short of the end of her snout, but the grip was powerful; Hamid surrendered immediately. The Blab jumped off him, chuckling triumph, then grabbed his sleeve to help him up. He stood up, rubbing his nose gingerly. "Okay, monster, let's get going." He waved downhill, toward Ann Arbor Town.

"Ha, ha! For sure. Let's get going!" The Blab danced down the rocks faster than he could hope to go. Yet every few seconds the creature paused an instant, checking that he was still following. Hamid shook his head, and started down. Damned if he was going to break a leg just to keep up with her. Whatever her homeworld, he guessed that winter around Marquette was the time of year most homelike for the Blab. Take her coloring: stark black and white, mixed in wide curves and swirls. He'd seen that pattern in pictures of ice pack seals. When there was snow on the ground, she was practically invisible.

She was fifty meters ahead of him now. From this distance, the Blab could almost pass for a dog, some kind of greyhound maybe. But the paws were too large, and the neck too long. The head looked more like a seal's than a dog's. Of course, she could bark like a dog. But then, she could also sound like a thunderstorm, and make something like human conversation— all at the same time. There was only one of her kind in all Middle America. This last week, he'd come to learn that her kind were almost as rare Out There. A Tourist wanted to buy her . . . and Tourists could pay with coin what Hamid Thompson had sought for more than half his twenty years.

Hamid desperately needed some good advice. It had been five years since he'd asked his father for help; he'd be damned if he did so now. That left the University, and Lazy Larry. . . .

By Middle American standards, Ann Arbor Town was *ancient*. There were older places: out by the landing zone, parts of Old Marquette still stood. School field trips to those ruins were brief—the prefab quonsets were mildly radioactive. And of course there was individual buildings in the present-day capital that went back almost to the beginning. But much of the University in Ann Arbor dated from just after those first permanent structures: the University had been a going concern for 190 years.

Something was up today, and it had nothing to do with Hamid's problems. As they walked into town, a couple of police helicopters swept in from Marquette, began circling the school. On the ground, some of Ham's favorite back ways were blocked off by University safety patrols. No doubt it was Tourist business. He might have to come in through the Main Gate, past the Math Building. *Yuck.* Even after ten years he loathed that place: his years as a supposed prodigy; his parents forcing him into math classes he just wasn't bright enough to handle; the tears and anger at home, till he finally convinced them that he was not the boy they thought.

They walked around the Quad, Hamid oblivious to the graceful buttresses, the ivy that meshed stone walls into the flute trees along the street. That was all familiar . . . what was new was all the Federal cop cars. Clusters of students stood watching the cops, but there was no riot in the air. They just seemed curious. Besides, the Feds had never interfered on campus before.

"Keep quiet, okay?" Hamid muttered.

"Sure, sure." The Blab scrunched her neck back, went into her doggie act. At one time they had been notorious on campus, but he had dropped out that summer, and people had other things on their minds today. They walked through the main gate without comment from students or cops.

The biggest surprise came when they reached Larry's slummy digs at Morale Hall. Morale wasn't old enough to be historic; it was old enough to be in decay. It had been an abortive experiment in brick construction. The clay had cracked and rotted, leaving gaps for vines and pests. By now it was more a reddish mound of rubble than a habitable structure. This was where the University Administration stuck tenured faculty in greatest disfavor; the Quad's Forgotten Quarter . . . but not today. Today the cop cars were piled two deep in the parking areas, and there were shotgun-toting guards at the entrance!

Hamid walked up the steps. He had a sick feeling that Lazy Larry might be the hardest prof in the world to see today. On the other hand, working with the Tourists meant Hamid saw some of these security people every day.

"Your business, sir?" Unfortunately, the guard was no one he recognized.

"I need to see my advisor . . . Professor Fujiyama." Larry had never been his advisor, but Hamid was looking for advice.

"Um." The cop flicked on his throat mike. Hamid couldn't hear much, but there was something about "that black and white off-planet creature." Over the last twenty years, you'd have to have been living in a cave never to see anything about the Blabber.

A minute passed, and an older officer stepped through the doorway.

"Sorry, son, Mr. Fujiyama isn't seeing any students this week. Federal business."

Somewhere a funeral dirge began playing. Hamid tapped the Blab's forepaw with his foot; the music stopped abruptly. "Ma'am, it's not school business." Inspiration struck: why not tell something like the truth? "It's about the Tourists and my Blabber."

The senior cop sighed. "That's what I was afraid you'd say. Okay, come along." As they entered the dark hallway, the Blabber was chuckling triumph. Someday the Blab would play her games with the wrong people and get the crap beat out of her, but apparently today was not that day.

They walked down two flights of stairs. The lighting got even worse, half-dead fluorescents built into the acoustic tiling. In places the wooden stairs sagged elastically under their feet. There were no queues of students squatting before any of the doors, but the cops hadn't cleared out the faculty: Hamid heard loud snoring from one of the offices. The Forgotten Quarter—Morale Hall in particular—was a strange place. The one thing the faculty here had in common was that they had been an unbearable pain in the neck to someone. That meant that both the most incompetent and the most brilliant were jammed into these tiny offices.

Larry's office was in the sub-basement, at the end of a long hall. Two more cops flanked the doorway, but otherwise it was as Hamid remembered it. There was a brass nameplate: "Professor L. Lawrence Fujiyama, Department of Transhuman Studies." Next to the nameplate, a sign boasted implausible office hours. In the center of the door was the picture of a piglet and the legend: "If a student appears to need help, then appear to give him some."

The police officer stood aside as they reached the door; Hamid was going to have to get in under his own power. Ham gave the door a couple of quick knocks. There was the sound of footsteps, and the door opened a crack. "What's the secret password?" came Larry's voice.

"Professor Fujiyama, I need to talk to—"

"That's not it!" The door was slammed loudly in Hamid's face.

The senior cop put her hand on Hamid's shoulder. "Sorry, son. He's done that to bigger guns than you."

He shrugged off her hand. Sirens sounded from the black and white creature at his feet. Ham shouted over the racket, "Wait! It's me, Hamid Thompson! From your Transhume 201."

The door came open again. Larry stepped out, glanced at the cops, then looked down at the Blabber. "Well, why didn't you say so? Come on in." As Hamid and the Blab scuttled past him, Larry smiled innocently at the Federal officer. "Don't worry, Susie, this is official business."

Fujiyama's office was long and narrow, scarcely an aisle between deep equipment racks. Larry's students (those who dared these depths) doubted the man could have survived on Old Earth before electronic datastorage. There must be tonnes of junk squirreled away on those shelves. The gadgets stuck out this way and that into the aisle. The place was a museum—perhaps literally; one of Larry's specialties was archeology. Most of the machines were dead, but here and there something clicked, something glowed. Some of the gadgets were Rube Goldberg jokes, some were early colonial prototypes . . . and a few were from Out There. Steam and water pipes covered much of the ceiling. The place reminded Hamid of the inside of a submarine.

At the back was Larry's desk. The junk on the table was balanced precariously high: a display flat, a beautiful piece of night black statuary. In Transhume 201, Larry had described his theory of artifact management: Last-In-First-Out, and every year buy a clean bed sheet, date it, and lay it over the previous layer of junk on your desk. Another of Lazy Larry's jokes, most had thought. But there really *was* a bed sheet peeking out from under the mess.

Shadows climbed sharp and deep from the lamp on Larry's desk. The cabinets around him seemed to lean inwards. The open space between them was covered with posters. Those posters were one small reason Larry was down here: ideas to offend every sensible faction of society. A pile of . . . something . . . lay on the visitor's chair. Larry slopped it onto the floor and motioned Hamid to sit.

"Sure, I remember you from Transhume. But why mention that? You own the Blabber. You're Huss Thompson's kid." He settled back in his chair.

I'm not Huss Thompson's kid! Aloud, "Sorry, that was all I could think to say. This is about my Blabber, though. I need some advice."

"Ah!" Fujiyama gave his famous polliwog smile, somehow innocent and predatory at the same time. "You came to the right place. I'm full of it. But I heard you had quit school, gone to work at the Tourist Bureau."

Hamid shrugged, tried not to seem defensive. "Yeah. But I was already a senior, and I know more American Thought and Lit than most graduates . . . and the Tourist caravan will only be here another half year. After that, how long till the next? We're showing them everything I could imagine they'd want to see. In fact, we're showing them more than there really *is* to see. It could be a hundred years before anyone comes down here again."

"Possibly, possibly."

"Anyway, I've learned a lot. I've met almost half the Tourists. But . . ." There were ten million people living on Middle America. At least a million had a romantic yearning to get Out There. At least ten thousand would give everything they owned to leave the Slow Zone, to live in a civilization that spanned thousands of worlds. For the last ten years, Middle America had known of the Caravan's coming. Hamid had spent most of those years—half his life, all the time since he got out of math—preparing himself with the skills that could buy him a ticket Out.

Thousands of others had worked just as hard. During the last decade, every department of American Thought and Literature on the planet had been jammed to the bursting point. And more had been going on behind the scenes. The government and some large corporations had had secret programs that weren't revealed till just before the Caravan arrived. Dozens of people had bet on the long shots, things that no one else thought the Outsiders might want. Some of those were fools: the world-class athletes, the chess masters. They could never be more than eighth rate in the vast populations of the Beyond. No, to get a ride you needed something that was odd . . . Out There. Besides the Old Earth angle, there weren't many possibilities—though that could be approached in surprising ways: there was Gilli Weinberg, a bright but not brilliant ATL student. When the Caravan reached orbit, she bypassed the Bureau, announced herself to the Tourists as a genuine American cheerleader and premier courtesan. It was a ploy pursued less frankly and less successfully by others of both sexes. In Gilli's case, it had won her a ticket Out. The big laugh was that her sponsor was one of the few non-humans in the Caravan, a Lothlrimarre slug who couldn't survive a second in an oxygen atmosphere.

"I'd say I'm on good terms with three of the Outsiders. But there are at least five Tour Guides that can put on a better show. And you know the Tourists managed to revive four more corpsicles from the original Middle America crew. Those guys are sure to get tickets Out, if they want 'em." Men and women who had been adults on Old Earth, two thousand light-years away and twenty thousand years ago. It was likely that Middle America had no more valuable export this time around. "If they'd just come a few years later, after I graduated . . . maybe made a name for myself."

Larry broke into the self-pitying silence. "You never thought of using the Blabber as your ticket Out?"

"Off and on." Hamid glanced down at the dark bulk that curled around his feet. The Blab was *awfully* quiet.

Larry noticed the look. "Don't worry. She's fooling with some ultrasound imagers I have back there." He gestured at the racks behind Hamid, where a violet glow played hopscotch between unseen gadgets. The boy smiled, "We may have trouble getting her out of here." He had several ultrasonic squawkers around the apartment, but the Blab rarely got to play with high-resolution equipment. "Yeah, right at the beginning, I tried to interest them in the Blab. Said I was her trainer. They lost interest as soon as they saw she couldn't be native to Old Earth. . . . These guys are *freaks*, Professor! You could rain transhuman treasure on 'em, and they'd call it spit! But give 'em Elvis Presley singing Bruce Springsteen and they build you a spaceport on Selene!"

Larry just smiled, the way he did when some student was heading for academic catastrophe. Hamid quieted, "Yeah, I know. There are good reasons for some of the strangeness." Middle America had nothing that would interest anybody rational from Out There. They were stuck nine light-years inside the Slow Zone: commerce was hideously slow and expensive. Middle American technology was obsolete and—considering their location—it could never amount to anything competitive. Hamid's unlucky world had only one thing going for it. It was a direct colony of Old Earth, and one of the first. Their greatship's tragic flight had lasted twenty thousand years, long enough for the Earth to become a legend for much of humankind.

In the Beyond, there were millions of solar systems known to bear human-equivalent intelligences. Most of these could be in more or less instantaneous communication with one another. In that vastness humanity was a speck—perhaps four thousand worlds. Even on those, interest in a first-generation colony within the Slow Zone was near zero. But with four thousand worlds, that was enough: here and there was a rich eccentric, a historical foundation, a religious movement—all strange enough to undertake a twenty-year mission into the Slowness. So Middle America should be glad for these rare mixed nuts. Over the last hundred years there had been occasional traders and a couple of Tourists caravans. That commerce had raised the Middle American standard of living substantially. More important to many—including Hamid—it was almost their only peephole on the universe beyond the Zone. In the last century, two hundred Middle Americans had escaped to the Beyond. The early ones had been government workers, commissioned scientists. The Feds' investment had not paid off: of all those who left, only five had returned. Larry Fujiyama and Hussein Thompson were two of those five.

"Yeah, I guess I knew they'd be fanatics. But most of them aren't even much interested in accuracy. We make a big thing of representing twenty-first-century America. But we both know what that was like: heavy industry moving up to Earth orbit, five hundred million people still crammed into North America. At best what we have here is like mid-twentieth-century America—or even earlier. I've worked very hard to get our past straight. But except for a few guys I really respect, anachronism doesn't seem to bother them. It's like just being here with us is the big thing."

Larry opened his mouth, seemed on the verge of providing some insight. Instead he smiled, shrugged. (One of his many mottos was, "If you didn't figure it out yourself, you don't understand it.")

"So after all these months, where did you dig up the interest in the Blabber?"

"It was the slug, the guy running the Tour. He just mailed me that he had a party who wanted to buy. Normally, this guy haggles. He—wait, you know him pretty well, don't you? Well, he just made a flat offer. A payoff to the Feds, transport for me to Lothlrimarre," that was the nearest civilized system in the Beyond, "and some ftl privileges beyond that."

"And you kiss your pet goodbye?"

"Yeah. I made a case for them needing a handler: me. That's not just bluff, by the way. We've grown up together. I can't imagine the Blab accepting anyone without lots of help from me. But they're not interested. Now, the slug claims no harm is intended her, but . . . do you believe him?"

"Ah, the slug's slime is generally clean. I'm sure he doesn't know of any harm planned . . . and he's straight enough to do at least a little checking. Did he say who wanted to buy?"

"Somebody—something named Ravna&Tines." He passed Larry a flimsy showing the offer. Ravna&Tines had a logo: it looked like a stylized claw. "There's no Tourist registered with that name."

Larry nodded, copied the flimsy to his display flat: "I know. Well, let's see. . . ." He puttered around for a moment. The display was a lecture model, with imaging on both sides. Hamid could see the other was searching internal Federal databases. Larry's eyebrows rose. "Hm*hm!* Ravna&Tines arrived just last week. It's not part of the Caravan at all."

"A solitary trader . . ."

"Not only that. It's been hanging out past the Jovians—at the slug's request. The Federal space net got some pictures." There was a fuzzy image of something long and wasp-waisted, typical of the Outsiders' ramscoop technology. But there were strange fins—almost like the wings on a sailplane. Larry played some algorithmic game with the display and the image sharpened. "Yeah. Look at the aspect ratio on those fins. This guy is carrying high-performance ftl gear. No good down here of course, but hot stuff across an enormous range of environment . . ." he whistled a few bars of Nightmare Waltz. "I think we're looking at a High Trader."

Someone from the Transhuman Spaces.

Almost every university on Middle America had a Department of Transhuman Studies. Since the return of the five, it had been a popular thing to do. Yet most people considered it a joke. Transhume was generally the bastard child of Religious Studies and an Astro or Computer Science department, the dumping ground for quacks and incompetents. Lazy Larry had founded the department at Ann Arbor—and spent much class time eloquently proclaiming its fraudulence. Imagine, trying to study what lay *beyond* the Beyond! Even the Tourists avoided the topic. Transhuman Space existed—perhaps it included most of the universe—but it was a tricky, risky, ambiguous thing. Larry said that its reality drove most of the economics of the Beyond . . . but that all the theories about it were rumors at tenuous second hand. One of his proudest claims was that he raised Transhuman Studies to the level of palm reading.

Yet now . . . apparently a trader had arrived that regularly penetrated the Transhuman Reaches. If the government hadn't sat on the news, it would have eclipsed the Caravan itself. And *this* was what wanted the Blab. Almost involuntarily, he reached down to pet the creature. "Y-you don't think there could really be anybody transhuman on that ship?" An hour ago he had been agonizing about parting with the Blab; that might be nothing compared to what they really faced.

For a moment he thought Larry was going to shrug the question off. But the older man sighed. "If there's anything we've got right it's that no transhuman can think at these depths. Even in the Beyond, they'd die or fragment or maybe cyst. I think this Ravna&Tines must be a human-equivalent intellect, but it could be a lot more dangerous than the average Outsider . . . the tricks it would know, the gadgets it would have." His voice drifted off;

he stared at the forty-centimeter statue perched on his desk. It was lustrous green, apparently cut from a flawless block of jade. *Green? Wasn't it black a minute ago?*

Larry's gaze snapped up to Hamid. "Congratulations. Your problem is a lot more interesting than you thought. Why would any Outsider want the Blab, much less a High Trader?"

". . . Well, her kind must be rare. I haven't talked to any Tourist who recognized the race."

Lazy Larry just nodded. Space is deep. The Blab might be from somewhere else in the Slow Zone.

"When she was a pup, lots of people studied her. You saw the articles. She has a brain as big as a chimp, but most of it's tied up in driving her tympana and processing what she hears. One guy said she's the ultimate in verbal orientation—all mouth and no mind."

"Ah! A student!"

Hamid ignored the Larryism. "Watch this." He patted the Blab's shoulder.

She was slow in responding; that ultrasound equipment must be fascinating. Finally she raised her head. "What's up?" The intonation was natural, the voice a young woman's.

"Some people think she's just a parrot. She can play things back better than a high-fidelity recorder. But she also picks up favorite phrases, and uses them in different voices—and almost appropriately. . . . Hey, Blab. What's that?" Hamid pointed at the electric heater that Larry had propped by his feet. The Blab stuck her head around the corner of the desk, saw the cherry glowing coils. This was not the sort of heater Hamid had in his apartment.

"What's that . . . that . . ." The Blab extended her head curiously toward the glow. She was a bit too eager; her nose bumped the heater's safety grid. *"Hot!"* She jumped back, her nose tucked into her neck fur, a foreleg extended toward the heater. "Hot! Hot!" She rolled onto her haunches, and licked tentatively at her nose. "Jeeze!" She gave Hamid a look that was both calculating and reproachful.

"Honest, Blab, I didn't think you would touch it. . . . She's going to get me for this. Her sense of humor extends only as far as ambushes, but it can be pretty intense."

"Yeah. I remember the Zoo Society's documentary on her." Fujiyama was grinning broadly. Hamid had always thought that Larry and the Blab had kindred humors. It even seemed that the animal's cackling became like the old man's after she attended a couple of his lectures.

Larry pulled the heater back and walked around the desk. He hunched down to the Blab's eye level. He was all solicitude now, and a good thing: he was looking into a mouth full of sharp teeth, and somebody was playing the Timebomb Song. After a moment, the music stopped and she shut her mouth. "I can't believe there isn't human equivalence hiding here somewhere. Really. I've had freshmen who did worse at the start of the semester. How could you get this much verbalization without intelligence to benefit from it?" He reached out to rub her shoulders. "You got sore shoulders, Baby? Maybe little hands ready to burst out?"

The Blab cocked her head. "I like to soar."

Hamid had thought long about the Heinlein scenario; the science fiction of Old Earth was a solid part of the ATL curriculum. "If she is still a child, she'll be dead before she grows up. Her bone calcium and muscle strength have deteriorated about as much as you'd expect for a thirty-year-old human."

"Hm. Yeah. And we know she's about your age." Twenty. "I suppose she could be an ego frag. But most of those are brain-damaged transhumans, or obvious constructs." He went back behind his desk, began whistling tunelessly. Hamid twisted uneasily in his chair. He had come for advice. What he got was news that they were in totally over their heads. He shouldn't be surprised; Larry was like that. "What we need is a whole lot more information."

"Well, I suppose I could flat-out demand the slug tell me more. But I don't know how I can force any of the Tourists to help me."

Larry waved breezily. "That's not what I meant. Sure, I'll ask the Lothlrimarre about it. But basically the Tourists are at the end of a nine light-year trip to nowhere. Whatever libraries they have are like what you would take on a South Seas vacation—and out of date, to boot. . . . And of course the federal government of Middle America doesn't know what's coming off to begin with. Heh, heh. Why else do they come to me when they're really desperate? . . . No, what we need is direct access to library resources Out There."

He said it casually, as though he were talking about getting an extra telephone, not solving Middle America's greatest problem. He smiled complacently at Hamid, but the boy refused to be drawn in. Finally, "Haven't you wondered why the campus—Morale Hall, in particular—is crawling with cops?"

"Yeah." *Or I would have, if there weren't lots else on my mind.*

"One of the more serious Tourists—Skandr Vrinimisrinithan—brought along a genuine transhuman artifact. He's been holding back on it for months, hoping he could get what he wants other ways. The Feds—I'll give 'em this—didn't budge. Finally he brought out his secret weapon. It's in this room right now."

Ham's eyes were drawn to the stone carving (now bluish green) that sat on Larry's desk. The old man nodded. "It's an ansible."

"Surely they don't call it that!"

"No. But that's what it is."

"You mean, all these years, it's been a lie that ftl won't work in the Zone?" *You mean I've wasted my life trying to suck up to these Tourists?*

"Not really. Take a look at this thing. See the colors change. I swear its size and mass do, too. This is a real transhuman artifact. Not an intellect, of course, but not some human design manufactured in Transhuman space. Skandr claims—and I believe him—that no other Tourist has one."

A transhuman artifact. Hamid's fascination was tinged with fear. This was something one heard of in the theoretical abstract, in classes run by crackpots.

"Skandr claims this gadget is 'aligned' on the Lothlrimarre commercial outlet. From there we can talk to any registered address in the Beyond."

"Instantaneously." Hamid's voice was very small.

"Near enough. It would take a while to reach the universal event horizon; there are some subtle limitations if you're moving at relativistic speeds."

"And the catch?"

Larry laughed. "Good man. Skandr admits to a few. This thing won't work more than ten light years into the Zone. I'll bet there aren't twenty worlds in the Galaxy that could benefit from it—but we are *definitely* on one. The trick sucks enormous energy. Skandr says that running this baby will dim our sun by half a percent. Not noticeable to the guy in the street, but it could have long-term bad effects." There was a short silence; Larry often did that after a cosmic understatement. "And from your standpoint, Hamid, there's one big drawback. The mean bandwidth of this thing is just under a six bits per minute."

"Huh? Ten seconds to send a single bit?"

"Yup. Skandr left three protocols at the Lothlrimarre end: ASCII, a Hamming map to a subset of English, and an AI scheme that guesses what you'd say if you used more bits. The first is Skandr's idea of a joke, and I wouldn't trust the third more than wishful thinking. But with the Hamming map, you could send a short letter—say five hundred English words—in a day. It's full-duplex, so you might get a good part of your answer in that time. Neat, huh? Anyway, it beats waiting twenty years."

Hamid guessed it would be the biggest news since first contact, one hundred years ago. "So . . . uh, why did they bring it to you, Professor?"

Larry looked around his hole of an office, smiling wider and wider. "Heh, heh. It's true, our illustrious planetary president is one of the five; he's been Out There. But I'm the only one with real friends in the Beyond. You see, the Feds are very leery of this deal. What Skandr wants in return is most of our zygote bank. The Feds banned any private sale of human zygotes. It was a big moral thing: 'no unborn child sold into slavery or worse.' Now they're thinking of doing it themselves. They really *want* this ansible. But what if it's a fake, just linked up to some fancy database on Skandr's ship? Then they've lost some genetic flexibility, and maybe they've sold some kids into hell—and got nothing but a colorful trinket for their grief.

"So. Skandr's loaned them the thing for a week, and the Feds loaned it to me—with close to *carte blanche*. I can call up old friends, exchange filthy jokes, let the sun go dim doing it. After a week, I report on whether the gadget is really talking to the Outside."

Knowing you, "I bet you have your own agenda."

"Sure. Till you showed up the main item was to check out the foundation that sponsors Skandr, see if they're as clean as he says. Now . . . well, your case isn't as important morally, but it's very interesting. There should be time for both. I'll use Skandr's credit to do some netstalking, see if I can find *anyone* who's heard of Blabbers, or this Ravna&Tines."

Hamid didn't have any really close friends. Sometimes he wondered if that was another penalty of his strange upbringing, or if he was just naturally unlikable. He had come to Fujiyama for help all right, but all he'd been expecting was a round of prickly questions that eventually brought *him* to some insight. Now he seemed to be on the receiving end of a favor of world-shaking proportions. It made him suspicious and very grateful all at once. He gabbled some words of abject gratitude.

Larry shrugged. "It's no special problem for me. I'm curious, and this week I've got the *means* to satisfy my curiosity." He patted the ansible. "There's a real favor I can do though: so far, Middle America has been cheated occasionally, but no Outsider has used force against us. That's one good thing about the Caravan system: it's to the Tourists' advantage to keep each other straight. Ravna&Tines may be different. If this is really a High Trader, it might just make a grab for what it wants. If I were you, I'd keep close to the Blabber. . . . And I'll see if the slug will move one of the Tourist barges over the campus. If you stay in this area, not much can happen without them knowing.

"Hey, see what a help I am? I did nothing for your original question, and now you have a whole, ah, shipload of new things to worry about. . . ."

He leaned back, and his voice turned serious. "But I don't have much to say about your original question, Hamid. If Ravna&Tines turn out to be decent, you'll still have to decide for yourself about giving up the Blab. I bet every critter that thinks it thinks—even the transhumans—worry about how to do right for themselves and the ones they love. I—uh, oh damn! Why don't you ask your pop, why don't you ask Hussein about these things? The guy has been heartbroken since you left."

Ham felt his face go red. Pop had never had much good to say about Fujiyama. Who'd have guessed the two would talk about him? If Hamid had known, he'd never have come here today. He felt like standing up, screaming at this old man to mind his own business. Instead, he shook his head and said softly, "It's kind of personal."

Larry looked at him, as if wondering whether to push the matter. One word, and Ham knew that all the pain would come pouring out. But after a moment, the old man sighed. He looked around the desk to where the Blab lay, eyeing the heater. "Hey, Blabber. You take good care of this kid."

The Blab returned his gaze. "Sure, sure," she said.

Hamid's apartment was on the south side of campus. It was large and cheap, which might seem surprising so near the oldest university around, and just a few kilometers south of the planetary capital. The back door opened on kilometers of forested wilderness. It would be a long time before there was any land development immediately south of here. The original landing zones were just twenty klicks away. In a bad storm there might be a little hot stuff blown north. It might be only fifty percent of natural background radiation, but with a whole world to colonize, why spread towns toward the first landings?

Hamid parked the commons bicycle in the rack out front, and walked quietly around the building. Lights were on upstairs. There were the usual motorbikes of other tenants. *Something* was standing in back, at the far end of the building. Ah. A Halloween scarecrow.

He and the Blab walked back to his end. It was past twilight and neither moon was in the sky. The tips of his fingers were chilled to numbness. He stuck his hands in his pockets, and paused to look up. The starships of the Caravan were in synch orbit at this longitude. They formed a row of bright dots in the southern sky. Something dark, too regular to be a cloud hung almost straight overhead. That must be the protection Larry had promised.

"I'm hungry."

"Just a minute and we'll go in."

"Okay." The Blab leaned companionably against his leg, began humming. She looked fat now, but it was just her fur, all puffed out. These temperatures were probably the most comfortable for her. He stared across the star fields. *God, how many hours have I stood like this, wondering what all those stars mean?* The Big Square was about an hour from setting. The fifth brightest star in that constellation was Lothlrimarre's sun. At Lothlrimarre and beyond, faster than light travel was possible—even for twenty-first-century Old Earth types. If Middle America were just ten more light years farther out from the galactic center, Hamid would have had all the Beyond as his world.

His gaze swept back across the sky. Most everything he could see there would be in the Slow Zone. It extended four thousand light years inward from here, if the Outsiders were to be believed. Billions of star systems, millions of civilizations—trapped. Most would never know about the outside.

Even the Outsiders had only vague information about the civilizations down here in the Slow Zone. Greatships, ramscoops, they all must be invented here again and again. Colonies spread, knowledge gained, most often lost in the long slow silence. What theories the Slow Zone civilizations must have for why nothing could move faster than light—even in the face of superluminal events seen at cosmic distances. What theories they must have to explain why human-equivalent intelligence was the highest ever found and ever created. Those ones deep inside, they might at times be the happiest of all, their theories assuring them they were at the top of creation. If Middle America were only a hundred light years further down, Hamid would never know the truth. He would love this world, and the spreading of civilization upon it.

Hamid's eye followed the Milky Way to the western horizon. The glow wasn't really brighter there than above, but he knew his constellations. He was looking at the galactic center. He smiled wanly. In twentieth-century science fiction, those star clouds were imagined as the homes of "elder races," godlike intellects. . . . But the Tourists call those regions of the galaxy, the Depths. The Unthinking Depths. Not only was ftl impossible there, but so was sentience. So they guessed. They couldn't know for sure. The fastest round-trip probe to the edge of the Depths took about ten thousand years. Such expeditions were rare, though some were well documented.

Hamid shivered, and looked back at the ground. Four cats sat silently just beyond the lawn, watching the Blab. "Not tonight, Blab," he said, and the two of them went indoors.

The place looked undisturbed: the usual mess. He fixed the Blab her dinner and heated some soup for himself.

"Yuck. This stuff tastes like *shit!*" The Blab rocked back on her haunches and made retching sounds. Few people have their own childhood obnoxiousness come back to haunt them so directly as Hamid Thompson did. He could remember using exactly those words at the dinner table. Mom should have stuffed a sock down his throat.

Hamid glanced at the chicken parts. "Best we can afford, Blab." He was running his savings down to zero to cover the year of the Tourists. Being a guide was such a plum that no one thought to pay for it.

"Yuck." But she started nibbling.

As Ham watched her eat, he realized that one of his problems was solved. If Ravna&Tines wouldn't take him as the Blab's "trainer," they could hike back to the Beyond by themselves. Furthermore, he'd want better evidence from the slug—via the ansible he could get assurances directly from Lothlrimarre—that Ravna&Tines could be held to promises. The conversation with Larry had brought home all the nightmare fears, the fears that drove some people to demand total rejection of the Caravan. Who knew what happened to those that left with Outsiders? Almost all Middle American knowledge of the Beyond came from less than thirty starships, less than a thousand strangers. Strange strangers. If it weren't for the five who came back, there would be zero corroboration. Of those five . . . well, Hussein Thompson was a mystery even to Hamid: seeming kind, inside a vicious mercenary. Lazy Larry was a mystery, too, a cheerful one who made it clear that you better think twice about what folks tell you. But one thing came clear from all of them: space is deep. There were millions of civilized worlds in the Beyond, thousands of star-spanning empires. In such vastness, there could be no single notion of law and order. Cooperation and enlightened self-interest were common, but . . . nightmares lurked.

So what if Ravna&Tines turned him down, or couldn't produce credible assurances? Hamid went into the bedroom, and punched up the news, let the color and motion wash over him. Middle America was a beautiful world, still mostly empty. With the agrav plates and the room-temperature fusion electrics that the Caravan had brought, life would be more exciting here then ever before. . . . In twenty or thirty years there would likely be another caravan. If he and the Blab were still restless—well, there was plenty of time to prepare. Larry Fujiyama had been forty years old when he went Out.

Hamid sighed, happy with himself for the first time in days.

• • •

The phone rang just as he finished with the news. The name of the incoming caller danced in red letters across the news display: *Ravna*. No location or topic. Hamid swallowed hard. He bounced off the bed, turned the phone pickup to look at a chair in an uncluttered corner of the room, and sat down there. Then he accepted the call.

Ravna was human. And female. "Mr. Hamid Thompson, please."

"T-that's me." *Curse the stutter.*

For an instant there was no reaction. Then a quick smile crossed her face. It was not a friendly smile, more like a sneer at his nervousness. "I call to discuss the animal. The Blabber, you call it. You have heard our offer. I am prepared to improve upon it." As she spoke, the Blab walked into the room and across the phone's field of view. Her gaze did not waver. Strange. He could see that the video transmit light was on next to the screen. The Blab began to hum. A moment passed and *then* she reacted, a tiny start of surprise.

"What is your improvement?"

Again, a half-second pause. Ravna&Tines were a lot nearer than the Jovians tonight, though apparently still not at Middle America. "We possess devices that allow faster than light communication to a world in the . . . Beyond. Think on what this access means. With this, if you stay on Middle America, you will be the richest man on the planet. If you choose to accept passage Out, you will have the satisfaction of knowing you have moved your world a good step out of the darkness."

Hamid found himself thinking faster than he ever had outside of a Fujiyama oral exam. There were plenty of clues here. Ravna's English was more fluent than most Tourists', but her pronunciation was awful. Human but awful: her vowel stress was strange to the point of rendering her speech unintelligible, and she didn't voice things properly: "pleess" instead "pleez," "chooss" instead of "chooz."

At the same time, he had to make sense of what she was saying and decide the correct response. Hamid thanked God he already knew about ansibles. "Miss Ravna, I agree. That is an improvement. Nevertheless, my original requirement stands. I must accompany my pet. Only I know her needs." He cocked his head. "You could do worse than have an expert on call."

As he spoke, her expression clouded. Rage? She seemed hostile toward him *personally*. But when he finished, her face was filled with an approximation of a friendly smile. "Of course, we will arrange that also. We had not realized earlier how important this is to you."

Jeeze. Even I can lie better than that! This Ravna was used to getting her own way without face-to-face lies, or else she had real emotional problems. Either way: "And since you and I are scarcely equals, we also need to work something out with the Lothlrimarre that will put a credible bond on the agreement."

Her poorly constructed mask slipped. "That is absurd." She looked at something off camera. "The Lothlrimarre knows nothing of us. . . . I will try to satisfy you. But know this, Hamid Thompson: I am the congenial, uh, *humane* member of my team. Mr. Tines is very impatient. I try to restrain him, but if he becomes enough desperate . . . things could happen that would hurt us all. Do you understand me?"

First a lie, and now chainsaw subtlety. He fought back a smile. *Careful. You might be mistaking raw insanity for bluff and bluster.* "Yes, Miss Ravna, I do understand, and your offer is generous. But . . . I need to think about this. Can you give me a bit more time?" *Enough time to complain to the Tour Director.*

"Yes. One hundred hours should be feasible."

After she rang off, Hamid sat for a long time, staring sightlessly at the dataset. What *was* Ravna? Through twenty thousand years of colonization, on worlds far stranger than Middle America, the human form had drifted far. Cross fertility existed between most of Earth's children, though they differed more from one another than had races on the home planet. Ravna looked more like an Earth human than most of the Tourists. Assuming she was of normal height, she could almost have passed as an American of Middle East descent: sturdy, dark-skinned, black-haired. There were differences. Her eyes had epicanthic folds, and the irises were the most intense violet he had ever seen. Still, all that was trivial compared to her manner.

Why hadn't she been receiving Hamid's video? Was she blind? She didn't seem so otherwise; he remembered her looking at things around her. Perhaps she was some sort of personality simulator. That had been a standard item in American science fiction at the end of the twentieth century; the idea passed out of fashion when computer performance seemed to top out in the early twenty-first. But things like that should be possible in the Beyond, and certainly in Transhuman Space. They wouldn't work very well down here, of course. Maybe she was just a graphical front end for whatever Mr. Tines was.

Somehow, Hamid thought she was real. She certainly had a human effect on him. Sure she had a good figure, obvious under soft white shirt and pants. And sure, Hamid had been girl crazy the last five years. He was so horny most of the time, it felt good just to ogle femikins in downtown Marquette stores. But for all-out sexiness, Ravna wasn't *that* spectacular. She had nothing on Gilli Weinberg or Skandr Vrinimisrinithan's wife. Yet, if he had met her at school, he would have tried harder to gain her favor than he had Gilli's . . . and that was saying *a lot.*

Hamid sighed. That probably just showed that *he* was nuts.

"I wanna go out." The Blab rubbed her head against his arm. Hamid realized he was sweating even though the room was chill.

"God, not tonight, Blab." He realized that there was a lot of bluff in Ravna&Tines. At the same time, it was clear they were the kind who might just *grab* if they could get away with it.

"I wanna go out!" Her voice came louder. The Blab spent many nights outside, mainly in the forest. That made it easier to keep her quiet when she was indoors. For the Blab, that was a chance to play with her pets: the cats—and sometimes the dogs—in the neighborhood. There had been a war when he and the Blab first arrived here. Pecking orders had been abruptly revised, and two of the most ferocious dogs had just disappeared. What was left was very strange. The cats were fascinated by the Blab. They hung around the yard just for a glimpse of her. When she was here they didn't even fight among themselves. Nights like tonight were the best. In a couple of hours both Selene and Diana would rise, the silver moon and the gold. On nights like this, when gold and silver lay between deep shadows, Hamid had seen her pacing through the edge of the forest, followed by a dozen faithful retainers.

But, *"Not tonight, Blab!"* There followed a major argument, the Blabber blasting rock music and kiddie shows at high volume. The noise wasn't the loudest she could make. That would have been physically painful to Ham. No, this was more like a cheap music player set way high. Eventually it would bring complaints from all over the apartment building. Fortunately for Hamid, the nearest rooms were unoccupied just now.

After twenty minutes of din, Hamid twisted the fight into a "game of humans." Like many pets, the Blab thought of herself as a human being. But unlike a cat or a dog or even a parrot, she could do a passable job of imitating one. The trouble was, she couldn't always find people with the patience to play along.

They sat across from each other at the dinette table, the Blab's forelegs splayed awkwardly across its surface. Hamid would start with some question—it didn't matter the topic. The Blab would nod wisely, ponder a reply. With most abstractions, anything she had to say was nonsense, meaningful only to tea-leaf readers or wishful thinkers. Never mind that. In the game, Hamid would respond with a comment, or laugh if the Blab seemed to be in a joke-telling behavior. The pacing, the intonation—they were all perfect for real human dialog. If you didn't understand English, the game would have sounded like two friends having a good time.

"How about an imitation, Blab? Joe Ortega. President Ortega. Can you do that?"

"Heh, heh." That was Lazy Larry's cackle. "Don't rush me. I'm thinking. I'm thinking!" There were several types of imitation games. For instance, she could speak back Hamid's words instantly, but with the voice of some other human. Using that trick on a voice-only phone was probably her favorite game of all, since her audience really *believed* she was a person. What he was asking for now was almost as much fun, if the Blab would play up to it.

She rubbed her jaw with a talon, "Ah yes." She sat back pompously, almost slid onto the floor before she caught herself. "We must all work together in these exciting times." That was from a recent Ortega speech, a simple playback. But even when she got going, responding to Hamid's questions, adlibbing things, she was still a perfect match for the President of Middle America. Hamid laughed and laughed. Ortega was one of the five who came back, not a very bright man but self-important and ambitious. It said something that even his small knowledge of the Outside was enough to propel him to the top of the world state. The five were very big fish in a very small pond—that was how Larry Fujiyama put it.

The Blab was an enormous show-off, and was quickly carried away by her own wit. She began waving her forelegs around, lost her balance and fell off the chair. "Oops!" She hopped back on the chair, looked at Hamid—and began laughing herself. The two were in stitches for almost half a minute. This had happened before; Hamid was sure the Blab could not appreciate humor above the level of pratfalls. Her laughter was imitation for the sake of congeniality, for the sake of being a person. "Oh, God!" She flopped onto the table, "choking" with mirth, her forelegs across the back of her neck as if to restrain herself.

The laughter died away to occasional snorts, and then a companionable silence. Hamid reached across to rub the bristly fur that covered the Blab's forehead tympanum. "You're a good kid, Blab."

The dark eyes opened, turned up at him. Something like a sigh escaped her, buzzing the fur under his palm. "Sure, sure," she said.

Hamid left the drapes partly pulled, and a window pane cranked open where the Blab could sit and look out. He lay in the darkened bedroom and watched her silhouette against the silver and gold moonlight. She had her nose pressed up to the screen. Her long neck was arched to give both her head and shoulder tympana a good line on the outside. Every so often her head would jerk a few millimeters, as if something very interesting had just happened outside.

The loudest sound in the night was faint roach racket, out by the forest. The Blab was being very quiet—in the range Hamid could hear—and he was grateful. She really was a good kid.

He sighed and pulled the covers up to his nose. It had been a long day, one where life's problems had come out ahead.

He'd be very careful the next few days; no trips away from Marquette and Ann Arbor, no leaving the Blab unattended. At least the slug's protection looked solid. *I better tell Larry about the second ansible, though.* If Ravna&Tines just went direct to the government with it . . . that might be the most dangerous move of all. For all their pious talk and restrictions on private sales, the Feds would sell their own grandmothers if they thought it would benefit the Planetary Interest. Thank God they already had an ansible—or almost had one.

Funny. After all these years and all the dreams, that it was the Blab the Outsiders were after. . . .

Hamid was an adopted child. His parents had told him that as soon as he could understand the notion. And somewhere in those early years, he had guessed the truth . . . that his father had brought him in . . . from the Beyond. Somehow Huss Thompson had kept that fact secret from the public.

Surely the government knew, and cooperated with him. In those early years—before they forced him into Math—it had been a happy secret for him; he thought he had all his parents' love. Knowing that he was really from Out There had just given substance to what most well-loved kids believe anyway—that somehow they are divinely special. His secret dream had been that he was some Outsider version of an exiled prince. And when he grew up, when the next ships from the Beyond came down . . . he would be called to his destiny.

Starting college at age eight had just seemed part of that destiny. His parents had been so confident of him, even though his tests results were scarcely more than bright normal. . . . That year had been the destruction of innocence. He wasn't a genius, no matter how much his parents insisted. The fights, the tears, their insistence. In the end, Mom had left Hussein Thompson. Not till then did the man relent, let his child return to normal schools. Life at home was never the same. Mom's visits were brief, tense . . . and rare. But it wasn't for another five years that Hamid learned to hate his father. The learning had been an accident, a conversation overheard. Hussein had been *hired* to raise Hamid as he had, to push him into school, to twist and ruin him. The old man had never denied the boy's accusations. His attempts to "explain" had been vague mumbling . . . worse than lies. . . . If Hamid was a prince, he must be a very hated one indeed.

The memories had worn deep grooves, ones he often slid down on his way to sleep. . . . But tonight there was something new, something ironic to the point of magic. All these years . . . it had been the Blab who was the lost princeling . . . !

There was a hissing sound. Hamid struggled toward wakefulness, fear and puzzlement playing through his dreams. He rolled to the edge of the bed and forced his eyes to see. Only stars shone through the window. The Blab. She wasn't sitting at the window screen anymore. She must be having one of her nightmares. They were rare, but spectacular. One winter's night Hamid had been wakened by the sounds of a full-scale thunderstorm. This was not so explosive, but . . .

He looked across the floor at the pile of blankets that was her nest. Yes. She was there, and facing his way.

"Blab? It's okay, baby."

No reply. Only the hissing, maybe louder now. *It wasn't coming from the Blab.* For an instant his fuzzy mind hung in a kind of mouse-and-snake paralysis. Then he flicked on the lights. No one here. The sound was from the dataset; the picture flat remained dark. *This is crazy.*

"Blab?" He had never seen her like this. Her eyes were open wide, rings of white showing around the irises. Her forelegs reached beyond the blankets. The talons were extended and had slashed deep into the plastic flooring. A string of drool hung from her muzzle.

He got up, started toward her. The hissing formed a voice, and the voice spoke. "I want her. Human, I want her. And I will have her." Her, the Blab.

"How did you get access? You have no business disturbing us." Silly talk, but it broke the nightmare spell of this waking.

"My name is Tines." Hamid suddenly remembered the claw on the Ravna&Tines logo. Tines. Cute. "We have made generous offers. We have been patient. That is past. I will have her. If it means the death of all you m-meat animals, so be it. But I *will* have her."

The hissing was almost gone now, but the voice still sounded like something from a cheap synthesizer. The syntax and accent were similar to Ravna's. They were either the same person, or they had learned English from the same source. Still, Ravna had seemed angry. Tines sounded flat-out nuts. Except for the single stutter over "meat," the tone and pacing were implacable. And that voice gave away more than anything yet about why the Outsider wanted his pet. There was a *hunger* in its voice, a lust to feed or to rape.

Hamid's rage climbed on top of his fear. "Why don't you just go screw yourself, comic monster! We've got *protection*, else you wou!dn't come bluffing—"

"Bluffing! *Bluffiiyowru—*" the words turned into choked gobbling sounds. Behind him, Hamid heard the Blab scream. After a moment the noises faded. "I do not bluff. Hussein Thompson has this hour learned what I do with those who cross me. You and all your people will also die unless you deliver her to me. I see a ground car parked by your . . . house. Use it to take her east fifty kilometers. Do this within one hour, or learn what Hussein Thompson learned—that *I do not bluff.*" And Mr. Tines was gone.

It has *to be a bluff! If Tines has that power why not wipe the Tourists from the sky and just grab the Blab?* Yet they were so stupid about it. A few smooth lies a week ago, and they might have gotten everything without a murmur. It was as if they couldn't imagine being disobeyed—or were desperate beyond reason.

Hamid turned back to the Blab. As he reached to stroke her neck, she twisted, her needle-toothed jaws clicking shut on his pyjama sleeve. "Blab!"

She released his sleeve, and drew back into the pile of blankets. She was making whistling noises like the time she got hit by a pickup trike. Hamid's father guessed those must be true Blabber sounds, like human sobs or chattering of teeth. He went to his knees and made comforting noises. This time she let him stroke her neck. He saw that she had wet her bed. The Blab had been toilet trained as long as he had. Bluff or not, this had thoroughly terrified her. Tines claimed he could kill everyone. Hamid remembered the ansible, a god-damned telephone that could dim the sun.

Bluff or madness?

He scrambled back to his dataset, and punched up the Tour Director's number. Pray the slug was accepting more than mail tonight. The ring pattern flashed twice, and then he was looking at a panorama of cloud tops and blue sky. It might have been an aerial view of Middle America, except that as you looked downwards the clouds seemed to extend forever, more and more convoluted in the dimness. This was a picture clip from the ten-bar level over Lothlrimarre. No doubt the slug chose it to soothe human callers, and still be true to the nature of his home world—a subjovian thirty thousand kilometers across.

For five seconds they soared through the canyons of cloud. *Wake up, damn you!*

The picture cleared and he was looking at a human—Larry Fujiyama! Lazy Larry did not look surprised to see him. "You got the right number, kid. I'm up here with the slug. There have been developments."

Hamid gaped for an appropriate reply, and the other continued. "Ravna&Tines have been all over the slug since about midnight. Threats and promises, mostly threats since the Tines critter took their comm. . . . I'm sorry about your dad, Hamid. We should've thought to—"

"What?"

"Isn't that what you're calling about? . . . Oh. It's been on the news. Here—" The picture dissolved into a view from a news chopper flying over eastern Michigan farmland. It took Hamid a second to recognize the hills. This was near the Thompson spread, two thousand klicks east of Marquette. It would be past sunup there. The camera panned over a familiar creek, the newsman bragging how On-Line News was ahead of the first rescue teams. They crested a range of hills and . . . where were the trees? Thousands of black lines lay below, trunks of blown-over trees, pointing inevitably inward, toward the center of the blast. The newsman babbled on about the meteor strike and how fortunate it was that ground zero was in a lake valley, how only one farm had been affected. Hamid swallowed. That farm . . . was Hussein Thompson's. The place they lived after Mom left. Ground zero itself was obscured by rising steam—all that was left of the lake. The reporter assured his audience that the crater consumed all the land where the farm buildings had been.

The news clip vanished. "It was no Middle American nuke, but it wasn't natural, either," said Larry. "A lighter from Ravna&Tines put down there two hours ago. Just before the blast, I got a real scared call from Huss, something about 'the tines' arriving. I'll show it to you if—"

"No!" Hamid gulped. "No," he said more quietly. How he had hated Hussein Thompson; how he had loved his father in the years before. Now he was gone, and Hamid would never get his feelings sorted out. "Tines just called me. He said he killed my—Hussein." Hamid played back the call. "Anyway, I need to talk to the slug. Can he protect me? Is Middle America really in for it if I refuse the Tines thing?"

For once Larry didn't give his "you figure it" shrug. "It's a mess," he said. "And sluggo's waffling. He's around here somewhere. Just a sec—" More peaceful cloud-soaring. Damn, damn, damn. Something bumped gently into the small of his back. The Blab. The black and white neck came around his side. The dark eyes looked up at him. "What's up?" she said quietly.

Hamid felt like laughing and crying. She was very subdued, but at least she recognized him now. "Are you okay, Baby?" he said. The Blabber curled up around him, her head stretched out on his knee.

On the dataset, the clouds parted and they were looking at both Larry Fujiyama and the slug. Of course, they were not in the same room; that would have been fatal to both. The Lothlrimarre barge was a giant pressure vessel. Inside, pressure and atmosphere were just comfy for the slug—about a thousand bars of ammonia and hydrogen. There was a terrarium for human visitors. The current view showed the slug in the foreground. Part of the wall behind him was transparent, a window into the terrarium. Larry gave a little wave, and Hamid felt himself smiling. No question who was in a zoo.

"Ah, Mr. Thompson. I'm glad you called. We have a very serious problem." The slug's English was perfect, and though the voice was artificial, he sounded like a perfectly normal Middle American male. "Many problems would be solved if you could see your way clear to give—"

"No." Hamid's voice was flat. "N-not while I'm alive, anyway. This is no business deal. You've heard the threats, and you saw what they did to my father." The slug had been his ultimate employer these last six months, someone rarely spoken to, the object of awe. None of that mattered now. "You've always said the first responsibility of the Tour Director is to see that no party is abused by another. I'm asking you to live up to that."

"Um. Technically, I was referring to you Middle Americans and the Tourists in my caravan. I know I have the power to make good on my promises with them. . . . But we're just beginning to learn about Ravna&Tines. I'm not sure it's reasonable to stand up against them." He swiveled his thousand-kilo bulk toward the terrarium window. Hamid knew that under Lothlrimarre gravity, the slug would have been squashed into the shape of a flatworm, with his manipulator fringe touching the ground. At one gee, he looked more like an overstuffed silk pillow, fringed with red tassles. "Larry has told me about Skandr's remarkable Slow Zone device. I've heard of such things. They are *very* difficult to obtain. A single one would have more than financed my caravan. . . . And to think that Skandr pleaded his foundation's poverty in begging passage. . . . Anyway, Larry has been using the 'ansible' to ask about what your Blabber really is."

Larry nodded. "Been at it since you left, Hamid. The machine's down in my office, buzzing away. Like Skandr says, it is aligned on the commercial outlet at Lothlrimarre. From there I have access to the Known Net. Heh, heh. Skandr left a *sizable* credit bond at Lothlrimarre. I hope he and Ortega aren't too upset by the phone bill I run up testing this gadget for them. I described the Blab, and put out a depth query. There are a million subnets, all over the Beyond, searching their databases for anything like the Blab. I—" His happy enthusiasm wavered, "Sluggo thinks we've dug up a reference to the Blabber's race. . . ."

"Yes, and it's frightening, Mr. Thompson." It was no surprise that none of the Tourists had heard of a blabber. The only solid lead coming back to Larry had been from halfway around the galactic rim, a nook in the Beyond that had only one occasional link with the rest of the Known Net. That far race had no direct knowledge of the Blabbers. But they heard rumors. From a thousand light-years below them, deep within the Slow Zone, there came stories . . . of a race matching the Blab's appearance. The race was highly intelligent, and had quickly developed the relativistic transport that was the fastest thing inside the Zone. They colonized a vast sphere, held an empire of ten thousand worlds—all without ftl. And the tines—the name seemed to fit—had not held their empire through the power of brotherly love. Races had been exterminated, planets busted with relativistic kinetic energy bombs. The tines' technology had been about as advanced and deadly as could exist in the Zone. Most of their volume was a tomb now, their story whispered through centuries of slow flight toward the Outside.

"Wait, wait. Prof Fujiyama told me the ansible's bandwidth is a tenth of a bit per second. You've had less than twelve hours to work this question. How can you possibly know all this?"

Larry looked a little embarrassed—a first as far as Hamid could remember. "We've been using the AI protocol I told you about. There's massive interpolation going on at both ends of our link to Lothlrimarre."

"I'll bet!"

"Remember, Mr. Thompson, the data compression applies only to the first link in the chain. The Known Net lies in the Beyond. Bandwidth and data integrity are very high across most of its links."

The slug sounded very convinced. But Hamid had read a lot about the Known Net; the notion was almost as fascinating as ftl travel itself. There was no way a world could have a direct link with all others—partly because of range limitations, mainly because of the *number* of planets involved. Similarly, there was no way a single "phone company" (or even ten thousand phone companies!) could run the thing. Most likely, the information coming to them from around the galaxy had passed through five or ten intermediate hops. The intermediates—not to mention the race on the far rim—were likely nonhuman. Imagine asking a quesiton in English to someone who also speaks Spanish, and that person asking the question in Spanish to someone who understands Spanish and passes the question on in German. This was a million times worse. Next to some of the creatures Out There, the slug could pass for human!

Hamid said as much. "F-furthermore, even if this *is* what the sender meant, it could still be a lie! Look at what local historians did to Richard the Third, or Mohamet Rose."

Lazy Larry smiled his polliwog smile, and Hamid realized they must have been arguing about this already. Larry put in, "There's also this, sluggo: the nature of the identification. The tines must have something like hands. See any on Hamid's Blabber?"

The slug's scarlet fringe rippled three quick cycles. Agitation? Dismissal? "The text is still coming in. But I have a theory. You know, Larry, I've always been a great student of sex. I may be a 'he' only by courtesy, but I think sex is fascinating. It's what makes the 'world go around' for so many races." Hamid suddenly understood Gilli Weinberg's success. "So. Grant me my expertise. My guess is the tines exhibit *extreme* sexual dimorphism. The males' forepaws probably are hands. No doubt it's the males who are the killers. The females—like the Blab—are by contrast friendly, mindless creatures."

The Blab's eyes rolled back to look at Hamid. "Sure, sure," she murmured. The accident of timing was wonderful, seeming to say *who is this clown?*

The slug didn't notice. "This may even explain the viciousness of the male. Think back to the conversation Mr. Thompson had. These creatures seem to regard their own females as property to exploit. Rather the ultimate in sexism." Hamid shivered. That *did* ring a bell. He couldn't forget the *hunger* in the tines's voice.

"Is this the long way to tell me you're not going to protect us?"

The slug was silent for almost fifteen seconds. Its scarlet fringe waved up and down the whole time. Finally: "Almost, I'm afraid. My caravan customers haven't heard this analysis, just the threats and the news broadcasts. Nevertheless, they are tourists, not explorers. They demand that I refuse to let you aboard. Some demand that we leave your planet immediately. . . . How secure is this line, Larry?"

Fujiyama said, "Underground fiberoptics, and an encrypted laser link. Take a chance, sluggo."

"Very well. Mr. Thompson, there is what you can expect from me: I can stay over the city, and probably defend against direct kidnapping—that unless I see a planetbuster coming. I doubt very much they have that set up, but if they do—well, I don't think even you would want to keep your dignity at the price of a relativistic asteroid strike.

"I can *not* come down to pick you up. That would be visible to all, a direct violation of my customers' wishes. On the other hand," there was another pause, and his scarlet fringe whipped about even faster than before, "if you should appear, uh, up here, I would take you aboard my barge. Even if this were noticed, it would be a *fait accompli.* I could hold off my customers, and likely our worst fate would be a premature and unprofitable departure from Middle America."

"T-that's very generous." *Unbelievably so.* The slug was thought to be an honest fellow—but a very hard trader. Even Hamid had to admit that the claim on the slug's honor was tenuous here, yet he was risking a twenty-year mission for it.

"Of course, *if* we reach that extreme, I'll want a few years of your time once we reach the Outside. My bet is that hard knowledge about your Blabber might make up for the loss of everything else."

A day ago, Hamid would have quibbled about contracts and assurances. Today, well, the alternative was Ravna&Tines. . . . With Larry as witness, they settled on two years indenture and a pay scale.

Now all he and the Blab had to do was figure how to climb five thousand meters straight up. There was one obvious way:

• • •

It was Dave Larson's car, but Davey owed him. Hamid woke his neighbor, explained that the Blab was sick and had to go into Marquette. Fifteen minutes later, Hamid and the Blab were driving through Ann Arbor Town. It was a Saturday, and barely into morning twilight; he had the road to himself. He'd half expected the place to be swarming with cops and military. If Ravna&Tines ever guessed how easy it was to intimidate Joe Ortega . . . If the Feds knew exactly what was going on, they'd turn the Blab over to Tines in an instant. But apparently the government was simply confused, lying low, hoping it wouldn't be noticed till the big boys upstairs settled their arguments. The farm bombing wasn't in the headline list anymore. The Feds were keeping things quiet, thereby confining the mindless panic to the highest circles of government.

The Blab rattled around the passenger side of the car, alternately leaning on the dash and sniffing in the bag of tricks that Hamid had brought. She was still subdued, but riding in a private auto was a novelty. Electronics gear was cheap, but consumer mechanicals were still at a premium. And without a large highway system, cars would never be the rage they had been on Old Earth; most freight transport was by rail. A lot of this would change because of the Caravan. They brought one hundred thousand agrav plates—enough to revolutionize transport. Middle America would enter the Age of the Aircar—and for the first time surpass the homeworld. So saith Joe Ortega.

Past the University, there was a patch of open country. Beyond the headlights, Hamid caught glimpses of open fields, a glint of frost. Hamid looked up nervously every few seconds. Selene and Diana hung pale in the west. Scattered clouds floated among the Tourist barges, vague grayness in the first light of morning. No intruders, but three of the barges were gone, presumably moved to orbit. The Lothlrimarre vessel floated just east of Marquette, over the warehouse quarter. It looked like the slug was keeping his part of the deal.

Hamid drove into downtown Marquette. Sky signs floated brightly amid the two-hundred-storey towers, advertising dozens of products—some of which actually existed. Light from discos and shopping malls flooded the eight-lane streets. Of course the place was deserted; it was Saturday morning. Much of the business section was like this—a reconstruction of the original Marquette as it had been on Earth in the middle of the twenty-first century. That Marquette had sat on the edge of an enormous lake, called Superior. Through that century, as Superior became the splash-down point for heavy freight from space, Marquette had become one of the great port cities of Earth, the gateway to the solar system. The Tourists said it was legend, ur-mother to a thousand worlds.

Hamid turned off the broadway, down an underground ramp. The Marquette of today was for show, perhaps one percent the area of the original, with less than one percent the population. But from the air it looked good, the lights and bustle credible. For special events, the streets could be packed with a million people—everyone on the continent that could be spared from essential work. And the place wasn't really a fraud; the Tourists knew this was a reconstruction. The point was, it was an *authentic* reconstruction, as could only be done by a people one step from the original source—that was the official line. And in fact, the people of Middle America had made enormous sacrifices over almost twenty years to have this ready in time for the Caravan.

The car rental was down a fifteen-storey spiral, just above the train terminal. *That* was for real, though the next arrival was a half hour away. Hamid got out, smelling the cool mustiness of the stone cavern, hearing only the echoes of his own steps. Millions of tonnes of ceramic and stone stood between them and the sky. Even an Outsider couldn't see through that . . . he hoped. One sleepy-eyed attendant watched him fill out the forms. Hamid stared at the display, sweating even in the cool; would the guy in back notice? He almost laughed at the thought. His first sally into crime was the least of his worries. If Ravna&Tines were plugged into the credit net, then in a sense they really *could* see down here—and the bogus number Larry had supplied was all that kept him invisible.

They left in a Millennium Commander, the sort of car a Tourist might use to bum around in olden times. Hamid drove north through the underground, then east, and when finally they saw open sky again, they were driving south. Ahead was the warehouse district . . . and hanging above it, the slug's barge, its spheres and cupolas green against the brightening sky. So huge. It looked near, but Hamid knew it was a good five thousand meters up.

A helicopter might be able to drop someone on its topside, or maybe land on one of the verandas—though it would be a tight fit under the overhang. But Hamid couldn't fly a chopper, and wasn't even sure how to rent one at this time of day. No, he and the Blab were going to try something a lot more straightforward, something he had done every couple of weeks since the Tourists arrived.

They were getting near the incoming lot, where Feds and Tourists held payments-to-date in escrow. Up ahead there would be cameras spotted on the roofs. He tinted all but the driver-side window, and pushed down on the Blab's shoulders with his free hand. "Play hide for a few minutes."

"Okay."

Three hundred meters more and they were at the outer gate. He saw the usual three cops out front, and a fourth in an armored box to the side. If Ortega was feeling the heat, it could all end right here.

They looked *real* nervous, but they spent most of their time scanning the sky. They knew something was up, but they thought it was out of their hands. They took a quick glance at the Millennium Commander and waved him through. The inner fence was almost as easy, though here he had to enter his Guide ID. . . . If Ravna&Tines were watching the nets, Hamid and the Blab were running on borrowed time now.

He pulled into the empty parking lot at the main warehouse, choosing a slot with just the right position relative to the guard box. "Keep quiet a little while, Blab," he said. He hopped out and walked across the gravel yard. Maybe he should move faster, as if panicked? But no, the guard had already seen him. *Okay, play it cool.* He waved, kept walking. The glow of morning was already dimming the security lamps that covered the lot. No stars shared the sky with the clouds and the barges.

It was kind of a joke that merchandise from the Beyond was socked away here. The warehouse was big, maybe two hundred meters on a side, but an old place, sheet plastic and aging wood timbers.

The armored door buzzed even before Hamid touched it. He pushed his way through. "Hi, Phil."

Luck! The other guards must be on rounds. Phil Lucas was a friendly sort, but not too bright, and not very familiar with the Blab. Lucas sat in the middle of the guard cubby, and the armored partition that separated him from the visitor trap was raised. To the left was a second door that opened into the warehouse itself. "Hi, Ham." The guard looked back at him nervously. "Awful early to see you."

"Yeah. Got a little problem. There's a Tourist out in the Commander." He waved through the armored window. "He's drunk out of his mind. I need to get him Upstairs and quietly."

Phil licked his lips. "Christ. Everything happens at once. Look, I'm sorry, Ham. We've got orders from the top at Federal Security: nothing comes down, nothing goes up. There's some kind of a ruckus going on amongst the Outsiders. If they start shooting, we want it to be at each other, not us."

"That's the point. We think this fellow is part of the problem. If we can get him back, things should cool off. You should have a note on him. It's Antris ban Reempt."

"Oh. *Him.*" Ban Reempt was the most obnoxious Tourist of all. If he'd been an ordinary Middle American, he would have racked up a century of jail time in the last six months. Fortunately, he'd never killed anyone, so his antics were just barely ignorable. Lucas pecked at his dataset. "No, we don't have anything."

"Nuts. Everything stays jammed unless we can get this guy Upstairs," Hamid paused judiciously, as if giving the matter serious thought. "Look, I'm going back to the car, see if I can call somebody to confirm this."

Lucas was dubious. "Okay, but it's gotta be from the top, Ham."

"Right."

The door buzzed open, and Hamid was jogging back across the parking lot. Things really seemed on track. Thank God he'd always been friendly with the cops running security here. The security people regarded most of the Guides as college-trained snots—and with some reason. But Hamid had had coffee with these guys more than once. He knew the system . . . he knew the incoming phone number for security confirmations.

Halfway across the lot, Hamid suddenly realized that he didn't have the shakes anymore. The scheme, the adlibbing, it almost seemed normal—a skill he'd never guessed he had. Maybe that's what desperation does to a fellow. . . . Somehow this was almost fun.

He pulled open the car door. "Back! Not yet." He pushed the eager Blab onto the passenger seat. "Big game, Blab." He rummaged through his satchel, retrieved the two comm sets. One was an ordinary head and throat model, the other had been modified for the Blab. He fastened the mike under the collar of his windbreaker. The earphone shouldn't be needed, but it was small; he put it on, turned the volume down. Then he strapped the other commset around the Blab's neck, turned off *its* mike, and clipped the receiver to her ear. "The game, Blab: Imitation. Imitation." He patted the commset on her shoulder. The Blab was fairly bouncing around the Commander's cab. "For sure. Sure, sure! Who, who?"

"Joe Ortega. Try it: 'We must all pull together . . .'"

The words came back from the Blab as fast as he spoke them, but changed into the voice of the Middle American President. He rolled down the driver-side window; this worked best if there was eye contact. Besides, he might need her out of the car. "Okay. Stay here. I'll go get us the sucker." She rattled his instructions back in pompous tones.

One last thing: He punched a number into the car phone, and set its timer and no video option. Then he was out of the car, jogging back to the guard box. This sort of trick had worked often enough at school. Pray that it would work now. Pray that she wouldn't ad lib.

He turned off the throat mike as Lucas buzzed him back into the visitor trap. "I got to the top. Someone—maybe even the Chief of Federal Security—will call back on the Red Line."

Phil's eyebrows went up. "That would do it." Hamid's prestige had just taken a giant step up.

Hamid made a show of impatient pacing about the visitor trap. He stopped at the outer door with his back to the guard. Now he really *was* impatient. Then the phone rang, and he heard Phil pick it up.

"Escrow One, Agent Lucas speaking, Sir!"

From where he was standing, Hamid could see the Blab. She was in the driver's seat, looking curiously at the dash phone. Hamid turned on the throat mike and murmured, "Lucas, this is Joseph Stanley Ortega."

Almost simultaneously, "Lucas, this is Joseph Stanley Ortega," came from the phone behind him. The words were weighted with all the importance Hamid could wish, and something else: a furtiveness not in the public speeches. That was probably because of Hamid's original delivery, but it didn't sound too bad.

In any case, Phil Lucas was impressed. "Sir!"

"Agent Lucas, we have a problem." Hamid concentrated on his words, and tried to ignore the Ortega echo. For him, that was the hardest part of the trick, especially when he had to speak more than a brief sentence. "There could be nuclear fire, unless the Tourists cool off. I'm with the National Command Authorities in deep shelter: it's that serious." Maybe that would explain why there was no video.

Phil's voice quavered. "Yes, sir." *He* wasn't in deep shelter.

"Have you verified—" *clicket* "—my ID?" The click was in Hamid's earphone; he didn't hear it on the guard's set. A loose connection in the head-piece?

"Yes, sir. I mean . . . just one moment." Sounds of hurried keyboard tap-ping. There should be no problem with a voiceprint match, and Hamid needed things nailed tight to bring this off. "Yes, sir, you're fine. I mean—"

"Good. Now listen carefully: The guide, Thompson, has a Tourist with him. We need that Outsider returned, *quickly and quietly.* Get the lift ready, and keep everybody clear of these two. If Thompson fails, millions may die. Give him whatever he asks for." Out in the car, the Blab was having a high old time. Her front talons were hooked awkwardly over the steering wheel. She twisted it back and forth, "driving" and "talking" at the same time: the apotheosis of life—to be taken for a person by real people!

"Yes, sir!"

"Very well. Let's—" *clicket-click* "—get moving on this." And on that last click, the Ortega voice was gone. *God damned cheapjack commset!*

Lucas was silent a moment, respectfully waiting for his President to con-tinue. Then, "Yes, sir. What must we do?"

Out in the Millennium Commander, the Blab was the picture of con-sternation. She turned toward him, eyes wide. *What do I say now?* Hamid re-peated this line, as loud as he dared. No Ortega. *She can't hear anything I'm saying!* He shut off his mike.

"Sir? Are you still there?"

"Line must be dead," Hamid said casually, and gave the Blab a little wave to come running.

"Phone light says I still have a connection, Ham. . . . Mr. President, can you hear me? You were saying what we must do. Mr. President?"

The Blab didn't recognize his wave. Too small. He tried again. She tapped a talon against her muzzle. *Blab! Don't ad lib!* "Well, uh," came Or-tega's voice, "don't rush me. I'm thinking. I'm thinking! . . . We must all pull together or else millions may die. Don't you think? I mean, it makes sense—" which it did not, and less so by the second. Lucas was making "uh-huh" sounds, trying to fit reason on the Blabber. His tone was steadily more puzzled, even suspicious.

No help for it. Hamid slammed his fist against the transp armor, and waved wildly to the Blab. *Come here!* Ortega's voice died in midsyllable. He turned to see Lucas staring at him, surprise and uneasiness on his face. "Something's going on here, and I don't like it—" Somewhere in his mind, Phil had figured out he was being taken, yet the rest of him was carried for-ward by the inertia of the everyday. He leaned over the counter, to get Hamid's line of view on the lot.

The original plan was completely screwed, yet strangely he felt no panic, no doubt; there were still options: Hamid smiled—and jumped across the counter, driving the smaller man into the corner of wall and counter. Phil's hand reached wildly for the tab that would bring the partition down. Hamid just pushed him harder against the wall . . . and grabbed the guard's pistol from its holster. He jammed the barrel into the other's middle. "Quiet down, Phil."

"*Son of a bitch!*" But the other stopped struggling. Hamid heard the Blab slam into the outer door.

"Okay. Kick the outside release." The door buzzed. A moment later, the Blab was in the visitor trap, bouncing around his legs.

"Heh heh heh! That was good. That was really good!" The cackle was Lazy Larry's but the voice was still Ortega's.

"Now buzz the inner door." The other gave his head a tight shake. Hamid punched Lucas's gut with the point of the pistol. "*Now!*" For an instant, Phil seemed frozen. Then he kneed the control tab, and the inner door buzzed. Hamid pushed it ajar with his foot, then heaved Lucas away from the counter. The other bounced to his feet, his eyes staring at the muzzle of the pistol, his face very pale. *Dead men don't raise alarums.* The thought was clear on his face.

Hamid hesitated, almost as shocked by his success as Lucas was. "Don't worry, Phil." He shifted his aim and fired a burst over Lucas's shoulder . . . into the warehouse security processor. Fire and debris flashed back into the room—and now alarms sounded everywhere.

He pushed through the door, the Blab close behind. The armor clicked shut behind them; odds were it would stay locked now that the security processor was down. Nobody in sight, but he heard shouting. Hamid ran down the aisle of upgoing goods. They kept the agrav lift at the back of the building, under the main ceiling hatch. Things were definitely not going to plan, but if the lift was there, he could still—

"There he is!"

Hamid dived down an aisle, jigged this way and that between pallets . . . and then began walking very quietly. He was in the downcoming section now, surrounded by the goods that had been delivered thus far by the Caravan. These were the items that would lift Middle America beyond Old Earth's twenty-first century. Towering ten meters above his head were stacks of room-temperature fusion electrics. With them—and the means to produce more—Middle America could trash its methanol economy and fixed fusion plants. Two aisles over were the raw agrav units. These looked more like piles of fabric than anything high-tech. Yet the warehouse lifter was built around one, and with them Middle America would soon make aircars as easily as automobiles.

Hamid knew there were cameras in the ceiling above the lights. Hopefully they were as dead as the security processor. Footsteps one aisle over. Hamid eased into the dark between two pallets. Quiet, quiet. The Blab didn't feel like being quiet. She raced down the aisle ahead of him, raking the spaces between the pallets with a painfully loud imitation of his pistol. They'd see her in a second. He ran the other direction a few meters, and fired a burst into the air.

"Jesus! How many did asshole Lucas let in?" Someone very close replied,

"That's still low-power stuff." Much quieter: "We'll show these guys some firepower." Hamid suddenly guessed there were only two of them. And with the guard box jammed, they might be trapped in here till the alarm brought guards from outside.

He backed away from the voices, continued toward the rear of the warehouse.

"Boo!" The Blab was on the pallets above him, talking to someone on the ground. Explosive shells smashed into the fusion electrics around her. The sounds bounced back and forth through the warehouse. Whatever it was, it was a cannon compared to his pistol. No doubt it was totally unauthorized for indoors, but that did Hamid little good. He raced forward, heedless of the destruction. "Get down!" he screamed at the pallets. A bundle of shadow and light materialized in front of him and streaked down the aisle.

A second roar of cannon fire, tearing through the space where he had just been. But something else was happening now. Blue light shone from somewhere in the racks of fusion electrics, sending brightness and crisp shadows across the walls ahead. It felt like someone had opened a furnace door behind him. He looked back. The blue was spreading, an arc-welder light that promised burns yet unfelt. He looked quickly away, afterimages dancing on his eyes, afterimages of the pallet shelves *sagging* in the heat.

The autosprinklers kicked on, an instant rainstorm. But this was a fire that water would not quench—and might even fuel. The water exploded into steam, knocking Hamid to his knees. He bounced up sprinting, falling, sprinting again. The agrav lift should be around the next row of pallets. In the back of his mind, something was analyzing the disaster. That explosive cannon fire had started things, a runaway melt in the fusion electrics. They were supposedly safer than meth engines—but they could melt down. This sort of destruction in a Middle American nuclear plant would have meant rad poisoning over a continent. But the Tourists claimed their machines melted clean—shedding low-energy photons and an enormous flood of particles that normal matter scarcely responded to. Hamid felt an urge to hysterical laughter; Slow Zone astronomers light-years away might notice this someday, a wiggle on their neutrino scopes, one more datum for their flawed cosmologies.

There was lightning in the rainstorm now, flashes between the pallets and across the aisle—into the raw agrav units. The clothlike material jerked and rippled, individual units floating upwards. Magic carpets released by a genie.

Then giant hands clapped him, sound that was pain, and the rain was gone, replaced by a hot wet wind that swept around and up. Morning light shown through the steamy mist. The explosion had blasted open the roof. A rainbow arced across the ruins. Hamid was crawling now. Sticky wet ran down his face, dripped redly on the floor. The pallets bearing the fusion electrics had collapsed. Fifteen meters away, molten plastic slurried atop flowing metal.

He could see the agrav lift now, what was left of it. The lift sagged like an old candle in the flow of molten metal. So. No way up. He pulled himself back from the glare, and leaned against the stacked agravs. They slid and vibrated behind him. The cloth was soft, yet it blocked the heat, and some of the noise. The pinkish blue of a dawn sky shown through the last scraps of mist. The Lothlrimarre barge hung there, four spherical pressure vessels embedded in intricate ramps and crenellations.

Jeeze. Most of the warehouse roof was just . . . gone. A huge tear showed through the far wall. *There!* The two guards. They were facing away from him, one half leaning on the other. Chasing him was very far from their minds at the moment. They were picking their way through the jumble, trying to get out of the warehouse. Unfortunately, a rivulet of silver metal crossed their path. One false step and they'd be ankle deep in the stuff. But they were lucky, and in fifteen seconds passed from sight around the outside of the building.

No doubt he could get out that way, too. . . . But that wasn't why he was here. Hamid struggled to his feet, and began shouting for the Blab. The hissing, popping sounds were loud, but not like before. If she were conscious, she'd hear him. He wiped blood from his lips and limped along the row of agrav piles. *Don't die, Blab. Don't die.*

There was motion everywhere. The piles of agravs had come alive. The top ones simply lifted off, tumbled upwards, rolling and unrolling. The lower layers strained and jerked. Normal matter might not notice the flood of never-never particles from the melt-down; the agravs were clearly not normal. Auras flickered around the ones trapped at the bottom. But this was not the eye-sizzling burn of the fusion electrics. This was a soft thing, an awakening rather than an explosion. Hamid's eyes were caught on the rising. Hundreds of them just floating off, gray and russet banners in the morning light. He leaned back. Straight up, the farthest ones were tiny specks against the blue. *Maybe—*

Something banged into his legs, almost dumping him back on the floor. "Wow. So loud." The Blab had found *him!* Hamid knelt and grabbed her around the neck. She looked fine! A whole lot better than he did anyway. Like most smaller animals, she could take a lot of bouncing around. He ran his hands down her shoulders. There were some nicks, a spattering of blood. And she looked subdued, not quite the hellion of before. "Loud. Loud," she kept saying.

"I know, Blab. But that's the worst." He looked back into the sky. At the rising agravs . . . at the Lothlrimarre barge. *It would be crazy to try . . .* but he heard sirens outside.

He patted the Blab, then stood and clambered up the nearest pile of agravs. The material, hundreds of separate units piled like blankets, gave beneath his boots like so much foam rubber. He slid back a ways after each step. He grabbed at the edges of the units above him, and pulled himself near the top. He wanted to test one that was free to rise. Hamid grabbed the top layer, already rippling in an unsensed wind. He pulled out his pocket knife, and slashed at the material. It parted smoothly, with the resistance of heavy felt. He ripped off a strip of the material, stuffed it in his pocket, then grabbed again at the top layer. The unit fluttered in his hands, a four-meter square straining for the sky. It slowly tipped him backwards. His feet left the pile. It was rising as fast as the unloaded ones!

"Wait for me! Wait!" The Blab jumped desperately at his boots. Two meters up, three meters. Hamid gulped, and let go. He crashed to the concrete, lay stunned for a moment, imagining what would have happened if he'd dithered an instant longer. . . . Still. He took the scrap of agrav from his pocket, stared at it as it tugged on his fingers. There was a pattern in the reddish-gray fabric, intricate and recursive. The Tourists said it was in a different class from the fusion electrics. The electrics involved advanced technology, but were constructable within the Slow Zone. Agrav, on the other hand . . . the effect could be explained in theory, but its practical use depended on instant-by-instant restabilization at atomic levels. The Tourists claimed there were billions of protein-sized processors in the fabric. This was an import—not just from the Beyond—but from Transhuman Space. Till now, Hamid had been a skeptic. Flying was such a prosaic thing. But . . . these things had no simple logic. They were more like living creatures, or complex control systems. They seemed a lot like the "smart matter" Larry claimed was common in Transhuman technology.

Hamid cut the strip into two different-sized pieces. The cut edges were smooth, quite unlike cuts in cloth or leather. He let the fragments go. . . . They drifted slowly upwards, like leaves on a breeze. But after a few seconds, the large one took the lead, falling higher and higher above the smaller. *I could come down just by trimming the fabric!* And he remembered how the carpet had drifted sideways, in the direction of his grasp.

The sirens were louder. He looked at the pile of agravs. Funny. A week ago he had been worried about flying commercial air to Westland. "You want games, Blab? This is the biggest yet."

He climbed back up the pile. The top layer was just beginning to twitch. They had maybe thirty seconds, if it was like the others. He pulled the fabric around him, tying it under his arms. "Blab! Get your ass up here!"

She came, but not quite with the usual glee. Things had been rough this morning—or maybe she was just brighter than he was. He grabbed her, and tied the other end of the agrav under her shoulders. As the agrav twitched toward flight, the cloth seemed to shrink. He could still cut the fabric, but the knots were tight. He grabbed the Blab under her hind quarters, and drew her up to his chest—just like Pop used to do when the Blab was a pup. Only now, she was big. Her forelegs stuck long over his shoulders.

The fabric came taut around his armpits. Now he was standing. Now—his feet left the pile. He looked *down* at the melted pallets, the silver metal rivers that dug deep through the warehouse floor. The Blab was making the sounds of a small boy crying.

They were through the roof. Hamid shuddered as the morning chill turned his soaked clothing icy. The sun was at the horizon, its brilliance no help against the cold. Shadows grew long and crisp from the buildings. The guts of the warehouse lay open below them; from here it looked dark, but lightning still flickered. More reddish-gray squares floated up from the ruins. In the gravel lot fronting the warehouse, there were fire trucks and armored vehicles. Men ran back and forth from the guard box. A squad was moving around the side of the building. Two guys by the armored cars pointed at him, and others just stopped to stare. A boy and his not-dog, swinging beneath a wrong-way parachute. He'd seen enough Feds 'n' Crooks to know they could shoot him down easily, any number of ways. One of the figures climbed into the armored car. If they were half as trigger happy as the guards inside the warehouse . . .

Half a minute passed. The scene below could fit between his feet now. The Blab wasn't crying anymore, and he guessed the chill was no problem for her. The Blab's neck and head extended over his shoulder. He could feel her looking back and forth. "Wow," she said softly. "Wow."

Rockabye baby. They swung back and forth beneath the agrav. Back and forth. The swings were getting wider each time! In a sickening whirl, the sky and ground traded places. He was buried head first in agrav fabric. He struggled out of the mess. They weren't hanging below the agrav now, they were *lying* on top of it. This was crazy. How could it be stable with them on top? In a second it would dump them back under. He held tight to the Blab . . . but no more swinging. It was as if the hanging-down position had been the unstable one. More evidence that the agrav was smart matter, its processors using underlying nature to produce seemingly unnatural results.

The damn thing really was a flying carpet! Of course, with all the knots, the four-meter square of fabric was twisted and crumpled. It looked more like the Blab's nest of blankets back home than the flying carpets of fantasy.

The warehouse district was out of sight beneath the carpet. In the spaces around and above them, dozens of agravs paced him—some just a few meters away, some bare specks in the sky. Westwards, they were coming even with the tops of the Marquette towers: brown and ivory walls, vast mirrors of windows reflecting back the landscape of morning. Southwards, Ann Arbor was a tiny crisscross of streets, almost lost in the bristle of leafless trees. The quad was clearly visible, the interior walks, the tiny speck of red that was Morale Hall. He'd had roughly this view every time they flew back from the farm, but now . . . there was nothing around him. It was just Hamid and the Blab . . . and the air stretching away forever beneath them. Hamid gulped, and didn't look down for a while.

They were still rising. The breeze came straight down upon them—and it seemed to be getting stronger. Hamid shivered uncontrollably, teeth chattering. How high up were they? Three thousand meters? Four? He was going numb, and when he moved he could hear ice crackling in his jacket. He felt dizzy and nauseous—five thousand meters was about the highest you'd want to go without oxygen on Middle America. He *thought* he could stop the rise; if not, they were headed for space, along with the rest of the agravs.

But he had to do more than slow the rise, or descend. He looked up at the Lothlrimarre's barge. It was much nearer—and two hundred meters to the east. If he couldn't move this thing sideways, he'd need the slug's active cooperation.

It was something he had thought about—for maybe all of five seconds—back in the warehouse. If the agrav had been an ordinary lighter-than-air craft, there'd be no hope. Without props or jets, a balloon goes where the wind says; the only control comes from finding the *altitude* where the wind and you want the same thing. But when he grabbed that first carpet, it really had slid horizontally toward the side he was holding. . . .

He crept toward the edge. The agrav yielded beneath his knees, but didn't tilt more than a small boat would. Next to him, the Blab looked over the edge, straight down. Her head jerked this way and that as she scanned the landscape. "Wow," she kept saying. Could she really understand what she was seeing?

The wind shifted a little. It came a bit from the side now, not straight from above. He really did have control! Hamid smiled around chattering teeth.

The carpet rose faster and faster. The downward wind was an arctic blast. They must be going up at fifteen or twenty klicks per hour. The Lothlrimarre barge loomed huge above them . . . now almost beside them.

God, they were *above* it now! Hamid pulled out his knife, picked desperately at the blade opener with numbed fingers. It came open abruptly—and almost popped out of his shaking hand. He trimmed small pieces from the edge of the carpet. The wind from heaven stayed just as strong. Bigger pieces! He tore wildly at the cloth. One large strip, two. And the wind eased . . . stopped. Hamid bent over the edge of the carpet, and stuffed his vertigo back down his throat. *Perfect.* They were directly over the barge, and closing.

The nearest of the four pressure spheres was so close it blocked his view of the others. Hamid could see the human habitat, the conference area. They would touch down on a broad flat area next to the sphere. The aiming couldn't have been better. Hamid guessed the slug must be maneuvering too, moving the barge precisely under his visitor.

There was a flash of heat, and an invisible fist slammed into the carpet. Hamid and the Blab tumbled—now beneath the agrav, now above. He had a glimpse of the barge. A jet of yellow-white spewed from the sphere, ammonia and hydrogen at one thousand atmospheres. The top pressure sphere had been breached. The spear of superpressured gas was surrounded by pale flame where the hydrogen and atmospheric oxygen burned.

The barge fell out of view, leaving thunder and burning mists. Hamid held onto the Blab and as much of the carpet as he could wrap around them. The tumbling stopped; they were upside down in the heavy swaddling. Hamid looked out:

"Overhead" was the brown and gray of farmland in late autumn. Marquette was to his left. He bent around, peeked into the sky. There! The barge was several klicks away. The top pressure vessel was spreading fire and mist, but the lower ones looked okay. Pale violet flickered from between the spheres. Moments later, thunder echoed across the sky. The slug was fighting back!

He twisted in the jumble of cloth, trying to see the high sky. To the north . . . a single blue-glowing trail lanced southwards . . . split into five separate, jigging paths that cooled through orange to red. It was beautiful . . . but somehow like a jagged claw sketched against the sky. The claw tips dimmed to nothing, but whatever caused them still raced forward. The attackers' answering fire slagged the north-facing detail of the barge. It crumpled like trash plastic in a fire. The bottom pressure vessels still looked okay, but if the visitors' deck got zapped like that, Larry would be a dead man.

Multiple sonic booms rocked the carpet. Things swept past, too small and fast to clearly see. The barge's guns still flickered violet, but the craft was rising now—faster than he had ever seen it move.

After a moment, the carpet drifted through one more tumble, and they sat heads up. The morning had been transformed. Strange clouds were banked around and above him, some burning, some glowing, all netted with the brownish-reds of nitrogen oxides. The stench of ammonia burned his eyes and mouth. The Blab was making noises through her mouth, true coughing and choking sounds.

The Tourists were long gone. The Lothlrimarre was a dot at the top of the sky. All the other agravs had passed by. He and the Blab were alone in the burning clouds. *Probably not for long.* Hamid began sawing at the agrav fabric—tearing off a slice, testing for an upwelling breeze, then tearing off another. They drifted through the cloud deck into a light drizzle, a strange rain that burned the skin as it wet them. He slid the carpet sideways into the sunlight, and they could breathe again. Things looked almost normal, except where the clouds cast a great bloody shadow across the farmland.

Where best to land? Hamid looked over the edge of the carpet . . . and saw the enemy waiting. It was a cylinder, tapered, with a pair of small fins at one end. It drifted through the carpet's shadow, and he realized the enemy craft was *close*. It couldn't be more than ten meters long, less than two meters across at the widest. It hung silent, pacing the carpet's slow descent. Hamid looked up, and saw the others—four more dark shapes. They circled in, like killer fish nosing at a possible lunch. One slid right over them, so slow and near he could have run his palm down its length. There were no ports, no breaks in the dull finish. But the fins—red glowed dim from within them, and Hamid felt a wave of heat as they passed.

The silent parade went on for a minute, each killer getting its look. The Blab's head followed the craft around and around. Her eyes were wide, and she was making the terrified whistling noises of the night before. The air was still, but for the faint updraft of the carpet's descent. Or was it? . . . The sound grew, a hissing sound like Tines had made during his phone call.

Only now it came from all the killers, and there were overtones lurking at the edge of sensibility, tones that never could have come from an ordinary telephone.

"Blab." He reached to stroke her neck. She slashed at his hand, her needle-teeth slicing deep. Hamid gasped in pain, and rolled back from her. The Blab's pelt was puffed out as far as he had ever seen it. She looked twice normal size, a very large carnivore with death glittering in her eyes. Her long neck snapped this way and that, trying to track all the killers at once. Fore and rear talons dragged long rips through the carpet. She climbed onto the thickest folds of the carpet, and *shrieked* at the killers . . . and collapsed.

For a moment, Hamid couldn't move. His hand, the scream: razors across his hand, icepicks jammed in his ears. He struggled to his knees and crawled to the Blabber. "Blab?" No answer, no motion. He touched her flank: limp as something fresh dead.

In twenty years, Hamid Thompson had never had close friends, but he had never been alone, either. Until now. He looked up from the Blabber's body, at the circling shapes.

Alone at four thousand meters. He didn't have much choice when one of the killer fish came directly at him, when something wide and dark opened from its belly. The darkness swept around them, swallowing all.

Hamid had never been in space before. Under other circumstances, he would have reveled in the experience. The glimpse he'd had of Middle America from low orbit was like a beautiful dream. But now, all he could see through the floor of his cage was a bluish dot, nearly lost in the sun's glare. He pushed hard against the clear softness, and rolled onto his back. It was harder than a one-handed pushup to do that. He guessed the mothership was doing four or five gees . . . and had been for hours.

When they had pulled him off the attack craft, Hamid had been semi-conscious. He had no idea what acceleration that shark boat reached, but it was more than he could take. He remembered that glimpse of Middle America, blue and serene. Then . . . they'd taken the Blab—or her body—away. *Who?* There had been a human, the Ravna woman. She had done something to his hand; it wasn't bleeding anymore. And . . . and there had been the Blabber, up and walking around. No, the pelt pattern had been all wrong. *That must have been Tines.* There had been the hissing voice, and some kind of argument with Ravna.

Hamid stared up at the sunlight on the ceiling and walls. His own shadow lay spread-eagled on the ceiling. In the first hazy hours, he had thought it was another prisoner. The walls were gray, seamless, but with scrape marks and stains, as though heavy equipment was used here. He thought there was a door in the ceiling, but he couldn't remember for sure. There was no sign of one now. The room was an empty cubical, featureless, its floor showing clear to the stars: surely not an ordinary brig. There were no toilet facilities—and at five gees they wouldn't have helped. The air was thick with the stench of himself. . . . Hamid guessed the room was an airlock. The transparent floor might be nothing more than a figment of some field generator's imagination. A flick of a switch and Hamid would be swept away forever.

The Blabber gone, Pop gone, maybe Larry and the slug gone. . . . Hamid raised his good hand a few centimeters and clenched his fist. Lying here was the first time he'd ever thought about killing anyone. He thought about it a lot now. . . . It kept the fear tied down.

"Mr. Thompson." Ravna's voice. Hamid suppressed a twitch of surprise: after hours of rage, to hear the enemy. "Mr. Thompson, we are going to free fall in fifteen seconds. Do not be alarmed."

So, airline courtesy of a sudden.

The force that had squished him flat these hours, that had made it an exercise even to breathe, slowly lessened. From beyond the walls and ceiling he heard small popping noises. For a panicky instant, it seemed as though the floor had disappeared and he was falling through. He twisted. His hand hit the barrier . . . and he floated slowly across the room, toward the wall that had been the ceiling. A door had opened. He drifted through, into a hall that would have looked normal except for the intricate pattern of grooves and ledges that covered the walls.

"Thirty meters down the hall is a latrine," came Ravna's voice. "There are clean clothes that should fit you. When you are done . . . when you are done, we will talk."

Damn right. Hamid squared his shoulders and pulled himself down the hall.

She didn't look like a killer. There was anger—tension?—on her face, the face of someone who has been awake a long time and has fought hard—and doesn't expect to win.

Hamid drifted slowly into the—conference room? bridge?—trying to size everything up at once. It was a large room, with a low ceiling. Moving across it was easy in zero gee, slow bounces from floor to ceiling and back. The wall curved around, transparent along most of its circumference. There were stars and night dark beyond.

Ravna had been standing in a splash of light. Now she moved back a meter, into the general dimness. Somehow she slipped her foot into the floor, anchoring herself. She waved him to the other side of a table. They stood in the half crouch of zero gee, less than two meters apart. Even so, she looked taller than he had guessed from the phone call. Her mass might be close to his. The rest of her was as he remembered, though she looked very tired. Her gaze flickered across him, and away. "Hello, Mr. Thompson. The floor will hold your foot, if you tap it gently."

Hamid didn't take the advice; he held onto the table edge and jammed his feet against the floor. He would have something to brace against if the time came to move quickly. "Where is my Blabber?" His voice came out hoarse, more desperate than demanding.

"Your pet is dead."

There was a tiny hesitation before the last word. She was as bad a liar as ever. Hamid pushed back the rage: if the Blab was alive, there was something still possible beyond revenge. "Oh." He kept his face blank.

"However, we intend to return you safely to home." She gestured at the star fields around them. "The six-gee boost was to avoid unnecessary fighting with the Lothlrimarre being. We will coast outwards some farther, perhaps even go into ram drive. But Mr. Tines will take you back to Middle America in one of our attack boats. There will be no problem to land you without attracting notice . . . perhaps on the western continent, somewhere out of the way." Her tone was distant. He noticed that she never looked directly at him for more than an instant. Now she was staring just to one side of his face. He remembered the phone call, how she seemed to ignore his video. Up close, she was just as attractive as before—more. Just once he would like to see her smile. *And somewhere there was unease that he could be so attracted by a murderous stranger.*

If only. "If only I could understand *why*. Why did you kill the Blab? Why did you kill my father?"

Ravna's eyes narrowed. "That cheating piece of filth? He is too tricky to kill. He was gone when we visited his farm. I'm not sure I have killed anyone on this operation. The Lothlrimarre is still functioning, I know that." She sighed. "We were all very lucky. You have no idea what Tines has been like these last days. . . . He called you last night."

Hamid nodded numbly.

"Well, he was mellow then. He tried to kill me when I took over the ship. Another day like this and he would have been dead—and most likely your planet would have been so too."

Hamid remembered the Lothlrimarre's theory about the tines's need. And now that the creature had the Blab. . . . "So now Tines is satisfied?"

Ravna nodded vaguely, missing the quaver in his voice. "He's harmless now and very confused, poor guy. Assimilation is hard. It will be a few weeks . . . but he'll stabilize, probably turn out better than he ever was."

Whatever that means.

She pushed back from the table, stopped herself with a hand on the low ceiling. Apparently their meeting was over. "Don't worry. He should be well enough to take you home quite soon. Now I will show you your—"

"Don't rush him, Rav. Why should he want to go back to Middle America?" The voice was a pleasant tenor, human sounding but a little slurred.

Ravna bounced off the ceiling. "I thought you were going to stay out of this! Of course the boy is going back to Middle America. That's his home; that's where he fits."

"I wonder." The unseen speaker laughed. He sounded cheerfully— *joyfully*—drunk. "Your name is shit down there, Hamid, did you know that?"

"Huh?"

"Yup. You slagged the Caravan's entire shipment of fusion electrics.

'Course you had a little help from the Federal Police, but that fact is being ignored. Much worse, you destroyed most of the agrav units. *Whee.* Up, up and away. And there's no way those can be replaced short of a trip back to the Outsi—"

"Shut up!" Ravna's anger rode over the good cheer. "The agrav units were a cheap trick. Nothing that subtle can work in the Zone for long. Five years from now they would all have faded."

"Sure, sure. I know that, and you know that. But both Middle America and the Tourists figure you've trashed this Caravan, Hamid. You'd be a fool to go back."

Ravna shouted something in a language Hamid had never heard.

"English, Rav, English. I want him to understand what is happening."

"He is going back!" Ravna's voice was furious, almost desperate. "We *agreed!"*

"I know, Rav." A little of the rampant joy left the voice. It sounded truly sympathetic. "And I'm sorry. But I was different then, and I understand things better now. . . . Hey, I'll be down in a minute, okay?"

She closed her eyes. It's hard to slump in free fall, but Ravna came close, her shoulders and arms relaxing, her body drifting slowly up from the floor. "Oh, Lord," she said softly.

Out in the hall, someone was whistling a tune that had been popular in Marquette six months ago. A shadow floated down the walls, followed by . . . *the Blab?* Hamid lurched off the table, flailed wildly for a handhold. He steadied himself, got a closer look.

No. Not the Blab. It was of the same race certainly, but this one had an entirely different pattern of black and white. The great patch of black around one eye and white around the other would have been laughable . . . if you didn't know what you were looking at: at last to see Mr. Tines.

Man and alien regarded each other for a long moment. It was a little smaller than the Blab. It wore a checkered orange scarf about its neck. Its paws looked no more flexible than his Blab's . . . but he didn't doubt the intelligence that looked back from its eyes. The tines drifted to the ceiling, and anchored itself with a deft swipe of paw and talons. There were faint sounds in the air now, squeaks and twitters almost beyond hearing. If he listened close enough, Hamid guessed he would hear the hissing, too.

The tines looked at him, and laughed pleasantly—the tenor voice of a minute before. "Don't rush me! I'm not all here yet."

Hamid looked at the doorway. There were two more there, one with a jeweled collar—the leader? They glided through the air and tied down next to the first. Hamid saw more shadows floating down the hall.

"How many?" he asked.

"I'm six now." He thought it was a different tines that answered, but the voice was the same.

The last three floated in the doorway. One wore no scarf or jewelry . . . and looked very familiar.

"Blab!" Hamid pushed off the table. He went into a spin that missed the door by several meters. The Blabber—it must be her—twisted skillfully around and fled the room.

"Stay away!" For an instant the tines's voice changed, held the same edge as the night before. Hamid stood on the wall next to the doorway and looked down the hall. The Blab was there, sitting on the closed door at the far end. Hamid's orientation flipped . . . the hall could just as well be a deep, bright-lit well, with the Blab trapped at the bottom of it.

"Blab?" He said softly, aware of the tines behind him.

She looked up at him. "I can't play the old games anymore, Hamid," she said in her softest femvoice. He stared for a moment, uncomprehending. Over the years, the Blab said plenty of things that—by accident or in the listeners' imagination—might seem humanly intelligent. Here, for the first time, he knew that he was hearing sense. . . . And he guessed what Ravna meant when she said the Blab was dead.

Hamid backed away from the edge of the pit. He looked at the other tines, remembered that their speech came as easily from one as the other. "You're like a hive of roaches, aren't you?"

"A little." The tenor voice came from somewhere among them.

"But telepathic," Hamid said.

The one who had been his friend answered, but in the tenor voice: "Yes, between myselves. But it's no sixth sense. You've known about it all your life. I like to talk a lot. Blabber." The squeaking and the hissing: just the edge of all they were saying to each other across their two-hundred-kilohertz bandwidth. "I'm sorry I flinched. Myselves are still confused. I don't know quite who I am."

The Blab pushed off and drifted back into the bridge. She grabbed a piece of ceiling as she came even with Hamid. She extended her head toward him, tentatively, as though he were a stranger. *I feel the same way about you,* thought Hamid. But he reached out to brush her neck with his fingers. She twitched back, glided across the room to nestle among the other tines.

Hamid stared at them staring back. He had a sudden image: a pack of long-necked rats beadily analyzing their prey. "So. Who is the real Mr. Tines? The monster who'd smash a world, or the nice guy I'm hearing now?"

Ravna answered, her voice tired, distant. "The monster tines is gone . . . or going. Don't you see? The pack was unbalanced. It was dying."

"There were five in my pack, Hamid. Not a bad number: some of the brightest packs are that small. But I was down from seven—two of myselves had been killed. The ones remaining were mismatched, and only one of them was female." Tines paused. "I know humans can go for years without contact with the opposite sex, and suffer only mild discomfort—"

Tell me about it.

"—but tines are very different. If a pack's sex ratio gets too lopsided, especially if there is a mismatch of skills, then the mind disintegrates. . . . Things can get very nasty in the process." Hamid noticed that all the time it talked, the two tines next to the one with the orange scarf had been nibbling at the scarf's knots. They moved quickly, perfectly coordinated, untying and retying the knots. *Tines doesn't need hands.* Or put another way, he already had six. Hamid was seeing the equivalent of a human playing nervously with his tie.

"Ravna lied when she said the Blab is dead. I forgive her: she wants you off our ship, with no more questions, no more hassle. But the Blabber isn't dead. She was *rescued* . . . from being an animal the rest of her life. And her rescue saved the pack. I feel so . . . happy. Better even than when I was seven. I can understand things that have been puzzles for years. Your Blab is far more language-oriented than any of my other selves. I could never talk like this without her."

Ravna had drifted toward the pack. Now she had her feet planted on the floor beneath them. Her head brushed the shoulder of one, was even with the eyes of another. "Imagine the Blabber as the verbal hemisphere of a human brain," she said to Hamid.

"Not quite," Tines said. "A human hemisphere can almost carry on by itself. The Blab by itself could never be a person."

Hamid remembered how the Blab's greatest desire had often seemed just to *be* a real person. And listening to this creature, he heard echoes of the Blab. It would be easy to accept what they were saying. . . . Yet if you turned the words just a little, you had enslavement and rape—the slug's theory with frosting.

Hamid turned away from all the eyes and looked across the star clouds. *How much should I believe? How much should I seem to believe?* "One of the Tourists wanted to sell us a gadget, an 'ftl radio.' Did you know that we used it to ask about the tines? Do you know what we found?" He told them about the horrors Larry had found around the galactic rim.

Ravna exchanged a glance with the tines by her head. For a moment the only sound was the twittering and hissing. Then Tines spoke. "Imagine the most ghastly villains of Earth's history. Whatever they are, whatever holocausts they set, I assure you much worse has happened elsewhere. . . . Now imagine that this regime was so vast, so effectively *evil* that no honest historians survived. What stories do you suppose would be spread about the races they exterminated?"

"Okay. So—"

"Tines are not monsters. On average, we are no more bloodthirsty than you humans. But we are descended from packs of wolf-like creatures. We are deadly warriors. Given reasonable equipment and numbers, we can outfight most anything in the Slow Zone." Hamid remembered the shark pack of attack boats. With one animal in each, and radio communication . . . no team of human pilots could match their coordination. "We were once a great power in our part of the Slow Zone. We had enemies, even when there was no war. Would you trust creatures who live indefinitely, but whose personalities may drift from friendly to indifferent—even to inimical—as their components die and are replaced?"

"And you're such a peach of a guy because you've got the Blab?"

"*Yes!* Though you liked . . . I know you would have liked me when I was seven. But the Blab has a lovely outlook; she makes it fun to be alive."

Hamid looked at Ravna and the pack who surrounded her. So the tines had been great fighters. That he believed. So they were now virtually extinct, having run into something even deadlier. That he could believe, too. Beyond that . . . he'd be a fool to believe anything. He could imagine Tines as a friend, he wanted Ravna as one. But all the talk, all the seeming argument— it could just as well be manipulation. One thing was sure: if he returned to Middle America, he would never know the truth. He might live the rest of his life safe and cozy, but he wouldn't have the Blab, and he would never know what had really happened to her.

He gave Ravna a lopsided smile. "Back to square one then. I want passage to the Beyond with you."

"Out of the question. I-I made that clear from the beginning."

Hamid pushed nearer, stopped a meter in front of her. "Why won't you look at me?" he said softly. "Why do you hate me so much?"

For a full second, her eyes looked straight into his. "I *don't* hate you!" Her face clouded, as if she were about to weep. "It's just that you're such a God *damned* disappointment!" She pushed back abruptly, knocking the tines out of her way.

He followed her slowly back to the conference table. She "stood" there, talking to herself in some unknown language. "She's swearing to her ancestors," murmured a tines that drifted close by Hamid's head. "Her kind is big on that sort of thing."

Hamid anchored himself across from her. He looked at her face. Young, no older than twenty it looked. But Outsiders had some control over aging. Besides, Ravna had spent at least the last ten years in relativistic flight. "You hired my—you hired Hussein Thompson to adopt me, didn't you?"

She nodded.

"Why?"

She looked back at him for a moment, this time not flinching away. Finally she sighed. "Okay, I will try but . . . there are many things you from the Slow Zone do not understand. Middle America is close to the Beyond, but you see out through a tiny hole. You can have even less concept of what lies beyond the Beyond, in the Transhuman reaches." She was beginning to sound like Lazy Larry.

"I'm willing to start with the version for five-year-olds."

"Okay." The faintest of smiles crossed her face. It was everything he'd guessed it would be. He wondered how he could make her do it again. " 'Once upon a time,' "—the smile again, a little wider!—"there was a very wise and good man, as wise and good as any mere human or human equivalent can ever be: a mathematical genius, a great general, an even greater peacemaker. He lived five hundred years subjective, and half that time he was fighting a very great evil."

The Tines put in, "Just a part of that evil chewed up my race for breakfast."

Ravna nodded. "Eventually it chewed our hero, too. He's been dead almost a century objective. The enemy has been very alert to keep him dead. Tines and I may be the last people trying to bring him back. . . . How much do you know about cloning, Mr. Thompson?"

Hamid couldn't answer for a moment; it was too clear where all this was going. "The Tourists claim they can build a viable zygote from almost any body cell. They say it's easy, but that what you get is no more than an identical twin of the original."

"That is about right. In fact, the clone is often *much* less than an identical twin. The uterine environment determines much of an individual's adult characteristics. Consider mathematical ability. There is a genetic component—but part of mathematical genius comes from the fetus getting just the right testosterone overdose. A little too much and you have a *dummy*."

"Tines and I have been running for a long time. Fifty years ago we reached Lothlrimarre—the back end of nowhere if there ever was one. We had a clonable cell from the great man. We did our best with the humaniform medical equipment that was available. The newborn *looked* healthy enough. . . ."

Rustle, hiss.

"But why not just raise the—child—yourself?" Hamid said. "Why hire someone to take him into the Slow Zone?"

Ravna bit her lip and looked away. It was Tines who replied: "Two reasons. The enemy wants you permanently dead. Raising you in the Slow Zone was the best way to keep you out of sight. The other reason is more subtle. We don't have records of your original memories; we can't make a perfect copy. But if we could give you an upbringing that mimicked the original's . . . then we'd have someone with the same outlook."

"Like having the original back, with a bad case of amnesia."

Tines chuckled. "Right. And things went very well at first. It was great good luck to run into Hussein Thompson at Lothlrimarre. He seemed a bright fellow, willing to work for his money. He brought the newborn in suspended animation back to Middle America, and married a woman equally bright, to be your mother."

"We had everything figured, the original's background imitated better than we had ever hoped. I even gave up one of my selves, a newborn, to be with you."

"I guess I know most of the rest," said Hamid. "Everything went fine for the first eight years," the happy years of a loving family, "till it became clear that I wasn't a math genius. Then your hired hand didn't know what to do, and your plan fell apart."

"It didn't have to!" Ravna slapped the table. The motion pulled her body up, almost free of the foot anchors. "The math ability was a big part, but there was still a chance—if Thompson hadn't welshed on us." She glared at Hamid, and then at the pack. "The original's parents died when he was ten years old. Hussein and his woman were supposed to disappear when the clone was ten, in a faked air crash. *That was the agreement!* Instead—" she swallowed. "We talked to him. He wouldn't meet in person. He was full of excuses, the clever bastard. 'I didn't see what good it would do to hurt the boy any more,' he said. 'He's no superman, just a good kid. I wanted him to be happy!' " She choked on her own indignation. "*Happy!* If he knew what we have been through, what the stakes are—"

Hamid's face felt numb, frozen. He wondered what it would be like to throw up in zero gee. "What—what about my mother?" he said in a very small voice.

Ravna gave her head a quick shake. "She tried to persuade Thompson. When that didn't work, she left you. By then it was too late; besides, that sort of abandonment is not the trauma the original experienced. But she did her part of the bargain; we paid her most of what we promised. . . . We came to Middle America expecting to find someone very wonderful, living again. Instead, we found—"

"—a piece of trash?" He couldn't get any anger into the question.

She gave a shaky sigh. ". . . No, I don't really think that. Hussein Thompson probably did raise a good person, and that's more than most can claim. But if you were the one we had hoped, you would be known all over Middle America by now, the greatest inventor, the greatest mover since the colony began. And that would be just the beginning." She seemed to be looking through him . . . remembering?

Tines made a diffident throat-clearing sound. "Not a piece of trash at all. And not just a 'good kid,' either. A part of me lived with Hamid for twenty years; the Blabber's memories are about as clear as a tines fragment's can be. Hamid is not just a failed dream to me, Rav. He's different, but I like to be around him almost as much as with . . . the other one. And when the crunch came—well, I saw him fight back. Given his background, even the original couldn't have done better. Hitching a ride on a raw agrav was the sort of daring that—"

"Okay, Tiny, the boy is daring and quick. But there's a difference between suicidal foolishness and calculated risk-taking. This late in life, there's no way he'll become more than a 'good man.' " Sarcasm lilted in the words.

"We could do worse, Rav."

"We *must* do far better, and you know it! See here. It's two years subjective to get out of the Zone, and our suspension gear is failed. I will *not* accept seeing his face every day for two years. He goes back to Middle America." She kicked off, drifted toward the tines that hung over Hamid.

"I think not," said Tines. "If he doesn't want to go, I won't fly him back."

Anger and—strangely—panic played on Ravna's face. "This isn't how you were talking last week."

"Heh heh heh." Lazy Larry's cackle. "I've changed. Haven't you noticed?"

She grabbed a piece of ceiling and looked down at Hamid, calculating.

"Boy. I don't think you understand. We're in a hurry; we won't be stopping any place like Lothlrimarre. There is one last way we might bring the original back to life—perhaps even with his own memories. You'll end up in Transhuman space if you come with us. The chances are that none of us will surv—" She stopped, and a slow smile spread across her face. Not a friendly smile. "Have you not thought what use your body might still be to us? You know nothing of what we plan. We may find ways of using you like a—like a blank data cartridge."

Hamid looked back at her, hoping no doubts showed on his face. "Maybe. But I'll have two years to prepare, won't I?"

They glared at each other for a long moment, the greatest eye contact yet. "So be it," she said at last. She drifted a little closer. "Some advice. We'll be two years cooped up here. It's a big ship. Stay out of my way." She drew back and pulled herself across the ceiling, faster and faster. She arrowed into the hallway beyond, and out of sight.

Hamid Thompson had his ticket to the Outside. Some tickets cost more than others. What much would he pay for his?

Eight hours later, the ship was under ram drive, outward bound. Hamid sat in the bridge, alone. The "windows" on one side of the room showed the view aft. Middle America's sun cast daylight across the room.

Invisible ahead of them, the interplanetary medium was being scooped in, fuel for the ram. The acceleration was barely perceptible, perhaps a fiftieth of a gee. The ram drive was for the long haul. That acceleration would continue indefinitely, eventually rising to almost half a gravity—and bringing them near light speed.

Middle America was a fleck of blue, trailing a white dot and a yellow one. It would be many hours before his world and its moons were lost from sight—and many days before they were lost to telescopic view.

Hamid had been here an hour—two?—since shortly after Tines showed him his quarters.

The inside of his head felt like an abandoned battlefield. A monster had become his good buddy. The man he hated turned out to be the father he had wanted . . . and his mother now seemed an uncaring manipulator. *And now I can never go back and ask you truly what you were, truly if you loved me.*

He felt something wet on his face. One good thing about gravity, even a fiftieth of a gee: it cleared the tears from your eyes.

He must be very careful these next two years. There was much to learn, and even more to guess at. What was lie and what was truth? There were things about the story that . . . how could one human being be as important as Ravna and Tines claimed? Next to the Transhumans, no human equivalent could count for much.

It might well be that these two believed the story they told him—*and that could be the most frightening possibility of all.* They talked about the Great Man as though he were some sort of messiah. Hamid had read of similar things in Earth history: twentieth-century Nazis longing for Hitler, the fanatics of the Afghan Jihad scheming to bring back their Imam. The story Larry got from the ansible could be true, and the Great Man might have been accomplice to the murder of a thousand worlds.

Hamid found himself laughing. *Where does that put me?* Could the clone of a monster rise above the original?

"What's funny, Hamid?" Tines had entered the bridge quietly. Now he settled himself on the table and posts around Hamid. The one that had been the Blab sat just a meter away.

"Nothing. Just thinking."

They sat for several minutes in silence, watching the sky. There was a wavering there—like hot air over a stove—the tiniest evidence of the fields that formed the ram around them. He glanced at the tines. Four of them were looking out the windows. The other two looked back at him, their eyes as dark and soft as the Blab's had ever been.

"Please don't think badly of Ravna," Tines said. "She had a real thing going with the almost-you of before. . . . They loved each other very much."

"I guessed."

The two heads turned back to the sky. These next two years he must watch this creature, try to decide. . . . But suspicions aside, the more he saw of Tines, the more he liked him. Hamid could almost imagine that he had not lost the Blab, but gained five of her siblings. And the bigmouth had finally become a real person.

The companionable silence stretched on. After a moment, the one that had been the Blab edged across the table and bumped her head against his shoulder. Hamid hesitated, then stroked her neck. They watched the sun and the fleck of blue a moment more. "You know," said Tines, but in the femvoice that was the Blab's favorite, "I will miss that place. And most of all . . . I will miss the cats and the dogs."

Janet Kagan

THE RETURN OF THE KANGAROO REX

Janet Kagan made her first short fiction sale in 1989, but has rapidly built a large and enthusiastic audience for her work, and has become a figure of note in the nineties. Although her debt to earlier writers of the offworld adventure tale, particularly James H. Schmitz (on whose work she is something of an authority, having contributed the introduction for the collection *The Best of James H. Schmitz*), is clear, she quickly developed a characteristic and flavorful voice of her own, and always brings her own quirky and individual perspective to whatever she's writing about, here breathing new life into the Exploring-a-Frontier-Planet story, a subgenre most commentators would have thought to be played out decades before. In fact, her linked series of stories about Mama Jason, of which "The Return of the Kangaroo Rex" is an example, later collected in book form as *Mirabile,* has proved to be one of the most popular series to run in *Asimov's Science Fiction* in recent years, with several of the stories winning the *Asimov's* Reader's Award Poll by large margins. Her first novel, a Star Trek novel called *Uhura's Song* was a nationwide bestseller, and her second novel *Hellspark* (*not* a Star Trek novel) was also widely acclaimed, and has been recently reissued. She is a frequent contributor to *Asimov's Science Fiction,* and has also sold to *Analog, Pulphouse,* and *Absolute Magnitude.* Her story "The Nutcracker Coup" won her a Hugo Award in 1993. She lives in Lincoln Park, New Jersey, with her husband, Ricky, several computers, and *lots* of cats, and is at work on a new novel.

In the wry and suspenseful story that follows, she takes us along to the frontier planet Mirabile to meet a woman whose job it is to cope with some very dangerous and very odd creatures, and follows her as she unravels a compelling biological mystery.

I'd been staring at the monitor so long all the genes were beginning to look alike to me. They shouldn't have, of course—this gene-read was native Mirabilan, so it was a whole new kettle of fish.

That's an American Guild expression, but it's the right one. At a casual look, had the critter been Earth-based, we'd have classed it as fish and left it at that. The problem was that it had taken a liking to our rice crop, and, if we didn't do something quick, nobody on Mirabile'd see a chow fun noodle ever again. So I went back to staring, trying to force those genes into patterns the team and I could cope with.

Moving the rice fields didn't guarantee we'd find a place free of them. In the first place, it encysted in dry ground, meaning you never knew where it'd pop up until you flooded the area. In the second place, it could leap like a salmon from the first place *to* the second place. It had already demonstrated its ability to spread from one field to the next. Susan had measured a twelve-foot leap.

The prospect got dimmer when Chie-Hoon caught them making that same leap from dry ground. Their limit was some five or six leaps until they hit water again, but that gave them quite a range.

It was as pretty a piece of native bioengineering as I've seen, one I could appreciate even if the rice growers couldn't. Wiping 'em out wholesale was not an option on *my* list, but I knew the farmers would be thinking along those lines if we didn't come up with something by next growing season.

I don't mess with the Mirabilan ecology any more than I have to. We don't know enough about it to know what we're getting into. Even if I thought we could do it, we'd be fools to try to wipe out any native species. The Earth-authentic species we've imported have played havoc enough with the Mirabilan ecology.

I wasn't paying much attention to anything but the problem at hand, so when Susan exclaimed, "Noisy! You look *awful*," I practically jumped out of my skin and busted my elbow turning my chair.

"Noisy" is Susan's pet name for Leonov Bellmaker Denness, and he *did* look awful. His white hair looked like something had nested in it; he was bleeding—no, *had* bled profusely—across the cheek; his shirt hung in tatters from the shoulder and there were raking claw-marks along his upper arms. Mike went scrambling for the emergency kit.

The only thing that spoiled the impact of all this disaster was that Leo was grinning from ear to ear. "Now, is that any way to greet an old friend?" he said to Susan. "Especially one who's come courting?"

He turned the grin on me and it got broader and brighter. Then he made me a deep formal bow and started in: "Ann Jason Masmajean, I, Leonov Bellmaker Denness, beg you to hear my petition."

I got to my feet and bowed back, just as deeply and formally, to let him know I'd be glad to hear him out. He made a second bow, deeper than the first, and went on: "I have brought you a gift in symbol of my intentions . . ."

Mike had the medical kit but he stood frozen. Chances were neither he nor Susan had ever seen a ship's-formal proposal except in the old films. The novelty of it kept either from interrupting. Just as well. I was enjoying the performance: Leo has flair.

Besides, I wouldn't dream of interrupting a man in the process of cataloguing my virtues, even if some of those "virtues" would have raised eyebrows in a lot of other people. I especially liked being called "reasonably stubborn."

At last Leo got to the wrap-up. "It is my hope that you will accept my gift and consider my suit." He finished off with yet another bow.

Seeing he was done spurred Mike and Susan into action. Susan held Leo down while Mike worked him over with alcohol swabs. "No respect for ritual," Leo complained, "Back 'em off, Annie, can't you? I'm not senile yet! I *did* clean the wounds."

Leo had spent years as a scout, so I didn't doubt his good sense. He'd hardly have lived to the ripe old age he had if he hadn't been cautious about infection in the bush.

To the two of them, he protested, "The lady hasn't answered yet."

"Back off," I told the kids.

They didn't until I advanced on them. Mike took two steps away from Leo, put his hands behind his back, and said to Susan, "*Now* he's going to get it." Susan nodded.

Leo just kept grinning, so I gave him a huge hug hello to make sure nothing was broken. The rest of him looked just fine, so I stepped back and bowed once more to meet the requirements of the ritual. "Leo Bellmaker Denness, I, Ann Jason Masmajean, am sufficiently intrigued to view your gift."

He crooked a finger and led me outside, Mike and Susan right behind. "In the back of the truck. *Don't* open that door until you've had a good look!"

So we climbed the back bumper and all crowded to the window for a good look. We didn't get one at first. Whatever it was was mad as all hell, and launched itself at the door hard enough to rattle the window and make the three of us jump back en masse. The door held.

Leo said, "It's been doing that all the way from Last Edges. Hasn't gotten through the door yet, but I'm a little worried it might hurt itself."

"It's not itself it wants to hurt," Susan said.

"You'd be pissed, too, if somebody wrestled you away from your mama and shoved you into the back of a truck headed god-knows-where," Leo said.

The door stopped rattling. I got a foot on the back bumper and hoisted myself up for a second try. Leo's present glared at me through the window and snarled. I snarled back in the same tone.

Since it was a youngster and I was an unknown, it backed off with a hop, letting me get a good look. In overall shape, it was kangaroo, but it had the loveliest set of stripes across the hips I'd ever seen—and the jaw! Oh, the jaw! It opened that jaw to warn me to keep back, and the head split almost to the ear, to show me the sharpest set of carnivore teeth in history.

"Oh, Leo," I murmured, stepping down from my perch. "That's the nicest present anybody's ever brought me." I gave him another big hug and a thorough kiss for good measure. "Leonov Bellmaker Denness, I accept both your gift and your suit."

He beamed. "I knew I got it right."

"Oh, shit!" said Mike, from behind me. "Susan! It's a goddam kangaroo rex!" He stared at Leo in disbelief. "Are you telling me this man brought you a *kangaroo rex* as a courting present?"

Susan, in turn, looked at *Mike* in disbelief. "It's perfect, you idiot! It means Noisy knows exactly what kind of person she is, and how to please her. Don't you understand *anything*?"

That would have devolved into a squabble—let a twenty-four-year-old and a sixteen-year-old discuss any subject and that's the usual outcome—but the kangaroo rex slammed against the door of the truck again and brought them both back to their senses.

"Leo," I said, "go on over to my house and get yourself cleaned up. We'll wrestle the thing into a cage. Then I want to hear all about it."

He nodded. "Sure. Two things first, though. Pick the right cage—I saw that thing jump a six-foot fence—then contact Moustafa Herder Kozlev or Janzen Herder Lizhi in Last Edges. I told Moustafa I'd make the official report on his Dragon's Tooth but I doubt he believes me." He examined a set of skinned knuckles. "Not when I punched him to keep him from shooting it."

"My hero," I said, meaning it.

He kissed my hand and vanished in the direction of my house. I turned to my available team-members and said, "Don't just stand there with your eyes hanging out of your heads. Let's get to work."

By the time we'd gotten an enclosure ready for the creature, Chie-Hoon and Selima had returned from up-country, where they'd been watching those damned hopping fish in the act. Just as well, because it took all five of us to maneuver the kangaroo rex safely out of the truck and into captivity.

Most of us wound up with bruises. It was still mad as all hell. It slammed each side of the fence in turn (didn't take it but two hops to cross the enclosure either) and once shot up and cracked its head on the overhead wire. That settled it down a bit. I sent Selima to get it some meat.

I couldn't take my eyes off the thing. I hadn't seen one for nine years.

"Another outbreak of kangaroo rexes," said Chie-Hoon, "Just what we needed. I assume it sprang from the kangaroos around Gogol?"

"Last Edges," I said. That didn't surprise me, the EC around Last Edges being almost identical to that around Gogol. "Contact Herders Kozlev and Lizhi up there. Tell them we've been notified. Find out if they've seen any more—"

"The usual drill," said Chie-Hoon.

"The usual drill."

Selima came back. She'd brought one of the snaggers Mike invented—let him do the honors of getting the cell sample while she distracted it with the meat. Or tried to. The snagger doesn't do more than pin-prick, but that was enough to rile the rex into slamming against the fence again, trying to get at Mike while he reeled the sample through the chain-link.

Mike jerked back but the sample came with him. He held it out to me. "Hardly necessary," he said. "I know what we're gonna find."

So did I. There was no doubt in my mind that the sample would match those from the last outbreak gene for gene. The kangaroo rex had settled down, wolfing at the meat Selima had tossed it. "It eats gladrats," said Selima, looking surprised. "It can't be *all* bad."

Not as far as I was concerned, it couldn't be all bad. If it was a Dragon's Tooth, it was a beautifully constructed one—completely viable.

That may need a word of explanation. . . . You see, when they shipped us off to colonize Mirabile, they were into redundancy. We got cold-storage banks of every conceivable species. (I use the "we" loosely; I'm third-generation Mirabilan myself.) But on top of that we also got the redundancy built right into the gene helices of all the stored species. Some bright-eyed geneticist back on Earth had apparently gotten *that* idea just before the expedition set off: genes within genes, helices tucked away inside other helices.

It was a good idea in theory. If we lost a species (*and* lost the ability to build it ourselves), sooner or later it would pop up spontaneously—all it needed was the right environmental conditions. Given the right EC, every hundredth turtle would lay an alligator egg.

In practice, it was a rotten idea. We'll never lack for alligators, not on Mirabile. They didn't tell us how to turn off those hidden helices, or if they did, the technique was only described in that part of ship's files we'd lost. So we Jasons have a running battle with cattle that are giving birth to reindeer and daffodils seeding iris (or worse—cockroaches).

Meanwhile, in the manner of all genes, the hidden genes *mixed*. While the turtle genes were reproducing turtles, the alligator genes tucked in with the turtle genes were mixing with god-knows-what. So given the right EC, we got chimera—familiarly known as Dragon's Teeth.

It was possible that the kangaroo rex was just an intermediate, a middle step between a kangaroo and anything from a gerbil to a water buffalo. Right now, however, it was a kangaroo rex, and impressive as all hell.

"You watch it, Mama Jason," Susan said. "I'll do the gene-read." She reached for the sample as if she had a vested interest in the beast herself. *She* figured she did, at least. Must have been all the times she'd made me tell the story of the first outbreak.

She may be the youngest and newest member of the team, but she can do a gene-read with the best of us. I handed the sample over.

Then I just stood there quietly and appreciated it. About three feet tall (not counting the tail, of course), it was already quite capable of surviving on its own. Which meant, more than likely, that its mama would very shortly move its sibling out of storage and into development. Chances were pretty good that one would be a kangaroo rex, too. Since the mama hadn't abandoned this one, it seemed unlikely she'd abandon another. I wondered if there were enough of them for a reliable gene pool.

The rex had calmed down now that it had eaten—now that most of the excitement was over. It was quietly investigating the enclosure, moving slowly on all fours. Hunched like that, it looked a lot like a mythological line-backer about to receive. With those small front legs, you never expect the thing (even a regulation kangaroo) to have the shoulders it does.

As it neared the side of the fence that I was gaping through, it yawned—

the way a cat does, just to let you know it has weapons. I stayed quiet and still. It didn't come any closer and it didn't threaten any further.

That was a good sign, as far as I was concerned. Either it was full or it didn't consider me prey. I was betting it didn't consider me prey. Still, it *was* nasty-looking, which wasn't going to help its case, and it was still a baby. Adult, if it were a true kangaroo rex, it would stand as high as its kangaroo mother—six or seven feet.

In the outbreak of them we'd had nine years back near Gogol, they'd been herd animals. There had been some twenty-odd, with more on the way, of course. Chie-Hoon tells me kangaroos come in "mobs," which seemed appropriate for the kangaroo rexes as well, if a little weak-sounding. And we'd wiped out the last group wholesale.

Oh, I'd yelled and screamed a lot. At the very least, I'd hoped we could stash the genes so we could pull them out if we ever needed the creature for some reason. I got voted down, and I got voted down, and finally I got shouted down.

This time would be different.

The kangaroo rex sat back on its tail and began to wash, using its tongue and paws as prettily as any cat. In the midst of cleaning its whiskers, it froze, glanced up briefly, then went back to preening.

That was the only warning I had that Leo was back. He hadn't lost the ability to move softly with the passage of years. He put his arm around me and I leaned into him, feeling a little more than cat-smug myself, though I hadn't done anything to deserve it. Maybe *because* I hadn't done anything to deserve it.

"Pretty thing," Leo said softly, so as not to startle it. "Now I understand why you wanted to keep them."

"This time we *are* keeping them," I said.

There was a clatter of the door behind me. The kangaroo rex bounced to the farthest side of the enclosure, hit the fence on the second bounce, and froze, jaws agape and threatening.

"I know what you're thinking, Annie," Mike said. "You'd better come talk to these guys first. You're not going to like what you hear."

Herders Jarlskog and Yndurain were not inclined toward leniency, especially not Jarlskog, who had worked himself up into a fine sense of outrage. To hear him tell it, you'd have thought a mob of rexes had eaten his entire flock, plus several of his children. So the entire town was already in an uproar.

I halfway agreed with their sentiments. I like the occasional lamb chop just as much as the next guy—especially the way Chris cooks them up at Loch Moose Lodge—and this was one of only seven flocks on all of Mirabile. Sheep here are labor-intensive. They can't be trusted to graze unattended: forever eating something native that'll poison them. So we keep only the seven flocks and we keep them on a strict diet of Earth fodder.

All this means that they have to be kept behind fences and that the plant life in there with 'em has to be policed regularly. That's one of the reasons all the flocks are on the fringes of the desert—it's easier to irrigate the plant life into submission.

The result of all this is that we eat a lot more kangaroo tail soup than we eat lamb curry. The kangaroos fend for themselves quite nicely, thank you, and there's no shortage of them.

Jarlskog wanted me to arrange an instant shortage of kangaroo rexes. So did Yndurain. In an hour's time, the rest of the town would start calling in with the same demand. I soothed them by telling them I'd have a team up there by the end of the day. In the meantime, they were to shoot only if they saw a rex actually in with the sheep.

They grumbled some but agreed. When I canceled the call, I turned to Leo. "What do you think? Will they go right out and shoot every kangaroo in sight?"

"No," he said. "Janzen and Moustafa are good kids. I think they can put a damper on the hysteria. Once I convinced Moustafa the rex was mine, he was even willing to help me catch it."

"It took a bit of convincing, though." I glanced significantly at his skinned knuckles.

He grinned and shrugged. "In the heat of passion." His face turned serious and he added, "He *will* shoot any roo that jumps that fence today, though, so if you want to head up there, now's the time."

Mike handed me a sheaf of hard copy. It was the list of everybody who lived in a hundred-mile radius of the spot where the rex had turned up. "Good news," he said. "We only have to worry about twenty families."

That is the only advantage I know of being underpopulated. For a moment, I considered not issuing a general alert. After all, for all we knew, there was only *one* kangaroo rex and it was in our backyard.

Mike read my mind and shook his head. "If you want to keep them, Annie, you better not risk having one of them eat some kid."

"It was only an idle thought," I told him. "Put out a notification. Keep the kids in, keep the adults armed. But add that I don't want them shot unless it's absolutely necessary."

Chie-Hoon said, "Annie, we're not going to go through this *again*, are we?"

"Damn straight, we are," I said, "and this time I intend to win! Who's coming with me?"

"Me," said Leo.

"And me," said Susan, looking up from her monitor. "It *is* the same kangaroo rex as last time, Mama Jason, only I've got two secondary helices here. They're both marsupial, but more than that I can't tell you offhand. It'll take the computer all night to search."

"Let me have a look first," Chie-Hoon said. "Maybe I'll recognize something. I have a vested interest in marsupials, after all."

Everybody's got to have a hobby. Chie-Hoon's is the Australian Guild, meaning Chie-Hoon knows more than anybody could ever want to know about the customs and wildlife of Earth's "Australia," which includes about ninety percent of the marsupials found in ship's records.

"Help yourself," I said. I'd never found the time to join any of the Earth Authentic Guilds myself—if I were looking for a hobby I rather thought I'd make it Leo—but this was the sort of thing that came in handy. "Since Leo volunteers to come along, we'll leave you to it."

We're habitually short-handed, and since I'd worked with Leo once before I knew he and I could handle just about anything that came up. As for Susan, well, Earth-authentic wild horses couldn't have kept her away.

Mike looked glum. "I get stuck with the fish, right?"

"And Selima," I pointed out, which brightened him up considerably. (I'm rather hoping those two will decide to help alleviate our underpopulation problem one of these fine days. I'm giving them every opportunity.) "We'll be in touch."

"We'll argue," Mike assured me.

We took my skimmer. Leo, being retired (hah!), no longer rates up-to-date equipment. We let Susan drive and scandalized her by necking in the back seat. When we'd caught up a bit on old times, we broke the clinch.

"Why will you argue?" Leo asked.

"You remember, Noisy. Mama Jason wanted to keep the kangaroo rexes the last time they cropped up. Mike and Chie-Hoon didn't."

"A *lot* of people didn't want them kept," I said. "I lost that round."

"It's not going to be any easier this time," Leo said. "Both those herders were—if you'll pardon the expression—hopping mad."

Susan giggled. So did I.

"I know. But I'm older and meaner this time around."

" 'Meaner'?" That was Susan. "Mama Jason, *last* time one of the damn things almost chewed your foot off!"

"D'you think I could forget something like that?" I leaned on the back of the seat and glared at her in the mirror. "That has nothing to do with it."

" 'You never know what might be useful in the long run.' I know," Susan said. "It's not as if we're going to pick up and go back to Earth if we run out of sheep, either."

I gave a sidelong glance at Leo. "Just what I needed; somebody who quotes my own words back at me. . . ."

"You've only yourself to blame," he said.

"Thanks," said Susan, to let us both know she took this little routine as a compliment. "Now tell me who took what side last time around, and what you expect them to do this time."

"It was me against them," I admitted. When Susan whistled, I stuck in, "I almost got Mike to go along with me, but in the end, that wouldn't have made any difference. Mike didn't have much pull then."

"Meaning he was about the same age I am now," said Susan, "so my opinion won't swing much weight either."

"I had intended to be tactful."

Leo raised an eyebrow at me. "That's not like you, Annie. Do you need the allies that badly? It occurs to me that you swing a bit more weight these days yourself."

"Oh, considerably. But that won't do me a lot of good unless I can convince people like Jarlskog and Yndurain that the rexes are worth keeping. For god's sake, Leo! What's to stop them from simply shooting down every one they see? *We* certainly haven't the hands to police every last bit of territory, especially not Last Edges or Gogol or the like."

Last Edges has a total population of fifty. That's minute, but it's five times the number of people I've got to work with.

"Most people understand enough about ecological balance to follow the guide-lines you folks set," Leo said, but with a bit of a rising inflection.

"If I tell them it's 'Earth-authentic,' sure. But this one isn't. Furthermore, nobody in his right mind likes it."

"*I* like it," Susan said. When I didn't respond to that, she said in a small amused voice, "Oh," then giggled, then sighed in resignation. "So what do we do?"

"Nothing, until we check out the situation locally."

The local situation hadn't simmered down while it waited for our arrival. Not that I'd expected it to, but I could see that both Susan and Leo had. A third of the adults were guarding the sheep field with guns. Another third, I imagine, was guarding the kids likewise. The rest turned out to be a combination welcoming committee and lynch mob. Read: *we* were welcome, the kangaroo rexes were most emphatically not.

I listened to the babble without a word for all of twenty minutes, motioning for Susan and Leo to do the same. Best to let them get as much of it out of their systems as possible while we waited for a couple of leaders to sort themselves out of the crowd—then we'd know who and what we were actually dealing with.

In the end, there were two surprises. The first was that someone was dispatched to "Go get Janzen. Right now." When Janzen arrived, Janzen got thrust to the fore. Janzen was about Susan's age. He looked at me, cocked an eyebrow at Leo, who nodded and grinned, then he grinned at me and stuck out his hand. That was when I noticed the striking resemblance the kid had to Leo. I cocked an eyebrow at Leo, whose grin got wider.

Janzen took care of shutting down the general noise level and introducing us to the population at large. Leo got introduced by his previous job description—as Leonov *Opener* Denness—and yes, Leo was Janzen's grandad. Both of which upped our status exactly the way Janzen had intended them to. At a bet, a lot of the local kids had been through a survival course or two with Leo.

The second surprise wasn't nearly as pleasant. The other speaker for the populace—read "loudmouth" in this case—was none other than Kelly Herder Sangster, formerly a resident of Gogol. She'd wanted the kangaroo rexes near Gogol wiped out and she wanted the same thing here and *now*.

I knew from experience how good she was at rousing rabble. She'd done it at Gogol. I could talk myself blue in the face, put penalties on the shooting of a rex, but I'd lose every one of them to "accidental" shootings if I couldn't get the majority of the crowd behind me.

Sangster squared off, aimed somewhere between me and Janzen, shoved back her hat, bunched her fists on her hips, and said, "They eat sheep. Next thing you know they'll be eating our kids! And Cryptobiology sends us somebody who loves Dragon's Teeth!"

She pointed an accusing finger at me. "When they attacked us in Gogol, *she* wanted to keep them! Whaddaya think about that?" The last was to the crowd.

The crowd didn't think much of that at all. There was much muttering and rumbling.

"I think," I said, waiting for the crowd to quiet enough to listen, "I'd like to know more about the situation before I make any decisions for or against."

I looked at Janzen. "You were the first to see it, I'm told. Did it eat your sheep?"

"No, it didn't," he said. That caused another stir and a bit of a calm. "It was in the enclosure—but it was chasing them, all of them, the way a dog does when it's playing. To be fair, I don't know what it would have done when it caught them. We caught it before we could find out." He looked thoughtful. "But it seems to me that it had plenty of opportunity to catch a sheep and didn't bother. Moustafa? What do you think?"

Moustafa rubbed his sore jaw, glowered at Leo, and said, very grudgingly, "You're right, Janzen. It was like the time Harkavy's dog got into the sheep pen—just chased 'em around. Plenty of time to catch 'em but didn't. Just wanted to see them run." He glowered once more. "But for a kangaroo, it's an adolescent. Maybe it hasn't learned to hunt yet. That might have been practice."

"I concede the point," I said, before Sangster could use it to launch another torpedo. "The next thing I need to know is, how many of them are there?"

As if prompted (perhaps he was, I hadn't been watching Leo for the moment), Janzen said, "For all I know, only the one." He looked hard at Sangster. "You see any?"

Sangster dropped her eyes. "No," she muttered, "not since Gogol." She raised her eyes and made a comeback, "No thanks to Jason Masmajean here."

Janzen ignored that. "Anybody else?"

"That doesn't mean a damn thing, Janzen, and you know it," someone said from the crowd. "For all we know, the entire next generation of kangaroos will be Dragon's Teeth—and *that* would be a shitload of kangaroo rexes!"

"I say we get rid of them while there's only one," Sangster put in. "I'm for loading my shotgun and cleaning the roos out *before* they sprout Dragon's Teeth!"

"Now I remember!" I said, before the crowd could agree with her, "*You're* the one that's allergic to roo-tail soup!"

"I'm not allergic—I just don't like it," she snapped back, before thinking it through.

"Well," said Janzen, "*I* like roo-tail soup, so I'd just as soon consider this carefully before I stick myself with nothing but vegetable for the rest of my life."

"Rest of your life . . ." Sangster sneered at him. "What the hell are you talking about?"

"I'll take that question," I said. "If you've a genuine outbreak of kangaroo rexes here, instead of a one-shot, then you'll have to destroy all the kangaroos. That's what was done at Gogol. Gogol can never let the kangaroo herds—"

" 'Mobs' " corrected Sangster, "Kangaroos come in mobs, not herds."

"Gogol can never let the kangaroos *mob* again. Any kangaroo found in that EC is shot. The environmental conditions there are such that sooner or later any kangaroo around Gogol will produce a kangaroo rex." I gave a long look through the crowd. "I won't lie to you: Last Edges has roughly the same EC as Gogol did. Which means you may have to face the same decision. As for me, I'd wait to find out if the rexes eat sheep before I decide to kill off all the roos."

"Sounds fair," said Janzen, almost too promptly. "How do we go about this?"

"First, I want a good look at your EC. I want to see, if you haven't scuffed it up too much, where you spotted the rex. Then we do a little scouting of the surrounding area." I grinned over my shoulder at Leo. "Luckily, we have somebody who's an old hand at that."

"Luckily," agreed Janzen.

"But I could also use some additional help." I looked straight at Sangster—I wanted her where I could keep an eye on her and where she couldn't rabble-rouse while I was busy. "What do you say, Sangster? Willing to put in a little effort?"

What could she say? She just said it with all the bad grace she could muster.

"Take Janzen, too," came a voice from the crowd. Aha! there were two factions already. "Yes," agreed another voice, "You go with 'em, Janzen. *You* like roo soup."

"In the meantime," I said, "stick to the precautions we already discussed. However—if anyone spots a rex, I want you to notify us immediately. Don't shoot it."

"Oh, yes, right. Don't shoot it," Sangster mocked.

I looked at her as if she were nuts. "Look," I said, "if there *are* more than one, it can lead us to the rest of the mob. Or would you rather just hunt them by guess and by golly? I don't have the time myself. Are *you* volunteering?"

That was the right thing to say, too. So I added one last filip. "Susan?" Susan edged forward. "Susan will be in charge of collecting the gene samples from each sheep, simply as a precaution."

This did not make Susan happy—she wanted to go haring off after the kangaroo rexes—but I knew she wouldn't argue with me in public. "Sample each?" she said.

"That's right. I don't want a single one lost. After all, who knows what genes they've got hidden in those? Might be, one of them can sprout the Shmoo."

That brought a bit of laughter—the Shmoo's a legendary creature that tastes like everything good and drops dead for you if you look at it hungry. The ultimate Dragon's Tooth, except that Sangster would never use that derogatory term for something she *approved* of.

The crowd approved our plan, especially the part about collecting gene samples from each sheep. It was a nuisance to do, but I knew it would settle them down. Herders know as well as anybody how desperately we need diversity within a species. I was offering to clone any sheep we lost to the rexes in the process of my investigation. That meant they'd lose the time it took to bring the sheep back to breeding age, but that they wouldn't lose any genetic variation.

Moustafa volunteered to help Susan with the sampling. So did a handful of others. Then the rest of the crowd dispersed, leaving us to get down to business at last.

Moustafa led the way to the sheep pen where Janzen and Leo had bagged my baby rex. The enclosure looked like every single one I've ever seen, identical to those at Gogol, identical to every other one in Last Edges as well, no doubt. It *sounded* like the crowd had—lots of milling, scuffling, and bleating.

The moment we rounded the corner and saw the sheep, I had to clamp my jaw hard to keep from laughing. The sheep were an eye-popping sky-blue, every single one of them! Susan *did* burst into laughter. I elbowed her hard in the ribs. "Don't you dare laugh at Mike's sheep," I told her.

Mike had been trying for a breed that could eat Mirabilan plant life without killing itself. What he'd gotten was a particularly hardy type that tasted just as good as the original, but sprouted that unbelievable shade of blue wool. Mike had promptly dubbed them "Dylan Thomas sheep," and offered them out to the herders. Janzen and Moustafa had obviously taken him up on the offer.

Susan simmered down, just barely, to giggles. "But, Mama Jason," she said, "all this fuss because a Dragon's Tooth might eat a Dragon's Tooth. . . ."

And at that Janzen laughed too. He looked at Susan. "I hadn't thought of it that way, but, now that you mention it, it is funny." He cocked an eyebrow at Moustafa, who sighed and said, "You always were nuts, Janzen. Yeah. It's funny."

Moustafa looked at me more seriously, though. "But we can't afford to lose many. It's not as if we've got a high population to play around with. We don't even dare interbreed them with the Earth-authentics until we've built up the flock to twice this size or more."

I nodded. The kid was as sensible as Janzen. I wasn't surprised he'd taken a shot at the rex. In his position, I probably would have too. Hell, I'd have done it if they'd been the Earth-authentics. Why mess around? "Okay, Susan," I said, "Start with this flock. Make sure you get one of each."

If the artificial wombs were free this winter, I'd see Mike's pet project doubled, whether we needed them or not. Pretty damn things once you got over the initial shock. They smelled godawful, of course, but what sheep doesn't? The wool made beautiful cloth and even more beautiful rugs. It was already something of a posh item all over Mirabile.

"All yours," I said to Susan, and she and Moustafa set to work.

I followed Leo along the fence, watching where I put my feet. When you've got an expert tracker, you stay out of his way and let him do his job. Janzen knew this just as well as I did, so he was the one, not me, who grabbed Sangster to keep her from overstepping Leo and messing up any signs of the rex.

It wasn't long before Leo stopped and pointed us off across the sheep field. I shouldered my gear and we set out to track the kangaroo rex.

Tracking a kangaroo isn't as easy as you might think, even with the help of a world-class tracker like Leo. (I'm not so bad at it myself. Neither is Janzen, as it turns out.) These kangaroos were reds (I don't mean the warning-light red that signals that some critter is about to chain up to something else; I mean a lovely tawny animal red) and *they* are world-class distance jumpers, especially when they're panicked. They had been by Moustafa's rifle shot, which meant they'd been traveling in leaps of fifteen to twenty feet. So it was check the launch spot, then cast about for the landing and subsequent relaunch.

It was only guesswork that we were following the rex's mother anyway. We wouldn't know her to look at her. Only a full gene-read could tell us that. I'd have to sample most of the roos in the mob to find out how many of them were capable of producing baby rexes.

Sangster bent down to uproot a weed or two. When I frowned at her for taking the time, she held out the plant to me and said, "That'll kill a sheep as sure as a kangaroo rex will."

Janzen looked over. "Surer," he said. "I still don't know if kangaroo rexes eat sheep." To me, he added, "But that will poison one. That's lambkill."

I almost laughed. Like any Mirabilan species we've had occasion to work with, it has a fancy Latin name, but this was the first I'd heard its common name. The fancy Latin name is an exact translation. Sounded like Granpa Jason's work to me.

Sangster stooped to pull another. Curious how small they were. Must mean they policed the fields *very* carefully. These were newly sprouted. I spotted one and pulled it myself, then stuck my head up and looked for Leo again. He'd found the next set of footprints.

Good thing the roos have such big feet. In this kind of wiry, springy scrub we wouldn't have had much chance otherwise. Leo wiped sweat from his forehead and pointed toward the oasis in the distance. "Chances are they'll be there, including our rex's mother. In this heat, they'll be keeping to the shade to conserve water." He glanced at Janzen. "Is that the only natural source of water in the area?"

Janzen nodded.

I squinted into the shimmer. The plants had that spiky look of Mirabilan vegetation. There was a distinct break between the Earth-authentic lichens and scrub, then a fence, then a broad strip of desert, then the dark green of the Mirabilan oasis. The broad strip of desert was maybe twenty hops for a roo, or looked that way from this angle.

"Even the roos are a problem," Sangster observed. "They can hop the fence—they bring the lambkill seeds in on their fur."

"It'd blow in from there," I said. "Same as it did at Gogol." I couldn't help it. I'd been wondering ever since I first spotted her in the crowd. "Herder Sangster, what made you leave Gogol?"

Sangster scowled, not exactly at me. "It's Crafter Sangster now. I lost my flock, seventy percent of it anyway."

Leo said, "To the kangaroo rexes?"

She just about glared him into the ground. "To the lambkill," she said. "After we got rid of the rexes and the roos that bred them, the lambkill was still there. Worse than ever, it seemed."

"Yes," Janzen put in. "When Moustafa and I were deciding where to raise Mike's flock of Thomas sheep, I did some checking in the various areas available. Something in the EC here makes the lambkill less prevalent . . . or less deadly perhaps. The death count attributable to it isn't nearly as high here as it is around Gogol." He cocked his head, which made his resemblance to Leo all the stronger. "Say! Maybe you could find out what the difference is?"

"Maybe I could," I said, making it clear I would certainly look into the problem. "But for now let's find those roos. I'll put Susan on soil and vegetation samples as soon as she's done with sheep."

To my surprise, he frowned. "Isn't she a little young . . . ?"

"When's *your* birthday?" I asked him. When he told me, I said, "Yeah, I guess from your point of view she is a little young. You've got two months on her."

"Oops," said Janzen. "Sorry."

"No skin off my nose," I told him.

Leo grinned and slapped Janzen on the shoulder. "Would be skin off *his* if Susan had heard him, though. Rightly, too." Leo put an easy arm around Janzen's shoulder. "Susan's the one who developed the odders, Janz. You know, the neo-otters that keep the canals around Torville free of clogweed?"

Janzen looked rightly impressed. Good for Leo, I thought, rub it in just enough so the lesson takes.

"Besides," Leo said, "if age had any bearing on who gets what job, Annie and I would be sitting in the shade somewhere sipping mint juleps and fanning ourselves. Now, could we get on with this before we all, young and old alike, melt?"

So we did. The strip of desert was wider than I'd thought. We'd need that spring as much as the roos did. Of course, they were quite sensibly lying in the shade (drinking mint juleps, no doubt, whatever *they* were—I'd have to remember to ask Leo about that later), going nowhere until the cool of evening.

We'd lost our specific roo (if we'd ever had her) on the broad rocky flat that lay between the strip of desert and the oasis. We paused in the first bit of welcoming shade.

Without a word, Leo signed the rest of us to wait while he moved farther in to scout the location of the mob without panicking it. I handed him the cell-sampler. If he saw anything that looked like a rex, I wanted an instant sample. I needed to know if more than one mother was breeding them.

For a long while, it was quiet, except for the sound of running water and the damned yakking of the chatterboxes. Every planet must have something like this—it's simply the noisiest creature in the EC. It keeps up a constant racket unless something disturbs it. When the chatterboxes shut up, you know you're in trouble. Most people think the chatterboxes are birds, and that's good enough most ways—they fly, they lay eggs, what more could you ask of birds?

I, for one, prefer that my birds have feathers. Technically speaking, feathers are required. The chatterboxes are a lot closer to lizards. I guess the closest Earth-authentic would be something like a pterodactyl, except that all the pterodactyl reconstructions in ship's files showed them brown or green. I wonder what the paleontologists back on Earth would have made of ours.

The chatterboxes, besides being noisy, are the most vivid colors imaginable—blues and reds and purples and yellows—and in some of the most tasteless combinations you can imagine. They make most Mirabilan predators violently ill, which shouldn't come as much of a surprise. The eggs are edible, though, and not just to *Mirabilan* predators.

We watched and listened to the chatterboxes, thinking all the while, I'm sure, that we ought to bring home some eggs if we lucked onto a nest.

Then Leo was back.

He leaned close and spoke in a quiet voice. The chatterboxes kept right on. "Annie, I've found the mob, but I didn't see anything that looked like a rex—nothing out of the ordinary at all. Just browsing kangaroos."

"Chances are, mine is the first one, then. Do you think we can all get a look without sending them in all directions?"

"Depends on *your* big feet."

"Thanks," I told him.

The whole bunch of us headed out as quietly as we knew how. I'd been worried about Sangster, but she'd obviously taken the kids' training course to heart—she was as quiet as the rest of us.

We worked our way through sharpscrub, dent-de-lion, careless weed, spurts, and stick-me-quick. It was mostly uphill. The terrain here was mostly rock with a very slender capping of soil. Leo brushed past a stand of creve-coeur and collected a shirtful of its nasty burrs, saving us all from a similar fate. I didn't envy him the task of picking them out.

At last Leo stopped us. Kneeling, he slid forward, motioning me to follow. Our faces inches apart, we peered through a small stand of lightenme.

There was the tiny trickle of stream that fed this oasis. In the shade of the surrounding trees lolled the mob of kangaroos, looking for the moment not so much like a mob as like a picnic luncheon. There were perhaps twenty in clear view, and not a striped hip among them. Still, that meant there were plenty more we couldn't see.

It was also quite possible that the mother of our rex had been ostracized because of her peculiar offspring. That happened often enough with Dragon's Teeth.

Beside me there was an intake of breath. The chatterboxes paused momentarily, then, to my relief, went right back to their chattering. Sangster pointed into the sharpscrub to my left.

I caught just the quickest glimpse of stripes, followed it to the end of its bound. As it knelt on its forepaws to drink from the stream, I could see it had the face and jaw of a red kangaroo, but the haunches were very faintly striped. I nodded to her. Good bet, that one. Different enough to be worth the first check.

Taking the cell-sampler back from Leo, I backed up—still on my hands and knees—and skinned around to get as close as I could. (Skinned being the operative word in that EC. My palms would never be the same.) Just at that moment, two of the adolescents started a kicking match.

Their timing was perfect. I took advantage of the distraction, rose, tiptoed forward, and potted Striped Rump with the sampler. It twitched and looked around but wasn't in the least alarmed. All it did was lean back on its tail and scratch the area with a forepaw, for all the world like a human slob.

Very slowly, I reeled in the sample. (I've startled too many creatures reeling in samples not to be aware of that problem.) Once I had it, I stashed it in my pack, reloaded, and popped a second roo, this time a male—all chest and shoulders, a good seven-footer. If the rexes got that big, I would be awfully hard put to convince anybody they should be kept.

Not that it looked menacing now. It was lying belly-up in the deep shade, with its feet in the air. Just now, it looked like some kid had dropped a stuffed toy.

I knew better: Mike had gotten into an altercation with a red that size once, and it had taken three hundred and forty-one stitches to repair the damage. Roos use their claws to dig for edible roots. They panic, those claws'll do just as efficient a job digging holes in your face.

Two sampled. I figured the best thing to do was keep sampling as long as I could. I got eleven more without incident. Then I almost walked into the fourteenth.

Its head jerked up from the vie-sans-joie it and its joey were browsing. The joey dived headfirst into mama's pouch.

I knew it was all over, so I shot the sampler at the mother point-blank, as the joey somersaulted to stare at me wide-eyed between its own hind feet. Mama took off like a shot.

Next thing I knew, the chatterboxes were in the air, dead silent except for the sound of their wings, and every kangaroo was bounding every which way.

Janzen and Leo were on their feet in the same moment, dragging Sangster to hers as well. Less chance of being jumped on if the roos were stampeding *away* from you. Leo bellowed at them, just to make sure.

Trouble is, you can't count on a roo to do anything but be the damn dumb creature it is—so three of them headed straight *for* Leo and company.

Janzen dived left. Still bellowing, Leo dived right. And there stood Sangster, right in the middle, unable to pick a direction. She took one step left, a second right—that little dance that people do in the street just before they bump into each other.

Striped Rump was still aimed straight for her.

I raised my shotgun and aimed for Striped Rump. "No, Annie!" Leo shouted. But I was thinking of Mike—I sighted.

Three things happened at once: Leo hooked a foot at Sangster's ankle and jerked her out of the path of the roo, Janzen bellowed louder than ever I'd heard Leo manage, and I squeezed the trigger.

Striped Rump touched one toe to the ground and reversed direction in mid-leap. My shot passed over its shoulder as it bounded away from Sangster. By the time the shot had finished echoing off the rocks, there wasn't a roo to be seen anywhere.

I charged over to where Leo was picking Sangster up and dusting her off. Polite full-body-check, that was. From his nod, she was just fine, so I spared a glance for Janzen, who seemed likewise.

"Dammit, woman!" Leo said. "What happened to 'Don't shoot unless it's absolutely necessary'? That was your likeliest prospect."

"The hell with you, Leo. *You've* never seen anybody mangled by a roo." It came out tired. The adrenaline rush was gone and the heat was suddenly unbearable. "I'm not in the mood to be scolded right now. You can do it later, when I'm ready to thank you for saving old Striped Rump."

I glared at Sangster. "If you're fit to travel, I vote we get the hell out of this sun and let me process my samples."

She opened her mouth, a little round O of a shape, as if to say something. Then she just nodded.

We slogged our way back across the sheep range. By the time we reached the shade of Janzen's digs, I was unpissed enough to growl at Leo, "What's a mint julep? Maybe I could use one."

Leo shot a sidelong glance at Janzen, who grinned and said, "You *know* I keep the mixings. You also know you're all welcome to stay at my place." He cocked his head slightly to the side, "If you don't tell Susan what an idiot I am."

"We'll let her find out on her own," Leo said.

Which settled that—and us as well.

I was almost into the welcome shade of Janzen's house when Sangster grabbed at my arm. I turned—the look on her face was downright ferocious. Here it comes again, I thought. Death to the kangaroo rex!

Instead, she demanded, "Why?" That ferocious look was still there.

I blinked. "Why *what*, dammit?"

"Why did you shoot at that damned roo?"

Some people just don't get it, ever. I shook my head and sighed. "Humans are the most endangered species on Mirabile," I said, "and you want to know why I fired?"

That was all I had the patience for. I turned on my heel, yanked away from her, and fairly dived into the coolness of Janzen's house, letting the door slam behind me as my final word on the subject.

The mint julep improved my outlook no end, so I keyed into Janzen's computer (rank hath its privileges) and entered the samples I'd picked up. While I was waiting for my readout, I checked my office files to see what the rest of the team had come up with.

First thing I got was a real pretty schematic of my kangaroo rex. It was an even neater bit of engineering than I'd thought at first—the teeth at the side of the jaws (they were two inches long!) worked across each other, like butchers' shears. What with the 180-degree jaw span, that would give it an awesome ability to shear bone. Sheep bone was well within its capabilities.

That still didn't mean it ate sheep, but it didn't help the cause any.

Next I got the gene-reads on the secondary helices. Didn't recognize either worth a damn. Neither had Chie-Hoon, because there was a note appended that said simply, "Annie: Sorry, neither of these looks familiar to me. We're checking them against ship's records now. Let you know what we find."

That'd be sometime the next day. A search and match takes entirely too much time, always assuming that there *is* a match. Lord only knew what was in those portions of ship's records we'd lost in transit.

The gene-read on Striped Rump was about what I'd expected, just a few twists off normal red kangaroo.

"Roo stew?" said a voice behind me.

"Sure," I said, without looking up, "still perfectly edible, despite those." I tapped the offending genes on the monitor.

"Janzen," said Leo's voice, "No point talking to her when she's reading genes. She's not talking about the same thing you are."

That was enough to make me turn away from the screen. I looked at Janzen. "Sorry," I said. "What was it you wanted to know?"

"I just asked if you'd mind having roo stew for dinner. I intend to eat a lot of roo while I still have the option."

"Say yes, Annie." That was Leo again. "Janzen and Moustafa make the best roo stew I've ever had. Even Chris couldn't beat their recipe."

Chris is the best chef on Mirabile. Like Susan, she's one of Elly's kids. She's one of the reasons Loch Moose Lodge is my favorite vacation spot.

"That's some recommendation! Can I get in on this?" That was Susan.

"I put the sheep samples in the truck, Mama Jason; all set for in vitro in case we need them. Is that your rex breeder? Sangster won't talk about what you guys found—what did you do to her? Threaten her with a corn crop that sprouts cockroaches?"

"One thing at a time," I said. "Janzen, yes, thank you. I'm extremely fond of roo myself. Will there be enough for Susan too, or shall I make her eat rations?"

Susan threatened to punch me. Janzen grinned at her and said, "Plenty enough, Susan. Now I know why Leo wants to hook up with Annie. Just his type."

To change the subject, I tapped the monitor again and said, "That's our most likely candidate for rex breeder. I was just about to check for secondary helices. You can watch over my shoulder—unless you want to watch how Janzen and Moustafa make stew. The recipe'd make a good birthday present for Chris . . . ?"

Susan looked horribly torn for a brief moment. Janzen grinned at her again and said, "I'll write out our recipe for you, Susan. You stick here and tell me what I need to know about the kangaroo rexes." The kid had a *lot* in common with his granddad.

While Susan pulled up a chair, I turned back to the monitor and started reading genes again. Yup, there was a secondary helix, all right. I split the screen, called up the gene-read on my kangaroo rex, and compared the two. No doubt about it. "Thanks for saving old Striped Rump, Leo. She's it."

I stored that to send back to the lab and called up the next sample. "Let's see how many other rex breeders we've got."

By the time Moustafa dished out the roo stew, I'd found two more rex breeders in the sample of thirteen. And they were all remarkably consistent about it.

"Hell," said Leo.

"Not exactly, Noisy," Susan said. "That means most likely the kangaroo rex is an intermediate for an Earth-authentic."

I was momentarily more interested in the stew than in anything else. It lived up to Leo's billing. I was still trying to place the spices Janzen and Moustafa used when Leo laid a hand on my arm to get my attention. "Mmmph?" I said, through a mouthful.

"You've got to train your assistants to use less jargon," he said.

I scooped up another forkful of stew and simply eyed Susan.

"Oops," she said. "Sorry, Noisy. A true Dragon's Tooth is usually a chimera—bits and pieces of the genetic material of two very different species. Even a plant-animal combination's possible. But it's not consistent.

"If we've got three roos that are going to at some time produce rexes, all of which are close enough genetically to interbreed, then most likely it's *not* a Dragon's Tooth. Most likely it's the first visible step on the chain up to another Earth-authentic." She waited anxiously to see if he'd gotten it this time. When he nodded, she dived back into her own dinner. "Great stew, Moustafa, Janzen. I'd sure hate it if we have to kill off the roos."

"Any idea just how big the roo population is?" I asked the two local kids.

They exchanged a glance. Moustafa said, "Couple hundred, maybe. It never occurred to me to count."

Janzen shook his head, meaning it hadn't occurred to him either, then he said, "You can get some idea after dinner. Once the sun goes down, most of them will be out in the pasture, browsing. If it were crops we were raising instead of sheep, they'd be a much bigger nuisance than they are now."

Susan raised a querying brow at him.

"Given any kind of a choice, the roos prefer their food tender, which means they go for young shoots. That'd play havoc with any food crop. Sheep will browse tough stuff that's inedible to most Earth-authentics, and they'll do it right down to the ground."

"Yeah," said Moustafa, "And they're too stupid to know what's poisonous and what isn't."

That reminded me. "Excuse me a minute," I said—but I took my bowl of stew with me while I went to the computer to call up the home team.

I got Mike, which was good luck, and there were no emergencies in the offing, which was better. "I need an EC workup on Gogol. Can you get me one by tomorrow evening?" At his look, I said, "It doesn't have to be complete—just a preliminary: quick and dirty is fine. We'll do a complete if anything interesting shows up." His look hadn't improved, so I added, "Take Selima. With two of you, it'll go faster and won't be quite as dirty."

That fixed the look right up. Ah, young love . . . ain't it handy? "Anything new I should know about?"

"Yeah." This time he grinned. "Your kangaroo rex didn't recognize lamb as edible."

Behind me, someone said, "All *right!*" on a note of triumph. I ignored that to eye Mike suspiciously. When he said nothing further, I voiced his implied, "But . . . ?"

"But it could learn that trick. Right now its idea of superb cuisine is chatterboxes, grubroots, and gladrats."

Interesting. Those were all Mirabilan, and all pests from our point of view. "That's certainly in its favor," I said. "They're all of a size too—nowhere near the size of sheep."

"Means nothing. There's only one rex on the premises. Who knows what size prey a mob of them will take on."

"I know," I said, "but that gives me more breathing space here." I thought about it a moment, then got an inspiration. "Mike? Try it on those damn jumping fish next time it looks hungry."

That brought a grin from Mike. "Annie," he said, "our luck's not *that* good this summer. Besides, the rexes wouldn't do well in that EC."

"Just try it. And shoot me that EC report as soon as you can." I broke the connection, picked up my bowl, and—still thinking about it—headed back for the dinner table. I almost ran Leo down. I looked around me. The whole troop had been looking over my shoulder. "Sit," I said, "my apologies. We will now give the stew the attention it deserves."

Which we did, and when we were done, it was time for Janzen and Moustafa to see to their sheep for the evening . . . and for me and Leo to place ourselves strategically in the fields to see how many roos showed up to browse—and how many of them were breeding rexes.

We ran into half a dozen of the locals and enlisted three. Susan dug out two more samplers, but those went to Leo and Susan herself. (We're short of equipment. I put that on the docket for winter, making more samplers or finding somebody who wanted the job.)

Sangster was nowhere to be seen. Despite Susan's earlier comment, I had no doubt she was off somewhere raising the level of hysteria. I could have kicked myself for not dragging Sangster in with us that afternoon, just to keep her out of trouble.

It would have been a lovely evening for hanky-panky. Too bad Leo was on the opposite edge of the field. With the sun going down, there was a bit of nip in the air. Dew had started to condense and I was wet to the knees, but I laid out a bit of tarp to sit on and to drag around my shoulders and settled down to count roos.

They weren't much worried about humans, as it turned out. At the moment, that was a plus. If the rexes had the same inclination, though, it would be just one more thing to worry about.

Susan I'd stationed roughly in eye-shot—at least, with the help of a good flashlight. But pretty soon I was so busy taking samples that I had no time for more than an occasional check on her. She was taking samples just as furiously as I was.

Moustafa's estimate had been in the hundreds, by which he'd meant maybe two hundred. I'd have guessed more. I counted nearly a hundred within the ring of light my flashlight produced. The flashlight bothered them not at all. They placidly munched at this, that, and the other. About as peaceful as a herd of cows and about as bright: one of the youngsters nibbled my tarp before I tapped its nose. Then it hopped back into mama's pouch and glared at me. Mama went on chewing, while I got samples of both.

In the cool of the evening, they were much more active. The youngsters chased and kicked each other and a lot of mock battles went down, reminding me of nothing so much as the way Susan and Mike behaved.

More than one of the youngsters had striped hips, so I crept as close as I dared while they were occupied with each other, to get samples specifically from them. Once again, a mock battle—great leaps in the air and powerful kicks from those hind legs—covered my movement.

Three older kangaroos paused to look up from their eating but they looked up at the antics of the youngsters with the same kind of wearied eye I had been known to turn on activities of that sort from our younger contingent. Satisfied that the kids weren't getting into any trouble, they went back to what they'd been doing—which was grubbing in the ground, presumably for roots.

You wouldn't believe those claws unless you saw them in action. Once again, I appreciated the muscular shoulders. I frankly didn't see why a kangaroo rex should seem any more ferocious—at first glance, anyhow—than a basic kangaroo. Watching them, I got a tickle in the back of my skull. The stuff they were grubbing up looked familiar. Nova-light is romantic, but not as good for some things as for others. I debated the wisdom of turning my flashlight on them for a better look.

Being old hands, *they* would not be so likely to take my intrusion as lightly as the joey had. I didn't want to start a stampede. There were just too many of them in the general neighborhood. I didn't relish the thought of being run down by several hundred pounds of panicked roo.

The elder roos looked up, suddenly wary. I abandoned my plan and followed their point. Some sort of disturbance at the edge of the mob, very near where I'd last seen Susan. And damned if I could see her now—there were too many adult roos between my position and hers.

The nearby roos got a bit skittish. Two of the adult males bounced once in Susan's direction, froze, and watched. A new mob had joined the browsing.

This was a smaller group. Dominant male, two females, and two matching joeys. Damned if the male didn't have that striped rump. I didn't dare edge closer, not with the nearby roos nervous already. I held my ground and hoped the quintet of likelies would pass near enough to Susan for her to get a safe shot at sampling them.

But they skirted Susan (now that my brain was working again, I decided I was glad they had) and headed in my direction. Closer examination told me that papa was a roo. Neither of the mamas was, though. To hell with the striped rump—these two were plain and simple kangaroo rexes—and most of the nearby roos didn't like it any more than I did.

Their movements were different. (Well, let's face it—they would be.) Except for the male, they weren't grazing. They were searching the grass for whatever small prey the rest of the roos startled into motion. I could see why they liked to hang around with the browsers. The browsing roos gave them cover and, as often as not, sent gladrats and grubroots right into those waiting jaws.

I couldn't recall when I'd ever heard anything eaten with a snap quite that impressive, either. I eased back down in the grass, hoping they'd get close enough that I could get shots at both the mothers and the joeys. I laid my rifle where I could reach it at a moment's notice and raised my sampler.

To my surprise, the roos around me, after whiffling the air a few times, settled back to their browsing. When the rexes came close, the roos eased away, but didn't panic. Not quite acceptable in polite society, I could see, but nothing to worry about so long as they kept to their own table.

One of the rex joeys pounced after something small in the grass. In the excitement of the chase, it headed straight for me. I popped it with the sampler on the spot and it jumped straight up in the air, came down bouncing the opposite direction, headed for mama. It made a coughing bark the like of which I never heard from a roo.

Mama made the same coughing sound, bounded *over* the joey, and the next thing I knew I was face to face with several hundred pounds of angry rex. The jaws snapped as I brought up my gun. Then something hit me in the shoulder with the force of a freight train. The gun went in one direction, I went in the other, rolling as best I could to keep from being kicked a second time by the papa roo.

A brilliant flash of light struck in our direction, illuminating the mama rex as she came after me. There was a yell and a shot from somewhere behind me. I may have imagined it, but I swear I felt that bullet pass inches from my right ear.

The mama rex stopped in her tracks—stunned, not shot. The rest of the mobs, roos and rexes alike, took off in all directions. The ground shook from their thundering kick-offs and landings.

I scrambled to my feet, the better to dodge if dodging was possible in that chaos. It was only then that I realized that some damn fool of a human had the kangaroo rex by the tail, hauling it back as it tried to bound away.

A second damn fool of a human grabbed for the rex's feet, dragging them out from under it so it couldn't kick.

Dammit! They'd forgotten the teeth!

I was moving before I even put a thought to it. Dived, landed roughly on the rex's head and grabbed it about the throat, pulling the jaw closed toward my chest and hanging on for dear life while the thing struggled for all it was worth. It had the worst damn breath of any creature I'd ever gotten that foolishly close to.

Through the haze and the brilliance of the artificial light, I saw somebody race up and plunge a hypodermic needle into the upturned haunch. The rex coughed its outrage and struggled twice as hard. I almost suffocated. I don't even want to think how close its snap came to my ear.

Somebody else was trying to loop a rope around those thrashing hind legs and not being very successful about it. I'd have let go, if I could have thought of a safe way of doing it.

Then all at once the struggle went out of the rex. It kicked weakly a few more times, then went limp, for all the world as if it were too hot a day to do anything but lie around in the shade.

The fellow with the rope said, "Took long enough!" and finished his tying—as neat as any cowboy on ship's film. He whipped another length of rope off his hip, came round to me, and wrapped the length about the jaw, sealing it temporarily shut. Then he stood up, dusted off his hands, and said, "Kelly, you're gonna have to come up with a better mousetrap. Damned if I'm gonna do *that* again!"

Sangster uncrimped herself from the rex's tail and stood to face him. "Thought the Texan Guild would be a damn sight better at hog-tying." The challenge in her voice was unmistakeable. "I guess the Australian Guild will have to handle the rest alone."

"Hell," said the Texan, in that peculiar drawl that identifies members of the guild, "just give us a chance to practice. These things move a sight different than a longhorn."

"You're on," said Sangster. "Now let's get this into the cage before the valium wears off." She turned to me and said, "We'll catch the rest of them for you."

Four of them hefted the limp rex onto their shoulders and started back toward town.

None of it was making sense, least of all Sangster's parting shot. Maybe that roo's kick had caught me in the side of the head after all and I just didn't know it. I felt like walking wounded.

Must have been stunned, because it wasn't until Leo and Susan picked up my gun and my cell sampler and caught my elbows on either side that I even remembered to make sure they were okay themselves.

Leo looked about like I felt. Susan was fine, bounding along, half in front of us, half trying to carry me by my elbow, as if she'd caught the bounds from the roos. "Mama Jason," she caroled as she bounced, "I'm so glad you're okay! That was about the most exciting thing that's ever happened to me, *ever!* Wasn't it, Noisy? Have you ever *seen* anything like that in your *life?* Just wait until I tell Chris and Elly and Mike. . . ."

None of that seemed to require any response from me, so I saved my breath for walking.

"*Are* we going to catch the rest of them?" she demanded at last. "What about the rex's joey? Shouldn't we find it? Maybe it wasn't weaned yet."

From the brief look I'd gotten at the joeys, chances were Susan was right. If the rex they'd shot full of valium lived, we'd still lose the rex joey.

But when we rounded the corner, we found a makeshift cage—a big one, much to my relief—built onto a transport trailer that sat right next to Sangster's house. In it was the mama rex, still groggy but unmuzzled now, *and* her joey. At least, I *hoped* it was hers. It was pretty damned angry, but was expending most of its energy to try to get a response out of mama.

The entire town of Last Edges and then some had turned out to gawk. Sangster lounged against the cage like she owned 'em both. When she saw us coming, she nodded and took a few steps to meet us.

"Earth used to have zoos," she said, with no preamble. Glancing at the Texan Guilder, she added, "Ramanathan checked out the references for us in ship's log." She folded her arms across her chest and, with an air of pronouncement, finished, "We've decided we don't mind if you keep them in a zoo. We'll catch the rest of them for you."

That was not what I'd had in mind at all. Still, I wasn't going to make any objection as long as it kept Sangster and her crew from shooting them on sight. "Who's funding this zoo," I said, "and who's going to catch the grubroots and gladrats to feed them?"

Sangster and the Texan exchanged glances. "We'll talk about it later," she said.

I'll just bet, I thought, but didn't say it. I shrugged and turned to plod back to Janzen's place. I needed a hot soak to get the kinks out. My shoulder was beginning to stiffen from the bruises I'd gotten. (At least, I hoped it wasn't worse than bruises.) "Get that joey something to eat," I said. "They were hunting when you interrupted them. Grubroots will do just fine. That's what it was after."

I left. Somebody would see to it—probably Janzen.

Sangster caught up with me at the door to Janzen's place. "I talked the Australian guild into cooperating. I can talk them into funding the zoo, too. Marsupials are *our* jurisdiction. Maybe the rex is an Earth-authentic that got lost with the missing ship's files."

"Maybe," I said, stopping to consider her. Damned strange woman. I was sure from her manner that she was still mad as all hell at me, so none of this made sense. "More likely an intermediate, ready to chain up to an Earth-authentic."

"We want them *off* the sheep range," she said. "It's this or kill the roos again. We talked the Texan Guild into helping us. We can get them all for your zoo."

What could I say? "Until the next batch chains up from the roos." I shrugged one more time.

Sangster scowled deeper. "I saved this pair for you. I talked them into making a zoo. Now we're even."

She practically spat that last at me, then she turned on her heel and stamped away, raising dust with her fury.

Even for *what?* I wondered. *Damn* strange woman, like I said before.

I woke up stiff all over. Susan was balanced on the edge of my cot, barely able to contain herself. "What?" I said.

"They caught the other mama rex and her joey last night, Mama Jason. We get to keep them after all."

"Zoo is *not* my idea of keeping them, dammit. Just sheer luck they haven't killed any of them yet, between the valium and beating them into submission." I tried to get coherent but I'm not ready for mornings, ever. "Read up on zoos—and I don't mean the cursory reading Sangster and her mates did. Zoos always held the *last* individuals of the species: they were a death sentence."

"Oh," she said. "Mike called. He and Selima are up at Gogol, doing that EC check you wanted. He'll have it this evening."

"Good. I want you to do the same here. That I want this evening, too."

"Betcha I'm faster than Mike."

"Better be cleaner, too," I said, "or faster doesn't count."

She grinned at me, bounded off the cot, and was out the door without another word. Guaranteed her report would be both faster and cleaner than Mike's—unless I called Mike and issued the same challenge, that is. I dragged myself out of bed. Breakfast first, to get the mind moving, then to the computer to see what, if anything, was new from the lab.

What was new was a note from Chie-Hoon. "Skipped an emergency meeting of the Australian Guild for this, Annie, so you'd better appreciate it." Appended were reconstructions of the two critters our rexes were planning to chain up to.

Chie-Hoon had a gift for that: take the gene chart and draw from it a picture of what the resulting animal would look like. There were no Latin names for 'em, which meant Chie-Hoon hadn't been able to find a gene-read for either in ship's records.

The first one was just a variant on roo. The second was, well, as weird a thing as I'd *ever* seen, including the Mirabilan jumping fish. It had the same jaw and jaw-span as the rexes, but it was a quadruped. The tail wasn't as thick (well, it didn't need the tail for balance the way the roos did) and the hip stripes continued up to the shoulders, narrowing as they went. Basic predator with camouflage stripes.

The pouch opening aimed toward the tail, instead of toward the head. Took me a moment to figure that out—kept the baby from falling out while the critter chased prey, probably also kept it from getting scratched up on creve-coeur in the same circumstances. What it boiled down to was a marsupial version of a wolf. Probably wouldn't stack up too well against the mammalian wolf (a species I'm rather partial to), but it was a fine off-the-wall bit of work nonetheless.

Then I went on to the note from Mike. As Susan had said, he and Selima were on their way. Susan *had* forgotten to pass along the final message . . . which was that my courting present thought the jumping fish were great toys but showed not the slightest interest in eating them. As Mike said, our luck's not *that* good this summer.

"How's the shoulder this morning, Annie?" Leo looked like he'd been up and around for hours already.

"Stiff," I said—and bless his sweet soul, he came right in to massage it—"I appreciate your courting gift all the more, now that I know what kind of fight you went through to catch it for me."

"All in the name of love," he said and I could feel his grin light up the room all around me even if I couldn't see it. "What can I do for you today?"

"Join me on a long, probably useless, but definitely exhausting walk around the sheep fields. Unless you could pick out the spot the Australian Guild grabbed the rex in the daylight?" Probably too much to hope for.

"I can pick it out," he said. "That big a scrabble left signs—and I know about where you were a few moments before."

"What would I do without you?"

So we headed out. The route took us past the caged rexes. Some fifteen people were still standing about staring in at them—some tourist attraction, all right. Safe but scary, as Leo had said once in another context.

I wanted to see how they were faring myself, so I shoved through the crowd. One of the gawkers had a stick and was using it to poke at the baby rex through the bars of the cage. Just to rile it and make its mother charge him.

As I got there, the mother was just rebounding off the wire. I snatched the stick out of the bastard's hand and slapped him a good one alongside the head with it. "You like that?" I demanded.

"Hell, no!" he said.

"Then what makes you think that creature does?"

"I—" He looked sheepish for a moment, then defiant. "I just wanted to see them move around some. They weren't doing anything."

"Roos don't do anything in this heat, either. That's their way of conserving water, you damn fool. Who raised you?"

Stunned, he told me.

"Well, they ought to be ashamed of themselves. They damn sure didn't teach you the sense god gave the rexes there."

"Hey! You can't talk about my raisers—"

"Then you oughta stop doing stupid things that lead me to believe they raised you wrong."

That did it. I watched him go all embarrassed.

"Sorry," he said at last. "Everybody else was doing it."

"Then prove to me that you're a cut better. First, you get the rexes some water, so they can replace what they've lost. Then you get that damned Australian Guild to move this into the shade. Then you can stand here and make sure nobody else beats up on the rexes. Then I'll revise my opinion of your raisers. Got that?"

"Yes, *ma'am!*"

Yes, *ma'am*, and he'd do it, too. I was satisfied he'd keep them from being harassed further.

Then I got a chance to look at the rexes. The other joey was dragging a foot. Hellfire and damnation, they'd broken its leg catching it. I roared at Leo, "Get Sangster and her damned Australians down here right now!"

So we spent most of the afternoon coaxing the injured joey out of the cage so we could splint its leg. Zoos, just love 'em. Hope the guy that invented 'em wound up in a cage all his own—in the sun.

Sangster and her mates were apologetic but clearly had no intention of giving up their plan to catch any more rexes that turned up for their zoo. Oughta be a damned law to protect animals from people.

It was cooling toward evening when Leo and I finally set out to look for the spot I had in mind. Something was still niggling me about that, but the whole struggle with the rex had shoved it completely out of my head. I was hoping if I saw the spot again, the same thought might come back.

Leo found it for me in record time. Would have taken me twice as long. He stood in the middle of the spot where the first rex had been when that blinding light and stunning shot hit it all at once. "Now you see if you can reconstruct your position from that," he said. "Just pretend I'm a kangaroo rex."

"You haven't got the jaw for it, Leo." I cast about and made some good guesses. They were good enough that I found bits of the broken cell sampler there. I flopped down next to the bits and glanced around. Nothing jogged my memory, so I closed my eyes and tried to see it again.

That worked: the roos (not the rexes) had been digging up plants just *there*. I hauled myself to my feet and went over to look.

The plants the roos had been grubbing up were still there, shriveled in the heat and utterly unrecognizable. Fine. I could still do a gene-read on them if I did it *now*. "Okay," I said, "Back to Janzen's. You can make me a mint julep. If this is what I hope it is, we'll toast Mirabile."

What with one thing and another, I didn't get my gene-read on the withered plants until after dinner. It was just what I expected it to be, so I put in a call to Mike out at Gogol. Mike and Selima couldn't be found for me (aha!) but they'd left their EC run in my file.

"Susan!" I yelled and she came running. "You finish that EC check for me?"

She looked smug. "On file," she said. "Did I beat Mike out?"

I cued up her file. "Mike's was filed roughly the same time as yours but then he had extra hands—Selima was with him."

"Oh," said Susan. "Well, it's only fair to say I had extra hands, too. Janzen helped me." That made her look smugger and set off a second *aha!*, which I did not voice, as much as I enjoyed it.

I read through Susan's EC on Last Edges, then went to Mike's from Gogol a second time, then pulled hard copy on both. "Gotcha," I said, as the reports stacked up in the printer. "Mint juleps all around, Leo!"

I handed Susan the sheaf of reports and said, "Read 'em. Then tell me how this EC differs from the EC at Gogol." I leaned back in my chair, accepted the mint julep from Leo, and waited to see if Susan would see it too.

After a while, Susan's head came up. She stared at me and her mouth worked, but nothing came out. She handed the sheaf of papers to Janzen, went to the computer, and called up the EC we'd done on Gogol all those years ago, the first time the kangaroo rexes had reared their ugly little heads. She nodded to herself, then pulled hard copy on that too.

She came back with it and added it to the pile Janzen was reading. Then she sat down and said, "To kill the rexes, they have to kill the roos—but if they kill the roos, the *sheep* die."

"What?" said Moustafa and tried to wrest the reports from Janzen, who didn't cooperate. "I don't see it, Susan. I don't know how to read these things."

She gave him a pitying look but explained: "There are only two significant differences between the EC here and the EC at Gogol. The first is that Gogol has no roos—or very few; they're shot on sight—and the second is that Gogol is awash in lambkill."

Moustafa made a stifled noise deep in his throat. Janzen said, "Does this mean I don't have to give up my roo-tail soup?"

"It means," I said, "that the roos eat the lambkill, which prevents your *sheep* from eating it. You may be willing to give up your roo-tail soup, but how many people in Last Edges are willing to give up their sheep—the way Sangster did after the roos were killed in Gogol?"

I raised my glass. "To Mirabile," I said.

It was Janzen who rang the meeting bell. And what with the Australian Guilders and the Texan Guilders—all of whom were antsy to be back on the range rounding up kangaroo rexes—we had a much larger turnout than expected. There was a lot of jostling and more than one case of bad manners. I had to wonder if the Texan Guild went so far as to call each other out for gunfights, but apparently not, as nobody did.

When they finally all simmered down, I explained the situation to them. I guess I expected them to forgive the rexes on the spot. I should know better at my age.

Sangster said, "Of *course*, the roos eat lambkill! They grub it out right down to the root—*anybody* could have told you that, for god's sake!"

"You don't get it," Janzen shot back. "Kill the roos and the *lambkill* kills the sheep! That's why you lost your flock at Gogol. D'you want the same thing to happen here? *I* sure as hell don't!"

There was a good loud mutter of agreement from the crowd on that one. Sangster stamped her foot and yelled for attention. After a while she got it, but it was a lot more hostile than she was used to.

"Stabilize the roos, then," she said. She glared at me. "You've done it before with domestic herds. Those guernseys that were dropping deer every other generation. You got those stabilized to where they chain up only once every ten years. Are you telling me you can't do the same for our roos—or can't you be bothered? Might mess up your beloved kangaroo rexes."

I didn't get a chance to answer. From the very back of the crowd came an agonized shout: "*No*, Annie! You can't stabilize them! You don't know what the rexes are chaining up to! I do! And you *can't* stabilize the roos!"

I peered over heads and could just barely make out a mop of straight black hair and piercing black eyes. By this time I'd recognized Chie-Hoon's voice, even though I'd never heard the kid quite so worked up about anything.

Before anybody'd had time to react to this, Chie-Hoon was standing on a chair, waving a banner-sized picture. I recognized it even from that distance: Chie-Hoon's own reconstruction of the weirder of the two critters our rexes were chaining up to, the one with the jaws.

"Mates!" shouted Chie-Hoon, and had the instant attention of every Australian Guild member there. (When one of the locals made to object to this interruption from a nonresident, he was swiftly stifled by a menacing look from a guilder.) "D'ya recognize this?" Chie-Hoon spread the picture wide and turned, slowly, on the chair to let every one of them have a good look.

"It's a Tasmanian wolf," said somebody—to which there was general agreement—then a swift reshuffling of the Australian Guild to get closer.

"Good on you, mate," said Chie-Hoon. "That's exactly right! *That's* what our rexes are chaining up to! It was extinct on Earth, but that doesn't make it any the less Earth-authentic. Speaking as a member of the Australian Guild, Annie, I won't have you stabilizing the rexes. Save the Tasmanian wolf!"

With that, Chie-Hoon raised a fist, dramatically, then shouted a second time, "Save the Tasmanian wolf!"

And before I knew what was happening, pandemonium reigned. The entire Australian Guild was chanting, "Save the Tasmanian wolf!" as if their own lives depended on it, with Kelly Crafter Sangster herself leading the chant.

Twenty minutes later, they released the uninjured rex and its mother, with promises to release the other pair as soon as the joey's leg had healed, and I was being threatened with dire consequences if I didn't return Leo's courting gift to the fields within the week.

"They won't let me keep my present," I said to Leo, grinning through my complaint.

"I know," he said, grinning just as much. "But they'll let you keep your kangaroo rexes. That's what counts."

"It was a great courting gift, Leo."

"I know."

"We'll have to see about re-establishing the kangaroos at Gogol, too, before we lose the rest of the sheep there to the lambkill."

"Don't you ever think about anything but work, woman?"

"Occasionally. Call Loch Moose Lodge and book us a room for the week. I need a vacation."

He started off to do just that. I had another thought. "Leo!"

"You're not changing your mind." That was an order.

"No, I'm not changing my mind. But it occurs to me that Chris always wanted to be a member of my team, if she could be the official cook. Tell her I'm bringing her a brace of fish." It was those damned jumping fish I had in mind. "If she can find a way to cook them that'll make them the hot item of the season, she's on the team."

He laughed. "You've just made Chris's day."

He turned to go again, but I caught him and gave him a good long kiss, just so he wouldn't forget to book the room while he was at it. "You made my year, Leo."

Now all I had to do was think of an appropriate courting present for *him*. Which wasn't going to be easy. What do you give a guy who gives you a kangaroo rex?

I'd think of something.

Walter Jon Williams

PRAYERS ON THE WIND

Walter Jon Williams was born in Minnesota and now lives in Albuquerque, New Mexico. His short fiction has appeared frequently in *Asimov's Science Fiction,* as well as in *The Magazine of Fantasy & Science Fiction, Wheel of Fortune, Global Dispatches, Alternate Outlaws,* and in other markets, and has been gathered in the collections *Facets* and *Frankensteins and Foreign Devils.* His novels include *Ambassador of Progress, Knight Moves, Hardwired, The Crown Jewels, Voice of the Whirlwind, House of Shards, Days of Atonement,* and *Aristoi.* His novel *Metropolitan* garnered wide critical acclaim in 1996 and was one of the most talked-about books of the year. His most recent book is a sequel to *Metropolitan, City on Fire.*

Williams is a highly eclectic writer, and the fact is, one Walter Jon Williams story is rarely much like any *other* Walter Jon Williams story. He's written a wider range of different *kinds* of stuff than almost any other writer of his generation, ranging from some of the best Alternate History stories of the eighties (including the deeply moving Alternate Civil War novella, following Edgar Allan Poe's career as a Confederate general, "No Spot of Ground," and the compassionate and melancholy look at the alternate and alternately entangled lives that might have been lead by Mary Wollstonecraft Shelley, Percy Bysshe Shelley, and Lord Byron, "Wall, Stone, Craft") to stories featuring scenarios quirky enough to rank with the most off-the-wall Waldropian stuff (sending H. G. Wells's invading Martians striding into the bizarre, ritualized, and mannered world of the Forbidden City in nineteenth-century China in "Foreign Devils," and, in "Red Elvis," presenting us with an Elvis Presley who grows up to become an inspirational socialist leader whose influence changes the course of modern history); he's written gritty Mean Streets hard-as-nails cyberpunk, in stories such as "Wolf Time" and "Video Star" and "Flatline," and in novels such as the *Hardwired* and *Voice of the Whirlwind;* he's written with depth and real ingenuity about the interaction of humankind with aliens, in the brilliant "Surfacing," as well as in novels such as *Angel Station;* he's written lighthearted, wryly amusing, socially satirical novels of manners, featuring the adventures of a Raffles-like thief in a future society, in *The Crown Jewels* and *House of Shards;* he's written dark, moody, intricate, involuted Machiavellian studies of Realpolitik in action, full of betrayals and counter-betrayals and counter-*counter* betrayals, such as "Solip:System" and "Erogenoscape." Williams also mixes genres with audacity and daring, mixing classical Chinese mythology with the chop-sockey fantasy of Hong Kong martial arts movies in the droll "Broadway Johnny," mixing sword and sorcery with the Hornblower-like sea story in "Consequences," having costumed superheroes grilled by the House Committee on Un-American Activities in the McCarthy–era America of the 1950s in "Witness," and mixing fantasy with technologically oriented "hard" science fiction in books such as *Metropolitan* and *City on Fire* successfully enough to be counted as one of the progenitors of an as yet nascent subgenre sometimes called "Hard Fantasy."

This breadth of range sometimes obscures the fact that Williams has also written some of the most inventive and Wide Screen Space Opera of recent times, including the monumental novel *Aristoi,* one of the most successful of Modern Space Operas. But then, Williams is a great fan of adventure writing, and even his most introspective stories are usually crammed with action; in this he strongly recalls his mentor, Roger Zelazny, and it's no accident that Walter was selected by Roger Zelazny himself to write a sequel to Zelazny's famous story "The Graveyard Heart"—and ended up producing by far the most successful Zelazny homage I've ever read, the complex and eloquent novella "Elegy for Angels and Dogs."

Zelazny's influence is also clear in the vivid and gorgeously colored story that follows, with Williams taking us deep into the far future and across the galaxy to a distant planet to detail the intricate workings of a *very* strange future society . . . a society caught at a moment of crisis that may destroy the very foundations of its civilization forever. . . .

Hard is the appearance of a Buddha.

—Dhammapada

Bold color slashed bright slices out of Vajra's violet sky. The stiff spring breeze off the Tingsum glacier made the yellow prayer flags snap with sounds like gunshots. Sun gleamed from baroque tracework adorning silver antennae and receiver dishes. Atop the dark red walls of the Diamond Library Palace, saffron-robed monks stood like sentries, some of them grouped in threes around ragdongs, trumpets so huge they required two men to hold them aloft while a third blew puff-checked into the mouthpiece. Over the deep, grating moan of the trumpets, other monks chanted their litany.

Salutation to the Buddha.
In the language of the gods and in that of the Lus,
In the language of the demons and in that of the men,
In all the languages which exist,
I proclaim the Doctrine.

Jigme Dzasa stood at the foot of the long granite stair leading to the great library, the spectacle filling his senses, the litany dancing in his soul. He turned to his guest. "Are you ready, Ambassador?"

The face of !urq was placid. "Lus?" she asked.

"Mythical beings," said Jigme. "Serpentine divinities who live in bodies of water."

"Ah," !urq said. "I'm glad we got that cleared up."

Jigme looked at the alien, decided to say nothing.

"Let us begin," said the Ambassador. Jigme hitched up his zen and began the long climb to the Palace, his bare feet slapping at the stones. A line of Gelugspa monks followed in respectful silence. Ambassador Colonel !urq climbed beside Jigme at a slow trot, her four boot heels rapping. Behind her was a line of Sangs, their centauroid bodies cased neatly in blue-and-gray uniforms, decorations flashing in the bright sun. Next to each was a feathery Masker servant carrying a ceremonial parasol.

Jigme was out of breath by the time he mounted the long stairway, and his head whirled as he entered the tsokhang, the giant assembly hall. Several thousand members of religious orders sat rigid at their stations, long lines of men and women: Dominicans and Sufis in white, Red Hats and Yellow Hats in their saffron zens, Jesuits in black, Gyudpas in complicated aprons made of carved, interwoven human bones. . . . Each sat in the lotus posture in front of a solid gold data terminal decorated with religious symbols, some meditating, some chanting sutras, others accessing the Library.

Jigme, !urq, and their parties passed through the vast hall that hummed with the distant, echoing sutras of those trying to achieve unity with the Diamond Mountain. At the far side of the room were huge double doors of solid jade, carved with figures illustrating the life of the first twelve incarnations of the Gyalpo Rinpoche, the Treasured King. The doors opened on silent hinges at the touch of equerries' fingertips. Jigme looked at the equerries as he passed—lovely young novices, he thought, beautiful boys really. The shaven nape of that dark one showed an extraordinary curve.

Beyond was the audience chamber. The Masker servants remained outside, holding their parasols at rigid attention, while their masters trotted into the audience chamber alongside the line of monks.

Holographic murals filled the walls, illustrating the life of the Compassionate One. The ceiling was of transparent polymer, the floor of clear crystal that went down to the solid core of the planet. The crystal refracted sunlight in interesting ways, and as he walked across the room Jigme seemed to walk on rainbows.

At the far end of the room, flanked by officials, was the platform that served as a throne. Overhead was an arching canopy of massive gold, the words AUM MANI PADME HUM worked into the design in turquoise. The platform was covered in a large carpet decorated with figures of the lotus, the Wheel, the swastika, the two fish, the eternal knot, and other holy symbols. Upon the carpet sat the Gyalpo Rinpoche himself, a small man with a sunken chest and bony shoulders, the Forty-First Incarnation of the Bodhisattva Bob Miller, the Great Librarian, himself an emanation of Avalokitesvara.

The Incarnation was dressed simply in a yellow zen, being the only person in the holy precincts permitted to wear the color. Around his waist was a rosary composed of 108 strung bone disks cut from the forty skulls of his previous incarnations. His body was motionless but his arms rose and fell as the fingers moved in a series of symbolic hand gestures, one mudra after another, their pattern set by the flow of data through the Diamond Mountain.

Jigme approached and dropped to his knees before the platform. He pressed the palms of his hands together, brought the hands to his forehead, mouth, and heart, then touched his forehead to the floor. Behind him he heard thuds as some of his delegation slammed their heads against the crystal surface in a display of piety—indeed, there were depressions in the floor worn by the countless pilgrims who had done this—but Jigme, knowing he would need his wits, only touched his forehead lightly and held the posture until he heard the Incarnation speak.

"Jigme Dzasa. I am pleased to see you again. Please get to your feet and introduce me to your friends."

The old man's voice was light and dry, full of good humor. In the seventy-third year of his incarnation, the Treasured King enjoyed good health.

Jigme straightened. Rainbows rose from the floor and danced before his eyes. He climbed slowly to his feet as his knees made popping sounds—twenty years younger than the Incarnation, he was a good deal stiffer of limb—and moved toward the platform in an attitude of reverence. He reached to the rosary at his waist and took from it a white silk scarf embroidered with a religious text. He unfolded the khata and, sticking out his tongue in respect, handed it to the Incarnation with a bow.

The Gyalpo Rinpoche took the khata and draped it around his own neck with a smile. He reached out a hand, and Jigme dropped his head for the blessing. He felt dry fingertips touch his shaven scalp, and then a sense of harmony seemed to hum through his being. Everything, he knew, was correct. The interview would go well.

Jigme straightened and the Incarnation handed him a khata in exchange, one with the mystic three knots tied by the Incarnation himself. Jigme bowed again, stuck out his tongue, and moved to the side of the platform with the other officials. Beside him was Dr. Kay O'Neill, the Minister of Science. Jigme could feel O'Neill's body vibrating like a taut cord, but the minister's overwrought state could not dispel Jigme's feeling of bliss.

"Omniscient," Jigme said, "I would like to present Colonel !urq, Ambassador of the Sang."

!urq was holding her upper arms in a Sang attitude of respect. Neither she nor her followers had prostrated themselves, but had stood politely by while their human escort had done so. !urq's boots rang against the floor as she trotted to the dais, her lower arms offering a khata. She had no tongue to stick out—her upper and lower palates were flexible, permitting a wide variety of sounds, but they weren't as flexible as all that. Still she thrust out her lower lip in a polite approximation.

"I am honored to be presented at last, Omniscient," !urq said.

Dr. O'Neill gave a snort of anger.

The Treasured King draped a knotted khata around the Ambassador's neck. "We of the Diamond Mountain are pleased to welcome you. I hope you will find our hospitality to your liking."

The old man reached forward for the blessing. !urq's instructions did not permit her to bow her head before an alien presence, so the Incarnation simply reached forward and placed his hand over her face for a moment. They remained frozen in that attitude, and then !urq backed carefully to one side of the platform, standing near Jigme. She and Jigme then presented their respective parties to the Incarnation. By the end of the audience the head of the Gyalpo Rinpoche looked like a tiny red jewel in a flowery lotus of white silk khatas.

"I thank you all for coming all these light-years to see me," said the Incarnation, and Jigme led the visitors from the audience chamber, chanting the sutra *Aum vajra guru Padma siddhi hum, Aum the diamond powerful guru Padma*, as he walked.

!urq came to a halt as soon as her party had filed from the room. Her lower arms formed an expression of bewilderment.

"Is that all?"

Jigme looked at the alien. "That is the conclusion of the audience, yes. We may tour the holy places in the Library, if you wish."

"We had no opportunity to discuss the matter of Gyangtse."

"You may apply to the Ministry for another interview."

"It took me twelve years to obtain this one." Her upper arms took a stance that Jigme recognized as martial. "The patience of my government is not unlimited," she said.

Jigme bowed. "I shall communicate this to the Ministry, Ambassador."

"Delay in the Gyangtse matter will only result in more hardship for the inhabitants when they are removed."

"It is out of my hands, Ambassador."

!urq held her stance for a long moment in order to emphasize her protest, then relaxed her arms. Her upper set of hands caressed the white silk khata. "Odd to think," she said, amused, "that I journeyed twelve years just to stick out my lip at a human and have him touch my face in return."

"Many humans would give their lives for such a blessing," said Jigme.

"Sticking out the lip is quite rude where I come from, you know."

"I believe you have told me this."

"The Omniscient's hands were very warm." !urq raised fingers to her forehead, touched the ebon flesh. "I believe I can still feel the heat on my skin."

Jigme was impressed. "The Treasured King has given you a special blessing. He can channel the energies of the Diamond Mountain through his body. That was the heat you felt."

!urq's antennae rose skeptically, but she refrained from comment.

"Would you like to see the holy places?" Jigme said. "This, for instance, is a room devoted to Maitreya, the Buddha That Will Come. Before you is his statue. Data can be accessed by manipulation of the images on his headdress."

Jigme's speech was interrupted by the entrance of a Masker servant from the audience room. A white khata was draped about the avian's neck. !urq's trunk swiveled atop her centaur body; her arms assumed a commanding stance. The clicks and pops of her own language rattled from her mouth like falling stones.

"Did I send for you, creature?"

The Masker performed an obsequious gesture with its parasol. "I beg the Colonel's pardon. The old human sent for us. He is touching us and giving us scarves." The Masker fluttered helplessly. "We did not wish to offend our hosts, and there were no Sang to query for instruction."

"How odd," said !urq. "Why should the old human want to bless our slaves?" She eyed the Masker and thought for a moment. "I will not kill you today," she decided. She turned to Jigme and switched to Tibetan. "Please continue, Rinpoche."

"As you wish, Colonel." He returned to his speech. "The Library Palace is the site of no less than twenty-one tombs of various bodhisattvas, including many incarnations of the Gyalpo Rinpoche. The Palace also contains over eight thousand data terminals and sixty shrines."

As he rattled through the prepared speech, Jigme wondered about the scene he had just witnessed. He suspected that "I will not kill you today" was less alarming than it sounded, was instead an idiomatic way of saying "Go about your business."

Then again, knowing the Sang, maybe not.

The Cabinet had gathered in one of the many other reception rooms of the Library Palace. This one was small, the walls and ceiling hidden behind tapestry covered with appliqué, the room's sole ornament a black stone statue of a dancing demon that served tea on command.

The Gyalpo Rinpoche, to emphasize his once-humble origins, was seated on the floor. White stubble prickled from his scalp.

Jigme sat cross-legged on a pillow. Across from him was Dr. O'Neill. A lay official, her status was marked by the long turquoise earring that hung from her left ear to her collarbone, that and the long hair piled high on her head. The rosary she held was made of 108 antique microprocessors pierced and strung on a length of fiberoptic cable. Beside her sat the cheerful Miss Taisuke, the Minister of State. Although only fifteen years old, she was Jigme's immediate superior, her authority derived from being the certified reincarnation of a famous hermit nun of the Yellow Hat Gelugspa order. Beside her, the Minister of Magic, a tantric sorcerer of the Gyud School named Daddy Carbajal, toyed with a trumpet made from a human thigh bone. Behind him in a semireclined position was the elderly, frail, toothless State Oracle—his was a high-ranking position, but it was a largely symbolic one as long as the Treasured King was in his majority. Other ministers, lay or clerical, sipped tea or gossiped as they waited for the Incarnation to begin the meeting.

The Treasured King scratched one bony shoulder, grinned, then assumed in an eyeblink a posture of deep meditation, placing hands in his lap with his skull-rosary wrapped around them. "Aum," he intoned. The others straightened and joined in the holy syllable, the Pranava, the creative sound whose vibrations built the universe. Then the Horse of the Air rose from the throat of the Gyalpo Rinpoche, the syllables *Aum mane padme hum*, and the others reached for their rosaries.

As he recited the rosary, Jigme tried to meditate on each syllable as it went by, comprehend the full meaning of each, the color, the importance, the significance. *Aum*, which was white and connected with the gods. *Ma*, which was blue and connected with the titans. *Ne*, which was yellow and connected with men. *Pad*, which was green and connected with animals. *Me*, which was red and connected with giants and demigods. *Hum*, which was black and connected with dwellers in purgatory. Each syllable a separate realm, each belonging to a separate species, together forming the visible and invisible universe.

"Hri!" called everyone in unison, signifying the end of the 108th repetition. The Incarnation smiled and asked the black statue for some tea. The stone demon scuttled across the thick carpet and poured tea into his golden bowl. The demon looked up into the Incarnation's face.

"Free me!" said the statue.

The Gyalpo Rinpoche looked at the statue. "Tell me truthfully. Have you achieved Enlightenment?"

The demon said nothing.

The Treasured King smiled again. "Then you had better give Dr. O'Neill some tea."

O'Neill accepted her tea, sipped, and dismissed the demon. It scuttled back to its pedestal.

"We should consider the matter of Ambassador !urq," said the Incarnation.

O'Neill put down her teacup. "I am opposed to her presence here. The Sang are an unenlightened and violent race. They conceive of life as a struggle against nature rather than search for Enlightenment. They have already conquered an entire species, and would subdue us if they could."

"That is why I have consented to the building of warships," said the Incarnation.

"From their apartments in the Nyingmapa monastery, the Sang now have access to the Library," said O'Neill. "All our strategic information is present there. They will use the knowledge against us."

"Truth can do no harm," said Miss Taisuke.

"All truth is not vouchsafed to the unenlightened," said O'Neill. "To those unprepared by correct study and thought, truth can be a danger." She gestured with an arm, encompassing the world outside the Palace. "Who should know better than we, who live on Vajra? Haven't half the charlatans in all existence set up outside our walls to preach half-truths to the credulous, endangering their own Enlightenment and those of everyone who hears them?"

Jigme listened to O'Neill in silence. O'Neill and Daddy Carbajal were the leaders of the reactionary party, defenders of orthodoxy and the security of the realm. They had argued this point before.

"Knowledge will make the Sang cautious," said Jigme. "They will now know of our armament. They will now understand the scope of the human expansion, far greater than their own. We may hope this will deter them from attack."

"The Sang may be encouraged to build more weapons of their own," said Daddy Carbajal. "They are already highly militarized, as a way of keeping down their subject species. They may militarize further."

"Be assured they are doing so," said O'Neill. "Our own embassy is kept in close confinement on a small planetoid. They have no way of learning the scope of the Sang threat or sending this information to the Library. We, on the other hand, have escorted the Sang ambassador throughout human space and have shown her anything in which she expressed an interest."

"Deterrence," said Jigme. "We wished them to know how extensive our sphere is, that the conquest would be costly and call for more resources than they possess."

"We must do more than deter. The Sang threat should be eliminated, as were the threats of heterodox humanity during the Third and Fifth Incarnations."

"You speak jihad," said Miss Taisuke.

There was brief silence. No one, not even O'Neill, was comfortable with Taisuke's plainness.

"All human worlds are under the peace of the Library," said O'Neill. "This was accomplished partly by force, partly by conversion. The Sang will not *permit* conversion."

The Gyalpo Rinpoche cleared his throat. The others fell silent at once. The Incarnation had been listening in silence, his face showing concentration but no emotion. He always preferred to hear the opinions of others before expressing his own. "The Third and Fifth Incarnations," he said, "did nothing to encourage the jihads proclaimed in their name. The Incarnations did not wish to accept temporal power."

"They did not speak against the holy warriors," said Daddy Carbajal.

The Incarnation's elderly face was uncommonly stern. His hands formed the teaching mudra. "Does not Shakyamuni speak in the *Anguttara Nikaya* of the three ways of keeping the body pure?" he asked. "One must not commit adultery, one must not steal, one must not kill any living creature. How could warriors kill for orthodoxy and yet remain orthodox?"

There was a long moment of uncomfortable silence. Only Daddy Carbajal, whose tantric Short Path teaching included numerous ways of dispatching his enemies, did not seem nonplussed.

"The Sang are here to study us," said the Gyalpo Rinpoche. "We also study them."

"I view their pollution as a danger." Dr. O'Neill's face was stubborn.

Miss Taisuke gave a brilliant smile. "Does not the *Mahaparinirvana-sutra* tell us that if we are forced to live in a difficult situation and among people of impure minds, if we cherish faith in Buddha we can ever lead them toward better actions?"

Relief fluttered through Jigme. Taisuke's apt quote, atop the Incarnation's sternness, had routed the war party.

"The Embassy will remain," said the Treasured King. "They will be given the freedom of Vajra, saving only the Holy Precincts. We must remember the oath of the Amida Buddha: 'Though I attain Buddhahood, I shall never be complete until people everywhere, hearing my name, learn right ideas about life and death, and gain that perfect wisdom that will keep their minds pure and tranquil in the midst of the world's greed and suffering.' "

"What of Gyangtse, Rinpoche?" O'Neill's voice seemed harsh after the graceful words of Scripture.

The Gyalpo Rinpoche cocked his head and thought for a moment. Suddenly the Incarnation seemed very human and very frail, and Jigme's heart surged with love for the old man.

"We will deal with that at the Picnic Festival," said the Incarnation.

From his position by the lake, Jigme could see tents and banners dotting the lower slopes of Tingsum like bright spring flowers. The Picnic Festival lasted a week, and unlike most of the other holidays had no real religious connection. It was a week-long campout during which almost the entire population of the Diamond City and the surrounding monasteries moved into the open and spent their time making merry.

Jigme could see the giant yellow hovertent of the Gyalpo Rinpoche surrounded by saffron-robed guards, the guards present not to protect the Treasured King from attackers, but rather to preserve his tranquility against invasions by devout pilgrims in search of a blessing. The guards—monks armed with staves, their shoulders padded hugely to make them look more formidable—served the additional purpose of keeping the Sang away from the Treasured King until the conclusion of the festival, something for which Jigme was devoutly grateful. He didn't want any political confrontations disturbing the joy of the holiday. Fortunately Ambassador !urq seemed content to wait until her scheduled appearance at a party given by the Incarnation on the final afternoon.

Children splashed barefoot in the shallows of the lake, and others played chibi on the sward beside, trying to keep a shuttlecock aloft using the feet alone. Jigme found himself watching a redheaded boy on the verge of adolescence, admiring the boy's grace, the way the knobbed spine and sharp shoulders moved under his pale skin. His bony ankles hadn't missed the shuttlecock yet. Jigme was sufficiently lost in his reverie that he did not hear the sound of boots on the grass beside him.

"Jigme Dzasa?"

Jigme looked up with a guilty start. !urq stood beside him, wearing hardy outdoor clothing. Her legs were wrapped up to the shoulder. Jigme stood hastily and bowed.

"Your pardon, Ambassador. I didn't hear you."

The Sang's feathery antennae waved cheerfully in the breeze. "I thought I would lead a party up Tingsum. Would you care to join us?"

What Jigme wanted to do was continue watching the ball game, but he assented with a smile. Climbing mountains: that was the sort of thing the Sang were always up to. They wanted to demonstrate they could conquer anything.

"Perhaps you should find a pony," !urq said. "Then you could keep up with us."

Jigme took a pony from the Library's corral and followed the waffle patterns of !urq's boots into the trees on the lower slopes. Three other Sang were along on the expedition; they clicked and gobbled to one another as they trotted cheerfully along. Behind toiled three Maskers-of-burden carrying food and climbing equipment. If the Sang noticed the incongruity demonstrated by the human's using a quadruped as a beast of burden while they, centauroids, used a bipedal race as servants, they politely refrained from mentioning it. The pony's genetically altered cloven forefeet took the mountain trail easily, nimbler than the Sang in their heavy boots. Jigme noticed that this made the Sang work harder, trying to outdo the dumb beast.

They came to a high mountain meadow and paused, looking down at the huge field of tents that ringed the smooth violet lake. In the middle of the meadow was a three-meter tower of crystal, weathered and yellow, ringed by rubble flaked off during the hard winters. One of the Sang trotted over to examine it.

"I thought the crystal was instructed to stay well below the surface," he said.

"There must have been a house here once," Jigme said. "The crystal would have been instructed to grow up through the surface to provide Library access."

!urq trotted across a stretch of grass, her head down. "Here's the beginning of the foundation line," she said. She gestured with an arm. "It runs from here to over there."

The Sang cantered over the ground, frisky as children, to discover the remnants of the foundation. The Sang were always keen, Jigme found, on discovering things. They had not yet learned that there was only one thing worth discovering, and it had nothing to do with old ruins.

!urq examined the pillar of crystal, touched its crumbling surface. "And over eighty percent of the planet is composed of this?" she said.

"All except the crust," Jigme said. "The crystal was instructed to convert most of the planet's material. That is why our heavy metals have to come from mined asteroids, and why we build mostly in natural materials. This house was probably of wood and laminated cloth, and it most likely burned in an accident."

!urq picked up a bit of crystal from the ring of rubble that surrounded the pillar. "And you can store information in this."

"All the information we have," Jigme said reverently. "All the information in the universe, eventually." Involuntarily, his hands formed the teaching mudra. "The Library is a hologram of the universe. The Blessed Bodhisattva Bob Miller was a reflection of the Library, its first Incarnation. The current Incarnation is the forty-first."

!urq's antennae flickered in the wind. She tossed the piece of crystal from hand to hand. "All the information you possess," she said. "That is a powerful tool. Or weapon."

"A tool, yes. The original builders of the Library considered it only a tool. Only something to help them order things, to assist them in governing. They did not comprehend that once the Diamond Mountain contained enough information, once it gathered enough energy, it would become more than the sum of its parts. That it would become the Mind of Buddha, the universe in small, and that the Mind, out of its compassion, would seek to incarnate itself as a human."

"The Library is self-aware?" !urq asked. She seemed to find the notion startling.

Jigme could only shrug. "Is the universe self-aware?"

!urq made a series of meditative clicking noises.

"Inside the Diamond Mountain," Jigme said, "there are processes going on that we cannot comprehend. The Library was designed to be nearly autonomous; it is now so large we cannot keep track of everything, because we would need a mind as large as the Library to process the information. Many of the energy and data transfers that we can track are very subtle, involving energies that are not fully understood. Yet we can track some of them. When an Incarnation dies, we can see the trace his spirit makes through the Library—like an atomic particle that comes apart in a shower of short-lived particles, we see it principally through its effects on other energies—and we can see part of those energies move from one place to another, from one body to another, becoming another Incarnation."

!urq's antennae moved skeptically. "You can document this?"

"We can produce spectra showing the tracks of energy through matter. Is that documentation?"

"I would say, with all respect, your case remains unproven."

"I do not seek to prove anything." Jigme smiled. "The Gyalpo Rinpoche is his own proof, his own truth. Buddha is truth. All else is illusion."

!urq put the piece of crystal in her pocket. "If this was *our* Library," she said, "we would prove things one way or another."

"You would see only your own reflection. Existence on the quantum level is largely a matter of belief. On that level, mind is as powerful as matter. We believe that the Gyalpo Rinpoche is an Incarnation of the Library; does that belief help make it so?"

"You ask me questions based on a system of belief that I do not share. How can you expect me to answer?"

"Belief is powerful. Belief can incarnate itself."

"Belief can incarnate itself as delusion."

"Delusion can incarnate itself as reality." Jigme stood in his stirrups, stretching his legs, and then settled back into his saddle. "Let me tell you a story," he said. "It's quite true. There was a man who went for a drive, over the pass yonder." He pointed across the valley, at the low blue pass, the Kampa La, between the mountains Tampa and Tsang. "It was a pleasant day, and he put the car's top down. A windstorm came up as he was riding near a crossroads, and his fur hat blew off his head into a thorn bush, where he couldn't reach it. He simply drove on his way.

"Other people walked past the bush, and they saw something inside. They told each other they'd seen something odd there. The hat got weathered and less easy to recognize. Soon the locals were telling travelers to beware the thing near the crossroads, and someone else suggested the thing might be a demon, and soon people were warning others about the demon in the bush."

"Delusion," said !urq.

"It *was* delusion," Jigme agreed. "But it was *not* delusion when the hat grew arms, legs, and teeth, and when it began chasing people up and down the Kampa La. The Ministry of Magic had to send a naljorpa to perform a rite of chöd and banish the thing."

!urq's antennae gave a meditative quiver. "People see what they want to see," she said.

"The delusion had incarnated itself. The case is classic: the Ministries of Science and Magic performed an inquiry. They could trace the patterns of energy through the crystal structure of the Library: the power of the growing belief, the reaction when the belief was fulfilled, the dispersing of the energy when chöd was performed." Jigme gave a laugh. "In the end, the naljorpa brought back an old, weathered hat. Just bits of fur and leather."

"The naljorpa got a good reward, no doubt," said !urq, "for bringing back this moldy bit of fur."

"Probably. Not my department, actually."

"It seems possible, here on Vajra, to make a good living out of others' delusions. My government would not permit such things."

"What do the people lose by being credulous?" Jigme asked. "Only money, which is earthly, and that is a pitiful thing to worry about. It would matter only that the act of giving is sincere."

!urq gave a toss of her head. "We should continue up the mountain, Rinpoche."

"Certainly." Jigme kicked his pony into a trot. He wondered if he had just convinced !urq that his government was corrupt in allowing fakirs to gull the population. Jigme knew there were many ways to Enlightenment and that the soul must try them all. Just because the preacher was corrupt did not mean his message was untrue. How to convince !urq of that? he wondered.

"We believe it is good to test oneself against things," !urq said. "Life is struggle, and one must remain sharp. Ready for whatever happens."

"In the *Parinibbana-sutra*, the Blessed One says that the point of his teaching is to control our own minds. Then one can be ready."

"Of course we control our minds, Rinpoche. If we could not control our minds, we would not achieve mastery. If we do not achieve mastery, then we are nothing."

"I am pleased, then," Jigme smiled, "that you and the Buddha are in agreement."

To which !urq had no reply, save only to launch herself savagely at the next climb, while Jigme followed easily on his cloven-hoofed pony.

The scent of incense and flowers filled the Gyalpo Rinpoche's giant yellow tent. The Treasured King, a silk khata around his neck, sat in the lotus posture on soft grass. The bottoms of his feet were stained green. Ambassador !urq stood ponderously before him, lower lip thrust forward, her four arms in a formal stance, the Incarnation's knotted scarf draped over her shoulders.

Jigme watched, standing next to the erect, angry figure of Dr. O'Neill. He took comfort from the ever-serene smile of Miss Taisuke, sitting on the grass across the tent.

"Ambassador Colonel, I am happy you have joined us on holiday."

"We are pleased to participate in your festivals, Omniscient," said !urq.

"The spring flowers are lovely, are they not? It's worthwhile to take a whole week to enjoy them. In so doing, we remember the words of Shakyamuni, who tells us to enjoy the blossoms of Enlightenment in their season and harvest the fruit of the right path."

"Is there a season, Omniscient, for discussing the matter of Gyangtse?"

Right to the point, Jigme thought. !urq might never learn the oblique manner of speech that predominated at the high ministerial levels.

The Incarnation was not disturbed. "Surely matters may be discussed in any season," he said.

"The planet is desirable, Omniscient. Your settlement violates our border. My government demands your immediate evacuation."

Dr. O'Neill's breath hissed out at the word *demand*. Jigme could see her ears redden with fury.

"The first humans reached the planet before the border negotiations were completed," the Incarnation said equably. "They did not realize they were setting in violation of the agreement."

"That does not invalidate the agreement."

"Conceded, Ambassador. Still, would it not be unjust, after all their hard labor, to ask them to move?"

!urq's antennae bobbed politely. "Does not your Blessed One admit that life is composed of suffering? Does the Buddha not condemn the demon of worldly desires? What desire could be more worldly than a desire to possess a world?"

Jigme was impressed. Definitely, he thought, she was getting better at this sort of thing.

"In the same text," said Jigme, "Shakyamuni tells us to refrain from disputes, and not repel one another like water and oil, but like milk and water mingle together." He opened his hands in an offering gesture. "Will your government not accept a new planet in exchange? Or better yet, will they not dispose of this border altogether, and allow a free commerce between our races?"

"What new planet?" !urq's arms formed a querying posture.

"We explore constantly in order to fulfill the mandate of the Library and provide it with more data. Our survey records are available through your Library access. Choose any planet that has not yet been inhabited by humans."

"Any planet chosen will be outside of our zone of influence, far from our own frontiers and easily cut off from our home sphere."

"Why would we cut you off, Ambassador?"

"Gyangtse is of strategic significance. It is a penetration of our border."

"Let us then dispose of the border entirely."

!urq's antennae stood erect. Her arms took a martial position. "You humans are larger, more populous. You would overwhelm us by sheer numbers. The border must remain inviolate."

"Let us then have greater commerce across the border than before. With increased knowledge, distrust will diminish."

"You would send missionaries. I know there are Jesuits and Gelugspa who have been training for years in hopes of obtaining converts or martyrdom in the Sang dominions."

"It would be a shame to disappoint them." There was a slight smile on the Incarnation's face.

!urq's arms formed an obstinate pattern. "They would stir up trouble among the Maskers. They would preach to the credulous among my own race. My government must protect its own people."

"The message of Shakyamuni is not a political message, Ambassador."

"That is a matter of interpretation, Omniscient."

"Will you transmit my offer to your government?"

!urq held her stance for a long moment. Jigme could sense Dr. O'Neill's fury in the alien's obstinacy. "I will do so, Omniscient," said the Ambassador. "Though I have no confidence that it will be accepted."

"I think the offer will be accepted," said Miss Taisuke. She sat on the grass in Jigme's tent. She was in the butterfly position, the soles of her feet pressed together and her knees on the ground. Jigme sat beside her. One of Jigme's students, a clean-limbed lad named Rabjoms, gracefully served them tea and cakes, then withdrew.

"The Sang are obdurate," said Jigme. "Why do you think there is hope?"

"Sooner or later the Sang will realize they may choose any one of hundreds of unoccupied planets. It will dawn on them that they can pick one on the far side of our sphere, and their spy ships can travel the length of human-occupied space on quite legitimate missions, and gather whatever information they desire."

"Ah."

"All this in exchange for one minor border penetration."

Jigme thought about this for a moment. "We've held onto Gyangtse in order to test the Sangs' rationality and their willingness to fight. There has been no war in twelve years. This shows that the Sang are susceptible to reason. Where there is reason, there is capability for Enlightenment."

"Amen," said Miss Taisuke. She finished her tea and put down the glass.

"Would you like more? Shall I summon Rabjoms?"

"Thank you, no." She cast a glance back to the door of the tent. "He has lovely brown eyes, your Rabjoms."

"Yes."

Miss Taisuke looked at him. "Is he your consort?"

Jigme put down his glass. "No. I try to forsake worldly passions."

"You are of the Red Hat order. You have taken no vow of celibacy."

Agitation fluttered in Jigme's belly. "The *Mahaparinirvana-sutra* says that lust is the soil in which other passions flourish. I avoid it."

"I wondered. It has been remarked that all your pages are such pretty boys."

Jigme tried to calm himself. "I choose them for other qualities, Miss Taisuke. I assure you."

She laughed merrily. "Of course. I merely wondered." She leaned forward from out of her butterfly position, reached out, and touched his cheek. "I have a sense this may be a randy incarnation for me. You have no desire for young girls?"

Jigme did not move. "I cannot help you, Minister."

"Poor Jigme." She drew her hand back. "I will offer prayers for you."

"Prayers are always accepted, Miss Taisuke."

"But not passes. Very well." She rose to her feet, and Jigme rose with her. "I must be off to the Kagyupas' party. Will you be there?"

"I have scheduled this hour for meditation. Perhaps later."

"Later, then." She kissed his cheek and squeezed his hand, then slipped out of the tent. Jigme sat in the lotus posture and called for Rabjoms to take away the tea things. As he watched the boy's graceful movements, he gave an inward sigh. His weakness had been noticed, and, even worse, remarked on.

His next student would have to be ugly. The ugliest one he could find.

He sighed again.

A shriek rang out. Jigme looked up, heart hammering, and saw a demon at the back of the tent. Its flesh was bright red, and its eyes seemed to bulge out of its head. Rabjoms yelled and flung the tea service at it; a glass bounced off its head and shattered.

The demon charged forward, Rabjoms falling under its clawed feet. The overwhelming smell of decay filled the tent. The demon burst through the tent flap into the outdoors. Jigme heard more shrieks and cries of alarm from outside. The demon roared like a bull, then laughed like a madman. Jigme crawled forward to gather up Rabjoms, holding the terrified boy in his arms, chanting the Horse of the Air to calm himself until he heard the teakettle hissing of a thousand snakes followed by a rush of wind, the sign that the entity had dispersed. Jigme soothed his page and tried to think what the meaning of this sudden burst of psychic energy might be.

A few moments later, Jigme received a call on his radiophone. The Gyalpo Rinpoche, a few moments after returning to the Library Palace in his hovertent, had fallen stone dead.

"Cerebral hemorrhage," said Dr. O'Neill. The Minister of Science had performed the autopsy herself—her long hair was undone and tied behind, to fit under a surgical cap, and she still wore her scrubs. She was without the long turquoise earring that marked her rank, and she kept waving a hand near her ear, as if she somehow missed it. "The Incarnation was an old man," she said. "A slight erosion in an artery, and he was gone. It took only seconds."

The Cabinet accepted the news in stunned silence. For all their lives, there had been only the one Treasured King. Now the anchor of all their lives had been removed.

"The reincarnation was remarkably swift," Dr. O'Neill said. "I was able to watch most of it on the monitors in real time—the energies remained remarkably focused, not dissipated in a shower of sparks as with most individuals. I must admit I was impressed. The demon that appeared at the Picnic Festival was only one of the many side effects caused by such a massive turbulence within the crystal architecture of the Diamond Mountain."

Miss Taisuke looked up. "Have you identified the child?"

"Of course." Dr. O'Neill allowed herself a thin-lipped smile. "A second-trimester baby, to be born to a family of tax collectors in Dulan Province, near the White Ocean. The fetus is not developed to the point where a full incarnation is possible, and the energies remain clinging to the mother until they can move to the child. She must be feeling . . . elevated. I would like to interview her about her sensations before she is informed that she is carrying the new Bodhisattva." Dr. O'Neill waved a hand in the vicinity of her ear again.

"We must appoint a regent," said Daddy Carbajal.

"Yes," said Dr. O'Neill. "The more so now, with the human sphere being threatened by the unenlightened."

Jigme looked from one to the other. The shock of the Gyalpo Rinpoche's death had unnerved him to the point of forgetting political matters. Clearly this had not been the case with O'Neill and the Minister of Magic.

He could not let the reactionary party dominate this meeting.

"I believe," he said, "we should appoint Miss Taisuke as Regent."

His words surprised even himself.

. . .

The struggle was prolonged. Dr. O'Neill and Daddy Carbajal fought an obstinate rearguard action, but finally Miss Taisuke was confirmed. Jigme had a feeling that several of the ministers only consented to Miss Taisuke because they thought she was young enough that they might manipulate her. They didn't know her well, Jigme thought, and that was fortunate.

"We must formulate a policy concerning Gyangtse and the Sang," Dr. O'Neill said. Her face assumed its usual thin-lipped stubbornness.

"The Omniscient's policy was always to delay," Miss Taisuke said. "This sad matter will furnish a further excuse for postponing any final decision."

"We must put the armed forces on alert. The Sang may consider this a moment in which to strike."

The Regent nodded. "Let this be done."

"There is the matter of the new Incarnation," Dr. O'Neill said. "Should the delivery be advanced? How should the parents be informed?"

"We shall consult the State Oracle," said Miss Taisuke.

The Oracle, his toothless mouth gaping, was a picture of terror. No one had asked him anything in years.

Eerie music echoed through the Oracular Hall of the Library, off the walls and ceiling covered with grotesque carvings—gods, demons, and skulls that grinned at the intent humans below. Chanting monks sat in rows, accompanied by magicians playing drums and trumpets all made from human bone. Jigme's stinging eyes watered from the gusts of strong incense.

In the middle of it all sat the State Oracle, his wrinkled face expressionless. Before him, sitting on a platform, was Miss Taisuke, dressed in the formal clothing of the Regency.

"In old Tibetan times, the Oracle used to be consulted frequently," Jigme told Ambassador !urq. "But since the Gyalpo Rinpoche has been incarnated on Vajra, the Omniscient's close association with the universe analogue of the Library has made most divination unnecessary. The State Oracle is usually called upon only during periods between Incarnations."

"I am having trouble phrasing my reports to my superiors, Rinpoche," said !urq. "Your government is at present run by a fifteen-year-old girl with the advice of an elderly fortune-teller. I expect to have a certain amount of difficulty getting my superiors to take this seriously."

"The Oracle is a serious diviner," Jigme said. "There are a series of competitive exams to discover his degree of empathy with the Library. Our Oracle was right at the top of his class."

"My government will be relieved to know it."

The singing and chanting had been going on for hours. !urq had long been showing signs of impatience. Suddenly the Oracle gave a start. His eyes and mouth dropped open. His face had lost all character.

Then something else was there, an alien presence. The Oracle jumped up from his seated position, began to whirl wildly with his arms outstretched. Several of his assistants ran forward carrying his headdress while others seized him, holding his rigid body steady. The headdress was enormous, all hand-wrought gold featuring skulls and gods and topped with a vast array of plumes. It weighed over ninety pounds.

"The Oracle, by use of intent meditation, has driven the spirit from his own body," Jigme reported. "He is now possessed by the Library, which assumes the form of the god Yamantaka, the Conqueror of Death."

"Interesting," !urq said noncommittally.

"An old man could not support that headdress without some form of psychic help," Jigme said. "Surely you must agree?" He was beginning to be annoyed by the Ambassador's perpetual skepticism.

The Oracle's assistants had managed to strap the headdress on the Oracle's bald head. They stepped back, and the Oracle continued his dance, the weighty headdress supported by his rigid neck. The Oracle dashed from one end of the room to the other, still whirling, sweat spraying off his brow, then ran to the feet of Miss Taisuke and fell to his knees.

When he spoke it was in a metallic, unnatural voice. "The Incarnation should be installed by New Year!" he shouted, and then toppled. When the assistant monks had unstrapped the heavy headdress and the old man rose, back in his body once more and rubbing his neck, the Oracle looked at Miss Taisuke and blinked painfully. "I resign," he said.

"Accepted," said the Regent. "With great regret."

"This is a young man's job. I could have broken my damn neck."

Ambassador !urq's antennae pricked forward. "This," she said, "is an unusually truthful oracle."

"Top of his class," said Jigme. "What did I tell you?"

The new Oracle was a young man, a strict orthodox Yellow Hat whose predictive abilities had been proved outstanding by every objective test. The calendar of festivals rolled by: the time of pilgrimage, the week of operas and plays, the kite-flying festival, the end of Ramadan, Buddha's descent from Tishita Heaven, Christmas, the celebration of Kali the Benevolent, the anniversary of the death of Tsongkhapa. . . . The New Year was calculated to fall sixty days after Christmas, and for weeks beforehand the artisans of Vajra worked on their floats. The floats—huge sculptures of fabulous buildings, religious icons, famous scenes from the opera featuring giant animated figures, tens of thousands of man-hours of work—would be taken through the streets of the Diamond City during the New Year's procession, then up onto Burning Hill in plain sight of the Library Palace where the new Incarnation could view them from the balcony.

And week after week, the new Incarnation grew, as fast as the technology safely permitted. Carefully removed from his mother's womb by Dr. O'Neill, the Incarnation was placed in a giant autowomb and fed a diet of nutrients and hormones calculated to bring him to adulthood. Microscopic wires were inserted carefully into his developing brain to feed the memory centers with scripture, philosophy, science, art, and the art of governing. As the new Gyalpo Rinpoche grew the body was exercised by electrode so that he would emerge with physical maturity.

The new Incarnation had early on assumed the lotus position during his rest periods, and Jigme often came to the Science Ministry to watch, through the womb's transparent cover, the eerie figure meditating in the bubbling nutrient solution. All growth of hair had been suppressed by Dr. O'Neill and the figure seemed smooth perfection. The Omniscient-to-be was leaving early adolescence behind, growing slim and cat-muscled.

The new Incarnation would need whatever strength it possessed. The political situation was worsening. The border remained unresolved—the Sang wanted not simply a new planet in exchange for Gyangtse, but also room to expand into a new militarized sphere on the other side of human space. Sang military movements, detected from the human side of the border, seemed to be rehearsals for an invasion, and were countered by increased human defense allotments. As a deterrent, the human response was made obvious to the Sang: Ambassador !urq complained continually about human aggression. Dr. O'Neill and Daddy Carbajal grew combative in Cabinet meetings. Opposition to them was scattered and unfocused. If the reactionary party wanted war, the Sang were doing little but playing into their hands.

Fortunately the Incarnation would be decanted within a week, to take possession of the rambling, embittered councils and give them political direction. Jigme closed his eyes and offered a long prayer that the Incarnation might soon make his presence felt among his ministers.

He opened his eyes. The smooth, adolescent Incarnation hovered before him, suspended in golden nutrient. Fine bubbles rose in the liquid, stroking the Incarnation's skin. The figure had a fascinating, eerie beauty, and Jigme felt he could stare at it forever.

Jigme saw, to his surprise, that the floating Incarnation had an erection. And then the Incarnation opened his eyes.

The eyes were green. Jigme felt coldness flood his spine—the look was knowing, a look of recognition. A slight smile curled the Incarnation's lips. Jigme stared. The smile seemed cruel.

Dry-mouthed, Jigme bent forward, slammed his forehead to the floor in obeisance. Pain crackled through his head. He stayed that way for a long time, offering prayer after frantic prayer.

When he finally rose, the Incarnation's eyes were closed, and the body sat calmly amid golden, rising bubbles.

The late Incarnation's rosary seemed warm as it lay against Jigme's neck. Perhaps it was anticipating being reunited with its former owner.

"The Incarnation is being dressed," Dr. O'Neill said. She stepped through the doors into the vast cabinet room. Two novice monks, doorkeepers, bowed as she swept past, their tongues stuck out in respect, then swung the doors shut behind her. O'Neill was garbed formally in a dress so heavy with brocade that it crackled as she moved. Yellow lamplight flickered from the braid as she moved through the darkened counsel chamber. Her piled hair was hidden under an embroidered cap; silver gleamed from the elaborate settings of her long turquoise earring. "He will meet with the Cabinet in a few moments and perform the recognition ceremony."

The Incarnation had been decanted that afternoon. He had walked as soon as he was permitted. The advanced growth techniques used by Dr. O'Neill appeared to have met with total success. Her eyes glowed with triumph; her cheeks were flushed.

She took her seat among the Cabinet, moving stiffly in the heavy brocade.

The Cabinet sat surrounding a small table on which some of the late Incarnation's possessions were surrounded by a number of similar objects or imitations. His rosary was around Jigme's neck. During the recognition ceremony, the new Incarnation was supposed to single out his possessions in order to display his continuance from the former personality. The ceremony was largely a formality, a holdover from the earlier, Tibetan tradition—it was already perfectly clear, from Library data, just who the Incarnation was.

There was a shout from the corridor outside, then a loud voice raised in song. The members of the Cabinet stiffened in annoyance. Someone was creating a disturbance. The Regent beckoned to a communications device hidden in an image of Kali, intending to summon guards and have the disorderly one ejected.

The doors swung open, each held by a bowing novice with outthrust tongues. The Incarnation appeared between them. He was young, just entering late adolescence. He was dressed in the tall crested formal hat and yellow robes stiff with brocade. Green eyes gleamed in the dim light as he looked at the assembled officials.

The Cabinet moved as one, offering obeisance first with praying hands lifted to the forehead, mouth, and heart, then prostrated themselves with their heads to the ground. As he fell forward, Jigme heard a voice singing.

> *Let us drink and sport today,*
> *Ours is not tomorrow.*
> *Love with Youth flies swift away,*
> *Age is nought but Sorrow.*
> *Dance and sing,*
> *Time's on the wing,*
> *Life never knows the return of Spring.*

In slow astonishment, Jigme realized that it was the Incarnation who was singing. Gradually Jigme rose from his bow.

Jigme saw that the Incarnation had a bottle in his hand. Was he drunk? he wondered. And where in the Library had he gotten the beer, or whatever it was? Had he materialized it?

"This way, boy," said the Incarnation. He had a hand on the shoulder of one of the doorkeepers. He drew the boy into the room, then took a long drink from his bottle. He eyed the Cabinet slowly, turning his head from one to the other.

"Omniscient—" said Miss Taisuke.

"Not yet," said the Incarnation. "I've been in a glass sphere for almost ten months. It's time I had some fun." He pushed the doorkeeper onto hands and knees, then knelt behind the boy. He pushed up the boy's zen, clutched at his buttocks. The page cast little frantic glances around the room. The new State Oracle seemed apoplectic.

"I see you've got some of my things," said the Incarnation.

Jigme felt something twitch around his neck. The former Incarnation's skull-rosary was beginning to move. Jigme's heart crashed in his chest.

The Cabinet watched in stunned silence as the Incarnation began to sodomize the doorkeeper. The boy's face showed nothing but panic and terror.

This is a lesson, Jigme thought insistently. This is a living Bodhisattva doing this, and somehow this is one of his sermons. We will learn from this.

The rosary twitched, rose slowly from around Jigme's neck, and flew through the air to drop around the Incarnation's head.

A plain ivory walking stick rose from the table and spun through the air. The Incarnation materialized a third arm to catch the cane in midair. A decorated porcelain bowl followed, a drum, and a small golden figurine of a laughing Buddha ripped itself free from the pocket of the new State Oracle. Each was caught by a new arm. Each item had belonged to the former Incarnation; each was the correct choice.

The Incarnation howled like a beast at the moment of climax. Then he stood, adjusting his garments. He bent to pick up the ivory cane. He smashed the porcelain bowl with it, then broke the cane over the head of the Buddha. He rammed the Buddha through the drum, then threw both against the wall. All six hands rose to the rosary around his neck; he ripped at it and the cord broke, white bone disks flying through the room. His extra arms vanished.

"Short Path," he said, turned and stalked out.

Across the room, in the long silence that followed, Jigme could see Dr. O'Neill. Her pale face seemed to float in the darkness, distinct amid the confusion and madness, her expression frozen in a racking, electric moment of private agony. The minister's moment of triumph had turned to ashes.

Perhaps everything had.

Jigme rose to comfort the doorkeeper.

"There has never been an Incarnation who followed the Short Path," said Miss Taisuke.

"Daddy Carbajal should be delighted," Jigme said. "He's a doubtob himself."

"I don't think he's happy," said the Regent. "I watched him. He is a tantric sorcerer, yes, one of the best. But the Incarnation's performance frightened him."

They spoke alone in Miss Taisuke's townhouse—in the lha khang, a room devoted to religious images. Incense floated gently in the air. Outside, Jigme could hear the sounds of celebration as the word reached the population that the Incarnation was among them once again.

A statue of the Thunderbolt Sow came to life, looked at the Regent. "A message from the Library Palace, Regent," it said. "The Incarnation has spent the evening in his quarters, in the company of an apprentice monk. He has now passed out from drunkenness."

"Thank you, Rinpoche," Taisuke said. The Thunderbolt Sow froze in place. Taisuke turned back to Jigme.

"His Omniscience is possibly the most powerful doubtob in history," she said. "Dr. O'Neill showed me the spectra—the display of psychic energy, as recorded by the Library, was truly awesome. And it was perfectly controlled."

"Could something have gone wrong with the process of bringing the Incarnation to adulthood?"

"The process has been used for centuries. It has been used on Incarnations before—it was a fad for a while, and the Eighteenth through Twenty-Third were all raised that way." She frowned, leaning forward. "In any case, it's all over. The Librarian Bob Miller—and the divine Avalokitesvara, if you go for that sort of thing—has now been reincarnated as the Forty-Second Gyalpo Rinpoche. There's nothing that can be done."

"Nothing," Jigme said. The Short Path, he thought, the path to Enlightenment taken by magicians and madmen, a direct route that had no reference to morality or convention. . . . The Short Path was dangerous, often heterodox, and colossally difficult. Most doubtobs ended up destroying themselves and everyone around them.

"We have had carnal Incarnations before," Taisuke said. "The Eighth left some wonderful love poetry behind, and quite a few have been sodomites. No harm was done."

"I will pray, Regent," said Jigme, "that no harm may be done now."

It seemed to him that there was a shadow on Taisuke's usual blazing smile. "That is doubtless the best solution. I will pray also."

Jigme returned to the Nyingmapa monastery, where he had an apartment near the Sang embassy. He knew he was too agitated to sit quietly and meditate, and so called for some novices to bring him a meditation box. He needed to discipline both body and mind before he could find peace.

He sat in the narrow box in a cross-legged position and drew the lid over his head. Cut off from the world, he would not allow himself to relax, to lean against the walls of the box for support. He took his rosary in his hands. "*Aum vajra sattva,*" he began, Aum the Diamond Being, one of the names of Buddha.

But the picture that floated before his mind was not that of Shakyamuni, but the naked, beautiful form of the Incarnation, staring at him from out of the autowomb with green, soul-chilling eyes.

"We should have killed the Jesuit as well. We refrained only as a courtesy to your government, Rinpoche."

Perhaps, Jigme thought, the dead Maskers' souls were even now in the Library, whirling in the patterns of energy that would result in reincarnation, whirling like the snow that fell gently as he and !urq walked down the street. To be reincarnated as humans, with the possibility of Enlightenment.

"We will dispose of the bodies, if you prefer," Jigme said.

"They dishonored their masters," said !urq. "You may do what you like with them."

As Jigme and the Ambassador walked through the snowy streets toward the Punishment Grounds, they were met with grins and waves from the population, who were getting ready for the New Year celebration. !urq acknowledged the greetings with graceful nods of her antennae. Once the population heard what had just happened, Jigme thought, the reception might well be different.

"I will send monks to collect the bodies. We will cut them up and expose them on hillsides for the vultures. Afterward their bones will be collected and perhaps turned into useful implements."

"In my nation," !urq said, "that would be considered an insult."

"The bodies will nourish the air and the earth," said Jigme. "What finer kind of death could there be?"

"Elementary. A glorious death in service to the state."

Two Masker servants, having met several times with a Jesuit acting apparently without orders from his superiors, had announced their conversion to Buddhism. !urq had promptly denounced the two as spies and had them shot out of hand. The missionary had been ordered whipped by the superiors in his Order. !urq wanted to be on hand for it.

Jigme could anticipate the public reaction. Shakyamuni had strictly forbidden the taking of life. The people would be enraged. It might be unwise for the Sang to be seen in public for the next few days, particularly during the New Year Festival, when a large percentage of the population would be drunk.

Jigme and the Ambassador passed by a row of criminals in the stocks. Offerings of flowers, food, and money were piled up below them, given by the compassionate population. Another criminal—a murderer, probably—shackled in leg irons for life, approached with his begging bowl. Jigme gave him some money and passed on.

"Your notions of punishment would be considered far from enlightened in my nation," !urq said. "Flogging, branding, putting people in chains! We would consider that savage."

"We punish only the body," Jigme said. "We always allow an opportunity for the spirit to reform. Death without Enlightenment can only result in a return to endless cycles of reincarnation."

"A clean death is always preferable to bodily insult. And a lot of your flogging victims die afterward."

"But they do not die during the flogging."

"Yet they die in agony, because your whips tear their backs apart."

"Pain," said Jigme, "can be transcended."

"Sometimes," !urq said, antennae twitching, "you humans are terrifying. I say this in absolute and admiring sincerity."

There were an unusual number of felons today, since the authorities wanted to empty the holding cells before the New Year. The Jesuit was among them—a calm, bearded, black-skinned man stripped to the waist, waiting to be lashed to the triangle. Jigme could see that he was deep in a meditative trance.

Suddenly the gray sky darkened. People looked up and pointed. Some fell down in obeisance, others bowed and thrust out their tongues.

The Incarnation was overhead, sitting on a wide hovercraft, covered with red paint and hammered gold, that held a small platform and throne. He sat in a full lotus, his elfin form dressed only in a light yellow robe. Snow melted on his shoulders and cheeks.

The proceedings halted for a moment while everyone waited for the Incarnation to say something, but at an impatient gesture from the floating throne things got under way. The floggings went efficiently, sometimes more than one going on at once. The crowd succored many of the victims with money or offers of food or medicine. There was another slight hesitation as the Jesuit was brought forward—perhaps the Incarnation would comment on, or stay, the punishment of someone who had been trying to spread his faith—but from the Incarnation came only silence. The Jesuit absorbed his twenty lashes without comment, was taken away by his cohorts. To be praised and promoted, if Jigme knew the Jesuits.

The whipping went on. Blood spattered the platform. Finally there was only one convict remaining, a young monk of perhaps seventeen in a dirty, torn zen. He was a big lad, broad-shouldered and heavily-muscled, with a malformed head and a peculiar brutal expression—at once intent and unfocused, as if he knew he hated something but couldn't be bothered to decide exactly what it was. His body was possessed by constant, uncontrollable tics and twitches. He was surrounded by police with staves. Obviously they considered him dangerous.

An official read off the charges. Kyetsang Kunlegs had killed his guru, then set fire to the dead man's hermitage in hopes of covering his crime. He was sentenced to six hundred lashes and to be shackled for life. Jigme suspected he would not get much aid from the crowd afterward; most of them were reacting with disgust.

"Stop," said the Incarnation. Jigme gaped. The floating throne was moving forward. It halted just before Kunlegs. The murderer's guards stuck out their tongues but kept their eyes on the killer.

"Why did you kill your guru?" the Incarnation asked.

Kunlegs stared at him and twitched, displaying nothing but fierce hatred. He gave no answer.

The Incarnation laughed. "That's what I thought," he said. "Will you be my disciple if I remit your punishment?"

Kunlegs seemed to have difficulty comprehending this. His belligerent expression remained unaltered. Finally he just shrugged. A violent twitch made the movement grotesque.

The Incarnation lowered his throne. "Get on board," he said. Kunlegs stepped onto the platform. The Incarnation rose from his lotus, adjusted the man's garments, and kissed him on the lips. They sat down together.

"Short Path," said the Incarnation. The throne sped at once for the Library Palace.

Jigme turned to the Ambassador. !urq had watched without visible expression.

"Terrifying," she said. "Absolutely terrifying."

Jigme sat with the other Cabinet members in a crowded courtyard of the Palace. The Incarnation was about to go through the last of the rituals required before his investiture as the Gyalpo Rinpoche. Six learned elders of six different religious orders would engage the Incarnation in prolonged debate. If he did well against them, he would be formally enthroned and take the reins of government.

The Incarnation sat on a platform-throne opposite the six. Behind him, gazing steadily with his expression of misshapen, twitching brutality, was the murderer Kyetsang Kunlegs.

The first elder rose. He was a Sufi, representing a three-thousand-year-old intellectual tradition. He stuck out his tongue and took a formal stance.

"What is the meaning of Dharma?" he began.

"I'll show you," said the Incarnation, although the question had obviously been rhetorical. The Incarnation opened his mouth, and a demon the size of a bull leapt out. Its flesh was pale as dough and covered with running sores. The demon seized the Sufi and flung him to the ground, then sat on his chest. The sound of breaking bones was audible.

Kyetsang Kunlegs opened his mouth and laughed, revealing huge yellow teeth.

The demon rose and advanced toward the five remaining elders, who fled in disorder.

"I win," said the Incarnation.

Kunlegs' laughter broke like obscene bubbles over the stunned audience.

"Short Path," said the Incarnation.

"Such a shame," said the Ambassador. Firelight flickered off her ebon features. "How many man-years of work has gone into it all? And by morning it'll be ashes."

"Everything comes to an end," said Jigme. "If the floats are not destroyed tonight, they would be gone in a year. If not a year, ten years. If not ten years, a century. If not a century . . ."

"I quite take your point, Rinpoche," said !urq.

"Only the Buddha is eternal."

"So I gather."

The crowd assembled on the roof of the Library Palace gasped as another of the floats on Burning Hill went up in flames. This one was made of figures from the opera, who danced and sang and did combat with one another until, burning, they came apart on the wind.

Jigme gratefully took a glass of hot tea from a servant and warmed his hands. The night was clear but bitterly cold. The floating throne moved silently overhead, and Jigme stuck out his tongue in salute. The Gyalpo Rinpoche, in accordance with the old Oracle's instructions, had assumed his title that afternoon.

"Jigme Dzasa, may I speak with you?" A soft voice at his elbow, that of the former Regent.

"Of course, Miss Taisuke. You will excuse me, Ambassador?"

Jigme and Taisuke moved apart. "The Incarnation has indicated that he wishes me to continue as head of the government," Taisuke said.

"I congratulate you, Prime Minister," said Jigme, surprised. He had assumed the Gyalpo Rinpoche would wish to run the state himself.

"I haven't accepted yet," she said. "It isn't a job I desire." She sighed. "I was hoping to have a randy incarnation, Jigme. Instead I'm being worked to death."

"You have my support, Prime Minister."

She gave a rueful smile and patted his arm. "Thank you. I fear I'll have to accept, if only to keep certain other people from positions where they might do harm." She leaned close, her whisper carrying over the sound of distant fireworks. "Dr. O'Neill approached me. She wished to know my views concerning whether we can declare the Incarnation insane and reinstitute the Regency."

Jigme gazed at Taisuke in shock. "Who supports this?"

"Not I. I made that clear enough."

"Daddy Carbajal?"

"I think he's too cautious. The new State Oracle might be in favor of the idea—he's such a strict young man, and, of course, his own status would rise if he became the Library's interpreter instead of subordinate to the Gyalpo Rinpoche. O'Neill herself made the proposal in a veiled manner—*if* such-and-such a thing proved true, how would I react? She never made a specific proposal."

Anger burned in Jigme's belly. "The Incarnation cannot be insane!" he said. "That would mean the Library itself is insane. That the Buddha is insane."

"People are uncomfortable with the notion of a doubtob Incarnation."

"What people? What are their names? They should be corrected!" Jigme realized that his fists were clenched, that he was trembling with anger.

"Hush. O'Neill can do nothing."

"She speaks treason! Heresy!"

"Jigme . . ."

"Ah. The Prime Minister." Jigme gave a start at the sound of the Incarnation's voice. The floating throne, its gold ornaments gleaming in the light of the burning floats, descended noiselessly from the bright sky. The Incarnation was covered only by a reskyang, the simple white cloth worn even in the bitterest weather by adepts of tumo, the discipline of controlling one's own internal heat.

"You *will* be my Prime Minister, yes?" the Incarnation said. His green eyes seemed to glow in the darkness. Kyetsang Kunlegs loomed over his shoulder like a demon shadow.

Taisuke bowed, sticking out her tongue. "Of course, Omniscient."

"When I witnessed the floggings the other day," the Incarnation said, "I was shocked by the lack of consistency. Some of the criminals seemed to have the sympathy of the officials, and the floggers did not use their full strength. Some of the floggers were larger and stronger than others. Toward the end they all got tired, and did not lay on with proper force. This does not seem to me to be adequate justice. I would like to propose a reform." He handed Taisuke a paper. "Here I have described a flogging machine. Each strike will be equal to the one before. And as the machine is built on a rotary principle, the machine can be inscribed with religious texts, like a prayer wheel. We can therefore grant prayers and punish the wicked simultaneously."

Taisuke seemed overcome. She looked down at the paper as if afraid to open it. "Very . . . elegant, Omniscient."

"I thought so. See that the machine is instituted throughout humanity, Prime Minister."

"Very well, Omniscient."

The floating throne rose into the sky to the accompaniment of the murderer Kunlegs' gross bubbling laughter. Taisuke looked at Jigme with desperation in her eyes.

"We must protect him, Jigme," she said.

"Of course."

"We must be very, very careful."

She loves him, too, he thought. A river of sorrow poured through his heart.

Jigme looked up, seeing Ambassador !urq standing with her head lifted to watch the burning spectacle on the hill opposite. "Very careful indeed," he said.

The cycle of festivals continued. Buddha's birthday, the Picnic Festival, the time of pilgrimage . . .

In the Prime Minister's lha khang, the Thunderbolt Sow gestured toward Taisuke. "After watching the floggings," it said, "the Gyalpo Rinpoche and Kyetsang Kunlegs went to Diamond City spaceport, where they participated in a night-long orgy with ship personnel. Both have now passed out from indulgence in drink and drugs, and the party has come to an end."

The Prime Minister knit her brows as she listened to the tale. "The stories will get offworld now," Jigme told her.

"They're already offworld."

Jigme looked at her helplessly. "How much damage is being done?"

"Flogging parties? Carousing with strangers? Careening from one monastery to another in search of pretty boys? Gracious heaven—the abbots are pimping their novices to him in hopes of receiving favor." Taisuke gave a lengthy shudder. There was growing seriousness in her eyes. "I'll let you in on a state secret. We've been reading the Sang's despatches."

"How?" Jigme asked. "They don't use our communications net, and the texts are coded."

"But they compose their messages using electric media," Taisuke said. "We can use the Library crystal as a sensing device, detect each character as it's entered into their coding device. We can also read incoming despatches the same way."

"I'm impressed, Prime Minister."

"Through this process, we were kept informed of the progress of the Sang's military buildup. We were terrified to discover that it was scheduled to reach its full offensive strength within a few years."

"Ah. That was why you consented to the increase in military allotments."

"Ambassador !urq was instructed not to resolve the Gyangtse matter, in order that it be used as a *casus belli* when the Sang program reached its conclusion. !urq's despatches to her superiors urged them to attack as soon as their fleet was ready. But now, with the increased military allotments and the political situation, !urq is urging delay. The current Incarnation, she suspects, may so discredit the institution of the Gyalpo Rinpoche that our society may disintegrate without the need for a Sang attack."

"Impossible!" A storm of anger filled Jigme. His hands formed the mudra of astonishment.

"I suspect you're right, Jigme." Solemnly. "They base their models of our society on their own past despotisms—they don't realize that the Treasured King is not a despot or an absolute ruler, but rather someone of great wisdom whom others follow through their own free will. But we should encourage !urq in this estimation, yes? Anything to give impetus to the Sang's more rational impulses."

"But it's based on a slander! And a slander concerning the Incarnation can never be countenanced!"

Taisuke raised an admonishing finger. "The Sang draw their own conclusions. And should we protest this one, we might give away our knowledge of their communications."

Anger and frustration bubbled in Jigme's mind. "What barbarians!" he said. "I have tried to show them truth, but . . ."

Taisuke's voice was calm. "You have shown them the path of truth. Their choosing not to follow it is their own karma."

Jigme promised himself he would do better. He would compel !urq to recognize the Incarnation's teaching mission.

Teaching, he thought. He remembered the stunned look on the doorkeeper's face that first Cabinet meeting, the Incarnation's cry at the moment of climax, his own desperate attempt to see the thing as a lesson. And then he thought about what !urq would have said, had she been there.

He went to the meditation box that night, determined to exorcise the demon that gnawed at his vitals. Lust, he recited, provides the soil in which other passions flourish. Lust is like a demon that eats up all the good deeds of the world. Lust is a viper hiding in a flower garden; it poisons those who come in search of beauty.

It was all futile. Because all he could think of was the Gyalpo Rinpoche, the lovely body moving rhythmically in the darkness of the Cabinet room.

The moan of ragdongs echoed over the gardens and was followed by drunken applause and shouts. It was the beginning of the festival of plays and operas. The Cabinet and other high officials celebrated the festival at the Jewel Pavilion, the Incarnation's summer palace, where there was an outdoor theater specially built among the sweet-smelling meditative gardens. The palace, a lacy white fantasy ornamented with statues of gods and masts carrying prayer flags, sat bathed in spotlights atop its hill.

In addition to the members of the court were the personal followers of the Incarnation, people he had been gathering during the seven months of his reign. Novice monks and nuns, doubtobs and naljorpas, crazed hermits, looney charlatans and mediums, runaways, workers from the spaceport . . . all drunk, all pledged to follow the Short Path wherever it led.

"Disgusting," said Dr. O'Neill. "Loathsome." Furiously she brushed at a spot on her brocaded robe where someone had spilled beer.

Jigme said nothing. Cymbals clashed from the stage, where the orchestra was practicing. Three novice monks went by, staggering under the weight of a flogging machine. The festival was going to begin with the punishment of a number of criminals, and any who could walk afterward would then be able to join the revelers. The first opera would be sung on a stage spattered with blood.

Dr. O'Neill stepped closer to Jigme. "The Incarnation has asked me to furnish him a report on nerve induction. He wishes to devise a machine to induce pain without damage to the body."

Heavy sorrow filled Jigme that he could no longer be surprised by such news. "For what purpose?" he asked.

"To punish criminals, of course. Without crippling them. Then his Omniscience will be able to order up as savage punishments as he likes without being embarrassed by hordes of cripples shuffling around the capital."

Jigme tried to summon indignation. "You should not impart unworthy motives to the Gyalpo Rinpoche."

Dr. O'Neill only gave him a cynical look. Behind her, trampling through a hedge, came a young monk, laughing, being pursued by a pair of women with whips. O'Neill looked at them as they dashed off into the darkness. "At least it will give *them* less of an excuse to indulge in such behavior. It won't be as much fun to watch if there isn't any blood."

"That would be a blessing."

"The Forty-Second Incarnation is potentially the finest in history," O'Neill said. Her eyes narrowed in fury. She raised a clenched fist, the knuckles white in the darkness. "The most intelligent Incarnation, the most able, the finest rapport with the Library in centuries . . . and look at what he is doing with his gifts!"

"I thank you for the compliments, Doctor," said the Incarnation. O'Neill and Jigme jumped. The Incarnation, treading lightly on the summer grass, had walked up behind them. He was dressed only in his white reskyang and the garlands of flowers given him by his followers. Kunlegs, as always, loomed behind him, twitching furiously.

Jigme bowed profoundly, sticking out his tongue.

"The punishment machine," said the Incarnation. "Do the plans move forward?"

Dr. O'Neill's dismay was audible in her reply. "Yes, Omniscient."

"I wish the work to be completed for the New Year. I want particular care paid to the monitors that will alert the operators if the felon's life is in danger. We should not want to violate Shakyamuni's commandment against slaughter."

"The work shall be done, Omniscient."

"Thank you, Dr. O'Neill." He reached out a hand to give her a blessing. "I think of you as my mother, Dr. O'Neill. The lady who tenderly watched over me in the womb. I hope this thought pleases you."

"If it pleases your Omniscience."

"It does." The Incarnation withdrew his hand. In the darkness his smile was difficult to read. "You will be honored for your care for many generations, Doctor. I make you that promise."

"Thank you, Omniscient."

"Omniscient!" A new voice called out over the sound of revelry. The new State Oracle, dressed in the saffron zen of a simple monk, strode toward them over the grass. His thin, ascetic face was bursting with anger.

"Who are these people, Omniscient?" he demanded.

"My friends, minister."

"They are destroying the gardens!"

"They are *my* gardens, minister."

"Vanity!" The Oracle waved a finger under the Incarnation's nose. Kunlegs grunted and started forward, but the Incarnation stopped him with a gesture.

"I am pleased to accept the correction of my ministers," he said.

"Vanity and indulgence!" the Oracle said. "Has the Buddha not told us to forsake worldly desires? Instead of doing as Shakyamuni instructed, you have surrounded yourself with followers who indulge their own sensual pleasures and your vanity!"

"Vanity?" The Incarnation glanced at the Jewel Pavilion. "Look at my summer palace, minister. It is a vanity, a lovely vanity. But it does no harm."

"It is nothing! All the palaces of the world are as nothing beside the word of the Buddha!"

The Incarnation's face showed supernal calm. "Should I rid myself of these vanities, minister?"

"Yes!" The State Oracle stamped a bare foot. "Let them be swept away!"

"Very well. I accept my minister's correction." He raised his voice, calling for the attention of his followers. A collection of drunken rioters gathered around him. "Let the word be spread to all here," he cried. "The Jewel Pavilion is to be destroyed by fire. The gardens shall be uprooted. All statues shall be smashed." He looked at the State Oracle and smiled his cold smile. "I hope this shall satisfy you, minister."

A horrified look was his only reply.

The Incarnation's followers laughed and sang as they destroyed the Jewel Pavilion, as they toppled statues from its roof and destroyed furniture to create bonfires in its luxurious suites. "Short Path!" they chanted. "Short Path!" In the theater the opera began, an old Tibetan epic about the death by treachery of the Sixth Earthly Gyalpo Rinpoche, known to his Mongolian enemies as the Dalai Lama. Jigme found a quiet place in the garden and sat in a full lotus, repeating sutras and trying to calm his mind. But the screams, chanting, songs, and shouts distracted him.

He looked up to see the Gyalpo Rinpoche standing upright amid the ruin of his garden, his head raised as if to sniff the wind. Kunlegs was standing close behind, caressing him. The light of the burning palace danced on his face. The Incarnation seemed transformed, a living embodiment of . . . of what? Madness? Exultation? Ecstasy? Jigme couldn't tell, but when he saw it he felt as if his heart would explode.

Then his blood turned cold. Behind the Incarnation, moving through the garden beneath the ritual umbrella of a Masker servant, came Ambassador !urq, her dark face watching the burning palace with something like triumph.

Jigme felt someone near him. "This cannot go on," said Dr. O'Neill's voice, and at the sound of her cool resolution terror flooded him.

"*Aum vajra sattva,*" he chanted, saying the words over and over, repeating them till the Jewel Pavilion was ash and the garden looked as if a whirlwind had torn through it, leaving nothing but tangled ruin.

Rising from the desolation, he saw something bright dangling from the shattered proscenium of the outdoor stage.

It was the young State Oracle, hanging by the neck.

"!urq's despatches have grown triumphant. She knows that the Gyalpo Rinpoche has lost the affection of the people, and that they will soon lose their tolerance." Miss Taisuke was decorating a Christmas tree in her lha khang. Little glowing buddhas, in their traditional red suits and white beards, hung amid the evergreen branches. Kali danced on top, holding a skull in either hand.

"What can we do?" said Jigme.

"Prevent a coup whatever the cost. If the Incarnation is deposed or declared mad, the Sang can attack under pretext of restoring the Incarnation. Our own people will be divided. We couldn't hope to win."

"Can't Dr. O'Neill see this?"

"Dr. O'Neill desires war, Jigme. She thinks we will win it whatever occurs."

Jigme thought about what interstellar war would mean; the vast energies of modern weapons deployed against helpless planets. Tens of billions dead, even with a victory. "We should speak to the Gyalpo Rinpoche," he said. "He must be made to understand."

"The State Oracle spoke to him, and what resulted?"

"You, Prime Minister—"

Taisuke looked at him. Her eyes were brimming with tears. "I have *tried* to speak to him. He is interested only in his parties, in his new punishment device. It's all he will talk about."

Jigme said nothing. His eyes stung with tears. Two weeping officials, he thought, alone on Christmas Eve. What more pathetic picture could possibly exist?

"The device grows ever more elaborate," Taisuke said. "There will be life extension and preservation gear installed. The machine can torture people for *lifetimes!*" She shook her head. Her hands trembled as they wiped her eyes. "Perhaps Dr. O'Neill is right. Perhaps the Incarnation needs to be put away."

"Never," Jigme said. "Never."

"Prime Minister." The Thunderbolt Sow shifted in her corner. "The Gyalpo Rinpoche has made an announcement to his people. 'The Short Path will end with the New Year.' "

Taisuke wiped her eyes on her brocaded sleeve. "Was that the entire message?"

"Yes, Prime Minister."

Her eyes rose to Jigme's. "What could it mean?"

"We must have hope, Prime Minister."

"Yes." Her hands clutched at his. "We must try to have hope."

Beneath snapping prayer flags, a quarter-size Jewel Pavilion made of flammable lattice stood on Burning Hill. The Cabinet was gathered inside it, flanking the throne of the Incarnation. The Gyalpo Rinpoche had decided to view the burning from inside one of the floats.

Kyetsang Kunlegs, grinning with his huge yellow teeth, was the only one of his followers present. The others were making merry in the city.

In front of the sham Jewel Pavilion was the new torture machine, a hollow oval, twice the size of a man, its skin the color of brushed metal. The interior was filled with mysterious apparatus.

The Cabinet said the rosary, and the Horse of the Air rose up into the night. The Incarnation, draped with khatas, raised a double drum made from the tops of two human skulls. With a flick of his wrist, a bead on a string began to bound from one drum to the other. With his cold green eyes he watched it rattle for a long moment. "Welcome to my first anniversary," he said.

The others murmured in reply. The drum rattled on. A cold winter wind blew through the pavilion. The Incarnation looked from one Cabinet member to the other and gave his cruel, ambiguous smile.

"On the anniversary of my ascension to the throne and my adoption of the Short Path," he said, "I would like to honor the woman who made it possible." He held out his hand. "Dr. O'Neill, the Minister of Science, whom I think of as my mother. Mother, please come sit in the place of honor."

O'Neill rose stone-faced from her place and walked to the throne. She prostrated herself and stuck out her tongue. The Treasured King stepped off the platform, still rattling the drum; he took her hand, helped her rise. He sat her on the platform in his own place.

Another set of arms materialized on his shoulders; while the first rattled the drum, the other three went through a long succession of mudras. Amazement, Jigme read, fascination, the warding of evil.

"My first memories in this incarnation," he said, "are of fire. Fire that burned inside me, that made me want to claw my way out of my glass womb and launch myself prematurely into existence. Fires that aroused lust and hatred before I knew anyone to hate or lust for. And then, when the fires grew unendurable, I would open my eyes, and there I would see my mother, Dr. O'Neill, watching me with happiness in her face."

Another pair of arms appeared. The Incarnation looked over his shoulder at Dr. O'Neill, who was watching him with the frozen stare given a poison serpent. The Incarnation turned back to the others. The breeze fluttered the khatas around his neck.

"Why should I burn?" he said. "My memories of earlier Incarnations were incomplete, but I knew I had never known such fire before. There was something in me that was not balanced. That was made for the Short Path. Perhaps Enlightenment could be reached by leaping into the fire. In any case, I had no choice."

There was a flare of light, a roar of applause. The first of the floats outside exploded into flame. Fireworks crackled in the night. The Incarnation smiled. His drum rattled on.

"Never had I been so out of balance," he said. Another pair of arms materialized. "Never had I been so puzzled. Were my compulsions a manifestation of the Library? Was the crystal somehow out of alignment? Or was something else wrong? It was my consort Kyetsang Kunlegs who gave me the first clue." He turned to the throne and smiled at the murderer, who twitched in reply. "Kunlegs has suffered all his life from Tourette's syndrome, an excess of dopamine in the brain. It makes him compulsive, twitchy, and—curiosly—brilliant. His brain works too fast for its own good. The condition should have been diagnosed and corrected years ago, but Kunlegs' elders were neglectful."

Kunlegs opened his mouth and gave a long laugh. Dr. O'Neill, seated just before him on the platform, gave a shiver. The Incarnation beamed at Kunlegs, then turned back to his audience.

"I didn't suffer from Tourette's—I didn't have all the symptoms. But seeing poor Kunlegs made it clear where I should look for the source of my difficulty." He raised the drum, rattled it beside his head. "In my own brain," he said.

Another float burst into flame. The bright light glowed through the wickerwork walls of the pavilion, shone on the Incarnation's face. He gazed into it with his cruel half-smile, his eyes dancing in the firelight.

Dr. O'Neill spoke. Her voice was sharp. "Omniscient, may I suggest that we withdraw? This structure is built to burn, and the wind will carry sparks from the other floats toward us."

The Incarnation looked at her. "Later, honored Mother." He turned back to the Cabinet. "Not wanting to bother my dear mother with my suspicions, I visited several doctors when I was engaged in my visits to town and various monasteries. I found that not only did I have a slight excess of dopamine, but that my mind also contained too much serotonin and norepinephrine, and too little endorphin."

Another float burst into flame. Figures from the opera screamed in eerie voices. The Incarnation's smile was beatific. "Yet my honored mother, the Minister of Science, supervised my growth. How could such a thing happen?"

Jigme's attention jerked to Dr. O'Neill. Her face was drained of color. Her eyes were those of someone gazing into the Void.

"Dr. O'Neill, of course, has political opinions. She believes the Sang heretics must be vanquished. Destroyed or subdued at all costs. And to that end she wished an Incarnation who would be a perfect conquering warrior-king—impatient, impulsive, brilliant, careless of life, and indifferent to suffering. Someone with certain sufficiencies and deficiencies in brain chemistry."

O'Neill opened her mouth. A scream came out, a hollow sound as mindless as those given by the burning floats. The Incarnation's many hands pointed to her, all but the one rattling the drum.

Laughing, Kyetsang Kunlegs lunged forward, twisting the khata around the minister's neck. The scream came to an abrupt end. Choking, she toppled back into his huge lap.

"She is the greatest traitor of all time," the Incarnation said. "She who poisoned the Forty-First Incarnation. She who would subvert the Library itself to her ends. She who would poison the mind of a Bodhisattva." His voice was soft, yet exultant. It sent an eerie chill down Jigme's back.

Kunlegs rose from the platform holding Dr. O'Neill in his big hands. Her piled-up hair had come undone and trailed across the ground. Kunlegs carried her out of the building and into the punishment machine.

The Incarnation's drum stopped rattling. Jigme looked at him in stunned comprehension.

"She shall know what it is to burn," he said. "She shall know it for many lifetimes."

Sparks blew across the floor before the Incarnation's feet. There was a glow from the doorway, where some of the wickerwork had caught fire.

The machine was automatic in its function. Dr. O'Neill began to scream again, a rising series of shrieks. Her body began to rotate. The Incarnation smiled. "She shall make that music for many centuries. Perhaps one of my future incarnations shall put a stop to it."

Jigme felt burning heat on the back of his neck. O'Neill's screams ran up and down his spine. "Omniscient," he said. "The pavilion is on fire. We should leave."

"In a moment. I wish to say a few last words."

Kunlegs came loping back, grinning, and hopped onto the platform. The Incarnation joined him and kissed him tenderly. "Kunlegs and I will stay in the pavilion," he said. "We will both die tonight."

"No!" Taisuke jumped to her feet. "We will not permit it! Your condition can be corrected."

The Incarnation stared at her. "I thank you, loyal one. But my brain is poisoned, and even if the imbalance were corrected I would still be perceiving the Library through a chemical fog that would impair my ability. My next Incarnation will not have this handicap."

"Omniscient!" Tears spilled from Taisuke's eyes. "Don't leave us!"

"You will continue as head of the government. My next Incarnation will be ready by the next New Year, and then you may retire to the secular life I know you wish to pursue in this lifetime."

"No!" Taisuke ran forward, threw herself before the platform. "I beg you, Omniscient!"

Suddenly Jigme was on his feet. He lurched forward, threw himself down beside Taisuke. "Save yourself, Omniscient!" he said.

"I wish to say something concerning the Sang." The Incarnation spoke calmly, as if he hadn't heard. "There will be danger of war in the next year. You must all promise me that you won't fight."

"Omniscient." This from Daddy Carbajal. "We must be ready to defend ourselves!"

"Are we an Enlightened race, or are we not?" The Incarnation's voice was stern.

"You are Bodhisattva." Grudgingly. "All know this."

"We are Enlightened. The Buddha commands us not to take life. If these are not facts, our existence has no purpose, and our civilization is a mockery." O'Neill's screams provided eerie counterpoint to his voice. The Incarnation's many arms pointed at the members of the Cabinet. "You may arm in order to deter attack. But if the Sang begin a war, you must promise me to surrender without condition."

"Yes!" Taisuke, still facedown, wailed from her obeisance. "I promise, Omniscient."

"The Diamond Mountain will be the greatest prize the Sang can hope for. And the Library is the Buddha. When the time is right, the Library will incarnate itself as a Sang, and the Sang will be sent on their path to Enlightenment."

"Save yourself, Omniscient!" Taisuke wailed. The roar of flames had drowned O'Neill's screams. Jigme felt sparks falling on his shaven head.

"Your plan, sir!" Daddy Carbajal's voice was desperate. "It might not work! The Sang may thwart the incarnation in some way!"

"Are we Enlightened?" The Incarnation's voice was mild. "Or are we not? Is the Buddha's truth eternal, or is it not? Do you not support the Doctrine?"

Daddy Carbajal threw himself down beside Jigme. "I believe, Omniscient! I will do as you ask!"

"Leave us, then. Kyetsang and I wish to be alone."

Certainty seized Jigme. He could feel tears stinging his eyes. "Let me stay, Omniscient!" he cried. "Let me die with you!"

"Carry these people away," said the Incarnation. Hands seized Jigme. He fought them off, weeping, but they were too powerful: he was carried from the burning pavilion. His last sight of the Incarnation was of the Gyalpo Rinpoche and Kunlegs embracing one another, silhouetted against flame, and then everything dissolved in fire and tears.

And in the morning nothing was left, nothing but ashes and the keening cries of the traitor O'Neill, whom the Bodhisattva in his wisdom had sent forever to Hell.

Jigme found !urq there, standing alone before O'Neill, staring at the figure caught in a webwork of life support and nerve stimulators. The sound of the traitor's endless agony continued to issue from her torn throat.

"There will be no war," Jigme said.

!urq looked at him. Her stance was uncertain.

"After all this," Jigme said, "a war would be indecent. You understand?"

!urq just stared.

"You must not unleash this madness in us!" Jigme cried. Tears rolled down his face. "Never, Ambassador! Never!"

!urq's antennae twitched. She looked at O'Neill again, rotating slowly in the huge wheel. "I will do what I can, Rinpoche," she said.

!urq made her lone way down Burning Hill. Jigme stared at the traitor for a long time.

Then he sat in the full lotus. Ashes drifted around him, some clinging to his zen, as he sat before the image of the tormented doctor and recited his prayers.

Maureen F. McHugh

THE MISSIONARY'S CHILD

Born in Ohio, Maureen F. McHugh spent some years living in Shijiazhuang in the People's Republic of China, an experience that has been one of the major shaping forces on her fiction to date. Upon returning to the United States, she made her first sale in 1989, and has since made a powerful impression on the SF world of the nineties with a relatively small body of work, becoming a frequent contributor to *Asimov's Science Fiction,* as well as selling to *The Magazine of Fantasy & Science Fiction, Alternate Warriors, Aladdin,* and other markets.

Not prolific by the high-production sausage-factory standards of the field, McHugh has nevertheless enjoyed the distinction of publishing some of the very best stories of the late eighties and nineties, especially such profound and disturbing stories as "Protection," "Nekropolis," and "The Lincoln Train," which won her a Hugo Award in 1996, although even her "second-string" stories such as "Baffin Island," "The Queen of Marincite," "Whispers" (with David B. Kisor), "In the Air," "The Beast," and "A Coney Island of the Mind" would be the envy of many another writer. Many of these stories take her into territories far beyond the range of the Planetary Adventure, but she can write those too when she sets her mind to it, as well or better than it's ever been done by anybody, as shown by stories such as "Strings," the recent Nebula finalist "The Cost to Be Wise," and the suspenseful, sly, and sardonic adventure that follows, "The Missionary's Child," a story with strong echoes of Ursula K. Le Guin, Joanna Russ, James Tiptree, Jr., and others, but one which demonstrates a voice and vision that are McHugh's alone. A story that shows us that sometimes even when you are determinedly minding your own business, it's hard to stay out of trouble . . . and that sometimes it's when you're *not* looking for anything that you find something that's the most worth finding. . . .

Although she's expert at shorter lengths, much of McHugh's reputation has been made with her novels. In 1992 she published one of the year's most widely acclaimed and talked-about first novels, *China Mountain Zhang,* which won the Locus Award for Best First Novel, the Lambda Literary Award, and the James Tiptree Jr. Memorial Award, and which was named a *New York Times* Notable Book as well as being a finalist for the Hugo and Nebula awards. Her most recent book, the novel *Half the Day Is Night,* received similar critical acclaim. Upcoming is a new novel, *Mission Child,* set on the same world as "The Missionary's Child" and "The Cost to Be Wise." She lives in Twinsburg, Ohio, with her husband, her son, and a golden retriever named Smith.

"Are you blind?" the woman asks.

I'm looking right at her. "No," I say, "I'm foreign."

Affronted, the woman straightens up in a swirl of rose-colored robe and chouli scent, clutching her veil. Here in the islands, they don't see very many blond-haired, blue-eyed barbarians; people have asked me if I can see normally, if all northerners are blue-eyed. But this is the first time someone has ever asked me that. Maybe she thinks that my eyes are filmed, like the milky-white of old people.

She thought I was begging—I must look pretty tattered. I should have said yes, then I could go get something to drink, get out of the sun. I'm sitting down by the water. I'm broke, and I've been hungry for awhile, and I'm listless and a little stupid from the heat and lack of food. I feel fifty instead of thirty-one.

I should go back to the hiring area, wait around with a couple of other thugs for some sort of nasty work. I should oil my sword. It's a waste of time; no one needs a mercenary here, the Celestial Prince doesn't hire foreigners in his army.

But I don't want to go back. Up in the market, some yammerhead had been rattling on about our Cousins from the stars. The Cousins haven't come to the islands in any numbers yet, and I'll wager he's never met any. Listening to this stonker gave me a headache. Wouldn't he be surprised if he knew that the Cousins think of us all about the way the woman who asked me if I was blind thinks of me. They think that we're barbarians. They think that we're stupid because we call what they do magic instead of *science*. Or they feel sorry for us.

I know better than thinking bitter; time to head back to the market, see if anybody will hire a tokking foreigner to dig ditches or something.

But I sit, my head aching with hunger and heat, too stupid to do anything about it. And I'm still sitting there a dine later, the sun is still high in the sky baked the color of celedon. Not awake, not asleep.

I'm going to have to start selling my gear, the slow road to starvation.

I open my eyes and watch a ship come in on the deep green sea. It has red eyes rimmed in violet and violet sails; from far away, I can see a person wearing dark clothes that are all of one piece. A Cousin, standing at the prow. On the boathouse there is a light, star-magic, like a third eye, blind and white. Here in the islands, when you see Cousins, they are with the rich and the powerful.

What would the Cousin think if I spoke a little of his/her language? I only remember a few phrases. "Hello," "My name is," and a phrase from my lessons, "Husband and wife Larkin have three children, a boy and two girls."

Would the Cousin be curious enough to take me aboard? Recognize the debt for what the Cousins did to my kin, help me get back to the mainland?

The ship docks, three guildmen and a Cousin disembark, and come down the quay. Southerners will stare at any foreigner, but they stare double at a Cousin, and who can blame them? The Cousin is a woman, with her hair uncovered, dressed like a man, but not looking like a man, no. That amuses me. Southern women pull their veils around their mouths and stop to watch.

She comes down the quay with studied indifference. I can understand that; what does one do when people stare day after day? Pretend not to notice.

She is tall, taller than me, but Cousins are usually tall, and I'm shorter than many men. She looks up directly at me while I am smiling, by chance. The length of a man between us. I can see that she has light eyes.

"Hello," I say in the trade language of the Cousins. The word just pops out.

It stops her, though, like a roped stabros calf. "Hello," she says, in the same tongue. Consternation among the guildmen; two in dark red and one in green, all with shaven heads dull with the graphite sheen of stubble. "You speak lingua?" she says.

"A little," I say.

Then she rattles on, asking me something, "where da-da da-da da."

I shrug. Search my memory. My lessons in lingua were a lifetime ago; I remember almost nothing. Something comes to me that I often said in class: "I don't understand," I say, "I speak little."

"Where did you learn?" she says in Suhkhra, the language of the southerners. "Starport?"

"Up north." No real answer. Already I'm sorry I spoke. Bad *enough* to be a tokking foreigner; worse to be a spectacle. And my head aches, and I am tired from three days' lack of food.

"Did you work at the port?" she asks, probing.

"No," I say. Flat.

She frowns. Then, like a boat before bad winds, she comes across in another direction. She speaks in my own language, the language of home. "What is your name?" She is careful and stilted in that one phrase.

"Jahn," I say, probably the commonest name among northern men. "What is yours?" I ask, without regard for courtesy.

"Sulia," she says. "Jahn, what kin-kind?"

"My kin are all dead," I say, "Jahn no-kin-kind."

But she shakes her head. "I'm sorry," she says in Suhkhra, "I don't understand. I speak very little Krerjian. What did you say your name was?"

"Jahn Sckarline," I say. And then, in my own tongue, "Go away." Because I am tired of her, tired of everything, tired of starving.

She isn't listening, and probably doesn't understand anyway. "Sckarline," she says. "I thought everyone from Sckarline—"

"Is dead," I say. "Thank you, Cousin. I am pleased you keep my kin-name." It's awkward to say in Suhkra. The Suhkra aren't good at irony anyway.

"Sulia Cousin," one of the guildmen says deferentially, "they are waiting for us."

She shakes him off. "I know about the settlement at Sckarline," she says to me. "You're a mission boy. You have an education. Why don't you work at a port?"

"And live in a *ghetto?*" The word comes back to me in her trade lingua. "With the other *natives?*"

"Isn't it better to get a tech job than to live like this?" she asks.

Better than a shantytown, I think, huddled together while the starships come screaming overhead, making one's teeth ache and one's goods rattle?

I look at her, she looks at me. I search my memory for the words in lingua, but my mind isn't sharp and it was too long ago. "Go away," I finally say in Suhkhra, "people are waiting."

She stands there hesitant, but the guildman does not. He strides forward and smacks me hard in the side of my head for my disrespect. I know better than to defend myself. Oh, Heth, my poor head! Southerners are a bad lot, they have no concept of a freeman.

So, having been knocked over, I stay still, with my nose near the stones, waiting to see if he'll hit me again, smelling dust, and sea, and the smell of myself, which is probably very distasteful to everyone else.

He crouches down, and I wait to be smacked again, empty-headed. But it isn't him, it's her. "What are you doing here?" she asks. She probably means how did you come here, but I find myself wondering, what am I doing here? Looking for work. Trying to get passage home. But home is gone, should never have existed in the first place.

What does any person do in a lifetime? I give her an answer out of the Proverbs. "Putting off death," I say. "Go away, before you complicate my task—you people have done enough to me."

She looks unhappy. Cousins are like that, a sentimental people. "If I could help you, I would," she says.

"I know," I say, "but your help would make me *need* you. And then I would be just one more local on one more backward world." Everywhere the Cousins go across the sky, it's the same. Wanji used to tell us about her people, about the Cousins. About other worlds like ours. Where two cultures meet, she said, one of them usually gives way.

The Cousin searches through her pockets, puts a coin, a rectangular silver piece, in the dust. I wait, not moving, until they go on.

I pick up the coin. A proud person would throw it after her. I'm not proud, I'm hungry. I take it.

In the market, it's rabbit and duck day—kids herding ducks with long switches, cages of rabbits for sale, hanging next to that cheap old staple, thekla lizard drying in strips. I dodge past tallgrass poles with craken-dyed cloth hanging startling yellow, and cut through between two vegetable stands. Next to the hiring area, they're grilling stabos jerky on sticks, and selling pineapple slices dipped in saltwater to make them sweeter.

I use the Cousin's silver to buy noodles and red peanut paste, spicy with proyakapiti, and I eat slowly. I'm three days empty of food, and if I eat too fast, I'll be sick. I learned about going without food during a campaign, when I first started soldiering. On the long walk to Bashtoy. I know all about the different kinds of hunger; the first sharp stabs of appetite, then the strong hunger, how your stomach hurts after awhile, and then how you forget, and then how hunger comes back, like swollen joints in an old woman. And how it wears you down, how you become tired and stupid, and how then finally it leaves you altogether, and your jaw bone softens until your teeth rock in their sockets, and you have been hungry so long you don't know what it means anymore.

The yammerhead is on the other side of the hiring area, still going on about how the guilds monopolize the Cousins. How the guilds were nothing until ten years ago, when the Cousins came and brought magic, and then no one could trade without permission of the guild. I close my eyes, feeling sleepy after food, and I can see the place where I grew up. I was born in Sckarline, a magic town. I remember the white houses, the power station where Ayuedesh taught boys to cook stabos manure and get swamp air from it, then turned that into power that sang through copper and made light. At night, we had light for three or four dine after sunset. Phrases in the lingua the Cousins speak, *Appropriate Technology*.

I am lost in Sckarline, looking for my mother, for kin. I see Trevin, and I follow him. He's way ahead, in leggings, in dark blue with fur on his shoulders. But the way he leads me is wrong, the buildings are burned, just blackened crossbeams jutting up, he is leading me toward—

"I'm looking for a musician." I jerk awake.

A flat-faced southerner waiting for hire says, "Musicians are over there." People who wait here are like me, looking for anything.

A portly man with a wine-colored robe says, "I'm looking for a musician who knows a little about swords."

"What kind of musician?" I ask. I always talk quietly, it's a failing, and the portly man doesn't hear me. He cocks his head.

"What kind of musician?" the flat-faced southerner repeats.

"Doesn't matter." The portly man shrugs, hawks so loudly it sounds as if he's clearing his tokking head, and spits.

Tokking southerners. They spit all the time, it drives me crazy. I hear them clear their throat, and I cringe and start looking to step out of the way. Heth knows I'm not squeamish, but they *all* do it, men, women, children.

"Sikha," the portly man offers. A sikha is a kind of southern lute, only they pick the strings on the neck as well as the ones on the body.

"How about flute?" I offer.

"Flute?" the portly man says. His robe is of good quality, but stained, and he has a negligent air. The robe gapes open to the belted waist, showing his smooth chest and the soft flab like breasts. "You play the flute, northerner?"

No, I want to say, I just wanted to help us think of some instruments. Patience. "Yes," I say, "I play the flute."

"Let's hear you."

So I dig out my wooden flute and make pretty sounds. He waves his hands and says, "How good are you with a sword?"

I dig into my pack and pull my cloak out of the bottom. It's crushed and wrinkled, people don't wear cloaks much in the south, but I spread it out so that he can see the badge on the breast: a white mountain against a red background. The survivors of the March to Bashtoy got them—that, and sixty gold coins. The sixty gold coins have been gone for a couple of years, but the badge is still on the cloak.

People murmur. The portly man doesn't know badges, he's not a fighter, but the flat-faced southerner does, and it shows in the sudden respect in his face, and that ends any question of my swordplay—which is fine because, badge or no badge, I'm only mediocre at swordplay. I'm just not tall enough or big enough.

Surviving a campaign is as much a matter of luck and cleverness as skill with a sword, anyway.

But that's why Barok hires me to play flute at his party.

He offers me twenty in silver, which is too much money. He pays me five right away. He must want me to be a bodyguard, and that means that he thinks that he'll *need* one. I like guard duty, or, better than that, something like being a sailor. But I didn't realize until I jumped ship that, here in the Islands, not just *anybody* can be a sailor. I shouldn't take this job, it sounds like trouble, but I've got to do something.

All boat trade except local fishing is controlled by the four Navigation Orders, all the Cousins's magic by the two Metaphysical Orders. I don't pay much attention to Magic; I'm just a whistler, a mercenary. I have three spells myself (but simple ones), that Ayuedesh Engineer, the old Cousin, wired into my skull when we knew that Scathalos High-on was going to attack Sckarline. A lot of good spells did us in the end, with all of two twenties of us and four Cousins, everybody in Sckarline who could fight at all, against the Scathalos High-on, Kin-leader's army.

I am supposed to report my spells to the Metaphysical Orders, but I'm not *that* stupid. Just stupid enough to come *here*.

A man who hires a sword to play music must have unusual parties, and I wait to hear what he wants of me.

"You'll need better clothes," he says. "And bathe, would you?"

I promise to meet him in the market in three dine or so. And then I finger the coppers left from the Cousin's silver and the five silver coins he's given me. First I go to the bath house, and I pay for a private bath. I hate bath houses. It is not, as the southerners all think, that northerners hate to bathe; I just find bath houses . . . uncomfortable. Even in a private room, I strip furtively, keeping my back to the door. But Heth, it is good to be clean, to not itch! I even wash my clothes, wring them out as best I can. The water runs black, and I have to put on wet clothes, but I imagine they'll dry fast enough.

Back at the market, I find a stall that sells used clothes. I go through piles until I find a black jacket with a high neck, fairly clean. And I have my hair trimmed.

I use much of my three dine and about half of the Cousin's silver, but when the time comes, I am back at the hiring area, cleaner, neater, with Barok's five silver still in my pocket, and ready to earn the other fifteen silver. And I don't wait long for my employer, who looks me over and spits, by which he means I have passed inspection.

I assume from his lavish way with silver and his manner that we will head to one of the better parts of town. After all, a lot of silver went into the feeding of that smooth belly and flaccid chest. But we head down toward where the river meets the ocean. It's a wide, tame river, enclosed by stone walls and arched—so they claim—by fourteen stone bridges. But this far down, all poor. The closer we get, the more rank it smells. We go down a stone stairs to the water, past women washing clothes, and out onto a small city of permanently moored boats.

The sunbleached boats have eyes painted on the prows, even though they never go anywhere. They're homes to families, each living the length of my arm from the next, all piled up together with brown dusty chickens, laundry flapping, brown children running from boat to boat, wearing nothing but a yellow gourd on a rope tied around their waist (if they fall overboard, the gourd floats, holding them up until some adult can fish them out of the water).

I've never been out here before; it's a maze, and it would be worth my life to step on these boats alone. Even walking with Barok, I feel the men's eyes follow me with hard gazes. We cross from boat to boat, they rise and fall under our feet. The boats bob, the green river stinks of garbage and rotting fish, and my poor head swirls a bit. I've been here two and half years, I speak the language, but only southerners can live piled up on top of each other this way.

Out near where the middle is kept clear for river traffic, we climb a ramp up onto a larger boat, maybe the length of five men head to foot, the home of Barok. A tiny brown woman wrapped in blue is shoving charcoal into a tampis jar, a jar with a place in the bottom to put fuel to heat the stuff cooking in the top. It's a big tampis jar. I smell meat; there's smooth creamy yogurt in a blue and white bowl next to her. I'm hungry again. She glances up, and looks back down. Barok ignores her and steps over a neat pyramid of pale lavender boxfruit, one split to show the purple meat. As I step over them, I reach down and hook one.

"Hie!" she snaps, "that is not for you!"

Barok doesn't even look back, so I wink at her and keep walking.

"Yellow-haired dog-devil!" she shrieks. I follow Barok down into the hold, now a good-sized apartment, if rather warm, and get my first surprise. There's a young girl, bare-armed and bare-haired, sitting at the table, drawing with brush and paper.

"Shell-sea," Barok growls.

So intent she is that she ignores him for a moment, and I get a chance to see what she's drawing—a long squiggling line that she's tracing as if every twist and curve has meaning. Which it clearly doesn't, since it meanders all over the page.

"Shell-sea! Take it in the back!"

She says sullenly, "It's too hot back there," and then looks up. I'm blond and sunburned, quite a sight for a southern girl who has probably never seen someone who didn't have dark hair in her life. She stares at me as she gathers her papers, and then walks to the back, her eyebrows knit into a dark line, clumping her feet heavily, like someone whose wits aren't right.

Barok watches her go as if he doesn't like the taste of something. "My guests will be here later. Wait on deck."

"What am I supposed to do?" I ask.

"Play music and watch the guests," he says.

"That's all?" I ask. "You're paying me twenty in silver to watch?" He starts to answer sharply, and I say, "If you tell me what to watch *for*, I might do a better job."

"You watch for trouble," he says. "That's enough."

This is bad, my stomach knows. An employer who doesn't trust his guests or his employees is like a dog with thrum—*everyone* gets bitten. I could quit, hand him back the five silvers, take the boxfruit, and go. I still have a little less than half of the Cousin's silver; I can do fine on that for a week, if I sleep down on the docks.

"There's food on the stern deck; help yourself, and ignore the woman if she complains."

So I keep the job. Stomach-thinking. Heth says in the Proverbs that our life hinges on little things. That's certainly true for me.

I eat slowly and carefully; I know that if I eat too much, I'll be sleepy. But I fill my pack with boxfruit, pigeon's egg dumplings, and red peanuts. Especially red peanuts—a person can live a long time on red peanuts. While I'm eating, Shell-sea comes up and sits on the stern to watch me. As I said, I'm not tall, most men have a bit of reach on me, and she's nearly my height. She's wearing a school uniform, the dark red of one of the orders, and her thick hair is tied back with a red cord. The uniform would be fine on a young girl, but only emphasizes that she's not a child. She's too old for bare arms, for uncovered hair, too old for the cord that belts the robe high under her small breasts. She is probably just past menses.

After I eat, I use a bucket to rinse my hands and face. After awhile she says, "Why don't you take off your shirt when you wash?"

"You are a forward child," I say.

She has the grace to blush, but she still looks expectant. She wants to see how much hair I have on my chest. Southerners don't have much body hair.

"I've already bathed today," I say. Southerners waiting to see if I look like a hairy termit make me very uncomfortable. "Why do you have such an unusual name?" I ask.

"It's not a name, it's a nickname." She stares at her bare toes and they curl in embarrassment. I thought she was a bit of a half-wit, but away from Barok she's quick enough, and light on her feet.

I wonder if she's his fancy girl. Most southerners don't take a pretty girl until they already have a first wife.

"Shell-sea? Why do they call you that?"

"Not 'Shell-sea'," she says, exasperated, *Chalcey*. What kind of name is 'Shell-sea'? My name is Chalcedony. I bet you don't know what that is."

"It's a precious stone," I say.

"How did you know?"

"Because I've been to the temple of Heth in Thelahckre," I say, "and the Shesket-lion's eyes are two chunks of chalcedony." I rinse my bowl in the bucket, then dump the water over the side; the soap scums the green water like oil. I'd been to a lot of places, trying to find the right place. The islands hadn't proven to be any better than the city of Lada on the coast. And Lada no better than Gibbun, which was supposed to be full of work, but the work was all for the new star port that the Cousins were building. My people forgetting their kin, living in slums. And Gibbun no better than Thelahckre.

"Why don't you have a beard?" she asks. Southerners can't grow beards until they're old, and then only long, bedraggled, wispy white things. They believe that all northerner men have them down to their belts.

"Because I don't," I say, irritated. "Why do you live with Barok?"

"He's my uncle."

We both stop then to watch a ship come down the river to the bay. Like the one the Cousin came in on, it has red eyes rimmed in violet, and violet sails. " 'Temperance,' " I read from the side.

Chalcey glances at me out of the corner of her eye.

I smile. "Yes, some northerners can even read."

"It's a ship of the Brothers of Succor," she says. "I go to the school of the Sisters of Clarity."

"And who are the Sisters of Clarity?" I ask.

"I thought you knew everything," she says archly. When I don't rise to this, she says, "The Sisters of Clarity are the sister order to the Order of Celestial Harmony."

"I see," I say, watching the ship glide down the river.

Testily, she adds. "Celestial Harmony is the first Navigation Order."

"Do they sail to the mainland?"

"Of course," she says, patronizing.

"What does it cost to be a passenger? Do they ever hire cargo-handlers or bookkeepers or anything like that?" I know the answer, but I can't help myself from asking.

She shrugs, "I don't know, I'm a student." Then, sly again, "I study drawing."

"That's wonderful," I mutter.

Passage *out* of here is my major concern. No one can work on a ship who isn't a member of a Navigational Order, and no order is likely to take a blond-haired northerner with a sudden vocation. Passage is expensive. Even food doesn't keep me from being depressed.

The guests begin to arrive just after sunset, while the sky is still indigo in the west. I'm in the hold with two food servers. I'm sweltering in my jacket, they're (both women) serene in their blue robes. I play simple songs. Barok comes by and says to me, "Sing some northern thing."

"I don't sing," I say.

He glares at me, but I'm not about to sing, and he can't replace me now, so that's that. But I feel guilty, so I try to be flashy, playing lots of trills, and some songs that I think might sound strange to their ears.

It's a small party, only seven men. Important men, because five boats clunk against ours. Or rich men. It's hard for me to make decisions about southerners, they act differently and I don't know what it means. For instance, southerners never say "no." So at first, I decided that they were all shifty bastards, but eventually I learned how to tell a "yes" that meant *no* from a "yes" that meant *yes*. It's not so hard—if you ask a shopkeeper if he can get you ground proyakapiti, and he says, "yes," then he *can*. If he giggles nervously and then says "yes," he's embarrassed, which means that he doesn't want you to know that he *isn't* able to get it, so you smile and say that you will be back for it later. He knows you are lying, you know he knows; you are both vastly relieved.

But these men smile and shimmer like oil, and Barok smiles and shimmers like oil, and I don't know what's cast, only that if tension were food, I could cut thick slices out of the air and dine on it.

There are no women except servers. I don't know if there are ever women at southern parties, because this is my first one. If a southern man toasts another, he cannot decline the toast without looking like a gelded sta-bos, so they drink a great deal of wine. After awhile, it seems to me that a man in green, ferret-thin, and a man in yellow are working together to get Barok drunk. If one of them toasts Barok, a bit later the other one does too. Barok would be drinking twice as much as they are, except that Barok himself toasts his guests, especially the ferret, a number of times, so it's hard to say. Besides, Barok is portly and can drink a great deal of wine.

But the servers are finished and cleaning up on deck, and Barok is near purple himself when he finally raps on the table for silence. I stop playing, and tap the bare sword under the serving table behind me with my foot, just to know where it is.

Barok clears a space on the long thin banquet table and claps his hands. Chalcey comes in, dressed in a robe the color of her school uniform, but with her arms and hair decently covered. The effect is nice, or would be if she didn't have that sullen, half-wit face she wears around her uncle.

She puts two rolled papers on the table, and then draws her veil close around her chin and crouches down like a proper girl. Barok opens one of the rolls, and I crane my head before the men close around it. All I get is a glimpse of one of Chalcey's squiggly-line drawings, with some writing on it. The men murmur. The man in yellow says, "What is this?"

"Galgor coast," Barok points, "Lesian and Cauldor Islands, the Liliana Strait."

Charts? Navigation charts of the Islands? How could Barok have gotten . . . or rather, how could Chalcey have drawn . . . She is studying drawing with an Order, though, isn't she? *Chalcey* drew the charts? But the Cousins have sold magic to the Navigational Orders to make sure students *can't* take out so much as a piece of paper. How does she get them out of the school?

The ferret spits on the wooden floor and I wince. "What else have you got?" the ferret asks, brusque, rude.

"Only the Liliana Straits and the Hekkhare Cove," Barok says.

"Hekkhare!" the man in blue says, "I can buy *that* off any fisherman."

"Ah, but you can compare this chart with your own charts of Hekkhare to see how my source is. And there are more coming, I can assure you." Barok fairly oozes.

"These look as if they were drawn by an amateur," ferret says. Chalcey sticks out her lower lip and beetles her eyebrows. She needs a mother around to tell her not to do that.

"If you want pretty, go to the market and buy a painting," Barok says.

"I'm not interested in artistry, I'm interested in competence," ferret snaps. "What's to say you didn't copy Hekkhare from some fisherman?" A black market in navigation charts! Maybe Barok would be able to steer me to someone who smuggled, or whatever they did with them. I might be able to work my passage out of here. "I'd like to know a little more about this source," ferret says, tapping his teeth.

"It's within one of the Orders," Barok says, "that's all I can tell you."

Yellow robe says, "You're telling me that a member of the order would sell charts? That they can counter the spellbind?"

"I didn't say a 'member of the order,' " Barok says, "I said someone *within* the order."

"This stinks," ferret says, and silently I agree.

Barok shrugs. "If you don't want them, don't take them." But the dome of his forehead is slick and shining in the lamplight.

Ferret looks at Barok. The ferret is the power in this room; the others wait on him, Barok talks to him, yellow is his flunky. These men came in boats; boats that *go* somewhere in these islands mean money, and maybe some influence with the Navigational Order. And Barok—Barok lives in a slum. A two-bit nothing trying to sell to the big lizards. Oh, Heth, I am in trouble!

Ferret contemplates, and the others wait. "All right, I'll take these to verify their validity. If these prove accurate, we'll see about the next set."

"No," Barok says, "I'm giving you Hekkhare; you pay me the 200 for Liliana."

"What if I just take the charts?" ferret asks.

"You don't know my source," Barok says, desperate.

"So? Who *else* would you sell them to? The Orders?" the ferret says, bored.

"Two hundred for Liliana," Barok says stubbornly.

Ferret rolls the charts up. "I don't think so," he says blandly.

My knees turn to water. I've fought in battle, scared off a thief in a warehouse once, but never done anything like this. Still, I start to crouch for my sword.

"Tell your barbarian to be still," ferret snaps. Yellow has a knife, so do the others. I don't need to be told again.

"These aren't free!" Barok says, "I have expenses, I—I owe people money, Sterler. I don't pay people, you'll never get another chart! They're good, I swear they're good!"

"We'll negotiate the next ones," the ferret says, and nods at the rest. They rise and start to go.

I know that Barok is going to lunge, although it is a tokking stupid thing to do. But he does it, his hands hooked to claw at ferret. I think he only wants the charts, that he can't bear to see them go, but yellow reacts instantly. I see the flash of metal from under his robe, but I don't think Barok does. It isn't a good blow, they are all drunk, and Barok is a fleshy man. The knife handle stands out of his belly at about his liver, and Barok staggers back against the table. For a moment, he doesn't know about the knife—sometimes a knife-wound feels just like a punch.

"You can't have it," he says, "I'll tell them about you!" Then he sees the knife, and the wine-colored stain on his dark robe, and his mouth opens, pink and wet and helpless.

"Find out his source," the ferret says.

Chalcey is staring, blank-faced. I do not want her to see. I remember what it is like to see.

Yellow robe takes the knife handle and holds on to it, his face only a foot or so from Barok's. I smell shit. Barok looks at him, his face slack with disbelief, and starts to blubber. Some men's minds snap when they die.

"Who gets them for you?" yellow robe asks.

Arterial blood, dark and mixed with stomach blood, pumps out around the knife. Barok is silent. Maybe Barok is refusing to betray his niece, but I think the truth is that he has lost his wits. He has certainly voided his bowels. When yellow robe twists the knife, he screams, and then blubbers some more, his saliva not yet bloodied. He wants to go to his knees, but yellow robe has the knife handle, and Barok's hung on that blade like meat on a hook.

Chalcey is crouched, wrapped in her veil. She edges backward away from the men, her hands behind her, scooting backward like a crab until she bumps into my legs and stifles a little scream.

Ferret turns to us. "What do you know?"

I shrug casually, or as casually as I can. "I was hired today; he wouldn't tell me what he hired me for."

He looks down at Chalcey. I say, "He hired her right after he hired me."

Barok begins to say, over and over again, "Stop it, stop it, please stop it," monotonously, his hands making little clutching motions at his belly, but afraid of the knife.

"Tell me your source," yellow robe says.

Barok doesn't seem to understand. "Stop it, please stop it," he whimpers. *Die*, I think. Die before you say anything, you fat old man!

"Tok it," ferret says. "You've ruined it."

I whisper to Chalcey, "Scream and try to run up the stairs."

She rolls her eyes at me, but doesn't move.

Yellow robe shouts in Barok's face, "Barok! Listen to me!" He slaps the dying man. "Who is your source? You want it to stop? Tell me your source!"

"Help me," Barok whispers. There is blood in his mouth, now. The shadows from the lamps are hard, the big red-robed belly is in the light, and he is starting to spill flesh and bowels. The smell is overwhelming; one of the men turns and vomits, and adds that to the stench.

"Tell me where you get the charts, we'll get you a healer," yellow robe says. A lie, it's too late for a healer. But a dying man has nothing to lose by believing a lie. His eyes flicker toward Chalcey. Does he even know what is happening, understand what they are demanding? He licks his lips as if about to speak. I can't let him speak. So I whistle, five clear discordant notes, to waken one of the spells in my skull, the one that eats power, light and heat, and all the lights go out.

Black. Star-magic is easy to do, hard to engineer.

"TOK!" someone shouts in the dark, and Barok screams, a high, white noise. Things fall, I push Chalcey toward the stairs and grab my sword. I'm almost too frightened to move myself; maybe if it wasn't for Chalcey, I wouldn't, but sometimes responsibility lifts me above my true nature.

I collide with someone in the dark, slap at their face with my sword, and feel something hook in my jacket, tear at my shirt and the bindings I wear under it, then burn in my side. Then the person is gone. Ferret is screaming, "The stairs! Block the stairs!" when I fall over the bottom step.

The darkness only lasts a handful of heartbeats. It's a whistler spell, better against real power like the Cousin's lights than against natural things like a lamp, and it always makes me tired later. I turn at the stairs just as the lights come back. Blinded for a moment, I slap with my sword for the flame and knock it flying. Burning oil sprays across the room, I see blue robe cover his face, and, gods help him, poor Barok squirming on the floor.

The boat is tinder dry, and instantly the pools of oil from the lamp are full of licking blue flames. I run up the stairs. Chalcey is standing—not by the gangplank but next to the rail. My pack is there, and in the pack the cloak with the badge, and my chain vest and bracers—all I own in the world. I go for the girl and the pack, my shield arm clenched against my burning side. Ferret and the others will come boiling out of the hold like digger bees at any moment. I look down over the railing and see one of the sailboats, a soft Cousins' light clipped to the mast, and, in the glow, a green-robed adolescent with a cleric's shaven head, looking up at me. I grab Chalcey's arm and shout, "Jump!" and we land on top of the poor bastard, Chalcey's shrieking and my oomph! drowning the boy's bleat of surprise. Chalcey tumbles, but I have aimed truer, breaking his arm and probably his collar bone, so that he lies stunned and wide-eyed. I pitch him out of the boat. He is struggling in the water as I shove us off. I hope to Heth he can swim; I can't.

Our boat has a simple, single sail; it's a pleasure boat rather than a real fisherman's boat, but it will have to do. I run the sail up awkwardly. The wind will drive us downriver, toward the harbor. I don't see the boats of the others.

There is no pursuit. I think that ferret and the others have cut across the gangplank rather than make for the sailboats. I crouch next to the tiller and gingerly explore my injury with my fingers, a long flat scrape that crossed the ribs before the shirt and bindings and jacket hung it up. It bleeds freely, but it's not deep.

Chalcey curls in the prow of the boat, looking back toward her uncle's boat. The fire must have eaten the wood in huge bites. When we reach the bridge, I look back and see that the boat has been cut away and floats free in the river, burning bright and pouring out black, oily smoke. Two sailboats skitter away like dragonflies, silhouettes against the flames. Then we are enveloped in black smoke and ash which hides the boat from us, and hides us from everyone else.

Coughing and hacking, and, Heth forgive me, spitting, I keep us in the smoke as long as I can.

When we are almost out of the harbor, Chalcey asks, "Where are we going?"

"I don't know," I say. "I wish we had one of your charts."

It's a clear night, we have a brisk breeze and no moon yet. A good night to escape. I follow the coast, away from the city. On the shore, dogs bark at us, and to each other, distant and lonely. The sound chains along the coast as we sail.

"Was that magic?" Chalcey says.

"Was what magic," I say absently. I'm tired and not feeling well; it is painful to cough and spit ash and soot when your side is cut open.

"When it got dark. When you whistled."

I nod in the darkness, then realize she can't see it. "Yes, that was a little magic."

"Are you a mage?"

Do I *look* like a mage? Would I be living this way if I could smelt metal, and make starstuff in bright colors, and machines and lights? "No, little-heart," I say, talking sweet because my thoughts are not nearly so patient, "I'm just a whistler. A fighter with no money and only a little skill."

"Do you think they'll get a healer for my uncle?"

No answer to give but the truth. "Chalcey, your uncle is dead."

She doesn't say anything for a long time, and then she starts to cry. It's chilly, and she's tired and frightened. It doesn't hurt her to cry. Maybe I cry a little, too; it wouldn't be the first time.

We bob along, the waves going *chop, chop, chop* against the prow of the lit-tle boat. Dogs bark, to us and to each other. Along our left, the lights from the city are fewer and fewer, the houses darker and smaller. It smells like broom trees out here, not city. In the wake of our little sailboat, craken phosphoresce. I wonder, since their light is blue, why is craken dye yellow?

Chalcey speaks out of the dark, "Could we go to my grandmother?"

"I don't know, sweet, where is your grandmother?"

"Across the Liliana Strait. On Lesian."

"If I knew where it was, I could try, even without a chart, but I'm a for-eigner, littleheart."

"I can draw a chart. I drew those charts."

She sounds like a little girl. I smile tiredly into the darkness. "But I don't have anything for you to copy."

"I don't need to copy," she says. "They're in my *head*. If I have drawn a chart, even once, I never forget it. That's why my Uncle Barok brought me to the Order to go to school. But we've only practiced with Hekkhare and now Liliana Strait."

"So you drew those charts from your head?" I ask.

"Of course." She tosses her hair, her veil around her shoulders, and I can see her against the sky, just for the moment the imperious and sly girl who tried to impress the northern barbarian. "Everybody thinks that the charts are safe, all the paper and everything is spellbound. But I don't carry any pa-pers or anything; it's all in my head."

"Chalcey," I breathe. "Can you draw one?"

"We don't have any paper, and it's dark."

"We'll land in a few hours and get some sleep. Then you can use my knife and draw it on the bottom of the boat."

"On the bottom of the boat?" She is diffident.

But I'm elated. Two people hiding from the rest of the island, in a small sailboat not meant for the open sea, going on a young girl's memory of a chart. But it's better than *Barok's* choices.

We have a fair breeze, the little sailboat is quiet except for the slap of the sail. The water is close, right at my hand. Chalcey says she's cold. I tell her to dig my cloak out of my pack and see if she can get some sleep.

I think she sleeps awhile. I keep pushing us on, thinking to go a little farther before we rest, passing places to pull the boat up, until I see the line of gray that means dawn and take us into a stream that cuts down to the ocean.

"Chalcey," I say, "when the boat stops, jump out and pull."

We come aground, and I try to stand up, and nearly fall over. My legs are numb from crouching, and my side has stiffened in the night.

"What's wrong?" Chalcey says, holding the prow to get out.

"Nothing," I say, "be careful when you get out of the boat."

The cold water is up to my waist and makes me gasp, but at the prow, Chalcey is in water only to her shins. I grit my teeth and push, sliding against the uneven bottom, and she pulls, and together we get the boat well aground. I lash it to a tree, the tide is still coming in and I don't want to lose it, and then I grab my pack and stumble up the bank.

I should check the area, but I ache and I'm exhausted, so tired. I'm a little dizzy, so I promise myself I'll only rest for a minute. I prop my head against the pack and close my eyes. The world swirls. . . .

Some tokking hero, I think, and then laugh. That's one quality to which I have never aspired.

We're in heavy trees, tall pale yellow fronds of broom trees, heavily tasseled at this time of year. I'm covered with chukka bites, and the cut in my side is hot; I can feel my pulse beating in it.

There's no sign of Chalcey.

I lever myself painfully up on my elbow and listen. Nothing. Could she have wandered off and gotten lost?

"Chalcey," I hiss.

No answer.

"Chalcey!" I say, louder.

"Here!" comes a voice from over the bank, and then her head pops up, floating above the soft lemon brush as if it had been plopped on a bush. Maybe I'm feverish.

"Are you in the water?" I ask.

"No," she says, "I'm in the boat. What's your name, anyway?"

"Jahn," I say.

"I took your knife, but you didn't wake up. Are you—" she hesitates, wide-eyed, and my heart lurches, "I mean, is your hurt bad?"

"No," I say, attempting to sit up naturally and failing.

"I drew a chart in the bottom of the boat, and then I used mud to make the lines darker." She shakes her head, "Drawing with a knife isn't the same as drawing with a pen."

She comes up on the bank, and we breakfast on boxfruit and red peanuts out of my pack. Breakfast and water improve my spirits immensely. I check Chalcey's drawing. She clenches her hands nervously while I look at it. As soon as a wave puts a little water in the bottom of the boat, the mud will wash out of the lines, and I have no way of judging how accurate it might be anyway, but I tell her it looks wonderful.

To hide her pleasure, she turns her head and spits matter-of-factly into the stream. I wince, but don't say anything.

We have nothing to store water in.

"How far is it to Lesian?" I ask.

She thinks it's about two days. "Jahn," she says, self-conscious about my name, "where did you learn your magic?"

"One of the Cousins put copper and glass in the bones of my head," I say. Not exactly true, but close enough.

That silences questions for awhile.

We get some good drinks of water and relieve ourselves, and maybe she prays to her deities, I don't know. Then we raise our pineapple-green sail, and we are off.

She chatters awhile about school. I like listening to her chatter. When it gets hot at midday, I have her spread my cloak across the prow and crawl into the shade underneath it. I stay with the tiller and wish for a hat. I've been browned by the sun, but the light off the green water is blinding and bright, and my nose suffers.

She sleeps during the heat of the day, and I nod. We are headed for a promontory which marks where we cut across the strait. In the afternoon, we have some bruised boxfruit out of my pack, which helps our thirst a bit. The way west is suddenly blocked by a spit of land; if Chalcey's drawing can be trusted, that's our promontory. Chalcey's chart indicates that it's not good to go ashore here, otherwise I'd stop for fresh water. We head for open sea, and I pray that the breeze holds up. I'm stiff, and tacking accurately all the way across is probably beyond my navigational skills.

I'm thirsty; Chalcey must be, too. She doesn't complain, but she gets quiet. The farther we go into the strait, the smaller the land behind us gets; the smaller the land, the quieter she gets. Once I ask her what the crossing was like when she came to live with her uncle. "It was a big boat," is all she'll say.

I'm light-headed from sun and thirst and fever by the time evening comes, and the cool is a relief. The sun goes down with the sudden swiftness of the south. I dig the pigeon's egg dumplings out of my pack, but they're too salty and just make me thirstier. Chalcey is hungry, though, and eats hers and half of mine.

"Jahn?" she says.

"Yes?"

"The Cousins—why do they call them that?"

"Because we are all kin," I say. "It is like in my home, when a place gets too big, and there isn't enough land to let all the stabos graze, part of the kin go somewhere else, and start a new home. Our many times elders were the Cousins. The stars are like islands for them. Some came here to live, but there was a war and the ships no longer came, and our elders' ships grew too old, and we forgot about the Cousins except for stories. Now they have found us again."

"And they help us?" she asks.

"Not really," I say. "They help the high-ons, mostly."

"What are 'high-ons'?" she asks. Southern doesn't have a word for high-ons, so I always just use the two southern words.

"High-ons, the old men who run things and have silver. Or the guilds, they are like high-ons."

"Were you a high-on?" she asks.

I laugh, which hurts my side. "No, littleheart," I say. "I am the unlucky child of unlucky parents. They believed that some of the Cousins would help us, would teach us. But the high-ons, they don't like it if anyone else has strength. So they sent an army and killed my kin. Things were better before the Cousins came."

"The Order says that the Cousins are good; they bring gifts."

"We *pay* for those gifts," I say. "With craken dye and ore and land. And with our own ways. Anywhere the Cousins come, things get bad."

It gets darker. Chalcey wraps herself in my cloak, and I hunch over the tiller. It isn't that the boat needs much sailing; there's a light wind and the sea is blessedly calm (someone seems to favor us, despite our attack on the green-robed boy to get this boat), but the boat is too small for me to go anywhere else, so I sit at the tiller.

The spray keeps the back of my left shoulder damp, and the breeze seems to leach the warmth out of me. My teeth start chattering.

"Chalcey?"

"What?" she murmurs sleepily from the prow.

"I am feeling a bit under, littleheart. Do you think you could sit with me and we could share the cloak?"

I can feel her hesitation in the dark. She's afraid of me, and that pains me. It's funny, too, considering. "I don't want anything other than warmth," I say gently.

She feels her way slowly from the prow. "It's *your* cloak," she says, "you can have it if you want."

"I think we can share it," I say. "Sit next to me, the tiller will be between us, and you can lean against me and sleep."

Gingerly, she sits down next to me, the boat rocking gently with her movements, and throws the cloak around our shoulders. She touches my arm on the tiller and jerks back. "You're hot," she says. Then she surprises me by touching my forehead. "You have a fever!"

"Don't worry about it," I say, oddly embarrassed. "Just sit here." She curls against me, and, after a few minutes, she leans her head on my shoulder. Her hair smells sweet. It's soothing to have her there. I try to keep the constellation southerners call the Crown to my right.

"How old are you?" she asks.

"Thirty-one," I say.

"That's not so old."

I laugh.

"Well," she is defensive, "you have white hair, but your face isn't old."

Sometimes I feel very old, and never more than now.

• • •

I jerk awake from scattered dreams of being back on Barok's boat. It's dawn. Chalcey stirs against my shoulder and settles again. I think about the sea, about our journey. Celestial navigation is not my strong point; I hope we haven't drifted too much. I hope that Chalcey's chart is good, and I wonder how much Barok will get paid for a boat with a chart carved on it, even if the chart isn't very good, but blue flames lick the chart, and I'm on Barok's boat again. . . .

I jerk awake. My fever feels low; because it's morning, I'm certain. I try to open my pack without disturbing Chalcey, but she's asleep against my right shoulder, and I'm awkward with my left hand and my side is stiff, so after a moment she straightens up. We have five boxfruit left, so we split one. I'm too thirsty for red peanuts, but Chalcey eats a few.

As the sun climbs, so does my fever, and I start dreaming even when my eyes are open. At one point, Trevin is in the boat with us, sitting there in his blue jerkin with the gray fur low on the shoulders, and I must be talking to him, because Chalcey says, "Who is Trevin?"

I blink and lean over the side and splash cold water on my sunburned face. When I sit up, I'm dizzy from the blood rushing to my head, but I know where I am. "Trevin was a friend," I say. "He's dead now."

"Oh," she says, and adds, with the callousness of youth, "How did he die?"

How did Trevin die? I have to think. "The flux," I say. "We were marching to Bashtoy, we were retreating, Trevin and I had decided to fight against Scalthalos High-on since he'd burned out Sckarline. It was winter, and we didn't have much to eat, and the people who got sick, many of them died." I add, "I joined the fight because of Trevin." I don't add, "I was in love."

When it gets hot, Chalcey soaks her veil in water and covers my head with it. I clutch the tiller. It seems that I am not sailing the boat so much as it is sailing me. She doles out the boxfruit, too, peeling them and splitting the purple segments.

"I think," she says, "that maybe I should look at your side."

"No," I say.

"Don't worry," she says, moving toward me in the boat.

"No," I snap.

"I could put some cool seawater on it," she says. "Saltwater is good for an injury."

"I don't take off my shirt," I say. I'm irrational and I know it, but I'm not going to take off my shirt. Not when someone is around. We were finally in Bashtoy and almost everyone I knew was dead, and the MilitiaMaster said, "Boy, what's your name?" and I didn't know that he was talking to me. "Boy!" he shouted, "what's your name!" and I stuttered "Jahn, sir." "We'll call you Jahn-the-clever," he said, "you're in my group now," and the others laughed, and after that I was Jahn-the-clever until they discovered that I was really clever, but I still wasn't going to take off my shirt.

My thoughts run like squirrels in a cage, and sometimes I talk out loud.

Trevin comes back. He asks, "Would you rather have grown up anywhere but Sckarline?"

Chalcey soaks her veil in water and tries to keep my face cool.

"Wanji taught us about the cities," I say, "and she was right. I've been there, Trevin." My voice is high. "Wherever the Cousins come, they use us, they live like Scalthalos High-on, and we clean their houses and are grateful for light and giz stick on Sixth-day night. People don't care about kin anymore, they don't care about anything. Wanji told us about culture clash, that the weaker culture dissolves."

"Wanji and Aneal, Ayuedesh and Kumar, they dedicated their lives to helping us," Trevin says.

"Aneal *apologized* to me, Trevin!" I say. "She apologized for the terrible wrong they had done! She said it would be better if they never came!"

"I know," he said.

"Jahn," Chalcey says. "Jahn, there's nobody here but *me!* Talk to me! Don't die!" She is crying. Her veil is wet, and so cold it takes my breath away.

Trevin didn't know. I never told him about Aneal apologizing, I never told anyone. I blink and he wavers, and I blink and blink and he goes away. "You're not Trevin," I say, "I'm arguing with myself."

It's bright and hot.

I have my head on my arm.

The sky is lavender and red, and there is a dark stripe across the water that I can't make go away, no matter how hard I blink. I think that the fever is making my vision go, or that the sun has made me blind, until Chalcey, crying, says that it is Lesian.

There is no place to land, so we head up the coast northeast until we come to a river. "Go up here!" Chalcey says. "I know this place! I know that marker!" She is pointing to a pile of stone. "My grandmother lives up here!"

The night comes down around us before we see a light, like a cooking fire. I call instructions to shift the sail in a cracked voice; Chalcey has quick hands, thank Heth.

I run the boat aground, and Chalcey leaps out, calling and pulling at the boat, but I can't move. People come down and stand looking at us, and Chalcey says that her grandmother is Llasey. In the village they know her grandmother, although her grandmother lives a long walk away. I have a confused sense of being helped out of the boat, and I tell them, "We have silver, we can pay." Blur of people in the dark, and then into a place where there is too much light.

Then they are forcing hot seawater between my teeth, I can't drink it, then I think, "It's broth." The fire flickers off a whitewashed wall, and a bareheaded woman says, "Let me help you."

I don't want them to take off my shirt. "Not my shirt!" I say, raising my hands. They are talking and I can't follow what they are saying, but with gentle persistent hands they deftly hold my wrists and peel off the torn jacket and the shirt. The gentle voice says, "What's *this?*" and cuts the bindings on my chest.

Chalcey says, startled, "What's *wrong* with him!" I turn my face away.

A woman smiles at me and says, "You'll be all right, dear." Chalcey stares at me, betrayed, and the woman says to her (and to me), "She's a woman, dear. She'll be all right, there's nothing wrong with her except a bit of fever and too much sun."

And, so, stripped, I slide defenseless into sleep, thinking of the surprise on Chalcey's face.

I sleep a great deal during the next two days, wake up and drink soup, and sleep again. Chalcey isn't there when I wake up, although there is a pallet of blankets on the floor. And perhaps if I wake up and hear her, I pretend to be asleep and soon sleep again. But eventually I can't sleep anymore. Tuwle, the woman with the gentle hands who has given me a bed, asks me if I want a shirt or a dress, and, running my hand over my cropped hair, I say a shirt. But I tell her to call me Jahnna.

They bring me my shirt, neatly mended. And they won't take my silver.

Finally, Chalcey comes to see me. I am sitting on the bed where I have slept so long, shucking beans. It embarrasses me to be caught in shirt and breeches, shucking beans, although I've shucked beans, mended clothes, done all manner of woman's work in men's clothes. But it has been a long time since I've felt so self-conscious.

She comes in, tentative as a bird, and says, "Jahn?"

So I say, "Sit down," and immediately regret it, since there is no place to sit but next to me on the bed.

We go through the old routine of "how are you feeling?" and "what have you been doing?" She holds her veil tightly, although the women here don't go veiled for everyday.

Finally she says, in a hurt little voice, "You could have *told* me."

"I haven't told anyone in years." In a way, I almost didn't think I *was* a woman anymore.

"But I'm not just *any*one!" She is vexed. And how could she know that in a fight you become close comrades, yes, but that we know nothing about each other?

The snap of beans seems very loud. I think of trying to explain, about cutting my hair off to fight with Trevin, and learning long before Trevin died that fighting makes people strangers to themselves. Heth says life hinges on little things, like the fact that I am tall for a woman and flat-chested, and when the MilitiaMaster at Bashtoy saw me, half-starved and shorthaired, he thought that I was a boy, and so after that I *was*. Snap. And I run my thumb down the pod and the beans spill into the bowl.

To break the silence, she says, "Your sunburn is almost gone," and, amazingly, she blushes scarlet.

I realize then how it is with her. She had fancied herself in love. "I'm sorry, littleheart," I say, "I didn't intend to hurt or embarrass you. I'm embarrassed, too."

She looks at me sideways. "What do you have to be embarrassed about?"

"It's a little like having no clothes on, everybody knowing, and now that my kin are gone, I am always a stranger, wherever I go—" but she is looking at me without comprehension, so I falter and say lamely, "It's hard to explain."

"What are you going to do now?" she asks.

I sigh. That is a question that has been on my mind a great deal. Here there is no chance of saving passage money to get back to the mainland. "I don't know."

"I told my grandmother about you," Chalcey says. "She said you could come and stay with us, if you would work hard. I said you were very strong." Again she blushes scarlet, and hurries on, "It's a little farm, it used to be better, but there's only my grandmother, but we could help, and I think we could be friends."

As I learned during the long walk to Bashtoy, you may be tokked, but if you just look to the immediate future, sometimes, eventually, you find the way.

"I'd like that, littleheart," I say, meaning every word. "I'd like to be friends."

The future, it seems, does indeed hinge on little things.

G. David Nordley

POLES APART

G. David Nordley is a retired air force officer and astronautical engineer who has become a frequent contributor to *Analog* in the last few years, winning that magazine's Analytical Laboratory readers' poll in 1992 for his story "Poles Apart"; he also won the same award for his story "Into the Miranda Rift" in 1993. He has also sold stories to *Asimov's Science Fiction, Tomorrow, Mindsparks,* and elsewhere. He lives in Sunnyvale, California.

Like Varley, Nordley is another writer who finds the solar system an exotic enough setting for adventures just as it is, as he's demonstrated with stories of exploration and conflict on a grand scale, such as "Into the Miranda Rift," "Crossing Chao Meng Fu," "Out of the Quiet Years," "Dawn Venus," "Comet Gypsies," "Alice's Asteroid," "The Day of Their Coming," "Messengers of Chaos," and others; many of these stories make effective use of the latest astronomical and space probe data, data that shows just how bizarre, complex, surprising, and mysterious a place our solar system really is, a far cry from the conception of the solar system as a dull collection of rock, ice, and cinders that was common in the seventies. He's also moved out of the solar system to the strange alien planet Trimus, a planet settled by three radically different alien races working in concert, for stories such as "Network," "Final Review," and the swashbuckling story of cultures and racial attitudes in conflict that follows, "Poles Apart," a story that owes much to the tradition of writers such as Hal Clement, James H. Schmitz, and H. Beam Piper, and yet which has been filtered through a wry, shrewd, hardheaded sensibility that's Nordley's alone.

Nordley has yet to publish a novel, although a fix-up of the "Trimus" stories shouldn't be that hard to produce. A story collection is also long overdue, although none is forthcoming. Until then, you'll just have to look for him in the magazines, where he will surely continue to deliver solid and suspenseful science fiction adventures, based in accurate science but with a strong Sense of Wonder kick, for years to come.

... to establish a single planetary society in which all three spacefaring races take equal part: to find and develop common standards of civilized behavior, which may serve as a model for galactic civilizations to come.

—Compact and Charter of the Planet Trimus, Preamble

The human ship, almost four Charter units long with a huge square cloth sail, was new to Lieutenant Drinnil'ib. What, he wondered, were primitivists doing this far north? He hailed the ship, but instead of a verbal response, his voice brought a scurrying of the small two-legged beings around its deck. Before he could repeat the hail, a sharp, explosive, report split the air and something with a singing line attached went "thwunk" into the sea beside him.

What in the name of the Compact? he thought. The line brushed over his nose and he stuck his tongue out to grab and examine it. The line came under tension, and he let it slide through his manipulators until the end came along.

Pollution! The thing was sharp. It nicked the muscular fingers on one fork of his tongue before he clamped down on the line with the other, forcing the humans to try to reel him in with it. That should slow things down a bit, he thought. He raised a front claw and wrapped the line around it to ease the strain on his tongue. Then he held the object in front of his eyes. It was solid metal of some sort, and barbed: something that could have killed him if it had hit him in the wrong spot.

The thought and his reaction were almost simultaneous; he snapped his tail and bent his body downward. Not an eighth of a heartbeat later a tinny pop reached him through the water and another of the things zapped by. They *were* trying to kill him!

He let go, pulled a knife from his pouch, and slashed the line between the barbed missile and his foot. Then he swam first toward and then away from the ship, holding the line with his foot, and felt a satisfying give in the line after it jerked taut. He had some momentary misgivings—humans were fragile and he might have hurt one. But perhaps not: the tension on the line resumed quickly. Another slash of the knife took care of that. Drinnil'ib shook the remains of the rope from his claw, dove beneath the ship, and kept pace just below its hull.

Reaching back to his pouch, he replaced the knife with his gun and contemplated the plank belly of the offending vessel. Two, he thought, could play perforation. It took ten explosive rounds to put a fair-sized hole in the hull; the layers of polluting timbers were a twelfth of a Charter unit thick. But when he was finished, the ship was leaking so badly it would have to head for port too quickly to bother any other Do'utian.

Satisfied, he breached the surface immediately behind the ship, fired a shot in the air and roared a challenge: "I am planetary monitor Lieutenant Drinnil'ib and you have just assaulted me. What in the name of eternal repudiation do you think you are doing?"

Shouts sounded and sails rose. He grabbed the rudder of the ship with his front foot and wiggled it vigorously. Finally a face surrounded by reddish hair appeared over the railing on the rear of the boat.

"What in hell are you doing here, Monitor?" it shouted at him. "This is primitive territory—you damn techs are supposed to leave us alone."

"Not when people start getting killed," Drinnil'ib replied in a more conversational tone. "You can play your games but you have to observe the limits."

"Don't screw around in what you techs can't understand," it yelled. "Just leave us alone!"

Drinnil'ib rocked the ship again. "You're going to sink right here if you don't acknowledge that you can't sail around shooting people wherever you are. It's against the Compact."

"All right, all right, I hear you. Shooting at you was a big mistake. But next time, stay out of human whaling waters, Fish-man."

The polluting idiot didn't seem to show a trace of remorse, however Drinnil'ib thought he might be misinterpreting their body language. Just to be sure they didn't misinterpret *his*, Drinnil'ib gave the harpoonists something very easy to understand: he emptied his lungs of moisture-filled air right at them, soaking the speaker and sails. Then he kicked the ship away in disgust and sounded. Ten Charter units deep Drin put the barb in an evidence wrap, exchanged his gun for his communicator, and filed his report. He'd just gotten an object lesson on how some of the killings might have happened, but he would need human help to get to the bottom of it. A good excuse to look up an old colleague. With measured beats of his muscular tail, he headed for the northern reaches of the western continent.

As the tide-locked satellite of a superjovian infrared primary, Trimus has three symmetry axes: north-south, east-west, and inner-outer. This gives it three sets of geographic poles and three distinct climatic regions that allow for all three species to live in comfort. The arctic and antarctic match similar regions on Do'utia. The cool region surrounding the far pole matches the climate of the most populated areas of Kleth. The Earth-like near hemisphere is warmed both by Aurum and Ember, and ranges from temperate near the east and west poles to tropical directly beneath Ember. Trimus's close orbit about Ember gives it an effective day which is about twice the day of the Kleth homeworld, one and a half

times that of Earth, and three times that of Do'utia. For the last, however, what counts is the 407–day polar season cycle produced by the half-radian inclination of Trimus's orbit to the local ecliptic, and this is almost the same as on Do'utia.
—Planet Monitor's Handbook, Introduction

The morning sun was a tiny red ball in the mists next to the great ruddy crescent of Ember, as Drinnil'ib propelled himself upstream toward the human city with powerful tail strokes. The murders, he thought, struck at the purpose of Trimunian civilization by pitting one species against another.

Trimus was supposed to be the galactic laboratory for peaceful interspecies cooperation. But Ember had circled Aurum eight-cubed times since its settlement, and only the collective memory of the Kleth and the mechanical memories of the Humans went back that far. Some, he knew, felt this purpose had faded along with the need for experiment; preempted by distances of time and space so great that the residents of Trimus no longer represented the cultures that sent them. If they ever had, he thought wryly. Beings who would leave their home worlds forever to take part in an idealistic interstellar experiment may have had more in common with each other than with their various contemporaries.

But as far as Drin was concerned, the millennial-old civilization of Trimus had become its own reason for existence. Forget the rest of the galaxy and their occasional starships: to survive in peace with each other and their planet, its residents had to put the discipline of reason ahead of the natural inclination to group things by shape. To be a monitor was a calling, and he had no greater loyalty than to his world and its ideals, except, perhaps, to reason itself.

Headquarters said that Mary Pierce would be waiting for him at the marina landing past the watchtower at the base of the main channel bar, wherever that was . . . there! He caught the echo and eased himself to the right and into the deep cool channel. The harbor bottom was a backwater fairyland of human bubbles and Earth-life reefs, and the channel led through that like a wide black road. At its end, the cigar shapes of human submarines lay in a neat row, safe on the bottom from the winter ice. He put his legs down, released a bubble to settle himself firmly on the concrete, and with even measured strides hoisted his body into the warm air of the eastern continent.

A tiny tailless being, much smaller than the arrogant, hairy-faced barbarian that had cursed him earlier, waited for him at the end of the ramp, covered with a form-hugging cloth that Drinnil'ib knew was an even better insulator than his doci-thick blubber.

"Afternoon, Drin?" it called, the high pitch indicating it was a human female.

"Greetings," he rumbled and reached forward with one of the branches of his tongue to shake her hand. The familiar taste of the air around her put him at ease. "Mary? I'm sorry but it must be eight years since we last met. It's really good to see you again."

Now that he knew it was her, it was easy to pick out the subtle individual characteristics of her almost naked simian face and match them to his memory; the slight bend in the cartilaginous growth that housed her nostrils, the upturned angle of the hair on the upper ridge of her eye sockets, and its yellow-white color framing her face. It was a clean face, unmarred by any unnatural growth or scar, and he knew other humans considered her beautiful. He would agree, judging from the esthetics of functionality, and also from the esthetics of the curve.

"You look pretty magnificent yourself, chum," she responded, but then shook her head. "I only wish the occasion was a happier one."

He bobbed his massive head in the planetary convention of assent. "Five more dead, four Do'utian and one human."

"Butchered?"

"Neatly, intelligently, as last time, except the human. The sea left too little of him to tell. But this," he held up the barbed projectile, "may be at the bottom of it."

"Primitivist hunters?"

Drinnil'ib hooted. "Not primitive enough, it seems. This was propelled by chemical explosives."

There were always some from every species, from every generation, romantics who wanted to live in the reserved areas by their instincts without having to learn the science and culture that got their ancestors to Trimus. A disease of the character, he thought, which could not be eliminated without eliminating character itself.

"I am sorry, Drin," Mary said, "for what our children have done. They form communities, the communities evolve, get recruits, and no one seems to care. Some of those places haven't been visited in a century."

Drin gave a sigh of toleration. "It is in your nature to hunt and in ours to endure the hazards of the sea. But without a trained intellect to guide, any race . . ."

She shook her tiny head in negation. "Some things are *wrong*, and always have been. Everywhere for everyone. Killing is one. They know the Compact, that's a minimum for letting them go out there. So it's up to us to find which 'they' are responsible and take corrective action." She shrugged her shoulders and spread her arms. "A policeman's lot is not a happy one."

A quote he didn't recognize, but one that fit. Lieutenant Drin bobbed his head again.

"Oh, the duty can be interesting."

"Ha! Well, my sub's ready to go; we can leave any time," she said. "But I thought you might like to try Cragun's sushi before we head out." She bared the exquisite miniature ivory chisels of her teeth to him in a human gesture of good feeling. Was there, he wondered, some art in this reminder that both of them were occasional carnivores? He would have to ask her on the journey. Meanwhile, the sushi sounded most pleasant. He hoped they could find a cubic doci of their rice wine to go with it. About one of their traditional "gallons," if he recalled: "And a, um, gallon or two of, um, sake? To go with it?"

She laughed. "Just what I was thinking, Drin. Let's go."

The "Charter unit" is identical to the Kleth "glide," precisely eight to the eighth times the wavelength of the strongest line of neutral sodium (also approximately the peak wavelength of Aurum's spectrum). This is about a traditional Do'utian "tail," once related to the length of the average Do'utian, or almost ten human "meters," once defined as 1/23,420 (1/10,000, base 10) the distance from the equator of Earth to its north pole. The common "doci" (from duo-octi) is 1/100 of this, about the size of the adult hand of any of the three races.

—Planet Monitor's Handbook, Appendix C

Glensville, on the northing Graham River, was easily cool enough in winter to be a congenial tropical vacation spot. He just had to remember to move slowly to avoid building up too much body heat. Great banks of melting snow lined the road, and ice covered the dozen park lakes scattered among the stone and wood human hives. Cheerful humans sliding on long flat boards attached to their feet waved to him as he ambled down the main road with Mary.

Cragun's was one of the few above-water taverns on the eastern continent that was set up to serve Do'utians. There were two there when he arrived with Mary: the poet Shari'inadel and a large Do'utian man with fresh white scars on his flukes and a deep, raw crescent behind his blowhole. Those were unusual wounds for this area—the sort of wound that one got in a beak fight with another Do'utian. So, Drin thought, this Do'utian must be a primitivist of sorts—the kind that got his jollies on the southern beaches and came back every now and then to partake of the benefits of civilization.

The other turned its head, saw him, and hissed. Most impolite, and for what reason? Drin's lack of scars? His civilized bearing? His human companion? But this was a human town!

"I do not know you," Drin stated formally. "I am Monitor Lieutenant Drinnil'ib and I ask respect."

"Gota'lannshk. The sea has been generous with you, pretty monitor. But don't press your luck, beachmeat." The voice was a slurring, low-pitched rumble.

Drunk. Spoiling for a fight. Drin gave the other a sharp warning hiss, then turned away to ignore the reaction and cool his own rising irritation. He heard no response.

"You don't like him, do you?" Mary whispered.

"I've never met the man," Drin replied, beak shut, letting the words escape softly through the fleshy corner of his mouth. "But what he is does not swim well in my thoughts. His companion is a poet, named Shari. I know the family—she's their first egg in two centuries, and quite indulged. She could be just the sort of dissatisfied romantic that runs off for glandular adventures in the south, and then lives to regret it. I think she is being 'offered' a place in that ogre's harem."

"Her choice, isn't it?" Mary asked.

"Choice implies an intellectual process, but he's playing on her instincts. Look at that one, and do not judge human rustics so harshly. He appears to have engaged in mortal combat for the fun of it."

Mary coughed. "Drin, Cragen's has some giant squid fresh from the farm. I'll split it with you, 999 parts to you, 1 to me."

"Can you eat that much?" Drin rumbled. After his journey, a meal ashore would be welcome.

"Try me!"

"You're on." Drin made the order. "Someday I'd like to try this squid in its native ocean, though." A fantasy of his; when would he ever find time in his life for a round trip of ninety years?

"That's where you'd have to eat it. You're too fat to walk around on Earth." She had a point. Twice the gravity of Trimus would have disadvantages, and he had been gaining a bit lately. Well, he'd swim that off on this trip.

"Maybe you underestimate me," he rumbled. Cragen's did not, however. The squid arrived—more than enough for even his appetite.

They talked strategy. The nearest concentration of humans who might know something lived on the islands near the warm inner pole. Whether or not these folk pinpointed the murderers, Drin made clear that he would need to talk to the Do'utian exiles near the south pole; to placate, to gather evidence, or both. Then would come the older human communities on the southern edge of the undeveloped West Continent.

"Cities of stone, ships of wood. Reports of warfare and slavery." Mary shook her head. "At the very least, they need to be reminded of the Compact."

"That was certainly my experience," Drin agreed.

A common civilization requires a common language, common measurements, and places where all three species can meet comfortably. Human English shall be the common language because it is the only language all three races can pronounce acceptably. Numbers and measurements shall be in the Kleth octal system, which is easiest to learn, is compatible with cybernetic binary systems, and is more widespread than human base ten or Do'utian base twelve. Common architecture will follow Do'utian proportions, so that Do'utians will not be excluded from the social interaction needed for a common civilization.
—The Compact and Charter of Planet Trimus, Article 6

The journey to the inner pole archipelago left Drin fit and trim, and he enjoyed the taste of the exotic tropical fish. But to reach the island, they left the cold south-flowing bottom current and he felt like he was gliding through a hot bath. He looked forward to the south polar waters, and sent an almost joyful greeting to Mary when he caught the wake-sound of her submarine returning from her inquiries.

Nominally, the archipelago would have been reserved for Kleth primitivists, but they were very few and needed little land, so warm-loving human refugees from technological civilization had gradually spread among the islands. Here, near the inner pole, the infrared radiation from Ember came in almost directly overhead, almost doubling the distant orange sun's modest daily contribution. The more or less permanent high-pressure system kept skies clear unless the night fog rolled in. But it was clear tonight, and the gibbous, pink-belted almost-star dominated the zenith.

"Were there any witnesses?" Drin asked as Mary came alongside. She was lounging on the deck behind the submarine's pilot house, and the last rays of setting Aurum painted her a rich gold. She had no need for her insulating garment, and he watched muscles play under her thin epidermis as she got up to greet him. A strange shape, yet one that fit its owner as well as any in nature.

"No witnesses—not really that many people around. I found one man who heard about some whalers and got him to tell me he's seen them even in tropical waters. Says they're operating out of a city on a half-flooded volcanic island off the southern edge of the West Continent reserve. I checked the recon and there *is* some sort of primitive city there. Hasn't been visited by monitors for years."

"Were the people forthcoming?"

She shook her head. "There aren't many people here, and those who are here act frightened. I had to offer, well, an incentive to the only person who admitted knowing anything."

"I'm surprised the area isn't more heavily populated. This must be close to the original human climate, you don't seem to need artificial insulation here."

"No, we don't. And it does feel good!" She shook herself and her flesh rippled in a way that reminded him of a jellyfish, but much faster. "But it's enervating. Most people's minds need more stimulation from their environment. The people who live here don't even ask to replace the occasional death—children are too much work. They just live for pleasure."

Ages ago, Drin remembered, humans had arranged their genes to be infertile without deliberate medical intervention as a population-control measure to go along with anti-aging measures. The idea of being constantly driven to act out the reproduction process horrified him, but humans apparently enjoyed it. Of course it wasn't as messy with them.

Mary shook herself again. "Cooling off now, though. Time to kiss lotus land good-bye."

She waved and vanished down the submarine's hatch. They sounded together and slanted west toward the cold current and their joint adventure.

Half a day later his dorsal ganglia were running things while he was deep in thought about just how primitive things could get. He understood much of the attraction of the undeveloped areas. All space-faring people were descendants of those for whom the unbuilt beach and the untrod planet exerted an irresistible call. But his last trip had been eye-opening in other ways.

He had little basis for comparing what he'd seen to the depth of cultural degeneration Mary said she had experienced on her hothouse island, but all the same, he shuddered to think of what she would find on the shores of the south polar continent. At least humans without machines could still construct buildings. Ancient Do'utian women had mated and calved on the open beach. Without shelter, their retrogressing descendents would have no choice but to do the same. Despite himself, a shudder of prurient interest ran from his chest through his tail at the thought of beaches of nubile young mothers, blatantly receptive in the free air.

"Lieutenant Drin?" Daydreaming! How long had Mary been calling him?

With the flick of the tail, he glided over to the submarine and brought his right eye up to the center of the diamond hull. Its electric drive fields made him tingle as they pushed seawater toward its tail.

"Lost in thought, I'm afraid. What do you have?"

Mary was back in her artificial skin and all business. "Here's the recon on that primitive city." A relief map appeared on the holoscreen next to her. The flooded caldera surrounded a lagoon on three sides, and the forth appeared to be filled in by a simple stone dike. Large and small masonry buildings lined the shore of the lagoon.

"Mary, I think the cold current must flow by there, see the trench to the south?"

"Yes. Good eating?"

"It should be, and if so, we should find some Do'utian primitives nearby. I suggest we stay with the plan, head south first and gain what intelligence we can from the victim population before confronting this set of potential perpetrators. . . . Mary?"

"Yes, Drin?"

"In our early days, there were tests for reproductive rights. Death swims and beach fights. Bloodlust beyond reason. These occasional hunting deaths seem, in a way, like some of those old tests. I fear I will not be proud of how some of the Do'utian back-to-nature crowd might be living."

"Do you fear more than embarrassment?"

Yes, he needed to say. Yes I fear my own primitive instincts. So why did he hesitate to tell her? Mary was a friend and colleague, and any infirmity on his part could affect the mission.

"Mary . . . we have never needed to revise our mating instincts. In our cities, with the privacy of our rooms, there is no need. In fact, we must make an effort to replace those of our colony who are lost by accident—an embarrassing and very private effort for both beings concerned. But with everything out in the open . . . I'm not sure how I will—"

Peals of musical laughter twinkled like bells from the hull of her ship, for so long that Drin became concerned for her health. Finally, she pressed herself to the transparent hull.

"Drin, my friend . . . look, don't tell what I'm going to tell you to any other human, especially the other monitors, OK?"

"My word on it," Drin said, curiousity clawing at him.

"Well," she laughed, "in order to be accepted and get information I kind of went native. I allowed—hell, Drin, I enticed—my source to perform our mating act with me. I mean I was all there, and he was all there, and it just felt like the natural thing to do. In the line of duty, I told myself."

Drin swam in silence for a while thinking that to say the wrong thing would be harmful to his friend. But he soon realized that to say nothing at all could seem even worse. He reviewed what he knew of human mating. "Was this person physically suitable?"

This occasioned more laughter. "He was. Oh, yes. Exceedingly so."

"And you left this pleasure to return to your duty with me? I find this very admirable and hope, to the extent that we can compare our temptations, that I shall be able to exhibit similar moral strength."

"Moral strength? Drin, you are a forked-tongued devil."

After a moment, he realized this was a compliment. He gently pressed a shoulder to the window so that only the eighth of a doci or so of diamond hull separated their bodies. He easily felt the warmth of her flesh through this transparent, uninsulated section. This communication of friendship had no intellectual hazards.

But his mind returned to duty. "Perhaps," he rumbled after a while, "we should ask the Kleth Monitors for backup in case we find we need eyes overheard when we visit this city. I know a certain Officer Do Tor who has a sense of humor and does not dump everything into their racial memory."

"Perhaps," Mary laughed again. "I think I met him when the last starship visited, six years ago. Gold wings, silver crest? Flighty little yellow thing under his claw?"

"The very one."

"Why not? The more the merrier."

Following planetary engineering, only the north, east, and outer poles will be intensively settled. The remainder of the planet will be reserved for biological study and kept free of large settlements or significant technological effluents. The primary objective will be to observe how the three merged ecosystems evolve from their original design point. Low-intensity visitation, consistent with these objectives, may be tolerated by those who wish to experience life in the wild.

—The Compact and Charter of Planet Trimus, Article 12

"I have never seen such a cold, desolate wasteland of rocks in my life," Mary remarked as they approached an outrageously voluptuous antarctic beach. A fish for every taste, Drin thought.

She had parked the submarine and rode on his neck toward the shore-line, her warm thighs smooth against his sandy outer skin. The idea that she often had eggs, of a sort, waiting in a part of her body so near to him gave him ridiculous and perverted thoughts—thoughts that unwontedly stimu-lated certain secretory organs below the tips of his fingers. Some, he had heard, had experimented with interspecies stimulation and considered it a form of art. Thank providence, he thought, that such thoughts on his part could remain private. But if Mary ever said that *she* wanted . . . No, *no*. Consign that idea to the abyss. Too much chance of giving offense.

It didn't help at all, as they neared the beach, that he could see at least four unabashedly pregnant young Do'utian women lolling thick-necked on the smooth pebbles in the sun. The beachmaster was nowhere to be seen, a circumstance that ran his biological thermometer well past its set point. He wondered if Mary understood how hard this would be for him?

"That beach is an indolent paradise for us, I'm afraid. I'd much rather talk to the head man than that naked harem, but he's left them unprotected. This isn't good. Uh, Mary, if they become aggressive with me, it might be best if I just let nature . . ."

She patted the top of his head, firmly enough for him to notice.

"I'll never say a thing. Promise." She put her arms around his neck, as far as they would go, and pressed the soft parts of her body against the back of his head, laughing. It was not at all unpleasant. Then, suddenly, she stopped.

"Drin," she spoke quickly, "to your left. What is that in the—DRIN!"

Instantly, he rolled his eyes around and slipped his tongue into his pouch, triggering his sonar with one manipulator and grabbing his weapon with the other. Then he saw, and knew instantly that it was too late to do anything.

A tall pole, perhaps half a Charter unit high, supported a white pennant at its end, snapping in the offshore breeze. The other end was firmly buried in the side of the corpse of a Do'utian man, bloated, floating in the swell. He shuddered as the wind shifted and brought the scent of death to him.

"Are you OK?" asked Mary.

"Yes. But I would prefer to approach this upwind. How are you?"

She was a trained monitor, and, he hoped, not as affected due to the dif-ference in species. Fortunately for him, the wind shifted again.

"I'm fine. Look, why don't I check out the victim and the murder weapon while you interview?"

It made sense, but he was hoping for her presence to bolster his resolve not to be swept away by instinct on the beach. He belched in self-disgust; was he not master of himself?

"Very well, Mary. I'll take you over to it, I need to get closer anyway. I suspect the victim was the beachmaster here, and if so, these women have been widowed. I should be able to tell from his scent—he will have marked them. Widowing can be a very painful death sentence in primitive circum-stances; an unbirthed egg turns poisonous in a month or so."

"So my human primitives kill five Do'utians with one harpoon?"

"Mary, they are not *your* primitives," he rumbled. "Don't take so much on yourself. It's not very professional." He extended his tongue behind him and placed manipulators on both her shoulders. "Besides, there are no reports of harems dying because of the other murders." The thought struck him: why not? "We don't know the whole story," he finished. No, indeed.

He felt her five thin bony fingers cover his three thick muscular ones. She grasped tightly, and he could feel some warmth, though not taste her skin, through her water suit. He could not fathom what feelings ran through that alien mind nor what awful images from her past this fresh corpse might conjure. But he could recognize sadness in her, and try to give sympathy.

His own feelings were proving harder to manage. There was a primal urge in his species to avoid their dead, and thus, the evolutionists believed, avoid whatever circumstances might have led to death. Then there was what waited for him on the beach. He shuddered.

"I can tell you'd rather not go any closer, Drin." A splash surprised him, and Mary swam in front of his left eye. Humans, in general, were clumsy in the water. But they were fearless and some like Mary were competent, if slow. "I'll take it from here. Looks like about as far to the corpse as to the beach. No problem; I'll just swim in when I'm done, or I'll buzz for you if I need backup. OK?"

He rumbled an assent, she bared her teeth to him, flipped and started pulling herself through the water toward the victim, climbing through the waves with steady pulls of her front limbs. The wonder, he reflected, was not that his simian friends were slow in the water, but that they could swim at all, and even appear graceful, in their own way, while doing so.

"I'll be expecting you. Take care," he called after her. Then, with mixed feelings, he sent himself toward the beach.

The approach was not the simple landing of a human boat ramp. Jagged rocks were all over. The beachmaster had chosen well: an adult Do'utian needed care to reach the shore. Drin exhaled and settled firmly on the bottom to ignore the random swells. Legs extended, he picked his way carefully along, a Charter unit below the surface, while holding his sonar transceiver high over his head, hearing the image it received through his earphones. There! A sandy path opened through the rocks. He followed it. It zigzagged to an open gravelly area under the breakers that seemed safe enough, but he chose to pick his way through the smooth stones along its side just in case. Carefully, he emerged onto the beach.

The women crowded together as soon as they saw him. Very well, he'd take it slowly.

First though, he traced his route with a sharp tongue tip on his comset's screen and sent the resulting image to Mary. While she could float over larger outlaying rocks that would disembowel him, there seemed to be only one place where the breakers might not dash her to pieces. He also sent a brief report to Monitor Central and inquired about the status of his request for Kleth support. Scheduled, they told him.

Chores done, he returned his attention to the widowed harem. Widowed because they had been very clearly scented by the dead beachmaster, and the deceased's neobarbarism seemed to have extended to marking them physically as well as with his scent—some of the scars were still unhealed.

A medical team would be needed. While, contrary to his initial assessment, only two of them were gravid; with the beachmaster gone they would both be needing egg relief soon. Also, all four were clearly undernourished.

He filed a quick report for Do Tor on his comm unit, then walked forward to them slowly, mouth politely open, tongue and manipulators spread to signal peaceful intent. Still, they cowered. They were young, very young, despite scars and abrasions on their hides that most of his people wouldn't acquire in eight times eight times eight years, and would probably remove if they did.

"I'm Lieutenant Drinnil'ib from the Monitors. I don't mean any harm," he said. "I'd just like you to answer some questions."

It must be the smell of the beachmaster's death that frightened them into silence. He had come close enough to carry some of it, and they probably thought he was responsible.

They keened and backed away as he approached. But a cliff surrounded the beach, and soon they could back up no farther.

If they could smell the death, then there was no reason to try to keep it a secret. He was hoping to avoid the legendary consequences. Nonsense, he told himself. These must be at least semi-educated people, living in primitive conditions by choice.

"I'm sorry to have to bring you this news. I've come from the North Pole colony investigating the reported deaths of several people in this back-to-nature area. I'm afraid I have one more to investigate. By what I smell, the latest victim was your husband. I'm sorry. I assure you I had nothing to do with his death before the fact." Lieutenant Drinnil'ib reached into his pouch and produced his badge, a holoprint two docis on edge—big enough for them to see easily. It gave off his scent as well.

The smallest of the harem, with deep black scars on her forelimbs, finally walked forward, then lowered herself to her belly in supplication.

"No," he protested. "I don't want you to do that. Stand up! Speak to me, please."

She keened again, then opened her mouth wide. It took him a few heartbeats to register what he saw, and then a few more for the horror of it to sink in. Where the two branches of her tongue should have been, where the manipulators that signified their species' rise from the beach should have curled, was nothing but a blackened stump, so short it would be useless for feeding or speaking.

He quickly pulled in his own tongue and lowered his belly to the gravel, to be on her level. Then he gently touched his beak to hers in sympathy. She shut her eyes and lowered her beak in sadness, and he did the same. When he looked up again, the other three had joined them. The gravid ones were looking at him expectantly. Oh-oh.

"Look," he explained, "I'm not part of your culture. I'm a Monitor. This is strictly a professional visit." Their eyes showed no comprehension, and their bodies began to sway back and forth on their legs. They came closer, swaying and keening. The first female kept nuzzling him. He tried to back away, but froze.

From then on, he noted his body's response with what was almost detachment. Body temperature up. A tightness at the base of his tail. He wanted to keep his mouth shut to avoid tasting whatever chemicals they were putting out, but a groan worked its way out from deep inside him, his beak yawned open involuntarily as reason left his brain. The women were beside him, keening, holding him between their bodies, their beaks locked wide open, pressing his most private areas. The need to give overwhelmed him. He let his tongue caress their tails, almost as if it were someone else's.

He never saw the eggs emerge from their throats, but rather felt the smooth bumps against his underside, an emptying feeling in the base of his tail, and a slight coolness in that area as his consciousness slowly faded back in.

Afterward, of course, he remembered everything with the humiliating clarity of a terapixel hologram. Especially when he looked back at two white eggs covered with sticky yellow goo. And especially when he looked up and saw little Mary Pierce standing about eight Charter units away, mouth open in what must have been a look of horror.

Setting aside his embarrassment and disgust, he tried to remember what needed to be done. Back home, in a hospital, the eggs would be sprayed clean and anointed with all sorts of healthy fluids, wrapped in germicidal barriers, and placed in an incubator. The nearest thing to an incubator they had here was a Do'utian pouch. His was full of other things, but the women had pouches, too.

It was then that he realized that since none of the women had tongues, he would have to place the eggs in their pouches himself. He shut his eyes, moaned, and buried his beak in the sand again. He couldn't do this.

"It's OK," he heard Mary say. "I'm afraid I don't remember what the handbook says about Do'utian midwifery, but if there's anything I can do, just tell me."

He lifted his head up. "The handbook doesn't say anything. It's supposed to be too private. But . . . but the eggs need to be cleaned off and placed in the women's pouches. They can't do it themselves because their former husband disabled them. I'm . . . I'm afraid I'm not up to it."

"No problem, buddy. I think they accept me. Must be your scent all over me. Is it OK if I wash the eggs in the sea?"

"Yes, I think so."

She did this quickly and efficiently, taking each egg in turn, cradling and talking to it as if it was a fresh-born human. Drin refrained from telling her that there would be nothing inside the eggs to hear her for eight-squared days. Done with the washing, Mary took the smaller egg and approached one of the formerly gravid women, who looked accusingly at Drin and backed away. Then a strange thing happened. The smaller Do'utian woman quickly moved in front of Mary and offered her own pouch.

When that member of the harem had accepted both eggs, she came over to Drin and slowly scratched the sand with her beak. It soon became clear that she was writing. When she backed away, Drin could read, fairly clearly. "I GRI'IL."

"You can understand me?" Drin asked, wonderingly. Obviously, she could not speak.

She nodded.

"Your name is Gri'il?"

She nodded again.

"Do you want to leave?"

Gri'il did nothing, then nodded slowly, followed by a vigorous head shake. Something wrong.

"Will you follow me back to the North Pole? To civilization?"

She was still a very long time. Then she began painfully scratching the gravel again. What she wrote was "DANGR HUNTRS."

Mary saw this, went up to Gri'il, wrapped herself around the Do'utian woman's foreleg, and began her own type of keening. Soon, they had all joined in.

"I'm going to get some fish for everyone," Drin said to no one in particular, and trotted back to the shore. The mutilated Do'utian's were ill nourished and couldn't feed themselves. Besides, he needed something to do alone. Away from all women of whatever species.

Individuals who wish to visit or reside in the wild regions, alone or in small groups, may do so without interference so long as they respect the rights of others and do not significantly disturb the environment. Introduction of chemical industry is specifically prohibited. Alternative societies are permitted so long as the individuals who join such societies are free to leave such when they wish. Do not interfere with suicide, or risk-taking that amounts to such. However, murder will be treated no differently than in the civilized areas.

—Planet Monitor's Handbook
Law In Reserved Areas

"Gri, Ohghli, Donota, Notri, do I have it right?" Mary asked. Human memories, Drin thought, were amazingly poor considering their technological prowess—on the other hand, perhaps necessity had made them superlative inventors.

Drin rocked her submarine by putting a little extra into his next propulsive tail-stroke. "Your memory is either much worse than I think or you find a certain humor in my situation. I think I would rather not have my thoughts in that current so often."

"My apologies." The comset relayed the drop of pitch in her voice that Drin associated with increasing concern. "But they're your wives now, aren't they?"

"No! I have made no commitment. There is no registration. Except for

Gri'il, none of them seems to have any intellectual understanding of their lives, or that of the broader race. None of them is a suitable mate."

"I'd guess it will be hard for them to understand that," Mary suggested, more right than she could know.

"Very hard. I approached them under circumstances that make biological bonding almost inevitable in nature. And Gri'il took the eggs. . . ."

"She seems the responsible type, and educated somehow."

"She will have a tale to tell. I suspect she is a truant who dove into the back-to-nature business just a little deeper than her inherent depth. The others, I think, must have been born here. They seem virtually feral."

"What will happen to them?"

"I think Gri'il will return to civilization, sadder but wiser. The feral women . . . I don't know. The experts will have to decide—they may be happier as they are."

"Mutilated?"

"No, we'll fix that. But, they may be unable to adapt to civilization now. I cannot know their minds, or even if they have developed what you and I would recognize as a mind."

"That's heartless," Mary accused. "They love you."

"You don't understand the biology. I think our conversation should find different currents now."

But it didn't. Mary's attempt at matchmaking left him in no mood for conversation at all. There was silence instead, a silence that should have been filled with plans as they approached the primitivist human settlement.

It was shockingly big, even by his standards. Primitivism in humans, Drin realized at the sight, didn't really mean living without technology. It meant living with a technology so primitive that it could be sustained without any meaningful education at the expense of ceaseless, boring labor; a technology of hand-hewn planks, poles, and rough-cut stones in huge piles, piles made all the larger by beings who evolved with twice the local gravity.

The entrance to their harbor had been choked down to a canal by massive stone walls and guarded by massive wooden gates. The stream that issued from this was putrid. Drin turned away.

"Pollution! Mary, I think I would prefer to walk in."

"Understood. There must be two thousand people in this place, and that's the only outlet. The air isn't a whole lot better—lots of smoke. It's a couple of degrees over freezing; cool enough for you?"

"A nice balmy day."

"Why don't you try riding on top of the sub? You'll have to keep your tail off the rear electrodes."

Drin released a bubble of humor; the idea of him riding on a human submarine was indeed bizarre. But the water stunk like rotting carrion. "If you can steer without your forward fins, I could hang onto those with my forelegs. Then my tail wouldn't reach the electrodes."

"The sub says that's no problem. Climb aboard."

He swam into position, curled his front toes around the rounded edge of the flexidiamond fins and released some buoyancy gas to hold himself down. The submarine rose under him and broke the surface. The air stank as advertised, but only when he opened his mouth.

Soon Mary climbed out of the nose hatch to join him. She'd put her monitor uniform jumpsuit on over her insulated tights and looked academy sharp. Remembering that humans relied almost exclusively on visual identification, he pulled his monitor badges out of his pouch and stuck them on his front shoulders.

In front of them across the harbor entrance lay the top of the harbor wall, with an opening just a little wider than the submarine, the massive wooden gate was solid above water and dwarfed even Drin. It was guarded by heavy-set humans in thick-belted robes around which were buckled long, heavy, cutting tools; called swords, if he remembered correctly.

"Open the gate," Mary yelled. The men did nothing. Drin tapped her on the shoulder with his tongue to warn her, and she covered her ears. He took a large breath.

"PLANET MONITORS. OPEN THE GATE!" Drin yelled, two octaves lower than Mary, pouring air from his bladder as well as his lungs. The human guardhouse resonated nicely with his undertones and a satisfying crash emerged from its open door. Various stones and pieces of rotten mortar came clattering down the sides of the wall. One of the men extended his hands, palms out as if to plead for patience, while the other dipped into the now-steady guardhouse and emerged with a pair of colored flags. He faced the harbor and started waving them in various incomprehensible patterns.

Soon, they heard a screeching and groaning of hidden wheels and levers as the left gate swung ponderously open. From aerial holos, Drin knew the breakwater was eight squared Charter units thick, but even so, the narrow canyon revealed by the opening gate made him shudder a bit. He slipped a branch of his tongue out the corner of his mouth into his pouch, and wrapped its fingers around his weapon. When the noises stopped, the submarine nosed through the half-opened gate. It had only a few doci's of clearance on either side, but it maintained this clearance with mathematical precision as it moved smartly into the channel.

About halfway through, a red-robed human man jumped onto the hull from a ladder just inside the gate, landing without stumbling despite the vessel's speed. He looked at Drin, then at Mary, apparently unsure of whom was in charge; the male Do'utian or the female human.

"Who are you?" Drin rumbled. The man shook and looked around, as if for somewhere to jump, and finding nowhere, finally faced Drin.

"Yohin Bretz a Landend. I'm . . . I'm your harbor pilot. We've got to go to city gate. Lord Thet will talk to you there."

"Yohin Bretz a Landend," Mary said, "I'm Mary Pierce from the monitor bureau. This is Lieutenant Drinnil'ib, my colleague. This is my boat; Lieutenant Drin doesn't need one. We are here to investigate the deaths of several Do'utian primitivists in this region."

"Huh? Whalers playing games with the fish-people, I'd guess." Bretz looked down at the submarine. "What do you draw?"

"Draw?" Mary clearly didn't recognize the term. Drin did, from his readings in human nautical literature, but kept silent so as not to embarrass his partner.

"Yeah, *draw*. How far down is the bottom of this thing?"

"About a third of a Charter unit," she answered.

"What's that in meters?" A human chauvinist, Drin thought.

"It's a little over three of the old meters."

"Uh-huh. So the keel's about twice your height below the waterline?"

"Yes."

The pilot shook his head. "You'd displace thirty ton less without the fish-man on board, I'd guess, and ride a meter higher. Well, no problem, the channel's deep enough, but you'll have to stay in it. You've got to go hard aport as soon as you're out of the dike canal and steer for the big stone mill you'll see on the shore. Bear a bit to the port of it to lead the current, if I were you."

Drin rumbled a bit, and Mary smiled, recognizing his laugh. The submarine could follow the channel on sonar or with blue light without any help from the pilot.

"We'll do just fine," Mary said, "thank you. Now you can call me Mary, what can I call you?"

"Yohin, or Mr. Bretz to be polite."

They emerged into the harbor, a roughly circular body of fetid water. The air was thick with the smell of fish and dark with wood smoke. Now and then a flake of white ash would fall on them. Rough wooden human buildings lined the shore except for the far end. There, across the middling stream that struggled to flush the place, was a large stone wall, more vertical and smoothly finished than the dike across the harbor entrance.

Against this dock were tied wooden ships including several small round vessels not much longer than Drin himself, set with triangular sails, and a massive square-sailed ship—perhaps ten Charter units long. The last also had a strange, forward-projecting bow and two rows of oars with which it could presumably maneuver without wind.

"Hey, we're in the harbor!" Yohin shouted. "Don't you have to do something to turn this boat? How the . . . ?" His eyes went wide as the submarine turned to the channel without Mary doing anything. Drin rumbled again.

"Tell me, Mr. Bretz," Mary laughed, "are you happy here?"

"It puts bread on the table. Feeds me and my wife, gets me some respect. Even got a couple of slaves. I've been doing it 150 years. Yeah, I'm happy. Don't need any fancy stuff."

"Slaves?" Mary asked. "You have slaves?"

"Sure," Yohin said. "Someone's got to do the work while I'm out piloting. Be a shame if my wife had to, and I'm too tired after a day of this."

"Are the slaves happy?"

"I feed 'em well. They don't know anything else, so why shouldn't they be?"

Drin hissed. This manifestation of disgust, he realized, was wasted on this human pilot. "Do your slaves want to be slaves?" he asked. Yohin turned to him in surprise.

"They were captured fair and square. They know the game. What business is it of yours, Mister, excuse me, *Lieutenant* fish-man?"

"The primitive lifestyle is supposed to be voluntary. No one should be compelled to live like this."

"Look, I didn't set this up. But if you come after my slaves, you got an argument with me. Maybe from them, too. What would you do with them? Send them to some machine school so they can contemplate their navels for the rest of eternity? They're better off working for me.

"Now, lady," the pilot waved his hand at the other side of the harbor, "you've got to turn this tub sharp starboard and make dead on for the flagpole on the end of the fort . . . however you do it."

The submarine turned as if to the pilot's command, and he nodded judiciously.

"Never knew a woman could run a boat. But you do OK."

"I've got a lot of help," Mary said. "Yohin, I can imagine you doing this in one of those sailing ships with the wind blowing, using only your judgment and what you can see from the surface. I respect the skill you need to do that."

The pilot nodded his head and bared his teeth again. Mary, Drin realized, was gaining trust.

This human, Drin thought, had found whatever Gri'il had been seeking when she left civilization for the beach. The question was whether the failures should be allowed with the successes, particularly if the failures were involuntary.

"You said something about the whalers playing games with the Do'utians. What kind of games?"

"I heard there's a deal where the fishmen try to outfox the whalers. Them that lose are meat, but word is that's how they want it."

Drin rumbled his skepticism.

"Who sets up these games?" Mary asked.

"How the hell should I know? Maybe Lord Thet does. You can ask him, we're almost there."

The submarine's hull was well below the level of the dock, due in part to Drin's massive presence. From sea level, he couldn't see the rest of the top of the dock. The angle got worse as they fetched up next to the stones.

Carefully, using the wall as an additional point of balance, he swung his tail over the side and reared up on his hind legs, hooked the rippled pads of his front toes over the edge of the stone wall, bringing his head above dock level.

The man waiting for them on the dock by the city gate was probably Lord Thet. He was a head taller than Mary, gray-robed, and had thick black hair all over his face so that only the eyes and the nostril wattle showed when his mouth was shut. His robe covered either armor or what would, for a human, be an exceptionally large body. Others of his kind, holding metal-tipped spears, stood beside him. Perhaps fifty humans carrying some sort of primitive wood and cord weapons stood well back of the primitivist leader.

Mary was able to scramble up his back and jump from his shoulder to the stone platform. Undignified, but it got the job done. There was a fair amount of wind and harbor noise, but Mary left her comset on her belt, where it could see and record everything. Drin listened through his ear-phone.

"Hello, I'm Mary Pierce, Planetary Monitor."

"You are not wanted here," Lord Thet stated—with aggressive impo-liteness, Drin thought.

"Your name?" Mary asked.

The man remained silent, but the comset camera got a good look at him and the Monitor net quietly relayed the information through their ear-phones. He'd left civilization early in life and, despite his commanding presence, was largely ignorant of things beyond what he controlled.

"You are Jacob Lebbretzky, otherwise known as 'Lord Thet' according to your voice and features. I'll be gone fairly quickly if you answer my ques-tions," she told him.

"Don't overestimate your authority, Monitor. Your superiors are not that interested in us and your charter is open to interpretation."

Wishful thinking on his part, Drin felt—while the Monitors would bend over backward not to be overbearing, there was no question about the final outcome.

But only he and Mary were here right now, things were nowhere near final, and if this egomaniac idiot had talked himself into believing he could get away with minor violence . . . or if someone else had talked him into be-lieving . . .

Drin spoke quickly with his beak shut so that only Mary could hear him on her earphone. "Mary, this fool could be dangerous. He's gotten so big he's forgotten what's backing us up."

She raised a hand to acknowledge him, but continued to face Lord Thet. "Someone's killed at least four Do'utian primitivists," she told him.

"Have the fish-men accused us?"

"We found the bodies."

"Death happens. Only the untested live forever."

An ancient Do'utian philosophy, Drin thought. Why was he hearing it from an ignorant human primitivist? Do'utians did not die of old age, but reproduced slowly enough that in the natural state, mating battles, disease, and accidents of the hostile sea were enough to maintain a population bal-ance. But humans had eliminated aging and limited fertility with genetic en-gineering in historic times.

"You hunt them, don't you?" Mary pressed. "Your people hunt them in ships, as if they were animals."

Lebbretzsky was silent for a heartbeat or so, then said, "The contest is more even than that. There is no opportunity for heroism on either side without the opportunity for death. And the deaths let us raise new children uncontaminated by your machine culture."

This made Drin hiss as he thought of the stinking harbor, the human slaves, and the feral Do'utian women in his "harem." The sound got the momentary attention of the human, who probably had no idea of what it signified.

"Mr. Lebbretzsky," Mary responded, "I take your statement to mean that you know what I'm talking about. It has to stop, and the persons responsible must be reeducated. If you attempt to conceal them, then you will be a candidate for reeducation yourself."

Drin saw the man raise his arm as if to strike Mary, then put it down. Lebbretzsky, Drin realized, might be so ignorant and so deeply into these murders that he felt he had nothing to lose in an attack on a Monitor. Drin slipped a manipulator into his pouch holster for the second time. The movement of his tongue seemed to go unnoticed, or at least uncomprehended.

"Woman. Tell your superiors that your presence is an insult. Tell them that their interference with our culture is an interference of our rights to live and die the way we want. Tell them that we have not murdered anyone, and that the next time they want questions answered, not to send women and fish to ask them."

"Pollution!" Drin sent. "The victims were stabbed and butchered! But be careful, Mary."

The man continued: "There are no murders, woman Monitor. Now get out of here, or we will do what we can to eject you. You may have better weapons, but we are not afraid to die."

"Drin, better call that Kleth backup," Mary said aloud. Drin almost rejoined that he had done that hours ago—then realized that Mary was saying that for Lebbretzsky's benefit.

"Lebbretzsky," she continued, "I don't care what you think it is; attacking and killing Do'utians with harpoons is murder just as much as if you did it to me. The cultural group can deal with the whys later, but my job is to stop it, now. Who has been doing it? Where are they?"

Drin tensed. Mary, in her fearless eagerness to erase what she saw as a blot on her race, was pushing a bull on its own beach. Wrong species, but in this case, Drin feared some convergent evolution. As if to confirm his thoughts, the big human drew a long knife. Mary backed quickly away from him and got her gun out. Drin put a manipulator in his pouch and keyed his comset by feel. He dumped everything they had so far into the Monitor net—just in case he and Mary didn't survive her abuse of Lord Thet's hospitality.

"All right," Mary yelled. "Lebbretzsky, drop the weapon and lie down. You are in custody. You can arrange representation after you've been secured."

"Mary . . ." Drin sent. Too late. Lebbretzsky's hand seemed to flick and the knife flew at Mary. Her gun got it on doppler, flashed, and a smart bullet locked on the thing and knocked it out of the air. The two humans stared at each other in silence for a few seconds as if in a momentary stalemate. But here and now Lebbretzsky had overwhelming numbers. He made some kind of a signal and a hundred darts flew at Mary, some at Drin. He and Mary both fired as fast as their weapons could, but Mary was hit.

"Got my leg," she said with professional calmness. "Drin, let's get out of here."

Drin roared and with the occasional supreme effort his race could summon, pulled himself over the edge of the dock and scrambled toward Mary. The human archers paused in surprise and he flung his tongue out to his injured partner. He was just able to grab her leg with one manipulator and was pulling her to him when the primitivists started shooting again. He reeled Mary in with one manipulator while the other sent smart bullets at the legs of the crossbow archers.

Mary, a small moving target, wasn't hit again. But despite both their guns knocking dozens of darts off their trajectories, he was hit himself. The darts irritated like the spines of the giant dagger snail, but none seemed to reach below his layer of fat, and none had hit his eyes.

Some of the men with swords charged at him. He waited until they were too close, then quickly turned and swept the polluting snailbrains over the side of the dock with his tail. Then, with Mary firmly in his beak, he leapt into the harbor after them.

"Hold your breath," he said on the way down. He landed so as to spray as much water around as possible.

Momentarily sheltered by confusion and the high wall, he had time to help Mary into the submarine hatch. Then, thinking of the large harpoon he'd seen in the erstwhile beachmaster, Drin headed, fast and direct, for the harbor entrance. He sprinted through the harbor with a surface-racing tail-stroke, and used his legs to help him over the shallow spots. This time, he didn't even notice the dirty water.

A look back told him the human primitivists were busy with their colored flags again, and when he ducked under water he could hear the sound of the harbor gate creaking shut. Another look above water showed him that the large ship with oars was underway and pursuing them.

He reached the canal through the harbor wall well before the submarine, and sped to its end. But the massive gate was already closed and locked. He put his beak against it and pressed as hard as he could, and the thrusts of his tail sent waves of brackish brown water back down the channel. The gates hardly noticed.

He surfaced and scouted the channel walls. They were not quite vertical, perhaps widening half a Charter unit over two Charter units of rise, and the cobbled surface provided plenty of claw holds. It would not be out of the question to attempt to climb it.

But first he tried bellowing at the watchmen to open the gate. Not to his surprise, they refused. He did, however, have the satisfaction of seeing their little guardhouse collapse from resonance. Looking back, he saw the submarine enter the channel with the oar ship in hot pursuit.

"Mary, what's your status?" he sent.

"I got the dart out, patched the wound and patched the suit. Hurts like hell. I won't be running around for a while. I'm a little worried about that ram."

"Ram?"

"That rowboat with the solid nose that's chasing me. It's got to weigh a cube, it's moving fast, it's built to bash things, and it doesn't have any brakes. How are you doing on that gate?"

Weigh a cube? That was about eight-times-four as much as his body. Pollution!

"No luck at all," he sent. "Any chance your submarine can ram it open?"

"I'll try the underwater grate. That has to be the weak point."

Drin moved to the side of the canal and watched the humped deck of the submarine flow by him. Its wake grew, then disappeared. There was silence for a heartbeat, than a muffled boom. The gate held.

"Mary?" he asked.

"I'm OK, considering. Might have done some damage. Going to back off for another try."

She did, but that was no more successful than the first.

"Drin, if you can climb out of this, you'd better get going."

The primitivist ram had entered the canal at full speed. Clearly, they were going to try to crush both Drin and the submarine between the ram and the gate, regardless of what damage that did to the latter two. The slaves rowing the ram, he realized, probably didn't know their ship was charging at a locked gate. And its officers must believe, wrongly, that destroying Drin and Mary gave them a chance to avoid reeducation.

But there was no chance to discuss it with them now. Drin threw himself at the canal wall and his legs found claw holds on the rocks under water. Carefully, he heaved himself up the near vertical embankment. But as soon as he tried to put any weight at all on his forelegs, claws slipped on the damp mossy covering of the stones near the waterline, and he tumbled back into the canal. He tried it once more, then saw the submarine break the surface and start accelerating backward at the ram.

"Mary!" he bellowed, forgetting the comset.

"I got us into this, I baited them. I'd rather go down fighting." Despite the brave words, her voice trembled. "Good luck, friend."

He clung half in and out of the water like a paralyzed lungfish and watched the two human vessels collide. There was a tremendous thundering boom as they hit, followed by cracking and splintering sounds. In seeming slow motion, the ram rode up over the submarine and the rock walls transmitted an eerie hollow grating sound to him as the submarine's keel scraped along the canal's stone bottom. The combined wreck grated down the channel with scarcely diminished speed like a piston toward the massive gate.

There was too little room for him to remain where he was. He released his hold, slipped back into the water, and swam for the gate. Maybe everything would grind to a halt before it got there.

Underwater, Drin heard a sudden, ear-piercing crack. Pollution! he thought, the hull of the submarine must have broken. He surfaced and looked back. Both ends of the submarine stuck out of the water. The primitivist ship rode farther up on one of the pieces and then fell off to the side, gouging its ram into the side of the canal. Its stern hit the other side and, with a great screeching and rending, the keel of the ram snapped, leaving the broken human ship stopped sideways in the channel. Men, some of them skewered by splintered oars, tumbled from the broken vessel like fish from a torn net. The mess ground to a halt just a Charter unit from the gate.

"Mary?" he sent. There was no answer. Flames, from spilled heating fires aboard the ram, or discharging power leads on the submarine, began spreading in the above-water wreckage.

Drin threw himself into the devastation, prying blood-stained pieces of the ram away from the broken submarine hull. There was movement all around him, and he saw that the human survivors were having no better luck than he in climbing the slippery canal sides. Hoping that the time it took would not prove critical, Drin seized the still upright mast in his beak, snapped it with a vicious twist of his body, and let it fall so that its top rested on the dike above.

"CLIMB!" he roared to anyone who would listen.

Some of the astonished humans caught on and began scrambling up the mast to safety above. One was a large red-bearded man—the same one, he realized, that had mocked him from the decks of another ship only weeks ago. They stared at each other in a frozen moment of recognition, but Drin had more than an arrest on his mind.

Ignoring minor burns and lacerations, Drin clawed away the remains of a lower deck to expose the broken pressure hull of the submarine. It was filled with water. Drin stuck his tongue in and located the cockpit from feel and memory. Mary was not in the seat, but he could scent her blood. He felt around the tiny compartment, using both branches. He found her underwater gear, and, presuming success, grabbed it. A few more precious seconds, and he found Mary motionless in a small air pocket near the back of the cockpit.

With both branches wrapped around her, he strained to pull her up like a hatchling, into his mouth. With her legs sticking painfully down his throat, he was just able to close his beak over her head. Then he smashed his way out of the wreck, inhaled an hour's worth of air, and dove back into the putrid water. Over-buoyant, he swam down to the wooden grid and held on with his legs.

There was hardly room for both Mary and his tongue, so, with the skill of a contortionist, he managed to slip a loop of the tongue out the fleshy corner of his mouth, leaving the ends of the manipulator branches inside. Drin lowered his head and squeezed water from her lungs. They reinflated on their own as he forced the water from his mouth with air from his bladder. He squeezed again. She moved. Conscious? He hoped she would understand quickly enough not to panic.

He felt her hand pat one of his fingers. It seemed a controlled, understanding, gesture. He turned his attention to his external predicament.

With gloom and debris in the water, and Aurum low in the antarctic sky, he should be invisible from above. He began exploring the bottom of the gate where the submarine had smashed into it. Here and there, an outer buffer of great tree trunks had been smashed to kindling. But nothing behind had broken enough to let him through.

There was purposeful movement inside his mouth. "Drin, I've got my gills on. You can let me out now." Mary's voice in his ear was the best news he'd had since he'd come into the primitivist cesspool. Using his tongue to keep her from bobbing to the surface, he expelled the bubble of air from his mouth, then let her float free.

"How do you feel?" he asked.

"Lousy. No broken bones, I think. Tired. I've still got a little fluid in my lungs." She drifted slowly over to the grate and surveyed the damaged gate. "I guess I didn't put a hole in this thing."

"It appears not."

Trapped. They were both silent.

"Uh, Drin? Can you think of any way we could make them think I did break through? If they think we're already gone maybe they'll open the gate to come after us, or to clear the floating debris."

The grate was too fine for even Mary to squeeze through—it was probably designed with human sappers in mind. His tongue could just fit, but wasn't long enough. But maybe . . .

"I could try to blow a bubble with some debris through the grate and out the other side."

"Hey, go for it!"

He did it, placing his blowhole against one of the spaces between the beams of an undamaged section and blew. Some of it escaped on their side, but not much—some must have gone through. They waited for a subjective eternity. He was on the point of suggesting another frontal assault when they heard a hideous, hollow, creak.

They waited. Nothing.

Then another creak. Drin thought he could detect a slight shudder.

"I think they're trying to open it," he said. "You might have jammed it a bit when you rammed it. That's a case of an emotional, spur of the moment action that did exactly the opposite of—"

"Drin, your folk's eyes are built for hindsight. Why don't you stop philosophizing and just try to help them open the gate?"

Of course. With a firm clawhold on the bottom stones, and not having to fight gravity, Drin could apply his full strength. He waited until a creak signified another attempt to open the gate, then *pushed*. Slowly it began to move. There was a crack and a grind as something let go. Drin released his hold immediately, and the gate began to swing open on its own.

Hiding on the bottom beneath flotsam from the wreck, they drifted with the current out through the opening. Then, with Mary hanging onto a leg, he swam hard for clear water until he judged they were well over Lord Thet's horizon. He surfaced, turned on his back and sheltered Mary between his legs as he would a hatchling, and let horizon-grazing Ember and Aurum do what they could to warm her, while he took great breaths through his mouth to rid himself of heat and to pay his oxygen debt.

Mary was quiet for a while, exhausted, Drin surmised. So it startled him when she suddenly sat up and yelled: "Look, Drin, contrails!"

Do Tor had finally arrived.

Among all races, when violence is obviously futile, reason is encouraged. For this reason, where there is the likelihood of an irrational physical confrontation, the inclusion of a large Do'utian Monitor is highly recommended. Humans excel where strength is needed in confined places. And, where overhead intelligence and logistic agility are required, the Kleth can make a major contribution—but care should be taken to avoid endangering Kleth individually.

—Planet Monitor's Handbook,
Team Composition

. . . their mating bond is such that individuals become physiologically dependent on each other. A Kleth seldom survives the death of a mate, nor is their any record of one wanting to do so. Efforts to sustain life in these circumstances are always futile and should not be attempted.

—Planet Monitor's Handbook,
Medical Appendix

The Kleth aircraft met them just over the horizon from Lord Thet's city, on the beach of an uninhabited island dominated by a huge granite crag that gave shelter from the circumpolar wind. After greetings, Team Leader Do Tor and his mate started unloading supplies.

Mary was exhausted, so Drin scraped a deep pit in the sand for her, gathered wood, and lit a fire. Then, despite her exhaustion, and still limping from her wound, she insisted on washing her clothes and body in the frigid polar water, and turned an amazing shade of blue before she got back to the fire.

"D-don't worry," she told him as she shook convulsively under a blanket in front of the fire, "It's-s h-how we get our b-body heat b-back up."

Do Tor and his mate stretched their wings to catch some fish for her, and jibbered with amusement as she threw away all the good parts and heated the remaining muscle almost to the point of decomposition on a flat stone she put by the fire. Drin looked forward to having a good long feed later that night, in his own manner, on his way back to Gri'il's beach.

"Sorry late. Assumed you'd just leave Thet and wait for us," the Klethan said in a guttural, sing-song English that was actually lower pitched than Mary's, despite his being less than half her mass.

"We tried," Mary laughed. "Things got in the way. We surface dwellers have certain problems about just flying away when things turn sour."

"Don't understand why primitivists had so much technology."

"Lack of interest on our part. Ignorance of the Charter and evolutionary pressure on theirs," Drin offered. "The best fighters end up in charge, and the best fighters are, more often than not, those with the best weapons. Also, if you can't make it clever, make it big." It would be a long while before he would forget the huge ram bearing down on him. "I doubt that Lord Thet or many of his people even understand why the Charter prohibits development in these areas; they've rebelled against anything resembling a scientific education."

"For humans, there is an inherent contradiction between 'back to nature' and 'no technology,'" Mary contributed, "because human nature *is* to make and use tools. So what happens is that the primitivists reinvent the wheel using primitive technology that, per capita, pollutes unmercifully and requires gobs of labor." Mary picked up a stone and threw it out of sight. "So then you get leadership dominance games that the most ruthless win, with slave labor of one sort or another for the losers. That works well long enough for the glandular bullies to start assembling miniature empires, and then . . ." She shook her head. "Allowing this Lord Thet set-up was taking noninterference too far, in my view. But that's up to the council. Anyway, we have our killers."

"Maybe," Drin demurred. "But I don't think this is a one-species issue." From a philosophical standpoint he certainly didn't want it to be human versus Do'utian, but something more than that was bothering him. "I'm not sure we have the whole story. In defending his hunting, the human Jacob Lebretzsky seemed to include the Do'utian primitivists in his defense."

"Do'utians help get selves butchered?" Do Tor clucked. "Strange thing, I think."

"If you think in groups, yes. But that isn't the natural Do'utain way to think." Drin moved his head slightly from side to side in mild negation. "I want to ask Gri'il some questions and learn more about this murdered beachmaster and his harem. I may have made some unfair assumptions about the last victim."

"Name was Glodego'alah, by the way," Do Tor added. "Left the north pole as a disillusioned student eight cubed great revolutions ago. Not happy as primitivist, either, but responsible. Took care of harem. Good being. We did our homework." The Kleth held its hard translucent wings out in a gesture of pride.

"Oh yes," his mate said, the first words she uttered, surprising Drin. Until now, Go Ton had been inert, folded up. One partner or the other might dominate, but they were always together. Divorce was unknown, as were widows or widowers. Go Ton's contribution was unusually forward, for a subordinate Klethan. But Monitor couples were known to be more independent.

"Did you bring the Do'utian interface coronet?" Drin asked.

"Not so late, otherwise." Do Tor rummaged in the pile of unloaded supplies and found a glasscloth package the size of a folded human tent. "Here."

Drin placed it in his pouch. Its woven-in antennae picked up and decoded motor nerve impulses—even those sent to absent peripheries. Now, not only could he ask questions of Gri'il; she would be able to answer.

There were also a tent and collapsible kayak for Mary. The tent fit nicely in the hollow he had dug, and she opened it up with its door to the fire. As it resumed its memorized shape, she turned to her fellow monitors.

"This," she said, "is camping. It's what most of us have in mind when we think of going back to nature, or living in a primitive situation. But, as you see, it's not primitive at all. And it's not social, we usually try to get away from other people when we do this. What's happened back at Thet just hasn't really registered with my people. I—"

"Mary, why should it register with you any more than with the rest of us?" Drin interrupted. "You have no special responsibility for them just because they happen to be human. There is no need to apologize."

"Oh yes, Go Ton agrees," Do Tor's mate spoke up. "We are one civilization on this world. Whole purpose of Planet Trimus. Eight-cubed years of lives meaningless if not. Eyes of Trimus we are. We should have noticed violations before dead bodies appear."

"Any Do'utian can smell that place in currents an eighth of the way around the planet. We ignored it," Drin said.

"Th-thanks," Mary said. "I just . . ." She shook her head and made sounds of human sadness, though Drin thought it was more in relief. He flicked out his tongue and wrapped his fingers around her hand, and she rewarded the gesture by squeezing him gently back, and baring her teeth in a big smile.

"We all go to the beach tomorrow, and gain more understanding," Do Tor said. "Now rest."

"You rest," Drin answered, reminding him that Do'utians didn't sleep in the eternal days of a polar summer. "I need to eat, feed the harem, and keep my injuries in water until they heal more. I will see you there at the beach. Take care, Mary."

She hugged his fingers to her, careless of her wrap, and his most sensitive organs were pressed into the alien heat and smell of her. He was overwhelmed for a moment, then she released him. "Yeah, you too," she said.

He backed away from the fire carefully, to avoid upsetting anything. Clear, he turned. And as his body turned toward the water, his mind followed, thinking ahead to his duties. His cuts and bruises were beginning to hurt, true. But something in the back of his mind was pushing him, something perhaps as powerful as the instinctual desire to join with the harem that chose him as their provider and their protector. It did not make sense to him that humans—even as degenerate as Lord Thet and his gang—would or could suddenly start preying on Do'utians, even given the sort of general philosophical license primitivism in both species seemed to grant. Something less random and more evil was happening. Perhaps Gri'il could help him.

The Planetary Civilization must be permitted to evolve, and experiments must be encouraged, for only through change is knowledge expanded.
                                    —The Compact and Charter of Planet Trimus, Article 5

Aurum stood high above Ember when Drin returned to the harem beach with his mouth full of fish, and the star had moved a dociradian west by the time he finished the simple duty of placing the fish into throats. Once done, he unpacked the neural interface cap and approached Gri'il.

Even now she hesitated, putting her nose to the beach. Despite everything that had happened, her distaste for this artificiality was evident. But then, apparently recognizing the necessity, she raised her head and came to him. He fitted the cap over her.

"It will take a while to calibrate itself. There will be a bit of a delay to start with, but you'll get used to it. Now, just tell me your name, as if you were whole again. Repeat it until the computer in the cap gets it right."

It produced an intelligible "Gri'illaboda" after about six tries, and she got used to it in a few more. Finally, she could speak through the device more or less naturally.

"OK," Drin said. "I'm going to record this, so why don't we start by having you say who you are?"

"I am Gri'illaboda, co-mate of Drinnil'ib."

Great. Just great. "I am sorry, Gri'il. I am a planetary monitor, and not a primitivist. I care for you, yes—but more as a senior family member, not as a mate."

"You replaced our beachmaster, mated with my co-mates."

"It was not my choice. I did not seek you or them to mate."

She was silent for a few heartbeats. He could hear the waves and the sea birds.

"Drinnil'ib, I was the daughter of Slora'analta and Broti'ilita. Did you know either of those?"

"The historian."

"Who told the old tales of the free seas and made a romantic out of his daughter. I was bored with school. I met a free rover. He took me here, quickened my ovaries . . . then took my tongue."

"Glodego'alah?"

"Never. Glodego'alah was a tourist who saw what had happened, fought the free rover for us, then took us here to be safe. But he paid for his charity in a way that happens all too often here."

"Then I am sorry for what I thought about Glodego'alah. We are seeking the humans who killed him, and four others who were killed. Did you know any of them? Did they have families here?"

"Glodego'alah remarked once that harems change masters easily because of such human predation. Their ships come in the channels between the islands and the ice pack where beachmasters gather fish."

Drin nodded. "I came close to being a victim myself on my way back from my initial investigation. It is easy enough for them—I suspected nothing until they shot at me. I would think someone down here would warn the humans not to do this."

Gri'il huffed in derision. "The sea lords don't interfere. They say the humans take the weak and the race gets stronger, and that the inbred softness of civilization is thus cleansed from our blood. But Glodego'alah was not soft."

"No, I'm sure he wasn't. Who are these 'sea lords'?"

"They are the free rovers, the ones who take from both poles what they want. They live like beachmasters at the south pole, then swim north and have all the luxuries of civilization. They are . . . the human word is hypocrites."

"And if they don't come back?"

"A harem doesn't stay unmastered long here. A sea lord shows up soon enough to claim a missing master's family. They seem to know, somehow, when one isn't coming back."

Her passiveness disturbed him, but perhaps it was simply adjustment. Early Do'utian history wasn't any prettier than early human history. Less so, in some respects. And the Kleth, of course, were cannibals well into their spacefaring days. Drin shuddered, wondering at his fascination with such things. But he had to ask; it might be important.

"Gri'il, how was your tongue to be taken?" Did she just submit to such an amputation?

"The sea lord who ran off my first mate, said it was traditional. He demanded this after the first mating, then he said he would not take my egg unless I submitted. Also . . . I can't explain. I sometimes feel a need to surrender myself, to let the tides of providence have their way with my flesh. At any rate, I did not resist. In my state at the time, he was God."

Submit to mutilation, or die. Such was her natural paradise. What polluting monster would . . .

"His name?"

"Gota'lannshk." The same ruffian he encountered at Cragen's? Drin hissed in disgust.

"You know of him?"

"We met. Look, Gri'il, will you come back to the North with me? For treatment."

"We are bound to you. I need to stay with you, to submit to you. And I have the eggs, remember? Or are you so civilized that that doesn't matter?"

The eggs probably shouldn't be hatched, Drin thought. Two fathers. No tests. No family. No birth allocation.

"Gri'il, compulsions are subject to medical intervention. My duty is to try to right the wrongs done so far, if I can, and prevent others from being done. Can you get the others to come?" And how many more were there out in those islands. Should they save them all? By force if needed?

"If it is clear that we are leaving, they will come, for whatever good it will do them."

"We'll regenerate their tongues, teach them to speak, send them to school."

"They were hatched out here. Their minds were untrained during the crucial years."

Truly feral. He feared as much. "Still, we have to try. We can find a deserted northern island for your co-mates, and arrange for them to be watched. But what about you? Now that this has happened, can't you see your way back to—"

"To what? We live with the humans and the Kleth on this planet at the expense of ceasing to live like Do'utians, at the expense of always pulling against our own inner nature. And the stars are too far apart for it to matter. I showed my tail to all of that. Say what you want. I lived. I swam in the wild currents. I did it on the beach. You want me to go back to that northern emotional straitjacket and listen to all those proper titters and I told you so's? I'd rather die!"

And her present state was not a humiliation? But her age-old argument, Drin thought, was unanswerable. The civilization of Trimus was for those who thought it mattered.

"We don't want to tell you how to live. I'm sure your privacy would be respected, and protected."

"Like in a zoo! Drinnil'ib, you rescued us, fed us. Don't you want us? Don't you feel the need to own and protect us? Or in the name of your Compact have you let the humans reengineer your sex?"

Drin groaned. He wanted her enough, but he did not *want* to want her. At least not as she was now. The whine of fans reached him before he could find a suitable way to explain that. Mary! Relief flowed through him. The aircraft settled on its fans, the hatch popped, and Drin walked over to greet his partner, leaving Gri'il with her beak in the gravel.

But Mary was nowhere in sight.

"Mary?" he called, worried.

Do Tor opened the canopy, jibbered to his machine, and the cargo door popped open. Of course, Drin realized. There was no room in the Kleth cockpit for a human, and indeed, it took Mary a while to unfold herself from the cramped space.

"I'm here, Drin."

"It's good to see you!" He explained about the sea lords. "So I think your human hunters have Do'utian accomplices, at least in principle. But things still don't swim well in my mind."

"The strongest, fastest, or most clever survive. I can see that, I guess. You think the Sea Lords were using Lord Thet to cull their herd, so to speak?"

"That seems to fit."

"Well, Lord Thet's gang of wannabe barbarians seems to be only too happy to help. Your people are the most challenging hunt in the ocean, they probably think."

"Brings up the question of whether we have right to interfere," Do Tor observed.

"To save lives?" Drin protested. "Of course we do."

Mary sighed and gestured to the sky. "Drin, there are now many beings out there who can trace their origins to our home worlds, but who have engineered so much into themselves that they look on *us* as primitivists. They could make a problem like Lord Thet vanish in an instant with no loss of life—but would we want that?"

"Those who didn't get killed might appreciate it."

Mary shook her head. "The parts of our natures that lead to this mess could easily be changed, but then what would we be? Death, even random death, may have a justifiable role in society that transcends individual needs. Perhaps, to keep our identity, we need to learn to accept that."

"I think," Drin asserted, perhaps a little more loudly than necessary, "that such issues should be debated by the planetary council and that *our* job is to not let anyone else get killed until they do and decide . . . whatever. Now, I have four physically mutilated and three of them intellectually mutilated—Do'utian women to bring back to where they can be properly protected and cared for. Let's do that and sort the rest out later."

"Agreed," Do Tor chuckled. Mary nodded quietly.

"Gri'il," Drin said, "is there any way the others can be told of how long a journey this will be?"

"They will follow you if I do," she said, coldly, it seemed. "But the hunters will be watching."

"And the planet will be watching them!" Drin proclaimed. "They won't dare do anything."

"I will ride with you," Mary said. "In full uniform. At least they'll know what they're playing with."

Drin didn't remind her of how persuasive her uniform and submarine were at Thet harbor.

"We'll fly cover with loud voices and guns," Do Tor said, spreading his wings. "Aircraft can fly itself, so that makes three above."

"Oh yes," his mate chimed. So it was decided. A convoy North.

Drin led the way into the water the next morning with Mary's warm legs and arms comfortably around his neck. They'd fashioned a light glasscloth collar for him that she could grasp and so hold her position in the current of his passage. This was no irritation, but the bulge of an appliance she had constructed to protect her wounded knee was a noticeable reminder of their vulnerability in these waters—many more monitors would be needed to handle Lord Thet and his allies without loss of life.

Gri'il came quietly after him, and as predicted, the harem followed.

It was a fine gray day with favorable surface winds, and light, cooling surface squalls. A brackish current flowed north here from the ice cap on the largest southern island, overlying warmer saline water flowing from an inner pole drainage basin, and so the Do'utians had made good time without becoming overtired.

By the morning of the second day, Lord Thet's domain was well behind them, and they glided through the waves halfway into reef-crowded tropical waters. A volcanic island with wide black beaches lay to their left, and a reef to their right, but the channel was fairly deep. Drin was just beginning to relax and enjoy the scenery when the human ships appeared.

"Don't think they're hunters," Do Tor sent. "Big Do'utian male right with them, no shooting."

"Can you describe him?" Drin asked.

"One and three-eighths Charter unit long. Big white crescent-shaped scar behind the blowhole. Do you know him?"

"If it's who I think it is, I've smelled him before. A harem-coveting sea lord with his tail across two beaches. It's time to ask that rogue a few questions."

Gri'il and her co-mates keened as if they were being mortally wounded.

"It sounds like our refugees have smelled him before as well," he continued. "I'd better let those humans know what we're about. Ready, Mary?"

"Gills on." He felt her arms as well as her legs encircle his neck, and her hands grasp the collar. She was secure. He dove and, slamming the ocean back and forth with his tail, headed toward the lead human ship much faster than he could manage on the surface.

About ten Charter units from the hull, he broke water again. So did his harem—he'd forgotten to tell Gri'il to stay back. It shouldn't be necessary, but he was uneasy.

"Mary, I'm not sure how much comfort we should take from Gota'lannshk being present."

"Why would they shoot at us and not him?"

"Why is there a sea lord always ready to inherit the harem of a victim? Why did Gota'lannshk seem to know that I'd had a close call with these hunters when we met him at Cragen's?"

"Lord Thet—"

"Mary, I don't want to insult your species, but I don't think that idiot has been running this atrocity."

"Huh? Why?"

"Later. I just hope these people have sense enough to keep out of this." Drin inhaled and boomed as authoritatively as he could, "Human ship, we are Planet Monitors escorting citizens on an official mission. We need to ask your companion some questions. Please do not interfere. I say again, do not interfere."

Mary waved at them and smiled.

The report of the harpoon gun reached him first, then Mary's scream and the sharp, deep pain in his neck.

"Look out!" Do Tor yelled over the radio link.

The taste of blood was in his throat. He dove and heard a sharp smack on the water over him. Instinct said to head for the very bottom, but Mary, if she were still alive—he could no longer feel any pressure from her legs—wouldn't survive that. Despite the pain, he pushed water hard and got about eight-squared Charter units away from the ship before he surfaced again.

"Mary?" he called. If those polluting, suicidal, feral idiots had killed her . . .

There was no answer. Oblivious of his wound, he turned back toward the ship, rage building.

"Do Tor, I can't see behind my head. What's happened to Mary?" Did the Kleth follow him?

"Drin. Long spear in your neck. Went through Mary first, through her leg. Not necessarily fatal wound, but suggest you make for nearest island. Go Ton will go with you. West, Drin, *now*. I've called aircraft down. That ship will not fire again. Go!"

As if to contradict the Kleth, the harpoon gun fired again and the lance slapped the water beside him. He could hear warning blasts from the aircraft and Go Ton squawking at the top of her lungs, telling the human ship to stop shooting. In the name of eternal repudiation, the murderers would pay for this! He started swimming toward the ship.

He felt, more than saw, a Do'utian charge under him directly at the human vessel.

"GRI'IL, NO!" he bellowed hopelessly, much too late.

The impact boomed out, sound reaching him underwater before through the air. Then, beneath, he heard the creaking and cracking of wood and the screams of humans underwater.

"Drin!" Do Tor screamed. "Get to that island, now. I take care of this. I will mark them. They will not escape, not melt into primitivist population. I mark. Go, now, save yourself. Save Mary."

"Drin," a soft voice called. "I'm awake. It hurts like hell, but if you have to go back for her, I understand. I can take it."

Reason returned. "Mary. No. I'll have to trust Do Tor." There was no way Gri'il could have survived that impact. No way that he would have. And the eggs . . . it was better that way. Perhaps Gri'il had known that. But his wound had little to do with the effort it took to push himself toward the island.

A whistle and some kind of explosion sounded behind him. Then another. He could hear loudspeakers. Killing for killing—perhaps they would understand *that*. Then, somewhere from the back of his mind, between the currents of pain and grief, a thought formed in an eddy of cold fear. Gota'lannshk had disappeared when the shooting started. To where?

The island was a long swim on the surface and he gagged on his blood by the time he got there. Go Ton was waiting at water's edge, alone, with a med kit that must have weighed as much as she did.

"Come on, just a few steps farther, above the tide line," she urged.

He did that, then he was on his belly, his tail still in moist sand. Go Ton fluttered to the top of his head, out of sight. He heard the buzz of a bone saw, and the shaft of the harpoon soon tumbled to the ground. There was a yelp, quickly stifled, from Mary. Then a numbness started spreading through the wound. Soon he felt as if he didn't know what had happened to him, that all that was wrong with him was a stiff neck.

"Now, Mary," Go Ton said, "I know it looks awful, but I think it best to leave that piece in your leg alone until help arrives. Human aircraft will be here in eight-fourth beats. Might do more harm than good if I try to remove it now."

"I understand," she said, "this sounds ridiculous, but right now I feel OK, except my leg is dead to the world. I'll be all right as long as I don't look at it. Can you help me down?"

"Not alone. Lieutenant Drin, can you lend a tongue?"

His tongue still worked; the barb had not gone in that deeply, perhaps in part because Mary's leg had slowed its entry. He reached back, and between the three of them, they were able to lower Mary down to the sand.

"Where's Do Tor?" she asked.

Pollution! She'd forgotten, Drin realized, and he couldn't warn her with his tongue extended so far.

"He's with the aircraft cleaning up the mess with the human ships," Go Ton responded, shakily. "He should have everything well in hand and be back with us soon."

"You've been too busy helping us to check!" Mary said. "I'll contact him, let him know we made it, and find out how things are."

"Please do not do that," Go Ton pleaded.

Just a little farther, Drin thought. There! Mary was safely down, and he could speak again.

"But, I know how much he means to you—" Mary started, oblivious to the danger.

"That's *why*, Mary," Drin interrupted, "for the sake of providence, think!" The Kleth team had taken the ultimate risk for them, and Go Ton's position was precarious. She would live as long as she believed her mate alive. But if everything was *not* fine with Do Tor, that would effectively eliminate Go Ton as well. "We need Go Ton just now."

"Oh!" Mary said. Everyone was quiet for a heartbeat. Then Mary continued, her voice with a certain forced steadiness. "Go Ton. Uh, that human garbage doesn't have any weapon that can hurt Do Tor. He'll be fine."

That human garbage shouldn't, Drin thought, have had any weapon that could have hurt him or Mary. But here they were.

"Drin, I am stiff-winged on Do'utian first aid," Go Ton said, firmly changing the subject, "but I think the spear should come out of you now. It is the sort that works its way in deeper every time you move, and without Mary's body holding it back . . ."

"Do it." Before the anesthetic, Drin could sense how close the barb had worked itself toward his central nervous column. He had arteries and blood to spare, but didn't want to stop breathing just yet.

"If you could roll on your side . . ." Go Ton asked. He complied, then lay silently, feeling little tugs and tears in his flesh and tried to imagine one of Go Ton's tiny thin horny arms deep in his flesh with knives, cutting a passage for the barbed spearhead.

Then the Kleth said: "Mary, need help. The strength of your arms."

Using the discarded shaft of the spear as a crutch, Mary hobbled around behind him, patting him on the beak as she went by.

A little later, he heard her say "oof," felt a sharp pull, and saw Mary fall backward into his field of view again—her arms bloody up to the elbows, her hands clutching the cruel barbed spearhead. Go Ton remained behind him; little tugs and pulls continued for another eight-cubed heartbeats.

"Now that's all closed as well as I can do it," Go Ton said.

"Thank you," Drin said, and rolled slowly back onto his belly. "Did the harem follow us here?" The thought of them reminded him of Gri'il. He shut his eyes and let the empty feeling pass.

"Yes, they're huddled together in shallows behind you," Go Ton answered. "They seem very sad, beaks in sand, but are unhurt, I think."

Drin was thinking that Do Tor should have been back by now, and searching his memory for any kind of convention for handling the worst-case situation. There would come a point when, if the news were bad, Go Ton would have to be told, and nature would have to take its course. To do otherwise would be to not respect the decision her people had made to not change this part of their genetic make up. Perhaps the best thing would be to wait until she asked herself. If . . .

The challenge roar echoed off the lava cliffs and caught them all by surprise.

In an instant, before he even realized what it meant, Drin's heart doubled the strength of its beats and he could feel the effects of various body chemicals, not greatly different from those that had hit him when he fertilized the feral eggs. That primordial insult deserved an equally primitive response. But he made himself stay still, and without moving his injured neck, he swiveled an eye to the direction of the noise. Far down the beach, a big, scarred male.

"Same Do'utian we saw with the human hunting ships," Go Ton said from above.

"Gota'lannshk," Drin rumbled, in no shape or mood to play primitive beachmaster games. "His beak is dripping with this. Tell that idiot to stay away from us, before I kill him!"

"Drin," Mary whispered, almost inaudibly, "he's bigger than you, and with your wound you'll kill yourself before you get to him. Try to calm down. Think. If he inherited Glodego'alah's harem, and he was connected with the human hunters—"

"*Precisely*, Mary. A lot easier to get Lord Thet's people to eliminate his rivals than fighting for a harem on the beach the old-fashioned way. These murders were no game of survival of the fittest, or even of macabre chance. Those polluting idiot sea rovers carefully selected the hunting victims and no doubt led Lord Thet's ships right to them. Lord Thet probably lost a few selected men as well, just to keep things even, gain birth allocations, and reduce the number of his political rivals." Drin's anger increased. He should turn the murderer into snail meat. His breath came faster.

"So," Mary said, "the whalers get their hunt, their flesh, and think they're just playing by some tough rules. But it's all fixed ahead of time. Premeditated. Drin, stay down, please. Drin? Drin! Give me your gun."

The Do'utian sea rover bellowed again and blind rage started working its way through Drin. The nerve of that cow stealer! He heaved himself to his feet, oblivious of the wound.

"DRIN!" Mary screamed. "Give me your gun! Drin. Your gun! Now!"

In some small corner of his consciousness, Mary's words got through. Somehow, as he began to rock back and forth on his legs, he sent his tongue into his pouch and retrieved the weapon for Mary, dropping it almost absentmindedly on the sand next to her. That popgun was never, he thought with a last wisp of clarity, meant to stop a charging Do'utian.

He got a whiff of the challenger, ripe with arrogance. He heard his cows keen and smelled their fright. Dimly, he remembered there were things one was supposed to do in beak-to-beak combat, things that used the opponent's charge against him. Ways to use the tail as well as the head to put the other on the sand, but that all seemed very fuzzy and far away just now. All he wanted was to charge and bite the throat.

Hardly even aware that he was doing it, Drin lifted a clawed front leg, dug it deep into sand, and bellowed. The sun was high; it was a good time to taste blood.

The other began its charge. He stomped forward to meet it. Somewhere behind him he heard a series of sharp, high-frequency sounds begin at regular intervals. He didn't care, his body was aflame, producing heat many times faster than he could lose it. He didn't care. It felt good. He felt the wind of his passage build up, giving him some relief. Somehow, both hind legs moved together while both front legs hit slightly apart. The beach shook beneath him. He fixed his eyes on the other's neck, looking for an opening, looking for where the cycle of its charging stride exposed the throat to Drin's beak.

But its neck kept getting lower to the beach. Its charge seemed to become unbalanced and slow. His opponent screamed now in protest and its scent changed from challenge to fear and danger. It keened and shrieked and wavered from side to side.

With the danger call, a bit of consciousness returned to Drin, and he swerved at the last heartbeat, avoiding a collision that could have ripped open his stitched-up insides and left him to bleed to death.

The sea lord collapsed into the sand in front of him, plowing a furrow two Charter units long with its gaping beak. He passed by the hulk in an instant and into an eerie silence. The bellows and the sharp sounds had ended; only the surf and the thunder of his own mad rush sounded on the beach.

Burning inside, Drin exhaled gales, bent his path into the sea and let momentum carry him into the cold water, sliding forward until it covered him. A very gentle bend of his tail brought his head back to the shore.

The drama was not over. The fallen sea lord groaned and snapped at sand. Its right foreleg was covered with blood and bent at a wrong angle. Its hind legs pushed sand uselessly, trying to propel it somewhere. Then it used its tail to turn itself over, trying to roll to the cooling waters of the sea. Once, twice, it rolled. But, as Drin settled himself into the life-giving cold water, the sea rover stopped rolling. Its tail rose majestically and thudded into the sand. Once, twice.

At the last, it threw its tongue at Mary, falling far short. "Dirty human cow," Gota'lannshk screamed at her. Then . . . nothing.

Heat death.

Drin lay in the shallows panting. Fiery pain shot through him. He could taste his own blood again; some of Go Ton's handiwork had come loose. He saw Mary prone, the shaft of the harpoon still projecting bloodily from her leg, her elbows in the sand, his gun in her hands, still aimed at the sea rover. She must have put a hundred bullets in his opponent's knee, but now she shook and moaned. He knew that killing a Do'utian over this was the very last thing she had wanted.

He wished to comfort her, but he was tired. Very, very tired.

His next awareness was of a hotness on his neck. He opened his right eye and looked back. Mary was there, flattened against his neck, gently calling his name.

"Mary," he managed to say, as softly as he had ever said anything, "I'm awake. I'll be OK."

She was apparently having trouble breathing, but turned to his eye and said, "Oh, Drin. Oh, Drin. It's—it's so hard to get my arms around you." Despite her appearance, he somehow knew she was happy.

Noise and smell intruded. The sky over the island beach was filled with both aircraft and Kleth. The death smell of Glodego'alah was there, among the smell of many beings, and the sound of many voices, Kleth, human, and Do'utian. He recognized Do Tor's and Go Ton's among them, and took a ragged but deep breath of satisfaction. Everyone had come through, and, like rational, civilized beings, they were all discussing what was to be done next.

Robert Reed

GUEST OF HONOR

Robert Reed sold his first story in 1986, and quickly established himself as a frequent contributor to *The Magazine of Fantasy & Science Fiction* and *Asimov's Science Fiction,* as well as selling many stories to *Science Fiction Age, Universe, New Destinies, Tomorrow, Synergy, Starlight,* and elsewhere.

Reed may be one of the most prolific of today's young writers, particularly at short-fiction lengths, seriously rivaled for that position only by authors such as Stephen Baxter and Brian Stableford. And—also like Baxter and Stableford—he manages to keep up a very high standard of quality while being prolific, something that is not at all easy to do. Almost every year throughout the mid-to-late nineties, he has produced at least two or three stories that would be good enough to get him into a Best of the Year anthology under ordinary circumstances, and some years he has produced four or five of them, and so often the choice is not whether or not to use a Reed story, but rather which Reed story to use—a remarkable accomplishment. Reed stories such as "The Utility Man," "Birth Day," "Blind," "A Place With Shade," "The Toad of Heaven," "Stride," "The Shape of Everything," "Guest of Honor," "Decency," "Waging Good," and "Killing the Morrow," among at least a half-dozen others equally as strong, count as among some of the best short work produced by anyone in the eighties and nineties. Nor is he non-prolific as a novelist, having turned out eight novels since the end of the eighties, including *The Leeshore, The Hormone Jungle, Black Milk, The Remarkables, Down the Bright Way, Beyond the Veil of Stars, An Exaltation of Larks,* and, most recently, *Beneath the Gated Sky.*

In spite of this large and remarkable body of work, though, Reed remains largely ignored and overlooked when the talk turns to the hot new writers of the nineties, and only recently is he beginning to get on to major award ballots with stories like "Chrysalis," which is on the final Nebula ballot as I type these words. Like Walter Jon Williams and Bruce Sterling, no one Robert Reed story is ever much like another Robert Reed story in tone or subject matter, and it may be that this versatility counts against him as far as building a reputation is concerned. John Clute, in *The Encyclopedia of Science Fiction,* noting that none of Reed's novels "share any background material or assumptions whatsoever," suggests that "today's sf readers tend to expect a kind of brand identity from authors, and it may be for this reason that Reed has not yet achieved any considerable fame."

It seems unfair that the range of an artist's palette should count against him—but Reed's name *is* slowly percolating into the public awareness here at the end of the nineties, and I suspect that he will become one of the big names of the first decade of the new century coming up on the horizon.

Much of Reed's output takes him beyond our purview here, into fantasy, horror, and other types of science fiction (including some stuff strongly reminiscent of *Galaxy*-era social satire), but a great deal of his output *is* strongly centered within the traditions of the Space Adventure. In fact, like some other young writers of the nineties, including Paul J. McAuley and Stephen Baxter, Reed is producing some of the most inventive and colorful of Modern Space Opera, stuff set on a scale so grand and played out across such immense vistas of time that it makes the "Superscience" stuff of the thirties look pale and conservative by comparison: his sequence of novellas for *Asimov's*, for instance, "Sister Alice," "Brother Perfect," and "Mother Death," detailing internecine warfare and intricate political intrigues between families of Immortals with powers and abilities so immense that they are for all intents and purposes gods, or the sequence of stories unfolding in *F&SF, Science Fiction Age,* and *Asimov's,* including "The Remoras," "Aeon's Child," and "Marrow," involving the journeyings of an immense spaceship the size of Jupiter, staffed by dozens of exotic alien races, that is engaged in a multimillion-year circumnavigation of the galaxy.

And in the poignant and haunting story that follows, he shows us that while being the guest of honor at an important and high-powered function is usually a position to be desired, in Reed's decadent future world of ultrarich immortals, it's an honor you might be well advised to avoid—if you *can.*

Reed lives in Lincoln, Nebraska, where he's at work on a novel-length version of his 1997 novella, "Marrow."

One of the robots offered to carry Pico for the last hundred meters, on its back or cradled in its padded arms; but she shook her head emphatically, telling it, "Thank you, no. I can make it myself." The ground was grassy and soft, lit by glowglobes and the grass-colored moon. It wasn't a difficult walk, even with her bad hip, and she wasn't an invalid. She could manage, she thought with an instinctive independence. And as if to show them, she struck out ahead of the half-dozen robots as they unloaded the big skimmer, stacking Pico's gifts in their long arms. She was halfway across the paddock before they caught her. By then she could hear the muddled voices and laughter coming from the hill-like tent straight ahead. By then she was breathing fast for reasons other than her pain. For fear, mostly. But it was a different flavor of fear than the kinds she knew. What was happening now was beyond her control, and inevitable . . . and it was that kind of certainty that made her stop after a few more steps, one hand rubbing at her hip for no reason except to delay her arrival. If only for a moment or two . . .

"Are you all right?" asked one robot.

She was gazing up at the tent, dark and smooth and gently rounded. "I don't want to be here," she admitted. "That's all." Her life on board the *Kyber* had been spent with robots—they had outnumbered the human crew ten to one, then more—and she could always be ruthlessly honest with them. "This is madness. I want to leave again."

"Only, you can't," responded the ceramic creature. The voice was mild, unnervingly patient. "You have nothing to worry about."

"I know."

"The technology has been perfected since—"

"*I know.*"

It stopped speaking, adjusting its hold on the colorful packages.

"That's not what I meant," she admitted. Then she breathed deeply, holding the breath for a moment and exhaling, saying, "All right. Let's go. Go."

The robot pivoted and strode toward the giant tent. The leading robots triggered the doorway, causing it to fold upward with a sudden rush of golden light flooding across the grass, Pico squinting and then blinking, walking faster now and allowing herself the occasional low moan.

"Ever wonder how it'll feel?" Tyson had asked her.

The tent had been pitched over a small pond, probably that very day, and in places the soft, thick grasses had been matted flat by people and their robots. So many people, she thought. Pico tried not to look at any faces. For a moment, she gazed at the pond, shallow and richly green, noticing the tamed waterfowl sprinkled over it and along its shoreline. Ducks and geese, she realized. And some small, crimson-headed cranes. Lifting her eyes, she noticed the large, omega-shaped table near the far wall. She couldn't count the place settings, but it seemed a fair assumption there were sixty-three of them. Plus a single round table and chair in the middle of the omegao—*my table*—and she took another deep breath, looking higher, noticing floating glowglobes and several indigo swallows flying around them, presuambly snatching up the insects that were drawn to the yellow-white light.

People were approaching. Since she had entered, in one patient rush, all sixty-three people had been climbing the slope while shouting, "Pico! Hello!" Their voices mixed together, forming a noisy, senseless paste. "Greetings!" they seemed to say. "Hello, hello!"

They were brightly dressed, flowing robes swishing and everyone wearing big-rimmed hats made to resemble titanic flowers. The people sharply contrasted with the gray-white shells of the robot servants. Those hats were a new fashion, Pico realized. One of the little changes made during these past decades . . . and finally she made herself look at the faces themselves, offering a forced smile and taking a step backward, her belly aching, but her hip healed. The burst of adrenaline hid the deep ache in her bones. Wrestling one of her hands into a wave, she told her audience, "Hello," with a near-whisper. Then she swallowed and said, "Greetings to you!" Was that her voice? She very nearly didn't recognize it.

A woman broke away from the others, almost running toward her. Her big, flowery hat began to work free, and she grabbed the fat, petalish brim and began to fan herself with one hand, the other hand touching Pico on the shoulder. The palm was damp and quite warm; the air suddenly stank of overly sweet perfumes. It was all Pico could manage not to cough. The woman—what was her name?—was asking, "Do you need to sit? We heard . . . about your accident. You poor girl. All the way fine, and then on the last world. Of all the luck!"

Her hip. The woman was jabbering about her sick hip.

Pico nodded and confessed, "Sitting would be nice, yes."

A dozen voices shouted commands. Robots broke into runs, racing one another around the pond to grab the chair beside the little table. The drama seemed to make people laugh. A nervous, self-conscious laugh. When the lead robot reached the chair and started back, there was applause. Another woman shouted, "Mine won! Mine won!" She threw her hat into the air and tried to follow it, leaping as high as possible.

Some man cursed her sharply, then giggled.

Another man forced his way ahead, emerging from the packed bodies in front of Pico. He was smiling in a strange fashion. Drunk or drugged . . . what was permissible these days? With a sloppy, earnest voice, he asked, "How'd it happen? The hip thing . . . how'd you do it?"

He should know. She had dutifully filed her reports throughout the mission, squirting them home. Hadn't he seen them? But then she noticed the watchful, excited faces—no exceptions—and someone seemed to read her thoughts, explaining, "We'd love to hear it *firsthand*. Tell, tell, tell!"

As if they needed to hear a word, she thought, suddenly feeling quite cold.

Her audience grew silent. The robot arrived with the promised chair, and she sat and stretched her bad leg out in front of her, working to focus her mind. It was touching, their silence . . . reverent and almost childlike . . . and she began by telling them how she had tried climbing Miriam Prime with two other crew members. Miriam Prime was the tallest volcano on a super-Venusian world; it was brutal work because of the terrain and their massive lifesuits, cumbersome refrigeration units strapped to their backs, and the atmosphere thick as water. Scalding and acidic. Carbon dioxide and water made for a double greenhouse effect. . . . And she shuddered, partly for dramatics and partly from the memory. Then she said, "Brutal," once again, shaking her head thoughtfully.

They had used hyperthreads to climb the steepest slopes and the cliffs. Normally hyperthreads were virtually unbreakable; but Miriam was not a normal world. She described the basalt cliff and the awful instant of the tragedy; the clarity of the scene startled her. She could feel the heat seeping into her suit, see the dense, dark air, and her arms and legs shook with exhaustion. She told sixty-three people how it felt to be suspended on an invisible thread, two friends and a winch somewhere above in the acidic fog. The winch had jammed without warning, she told; the worst bad luck made it jam where the thread was its weakest. This was near the mission's end, and all the equipment was tired. Several dozen alien worlds had been visited, many mapped for the first time, and every one of them examined up close. As planned.

"Everything has its limits," she told them, her voice having an ominous quality that she hadn't intended.

Even hyperthreads had limits. Pico was dangling, talking to her companions by radio; and just as the jam was cleared, a voice saying, "There . . . got it!", the thread parted. He didn't have any way to know it had parted. Pico was falling, gaining velocity, and the poor man was ignorantly telling her, "It's running strong. You'll be up in no time, no problem. . . ."

People muttered to themselves.

"Oh my," they said.

"Gosh."

"Shit."

Their excitement was obvious, perhaps even overdone. Pico almost laughed, thinking they were making fun of her storytelling . . . thinking, *What do they know about such things?* . . . Only, they were sincere, she realized a moment later. They were enraptured with the image of Pico's long fall, her spinning and lashing out with both hands, fighting to grab anything and slow her fall any way possible—

—and she struck a narrow shelf of eroded stone, the one leg shattered and telescoping down to a gruesome stump. Pico remembered the painless shock of the impact and that glorious instant free of all sensation. She was alive, and the realization had made her giddy. Joyous. Then the pain found her head—a great nauseating wave of pain—and she heard her distant friends shouting, "Pico? Are you there? Can you hear us? Oh, Pico . . . *Pico?* Answer us!"

She had to remain absolutely motionless, sensing that any move would send her tumbling again. She answered in a whisper, telling her friends that she was alive, yes, and please, please hurry. But they had only a partial thread left, and it would take them more than half an hour to descend . . . and she spoke of her agony and the horror, her hip and leg screaming, and not just from the impact. It was worse than mere broken bone, the lifesuit's insulation damaged and the heat bleeding inward, slowly and thoroughly cooking her living flesh.

Pico paused, gazing out at the round-mouthed faces.

So many people and not a breath of sound; and she was having fun. She realized her pleasure almost too late, nearly missing it. Then she told them, "I nearly died," and shrugged her shoulders. "All the distances traveled, every imaginable adventure . . . and I nearly died on one of our last worlds, doing an ordinary climb. . . ."

Let them appreciate her luck, she decided. *Their luck.*

Then another woman lifted her purple flowery hat with both hands, pressing it flush against her own chest. "Of course you survived!" she proclaimed. "You wanted to come home, Pico! You couldn't stand the thought of *dying.*"

Pico nodded without comment, then said, "I was rescued. Obviously." She flexed the damaged leg, saying, "I never really healed," and she touched her hip with reverence, admitting, "We didn't have the resources on board the *Kyber*. This was the best our medical units could do."

Her mood shifted again, without warning. Suddenly she felt sad to tears, eyes dropping and her mouth clamped shut.

"We worried about you, Pico!"

"All the time, dear!"

". . . in our prayers . . . !"

Voices pulled upon each other, competing to be heard. The faces were smiling and thoroughly sincere. Handsome people, she was thinking. Clean and civilized and older than her by centuries. Some of them were more than a thousand years old.

Look at them! she told herself.

And now she felt fear. Pulling both legs toward her chest, she hugged herself, weeping hard enough to dampen her trouser legs; and her audience said, "But you made it, Pico! You came home! The wonders you've seen, the places you've actually touched . . . with those hands. . . . And we're so proud of you! So proud! You've proven your worth a thousand times, Pico! You're made of the very best stuff—!"

—which brought laughter, a great clattering roar of laughter, the joke obviously and apparently tireless.

Even after so long.

They were Pico; Pico was they.

Centuries ago, during the Blossoming, technologies had raced forward at an unprecedented rate. Starships like the *Kyber* and a functional immortality had allowed the first missions to the distant worlds, and there were some grand adventures. Yet adventure requires some element of danger; exploration has never been a safe enterprise. Despite precautions, there were casualties. People who had lived for centuries died suddenly, oftentimes in stupid accidents; and it was no wonder that after the first wave of missions came a long moratorium. No new starships were built, and no sensible person would have ridden inside even the safest vessel. Why risk yourself? Whatever the benefits, why taunt extinction when you have a choice.

Only recently had a solution been invented. Maybe it was prompted by the call of deep space, though Tyson used to claim, "It's the boredom on Earth that inspired them. That's why they came up with their elaborate scheme."

The near-immortals devised ways of making highly gifted, highly trained crews from themselves. With computers and genetic engineering, groups of people could pool their qualities and create compilation humans. Sixty-three individuals had each donated moneys and their own natures, and Pico was the result. She was a grand and sophisticated average of the group. Her face was a blending of every face; her body was a feminine approximation of their own varied bodies. In a few instances, the engineers had planted synthetic genes—for speed and strength, for example—and her brain had a subtly different architecture. Yet basically Pico was their offspring, a stewlike clone. The second of two clones, she knew. The first clone created had had subtle flaws, and he was painlessly destroyed just before birth.

Pico and Tyson and every other compilation person had been born at adult size. Because she was the second attempt, and behind schedule, Pico was thrown straight into her training. Unlike the other crew members, she had spent only a minimal time with her parents. Her sponsors. Whatever they were calling themselves. That and the long intervening years made it difficult to recognize faces and names. She found herself gazing out at them, believing they were strangers, their tireless smiles hinting at something predatory. The neat white teeth gleamed at her, and she wanted to shiver again, holding the knees closer to her mouth.

Someone suggested opening the lovely gifts.

A good idea. She agreed, and the robots brought down the stacks of boxes, placing them beside and behind her. The presents were a young tradition; when she was leaving Earth, the first compilation people were returning with little souvenirs of their travels. Pico had liked the gesture and had done the same. One after another, she started reading the names inscribed in her own flowing handwriting. Then each person stepped forward, thanking her for the treasure, then greedily unwrapping it, the papers flaring into bright colors as they were bent and twisted and torn, then tossed aside for the robots to collect.

She knew none of these people, and that was wrong. What she should have done, she realized, was go into the *Kyber*'s records and memorize names and faces. It would have been easy enough, and proper, and she felt guilty for never having made the effort.

It wasn't merely genetics that she shared with these people; she also embodied slivers of their personalities and basic tendencies. Inside Pico's sophisticated womb, the computers had blended together their shrugs and tongue clicks and the distinctive patterns of their speech. She had emerged as an approximation of every one of them; yet why didn't she feel a greater closeness? Why wasn't there a strong, tangible bond here?

Or was there something—only, she wasn't noticing it?

One early gift was a slab of mirrored rock. "From Tween V," she explained. "What it doesn't reflect, it absorbs and reemits later. I kept that particular piece in my own cabin, fixed to the outer wall—"

"Thank you, thank you," gushed the woman.

For an instant, Pico saw herself reflected on the rock. She looked much older than these people. Tired, she thought. Badly weathered. In the cramped starship, they hadn't the tools to revitalize aged flesh, nor had there been the need. Most of the voyage had been spent in cold-sleep. Their waking times, added together, barely exceeded forty years of biological activity.

"Look at this!" the woman shouted, turning and waving her prize at the others. "Isn't it lovely?"

"A shiny rock," teased one voice. "Perfect!"

Yet the woman refused to be anything but impressed. She clasped her prize to her chest and giggled, merging with the crowd and then vanishing.

They look like children, Pico told herself.

At least how she imagined children to appear . . . unworldly and spoiled, needing care and infinite patience. . . .

She read the next name, and a new woman emerged to collect her gift. "My, what a large box!" She tore at the paper, then the box's lid, then eased her hands into the dunnage of white foam. Pico remembered wrapping this gift—one of the only ones where she was positive of its contents—and she happily watched the smooth, elegant hands pulling free a greasy and knob-faced nut. Then Pico explained:

"It's from the Yult Tree on Proxima Centauri 2." The only member of the species on that strange little world. "If you wish, you can break its dormancy with liquid nitrogen. Then plant it in pure quartz sand, never anything else. Sand, and use red sunlight—"

"I know how to cultivate them," the woman snapped.

There was a sudden silence, uneasy and prolonged.

Finally Pico said, "Well . . . good . . ."

"Everyone knows about Yult nuts," the woman explained. "They're practically giving them away at the greeneries now."

Someone spoke sharply, warning her to stop and think.

"I'm sorry," she responded. "If I sound ungrateful, I mean. I was just thinking, hoping . . . I don't know. Never mind."

A weak, almost inconsequential apology, and the woman paused to feel the grease between her fingertips. •

The thing was, Pico thought, that she had relied on guesswork in selecting these gifts. She had decided to represent every alien world, and she felt proud of herself on the job accomplished. Yult Trees were common on Earth? But how could she know such a thing? And besides, why should it matter? She had brought the nut and everything else because she'd taken risks, and these people were obviously too ignorant and silly to appreciate what they were receiving.

Rage had replaced her fear.

Sometimes she heard people talking among themselves, trying to trade gifts. Gemstones and pieces of alien driftwood were being passed about like orphans. Yet nobody would release the specimens of odd life-forms from living worlds, transparent canisters holding bugs and birds and whatnot inside preserving fluids or hard vacuums. If only she had known what she couldn't have known, these silly brats . . . And she found herself swallowing, holding her breath, and wanting to scream at all of them.

Pico was a compilation, yet she wasn't.

She hadn't lived one day as these people had lived their entire lives. She didn't know about comfort or changelessness, and with an attempt at empathy, she tried to imagine such an incredible existence.

Tyson used to tell her, "Shallowness is a luxury. Maybe the ultimate luxury." She hadn't understood him. Not really. "Only the rich can master true frivolity." Now those words echoed back at her, making her think of Tyson. That intense and angry man . . . the opposite of frivolity, the truth told.

And with that, her mood shifted again. Her skin tingled. She felt nothing for or against her audience. How could they help being what they were? How could anyone help their nature? And with that, she found herself reading another name on another unopened box. A little box, she saw. Probably another one of the unpopular gemstones, born deep inside an alien crust and thrown out by forces unimaginable . . .

There was a silence, an odd stillness, and she repeated the name.

"Opera? Opera Ting?"

Was it her imagination, or was there a nervousness running through the audience? Just what was happening—?

"Excuse me?" said a voice from the back. "Pardon?"

People began moving aside, making room, and a figure emerged. A male, something about him noticeably different. He moved with a telltale lightness, with a spring to his gait. Smiling, he took the tiny package while saying, "Thank you," with great feeling. "For my father, thank you. I'm sure he would have enjoyed this moment. I only wish he could have been here, if only . . ."

Father? Wasn't this Opera Ting?

Pico managed to nod, then she asked, "Where is he? I mean, is he busy somewhere?"

"Oh no. He died, I'm afraid." The man moved differently because he was different. He was young—even younger than I, Pico realized—and he shook his head, smiling in a serene way. Was he a clone? A biological child? What? "But on his behalf," said the man, "I wish to thank you. Whatever this gift is, *I* will treasure it. I promise you. I know you must have gone through hell to find it and bring it to me, and thank you so very much, Pico. Thank you, thank you. Thank you!"

Death.

An appropriate intruder in the evening's festivities, thought Pico. Some accident, some kind of tragedy . . . something had killed one of her sixty-three parents, and that thought pleased her. There was a pang of guilt woven into her pleasure, but not very much. It was comforting to know that even these people weren't perfectly insulated from death; it was a force that would grasp everyone, given time. Like it had taken Midge, she thought. And Uoo, she thought. *And Tyson.*

Seventeen compiled people had embarked on *Kyber*, representing almost a thousand near-immortals. Only nine had returned, including Pico. Eight friends were lost. . . . *Lost* was a better word than *death*, she decided. . . . And usually it happened in places worse than any Hell conceived by human beings.

After Opera—his name, she learned, was the same as his father's—the giving of the gifts settled into a routine. Maybe it was because of the young man's attitude. People seemed more polite, more self-contained. Someone had the presence to ask for another story. Anything she wished to tell. And Pico found herself thinking of a watery planet circling a distant red-dwarf sun, her voice saying, "Coldtear," and watching faces nod in unison.

They recognized the name, and it was too late. It wasn't the story she would have preferred to tell, yet she couldn't seem to stop herself. Coldtear was on her mind.

Just tell parts, she warned herself.

What you can stand!

The world was terran-class and covered with a single ocean frozen on its surface and heated from below. By tides, in part. And by Coldtear's own nuclear decay. It had been Tyson's idea to build a submersible and dive to the ocean's remote floor. He used spare parts in *Kyber*'s machine shop—the largest room on board—then he'd taken his machine to the surface, setting it on the red-stained ice and using lasers and robot help to bore a wide hole and keep it clear.

Pico described the submersible, in brief, then mentioned that Tyson had asked her to accompany him. She didn't add that they'd been lovers now and again, nor that sometimes they had feuded. She'd keep those parts of the story to herself for as long as possible.

The submersible's interior was cramped and ascetic, and she tried to impress her audience with the pressures that would build on the hyperfiber hull. Many times the pressure found in Earth's oceans, she warned; and Tyson's goal was to set down on the floor, then don a lifesuit protected with a human-shaped force field, actually stepping outside and taking a brief walk.

"Because we need to leave behind footprints," he had argued. "Isn't that why we've come here? We can't just leave prints up on the ice. It moves and melts, wiping itself clean every thousand years or so."

"But isn't that the same below?" Pico had responded. "New muds rain down—slowly, granted—and quakes cause slides and avalanches."

"So we pick right. We find someplace where our marks will be quietly covered. Enshrouded. Made everlasting."

She had blinked, surprised that Tyson cared about such things.

"I've studied the currents," he explained, "and the terrain—"

"Are you serious?" Yet you couldn't feel certain about Tyson. He was a creature full of surprises. "All this trouble, and for what—?"

"Trust me, Pico. Trust me!"

Tyson had had an enormous laugh. His parents, sponsors, whatever—an entirely different group of people—had purposefully made him larger than the norm. They had selected genes for physical size, perhaps wanting Tyson to dominate the *Kyber*'s crew in at least that one fashion. If his own noise was to be believed, that was the only tinkering done to him. Otherwise, he was a pure compilation of his parents' traits, fiery and passionate to a fault. It was a little unclear to Pico what group of people could be so uniformly aggressive; yet Tyson had had his place in their tight-woven crew, and he had had his charms in addition to his size and the biting intelligence.

"Oh Pico," he cried out. "What's this about, coming here? If it's not about leaving traces of our passage . . . then *what?*"

"It's about going home again," she had answered.

"Then why do we leave the *Kyber?* Why not just orbit Coldtear and send down our robots to explore?"

"Because . . ."

"Indeed! Because!" The giant head nodded, and he put a big hand on her shoulder. "I knew you'd see my point. I just needed to give you time, my friend."

She agreed to the deep dive, but not without misgivings.

And during their descent, listening to the ominous creaks and groans of the hull while lying flat on their backs, the misgivings began to reassert themselves.

It was Tyson's fault, and maybe his aim.

No, she thought. It was most definitely his aim.

At first, she thought it was some game, him asking, "Do you ever wonder how it will feel? We come home and are welcomed, and then our dear parents disassemble our brains and implant them—"

"Quiet," she interrupted. "We agreed. Everyone agreed. We aren't going to talk about it, all right?"

A pause, then he said, "Except, I know. How it feels, I mean."

She heard him, then she listened to him take a deep breath from the close, damp air; and finally she had strength enough to ask, "How can you know?"

When Tyson didn't answer, she rolled onto her side and saw the outline of his face. A handsome face, she thought. Strong and incapable of any doubts. This was the only taboo subject among the compilations—"How will it feel?"—and it was left to each of them to decide what they believed. Was it a fate or a reward? To be subdivided and implanted into the minds of dozens and dozens of near-immortals . . .

It wasn't a difficult trick, medically speaking.

After all, each of their minds had been designed for this one specific goal. Memories and talent; passion and training. All of the qualities would be saved—diluted, but, in the same instant, gaining their own near-immortality. Death of a sort, but a kind of everlasting life, too.

That was the creed by which Pico had been born and raised.

The return home brings a great reward, and peace.

Pico's first memory was of her birth, spilling slippery-wet from the womb and coughing hard, a pair of doctoring robots bent over her, whispering to her, "Welcome, child. Welcome. You've been born from *them* to be joined with *them* when it is time. . . . We promise you . . . !"

Comforting noise, and mostly Pico had believed it.

But Tyson had to say, "I know how it feels, Pico," and she could make out his grin, his amusement patronizing. Endless.

"How?" she muttered. "How do you know—?"

"Because some of my parents . . . well, let's just say that I'm not their first time. Understand me?"

"They made another compilation?"

"One of the very first, yes. Which was incorporated into them before I was begun, and which was incorporated into me because there was a spare piece. A leftover chunk of the mind—"

"You're making this up, Tyson!"

Except, he wasn't, she sensed. Knew. Several times, on several early worlds, Tyson had seemed too knowledgeable about too much. Nobody could have prepared himself that well, she realized. She and the others had assumed that Tyson was intuitive in some useful way. Part of him was from another compilation? From someone like them? A fragment of the man had walked twice beside the gray dust sea of Plicker, and it had twice climbed the giant ant mounds on Proxima Centauri 2. It was a revelation, unnerving and hard to accept; and just the memory of that instant made her tremble secretly, facing her audience, her tired blood turning to ice.

Pico told none of this to her audience.

Instead, they heard about the long descent and the glow of rare life-forms outside—a thin plankton consuming chemical energies as they found them—and, too, the growing creaks of the spherical hull.

They didn't hear how she asked, "So how does it feel? You've got a piece of compilation inside you . . . all right! Are you going to tell me what it's like?"

They didn't hear about her partner's long, deep laugh.

Nor could they imagine him saying, "Pico, my dear. You're such a passive, foolish creature. That's why I love you. So docile, so damned innocent—"

"Does it live inside you, Tyson?"

"It depends on what you consider life."

"Can you feel its presence? I mean, does it have a personality? An existence? Or have you swallowed it all up?"

"I don't think I'll tell." Then the laugh enlarged, and the man lifted his legs and kicked at the hyperfiber with his powerful muscles. She could hear, and feel, the solid impacts of his bootheels. She knew that Tyson's strength was nothing compared to the ocean's mass bearing down on them, their hull scarcely feeling the blows . . . yet some irrational part of her was terrified. She had to reach out, grasping one of his trouser legs and tugging hard, telling him:

"Don't! Stop that! Will you please . . . quit!?"

The tension shifted direction in an instant.

Tyson said, "I was lying," and then added, "About knowing. About having a compilation inside me." And he gave her a huge hug, laughing in a different way now. He nearly crushed her ribs and lungs. Then he spoke into one of her ears, offering more, whispering with the old charm, and she accepting his offer. They did it as well as possible, considering their circumstances and the endless groaning of their tiny vessel; and she remembered all of it while her voice, detached but thorough, described how they had landed on top of something rare. There was a distinct *crunch* of stone. They had made their touchdown on the slope of a recent volcano—an island on an endless plain of mud—and afterward they dressed in their lifesuits, triple-checked their force fields, then flooded the compartment and crawled into the frigid, pressurized water.

It was an eerie, almost indescribable experience to walk on that ocean floor. When language failed Pico, she tried to use silence and oblique gestures to capture the sense of endless time and the cold and darkness. Even when Tyson ignited the submersible's outer lights, making the nearby terrain bright as late afternoon, there was the palpable taste of endless dark just beyond. She told of feeling the pressure despite the force field shrouding her; she told of climbing after Tyson, scrambling up a rough slope of youngish rock to a summit where they discovered a hot-water spring that pumped heated, mineral-rich water up at them.

That might have been the garden spot of Coldtear. Surrounding the spring was a thick, almost gelatinous mass of gray-green bacteria, pulsating and fat by its own standards. She paused, seeing the scene all over again. Then she assured her parents, "It had a beauty. I mean it. An elegant, minimalist beauty."

Nobody spoke.

Then someone muttered, "I can hardly wait to remember it," and gave a weak laugh.

The audience became uncomfortable, tense and too quiet. People shot accusing looks at the offender, and Pico worked not to notice any of it. A bitterness was building in her guts, and she sat up straighter, rubbing at both hips.

Then a woman coughed for attention, waited, and then asked, "What happened next?"

Pico searched for her face.

"There was an accident, wasn't there? On Coldtear . . . ?"

I won't tell them, thought Pico. Not now. Not this way.

She said, "No, not then. Later." And maybe some of them knew better. Judging by the expressions, a few must have remembered the records. Tyson died on the first dive. It was recorded as being an equipment failure—Pico's lie—and she'd hold on to the lie as long as possible. It was a promise she'd made to herself and kept all these years.

Shutting her eyes, she saw Tyson's face smiling at her. Even through the thick faceplate and the shimmering glow of the force field, she could make out the mischievous expression, eyes glinting, the large mouth saying, "Go on back, Pico. In and up and a safe trip to you, pretty lady."

She had been too stunned to respond, gawking at him.

"Remember? I've still got to leave my footprints somewhere—"

"What are you planning?" she interrupted.

He laughed and asked, "Isn't it obvious? I'm going to make my mark on this world. It's dull and nearly dead, and I don't think anyone is ever going to return here. Certainly not to *here*. Which means I'll be pretty well left alone—"

"Your force field will drain your batteries," she argued stupidly. Of course he knew that salient fact. "If you stay here—!"

"I know, Pico. I know."

"But why—?"

"I lied before. About lying." The big face gave a disappointed look, then the old smile reemerged. "Poor, docile Pico. I knew you wouldn't take this well. You'd take it too much to heart . . . which I suppose is why I asked you along in the first place. . . ." and he turned away, starting to walk through the bacterial mat with threads and chunks kicked loose, sailing into the warm current and obscuring him. It was a strange gray snow moving against gravity. Her last image of Tyson was of a hulking figure amid the living goo; and to this day, she had wondered if she could have wrestled him back to the submersible—an impossibility, of course—and how far could he have walked before his force field failed.

Down the opposite slope and onto the mud, no doubt.

She could imagine him walking fast, using his strength . . . fighting the deep, cold muds . . . Tyson plus that fragment of an earlier compilation— and who was driving whom? she asked herself. Again and again and again.

Sometimes she heard herself asking Tyson, "How does it feel having a sliver of another soul inside you?"

His ghost never answered, merely laughing with his booming voice.

She hated him for his suicide, and admired him; and sometimes she cursed him for taking her along with him and for the way he kept cropping up in her thoughts. . . . "Damn you, Tyson. Goddamn you, goddamn you . . . !"

No more presents remained.

One near-immortal asked, "Are we hungry?", and others replied, "Famished," in one voice, then breaking into laughter. The party moved toward the distant tables, a noisy mass of bodies surrounding Pico. Her hip had stiffened while sitting, but she worked hard to move normally, managing the downslope toward the pond and then the little wooden bridge spanning a rocky brook. The waterfowl made grumbling sounds, angered by the disturbances; Pico stopped and watched them, finally asking, "What kinds are those?" She meant the ducks.

"Just mallards," she heard. "Nothing fancy."

Yet, to her, they seemed like miraculous creatures, vivid plumage and the moving eyes, wings spreading as a reflex and their nervous motions lending them a sense of muscular power. A vibrancy.

Someone said, "You've seen many birds, I'm sure."

Of a sort, yes . . .

"What were your favorites, Pico?"

They were starting uphill, quieter now, feet making a swishing sound in the grass; and Pico told them about the pterosaurs of Wilder, the man-sized bats on Little Quark, and the giant insects—a multitude of species— thriving in the thick, warm air of Tau Ceti I.

"Bugs," grumbled someone. "Uggh!"

"Now, now," another person responded.

Then a third joked, "I'm not looking forward to *that*. Who wants to trade memories?"

A joke, thought Pico, because memories weren't tradable properties. Minds were holographic—every piece held the basic picture of the whole—and these people each would receive a sliver of Pico's whole self. Somehow that made her smile, thinking how none of them would be spared. Every terror and every agony would be set inside each of them. In a diluted form, of course. The *Pico-ness* minimized. Made manageable. Yet it was something, wasn't it? It pleased her to think that a few of them might awaken in the night, bathed in sweat after dreaming of Tyson's death . . . just as she had dreamed of it time after time . . . her audience given more than they had anticipated, a dark little joke of her own. . . .

They reached the tables, Pico taking hers and sitting, feeling rather self-conscious as the others quietly assembled around her, each of them knowing where they belonged. She watched their faces. The excitement she had sensed from the beginning remained; only, it seemed magnified now. More colorful, more intense. Facing toward the inside of the omega, her hosts couldn't quit staring, forever smiling, scarcely able to eat once the robots brought them plates filled with steaming foods.

Fancy meals, Pico learned.

The robot setting her dinner before her explained, "The vegetables are from Triton, miss. A very special and much-prized strain. And the meat is from a wild hound killed just yesterday—"

"Really?"

"As part of the festivities, yes." The ceramic face, white and expressionless, stared down at her. "There have been hunting parties and games, among other diversions. Quite an assortment of activities, yes."

"For how long?" she asked. "These festivities . . . have they been going on for days?"

"A little longer than three months, miss."

She had no appetite; nonetheless, she lifted her utensils and made the proper motions, reminding herself that three months of continuous parties would be nothing to these people. Three months was a day to them, and what did they do with their time? So much of it, and such a constricted existence. What had Tyson once told her? The average citizen of earth averages less than one off-world trip in eighty years, and the trends were toward less traveling. Spaceflight was safe only to a degree, and these people couldn't stand the idea of being meters away from a cold, raw vacuum.

"Cowards," Tyson had called them. "Gutted, deblooded cowards!"

Looking about, she saw the delicate twists of green leaves vanishing into grinning mouths, the chewing prolonged and indifferent. Except for Opera, that is. Opera saw her and smiled back in turn, his eyes different, something mocking about the tilt of his head and the curl of his mouth.

She found her eyes returning to Opera every little while, and she wasn't sure why. She felt no physical attraction for the man. His youth and attitudes made him different from the others, but how much different? Then she noticed his dinner—cultured potatoes with meaty hearts—and that made an impression on Pico. It was a standard food on board the *Kyber*. Opera was making a gesture, perhaps. Nobody else was eating that bland food, and she decided this was a show of solidarity. At least the man was trying, wasn't he? More than the others, he was. He was.

Dessert was cold and sweet and shot full of some odd liquor.

Pico watched the others drinking and talking among themselves. For the first time, she noticed how they seemed subdivided—discrete groups formed, and boundaries between each one. A dozen people here, seven back there, and sometimes individuals sitting alone—like Opera—chatting politely or appearing entirely friendless.

One lonesome woman rose to her feet and approached Pico, not smiling, and with a sharp voice, she declared, "Tomorrow, come morning . . . you'll live forever . . . !"

Conversations diminished, then quit entirely.

"Plugged in. Here." "She was under the influence of some drug, the tip of her finger shaking and missing her own temple. "You fine lucky girl . . . Yes, you are . . . !"

Some people laughed at the woman, suddenly and without shame.

The harsh sound made her turn and squint, and Pico watched her straightening her back. The woman was pretending to be above them and uninjured, her thin mouth squeezed shut and her nose tilting with mock pride. With a clear, soft voice, she said, "Fuck every one of you," and then laughed, turning toward Pico, acting as if they had just shared some glorious joke of their own.

"I would apologize for our behavior," said Opera, "but I can't. Not in good faith, I'm afraid."

Pico eyed the man. Dessert was finished; people stood about drinking, keeping the three-month-old party in motion. A few of them stripped naked and swam in the green pond. It was a raucous scene, tireless and full of happy scenes that never seemed convincingly joyous. Happy sounds by practice, rather. Centuries of practice, and the result was to make Pico feel sad and quite lonely.

"A silly, vain lot," Opera told her.

She said, "Perhaps," with a diplomatic tone, then saw several others approaching. At least they looked polite, she thought. Respectful. It was odd how a dose of respect glossed over so much. Particularly when the respect wasn't reciprocated, Pico feeling none toward them. . . .

A man asked to hear more stories. Please?

Pico shrugged her shoulders, then asked, "Of what?" Every request brought her a momentary sense of claustrophobia, her memories threatening to crush her. "Maybe you're interested in a specific world?"

Opera responded, saying, "Blueblue!"

Blueblue was a giant gaseous world circling a bluish sun. Her first thought was of Midge vanishing into the dark storm on its southern hemisphere, searching for the source of the carbon monoxide upflow that effectively gave breath to half the world. Most of Blueblue was calm in comparison. Thick winds; strong sunlight. Its largest organisms would dwarf most cities, their bodies balloonlike and their lives spent feeding on sunlight and hydrocarbons, utilizing carbon monoxide and other radicals in their patient metabolisms. Pico and the others had spent several months living on the living clouds, walking across them, taking samples and studying the assortment of parasites and symbionts that grew in their flesh.

She told about sunrise on Blueblue, remembering its colors and its astounding speed. Suddenly she found herself talking about a particular morning when the landing party was jostled out of sleep by an apparent quake. Their little huts had been strapped down and secured, but they found themselves tilting fast. Their cloud was colliding with a neighboring cloud—something they had never seen—and of course there was a rush to load their shuttle and leave. If it came to that.

"Normally, you see, the clouds avoid each other," Pico told her little audience. "At first, we thought the creatures were fighting, judging by their roaring and the hard shoving. They make sounds by forcing air through pores and throats and anuses. It was a strange show. Deafening. The collision point was maybe a third of a kilometer from camp, our whole world rolling over while the sun kept rising, its bright, hot light cutting through the organic haze—"

"Gorgeous," someone said.

A companion said, "Quiet!"

Then Opera touched Pico on the arm, saying, "Go on. Don't pay any attention to them."

The others glanced at Opera, hearing something in his voice, and their backs stiffening reflexively.

And then Pico was speaking again, finishing her story. Tyson was the first one of them to understand, who somehow made the right guess and began laughing, not saying a word. By then everyone was on board the shuttle, ready to fly; the tilting stopped suddenly, the air filling with countless little blue balloons. Each was the size of a toy balloon, she told. Their cloud was bleeding them from new pores, and the other cloud responded with a thick gray fog of butterflylike somethings. The somethings flew after the balloons, and Tyson laughed harder, his face contorted and the laugh finally shattering into a string of gasping coughs.

"Don't you see?" he asked the others. "Look! The clouds are enjoying a morning screw!"

Pico imitated Tyson's voice, regurgitating the words and enthusiasm. Then she was laughing for herself, scarcely noticing how the others giggled politely. No more. Only Opera was enjoying her story, again touching her arm and saying, "That's lovely. Perfect. God, precious . . . !"

The rest began to drift away, not quite excusing themselves.

What was wrong?

"Don't mind them," Opera cautioned. "They're members of some new chastity faith. Clarity through horniness, and all that." He laughed at them now. "They probably went to too many orgies, and this is how they're coping with their guilt. That's all."

Pico shut her eyes, remembering the scene on Blueblue for herself. She didn't want to relinquish it.

"Screwing clouds," Opera was saying. "That is lovely."

And she thought.

He sounds a little like Tyson. In places. In ways.

After a while, Pico admitted. "I can't remember your father's face. I'm sure I must have met him, but I don't—"

"You did meet him," Opera replied. "He left a recording of it in his journal—a brief meeting—and I made a point of studying everything about the mission and you. His journal entries; your reports. Actually, I'm the best-prepared person here today. Other than you, of course."

She said nothing, considering those words.

They were walking now, making their way down to the pond, and sometimes Pico noticed the hard glances of the others. Did they approve of Opera? Did it anger them, watching him monopolizing her time? Yet she didn't want to be with *them*, the truth told. Fuck them, she thought; and she smiled at her private profanity.

The pond was empty of swimmers now. There were just a few sleepless ducks and the roiled water. A lot of the celebrants had vanished, Pico realized. To where? She asked Opera, and he said:

"It's late. But then again, most people sleep ten or twelve hours every night."

"That much?"

He nodded. "Enhanced dreams are popular lately. And the oldest people sometimes exceed fifteen hours—"

"Always?"

He shrugged and offered a smile.

"What a waste!"

"Of time?" he countered.

Immortals can waste many things, she realized. But never time. And with that thought, she looked straight at her companion, asking him, "What happened to your father?"

"How did he die, you mean?"

A little nod. A respectful expression, she hoped. But curious.

Opera said, "He used an extremely toxic poison, self-induced." He gave a vague disapproving look directed at nobody. "A suicide at the end of a prolonged depression. He made certain that his mind was ruined before autodocs and his own robots could save him."

"I'm sorry."

"Yet I can't afford to feel sorry," he responded. "You see, I was born according to the terms of his will. I'm 99 percent his clone, the rest of my genes tailored according to his desires. If he hadn't murdered himself, I wouldn't exist. Nor would I have inherited his money." He shrugged, saying, "Parents," with a measured scorn. "They have such power over you, like it or not."

She didn't know how to respond.

"Listen to us. All of this death talk, and doesn't it seem out of place?" Opera said, "After all, we're here to celebrate your return home. Your successes. Your gifts. And you . . . you on the brink of being magnified many times over." He paused before saying, "By this time tomorrow, you'll reside inside all of us, making everyone richer as a consequence."

The young man had an odd way of phrasing his statements, the entire speech either earnest or satirical. She couldn't tell which. Or if there was a *which*. Maybe it was her ignorance with the audible clues, the unknown trappings of this culture. . . . Then something else occurred to her.

"What do you mean? 'Death talk . . .' "

"Your friend Tyson died on Coldtear," he replied. "And didn't you lose another on Blueblue?"

"Midge. Yes."

He nodded gravely, glancing down at Pico's legs. "We can sit. I'm sorry; I should have noticed you were getting tired."

They sat side by side on the grass, watching the mallard ducks. Males and females had the same vivid green heads. Beautiful, she mentioned. Opera explained how females were once brown and quite drab, but people thought that was a shame, and voted to have the species altered, both sexes made equally resplendent. Pico nodded, only halfway listening. She couldn't get Tyson and her other dead friends out of her mind. Particularly Tyson. She had been angry with him for a long time, and even now her anger wasn't finished. Her confusion and general tiredness made it worse. Why had he done it? In life the man had had a way of dominating every meeting, every little gathering. He had been optimistic and fearless, the last sort of person to do such an awful thing. Suicide. The others had heard it was an accident—Pico had held to her lie—but she and they were in agreement about one fact. When Tyson died, at that precise instant, some essential heart of their mission had been lost.

Why? she wondered. Why?

Midge had flown into the storm on Blueblue, seeking adventure and important scientific answers; and her death was sad, yes, and everyone had missed her. But it wasn't like Tyson's death. It felt honorable, maybe even perfect. They had a duty to fulfill in the wilderness, and that duty was in their blood and their training. People spoke about Midge for years, acting as if she were still alive. As if she were still flying the shuttle into the storm's vortex.

But Tyson was different.

Maybe everyone knew the truth about his death. Sometimes it seemed that, in Pico's eyes, the crew could see what had really happened, and they'd hear it between her practiced lines. They weren't fooled.

Meanwhile, others died in the throes of life.

Uoo—a slender wisp of a compilation—was incinerated by a giant bolt of lightning on Miriam II, little left but ashes, and the rest of the party continuing its descent into the superheated Bottoms and the quiet Lead Sea.

Opaltu died in the mouth of a nameless predator. He had been another of Pico's lovers, a proud man and the best example of vanity that she had known—until today, she thought—and she and the others had laughed at the justice that befell Opaltu's killer. Unable to digest alien meats, the predator had sickened and died in a slow, agonizing fashion, vomiting up its insides as it staggered through the yellow jungle.

Boo was killed while working outside the *Kyber*, struck by a mote of interstellar debris.

Xon's lifesuit failed, suffocating her.

As did Kyties's suit, and that wasn't long ago. Just a year now, ship time, and she remembered a cascade of jokes and his endless good humor. The most decent person on board the *Kyber*.

Yet it was Tyson who dominated her memories of the dead. It was the man as well as his self-induced extinction, and the anger within her swelled all at once. Suddenly even simple breathing was work. Pico found herself sweating, then blinking away the salt in her eyes. Once, then again, she coughed into a fist; then finally she had the energy to ask, "Why did he do it?"

"Who? My father?"

"Depression is . . . should be . . . a curable ailment. We had drugs and therapies on board that could erase it."

"But it was more than depression. It was something that attacks the very old people. A kind of giant boredom, if you will."

She wasn't surprised. Nodding as if she'd expected that reply, she told him, "I can understand that, considering your lives." Then she thought how Tyson hadn't been depressed or bored. How could he have been either?

Opera touched her bad leg, for just a moment. "You must wonder how it will be," he mentioned. "Tomorrow, I mean."

She shivered, aware of the fear returning. Closing her burning eyes, she saw Tyson's walk through the bacterial mat, the loose gray chunks spinning as the currents carried them, lending them a greater sort of life with the motion. . . . And she opened her eyes, Opera watching, saying something to her with his expression, and her unable to decipher any meanings.

"Maybe I should go to bed, too," she allowed.

The park under the tent was nearly empty now. Where had the others gone?

Opera said, "Of course," as if expecting it. He rose and offered his hand, and she surprised herself by taking the hand with both of hers. Then he said, "If you like, I can show you your quarters."

She nodded, saying nothing.

It was a long, painful walk, and Pico honestly considered asking for a robot's help. For anyone's. Even a cane would have been a blessing, her hip never having felt so bad. Earth's gravity and the general stress were making it worse, most likely. She told herself that at least it was a pleasant night, warm and calm and perfectly clear, and the soft ground beneath the grass seemed to be calling to her, inviting her to lie down and sleep in the open.

People were staying in a chain of old houses subdivided into apartments, luxurious yet small. Pico's apartment was on the ground floor, Opera happy to show her through the rooms. For an instant, she considered asking him to stay the night. Indeed, she sensed that he was delaying, hoping for some sort of invitation. But she heard herself saying, "Rest well, and thank you," and her companion smiled and left without comment, vanishing through the crystal front door and leaving her completely alone.

For a little while, she sat on her bed, doing nothing. Not even thinking, at least in any conscious fashion.

Then she realized something, no warning given; and aloud, in a voice almost too soft for even her to hear, she said, "He didn't know. Didn't have an idea, the shit." Tyson. She was thinking about the fiery man and his boast about being the second generation of star explorers. What if it was all true? His parents had injected a portion of a former Tyson into him, and he had already known the early worlds they had visited. He already knew the look of double sunrises on the desert world orbiting Alpha Centauri A; he knew the smell of constant rot before they cracked their airlocks on Barnard's 2. But try as he might—

"—he couldn't remember how it feels to be disassembled." She spoke without sound. To herself. "That titanic and fearless creature, and he couldn't remember. Everything else, yes, but not that. And not knowing had to scare him. Nothing else did, but that terrified him. The only time in his life he was truly scared, and it took all his bluster to keep that secret—!"

Killing himself rather than face his fear.

Of course, she thought. Why not?

And he took Pico as his audience, knowing she'd be a good audience. Because they were lovers. Because he must have decided that he could convince her of his fearlessness one last time, leaving his legend secure. Immortal, in a sense.

That's what you were thinking . . .

. . . wasn't it?

And she shivered, holding both legs close to her mouth, and feeling the warm misery of her doomed hip.

She sat for a couple more hours, neither sleeping nor feeling the slightest need for sleep. Finally she rose and used the bathroom, and after a long, careful look through the windows, she ordered the door to open, and stepped outside, picking a reasonable direction and walking stiffly and quickly on the weakened leg.

Opera emerged from the shadows, startling her.

"If you want to escape," he whispered, "I can help. Let me help you, please."

The face was handsome in the moonlight, young in every fashion. He must have guessed her mood, she realized, and she didn't allow herself to become upset. Help was important, she reasoned. Even essential. She had to find her way across a vast and very strange alien world. "I want to get back into orbit," she told him, "and find another starship. We saw several. They looked almost ready to embark." Bigger than the *Kyber*, and obviously faster. No doubt designed to move even deeper into the endless wilderness.

"I'm not surprised," Opera told her. "And I understand."

She paused, staring at him before asking, "How did you guess?"

"Living forever inside our heads . . . That's just a mess of metaphysical nonsense, isn't it? You know you'll die tomorrow. Bits of your brain will vanish inside us, made part of us, and not vice versa. I think it sounds like an awful way to die, certainly for someone like you—"

"Can you really help me?"

"This way," he told her. "Come on."

They walked for an age, crossing the paddock and finally reaching the wide tube where the skimmers shot past with a rush of air. Opera touched a simple control, then said, "It won't be long," and smiled at her. Just for a moment. "You know, I almost gave up on you. I thought I must have read you wrong. You didn't strike me as someone who'd go quietly to her death. . . ."

She had a vague, fleeting memory of the senior Opera. Gazing at the young face, she could recall a big, warm hand shaking her hand, and a similar voice saying, "It's very good to meet you, Pico. At last!"

"I bet one of the new starships will want you." The young Opera was telling her, "You're right. They're bigger ships, and they've got better facilities. Since they'll be gone even longer, they've been given the best possible medical equipment. That hip and your general body should respond to treatments—"

"I have experience," she whispered.

"Pardon me?"

"Experience." She nodded with conviction. "I can offer a crew plenty of valuable experience."

"They'd be idiots not to take you."

A skimmer slowed and stopped before them. Opera made the windows opaque—"So nobody can see you"—and punched in their destination, Pico making herself comfortable.

"Here we go," he chuckled, and they accelerated away.

There was an excitement to all of this, an adventure like every other. Pico realized that she was scared, but in a good, familiar way. Life and death. Both possibilities seemed balanced on a very narrow fulcrum, and she found herself smiling, rubbing her hip with a slow hand.

They were moving fast, following Opera's instructions.

"A circuitous route," he explained. "We want to make our whereabouts less obvious. All right?"

"Fine."

"Are you comfortable?"

"Yes," she allowed. "Basically."

Then she was thinking about the others—the other survivors from the *Kyber*—wondering how many of them were having second or third thoughts. The long journey home had been spent in cold-sleep, but there had been intervals when two or three of them were awakened to do normal maintenance. Not once did anyone even joke about taking the ship elsewhere. Nobody had asked, "Why do we have to go to Earth?" The obvious question had eluded them, and at the time, she had assumed it was because there were no doubters. Besides herself, that is. The rest believed this would be the natural conclusion to full and satisfied lives; they were returning home to a new life and an appreciative audience. How could any sane compilation think otherwise?

Yet she found herself wondering.

Why no jokes?

If they hadn't had doubts, wouldn't they have made jokes?

Eight others had survived the mission. Yet none were as close to Pico as she had been to Tyson. They had saved each other's proverbial skin many times, and she did feel a sudden deep empathy for them, remembering how they had boarded nine separate shuttles after kisses and hugs and a few careful tears, each of them struggling with the proper things to say. But what could anyone say at such a moment? Particularly when you believed that your companions were of one mind, and, in some fashion, happy. . . .

Pico said, "I wonder about the others," and intended to leave it at that. To say nothing more.

"The others?"

"From the *Kyber*. My friends." She paused and swallowed, then said softly, "Maybe I could contact them."

"No," he responded.

She jerked her head, watching Opera's profile.

"That would make it easy to catch you." His voice was quite sensible and measured. "Besides," he added, "can't they make up their own minds? Like you have?"

She nodded, thinking that was reasonable. Sure.

He waited a long moment, then said, "Perhaps you'd like to talk about something else?"

"Like what?"

He eyed Pico, then broke into a wide smile. "If I'm not going to inherit a slice of your mind, leave me another story. Tell . . . I don't know. Tell me about your favorite single place. Not a world, but some favorite patch of ground on any world. If you could be anywhere now, where would it be? And with whom?

Pico felt the skimmer turning, following the tube. She didn't have to consider the question—her answer seemed obvious to her—but the pause was to collect herself, weighing how to begin and what to tell.

"In the mountains on Erindi 3," she said, "the air thins enough to be breathed safely, and it's really quite pretty. The scenery, I mean."

"I've seen holos of the place. It is lovely."

"Not just lovely." She was surprised by her authority, her self-assured voice telling him, "There's a strange sense of peace there. You don't get that from holos. Supposedly it's produced by the weather and the vegetation. . . . They make showers of negative ions, some say. . . . And it's the colors, too. A subtle interplay of shades and shadows. All very one-of-a-kind."

"Of course," he said carefully.

She shut her eyes, seeing the place with almost perfect clarity. A summer storm had swept overhead, charging the glorious atmosphere even further, leaving everyone in the party invigorated. She and Tyson, Midge, and several others had decided to swim in a deep-blue pool near their campsite. The terrain itself was rugged, black rocks erupting from the blue-green vegetation. The valley's little river poured into a gorge and the pool, and the people did the same. Tyson was first, naturally. He laughed and bounced in the icy water, screaming loud enough to make a flock of razor-bats take flight. This was only the third solar system they had visited, and they were still young in every sense. It seemed to them that every world would be this much fun.

She recalled—and described—diving feet first. She was last into the pool, having inherited a lot of caution from her parents. Tyson had teased her, calling her a coward and then worse, then showing where to aim. "Right here! It's deep here! Come on, coward! Take a chance!"

The water was startlingly cold, and there wasn't much of it beneath the shiny flowing surface. She struck and hit the packed sand below, and the impact made her groan, then shout. Tyson had lied, and she chased the bastard around the pool, screaming and finally clawing at his broad back until she'd driven him up the gorge walls, him laughing and once, losing strength with all the laughing, almost tumbling down on top of her.

She told Opera everything.

At first, it seemed like an accident. All her filters were off; she admitted everything without hesitation. Then she told herself that the man was saving her life and deserved the whole story. That's when she was describing the lovemaking between her and Tyson. That night. It was their first time, and maybe the best time. They did it on a bed of mosses, perched on the rim of the gorge, and she tried to paint a vivid word picture for her audience, including smells and the textures and the sight of the double moons overhead, colored a strange living pink and moving fast.

Their skimmer ride seemed to be taking a long time, she thought once she was finished. She mentioned this to Opera, and he nodded soberly. Otherwise, he made no comment.

I won't be disembodied tomorrow, she told herself.

Then she added, *Today, I mean today.*

She felt certain now. Secure. She was glad for this chance and for this dear new friend, and it was too bad she'd have to leave so quickly, escaping into the relative safety of space. Perhaps there were more people like Opera . . . people who would be kind to her, appreciating her circumstances and desires . . . supportive and interesting companions in their own right. . . .

And suddenly the skimmer was slowing, preparing to stop.

When Opera said, "Almost there," she felt completely at ease. Entirely calm. She shut her eyes and saw the raw, wild mountains on Erindi 3, storm clouds gathering and flashes of lightning piercing the howling winds. She summoned a different day, and saw Tyson standing against the storms, smiling, beckoning for her to climb up to him just as the first cold, fat raindrops smacked against her face.

The skimmer's hatch opened with a hiss.

Sunlight streamed inside, and she thought: *Dawn. By now, sure . . .*

Opera rose and stepped outside, then held a hand out to Pico. She took it with both of hers and said, "Thank you," while rising, looking past him and seeing the paddock and the familiar faces, the green ground and the giant tent with its doorways opened now, various birds flying inside and out again . . . and Pico most surprised by how little she was surprised, Opera still holding her hands, and his flesh dry, the hand perfectly calm.

The autodocs stood waiting for orders.

This time, Pico had been carried from the skimmer, riding cradled in a robot's arms. She had taken just a few faltering steps before half-crumbling. Exhaustion was to blame. Not fear. At least it didn't feel like fear, she told herself. Everyone told her to take it easy, to enjoy her comfort; and now, finding herself flanked by autodocs, her exhaustion worsened. She thought she might die before the cutting began, too tired now to pump her own blood or fire her neurons or even breathe.

Opera was standing nearby, almost smiling, his pleasure serene and chilly and without regrets.

He hadn't said a word since they left the skimmer.

Several others told her to sit, offering her a padded seat with built-in channels to catch any flowing blood. Pico took an uneasy step toward the seat, then paused and straightened her back, saying, "I'm thirsty," softly, her words sounding thoroughly parched.

"Pardon?" they asked.

"I want to drink . . . some water, please . . . ?"

Faces turned, hunting for a cup and water.

It was Opera who said, "Will the pond do?" Then he came forward, extending an arm and telling everyone else, "It won't take long. Give us a moment, will you?"

Pico and Opera walked alone.

Last night's ducks were sleeping and lazily feeding. Pico looked at their metallic green heads, so lovely that she ached at seeing them, and she tried to miss nothing. She tried to concentrate so hard that time itself would compress, seconds turning to hours, and her life in that way prolonged.

Opera was speaking, asking her, "Do you want to hear why?"

She shook her head, not caring in the slightest.

"But you must be wondering why. I fool you into believing that I'm your ally, and I manipulate you—"

"Why?" she sputtered. "So tell me."

"Because," he allowed, "it helps the process. It helps your integration into us. I gave you a chance for doubts and helped you think you were fleeing, convinced you that you'd be free . . . and now you're angry and scared and intensely alive. It's that intensity that we want. It makes the neurological grafts take hold. It's a trick that we learned since the *Kyber* left Earth. Some compilations tried to escape, and when they were caught and finally incorporated along with their anger—"

"Except, I'm not angry," she lied, gazing at his self-satisfied grin.

"A nervous system in flux," he said. "I volunteered, by the way."

She thought of hitting him. Could she kill him somehow?

But instead, she turned and asked, "Why this way? Why not just let me slip away, then catch me at the spaceport?"

"You were going to drink," he reminded her. "Drink."

She knelt despite her hip's pain, knees sinking into the muddy bank and her lips pursing, taking in a long, warmish thread of muddy water, and then her face lifting, the water spilling across her chin and chest, and her mouth unable to close tight.

"Nothing angers," he said, "like the betrayal of someone you trust."

True enough, she thought. Suddenly she could see Tyson leaving her alone on the ocean floor, his private fears too much, and his answer being to kill himself while dressed up in apparent bravery. A kind of betrayal, wasn't that? To both of them, and it still hurt. . . .

"Are you still thirsty?" asked Opera.

"Yes," she whispered.

"Then drink. Go on."

She knelt again, taking a bulging mouthful and swirling it with her tongue. Yet she couldn't make herself swallow, and after a moment, it began leaking out from her lips and down her front again. Making a mess, she realized. Muddy, warm, ugly water, and she couldn't remember how it felt to be thirsty. Such a little thing, and ordinary, and she couldn't remember it.

"Come on, then," said Opera.

She looked at him.

He took her arm and began lifting her, a small, smiling voice saying, "You've done very well, Pico. You have. The truth is that everyone is very proud of you."

She was on her feet again and walking, not sure when she had begun moving her legs. She wanted to poison her thoughts with her hatred of these awful people, and for a little while, she could think of nothing else. She would make her mind bilious and cancerous, poisoning all of these bastards and finally destroying them. That's what she would do, she promised herself. Except, suddenly she was sitting on the padded chair, autodocs coming close with their bright, humming limbs; and there was so much stored in her mind—worlds and people, emotions heaped on emotions— and she didn't have the time she would need to poison herself.

Which proved something, she realized.

Sitting still now.

Sitting still and silent. At ease. Her front drenched and stained brown, but her open eyes calm and dry.

George Turner

FLOWERING MANDRAKE

An Australian writer and critic of great renown, the late George Turner was for many years that country's most distinguished science fiction writer, and one of the few Australian SF writers to have established an international reputation that transcended parochial boundaries. Although he also published six mainstream novels, he was best known in the genre for the string of unsentimental, rigorous, and sometimes acerbic science fiction novels that he began to publish in 1978, including *Beloved Son, Vaneglory, Yesterday's Men, Brain Child, In the Heart or in the Head, Destiny Makers,* and the widely acclaimed *Drowning Towers,* which won the Arthur C. Clarke Award. His most recent novel was *Genetic Soldier.* His short fiction was collected in *A Pursuit of Miracles,* and he was the editor of an anthology of Australian science fiction, *The View from the Edge.*

During his lifetime Turner may have been considered to be the Grandmaster of Australian science fiction, and, true, he was decades older than his next most talked-about compatriot, Greg Egan . . . but even toward the end of his life he had lost none of his imagination or intellectual vigor, as he proved with the powerful and ingenious story that follows, a tale unsurpassed by any young Turks anywhere for the bravura sweep and daring of its conceptualization.

Turner died in 1997, at the age of eighty-two.

> Go, and catch a falling star,
> Get with child a mandrake root . . .
> —From the song, "Go, and catch", by John Donne

Four stars make Capella: two G-type suns sharing between them five times the mass of Terra's sol and two lesser lights seen only with difficulty from a system so far away.

Two of the fifteen orbiting worlds produced thinking life under fairly similar conditions but the dominant forms which evolved on each bore little resemblance to each other save in the possession of upright carriage, a head, and limbs for ambulation and grasping.

When, in time, they discovered each other's existence, they fought with that ferocity of civilized hatred which no feral species can or need to match.

The Red-Bloods fought at first because they were attacked, then because they perceived that the Green Folk were bent not on conquest but on destruction. The Green Folk fought because the discovery of Red-Blood dominance over a planet uncovered traits deep in their genetic structure. Evolution had been for them a million-year struggle against domination by emerging red-blooded forms and their eventual supremacy had been achieved only by ruthless self-preservation—the destruction of all competition. They kept small animals for various domestic and manufacturing purposes, even ate them at times for gourmet pleasure rather than need and feared them not at all, but the ancient enmity and dread persisted in racial defensiveness like a memory in the blood.

The discovery of a planet of Red-Bloods with a capacity for cultural competition wreaked psychological havoc. Almost without thought the Green Folk attacked.

Ships exploded, ancient cities drowned in fresh-sprung lava pits, atmospheres were polluted with death.

Beyond the Capellan system no sentient being knew of species in conflict. Galactic darkness swallowed the bright, tiny carnage.

Capella lay some forty-seven light-years from the nearest habitable planet, which its people called, by various forms of the name, Terra.

Only one member of crew, a young officer of the Fifth Brachiate, new to his insignia and with little seniority, but infinitely privileged over the Rootkin of his gunnery unit, escaped the destruction of *Deadly Thorn*. His name (if it matters, because it was never heard anywhere again) was Fernix, which meant in the Old Tongue, "journeying forest father."

When the Triple Alert flashed he was in the Leisure Mess, sucking at a tubule of the stem, taking in the new, mildly stimulating liquor fermented from the red fluid of animals. It was a popular drink, not too dangerously potent, taken with a flick of excitement for the rumor that it was salted with the life-blood of enemy captives. This was surely untrue but made a good morale boosting story.

Triple Alerts came a dozen a day and these bored old hands of the war no longer leapt to battle stations like sprouts-in-training. Some hostile craft a satellite's orbit distant had detected *Deadly Thorn* and launched a missile; deflector arrays would catch and return it with augmented velocity and the flurry would be over before they reached the doorway.

There was, of course, always the unlucky chance. Deflector arrays had their failings and enemy launchers their moments of cunning.

Fernix was still clearing his mouth when an instant of brilliant explosion filled space around *Deadly Thorn* and her nose section and Command Room blew out into the long night.

He was running, an automation trained to emergency, when the sirens screamed and through the remaining two-thirds of the ship the ironwood bulkheads thudded closed. He was running for his Brachiate Enclave, where his Root-kin waited for orders, when the second missile struck somewhere forward of him and on the belly plates five decks below.

A brutal rending and splintering rose under him and at his running feet the immensely strong deck-timbers tore apart in a gaping mouth that he attempted uselessly to cross in a clumsy, shaken leap. Off balance and unprepared, he felt himself falling into Cargo Three, the Maintenance Stores hold.

At the same moment ship's gravity vanished and the lighting system failed. *Deadly Thorn* was Dead Thorn. Fernix tumbled at a blind angle into darkness, arms across his head against crashing into a pillar or bulkhead at speed. In fact his foot caught in a length of rope, dragging him to a jarring halt.

Spread arms told him he had been fortunate to land on a stack of tarpaulins when it might as easily have been the sharp edges of tool boxes. Knowledge of the Issue Layout told him precisely where he was in the huge hold. There was a nub of escape pods in the wall not far to his left. He moved cautiously sideways, not daring to lose contact in null-gravity darkness but slithering as fast as he safely might.

Bulkheads had warped in the broken and twisted hull; both temperature and air pressure were dropping perceptibly.

He found the wall of the hold at the outer skin and moved slowly towards the vanished fore section until he felt the swelling of the nub of pods and at last the mechanism of an entry lock. Needing a little light to align the incised lines which would spring the mechanism, he pumped sap until the luminescent buds of his right arm shed a mild greenish radiance on the ironwood.

He thought momentarily, regretfully, of his Root-kin crew able to move only a creeper-length from their assigned beds, awaiting death without him. In this extremity he owed them no loyalty and they would expect none but they would, he hoped, think well of him. They were neuters, expendable and aware of it whereas he, Officer Class free-moving breeder, carried in him the gift of new life. There could be no question of dying with them though sentimental ballads wept such ideas; they, hard-headed pragmatists, would think it the act of an idiot. And they would be right.

He matched the lock lines and stepped quickly in as the fissure opened. As he closed the inner porte the automatic launch set the pod drifting gently into space.

He activated fresh luminescence to find the control panels and light switch. A low-powered light—perhaps forty watts—shone in the small space. To his eyes it was brilliant and a little dangerous; to a culture which made little use of metals, the power-carrying copper wires were a constant threat to wood, however tempered and insulated.

To discover where he was with respect to *Deadly Thorn*, he activated an enzyme flow through the ironwood hull at a point he judged would offer the best vision. As the area cleared he was able to see the lightless hulk occulting stars. The entire forward section was gone, perhaps blown to dust, and a ragged hole gaped amidships under the belly holds. If other pods floated nearby he could not see them.

Poised weightless over the controls, he checked the direction of the three-dimensional compass point in its bowl and saw that the homing beam shone steadily with no flicker from intervening wreckage. His way was clear and his duty certain, to return to the Home World carrying his spores of life.

A final, useless missile must have struck *Deadly Thorn* as he stretched for the controls and never reached them. A silent explosion dazzled his eyes, then assaulted his hearing as the shock wave struck the pod. A huge plate of *Deadly Thorn*'s armor loomed in the faint glow of his light, spinning lazily to strike the pod a glancing blow that set it tumbling end over end.

He had a split second for cursing carelessness because he had not strapped down at once. Then his curled up, frightened body bounced back and forth from the spinning walls until his head struck solidly and unconsciousness took him.

He came to in midair with legs bunched into his stomach and arms clasped around his skull. There was no gravity; he was falling free. But where?

Slow swimming motions brought him to a handhold but he became aware of a brutal stiffness in his right side. He pumped sap to make fingerlight, bent his head to the ribplates and saw with revulsion that he was deformed; the plates had been broken and had healed while he floated, but had healed unevenly in a body curled up instead of stretched. Surgery would rectify that—but first he must find a surgeon.

He was struck unpleasantly by the fact that even his botched joining would have occupied several months of the somatic shutdown which had maintained him in coma while the central system concentrated on healing. (He recalled sourly that the Red-Bloods healed quickly, almost on the run.)

Deity only knew where in space he might be by now.

But what had broken his body?

There were no sharp edges in the pod. Something broken, protruding spikes?

Shockingly, yes. The compass needle had been wrenched loose and the transparent, glassy tegument, black with his sap, lay shattered around it.

He thought, *I am lost*, but not yet with despair; there were actions to be taken before despair need be faced. He fed the hull, creating windows. Spaces cleared, opening on darkness and the diamond points of far stars. He found no sign of *Deadly Thorn*; he might have drifted a long way from her after the blast. He looked for the Home world, palely green, but could not find it; nor could he see the bluer, duller sister-world of the red-sapped, animal enemy.

Patiently he scanned the sky until a terrifying sight of the double star told him his search was done. It was visible still as a pair but as the twin radiances of a distant star. Of the lesser companions he could see nothing; their dimness was lost in the deep sky.

He had drifted unbelievably far. He could not estimate the distance; he remembered only from some long ago lecture that the double star might appear like this from a point beyond the orbit of the outermost planet, the dark fifteenth world.

The sight spoke not of months of healing but of years.

Only a brain injury . . .

Every officer carried a small grooming mirror in his tunic; with it Fernix examined the front and sides of his skull as well as he was able. Tiny swellings of healed fractures were visible, telling him that the braincase had crushed cruelly in on his frontal lobes and temples. Regrowth of brain tissue had forced them out again but the marks were unmistakable. In the collision with the wreckage of *Deadly Thorn* he had crashed disastrously into . . . what?

The whole drive panel was buckled and cracked, its levers broken off or jammed down hard in their guides. They were what had assaulted him. Acceleration at top level had held him unconscious until the last drops in the tank were consumed, releasing him then to float and commence healing.

Fearfully he examined the fuel gauges. The Forward Flight gauge was empty, its black needle flush with the bottom.

The Retro fuel gauge still showed full, indicating precisely enough to balance the forward gauge supply and bring the pod to a halt—enough, he realized drearily, to leave him twice as far from home as he now was, because the buckled panel had locked the steering jet controls with the rest. He could not take the pod into the necessary end for end roll. Only the useless deceleration lever still seemed free in its guides. The linkages behind the panel might still be operable but he had no means of reaching them and no engineering skill to achieve much if he did.

He was more than lost; he was coffined alive.

Something like despair, something like fear shook his mind as he eased himself into the pilot's seat, bruises complaining, but his species was not given to the disintegrative emotions. He sat quietly until the spasm subsided.

His actions now were culturally governed; there could be no question of what he would do. He was an officer, a carrier of breeding, and the next generation must be given every chance, however small, to be born. Very small, he thought. His pod could drift for a million years without being found and without falling into the gravity field of a world, let alone a livable world, but the Compulsion could not be denied. The Compulsion had never been stated in words; it was in the genes, irrevocable.

Calmly now, he withdrew the hull enzymes and blacked out the universe. He started the air pump and the quiet hiss of intake assured him that it was operative still. As the pressure tank filled with the withdrawn atmosphere he made the mental adjustment for Transformation. As with the

Compulsion, there were no words for what took place. Psychologists theorized and priests pontificated but when the time and the circumstance came together, the thing happened. The process was as intangible as thought, about whose nature there was also no agreement. The thought and the need and the will formed the cultural imperative and the thing happened.

Before consciousness left him, perhaps for ever, Fernix doused the internal heating, which was not run from the ruined drive panel.

Resuscitation he did not think about. That would take place automatically if the pod ever drifted close enough to a sun for its hull to warm appreciably, but that would not, could not happen. Deity did not play at Chance-in-a-Million with His creation.

Consciousness faded out. The last wisps of air withdrew. The temperature fell slowly; it would require several days to match the cold of space.

The Transformation crept over him as a hardening of his outer skin, slowly, slowly, until his form was sheathed in seamless bark. Enzymes clustered at the underside of his skin, fostering a hardening above and below until tegument and muscle took on the impermeability of ironwood. Officer of the Fifth Brachiate Fernix had become a huge, complex spore drifting in galactic emptiness.

He was, in fact, drifting at a surprising speed. A full tank expended at full acceleration had cut out with the pod moving at something close to six thousandths of the speed of light.

The pod's automatic distress signal shut down. It had never been heard amidst the radio noise of battle fleets. The interior temperature dropped towards zero and the vegetal computers faded out as ion exchange ceased. The pod slept.

Nearly eight thousand Terrestrial years passed before the old saying was disproved: Deity did indeed play at Chance-in-a-Million with His creation.

Vegetal computers were more efficient than a metal-working culture would readily believe, though they could not compete in any way with the multiplex machines of the animal foe—in any, that is, except one.

The pod's computers were living things in the sense that any plant is a living thing. They were as much grown as fashioned, as much trained as programmed, and their essential mechanisms shared one faculty with the entity in Transformation who slept in his armor: They could adopt the spore mode and recover from it in the presence of warmth.

They had no way of detecting the passage of millennia as they slept but their links to the skin of the pod could and did react to the heat of a G-type sun rushing nearer by the moment.

As the outer temperature rose, at first by microscopic increments, then faster and faster, the computer frame sucked warmth from the hull and, still at cryogenic levels, returned to minimal function.

At the end of half a day the chemical warming plant came silently into operation and the internal temperature climbed towards normal. Automatically the Life Maintenance computer opened the air tank to loose a jet of snow that evanesced at once into invisible gases.

The miracle of awakening came to Fernix. His outer tegument metamorphosed, cell by cell, into vegetal flesh as his body heat responded; first pores, then more generalized organs sucked carbon dioxide from the air and return from Transformation began.

Emergence into full consciousness was slow, first as an emptiness in which flashes of dreams, inchoate and meaningless, darted and vanished; then as a closer, more personal space occupied by true dreams becoming ever more lucid as metabolism completed its regeneration; finally as an awareness of self, of small pressures from the restricted pilot's seat, of sap swelling in capillaries and veins, of warmth and the sharp scent of too-pure air. His first coherent thought was that a good life caterer would have included some forest fragrance, mulch or nitrate, in the atmosphere tank.

From that point he was awake, in full muscular and mental control, more swiftly than a Red-Blood could have managed. (But the Red-Blood had no Transformation refuge that the scientists could discover; in deep cold or without air they died and quickly rotted. They were disgusting.)

He knew that only rising warmth could have recalled him.

A sun?

The Great Twin itself?

That was not possible.

Thanking Deity that the computers were not operated from the drive panel, he directed them to provide enzyme vision and in a moment gazed straight ahead at a smallish yellow sun near the center of the forward field.

So Deity did . . . He wasted no time on that beyond a transient thought that every chance must come to coincidence at some time in the life of the universe—and that he might as well be winner as any other.

He asked the navigating computer for details: distance, size, luminescence. Slowly, because vegetal processes cannot be hurried, the thing made its observations and calculations and offered them. Obediently it unrolled the stellar chart and almanac—and Fernix knew where he was.

And, he thought, little good *that* brings me.

This was a star not easily naked-eye visible from the Home world, but the astronomers had long ago pinpointed it and its unseen planets. He was forty-seven light-years from home (his mind accepted without understanding the abyss of time passed) on a course plunging him into the gravity well of an all-too-welcoming star at some thirty-two miles per second. The computer assured him that on his present course this yellow sun, though a child by comparison with the Great Twin, was powerful enough to grasp him and draw him into its atmosphere of flame.

But he had not come so far across time and space to die sitting still, eaten alive by a pigmy star.

He needed to buy time for thought. Deceleration alone was not enough for useful flight.

There was a blue-green planet, the almanac told him, which might possibly offer livable conditions. The hope was small in a universe where minute changes of temperature, orbit or atmosphere composition could put a world for ever beyond life, but the Deity which had guided him so finely and so far could surely crown His miracle with a greater one.

If he could achieve steering . . .

He was tempted to jimmy the cover off the Drive Panel and expose the linkages but common sense suggested that he would merely cause greater damage. He was coldly aware of ignorance and lack of mechanical talent; the maze of linkages would be to him just that—a maze, impenetrable.

Because he was untrained he failed for several hours to hit on the possibility that the the computer, once programmed to act rather than simply inform the pilot, might operate directly on the machine structures, bypassing linkages and levers. The entertainment media had imprinted him and all but those who actually operated space craft with a mental picture of pilots working by manual control, whereas it might be necessary only to tell the computer what he wanted.

That turned out to be anything but simple. As a gunnery officer he considered himself computer competent but he slept several times before he penetrated the symbols, information needs and connections of the highly specialized machine. Like most junior officers he had been rushed through an inadequate basic training and sent into space innocent of the peacetime auxiliary courses, with no expertise in other than visual navigation.

But, finally, the steering jets turned the pod end for end, the main jet roared triumphantly and the little craft slowed at the limit of deceleration his consciousness could bear. Held firmly in his straps with an arm weighing like stonewood, he questioned the computer about trajectories and escape velocities and how it might take him to the third planet of the yellow star.

It balanced distance against fuel and calculated a slingshot rounding of the central sun which would bring him economically to his goal, his destiny. There would be, Fernix knew, only a single chance and choice.

A Miner's Mate is, more correctly, an Asteroid Mining Navigational and Mass Detection Buoy. One of them sat sedately above a group of fairly large iridium-bearing "rocks" in the Belt, providing guidance for the occasional incoming or outgoing scow and warning against rogue intruders—meteorites or small asteroids in eccentric orbits. It carried a considerable armament, including two fusion bombs capable of shattering a ten-million-ton mass, but large wanderers were rare and collision orbits rarer still. Its warnings commonly did little more than send miners scurrying to the sheltered side of their rock until the danger passed.

Since space debris travels at speeds of miles per second, the sensitivity radius of the Mate's radar and vision systems was necessarily large. It registered the incoming pod at a million kilometers. Being fully automatic, it had no intelligence to find anything peculiar in the fact that it saw the thing before the mass detectors noted its presence. It simply radioed a routine alert to the mines and thereafter conscientiously observed.

The Shift Safety Monitor at the communication shack saw the tiny, brilliant point of light on his screen and wondered briefly what sort of craft was blasting inwards from the outer orbits. Scientific and exploratory probes were continuously listed and there were none due in this area of the System. Somebody racing home in emergency? Automatically he looked for the mass reading and there was none. What could the bloody Mate be doing? The mass of metal that put out such a blast must be easily measurable.

The Monitor's name was John Takamatta; he was a Murri from Western Queensland. This particular group of mines was a Murri venture and he was a trained miner and emergency pilot, now taking his turn on the dreary safety shift. Like most of his people he rarely acted without careful observation first; he waited for the Mate to declare or solve its problem.

The Mate's problem was that it could not recognize timber or any substance that let most of its beam through and diffused it thoroughly in passage. There was metal present but not enough to contain the tubes for such a drive blast and there was ceramic, probably enough for linings, but the amorphous mass surrounding these was matter for conjecture and conjecture was outside its capacity.

However, it tried, feeding back to the Mines computer a flicker of figures which mimicked a state of desperate uncertainty and gave the impression of a large, fuzzy thing of indefinite outline secreting within it some small metal components and ceramic duct lining.

Takamatta tried to enlarge the screen image but the size of the light did not change. It was either very small or far away or both.

The Mate's hesitant figures hovered around something under a ton but no mass so slight could contain such brilliance. Yet it could only be a ship and there were no ships of that nursery size. He rang the dormitory for the off-duty, sleeping Computer Technician. Albert Tjilkamati would curse him for it but they were related, men of the same Dreaming, and the curse would be routinely friendly.

Albert came, cursed, watched, sent a few test orders to the Mate and decided that it was not malfunctioning, yet the oscillating, tentative figures suggested a human operator floundering with an observation beyond his competence. Once the analogy had occurred to him, he saw the force of it.

"Something it can't recognize, John. Its beam is being diffused and spread from inner surfaces—like light shining into a box of fog. The receptors don't understand. John, man, it's picked up something new in space! We'll be in the newscasts!"

He called Search and Rescue's advance base in the Belt.

The Search and Rescue Watch Officer knew Albert Tjilkamati; if he said "strange" and "unusual," then strange and unusual the thing was.

"OK, Albert; I'll send a probe. Get back to you later."

He eased a torpedo probe out of its hangar, instructed its computers and sent it to intercept the flight path of the stranger. The probe was mainly a block of observational and analytical equipment in a narrow, twelve-meter tube, most of which was fuel tank; it leapt across the sky at an acceleration that would have broken every bone in a human body.

Starting from a point five million kilometers retrograde from the orbit of the Murri Mines, it used the Miner's Mate broadcast to form a base for triangulation and discovered at once that the incoming craft was decelerating at a g-number so high that the probe would have to recalculate its navigating instructions in order to draw alongside. It would, in fact, have to slow down and let the thing catch up with it.

The Watch Officer asked his prime computer for enhancement of the fuzzy mass/size estimates of the Mate, but the machine could not decide what the craft was made of or precisely where its edges were.

At this point, as if aware of observation, the craft's blast vanished from the screen.

The Watch Officer was intrigued but not much concerned; his probe had it on firm trace and would not let go. He notified HQ Mars, which was providentially the nearest HQ to him, of an incoming "artificial object of unknown origin," accompanied by a full transcript of the Mate's data, stated: "Intelligence probe despatched" and sat back to contemplate the probable uproar at HQ Mars. The lunatic fringe would be in full babble.

The computer, not Fernix, had cut the pod's blast because its velocity had dropped to the effective rate for rounding the system's sun. There would be corrections later as approach allowed more accurate data on the star's mass and gravity but for two million kilometers the pod would coast.

Fernix drifted into sleep. Transformation sleep conferred no healing, being essentially a reduction of metabolism to preservative zero; nothing was lost or gained during the hiatus. So he had awakened still in reaction to the stress of escape from *Deadly Thorn* and now needed sleep.

He woke again to the stridency of an alarm. The computer flashed characters in urgent orange, proclaiming the presence of a mass in steady attendance above and to the right of the pod and no more than twice its length distant.

He realized sluggishly that the mass must be a ship; only a ship equipped with damping screens could have approached so closely without detection.

The thought brought him fully alert. He opened a narrow vision slit and at first saw nothing; then he observed the slender occulting of stars. The thing was in darkness and probably painted black, else the central sun should have glinted on its nose.

If this was an artifact of the local life, he needed to find out what he could about it, even at the risk of exposing himself—if that was indeed a risk. The crew might well be friendly. He primed a camera for minimum exposure and, to aid it, turned the pod's lighting up full and opened the vision slit to his head's width for a tenth of a second.

It was enough for the camera to take its picture. It was enough, also, for the other to shoot through the gap a beam of intense light to take its own picture and blind Fernix's weak eyes. He flung his arms across his face and grunted with pain until his sight cleared. He stayed in darkness with the slit closed. He reasoned that he had been photographed by a race whose vision stretched farther into the shortwave light spectrum than his and not so far into the gentler infrared.

When the ache in his eyes subsided he examined his own infra-red picture. It showed a slender needle of nondescript color, dull and nonreflective, without visible ports. The small diameter of the craft inclined him to think it was an unmanned reconnaissance probe. His evolutionary teaching dictated that an intelligent life form must perforce have its brain case and sensory organs raised well above ground level, and no such entity could have stood upright or even sat comfortably in that projectile.

He considered what action he might take.

He had been outplayed at the observation game and could do nothing about that. His weaponless pod was not equipped to fight, which was perhaps as well; nothing would be gained by antagonizing these unknown people. Evasive action was out of the question. His fuel supply was low and his computer's decisions had been made on limits too tight for any but last-ditch interference from himself; there was none for ad hoc maneuver.

He could take no action. The next move must come from outside.

Conclusion reached, he slept.

The Search and Rescue call sign squealed in the shack, the screen cleared and Takamarra looked up from his novel as the Watch Officer hailed him, "John, oh John, have we got something here! This one will puncture holes in your Dreaming!"

John said coldly, "Indeed." He was no traditionalist but did not appreciate light handling of his cultural mores by a white man.

Some fifteen seconds would pass before his reply reached S & R and fifteen more for the Watch Officer's response. In that time he digested the message and concluded that the unlikely was true, that the intruding craft was extra-systemic. Alien. And that the existence of life among the stars *could* have some effect on the credibility of Murri Dreaming.

Then he decided that it would not. Incursion of the white man and knowledge of a huge world beyond the oceans had altered most things in his people's lives but not that one thing, the Dreamings around which the Murri cultures were built. Science and civilization might rock on their foundations as the word went out, *We are not alone*, but the ancient beliefs would not shift by the quiver of a thought.

Willy Grant's voice said, "Get this carefully, John. Make notes. We need the biggest scow you've got because yours is the nearest mining group. We want to pick this little ship out of the sky but we can't get a magnetic grapple on it because what little metal there is appears to be shielded. The best bet is to clamp it in the loading jaws of your Number Three scow if it's available. The thing is only ten meters long and three wide, so it will fit in easily. The scow can dawdle sunwards and let the outsider catch up with it until they are matched for speed. Forty-eight hours at one point five-g should do it. This is an Emergency Order, John, so time and fuel compensation will be paid. Relay that to your Manager, but pronto. The scow's computer can talk to mine about course and speed and we'll have your Manager's balls in a double reef knot if he raises objections. Got it?"

"Got it, Willy." He repeated the message for check. "Hang on while I pass it." Minus the threat; the Elder might not appreciate blunt humor.

The Murri Duty Manager preserved the Old Man routine of unimpressed self-possession, which fooled nobody. He turned his eyes from his screen, contemplated infinity in his fingernails for a respectable sixty seconds, raised his white-bearded head with an air of responsible decision-making and said, "Number Three scow is empty and available. It shall be floated off. The S & R computer can then take over." He would not have had the nerve to say otherwise; nobody in space flouted S & R.

Grant, on the other screen, heard the message and beat down the temptation to wink at John; the tribal old dear would be outraged and so would his miners. The Murri were good blokes but in some areas you had to tread carefully. When the Manager had cut out, he said, "Now, John, this'll rock you from here to Uluru. Look!"

He displayed a picture of the intruder illuminated by the probe's beam. It was shaped roughly like an appleseed, symmetrical and smooth, its line broken only by what must be a surprisingly narrow jet throat. Its color seemed to be a deep brown, almost ebony.

"Now, get this!" He homed the viewpoint to a distance of a few inches from the hull. "What do you make of it?"

What John saw surprised him very much. The hull surface was grained like wood; there was even a spot where some missile (sand-grain meteoroid?) had gouged it to expose a slightly lighter color and what was surely a broken splinter end.

Willy carried on talking. You do not wait for an answer across a thirty-second delay. "Looks like wood, doesn't it? Well, see this!" The view roved back and forth from nose to tail, and the wave pattern of the grain flowed evenly along the whole length. "You'd think they grew the thing and lathed it out of a single block. And why not? A ship doesn't have to be built of steel, does it? I know timber couldn't stand the take-off and landing strains but how about if they are ferried up in bulk in a metal mother ship or built on asteroids and launched at low speed? Or there could be means of hardening and strengthening timber; we don't know because we've never needed to do it. But a race on a metal-poor world would develop alternative technologies. I'd stake a month's pay the thing's made of wood, John."

In John's opinion he would have won the bet.

Willy did not display the other picture, the shocker taken when the alien tried to photograph the probe. Under instruction he had given Takamatta enough to satisfy immediate curiosity without providing food for the idiot fantasy that flourishes when laymen are presented with too much mystery and too few answers.

Alone he studied the startling hologram, at life size, which his computer had built for him.

It seemed that the alien had also taken a shot of the probe just as the automatic camera took advantage of the widening slit in the intruder's hull. The thing's face—"face" for want of a word—stared at him over what was surely a camera lens.

The alien—being, entity, what you would—seemed generally patterned on an anthropoid model with a skin dappled in gray and green. The head and neck protruded above shoulders from which sprang arms or extensions of some kind—probably arms, Willy thought, because on the thing's camera rested what should be fingers, though they looked more like a bunch of aerial roots dropped by some variety of creeper but thicker and, judging by their outlandish grasping, more flexible than fingers.

In the narrow head he could discern no obvious bone structure under thick—flesh? The face was repulsive in the vague fashion of nightmare when the horror is incompletely seen. There was a mouth, or something in the place of a mouth—an orifice, small and round with slightly raised edges where lips should have been. He thought of a tube which would shoot forward to fix and suck. Nose there was none. The eyes—they had to be eyes—were circular black discs with little holes at their centers.

He guessed hazily that black eyes, totally receptive of all wavelengths of light, could be very powerful organs of vision, given the outlandish nervous system necessary to operate them. Or, perhaps the central holes were the receptors, like pinhole cameras.

Ears? Well . . . there were flaps on the sides of the head, probably capable of manipulation since the hologram showed one raised and one nearly flush with the gray and green flesh. A third flap, partly open, in what must be called the forehead and revealing under it an intricately shaped opening reminiscent of the outer ear, suggested all-around hearing with a capacity for blocking out sound and/or direction finding. A useful variation.

Hair there seemed to be none but on the crown of the bud-shaped skull sat a plain, yellowish lump like a skittish party hat, a fez six inches or so high and four wide. Yet it seemed to be part of the head, not a decoration. He could make nothing of it.

There remained the faintly purplish cape around the thing's shoulders. Or was it a cape? It hung loosely over both shoulders and its lower edges fell below the rim of the vision slit, but it was parted at the throat and he had an impression that what he saw at the parting was dappled flesh rather than a garment. On closer examination he thought that the "cape" was actually a huge flap of skin, perhaps growing from the back of the neck. He thought of an elephant's ears, which serve as cooling surfaces.

An idea that had been knocking for expression came suddenly into the light and he said aloud, "The thing's a plant!"

At once he was, however unwarrantably, certain that he looked on the portrait of a plant shaped in the caricature of a man. The "cape" was a huge leaf, not for cooling but for transpiration. The seemingly boneless skull and tentacular hands made vegetable sense; the thing would be infinitely flexible in body, acquiring rigidity as and where needed by hydrostatic pressure. He pondered root systems and acquired mobility as an evolutionary problem without a glimmer of an answer, but his impression would not be shifted.

The thing from out there was a motile vegetable.

The setting up of ore refineries on asteroids which were usually worked out in a few years would have been prohibitively expensive, so the main refinery had been located on Phobos, and there the output of all Belt companies was handled without need for the scows to make planetfall. The saving in expensive fuel was most of what made the ventures profitable. Nor was there any waste of manpower on those lonely voyages; the scows were computer-directed from float-off to docking.

An empty scow, not slowed by several hundred ton mass of ore, could accelerate at a very respectable g-rate. Number Three scow from the Murri outfit caught its prey dead on time, forty-eight hours after float-off. Forty-eight hours of silent flight, accompanied by a probe which made no move, took toll of nerves. Fernix slept and wondered and theorized from too little knowledge and slept again. At the second waking he fed, sparsely, not knowing how long his supplies must stretch; he injected a bare minimum of trace elements into the mulch tray with just enough water to guarantee ingestion, and rested his feet in it. The splayed pads protruded their tubules like tiny rootlets as his system drew up the moisture. He preferred mouth feeding but in the pod he had no choice.

The brief euphoria of ingestion passed and his mood flickered between fear and hope. Did the probe accompany him for a purpose unknown or did its controllers watch and wait to see what he would do?

He would do nothing. The vacillations of mood rendered him unfit to decide with proper reason. He writhed internally but sat still, did nothing.

His people, slow-thinking and phlegmatic, did not slip easily into neurosis but he was muttering and twitching when new outside action came. He switched into calm observation and appraisal.

The alarm indicated a new presence in space, ahead of him but drawing close. He chanced a pinhole observation in the direction of the new mass but could see nothing. Whatever the thing was, either he was closing on it or it waited for him. His computer reported that the mass was losing some speed and he decided that it intended to match his course.

His instruments described it as long in body and large in diameter but not of a mass consistent with such size. An empty shell? Such as a cargo vessel with cleared holds?

Shortly he found that the probe had vanished and a quite monstrous ship was slipping back past him; the light of the system's sun shone on its pitted, blue-painted nose. It was old in space and about the size of a raiding destroyer but showed no sign of armament.

It slipped behind him and took up a steady position uncomfortably close to him. He was tempted to discover what it would do if he accelerated or changed course, then thought of his thin-edge supply of fuel. Do nothing, nothing; pray for friendly beings.

He saw with a frisson of tension that it was moving swiftly up to him.

Looming close to collision point, it opened its forward hull in a vast black mouth and gullet, like the sea monsters of his baby tales.

Its forward surge engulfed his pod, swallowed it whole and closed about it as something (grasping bands?) thudded on the pod's shell and held captor and prey to matched speeds. He was imprisoned in a vast, empty space, in darkness.

After a while he cleared the pod's entire shell, turning it into a transparent seed hanging in a white space illuminated by his interior lights. White, he thought, for optimum lighting when they work in here.

The space was utterly vacant. At the far end, roughly amidships he calculated, vertical oblong outlines were visible against her white paint—entry hatches. So the entities stood upright; he had expected no less. Evolutionary observation and theory (formulated so long ago, so far away) suggested that an intelligent, land-based being must stand erect, that it should carry brain and major sensory organs at its greatest height, that it should possess strong limbs for locomotion and grasping in limited number according to the law of minimum replication, that it—

—a dozen other things whose correctness he should soon discover in fact.

He saw that his pod was clamped above and below in a vise powerful enough to hold it steady in a turbulent maneuver. It was, his instruments told him, basically iron, as was the hull of the ship.

He was not sure whether or not he should envy a race which could be so prodigal of metal. Their technologies would be very different from those of the Home World.

He waited for them but they did not come.

Could their ship be unmanned, totally remote-controlled? His people had a few such—had had a few such—but their radio-control techniques had been primitive and doubtful. Given unlimited iron and copper for experiment . . .

He waited.

Suddenly the pod was jerked backward as the captor vessel decelerated at a comfortable rate; he could have withstood twice as much.

Homing on a world nearby? He could not tell; his instruments could not penetrate the metal hull.

He thought, I am learning the discipline of patience.

The crew of a ship approaching Phobos would have seen few surface installations though the moonlet housed the HQ Outer Planets Search and Rescue, an Advanced College of Null-Gravity Science, the Belt Mining Co-Operative Ore Refineries, a dozen privately owned and very secretive research organizations and, most extensive of all, the Martian Terra-forming Project Laboratories and Administrative Offices.

All of these were located inside the tunnelled and hollowed rock that was Phobos.

It had been known for a century or more that the moonlet was slowly spiralling inwards for a long fall to Mars and Martian Terraforming did not want some six thousand cubic kilometers of solid matter crashing on the planet either before or after its hundred-year work was completed. So the interior had been excavated to the extent of nearly twenty per cent of the total mass (the engineers had vetoed more less stress changes break the rock apart) and the detritus blasted into space at high velocity. The change in mass, even after the installation of men and machinery, had slowed the inward drift but more brutal measures would eventually have to be taken, and one College research unit was permanently engaged in deciding what such measures might be (brute force is easily said) and how they might be applied (less easily said).

Phobos, swinging six thousand kilometers above the Martian surface, was a busy hive where even gossip rarely rose above the intellectual feuds and excitements of dogged dedication—

—until a junior ass in S & R cried breathlessly, careless of eager ears, "Bloody thing looks like a lily pad with head and chest. A plant, bejesus!"

After that, S & R had trouble preventing the information being broadcast throughout the System, but prevent if they did. The last thing a troubled Earth needed as it emerged from the Greenhouse Years and the Population Wars was the political, religious and lunatic fringe upheaval expectable on the cry of *We are not alone.*

Possum Takamatta, John's younger brother, a Communications Operative with S & R, pondered the hologram transmitted from the Belt and asked, "Just what sense do they think an ecologist might make of that?"

"God knows," said ecologist Anne Spriggs of Waterloo, Iowa, and Martian Terraforming, who was as pink-and-white as Possum was deep brown-black, "but I know some botany, which is more than anyone else around here does, so I just might make a useful contribution, read guess."

"With no tame expert at hand, they're desperate?"

"Possum, wouldn't you be desperate?"

"Why? I'm just interested. My people knew that 'more things in heaven and earth' line twenty thousand years before Shakespeare. You got any ideas?"

"No, only questions."

"Like?"

"Is it necessarily a plant because it reminds us of a plant? If it is, how does a rooted vegetable evolve into a motile form?"

"Who says it's motile? We've only got this still picture."

"It has to be to go into space. It couldn't take a garden plot with it."

"Why not? A small one, packed with concentrates, eh? And why should it have to become motile? Might have descended from floating algae washed up in swamplands with plenty of mud. Developed feet instead of roots, eh?'

Anne said with frustration, "So much for the ecologist! The local screen-eye has more ideas than I do."

He tried soothing because he liked Anne. "You're hampered by knowledge, while I can give free rein to ignorance."

She was not mollified. "Anyway, is it plant or animal? Why not something new? Who knows what conditions formed it or where it's from?"

"From at least Alpha Centauri; that's the nearest. It came in at thirty k per second, and decelerating; if that was anything like its constant speed it's been on its way for centuries. That's a long time for one little lone entity."

"Why not FTL propulsion?"

"Come off it, girl! Do you credit that shit?"

"Not really."

"Nor does anyone else. If it came from anywhere out there, then it's an ancient monument in its own lifetime."

"In the face of that," she said, "I feel monumentally useless. What in hell am I good for?"

"Marry me and find out."

"In a humpy outside Alice Springs?"

"I've a bloody expensive home in Brisbane."

"And I've a fiancé in Waterloo, Iowa."

"The hell you say!"

"So watch it, Buster!" She planted a kiss on the tip of his ear. "That's it. Everything else is off limits."

"In Australia we say out of bounds."

"In Australia you also say sheila when you mean pushover."

Not quite right but near enough and she certainly made better viewing than the mess on the screen.

In another part of the cavern system the Base Commander S & R held a meeting in an office not designed to hold thirteen people at once—himself and the twelve managers of the moonlet's private research companies. Commander Ali Musad's mother was Italian, his father Iraqi and himself a citizen of Switzerland; S & R took pride in being the least racially oriented of all the service arms.

He had set the office internal g at one-fifth, enough to keep them all on the floor, however crowded; it is difficult to dominate a meeting whose units sit on walls and ceiling and float away at a careless gesture.

He said, "I have a problem and I need your help. As Station senior executive I can give orders to service groups and enforce them; of you ladies and gentlemen representing civilian projects I can only ask."

They resented his overall authority. They remained silent, letting him wriggle on his own hook, whatever it was. Then they might help, cautiously, if advantage offered.

"Some of you will have heard of a . . . presence . . . in space. A foolish boy talked too loudly in a mess room and no doubt the whisper of what he said has gone the rounds."

That should have produced a murmur but did not. Only Harrison of Ultra-Micro asked, "Something about a green man in a sort of lifeboat?"

"Something like that."

"I didn't pay attention. Another comedian at work or has someone picked up a phantom image from a dramacast?"

"Neither. He's real."

Someone jeered softly, someone laughed, most preferred a skeptical lift of eyebrows. Chan of Null-G Germinants suggested that managers had low priority on the rumor chain. "Ask the maintenance staff; they're the slush bearers."

Musad told them, "It isn't silly season slush; it's real; I've seen it. Talk has to be stopped."

Still they did not take him too seriously. "Can't stop gossip, Commander."

"I mean: Stop it getting off Phobos."

"Too late, Commander. If it's a little green men story it's gone out on a dozen private coms by now."

He said stiffly, "It hasn't. I've activated the censor network." The shocked silence was everything he could have desired. "Every com going out is being scanned for key words; anything containing them is being held for my decision."

He waited while anger ran its course of outrage and vituperation. They didn't give a damn about little green men but censorship was an arbitrary interference guaranteed to rouse fury anywhere across the System. The noise simmered down in predictable protests: ". . . abuse of power . . . justifiable only in war emergency . . . legally doubtful on international Phobos . . ."

Melanie Duchamp, the Beautiful Battleaxe of Fillette Bonded Aromatics, produced the growling English that browbeat boardrooms: "You will need a vairy good reason for this."

No honorific, he noted; Melanie was psyching herself for battle. "It was a necessary move. Now I am asking you to ratify it among your company personnel."

"Fat chance," said one, and another, "We'd have mutiny on our hands."

He had expected as much. "In that case I shall order it as a service necessity and take whatever blame comes." And leave them to accept blame if events proved his action the right one. "I can promise worse than mutiny if the news is not controlled."

At that at least they listened. He told them what he knew of the intruding ship, its contents and the speculation about its origin, and then: "Let this news loose on Earth and Luna and we'll have every whining, power-grabbing, politicking ratbag in the System here within days. I don't mean just the service arms and intelligence wood-beetles and scientists and power-brokers; I mean the churches and cults and fringe pseudo-sciences and rich brats with nothing better to do. I also mean your own company executives and research specialists and the same from your merchant rivals—to say nothing of the print and electronic media nosing at your secrets. How do you feel about it?"

It was Melanie who surrendered savagely. "I will support you—under protest."

"You don't have to cover your arse, Melanie. I'll take the flack."

"So? There will be lawsuits, class actions that will cost the companies millions."

"No! I will declare a Defense Emergency."

"Then God or Allah help you, Commander."

Harrison said, "You can't do it. You say the thing seems to be unarmed; how can you invoke defense?"

"Possible espionage by an alien intruder. If that won't do, the Legal Section will think up something else."

In the end they agreed if only because he left them no choice. Satisfied that they would keep the lid on civilian protest, he threw them a bone: He would call on them to supply experts in various fields not immediately available among the service personnel on Phobos, because he intended to bring the thing inside and mount as complete an examination as possible before allowing a squeak out of Phobos Communications.

They brightened behind impassive agreement. With their own men at the center of action they would be first with the news as history was made in their particular corners . . . with profit perhaps . . . and Wily Musad was welcome to the lawsuits.

When they had gone he summoned his secretary. "All on record?"

"Yes, sir."

"Am I covered?"

"I think so. They will cooperate in case you retaliate by leaving them out of the selection of expert assistance. Which means that you must take at least one from each firm, however useless."

"Yes. Many messages intercepted?"

"Seven for your attention. Three to media outlets. It seems we have some unofficial stringers aboard."

"The buggers are everywhere. I don't want media complaints when they find out that their lines were stopped. They stir up too much shit." He recalled too late that Miss Merritt was a Clean Thinker. "Sorry."

She was unforgiving. "Nevertheless there will be complaints." Her tone added, And serve you right. Clean Thinkers held that censorship was unnecessary in a right-minded community—and so was crude language.

"I think the courts will uphold me."

"No doubt, sir. Will that be all?"

"Yes, Miss Merritt." And to hell with you, Miss Merritt, but you are too efficient to be returned to the pool.

•   •   •

The Number Three scow drifted down through darkness to hover over the moonlet's docking intake, a square hole like a mineshaft, that came suddenly alive with light.

The docking computer took control, edged the huge scow, precisely centered, through the intake and closed the entry behind it.

A backup computer waited, ready to take over in the event of malfunction, and a human operator waited with finger on override, prepared to assume manual control at an unpredictable, unprogrammable happening. This was a first in the history of the human race and almost anything, including the inconceivable, might occur.

Nothing did.

The computer took the scow evenly through the second lock, closed it, moved the vessel sideways through the Repair and Maintenance Cavern to the largest dock and set it smoothly belly-down on the floor. Then, because nobody had thought to tell it otherwise, it followed normal procedure and switched on one-eighth g in the floor area covered by the vessel, sufficient to ensure cargo stability.

Watching in his office screen, Musad cursed somebody's thoughtlessness—his own, where the buck stopped—and opened his mouth for a countermanding order. Then he thought that any damage was already done. Anyway, why should there be damage? No world with an eighth g would have produced a life form requiring an atmosphere, and the probe had certainly reported an atmosphere of sorts. Whatever lived inside the . . . lifeboat? . . . should be comfortable enough.

He shut his mouth and called Analysis. "Full scan, inside and out. There is a living being inside; take care."

Analysis knew more than he about taking care and had prepared accordingly. The first necessity was to establish the precise position of the thing inside—being, entity, e-t, what you would—and ascertain that it was or was not alone. So: a very delicate selection of penetrating radiation in irreducibly small doses, just enough to get a readable shadow and keep it in view.

Analysis had far better instrumentation than the comparatively crude probe and established at once that the thing was alive and moving its . . . limbs? . . . While remaining in seated position facing the nose of the vessel. Able now to work safely around the thing, visitor, whatever, Analysis unleashed its full battery of probe, camera, resolution and dissection.

The results were interesting, exciting, even breathtaking, but no scrap of evidence suggested where the little ship might have come from.

Musad was an administrator, not a scientist; Analysis gave him a very condensed version of its immensely detailed preliminary report—blocked out, scripted, eviscerated, rendered down and printed for him in under three hours—highlighting the facts he had called for most urgently:

The living entity in the captive vessel would be, when it stood, approximately one and a half meters tall. It showed the basic pentagonal structure—head and four limbs—which might well represent an evolutionary optimum design for surface dwellers in a low-g Terrene range. There was a rudimentary skeletal structure, more in the nature of supportive surface plates than armatures of bone, and the limbs appeared tentacular rather than jointed. This raised problems of push-pull capability with no answers immediately available.

Spectroscopic reading was complicated by the chemical structure of the vessel's hull, but chlorophyll was definitely present in the entity as well as in the hull, and the bulky "cape" on its shoulders showed the visual characteristics of a huge leaf. It was certainly a carbon-based form and seemed to be about ninety per cent water; there was no sign of hemoglobin or any related molecule.

The atmosphere was some forty per cent denser than Terrene air at sea level, a little light in oxygen but heavy with water vapor and carbon dioxide.

Tentative description: Highly intelligent, highly evolved, motile plant species.

We always wondered about aliens and now we've got one. What does he eat? Fertilizer? Or does that snout work like a Venus fly trap?

The small amounts of iron in the vessel—tank linings and a few hand tools—argued a metal-poor environment, ruling out any Sol-system planet as a world of origin.

As if they needed ruling out!

The ceramic lining of the jet would require longer evaluation but appeared to be of an unfamiliar crystalline macro-structure. All the other parts of the vessel, including the hull, were timber. There was nothing unusual about the composition of the various woods but a great deal unusual about about the treatments they had undergone, presumably for hardening and strengthening; no description of these could be hazarded without closer examination. (There followed a dissertation on the possible technology of a timber-based culture. Musad skipped over it.)

Dating procedures were at best tentative on materials whose isotopic balance might not match Terrene counterparts, but guesstimates gave a pro tem figure of between seven and ten thousand Terrene years. The signatories declined to draw any conclusions as to the age of the vegetal pilot or where he might have originated.

And all it does is sit there, sit there, sit there, occasionally moving a tentacle in some unguessable activity. So: What next?

He was taken by an idea so absurd that it would not go away, an idea which might, just might stir the creature into some action. It was a sort of "welcome home" idea—rather, an introduction . . .

He called the Projection Library.

Fernix slept and woke while the deceleration held him comfortably in his seat. He slept again and woke, nerves alert, when deceleration ceased.

He opened a tiny vision hole but saw only his prison still closed around him.

Shortly there was a perceptible forward motion and the slightest of centrifugal effects as the direction changed several times. Then his captor ship settled, gently for so large a transport. His pod shook momentarily and was still.

Suddenly there was gravity, not much of it but enough to aid balance and movement.

Not that he had any intention of moving; he could not afford movement. He needed energy. Food alone was not enough; his thousands of chloroplasts needed sunlight for the miracle of conversion to maintain body temperature, muscle tone, even the capacity to think effectively. There was a spectrum lamp aboard but its batteries would operate for only a limited time; a pod was not intended for pan-galactic voyaging.

Yet full alertness could be demanded of him at any moment; he must pump his body resources to a reasonable ability for sustained effort. He used a third of the lamp's reserve, switched it off and continued at rest in the pilot seat.

There was little assessment he could make of his position. His captors had demonstrated no technological expertise (beyond a squandering of metal) which could not have been duplicated on the Home World, nor had they attempted to harm him. So they were civilized beings, reasonably of a cultural status with which he could relate.

On the panel, radiation detectors flickered at low power. He was, he guessed, being investigated. So, this race was able to operate its instruments *through* the metal hull outside. That proved little; a race evolving on a metal-rich world would naturally develop along different lines of scientific interest from one grown from the forests of Home. Different need not mean better.

It was an exciting thought, that on another world a people had emerged from the nurturing trees to conquer the void of space.

The thought was followed by another, more like a dream, in which his people had traversed the unimaginable distance between stars to colonize this faraway system, facing and overcoming the challenges of worlds utterly variant from their own, inventing whole new sciences to maintain their foothold on the universe.

The open-minded intelligence can contemplate the unfamiliar, the never conceived, and adapt it to new modes of survival.

He had arrived by freakish accident; could not his people have made the crossing during the eons while he crept through space in free fall? The idea of using Transformation for survival while a ship traversed the years and miles had been mooted often.

His reverie was broken by a squealing hiss from outside the pod.

Outside. They were supplying his prison with an atmosphere.

Chemist Megan Ryan was the first to curse Musad for mishandling the approach to the alien ship. Suited up and ready to examine the hull, she heard someone at the closed-circuit screen ask, "What the hell's going on? They've let air into the scow."

She clawed the man out of the way and punched Musad's number to scream at him, "What do you think you're bloddy well doing?"

"And who do you think you're talking to, Captain-Specialist?"

She took a deep, furious breath. "To you . . . sir. Who ordered air into the scow?"

"I did." His tone said that if she objected, her reason had better be fool-proof.

"But why, why, why?" She was close to stuttering with rage.

His administrative mind groped uneasily at the likelihood of an error of unscientific judgment and decided that this was not a moment for discipline. "To provide air and temperature for the investigating teams to work in. What else?"

She swallowed, conscious of a red face and tears of frustration. "Sir, that ship has been in space for God only knows how long, in the interstellar deep. Its timber hull will have collected impact evidence of space-borne elements and zero-temperature molecules. That evidence will by now have been negated by temperature change and highly reactive gases. Knowledge has been destroyed."

She was right and he would hear about it later from higher echelons; he simply had not thought from a laboratory standpoint. "I'm sorry, Meg, but my first priority for investigation is the traveller rather than the ship. He represents more urgent science than a little basic chemistry."

The wriggling was shameful and he knew it; he had forgotten everything outside the focus of his own excitement, the alien.

She was glaring still as he cut her off.

He spoke to the Library: "Have you got much?"

"A good representative selection, sir. Vegetable environments from different climates. As you requested, no human beings."

"Good. I don't want humans presented to him in stances and occupations he—it—won't understand. Get a computer mockup ready—a naked man, good physique, in a space suit. Set it up so that the suit can be dissolved from around him. I want a laboratory effect, emotionally distancing, to reduce any 'monster' reaction."

"Yes, sir," the screen murmured.

"He's put out a probe of some sort," said another screen. "Sampling the air maybe."

Musad turned to screen 3 and the alien ship. The temperature in the hold had risen to minus thirty Celsius and vapor was clearing rapidly from the warming air. Visibility was already good.

When the air reached normal temperature and pressure for their planet, Fernix reasoned, they would come for him.

They did not come, though temperature and pressure levelled off. He was disappointed but accepted that there would be circumstances which he could not at present comprehend.

He extended a hull probe for atmosphere analysis, to find the outside pressure very low while the water vapor content hovered at the "dry" end of the scale and the carbon dioxide reading was disturbingly light. He could exist in such an atmosphere only with difficulty and constant re-energizing. Acclimatization would take time.

Through the generations, he reasoned, his people would have made adaptation, for the vegetal germ was capable of swift genetic change. There would be visible differences by now—of skin, of stature, of breathing areas—but essentially they would be his people still. . . .

He saw a flash of colored movement outside his spyhole and leaned forward to observe.

In the prison space, a bare armslength from the pod's nose, a silver-green tree flickered into existence, took color and solidity to become a dark, slender trunk rising high before spreading into radiating fronds. His narrow field of vision took in others like it on both sides and beyond, ranged at roughly equal distances. Beyond them again, a broad river. The palmate forms were familiar (mutations, perhaps, of ancestral seeds carried across the void?) as was the formal arrangement on a river bank, the traditional files of the rituals of Deity.

As he watched, the scene changed to a vista of rolling highlands thickly covered with conical trees of the deep green of polar growths, and in the foreground a meadow brilliant with some manner of green cover where four-legged, white beasts grazed. Their shape was unfamiliar, but his people had used grazing beasts throughout historical time; children loved them and petted them and wept when they were slaughtered. Only the anthropoid monsters from the sister world could terrify the young and rouse the adults to protective fury.

As the picture faded he wondered had the man-beasts been utterly destroyed. Some would have been preserved for study . . . mated in zoos . . . exhibited . . .

A new view faded in and the hologram placed him at the edge of a great pond on whose surface floated green pads three or four strides across their diameter. He recognized water-dwelling tubers though the evolved details were strange, as were the flitting things that darted on and above them. Forms analogous to insects he guessed, thinking that some such line was an almost inevitable product of similar environment.

Cautiously he opened the vision slit wider and saw that the huge picture extended away and above as though no walls set limits to it. He looked upwards to an outrageously blue, cloudless sky that hurt his eyes. This world, without cloud cover, would be different indeed.

He realized with a burst of emotion, of enormous pride and fulfilment, that he was being shown the local planet of his people, accentuating the similarities that he would recognize, welcoming him Home as best they could.

The picture changed again and this time he wept.

His pod lay now in the heart of a jungle clearing, brilliant-hued with flowers and fungi that stirred memory though none were truly familiar. Tall, damp trunks lifted to the light, up to the tight leaf cover where the branching giants competed for the light filtered down through cloud cover. For there was cloud cover here, familiarly gray, pressing down and loosing its continuous drizzle to collect on the leaves and slide groundwards in silver-liquid tendrils. Bright insect-things darted, and larger things that flapped extensions like flattened arms to stay aloft in surprisingly effective fashion. These were strange indeed as were the four-legged, furry things that leapt and scurried on the ground, chewing leaves and grubbing for roots.

The whole area could have been a corner of his ancestral estate, transformed yet strangely and truly belonging. He had been welcomed to a various but beautiful world.

With the drunken recklessness of love and recognition he activated the enzyme control and cleared the entire hull of the pod for vision. It was as though he stood in the heart of a Home playground, amid surroundings he already loved.

Soon, soon his people of these new, triumphant years must show themselves . . .

. . . and as though the desire had triggered the revelation, the jungle faded away and a single figure formed beyond the nose of the pod, floating in darkness as only a hologram could, hugely bulky in its pressure suit, face hidden behind the filtering helmet plate but wholly human in its outward structure of head and arms and motor limbs.

He left the seat to lean, yearning, against his transparent hull, face pressed to the invisible surface, arms spread in unrestrained blessing.

The figure spread its arms in a similar gesture, the ancient gesture of welcome and peace, unchanged across the void and down the centuries.

The outlines of the pressure suit commenced to blur, to fade, revealing the creature within.

The naked body was white, stiff-limbed, fang-mouthed, bright-eyed with recognition of its helpless, immemorial foe.

It floated, arms outstretched, in mockery of the ritual of peace.

The Red-Blood.

The enemy.

When the first hologram appeared—the Nile-bank scene of the planting program for binding the loosening soil—Musad watched for reaction from the ship but there was none.

The Swedish panorama, its forest of firs contrasted with the feeding sheep, pleased him better. On any habitable world there must be some environment roughly correlating with this, some scene of bucolic peace.

Then came the Victoria lilies and their pond life— A screen voice said, "It's opened the vision slit a little bit. It's interested."

It? Too clinical. Musad would settle for he. Could be she, of course, or some exotic gender yet unclassified.

The fourth scene, the jungle display, brought a dramatic result. The entire hull of the ship became cloudy, then translucent and—vanished. The interior was revealed from nose to jet.

Musad did not bother scanning the internal fittings; a dozen cameras would be doing that from every angle. He concentrated on the alien.

It—*he* rose swiftly out of his chair, head thrust forward in the fashion of a pointing hound and stepped close to the invisible inner hull. He was not very tall, Musad thought, nor heavily muscled but very limber, as though jointless. (But how could a jointless being stand erect or exert pressure? His basically engineering-mind thought vaguely of a compartmentalized hydrostatic system, nerve-operated. Practical but slow in reaction time.) He lifted his tentacular arms, spreading the great "cape" like a leaf to sunlight, and raised them over his head in a movement redolent of ecstasy.

Could jungle, or something like it, be the preferred habitat? *He* was plainly enthralled.

The jungle scene faded and the hold was in darkness save for the low-level radiance of the little ship's interior lighting.

The computer's creation, man-in-space-suit, appeared forward of the ship, floating a meter above the floor. *He* leaned, in unmistakable fascination, close against the inner hull. *He* pressed his face against the invisible timber like a child at a sweetshop window and slowly spread his arms. His "hands" were bunches of gray-green hoses until the fingers separated and stiffened. Musad could see that the tubular members straightened and swelled slightly; he could detect no muscle but they had plainly hardened as they pressed against the wood. It seemed to Musad that he stood in a posture of unrestrained, longing welcome.

The Library operator must have caught the same impression and in a moment of inspiration had the space-suited figure duplicate the outspread stance of friendship. Then he began to fade the armor, baring the symbolic man within.

He remained perfectly still.

Musad advanced his viewpoint until the alien's face dominated his screen. The face changed slowly. Thin folds of skin advanced across the huge black eyes, closing until only small circles remained. The mouth tube retracted and simultaneously opened wide in another circle, a great "Oh!" of wonder and surprise. The face resembled nothing more than a child's drawing of a happy clown.

Musad pulled back the view and saw that the "cape" was now fully raised behind the head, like some vast Elizabethan jewelled collar, save that the leaf veins shone bright yellow.

"He's happy," Musad said to anyone who might hear him. "He's happy!"

He stepped slowly back from the hull, lowered an arm to one of the panels—and the dark hull was there again, lightless, impenetrable.

Musad could not, never did know that what he had seen was a rictus mask more deeply murderous than simple hatred could rouse and mold.

• • •

For Fernix recognition of the Red-Blood was more than a cataclysm; it was a trigger.

On the Home world, when the end came it was recognized.

An end was an end. Intellect lost overriding control and biological forces took over. Genetically dictated reactions awoke and the process of Final Change began.

Pollination, initiated in the peak years of adolescence and suspended until the Time of Flowering, was completed in a burst of inner activity. At the same time stimulant molecules invaded his cerebrum, clarifying and calming thought for the Last Actions. In the domed crown of his skull the bud stirred; the first lines of cleavage appeared faintly on the surface as the pressure of opening mounted. His people flowered once only in life—when, at the moment of leaving it, the pollen was gathered by exultant young partners while the dying one's children were born.

There would be none to gather pollen from Fernix but his salute should be as royal as his lineage.

The initial burst of killing rage against the Red-Blood ebbed slowly. Had the projection been indeed a physical Red-Blood he would have been unable to master the urge to murder; he would have been out of the pod and in attack without conscious thought, obeying an impulse prehistorically ancient. The fading of the thing helped return him to reason.

It had shown him in the opening of its mouth, in what the things called a "smile," that he was the helpless captive of enemy cruelty. The display of fangs had been the promise of the last insult to honorable extinction, the eating of his body before Final Change could translate him to Deity.

It did not seem to him irrational that he had so simply projected as fact his people's conquest of space and the new worlds; his psychology carried no understanding other than that the vegetal races were naturally dominant in the intellectual universe. The Home World scientists found it difficult to account for the evolution of thinking Red-Bloods on the neighbor planet; such things, they reasoned, could only be sports, the occasional creations of a blind chance, having no destiny.

Fernix, orthodox because he had no training beyond orthodoxy, could only grasp that his people must have been totally destroyed in that long ago war, overwhelmed by unimaginable disaster. Not they had conquered interstellar space but the Red-Bloods. He, Fernix, was alone in a universe empty of his kind.

He knew, as he regained mental balance, that Final Change had begun. There was no fear of death in his people's psychology, only an ineradicable instinct to perpetuate the species; Fernix felt already the changes in his lower limbs heralding the swift growth of embryonic offspring, motile units in one limb, rooted slave-kin in the other.

That they would be born only to die almost at once did not trouble him; he could not abort births governed by autonomic forces and he was not capable of useless railing against the inevitable. He had seen the terror of

Red-Bloods as death came to them and been unable to comprehend the working of brains which in extremity rendered their possessors useless and demented. How could such creatures have mastered the great void?

He settled again into the pilot's seat and with quick actions emptied the whole store of trace elements into the feeding bed and thrust his feet deep into the mulch.

With triumphant pleasure he opened the emergency carbon dioxide cock and drained the tank into the pod's atmosphere. His death would be such a flowering of insult as few had ever offered the Red-Bloods. The burst of mocking blossom, in the color of their own life fluid, would take his people out of history in a blaze of derisive laughter at their barbarian destroyers.

That was not all. One other gesture was possible—the winning of a last battle although the war was long over.

The alien had shut himself in. The shortwave team reported that he had resumed the pilot seat and as far as they could determine had moved little in several hours.

Anne Ryan blamed Musad and was careless who heard her. "It's a vegetable form and he lulls it into euphoria with holograms of arboreal paradise, then confronts it with a bone-and-meat structure as far outside its experience as it is outside ours! It's probably half-paralyzed with shock. It needs time to assimilate the unthinkable. We need a brain here, not a bloody bureaucrat."

Melanie's contribution seemed more vicious for being delivered in a strong Breton accent. "The thing showed its teeth! The plant was terrified. It has no teeth, only a sucking tube! So you bare teeth at it and it runs to hide! Who would not?"

Musad thought the woman had a point and that he had acted with more authority than prudence. But, what should be done on first contact with the unknowable? The only certainty had been that he must take some action; if he had ordered the scientists to leave the thing alone he would have had rebellion on his hands and eventually questions asked in political arenas; if he had given them their heads they would have mauled each other in battles for priority and he would have ended up cashiered for inefficient management of an undisciplined rabble.

Now, when he had no idea what to do, help came from his own S & R, from the shortwave investigation team. "Something's going on inside, sir, but we don't know what it means. In the first minutes after it closed off the vision we could see it—the shadow of it, that is—gesturing like an angry man. Then it went back to the seat and made motions like pressing little buttons or flicking small levers—maybe. We can't be sure because with so much wood it's hard to get even a shadow picture. At any rate it made some adjustments because the carbon dioxide component in its air went up to eight per cent. The water vapor content seems to have increased, too, and the temperature has risen from thirty-five degrees to forty-six."

"Hothouse conditions!"

"Super-hothouse, sir."

"What's he up to? Forcing his growth?"

"We think more likely some other growth it carries in there. Maybe it has seeds in that thing like a tub at its feet. That's if the things make seeds."

Seeds or sprouts or tubers or buds . . . What do you do when you don't know what you're dealing with? How do you even think?

The diffident, careful tones of the radiographer said, "Sir, it doesn't want any part of us."

"Seems so."

"If it won't come to us, sir, shouldn't we go to it?"

Musad had no false pride. "You have a suggestion, Sergeant?"

"We could put a duroplastic tent round its ship, sir, big enough to allow a bunch of scientists to work in space suits, and fill it with an atmosphere matching the alien's."

"Then?"

"Cut a hole in the hull, sir, and get it out. Cut the ship in half if necessary."

That should at least keep everybody quiet until the next decision—except, perhaps, the alien—and anything he did would be marginally preferable to stalemate. And—oh, God!—he would have to decide who to allow into the tent and who must wait his or her turn.

He noted the Sergeant's name; one man at least was thinking while the rest boiled and complained. Yet he hesitated to give a command which in itself would be controversial.

He was still hesitating when the Analysis team gave an update: "It hasn't moved from the chair in two hours. Now chest movement has ceased; it is no longer breathing. It is probably dead."

That settled it. He ordered positioning of the tent and matching of atmospheres. That done, they must recover the body before serious deterioration set in.

Fernix was not dead. Not quite. The complex overlapping of birth and death made the passing of his kind a drawn-out experience.

Fully aerated, he had ceased to breathe. The new ones in his lower limbs drew their nourishment from the mulch and no longer needed him, were in the process of detaching themselves. When they dropped free his life's duty, life's story, life's meaning would be complete . . .

. . . save for the one thing more, planned and prepared.

Now he could only wait with tentacle/finger curled for tightening, remaining perfectly still, having no reason to move, conserving strength for the final action.

His quietly sinking senses told him dully of sounds outside the pod and a fading curiosity wondered what they did out there. He thought of activating hull vision but the thought slipped away.

A sword of white fire cut a section from the hull alongside the control panels a long armslength from him and he was aware, without reacting as alertness ebbed (only the last command holding strength for its moment) of a suited figure entering the pod, followed by another. And another.

Red-Bloods. He no longer hated or cared. They would be dealt with.

One knelt by his lower limbs and unintelligible sounds dribbled from the grille in its helmet. He could not tell what it did.

Came the Last Pain, the splitting of cleavage lines in his bud sheath as the death flower swelled and bloomed from his ruined head.

At the moment of brain death his body obeyed the command stored in its nervous system for this moment. The curled tentacle/finger retracted, giving the computer its last command.

Under the tent the science teams went at it with a will. A small piece of timber was carved, with unexpected difficulty, from the alien craft's hull and rushed to a laboratory. The preliminary report came very quickly: ". . . a technique of molecular fusion—everything packed tight in cross-bonded grids. Not brittle but elastic beyond anything you'd believe. Take a real explosive wallop to do more than make it quiver and settle back."

The ceramic jet lining seemed impervious to common cutting methods and nobody wanted to use force at this stage. Soft radiation told little and they agreed that hard radiation should not be risked until they had found a means of excising small samples.

Chemanalysis had managed to create a computer mockup of the contents of the fuel tank, derived from hazy shortwave and sonar pictures, and was excited by a vision of complex molecular structures which promised incredible power output but must remain illogical until their catalysts were derived.

Carbon Dating, on safer ground with a piece of timber more or less analyzed, certified the ship eight thousand years old, give or take a hundred, which made no sense at all of the presence of a living thing within.

Well, it had been living, in some fashion, perhaps still was—in some fashion. But, centuries?

Then the section of hull was cut out and the first group went in. There was surprisingly little to see. The cabin was small because most of the vessel's volume was fuel storage and the living space was parsimoniously uncluttered. There was a timber panel with wooden keys mid-mounted like tiny seesaws, which might be on-off controls, another console-type installation that could reasonably be a keyboard and clusters of incomprehensible recording instruments—some circular, some square and some like bent thermometers. There was also a sort of dashboard set with small levers, badly smashed.

Ecologist Anne Spriggs of Waterloo, Iowa, surveyed the alien with the despair of a preserver arrived too late. The creature was an unpleasant sight, its gray and green skin muted in death to patched and streaky brown, its slender body collapsed upon itself until it resembled nothing so much as a stick-figure doll. It had died with a tentacle resting loosely around one of the on-off seesaw controls.

A tiny movement, low down, brought her kneeling cumbersomely to scrutinize the container of mulch on the floor beneath the creature's lower limbs. The limbs hung oddly above it, their exposed, footless termini lighter-colored than the body, as if only recently exposed. Broken off? Cut off? How and why?

Several brown sticks lay on the surface of the mulch. One of them wriggled. Despite an instant revulsion she reached a gloved hand to pick it up. It was a tuber of some kind, like a brown artichoke formed fortuitously with nubs for vestigial arms and legs and head, and spots for eyes.

Musad spoke in her helmet. "What have you there, Anne?"

"I think it's an embryo alien. It's like—" She shrugged and held it up.

He suggested, "A mandrake."

That was a somehow nasty idea, smelling of small evil.

A rending crack from the dead creature itself startled the suited figures crowding into the hull and those who watched through screens.

They were offered a miracle. The excrescence on the thing's skull opened flaps like huge sepals and a blood-red crimson bolt shot a meter's length of unfolding bloom free of the body. It unfurled not a single flower but a clustered dozen packed in and on each other, each opening the flared trumpet of a monstrous lily.

The flowers expanded in a drunken ecstasy of growth, bending down and over the dead thing that fed them until it was wrapped in a shroud of blood. From the hearts of the trumpets rose green stamens like spears, each crowned with a golden magnet of pollen.

And not another, Anne thought, for such a flourish of procreation to attract and join.

In the surprised stillness someone, somewhere, whistled softly and another hissed an indrawn breath of wonder. Melanie's voice spoke from her office deep in the moonlet, Breton roughness smoothed in awe; "I have never seen so lovely a thing."

An unidentified voice said, "Like a salute from somewhere out there."

And that, Musad thought, would be the line the media would fall on with crocodile tears: A Dying Salute from Infinity . . .

Then Anne Spriggs said with a touch of panic, "It moved!"

"What moved?"

"The body. It moved its hand. On the lever."

"A natural contraction," Musad said. "The whole external form appears to have shrunk."

Fernix had placed a slight delay on the ignition. He wanted the Red-Bloods to see his derisive flowering but he also wanted to be decently dead before the fury struck.

When the fuel spark finally leapt the ignition gap his life was over; he had timed his going with dignity. Home world would have honored him.

The jet roared, filling the scow's hold with a sea of fire before the craft skidded across the floor to crash through the soft steel of the imprisoning hull.

Those outside the scow had a microsecond's view of death in a blinding, incandescent torpedo that struck the rock wall of the Maintenance Cavern and disintegrated. The cloudburst of fuel from the shattered tank burgeoned in a twenty-thousand-degree ball of fire, engulfing and destroying the watchers in a hell-breath and licking its tongues of bellowing flame into the adjoining corridors and tunnels, a monstrous blast of heat driving death before it.

Thirty-seven scientists died and more than three hundred general personnel. Nearly a thousand others suffered serious burns.

The material damage ran to the total of a dozen national debts and the lawsuits of the private companies on Phobos made the fortunes of the lawyers on both sides.

Heads fell on the political chopping block, Musad's first among the offerings to the smug virtue of scapegoating.

First contact between intelligent cultures had been made.

Stephen Baxter

CILIA-OF-GOLD

Stephen Baxter made his first sale to *Interzone* in 1987, and since then has become one of that magazine's most frequent contributors, as well as making sales to *Asimov's Science Fiction, Science Fiction Age, Zenith, New Worlds,* and elsewhere. He's one of the most prolific of the new writers of the nineties, particularly at short lengths. In 1997, for instance, he probably published more short work in the genre than any other author (rivaled only by writers such as Robert Reed and Brian Stableford), at least eleven stories that I'm aware of, plus two or three non-genre stories—and, in spite of this prodigious output, managed to keep the overall quality amazingly high. His first novel, *Raft,* was released in 1991 to wide and enthusiastic response, and was rapidly followed by other well-received novels such as *Timelike Infinity, Anti-Ice, Flux,* and the H. G. Wells pastiche—a sequel to *The Time Machine*—*The Time Ships,* which won both the Campbell Memorial Award and the Philip K. Dick Award. His most recent books are the novels *Moonseed, Voyage,* and *Titan,* and the collections *Vacuum Diagrams: Stories of the Xeelee Sequence* and *Traces.*

Like many of his colleagues here in the late nineties—Greg Egan comes to mind, as do people like Paul J. McAuley, Michael Swanwick, Iain M. Banks, Bruce Sterling, Pat Cadigan, Brian Stableford, Gregory Benford, Ian McDonald, Gwyneth Jones, Vernor Vinge, Greg Bear, Geoff Ryman, and a half-dozen others—Stephen Baxter is busily engaged with revitalizing and reinventing the "hard-science" story for a new generation of readers.

And, like a few of those colleagues—Paul J. McAuley, for instance, or Walter Jon Williams—Baxter has a range that's broad enough to encompass several different styles of story, from Alternate History (in stories such as "Moon Six" and "Zemyla" and "War Birds," and novels such as *Voyage,* where he works out sometimes drastically different variants on how the space program would have turned out under different historical circumstances), to retro "Victorian SF" such as "Voyage to the King Planet," "The Ant-Men of Tibet," and *The Time Ships,* from the hardest of hard science fiction in stories such as "Planck Zero" and "Soliton Star" and *Raft,* to wide-screen Modern Space Opera of stunning scope and audacity of concept, such as the stories and novels of the "Xeelee Sequence." The influence of writers such as Wells, Larry Niven, and (especially) Arthur C. Clarke are clear enough in his work, but he is also involved in forging a new voice that's all his own.

Here he takes us to a mining colony on Mercury, in company with a troubleshooting mission that runs into troubles *considerably* more bizarre than anyone could ever have *anticipated* having to deal with. . . .

The people—though exhausted by the tunnel's cold—had rested long enough, Cilia-of-Gold decided.

Now it was time to fight.

She climbed up through the water, her flukes pulsing, and prepared to lead the group farther along the Ice-tunnel to the new Chimney cavern.

But, even as the people rose from their browsing and crowded through the cold, stale water behind her, Cilia-of-Gold's resolve wavered. The Seeker was a heavy presence inside her. She could *feel* its tendrils wrapped around her stomach, and—she knew—its probes must already have penetrated her brain, her mind, her *self.*

With a beat of her flukes, she thrust her body along the tunnel. She couldn't afford to show weakness. Not now.

"Cilia-of-Gold."

A broad body, warm through the turbulent water, came pushing out of the crowd to bump against hers: it was Strong-Flukes, one of Cilia-of-Gold's Three-mates. Strong-Flukes's presence was immediately comforting. "Cilia-of-Gold. I know something's wrong."

Cilia-of-Gold thought of denying it; but she turned away, her depression deepening. "I couldn't expect to keep secrets from you. Do you think the others are aware?"

The hairlike Cilia lining Strong-Flukes's belly barely vibrated as she spoke. "Only Ice-Born suspects something is wrong. And if she didn't, we'd have to tell her." Ice-Born was the third of Cilia-of-Gold's mates.

"I can't afford to be weak, Strong-Flukes. Not now."

As they swam together, Strong-Flukes flipped onto her back. Tunnel water filtered between Strong-Flukes's carapace and her body; her cilia flickered as they plucked particles of food from the stream and popped them into the multiple mouths along her belly. "Cilia-of-Gold," she said. "I *know* what's wrong. You're carrying a Seeker, aren't you?"

". . . Yes. How could you tell?"

"I love you," Strong-Flukes said. *"That's* how I could tell."

The pain of Strong-Flukes's perception was as sharp, and unexpected, as the moment when Cilia-of-Gold had first detected the signs of the infestation in herself . . . and had realized, with horror, that her life must inevitably end in madness, in a purposeless scrabble into the Ice over the world. "It's still in its early stages, I think. It's like a huge heat, inside me. And I can feel it reaching into my mind. Oh, Strong-Flukes . . ."

"Fight it."

"I can't. I—"

"You can. You *must.*"

The end of the tunnel was an encroaching disk of darkness; already Cilia-of-Gold felt the inviting warmth of the Chimney-heated water in the cavern beyond.

This should have been the climax, the supreme moment of Cilia-of-Gold's life.

The group's old Chimney, with its fount of warm, rich water, was failing; and so they had to flee, and fight for a place in a new cavern.

That, or die.

It was Cilia-of-Gold who had found the new Chimney, as she had explored the endless network of tunnels between the Chimney caverns. Thus, it was she who must lead this war—Seeker or no Seeker.

She gathered up the fragments of her melting courage.

"You're the best of us, Cilia-of-Gold," Strong-Flukes said, slowing. "Don't ever forget that."

Cilia-of-Gold pressed her carapace against Strong-Flukes's in silent gratitude.

Cilia-of-Gold turned and clacked her mandibles, signaling the rest of the people to halt. They did so, the adults sweeping the smaller children inside their strong carapaces.

Strong-Flukes lay flat against the floor and pushed a single eyestalk toward the mouth of the tunnel. Her caution was wise; there were species who could home in on even a single sound-pulse from an unwary eye.

After some moments of silent inspection, Strong-Flukes wriggled back along the Ice surface to Cilia-of-Gold.

She hesitated. "We've got problems, I think," she said at last.

The Seeker seemed to pulse inside Cilia-of-Gold, tightening around her gut. "What problems?"

"This Chimney's inhabited already. By *Heads.*"

Kevan Scholes stopped the rover a hundred yards short of the wall-mountain's crest.

Irina Larionova, wrapped in a borrowed environment suit, could tell from the tilt of the cabin that the surface here was inclined upward at around forty degrees—shallower than a flight of stairs. This "mountain," heavily eroded, was really little more than a dust-clad hill, she thought.

"The wall of Chao Meng-Fu Crater," Scholes said briskly, his radio-distorted voice tinny. "Come on. We'll walk to the summit from here."

"Walk?" She studied him, irritated. "Scholes, I've had one hour's sleep in the last thirty-six; I've traveled across ninety million miles to get here, via tugs and wormhole transit links—and you're telling me I have to *walk* up this damn hill?"

Scholes grinned through his faceplate. He was AS-preserved at around physical-twenty-five, Larionova guessed, and he had a boyishness that grated on her. *Damn it*, she reminded herself, *this "boy" is probably older than me.*

"Trust me," he said. "You'll love the view. And we have to change transports anyway."

"Why?"

"You'll see."

He twisted gracefully to his feet. He reached out a gloved hand to help Larionova pull herself, awkwardly, out of her seat. When she stood on the cabin's tilted deck, her heavy boots hurt her ankles.

Scholes threw open the rover's lock. Residual air puffed out of the cabin, crystallizing. The glow from the cabin interior was dazzling; beyond the lock, Larionova saw only darkness.

Scholes climbed out of the lock and down to the planet's invisible surface. Larionova followed him awkwardly; it seemed a long way to the lock's single step.

Her boots settled to the surface, crunching softly. The lock was situated between the rover's rear wheels: the wheels were constructs of metal strips and webbing, wide and light, each wheel taller than she was.

Scholes pushed the lock closed, and Larionova was plunged into sudden darkness.

Scholes loomed before her. He was a shape cut out of blackness. "Are you okay? Your pulse is rapid."

She could hear the rattle of her own breath, loud and immediate. "Just a little disoriented."

"We've got all of a third of a gee down here, you know. You'll get used to it. Let your eyes dark-adapt. We don't have to hurry this."

She looked up.

In her peripheral vision, the stars were already coming out. She looked for a bright double star, blue and white. There it was: Earth, with Luna.

And now, with a slow grandeur, the landscape revealed itself to her adjusting eyes. The plain from which the rover had climbed spread out from the foot of the crater wall-mountain. It was a complex patchwork of crowding craters, ridges and scarps—some of which must have been miles high—all revealed as a glimmering tracery in the starlight. The face of the planet seemed *wrinkled*, she thought, as if shrunk with age.

"These wall-mountains are over a mile high," Scholes said. "Up here, the surface is firm enough to walk on; the regolith dust layer is only a couple of inches thick. But down on the plain the dust can be ten or fifteen yards deep. Hence the big wheels on the rover. I guess that's what five billion years of a thousand-degree temperature range does for a landscape. . . ."

Just twenty-four hours ago, she reflected, Larionova had been stuck in a boardroom in New York, buried in one of Superet's endless funding battles. And now this . . . wormhole travel was bewildering. "Lethe's waters," she said. "It's so—desolate."

Scholes gave an ironic bow. "Welcome to Mercury," he said.

Cilia-of-Gold and Strong-Flukes peered down into the Chimney cavern.

Cilia-of-Gold had chosen the cavern well. The Chimney here was a fine young vent, a glowing crater much wider than their old, dying home. The water above the Chimney was turbulent, and richly cloudy; the cavern itself was wide and smooth-walled. Cilia-plants grew in mats around the Chimney's base. Cutters browsed in turn on the cilia-plants, great chains of them, their tough little arms slicing steadily through the plants. Sliding through the plant mats Cilia-of-Gold could make out the supple form of a Crawler, its mindless, tube-like body wider than Cilia-of-Gold's and more than three times as long. . . .

And, stalking around their little forest, here came the Heads themselves, the rulers of the cavern. Cilia-of-Gold counted four, five, six of the Heads, and no doubt there were many more in the dark recesses of the cavern.

One Head—close to the tunnel mouth—swiveled its huge, swollen helmet-skull toward her.

She ducked back into the tunnel, aware that all her cilia were quivering.

Strong-Flukes drifted to the tunnel floor, landing in a little cloud of food particles. "*Heads,*" she said, her voice soft with despair. "We can't fight Heads."

The Heads' huge helmet-skulls were sensitive to heat—fantastically so, enabling the Heads to track and kill with almost perfect accuracy. Heads *were* deadly opponents, Cilia-of-Gold reflected. But the people had nowhere else to go.

"We've come a long way to reach this place, Strong-Flukes. If we had to undergo another journey"—*through more cold, stagnant tunnels*—"many of us couldn't survive. And those who did would be too weakened to fight.

"No. We have to stay here—to *fight* here."

Strong-Flukes groaned, wrapping her carapace close around her. "Then we'll all be killed."

Cilia-of-Gold tried to ignore the heavy presence of the Seeker within her—and its prompting, growing more insistent now, that she *get away* from all this, from the crowding presence of people—and she forced herself to *think*.

Larionova followed Kevan Scholes up the slope of the wall-mountain. Silicate surface dust compressed under her boots, like fine sand. The climbing was easy—it was no more than a steep walk, really—but she stumbled frequently, clumsy in this reduced gee.

They reached the crest of the mountain. It wasn't a sharp summit: more a wide, smooth platform, fractured to dust by Mercury's wild temperature range.

"Chao Meng-Fu Crater," Scholes said. "A hundred miles wide, stretching right across Mercury's South Pole."

The crater was so large that even from this height its full breadth was hidden by the tight curve of the planet. The wall-mountain was one of a series that swept across the landscape from left to right, like a row of eroded teeth, separated by broad, rubble-strewn valleys. On the far side of the summit, the flanks of the wall-mountain swept down to the plain of the crater, a full mile below.

Mercury's angry sun was hidden beyond the curve of the world, but its corona extended delicate, structured tendrils above the far horizon.

The plain itself was immersed in darkness. But by the milky, diffuse light of the corona, Larionova could see a peak at the center of the plain, shouldering its way above the horizon. There was a spark of light at the base of the central peak, incongruously bright in the crater's shadows: that must be the Thoth team's camp.

"This reminds me of the Moon," she said.

Scholes considered this. "Forgive me, Dr. Larionova. Have you been down to Mercury before?"

"No," she said, his easy, informed arrogance grating on her. "I'm here to oversee the construction of Thoth, not to sightsee."

"Well, there's obviously a superficial similarity. After the formation of the main System objects five billion years ago, all the inner planets suffered bombardment by residual planetesimals. That's when Mercury took its biggest strike: the one which created the Caloris feature. But after that, Mercury was massive enough to retain a molten core—unlike the Moon. Later planetesimal strikes punched holes in the crust, so there were lava outflows that drowned some of the older cratering.

"Thus, on Mercury, you have a mixture of terrains. There's the most ancient landscape, heavily cratered, and the *planitia*: smooth lava plains, punctured by small, young craters.

"Later, as the core cooled, the surface actually shrank inward. The planet lost a mile or so of radius."

Like a dried-out tomato. "So the surface *is* wrinkled."

"Yes. There are *rupes* and *dorsa*: ridges and lobate scarps, cliffs a couple of miles tall and extending for hundreds of miles. Great climbing country. And in some places there are gas vents, chimneys of residual thermal activity." He turned to her, corona light misty in his faceplate. "So Mercury isn't really so much like the Moon at all. . . . Look. You can see Thoth."

She looked up, following his pointing arm. There, just above the far horizon, was a small blue star.

She had her faceplate magnify the image. The star exploded into a compact sculpture of electric blue threads, surrounded by firefly lights: the Thoth construction site.

Thoth was a habitat to be placed in orbit close to Sol. Irina Larionova was the consulting engineer contracted by Superet to oversee the construction of the habitat.

Thoth's purpose was to find out what was wrong with the Sun.

Recently, anomalies had been recorded in the Sun's behavior; aspects of its interior seemed to be diverging, and widely, from the standard theoretical models. Superet was a loose coalition of interest groups on Earth and Mars, intent on studying problems likely to impact the longterm survival of the human species.

Problems in the interior of mankind's only star clearly came into the category of things of interest to Superet.

Irina Larionova wasn't much interested in any of Superet's semi-mystical philosophizing. It was the work that was important, for her: and the engineering problems posed by Thoth were fascinating.

At Thoth, a Solar-interior probe would be constructed. The probe would be one Interface of a wormhole terminal, loaded with sensors. The Interface would be dropped into the Sun. The other Interface would remain in orbit, at the center of the habitat.

The electric-blue bars she could see now were struts of exotic matter, which would eventually frame the wormhole termini. The sparks of light moving around the struts were GUTships and short-haul tugs. She stared at the image, wishing she could get back to some real work.

Irina Larionova had had no intention of visiting Mercury herself. Mercury was a detail, for Thoth. Why would *anyone* come to Mercury, unless they had to? Mercury was a piece of junk, a desolate ball of iron and rock too close to the Sun to be interesting, or remotely habitable. The two Thoth exploratory teams had come here only to exploit: to see if it was possible to dig raw materials out of Mercury's shallow—and close-at-hand—gravity well, for use in the construction of the habitat. The teams had landed at the South Pole, where traces of water-ice had been detected, and at the Caloris Basin, the huge equatorial crater where—it was hoped—that ancient impact might have brought iron-rich compounds to the surface.

The tugs from Thoth actually comprised the largest expedition ever to land on Mercury.

But, within days of landing, both investigative teams had reported anomalies.

Larionova tapped at her suit's sleeve-controls. After a couple of minutes an image of Dolores Wu appeared in one corner of Larionova's faceplate. *Hi, Irina,* she said, her voice buzzing like an insect in Larionova's helmet's enclosed space.

Dolores Wu was the leader of the Thoth exploratory team in Caloris. Wu was Mars-born, with small features and hair grayed despite AntiSenescence treatments. She looked weary.

"How's Caloris?" Larionova asked.

Well, we don't have much to report yet. We decided to start with a detailed gravimetric survey. . . .

"And?"

We found the impact object. We think. It's as massive as we thought, but much—much—too small, Irina. It's barely a mile across, way too dense to be a planetesimal fragment.

"A black hole?"

No. Not dense enough for that.

"Then what?"

Wu looked exasperated. *We don't know yet, Irina. We don't have any answers. I'll keep you informed.*

Wu closed off the link.

Standing on the corona-lit wall of Chao Meng-Fu Crater, Larionova asked Kevan Scholes about Caloris.

"Caloris is *big*," he said. "Luna has no impact feature on the scale of Caloris. And Luna has nothing like the Weird Country in the other hemisphere. . . ."

"The what?"

A huge planetesimal—or *something*—had struck the equator of Mercury, five billion years ago, Scholes said. The Caloris Basin—an immense, ridged crater system—formed around the primary impact site. Whatever caused the impact was still buried in the planet, somewhere under the crust, dense and massive; the object was a gravitational anomaly which had helped lock Mercury's rotation into synchronization with its orbit.

"Away from Caloris itself, shock waves spread around the planet's young crust," Scholes said. "The waves focused at Caloris' antipode—the point on the equator diametrically opposite Caloris itself. And the land there was shattered, into a jumble of bizarre hill and valley formations. *The Weird Country* . . . Hey. Dr. Larionova."

She could *hear* that damnable grin of Schole's. "What now?" she snapped.

He walked across the summit toward her. "Look up," he said.

"Damn it, Scholes—"

There was a pattering against her faceplate.

She tilted up her head. Needle-shaped particles swirled over the wall-mountain from the planet's dark side and bounced off her faceplate, sparkling in corona light.

"What in Lethe is that?"

"Snow," he said.

Snow . . . On Mercury?

In the cool darkness of the tunnel, the people clambered over each other; they bumped against the Ice walls, and their muttering filled the water with crisscrossing voice-ripples. Cilia-of-Gold swam through and around the crowd, coaxing the people to follow her will.

She felt immensely weary. Her concentration and resolve threatened continually to shatter under the Seeker's assault. And the end of the tunnel, with the deadly Heads beyond, was a looming, threatening mouth, utterly intimidating.

At last the group was ready. She surveyed them. All of the people—except the very oldest and the very youngest—were arranged in an array which filled the tunnel from wall to wall; she could hear flukes and carapaces scraping softly against Ice.

The people looked weak, foolish, eager, she thought with dismay; now that she was actually implementing it her scheme seemed simple-minded. Was she about to lead them all to their deaths?

But it was too late for the luxury of doubt, she told herself. Now, there was no other option to follow.

She lifted herself to the axis of the tunnel, and clacked her mandibles sharply.

"Now," she said, "it is time. The most important moment of your lives. And you must *swim!* Swim as hard as you can; swim for your lives!"

And the people responded.

There was a surge of movement, of almost exhilarating *intent.* The people beat their flukes as one, and a jostling mass of flesh and carapaces scraped down the tunnel.

Cilia-of-Gold hurried ahead of them, leading the way toward the tunnel mouth. As she swam she could feel the current the people were creating, the plug of cold tunnel water they pushed ahead of themselves.

Within moments the tunnel mouth was upon her.

She burst from the tunnel, shooting out into the open water of the cavern, her carapace clenched firm around her. She was plunged immediately into a clammy heat, so great was the temperature difference between tunnel and cavern.

Above her the Ice of the cavern roof arched over the warm Chimney mouth. And from all around the cavern, the helmet-skulls of Heads snapped around toward her.

Now the people erupted out of the tunnel, a shield of flesh and chitin behind her. The rush of tunnel water they pushed ahead of themselves washed over Cilia-of-Gold, chilling her anew.

She tried to imagine this from the Heads' point of view. This explosion of cold water into the cavern would bring about a much greater temperature difference than the Heads' heat-sensor skulls were accustomed to; the Heads would be *dazzled*, at least for a time: long enough—she hoped—to give her people a fighting chance against the more powerful Heads.

She swiveled in the water. She screamed at her people, so loud she could feel her cilia strain at the turbulent water. *"Now!* Hit them now!"

The people, with a roar, descended toward the Heads.

Kevan Scholes led Larionova down the wall-mountain slope into Chao Meng-Fu Crater.

After a hundred yards they came to another rover. This car was similar to the one they'd abandoned on the other side of the summit, but it had an additional fitting, obviously improvised: two wide, flat rails of metal, suspended between the wheels on hydraulic legs.

Scholes helped Larionova into the rover and pressurized it. Larionova removed her helmet with relief. The rover smelled, oppressively, of metal and plastic.

While Scholes settled behind his controls, Larionova checked the rover's data desk. An update from Dolores Wu was waiting for her. Wu wanted Larionova to come to Caloris, to see for herself what had been found there.

Larionova sent a sharp message back, ordering Wu to summarize her findings and transmit them to the data desks at the Chao site.

Wu acknowledged immediately, but replied: *I'm going to find this hard to summarize, Irina.*

Larionova tapped out: *Why?*

We *think we've found an artifact.*

Larionova stared at the blunt words on the screen.

She massaged the bridge of her nose; she felt an ache spreading out from her temples and around her eye sockets. She wished she had time to sleep.

Scholes started the vehicle up. The rover bounced down the slope, descending into shadow. "It's genuine water-ice snow," Scholes said as he drove. "You know that a day on Mercury lasts a hundred and seventy-six Earth days. It's a combination of the eighty-eight-day year and the tidally locked rotation, which—"

"I know."

"During the day, the Sun drives water vapor out of the rocks and into the atmosphere."

"What atmosphere?"

"You really don't know much about Mercury, do you? It's mostly helium and hydrogen—only a billionth of Earth's sea-level pressure."

"How come those gases don't escape from the gravity well?"

"They do," Scholes said. "But the atmosphere is replenished by the solar wind. Particles from the Sun are trapped by Mercury's magnetosphere. Mercury has quite a respectable magnetic field: the planet has a solid iron core, which . . ."

She let Scholes' words run on through her head, unregistered. *Air from the solar wind, and snow at the South Pole . . .*

Maybe Mercury was a more interesting place than she'd imagined.

"Anyway," Scholes was saying, "the water vapor disperses across the planet's sunlit hemisphere. But at the South Pole we have this crater: Chao Meng-Fu, straddling the Pole itself. Mercury has no axial tilt—there are no seasons here—and so Chaos's floor is in permanent shadow."

"And snow falls."

"And snow falls."

Scholes stopped the rover and tapped telltales on his control panel. There was a whir of hydraulics, and she heard a soft crunch, transmitted into the cabin through the rover's structure.

Then the rover lifted upward through a foot.

The rover lurched forward again. The motion was much smoother than before, and there was an easy, hissing sound.

"You've just lowered those rails," Larionova said. "I knew it. This damn rover is a sled, isn't it?"

"It was easy enough to improvise," Scholes said, sounding smug. "Just a couple of metal rails on hydraulics, and Vernier rockets from a cannibalized tug to give us some push. . . ."

"It's astonishing that there's enough ice here to sustain this."

"Well, that snow may have seemed sparse, but it's been falling steadily—for five billion years . . . Dr. Larionova, there's a whole frozen ocean here, in Chao Meng-Fu Crater: enough ice to be detectable even from Earth."

Larionova twisted to look out through a viewport at the back of the cabin. The rover's rear lights picked out twin sled tracks, leading back to the summit of the wall-mountain; ice, exposed in the tracks, gleamed brightly in starlight.

Lethe, she thought. *Now I'm skiing. Skiing, on Mercury. What a day.*

The wall-mountain shallowed out, merging seamlessly with the crater plain. Scholes retracted the sled rails; on the flat, the regolith dust gave the ice sufficient traction for the rover's wide wheels. The rover made fast progress through the fifty miles to the heart of the plain.

Larionova drank coffee and watched the landscape through the viewports. The corona light was silvery and quite bright here, like moonlight. The central peak loomed up over the horizon, like some approaching ship on a sea of dust. The ice-surface of Chao's floor—though pocked with craters and covered with the ubiquitous regolith dust—was visibly smoother and more level than the plain outside the crater.

The rover drew to a halt on the outskirts of the Thoth team's sprawling camp, close to the foothills of the central peak. The dust here was churned up by rover tracks and tug exhaust splashes, and semi-transparent bubble-shelters were hemispheres of yellow, homely light, illuminating the darkened ice surface. There were drilling rigs, and several large pits dug into the ice.

Scholes helped Larionova out onto the surface. "I'll take you to a shelter," he said. "Or a tug. Maybe you want to freshen up before—"

"Where's Dixon?"

Scholes pointed to one of the rigs. "When I left, over there."

"Then that's where we're going. Come on."

Frank Dixon was the team leader. He met Larionova on the surface, and invited her into a small opaqued bubble-shelter nestling at the foot of the rig.

Scholes wandered off into the camp, in search of food.

The shelter contained a couple of chairs, a data desk, and a basic toilet. Dixon was a morose, burly American; when he took off his helmet there was a band of dirt at the base of his wide neck, and Larionova noticed a sharp, acrid stink from his suit. Dixon had evidently been out on the surface for long hours.

He pulled a hip flask from an environment suit pocket. "You want to drink?" he asked. "Scotch?"

"Sure."

Dixon poured a measure for Larionova into the flask's cap, and took a draught himself from the flask's small mouth.

Larionova drank; the liquor burned her mouth and throat, but it immediately took an edge off her tiredness. "It's good. But it needs ice."

He smiled. "Ice we got. Actually, we have tried it; Mercury ice is good, as clean as you like. We're not going to die of thirst out here, Irina."

"Tell me what you've found, Frank."

Dixon sat on the edge of the desk, his fat haunches bulging inside the leggings of his environment suit. "Trouble, Irina. We've found trouble."

"I know that much."

"I think we're going to have to get off the planet. The System authorities—and the scientists and conservation groups—are going to climb all over us, if we try to mine here. I wanted to tell you about it, before—"

Larionova struggled to contain her irritation and tiredness. "That's *not* a problem for Thoth," she said. "Therefore it's not a problem for me. We can tell Superet to bring in a water-ice asteroid from the Belt, for our supplies. You know that. Come on, Frank. Tell me why you're wasting my time down here."

Dixon took another long pull on his flask, and eyed her.

"There's *life* here, Irina," he said. "Life, inside this frozen ocean. Drink up; I'll show you."

The sample was in a case on the surface, beside a data desk.

The thing in the case looked like a strip of multicolored meat: perhaps three feet long, crushed and obviously dead; shards of some transparent shell material were embedded in flesh that sparkled with ice crystals.

"We found this inside a two-thousand-yard-deep core," Dixon said.

Larionova tried to imagine how this would have looked, intact and mobile. "This means nothing to me, Frank. I'm no biologist."

He grunted, self-deprecating. "Nor me. Nor any of us. Who expected to find life, on Mercury?" Dixon tapped at the data desk with gloved fingers. "We used our desks' medico-diagnostic facilities to come up with this reconstruction," he said. "We call it a *mercuric*, Irina."

A Virtual projected into space a foot above the desk's surface; the image rotated, sleek and menacing.

The body was a thin cone, tapering to a tail from a wide, flat head. Three parabolic cups—*eyes?*—were embedded in the smooth "face," symmetrically placed around a lipless mouth. . . . No, not eyes, Larionova corrected herself. Maybe some kind of sonar sensor? That would explain the parabolic profile.

Mandibles, like pincers, protruded from the mouth. From the tail, three fins were splayed out around what looked like an anus. A transparent carapace surrounded the main body, like a cylindrical cloak; inside the carapace, rows of small, hairlike cilia lined the body, supple and vibratile.

There were regular markings, faintly visible, in the surface of the carapace.

"Is this accurate?"

"Who knows? It's the best *we* can do. When we have your clearance, we can transmit our data to Earth, and let the experts get at it."

"Lethe, Frank," Larionova said. "This looks like a fish. It looks like it could *swim*. The streamlining, the tail—"

Dixon scratched the short hairs at the back of his neck and said nothing.

"But we're on Mercury, damn it, not in Hawaii," Larionova said.

Dixon pointed down, past the dusty floor. "Irina. It's not all frozen. There are *cavities* down there, inside the Chao ice-cap. According to our sonar probes—"

"Cavities?"

"Water. At the base of the crater, under a couple of miles of ice. Kept liquid by thermal vents, in crust-collapse scarps and ridges. Plenty of room for swimming . . . We speculate that our friend here swims on his back"—he tapped the desk surface, and the image swiveled—"and the water passes down, between his body and this carapace, and he uses all those tiny hairs to filter out particles of food. The trunk seems to be lined with little mouths. See?" He flicked the image to another representation; the skin became transparent, and Larionova could see blocky reconstructions of internal organs. Dixon said, "There's no true stomach, but there is what looks like a continuous digestive tube passing down the axis of the body, to the anus at the tail."

Larionova noticed a thread-like structure wrapped around some of the organs, as well as around the axial digestive tract.

"Look," Dixon said, pointing to one area. "Look at the surface structure of these lengths of tubing, here near the digestive tract."

Larionova looked. The tubes, clustering around the digestive axis, had complex, rippled surfaces. "So?"

"You don't get it, do you? It's *convoluted*—like the surface of a brain. Irina, we think that stuff must be some equivalent of nervous tissue."

Larionova frowned. *Damn it, I wish I knew more biology.* "What about this thread material, wrapped around the organs?"

Dixon sighed. "We don't know, Irina. It doesn't seem to fit with the rest of the structure, does it?" He pointed. "Follow the threads back. There's a broader main body, just here. We think maybe this is some kind of parasite, which has infested the main organism. Like a tapeworm. It's as if the threads are extended, vestigial limbs. . . ."

Leaning closer, Larionova saw that tendrils from the worm-thing had even infiltrated the brain-tubes. She shuddered; if this was a parasite, it was a particularly vile infestation. Maybe the parasite even modified the mercuric's behavior, she wondered.

Dixon restored the solid-aspect Virtual.

Uneasily, Larionova pointed to the markings on the carapace. They were small triangles, clustered into elaborate patterns. "And what's this stuff?"

Dixon hesitated. "I was afraid you might ask that."

"Well?"

". . . We think the markings are artificial, Irina. A deliberate tattoo, carved into the carapace, probably with the mandibles. Writing, maybe: those look like symbolic markings, with information content."

"Lethe," she said.

"I know. This fish was smart," Dixon said.

• • •

The people, victorious, clustered around the warmth of their new Chimney. Recovering from their journey and from their battle-wounds, they cruised easily over the gardens of cilia-plants, and browsed on floating fragments of food.

It had been a great triumph. The Heads were dead, or driven off into the labyrinth of tunnels through the Ice. Strong-Flukes had even found the Heads' principal nest here, under the silty floor of the cavern. With sharp stabs of her mandibles, Strong-Flukes had destroyed a dozen or more Head young.

Cilia-of-Gold took herself off, away from the Chimney. She prowled the edge of the Ice cavern, feeding fitfully.

She was a hero. But she couldn't bear the attention of others: their praise, the warmth of their bodies. All she seemed to desire now was the uncomplicated, silent coolness of Ice.

She brooded on the infestation that was spreading through her.

Seekers were a mystery. Nobody knew *why* Seekers compelled their hosts to isolate themselves, to bury themselves in the Ice. What was the point? When the hosts were destroyed, so were the Seekers.

Perhaps it wasn't the Ice itself the Seekers desired, she wondered. Perhaps they sought, in their blind way, something *beyond* the Ice. . . .

But there *was* nothing above the Ice. The caverns were hollows in an infinite, eternal Universe of Ice. Cilia-of-Gold, with a shudder, imagined herself burrowing, chewing her way into the endless Ice, upward without limit. . . . Was that, finally, how her life would end?

She hated the Seeker within her. She hated her body, for betraying her in this way; and she hated herself.

"Cilia-of-Gold."

She turned, startled, and closed her carapace around herself reflexively.

It was Strong-Flukes and Ice-Born, together.

Seeing their warm, familiar bodies, here in this desolate corner of the cavern, Cilia-of-Gold's loneliness welled up inside her, like a Chimney of emotion.

But she swam away from her Three-mates, backward, her carapace scraping on the cavern's Ice wall.

Ice-Born came toward her, hesitantly. "We're concerned about you."

"Then don't be," she snapped. "Go back to the Chimney, and leave me here."

"No," Strong-Flukes said quietly.

Cilia-of-Gold felt desperate, angry, confined. "You know what's wrong with me, Strong-Flukes. I have a *Seeker*. It's going to kill me. And there's nothing any of us can do about it."

Their bodies pressed close around her now; she longed to open up her carapace to them and bury herself in their warmth.

"We know we're going to lose you, Cilia-of-Gold," Ice-Born said. It sounded as if she could barely speak. Ice-Born had always been the softest, the most loving, of the Three, Cilia-of-Gold thought, the warm heart of their relationship. "And—"

"Yes?"

Strong-Flukes opened her carapace wide. "We want to be Three again," she said.

Already, Cilia-of-Gold saw with a surge of love and excitement, Strong-Flukes's ovipositor was distended: swollen with one of the three isogametes which would fuse to form a new child, their fourth. . . .

A child Cilia-of-Gold could never see growing to consciousness.

"*No!*" Her cilia pulsed with the single, agonized word.

Suddenly the warmth of her Three-mates was confining, claustrophobic. She had to get away from this prison of flesh; her mind was filled with visions of the coolness and purity of *Ice:* of clean, high *Ice.*

"Cilia-of-Gold. Wait. Please—"

She flung herself away, along the wall. She came to a tunnel mouth, and she plunged into it, relishing the tunnel's cold, stagnant water.

"Cilia-of-Gold! *Cilia-of-Gold!*"

She hurled her body through the web of tunnels, carelessly colliding with walls of Ice so hard that she could feel her carapace splinter. On and on she swam, until the voices of her Three-mates were lost forever.

We've dug out a large part of the artifact, Irina, Dolores Wu reported. *It's a mash of what looks like hull material.*

"Did you get a sample?"

No. We don't have anything that could cut through material so dense. . . . Irina, we're looking at something beyond our understanding.

Larionova sighed. "Just tell me, Dolores," she told Wu's data desk image.

Irina, we think we're dealing with the Pauli Principle.

Pauli's Exclusion Principle stated that no two baryonic particles could exist in the same quantum state. Only a certain number of electrons, for example, could share a given energy level in an atom. Adding more electrons caused complex shells of charge to build up around the atom's nucleus. It was the electron shells—this consequence of Pauli—that gave the atom its chemical properties.

But the Pauli principle *didn't* apply to photons; it was possible for many photons to share the same quantum state. That was the essence of the laser: billions of photons, coherent, sharing the same quantum properties.

Irina, Wu said slowly, *what would happen if you could turn off the Exclusion Principle, for a piece of baryonic matter?*

"You can't," Larionova said immediately.

Of course not. Try to imagine anyway.

Larionova frowned. What if one could lase mass? "The atomic electron shells would implode, of course."

Yes.

"All electrons would fall into their ground state. Chemistry would be impossible."

Yes. But you may not care . . .

"Molecules would collapse. Atoms would fall into each other, releasing immense quantities of binding energy."

You'd end up with a superdense substance, wouldn't you? Completely non-reactive, chemically. And almost unbreachable, given the huge energies required to detach non-Pauli atoms.

Ideal hull material, Irina . . .

"But it's all impossible," Larionova said weakly. "You *can't* violate Pauli."

Of course you can't, Dolores Wu replied.

Inside an opaqued bubble-shelter, Larionova, Dixon and Scholes sat on fold-out chairs, cradling coffees.

"If your mercuric was so smart," Larionova said to Dixon, "how come he got himself stuck in the ice?"

Dixon shrugged. "In fact it goes deeper than that. It looked to us as if the mercuric burrowed his way up into the ice, deliberately. What kind of evolutionary advantage could there be in behavior like that? The mercuric was certain to be killed."

"Yes," Larionova said. She massaged her temples, thinking about the mercuric's infection. "But maybe that thread-parasite had something to do with it. I mean, some parasites change the way their hosts behave."

Scholes tapped at a data desk; text and images, reflected from the desk, flickered over his face. "That's true. There are parasites which transfer themselves from one host to another—by forcing a primary host to get itself eaten by the second."

Dixon's wide face crumpled. "Lethe. That's disgusting."

"The lancet fluke," Scholes read slowly, "is a parasite of some species of ant. The fluke can make its host climb to the top of a grass stem and then lock onto the stem with its mandibles—and wait until it's swallowed by a grazing sheep. Then the fluke can go on to infest the sheep in turn."

"Okay," Dixon said. "But why would a parasite force its mercuric host to burrow up into the ice of a frozen ocean? When the host dies, the parasite dies too. It doesn't make sense."

"There's a lot about this that doesn't make sense," Larionova said. "Like, the whole question of the existence of life in the cavities in the first place. There's no *light* down there. How do the mercurics survive, under two miles of ice?"

Scholes folded one leg on top of the other and scratched his ankle. "I've been going through the data desks." He grimaced, self-deprecating. "A crash course in exotic biology. You want my theory?"

"Go ahead."

"The thermal vents—which cause the cavities in the first place. The vents are the key. I think the bottom of the Chao ice-cap is like the mid-Atlantic ridge, back on Earth.

"The deep sea, a mile down, is a desert; by the time any particle of food has drifted down from the richer waters above it's passed through so many guts that its energy content is exhausted.

"But along the Ridge, where tectonic plates are colliding, you have hydrothermal vents—just as at the bottom of Chao. And the heat from the Atlantic vents supports life: in little colonies, strung out along the mid-Atlantic Ridge. The vents form superheated fountains, smoking with deep-crust minerals that life can exploit: sulphides of copper, zinc, lead, and iron, for instance. And there are very steep temperature differences, and so there are high energy gradients—another prerequisite for life."

"Hmm." Larionova closed her eyes and tried to picture it. *Pockets of warm water, deep in the ice of Mercury; luxuriant mats of life surrounding mineral-rich hydrothermal vents, browsed by Dixon's mercuric animals.* . . . Was it possible?

Dixon asked, "How long do the vents persist?"

"On Earth, in the Ridge, a couple of decades. Here we don't know."

"What happens when a vent dies?" Larionova asked. "That's the end of your pocket world, isn't it? The ice chamber would simply freeze up."

"Maybe," Scholes said. "But the vents would occur in rows, along the scarps. Maybe there are corridors of liquid water, within the ice, along which mercurics could migrate."

Larionova thought about that for a while.

"I don't believe it," she said.

"Why not?"

"I don't see how it's possible for life to have *evolved* here in the first place." In the primeval oceans of Earth, there had been complex chemicals, and electrical storms, and . . .

"Oh, I don't think that's a problem," Scholes said.

She looked at him sharply. Maddeningly, he was grinning again. "Well?" she snapped.

"Look," Scholes said with grating patience, "we've two anomalies on Mercury: the life forms here at the South Pole, and Dolores Wu's artifact under Caloris. The simplest assumption is that the two anomalies are connected. Let's put the pieces together," he said. "Let's construct a hypothesis. . . ."

Her mandibles ached as she crushed the gritty Ice, carving out her tunnel upward. The rough walls of the tunnel scraped against her carapace, and she pushed Ice rubble down between her body and her carapace, sacrificing fragile cilia designed to extract soft food particles from warm streams.

The higher she climbed, the harder the Ice became. The Ice was now so cold she was beyond cold; she couldn't even feel the Ice fragments that scraped along her belly and flukes. And, she suspected, the tunnel behind her was no longer open but had refrozen, sealing her here, in this shifting cage, forever.

The world she had left—of caverns, and Chimneys, and children, and her Three-mates—were remote bubbles of warmth, a distant dream. The only reality was the hard Ice in her mandibles, and the Seeker heavy and questing inside her.

She could feel her strength seeping out with the last of her warmth into the Ice's infinite extent. And yet *still* the Seeker wasn't satisfied; still she had to climb, on and up, into the endless darkness of the Ice.

. . . But now—impossibly—there was something *above* her, breaking through the Ice. . . .

She cowered inside her Ice-prison.

Kevan Scholes said, "Five billion years ago—when the solar system was very young, and the crusts of Earth and other inner planets were still subject to bombardment from stray planetesimals—a ship came here. An interstellar craft, maybe with FTL technology."

"Why? Where from?" Larionova asked.

"I don't know. How could I know that? But the ship must have been massive—with the bulk of a planetesimal, or more. Certainly highly advanced, with a hull composed of Dolores's superdense Pauli construction material."

"Hmm. Go on."

"Then the ship hit trouble."

"What kind of trouble?"

"I don't *know.* Come on, Dr. Larionova. Maybe it got hit by a planetesimal itself. Anyway, the ship crashed here, on Mercury—"

"Right." Dixon nodded, gazing at Scholes hungrily; the American reminded Larionova of a child enthralled by a story. "It was a disastrous impact. It caused the Caloris feature. . . ."

"Oh, be serious," Larionova said.

Dixon looked at her. "Caloris *was* a pretty unique impact, Irina. Extraordinarily violent, even by the standards of the system's early bombardment phase. . . . Caloris Basin is *eight hundred miles* across; on Earth, its walls would stretch from New York to Chicago."

"So how did anything survive?"

Scholes shrugged. "Maybe the starfarers had some kind of inertial shielding. How can we know? Anyway the ship was wrecked; and the density of the smashed-up hull material caused it to sink into the bulk of the planet, through the Caloris puncture.

"The crew were stranded. So they sought a place to survive. Here, on Mercury."

"I get it," Dixon said. "The only viable environment, long term, was the Chao Meng-Fu ice cap."

Scholes spread his hands. "Maybe the starfarers had to engineer descendants, quite unlike the original crew, to survive in such conditions. And perhaps they had to do a little planetary engineering too; they may have had to initiate some of the hydrothermal vents which created the enclosed liquid-water world down there. And so—"

"Yes?"

"And so the creature we've dug out of the ice is a degenerate descendant of those ancient star travelers, still swimming around the Chao sea."

Scholes fell silent, his eyes on Larionova.

Larionova stared into her coffee. "A 'degenerate descendant.' After *five billion years?* Look, Scholes, on Earth it's only three and a half billion years since the first prokaryotic cells. And on Earth, whole phyla—groups of species—have emerged or declined over periods less than a *tenth* of the time since the Caloris Basin event. Over time intervals like that, the morphology of species flows like hot plastic. So how is it possible for these mercurics to have persisted?"

Scholes looked uncertain. "Maybe they've suffered massive evolutionary changes," he said. "Changes we're just not seeing. For example, maybe the worm parasite is the malevolent descendant of some harmless creature the starfarers brought with them."

Dixon scratched his neck, where the suit-collar ring of dirt was prominent. "Anyway, we've still got the puzzle of the mercuric's burrowing into the ice."

"Hmm." Scholes sipped his cooling coffee. "I've got a theory about that, too."

"I thought you might," Larionova said sourly.

Scholes said, "I wonder if the impulse to climb up to the surface is some kind of residual yearning for the stars."

"What?"

Scholes looked embarrassed, but he pressed on: "A racial memory buried deep, prompting the mercurics to seek their lost home world. . . . Why not?"

Larionova snorted. "You're a romantic, Kevin Scholes."

A telltale flashed on the surface of the data desk. Dixon leaned over, tapped the telltale and took the call.

He looked up at Larionova, his moon-like face animated. "Irina. They've found another mercuric," he said.

"Is it intact?"

"More than that." Dixon stood and reached for his helmet. "This one isn't dead yet. . . ."

The mercuric lay on Chao's dust-coated ice. Humans stood around it, suited, their faceplates anonymously blank.

The mercuric, dying, was a cone of bruised-purple meat a yard long. Shards of shattered transparent carapace had been crushed into its crystallizing flesh. Some of the cilia, within the carapace, stretched and twitched. The cilia looked differently colored from Dixon's reconstruction, as far as Larionova could remember: these were yellowish threads, almost golden.

Dixon spoke quickly to his team, then joined Larionova and Scholes. "We couldn't have saved it. It was in distress as soon as our core broke through into its tunnel. I guess it couldn't take the pressure and temperature differentials. Its internal organs seem to be massively disrupted. . . ."

"Just think." Kevan Scholes stood beside Dixon, his hands clasped behind his back. "There must be millions of these animals in the ice under our feet, embedded in their pointless little chambers. Surely none of them could dig more than a hundred yards or so up from the liquid layer."

Larionova switched their voices out of her consciousness. She knelt down, on the ice; under her knees she could feel the crisscross heating elements in her suit's fabric.

She peered into the dulling sonar-eyes of the mercuric. The creature's mandibles—prominent and sharp—opened and closed, in vacuum silence.

She felt an impulse to reach out her gloved hand to the battered flank of the creature: to *touch* this animal, this person, whose species had, perhaps, traveled across light-years—and five billion years—to reach her. . . .

But still, she had the nagging feeling that something was wrong with Scholes' neat hypothesis. The mercuric's physical design seemed crude. Could this really have been a starfaring species? The builders of the ship in Caloris must have had some form of major tool-wielding capability. And Dixon's earlier study had shown that the creature had no trace of any limbs, even vestigially. . . .

Vestigial limbs, she remembered. *Lethe.*

Abruptly her perception of this animal—and its host parasite—began to shift; she could feel a paradigm dissolving inside her, melting like a Mercury snowflake in the Sun.

"Dr. Larionova? Are you all right?"

Larionova looked up at Scholes. "Kevan, I called you a romantic. But I think you were almost correct, after all. *But not quite.* Remember we've suggested that the *parasite*—the infestation—changes the mercuric's behavior, causing it to make its climb."

"What are you saying?"

Suddenly, Larionova saw it all. "I don't believe this mercuric is descended from the starfarers—the builders of the ship in Caloris. I think the rise of the mercurics' intelligence was a *later* development; the mercurics grew to consciousness *here*, on Mercury. I *do* think the mercurics are descended from something that came to Mercury on that ship, though. A pet, or a food animal—Lethe, even some equivalent of a stomach bacteria. Five billion years is time enough for anything. And, given the competition for space near the short-lived vents, there's plenty of encouragement for the development of intelligence, down inside this frozen sea."

"And the starfarers themselves?" Scholes asked. "What became of them? Did they die?"

"No," she said. "No, I don't think so. But they, too, suffered huge evolutionary changes. I think they did devolve, Scholes; in fact, I think they lost their awareness.

"But one thing persisted within them, across all this desert of time. And that was the starfarers' vestigial will to *return*—to the surface, one day, and at last to the stars. . . ."

It was a will which had survived even the loss of consciousness itself, somewhere in the long, stranded aeons: a relic of awareness long since transmuted to a deeper biochemical urge—*a will to return home*, still embedded within a once-intelligent species reduced by time to a mere parasitic infection.

But it was a home which, surely, could no longer exist.

The mercuric's golden cilia twitched once more, in a great wave of motion which shuddered down its ice-flecked body.

Then it was still.

Larionova stood up; her knees and calves were stiff and cold, despite the suit's heater. "Come on," she said to Scholes and Dixon. "You'd better get your team off the ice as soon as possible; I'll bet the universities have their first exploratory teams down here half a day after we pass Earth the news."

Dixon nodded. "And Thoth?"

"Thoth? I'll call Superet. I guess I've an asteroid to order. . . ."

And then, she thought, *at last I can sleep. Sleep and get back to work.*

With Scholes and Dixon, she trudged across the dust-strewn ice to the bubble shelters.

She could feel the Ice under her belly . . . but above her *there was no Ice,* no water even, an infinite *nothing* into which the desperate pulses of her blinded eyes disappeared without echo.

Astonishingly—impossibly—she *was,* after all, above the Ice. How could this be? Was she in some immense upper cavern, its Ice roof too remote to see? Was this the nature of the Universe, a hierarchy of caverns within caverns?

She knew she would never understand. But it didn't seem to matter. And, as her awareness faded, she felt the Seeker inside her subside to peace.

A final warmth spread out within her. Consciousness splintered like melting ice, flowing away through the closing tunnels of her memory.

GONE TO GLORY

R. Garcia y Robertson made his first sale in 1987, and since has become a frequent contributor to *Asimov's Science Fiction* and *The Magazine of Fantasy & Science Fiction,* as well as selling several stories to *Amazing, Pulphouse,* and *Weird Tales,* and other markets.

Robertson has made something of a specialty of adventure writing and, in fact, may be one of the very best in the business when it comes to turning out vivid, headlong, fast-paced, colorful, inventive, swashbuckling, and yet keenly *intelligent* adventure stories. Since adventure writing is still widely considered to be synonymous with "junk" or throwaway writing by many genre critics, stuff not really worth considering (although a really good adventure story is actually harder to write in some ways than more introspective fiction), this may help to explain why Robertson's work, like Robert Reed's, has been largely and undeservedly ignored, and why he's rarely mentioned among the ranks of good new writers of the eighties and nineties—although a good case could be made that he's delivered more pure first-rate entertainment pound for pound than almost any other new writer of the last ten years.

L. Sprague de Camp was clearly one of the major influences on Robertson (although I suspect that George MacDonald Fraser, author of the *Flashman* series, was a strong influence as well), and, like de Camp, even the most swashbuckling of his adventures contains a generous measure of sly humor; also like de Camp, he makes intensive use of authentic and intensively researched historical settings, and clearly has a love for obscure and little-known corners of history. He's taken us to the bitter days of the Indian Wars on the American frontier in stories such as "The Moon of Popping Trees" and "The Other Magpie," to San Francisco's Chinatown during the Gold Rush days in "Four Kings and an Ace," to the turmoil of the French Revolution in "The Great Fear," to the Cretaceous period to stalk hungry dinosaurs in "The Virgin and the Dinosaur," to ancient Scandinavia in "The Wagon God's Wife," on a trip on a Mississippi paddle wheeler with Mark Twain in "Down the River," to London during the Blitz in "Wendy Darling, RFC," and to Greece in the days *before* history to deal with a fractious Hercules in "The Moon Maid"—among many other historical milieus that he has made his own.

Some of these stories are fantasy, and so outside our purview here, but his stories about the misadventures of Jake Bento and Peg and their bumbling crew of time-traveling documentary filmmakers—which includes the aforementioned "The Virgin and the Dinosaur" and "Down the River," as well as "On the Way to Gaugamela" and "Seven Wonders," as well as his recent novel *The Virgin and the Dinosaur*—have been extremely popular with *Asimov's* readers, as were his non-series time-travel stories "Gypsy Trade" and "Not Fade Away." He's also written baroque and inventive Space Opera or Space Adventures of various sorts, including "The Werewolves of Luna," "Into a Sunless Sea," "The Siren Shoals," "Cast on a Distant Shore," "Fair Verona," "Starfall," and the exuberant picaresque adventure that follows, "Gone to Glory," which takes us out across the boundless prairies of an exotic and dangerous alien world, in search of answers that it would be safer *not* to find. . . .

Robertson's books include, *The Spiral Dance, The Virgin and the Dinosaur, Atlantis Found,* and, most recently, *American Woman.* His most recent book is his first short-story collection, *The Moon Maid and Other Stories.* Several of his recent stories, including "Gypsy Trade," have been optioned for the movies, although none of them have made it to the screen as yet. He was born in Oakland, California, has a Ph.D. in the history of science and technology, and, before becoming a full-time writer, taught those subjects at UCLA and Villanova. He lives in Mt. Vernon, Washington.

Let's hope that as the years to come take us into the new century, Robertson gets some of the respect and attention he deserves. In the meantime, if you're looking for first-class adventure fiction, watch for his name—you're unlikely to be disappointed.

THE SAD CAFE

Defoe sat at one of the Sad Cafe's outdoor tables, soaking up gin slings and watching an energetic couple attempting to mate in midair, wearing nothing but gossamer wings and happy smiles. This pair of human mayflies had to be used to the exercise—neither showed a gram of fat or a bit of shame.

The four-hundred-year-old bistro stood in an open-air park on the Rue Sportif near Spindle's main axis, where g forces were low and the fun never slowed. Holodomes and hanging gardens arched overhead. Beyond the mating couple, halfway up Spindle's curve, nude bathers raised slow-motion splashes in a low-g pool. Not a shoddy spot for doing nothing. Defoe ordered his third (or maybe sixth) sloe gin sling from a roving cocktail bar, a barrel-shaped dispenser doing a lazy drunkard's walk between the tables, happily doling out drinks. Never asking for credit or expecting a tip. Human service was rarer than saber-tooth's teeth on Spindle.

Sipping his sloe gin, Defoe listened with mild disinterest to priority beeps coming over the comlink clipped to his ear. The first calls weren't for him, but they were coming fast and close together. Always a sad sign. Hoping not to be dragged too deeply into other people's troubles, he had his navmatrix decode the binary signals. The pilot's navmatrix grafted into the back of his skull was immune to alcohol. Defoe could down a dozen gin slings and still pilot a tilt-rotor VTOL in a blinding sandstorm or rendezvous with a starship—if the need arose. Only the need never arose. Not here. Not now.

First came a distress bulletin, direct from dirtside.

Then a standby alert.

Followed by a formal AID action request.

The final call was for him. Defoe answered in his off-duty voice.

Salome, his section head, came on-line. Her parents had been ultra-orthodox Satanists (who believed John the Baptist had it coming), and her strict religious upbringing made Salome controlled and precise, with barely a wayward impulse. Except for her hair, which tumbled in untamed curls and wild midnight-blue ringlets past her hips, almost to the floor. She sounded soft and winsome over the comlink, a sure sign HQ was in second-degree alarm—Salome never courted underlings unless she needed something. "There's an AID team down in Tuch-Dah country. They want us to send someone."

Defoe snickered. "Who's the lucky sucker?"

"AID wants an 'experienced surface hand.' Someone who knows the Tuch-Dah. You've been fortunate with them."

"Fortunate? Not hardly. Incredibly lucky would be nearer the mark." Not the sort of luck Defoe aimed to lean on.

Salome persisted. "But you have come through intact—always a plus—and saved us a lot of trouble." And saved the Tuch-Dah a lot of trouble, thought Defoe, not that the ungrateful bastards ever seemed to notice. "Besides, you're fresh up from the surface; it won't be so much of a shock."

"Right. With four months up-time coming." Up-time as in up here—on Spindle—where it was too perfect a day to contemplate work. Defoe had just done a solid eighteen weeks on Glory. Great-aunt Tillie in Alpha C would do duty dirtside before he went back early. "Last time AID lost a team, the problem solved itself—Tuch-Dahs sent their heads back in a leather bag."

"Marvelously considerate. But we can't always count on it. Take a couple of weeks," Salome suggested. "Clear this up, and we'll make it five months." That was double time. A rare offer. AID had to be in a fine panic.

"Make it six months," Defoe countered. *Every* day in paradise is perfect—so one is as good as another. He was demanding four days of up-time for every day dirtside—a splendid deal if he was so awfully essential.

"Find the team first," Salome told him primly. "Four weeks for going down to Glory. Four more for getting the job done." Defoe would get the extra days only if he delivered.

Bargaining with a Satanist was like dealing with the Devil. Centuries of persecution had turned a diabolically carefree sect into overcompensating overachievers. But it was always a comfort knowing that in the bad old days decent folk would have tied his boss to a stake and had her barbecued.

"I'll need a free hand," Defoe told her. "No interference from AID."

"That's your lookout. AID will be there—it's their team that's down. The way to avoid them is to get going and keep going."

"Sure thing." Defoe was already up and moving. "See you in Hell, Salome."

"Not unless you convert." He could hear her wicked smile. Another sign things were serious. Normally, Salome would never kid about religion.

Sloe gin and low gravity made the sidewalk seem to float in front of him. Rooftops and tree-lined arcades curved upward, vanishing into the light streaming down the length of the rotating habitat, reflected inward from mirrors set in the spinning well of stars. Spindle could amaze even sober senses.

Kids flashed past on the sidewalk, tanned young bodies in overdrive. Defoe passed feelie spas and low-g saunas. Happy holos invited him in. No more. Not now. Sorry, guys. Got to sober up and go to work.

Temptation abounded. And it was all free, from gaming orgies to organic feasts. Free as air to anyone who set foot on Spindle. Like an ancient Greek polis, Spindle made its own laws—but without the polis's slavery and infanticide—computers and birth lotteries took their place. No money. No credit. No theft, graft, or taxes. And like the ancient polis, Spindle had only two punishments that mattered. Death and exile. Now Defoe had to face both of these fates, for nothing except the right to return. Hardly fair, but the system lacked honest work.

At Port Orifice—the cavernous lock that let ships enter and exit—he drew emergency rations, heat caps, a thermal parka, bedroll, camp knife, folding mattock, climbing rope, canteen, and medikit. Telling the medikit to sober him up, he ticketed himself for the surface.

A call came through with his clearance. Salome's assistant, a pretty little catamite with painted lids and pierced nipples, purred into the comlink. "Hey, big boy. Is it true the Tuch-Dahs are cannibals?"

"No such luck." Defoe doubted Salome's kept boy had ever seen the surface. "They only eat people." Given conditions on Glory, Defoe thought cannibalism should at least be legal. Maybe even mandatory. If people were like hyenas, compelled to eat everything they killed, dirtside would be a safer place.

Salome's pet laughed wickedly. "Old Battle-ax wants to talk with you."

"Who?" The lock door dilated, cheerily welcoming Defoe aboard.

"Ellenor Battle. Boss dragon lady at AID."

Defoe stepped through the lock into the shuttle. "Tell 'em I've gone to Glory."

The oxyhydrogen shuttle lacked g-fields and cabin service; in-flight entertainment was a pair of tiny portholes. Defoe felt the backward jolt of retros. Spindle seemed to leap ahead; the sole fleck of civilization in this very outback system dwindled rapidly.

He had his navmatrix tap into the shuttle's moronic guidance system. Nerve endings merged with avionics—sensors, astrogation, and stabilization became extensions of sight, sound, and kinesthetics. A modest thrill. Pretty dry compared to real piloting. Defoe's previous employer had been an overprivileged idiot who wracked up a Fornax Skylark, stranding Defoe in-system. Delta Eridani was a dead end, producing nothing the wider universe needed. Traffic was all incoming. Subsidized AID shipments came in cosmic packing crates—robofreighters cannibalized at their destination.

Only a knack for steering through trouble (and putting up with Thals) earned Defoe part-time privileges on Spindle.

At the top of the stratosphere, the shuttle shifted her angle of attack. Acceleration gave way to the gentle persistent push of gravity. Through the near porthole Defoe saw the green-brown limb of the planet rising to greet him, edged by a thin corona of atmosphere. Cloud puffs hung over blue splotches—large lakes or inland seas. Knocking around the Near Eridani, he had seen worlds aplenty, some good, some bad, some merely uninhabitable. When humans first arrived, Glory had been an airless husk, pitted with craters. Relentless terraforming had made her almost livable. No worse than New Harmony, Elysium, Bliss, or any of a half-dozen made-to-order worlds. Either a shining success story, or a case of hideous ecocide. As a pilot, Defoe had to believe in terra-forming; starships needed places to go.

The shuttle came screeching in for a horizontal landing. Millions of kilometers of steppe, savanna, and lava desert allowed landing strips to be as long as needed. A groundhand undogged the hatch with a gleeful "Welcome to dirtside, land of enchantment—where falls can kill you, beasts can eat you, and Thals will snap your spine just to hear it pop. Watch your step, you are in two-thirds g."

Defoe nodded. He was used to gaining thirty kilos every time he went down to Glory. The strip was a study in spasmodic activity. Cargo pallets came dropping down from orbit, braked by big silver chutes, raising yellow clouds of dust. Semirigids landed and departed. SuperChimps sat like rows of sad monkeys, ready to help with the unloading. It had been cocktail time on Spindle; here it was early morning. Dun-colored hills stretched north and west of the field. Beyond the electrified perimeter, a solitary male moropus dug for steppe tubers. Hyenas trotted past, giving the moropus wide leeway—behind them, the Camelback Steppe disappeared into endless distance.

Waiting at the bottom of the landing ladder was a uniformed woman. Tall and athletic, with her steel-gray hair cut down to stubble, Ellenor Battle could easily have looked half her age—but she did not go for biosculpt or hair toner. Taking life as it came, she expected the universe to do the same. Defoe had dealt with Ellenor before, finding her as proud as Lucifer's aunt, a no-nonsense reminder that AID stood for the Agency for *Imperial* Development.

She gave him a liquid hydrogen greeting. "Welcome to Glory. You missed your briefing." Defoe confessed as much. Full-blown AID briefings were full of glaring oversights and ass-backward assumptions—besides, if the problem was solvable from orbit, AID would not have asked him down. But he listened dutifully to the facts as Ellenor saw them. "We have a semirigid and crew more than forty hours overdue. Orbital recon spotted the crash site in the TransAzur, Tuch-Dah territory. . . ."

"How many in the crew?"

"Three."

"All human?" A normal enough question, but Ellenor Battle took it badly, replying with a curt nod. Defoe never knew what was about to bother her. She was very like a Thal in that way—moody and demanding. Salome might worship Satan, but you at least knew where you stood.

A bang and a wail cut off conversation. SuperChimps were refueling the shuttle for her return to Spindle. Boiling LOX filled the collapsed tanks, screaming through the safety valves. With an irritated wave, Ellenor led him away from the ladder. Defoe matched her swift sure strides.

Two huge airship hangars dwarfed the clutter of buildings edging the strip. Outside the electrified perimeter sprawled Shacktown, one of those shameful slums-cum-animal-pens that sprang up around an Outback landing field. Cook smoke climbed lazily over dirty-naked Thal children searching through dung heaps for breakfast. Plastic honeycomb, narrow alleys, and open sewers gave Shacktown the look and smell of a slave labor camp—lacking only the camp's energy fences and city services.

The howl of liquid oxygen faded, and Ellenor went on, "A Thal came into Azur Station with a ship's recorder—hoping to trade it for booze. When the ship crashed, the survivors were attacked by Tuch-Dahs."

It had been a long time coming, Defoe decided, but all hell had finally broken out.

The main hangar was packed with nervous armed humans. Defoe was welcomed aboard by the Port Master, a local worthy who doubled as Mayor of Shacktown, charged with neglecting sanitation and handing out beer and bhang on election day. The hangar canteen had been opened for the duration. Drunk vigilantes brandished riot pistols, pepper grenades, and scoped sporting lasers—as though they could not decide whether they were faced with a prison break or a big game hunt. A Tuch-Dah uprising had the worst elements of both.

The quarter-kilometer hangar housed a giant rigid airship, the *Joie de Vivre*, belonging to a rancher named Helio from the Azur. Ellenor Battle pushed through the jittery throng with Defoe in tow, making for the control car. The gangway was guarded by a brace of armed Thals, meaner than normal Neanderthals, nearly as tall as Defoe, and twice as wide. They wore standard airship harnesses, supporting stubby grenade launchers and bandoliers of gas grenades. A pair of dire wolves strained on electronic leashes.

The liquored-up posse, loudly aiming to take on the entire Tuch-Dah nation, gave the two Thals ample space. It was easier to talk of annihilating ten thousand Neanderthals somewhere out on the steppe than to face down a couple of them sporting grim looks and civilized weapons.

What the Thals thought, Defoe could hardly guess. Heavy browridges hid their deep-set eyes.

A rigger appeared at the top of the gangway—a *Homo sapiens* with dark skin and a drooping mustache trained to blend into trim whiskers. Giving a sloppy sarcastic salute, he led them to the control car's lounge. He had a gasman's easy grace, accustomed to balancing on a catwalk in any sort of wind and weather. Crepe overshoes kept him from raising sparks. RIG'EM RIGHT was scrawled across the back of his bull-hide flight jacket, and he had the veteran gasman's grin—the small ironic smile that said he savored the insanity of making his living aboard a flying bomb.

Helio had that smile too. He sat by an open lounge window, eyes hidden by blue wraparound shades. Broad-shouldered as a Thal, the rancher was reckoned to be a dead shot. Surrounded by a breakfast buffet of cold capon and Azur caviar, he still looked deadlier than any dozen men outside.

Defoe pulled up a handwoven wicker seat, admiring the gold pattern in his plate.

Ellenor Battle tried to decline brunch, but Helio insisted. "It's no advantage to be uncomfortable."

No advantage indeed. Defoe let his host pour him some off-planet champagne. Relaxing under six tons of explosive hydrogen did not stop Helio from doing himself up right. Silk paneling framed slender lacquered columns.

"The first thing," Helio told his guests, "is to see this recorder—and the Thal who found it. We have the transmission from Azur Station. But what is that? A bunch of digital blips." He smiled behind his blue shades, kissing off the tips of his fingers. Electronic evidence was notoriously manipulatable—inadmissible in honest courts.

"So long as we get going." Ellenor Battle glared out the open window at the panicky mob scene below.

Defoe agreed. He too wanted to see the recorder—and the Thal who found it. But most immediately he had to get out of this idiotic atmosphere with its infectious panic. Once underway, things were bound to be better. Helio was supposed to understand Thals—and conditions in Tuch-Dah country—as well as anyone could pretend to. Besides, if there was any answer to the disappearance of the AID team, it was going to be "out there." Somewhere in the endless unknown that lay beyond the fringes of settlement, even on human-made planets. Defoe was fairly at peace with that. Hell, at the moment he made a dubious living off it.

Helio gave orders from the table, speaking through the open window and into the ship's comlink, letting the Port Master's young assistant come aboard, along with a couple of sober gunmen. The rest of the mob would be more of a threat to themselves than to the Tuch-Dahs. A gang of Super-Chimps hauled on the ground lines, and the cabin began to move.

As they cleared the hangar, Defoe had his navmatrix lock into the onboard systems. Everything read right. Gas pressure. Wind speed. Elevator alignment. Keel angle. When Helio gave the order to "up ship," the champagne in Defoe's glass did not so much as quiver. The sign of a good crew.

Shacktown and the landing strip fell away to windward. There was a hesitation as the big props started to turn, biting into thin air. Then airspeed picked up and they plowed along, powered by a cold-fusion reactor driving four paired propellers. The Camelback Steppe rolled placidly along a few hundred meters below. Springbok bounded off, alarmed by the airship's shadow.

Defoe decided he should see the recorder transmission from Azur Station, subjecting it to his own prejudices before hearing about it from others. Helio gave an airy wave. "Use my cabin. I have flying to do."

Ellenor Battle followed Defoe to the cabin, bent on seeing the recording again. Helio's private quarters were a sumptuous reminder of the good things to be had on Glory—hand-carved ivory and fine embroidery—luxuries that people on Spindle were too busy enjoying themselves to produce. And there was power to be had as well. Snappy service from human and semihuman attendants. Naked authority over Chimps, Thals, and Shacktown whores who would do nearly anything for next to nothing. Exotic animals roamed the endless veldt, ready to be hunted, killed, and butchered—the cabin was carpeted with a giant moropus hide, its head and claws attached. Defoe knew Dirtsiders who were not even tempted by the tame pleasures of Spindle, who snickered when he boarded a shuttle to go back.

The 3V imager made use of one whole bulkhead, turning curios and tapestries into a stereo tank.

Images leaped out. Defoe saw at once that the transmission wasn't a proper flight recording. The transmission had to come from an AID team member's personal recorder. First came establishing scenes—the semirigid taking off, steppe wildlife, a couple of male team members. Then came a terrible swift pan of breathtaking intensity. The recorder was sited on a small rise, aiming downslope. A low cairn of charred stones poked out of the steppe grass. Defoe flinched as rocket grenades and recoilless projectiles roared right at the recorder, a barrage so real that he almost dived out of his wicker seat, expecting to be showered with exploding shrapnel and shattered bric-a-brac. A ragged line of Thals came screaming out of the long grass, waving steel hatchets and hideous spiked clubs. They were Tuch-Dahs—no doubt there—Defoe recognized the garish paint and blood-freezing cries.

Willungha himself led the charge, atop a full-grown moropus—a tremendous horse-headed, long-necked beast with rhino-sized shoulders and tree-trunk limbs. Like Tars Tarkas aboard a wild thoat, the Neanderthal chieftain brayed commands, wielding a long thin lance. A grenade launcher in his rein hand looked like a tiny toy pistol.

Willungha's mount reared, waving clawed forefeet, and the recorder swung crazily, focusing for a second on the scene atop the knoll. Defoe could clearly make out the crash site. Kneeling among blackened girders and burnt grass was a woman, the third member of the AID team. She was small and brown-haired, in a rumpled uniform, taking painstaking aim with a recoilless pistol. Brown eyes stared intently over the sights, seeming to look right at Defoe. She squeezed off shot after shot as death stormed toward her.

The recorder jerked upward. Swaying grass tops framed empty blue sky.

A superbly ugly Tuch-Dah appeared, swinging a hideous curved club. The transmission ceased, replaced by braided hangings and a case of bone china.

Defoe turned to Lady Ellenor, saying, "That was fairly ghastly." Shutting her eyes, she gripped her wicker seat with white knuckles, letting out a short sharp gasp. He had thought Ellenor Battle would be fairly shockproof, especially on a second viewing—but without any warning, her feelings were showing. The woman was full of surprises.

Helio was in the lounge. Any flying he had done had not taken him away from the table. Breakfast had disappeared, but his glass still held champagne. Broken highlands had replaced the Camelback Steppe. Defoe's navmatrix knew the country; beyond these mesas lay the Sleeping Steppe. Then the Azur.

"Enjoy the show?" Helio's eyes were still hidden by blue shades, so it was hard to tell how he meant it.

Defoe nodded. A full-blown Tuch-Dah massacre. No wonder everyone from the Port Master on down was potted and praying. There were a thousand or so bona fide *Homo sapiens* on Glory. Plus maybe twice as many on Spindle who weren't much inclined to come down. Willungha could field twenty thousand club-wielding Tuch-Dah, if he cared to. There were ten million Thals spread over the planet.

Helio twirled the stem of his champagne glass. "Glory might have been a new Eden for ambitious youngsters from the Home Systems—but the task of terraforming was too real for them." Helio did not have to say that *he* had come here, giving up the easy life to raise bison and horses, risking his neck with archaic technology, making the planet not merely habitable but semi-inviting.

He clearly relished the irony of how hard it was to get people just to come down from Spindle. Yet the habitat was built as an interstellar slowboat, launched ages ago to seed the Delta Eridani system. A home for humans while Glory was being terraformed. But by the time Glory had a biosphere and a semibreathable atmosphere, the in-system humans had become perfectly adapted—to life on Spindle.

So AID had to go for Thals. Retrobred Neanderthals were shipped direct to Glory, to do the drudge work, overseeing SuperChimps, leveling landing strips, digging canals, tending great herds of herbivores. And the brutes had done a sterling job. Hell, they were still doing it. While backward types—like the Tuch-Dahs—bred like lemmings out on the vast steppes.

Defoe glanced over at Ellenor Battle. AID had planned this fiasco, from the first slowboats to the retrobreeding program that produced not just the Neanderthals, but a ready-made Cenozoic ecology as well.

She gave him a defiant glare, daring him to say that AID's multithousand-year program was a disaster. "The first colonists are on their way—ten thousand settlers, headed straight from Epsilon Eridani at near light speed. And a hundred thousand more are set to follow. And a million after that."

Epsilon E was less than twenty light-years away.

"Excellent." Helio emptied his champagne glass with an evil chuckle. "Willungha will have them for breakfast."

The rancher was right. Even a Navy cruiser with antimatter warheads could hardly cope with ten million Thals spread over an entire planet. (Currently the Navy had not so much as a captain's gig in-system.) The colonists could be armed, of course—but the Tuch-Dahs knew all about modern weapons. Dumping an armed mob of city-bred humans on a strange world, outnumbered ten thousand to one, with no way of telling the "good" Thals from the "bad" ones, would be a first-magnitude disaster. They might as well ship the weapons straight to Willungha, compliments of AID.

Ellenor Battle looked angrily out the lounge window, staring stiff-necked and imperious at the endless veldt. "There is room enough for humans and Neanderthals." As she saw it, AID was doing everyone a favor, bringing life to a dead world, making space for settlement, resurrecting a lost race, perhaps partly atoning for some ancient Cro-Magnon genocide.

Helio laughed heartily. "Tell that to Willungha. Maybe there is room. If the wild ones can be tamed, or pushed back. And the colonists kept near the strips. But no one is planning for that, eh?" He clearly thought someone should be.

"We have plans," Ellenor retorted.

Defoe thought of the lone AID woman in the recording, backed against the burnt-out wreck, coolly firing at the oncoming Thals. Whatever plans AID was hoarding had to beat that—in fact, they had better be damned slick.

The great blue-green ink blot of the Azur hove into sight. Azur Station stood at the near end, a small circle of dugouts and stock pens between the Blue Water Canal and an east-west fence line. All along the canal the Sleeping Steppe had been made to bloom, growing rice, melons, and sugarcane.

Azur's station chief met the airship. She was a big weatherbeaten woman named Cleo with flaming red hair, and scoped Centauri Special tucked under her arm—a sign of the times. A caravan was leaving her station, headed west along the fence line. The beasts of burden were low-humped retrobred camels, *Camelops hesternus*, as strong as Bactrians but more docile, with finer wool, also better eating.

Cleo had the recorder, and the Thal who had brought it, guarded by armed SuperChimps. The Thal did not understand Universal, or at least pretended not to—staring dumbly at the ring of narrow Cro-Magnon faces.

Helio tried signs. Grudgingly the Thal responded enough to indicate that he was *not* Tuch-Dah. He was Kee-too-Hee, from the marshes. He had found the recorder in a salt pan and trekked down to the station, hoping to get a reward. Instead he was being held prisoner and insulted. This did not altogether surprise him, but did not please him, either.

Ellenor Battle studied the recorder, then passed it to Defoe with a grim "What do you think?" The first time she had asked his opinion. Touched, he had his navmatrix go over the recorder. No sign of tampering. But this was an idiot box with sensors, playing back what was put in.

Defoe nodded at the Thal. "He's telling the truth. At least about not being Tuch-Dah. That circle and dot on his cheek is a Kee-too-Hee clan mark. Any right-thinking Tuch-Dah would cut his throat with a dull clamshell before claiming to be a Kee-too-Hee."

"But what was the recorder doing, sitting on a salt pan?" Ellenor sounded unconvinced. Rightly, so far as Defoe could see. "Give him his reward," she decided. "AID will pay. But don't let him go until we come back from the crash site."

The crash site lay across the Azur. Defoe watched the approach from the control car's foredeck, standing before wide wraparound windows. He felt Helio's firm hand on the elevators, anticipating changes in trim, keeping the keel angle constant. North of Azur Station, the shoreline became a maze of salt marsh teeming with spoonbills and wild boar. Then came the Azur itself, bright green in the shallows, deep blue in the center.

Helio pointed out his plantation, a great green delta thrust out into the sea. On the landward side, a long straight north-south fence kept his domestic herds from straying into Tuch-Dah country. West of the fence line was a knoll topped with a black smear left by the burned semirigid. Helio descended, dodging tall columns of vultures. Never a good sign.

Ellenor told Helio to turn out the *Joie*'s crew. "Have them go through the long grass around the knoll."

"Looking for what?" The rancher sounded skeptical.

"Whatever they find."

On the ground, Defoe was struck by how peaceful it seemed. This was the Saber-tooth Steppe, a silent mysterious savanna, its mystique as solid and tangible as a patch of unterraformed bedrock. The semirigid's small control car was intact, showing no sign of having come down hard. Blackened girders formed big looping curves. They might have been spares ready to be assembled into another ship.

Dire wolves sniffed out two bodies. "Burned beyond recognition" hardly conveyed the horror of the charred skeletons, jaws agape in final agony, held together by shreds of cooked flesh. Riggers watched Ellenor Battle go over the corpses with cool intensity, calling down DNA signatures and dental data from orbit. "This guy's kinda short," someone suggested. "Maybe he's a Thal."

"I don't know. Might be human."

"Human as you anyway."

"Just bein' hopeful."

Glad not to be needed, Defoe conducted his own search, using his navmatrix to find the low black cairn and the fold the Tuch-Dah had burst from. A rigger was down in the grass on his knees, a strip of gasbag fabric tied around his head like a bandanna holding his hair back. Defoe recognized RIG'EM RIGHT on the back of the man's jacket.

Seeing Defoe, he got up. His name was Rayson, which everyone shortened to Ray. He held up a small finned and pointed object. "There's a mess of these in the grass." Defoe recognized the spent projectile from a recoilless pistol. The young AID woman had been firing downslope from up by the wreck. Had she hit anything? Defoe looked for bloodstains.

Ray glanced upslope to where Ellenor Battle was working over the bodies, then walked around behind the fire-blackened cairn, opening his pants.

Defoe called out softly, "That's a shrine."

Taking a sharp step back, Ray zipped his pants. "Shit, I thought it was a barbecue pit." Just the sort of thing that got people in trouble in Tuch-Dah country—you could get brained by a Thal and never know why.

Finding no blood on the grass tops, Defoe stood up, studying the shoreline. The colder north shore marshes were thin, broken by shimmering white pans. Wind whipped fine dry grit off the pans, stinging his eyes, settling in skin creases. He licked the corners of his mouth, tasting tiny bits of the Saber-tooth Steppe. It was salty.

A dark object lay between the steppe and the sea, as still as the shrine. Defoe walked toward it, brittle shore grass crunching underfoot. The big still object was a bison, down on its knees. Vultures flapped off as Defoe approached. Tail, ears, eyes, and testicles were gone, but the bison was hideously alive, managing to lift its head, turning bloody sightless sockets toward Defoe.

"Damn." Ray was right behind him, letting out a low whistle. "I'll fix him." He produced a recoilless pistol with a folding stock. Shouldering it like a rifle, he fired.

The bison jerked at the impact, his head dropping, one horn gouging into the sandy pan. Defoe bent down, examining the dead beast; the tongue was torn out, the muzzle white with salt. There was more salt beneath the sand, where the horn had gone in. Looking east and west along the shore, Defoe saw spiraling columns of vultures.

Ellenor Battle pronounced the bodies to be *Homo sapiens sapiens.* Male. Two members of the AID team were accounted for. Cause of death unknown. "We should start a slow search, standard pattern, centered on the crash site."

Helio nodded and they set off again. As Glory's tight ten-hour day ended, Defoe sat in the lounge, trying to fit together everything he had seen—the mob scene in the hangar, the recording, the silent Thal, the crash site, and the dying bison. Delta Eridani had sunk down almost to the level of the steppe. The *Joie* was making gentle sweeps at less than thirty kph, twenty meters or so above the grass tops. He doubted they would turn up anything. That would be far too easy.

Gathering his things, Defoe climbed up to the keel. Tall hydrogen-filled gasbags swayed in semidarkness. A rigger with CATWALK CHARLIE on his jacket bossed a gang of SuperChimps.

Defoe made his way to the empty tail, unsealing an inspection hatch. Grass tops slid by less than twenty meters below. Unreeling a dozen meters of cable from a nearby winch, he swung his legs through the open hatch, letting the cable drop.

"Hope it wasn't something we said." Rigger Ray was standing on the keel catwalk.

Defoe shrugged. "I need room to work."

Ray sat down on a girder, eyeing the open hatch. This close to dusk, shaded by the giant tail, the hatch looked like a black hole whipping along in midair. "There's room aplenty down there. Just don't end up at the bottom of the food chain."

Defoe nodded. "I'll do my damnedest."

"Well, good-bye, an' good luck." Ray made it sound like, "Hope to hell you come back."

Defoe dropped through, slid down the cable, and let go. He had ample time to position himself. The most charming thing about Glory was the lazy falls at two-thirds g.

Steppe floated up to meet him.

Defoe hit, bounced, and scrambled to his feet. He stood staring up at the big tail of the dwindling airship. The *Joie de Vivre* kept to her search pattern, straining to complete the last leg before nightfall. When she dipped below a rise, he was alone.

Hip-high grass tops ran in every direction, prowled by tawny killers with knife-sized fangs. A cold undertaker's wind sent waves of color sweeping over the twilight steppe—deep blue, rust brown, old gold, and a dozen shades of green. Hyenas chuckled in the deepening gloom.

As Delta Eridani slid beneath the horizon, darkness rose up out of the grass roots, devouring the light. Night birds keened. Whoever said humans were the meanest animals—"the most dangerous game"—undoubtedly said it in daylight. Certainly it was never said at night, alone and unarmed on the Saber-tooth Steppe. Orienting himself by the strange stars of Eridani Sector, Defoe set out walking toward the distant fence line.

THE SABER-TOOTH STEPPE

Dew clung to the grass tops by the time Defoe found the fence line. He had slept once, to be roused stiff and sore by the cough of a saber-tooth. Throughout the dark morning hours, he heard the catlike predators that gave the steppe its name calling to each other. Dawn wind carried their smell, like the odor of a ship's cat in a confined cabin. At first light the calls ceased; he supposed the pride had made its kill.

The energy fence cut a shimmering line across the steppe, carrying a hefty neural frequency shock. Domestic herds grazed beyond it. Overgrazed, in fact. The far side looked like a low-cut lawn.

Defoe walked along the fence until he found a knot of horses, *Equus occidentalis*, tall as Arabians but heavier, with slender feet, reminding Defoe of zebras or unicorns. The lead mare even had zebra stripes across her withers.

The horses lifted their heads as he approached, staring at him and at the hip-high steppe grass. Defoe told his navmatrix to bypass the fence's gullible software. The air between the nearest pylons ceased to shimmer, but still carried the signal saying the fence was intact. Ripping up some long grass, Defoe stepped through, offering it to the lead mare. They were immediate friends. She took the grass, letting him mount.

Riding bareback, he guided her through the break in the fence. Her little herd trotted after them. Defoe set a leisurely course deeper into Tuch-Dah country. As his navmatrix moved out of range, the fence reestablished itself.

He saw springbok and pronghorn, but no bison or Tuch-Dahs. Steppe thinned into shortgrass prairie broken by black knobs of basalt. Curious antelope came right up to him, heads held high, showing off tiny horns and white throats. Brown somber eyes studied him intently. Defoe doubted they had ever been hunted by humans.

Seeing a spiraling column of vultures, Defoe made for it. It marked a bison kill, a lone bull set upon by hyenas. He got down to study the kill site. Drag marks mapped the struggle. The bison had been hit once and ripped completely apart, probably in seconds. Nothing remained but rags of hide and white bone-rich dung. Hyenas were more to be feared than overgrown cats; their bite was better than a panther's, and they weren't as picky as a saber-tooth pride.

A shadow swept over him, a gigantic condor-sized shape among the vultures, circling downward, parting the smaller birds, boring toward Defoe in a tight spiraling dive, hiding in the orange glare of Delta Eridani. Almost on top of him, the big shape sideslipped, spilling air. He recognized Ellenor Battle, wearing an ornithopter harness—a powered version of the wings people flew with on Spindle. She flew like she had been born with them, doing a low-level stall and landing feetfirst.

Never let down your guard on Saber-tooth Steppe. Defoe had been blissfully alone, sharing the day with vultures and a dead bison. Now without warning Ellenor Battle was standing over him, demanding an explanation. What excuse could he have for jumping ship, cutting fences, and stealing horses?

Defoe shrugged. "No one needed me just to fly around in circles aboard the *Joie de Vivre.*"

What fascinated him was her wings. A really fine pair. Falcoform Condors, solar assisted, seven-plus meters of extendible wingspan, with autoflaps and fingertip trim tabs. An energy pack in the small of her back powered the harness.

He nodded at the horses. "These are my tickets into Tuch-Dah country. What's your excuse for being here?" When it came to unwanted company, Glory could be more crowded than Spindle.

Ellenor slowly reached behind her back, taking the AID recorder from between her wings—it must have been strapped alongside the power pack. "I'm here because of this." She weighed it in her hands, then held it out. "It's my daughter's."

Defoe shooed aside some vultures and sat down. So, the woman on the AID team was another Battle. They did not look much alike, except perhaps in the shape of the face. But maybe Ellenor's hair used to be brown. More important, this explained her readiness to listen to reason.

"What *is* her name?" Defoe bore down lightly on the verb; no reason to assume she was dead.

"Lila. It's Hindu, and means the playful will of Heaven."

He took the recorder, turning it over in his hands. "So, why didn't your daughter have this with her during the attack?"

"I've been wondering. There might be some simple explanation."

"Might be." But Defoe doubted it. "That makes another strange circumstance about the crash and recording."

"What are the others?" Ellenor folded her wings, settling down across from him.

"First—no crash. That semirigid landed intact, then burned on the ground. Second, what sort of shot is Lila?"

"I taught her myself." There was pride in her voice and a recoilless pistol on her hip.

"So I supposed." He remembered how cool and unflinching Lila had looked—a lot like her mother. "But there was no blood on the grass. It is hard to believe every shot was a miss."

Ellenor nodded grimly.

Defoe got up, handed back the recorder, and dusted fine grains off his lap. The soil felt thin and silty. "Can you ride bareback?" Ellenor was not his first choice as a traveling companion, or even his fiftieth, but that was Glory for you.

"I was doing it before you were born." She fixed up a loop bridle, selected a mount, and they set off.

The prairie thinned further. Sandy patches showed between tufts of shriveled grass. More buzzards appeared, over more dead bison. More than even hyenas could eat. Defoe reined in, asking, "What do you make of this?"

Ellenor dismissed the apocalyptic scene. "A local die-off. We saw it from orbit. Lila's team was investigating."

Defoe shook his head. "I've been seeing signs of major drought ever since crossing the Azur. And real overgrazing as well. Helio's horses were frantic to cross the fence line."

Ellenor sniffed. "Is that a pilot's opinion, or are you a xenoecologist as well?"

"You don't have to be a xenoecologist to know a dead buffalo. The water table is falling. You can see the steppe salting up. Springbok and pronghorns are filtering in from out of the wild, replacing the bison."

Ellenor denied the Azur was in any trouble. "The sea is stabilized."

"Stabilized?" He reminded her the planet was still terraforming. "Shouldn't the Azur be growing?"

"A local shortfall," she insisted, shrugging off the buzzards and dead bison. "Another wet season and this will all be forgotten."

It did not seem that local to Defoe. Kilometers north of the Azur he could still smell salt on the breeze. Nor would the Tuch-Dah take a "local condition" so calmly—they had to live here. And they were not the types to forget and forgive. Anyone who endured a two-day Naming Fast knew Thals had god-awful long memories.

From time to time Ellenor took off, soaring aloft to do a turn around the landscape, looking for water. Near to dusk she found a dry bed winding through a sandy bottom. Dismounting, Defoe attacked the damp sand with his mattock. An hour of digging produced a small hole full of brackish liquid. He refilled his canteen, then let the horses drink.

Ellenor alighted on a cutbank, saying a rider was coming.

Defoe nodded. Dusk was when they could expect company. Gathering dry grass and brushwood, he made a bed for a fire. Then he took out a heat cap, a capsule the size of an oral antibiotic, breaking it and tossing it on the wood. It burned with an intense flame and acrid odor.

He watched the rider trot warily into camp, separating from the red-orange disk of Delta Eridani. It was Willungha, atop a giant male moropus. Thals did not have aerial recon and orbital scans, but not much that went on in Tuch-Dah country escaped Willungha's attention.

Despite rumors about him being a half-breed, or even *Homo sapiens*, the Tuch-Dah chieftain was pure Neanderthal, with bulging browridges, buckteeth, and a receding chin. That chin was the only weak thing about him. Willungha's huge head and shoulders topped a meter-wide chest; arms the size of Defoe's calves ended in hands strong enough to strangle a hungry saber-tooth (a perennial party-pleaser at Tuch-Dah fetes). An old scar ran along one gigantic thigh. In his youth, Willungha had been gored by a wounded bison, the horn going through his thigh. Hanging head down, with the horn tearing at his leg, Willungha had clamped his good leg and left arm around the beast's neck. Calmly drawing a sheath knife, he cut the bison's throat. Willungha's mount was an ancient cousin of the horse and rhino, intended to be a browser and pruner—recycling plant material into the soil. AID had never thought a moropus could be ridden.

He grunted a greeting.

Defoe did not attempt to answer. Instead he unhobbled the horses, laying the lead mare's halter rope ceremoniously before the Tuch-Dah. He kept back only a pair of mounts and a led horse for himself and Ellenor.

Willungha responded with a series of snorts. Wild Thals spoke a hideous concoction of clicks, hoots, and grunts, which some *Homo sapiens* claimed to understand, but none could imitate. To the Tuch-Dah, *Homo sapiens* were overwhelmingly deaf and totally dumb, hardly even a thinking species. Powerful and unpredictable maybe, able to tear up the landscape like a mad moropus. But reasoning? Even Willungha reserved judgment. He was tolerably familiar with "man the wise"—which explained his mixed opinion.

Having given gifts, Defoe moved to the next stop in the evening's entertainment, setting up the recorder by the fire so it would play on the cutbank. Using the eroded rock as a 3V screen, he had his navmatrix sort through the recorder's memory for the final images, including the Tuch-

Dah attack. When Willungha himself materialized atop his charging moropus, the chieftain gave a hoot and whistle. For all Defoe knew, it merely meant, "Hello." Or, "Handsome fellow, what?"

Lila appeared next, pistol in hand. Defoe froze the image. Walking up to the scene, he stabbed a finger at her, then made as if to look about— hopefully telling Willungha that he was looking for her.

The Tuch-Dah's eyes fixed him from within their deep sockets. Defoe repeated the signs. Wild Thals were not much impressed with off-planet marvels unless they could put them to use. Without as much as a grunt, Willungha headed off into the dark with his gift horses in tow.

Defoe leaped up, telling Ellenor, "We've got to follow." Willungha was the best lead they were likely to get.

They trekked through most of the short night. Badlands gave way to savanna. Tangerine dawn outlined the tops of black acacias.

Twenty-odd hours without sleep had Defoe dizzy with fatigue—wishing to God he could glaze over for a while. From upwind came the smell of burning dung, denoting a nomad camp.

Beneath the acacias stood a dark circle of yurts, surrounded by lowing herds. A crowd of Thals emerged to click and whistle their leader into camp. Defoe and Ellenor got no such cheery greetings, facing stony indifference leavened by the occasional dirty look.

While Ellenor sat with folded wings, Defoe listened to a lively exchange among the Thals, seeing fists waved in their direction. The discussion narrowed to a debate between Willungha and a tall brute with a broken nose and bold red-ocher tattoos. He must have outweighed Willungha by a couple of stone, but lacked the chieftain's sangfroid. Plug-ugly's part in the conversation consisted of low growls and grim looks.

Willungha ended the exchange, turning abruptly and striding over to where Defoe and Ellenor sat waiting. Squatting on his haunches, he made his position plain with signs and finger jabbing. They were free to search for their stray female, with a single exception. Defoe explained to Ellenor, "The only yurt we cannot enter belongs to Mean and Ugly over there." He nodded toward the tall Thal with the broken nose and ocher tattoos.

Ellenor frowned. "Logically that is the yurt we most want to examine."

Defoe nodded. Thals could be amazingly unsubtle. He fished out his medikit, knowing he would need a boost. Strapping the kit to his calf, he told it to give him the chemical equivalent of a week's rest. "I'll see what I can do about getting Plug-ugly's permission."

Stimulants hummed through his blood. The morning got brighter. A two-thirds-g bounce came back to his step. But Defoe hated relying on chemical imbalance; you could fool your body only so long. The Thal stood planted in front of his yurt, a skin hovel on wheels trimmed with camel tails. A bison hide hung over the doorway. Defoe strolled up with a hearty "How ya doin'?"

The Tuch-Dah merely spat. Since neither could speak the other's language, there was no need for formal insults. Defoe slid silently into migi game, arms hanging loose, spine aligned, right foot leading. Out the corner of his eye, he could see Willungha and the boys settling down to watch the fun.

Giving a roar, the Thal rushed at him, arms raised, bent on snapping the spindly Cro-Magnon in half. Defoe was well outweighed, and his sparring partner would be immune to any sort of body blow. He seized the big right wrist with his left hand. Pivoting sideways, he used the Neanderthal's momentum to sling the ogre over his hip, hacking as hard as he could at the immobilized right wrist. Mean and Ugly went butt-over-browridge into a heap against one wheel of his yurt.

Willungha's boys applauded with pant hoots.

The Thal bounded right back up, snarling like a wounded lion. Favoring his right hand, he lashed at Defoe with his left. Defoe parried with his forearm. A bad mistake—the glancing blow staggered him.

Grinning with feral glee, the Thal circled leftward, not even winded. The bastard had probably gotten his beauty sleep. Defoe's right forearm felt numb, and his lungs rasped—a sign the medikit had reached its limits. Much more of this, and the Thal would wear him down. Then stomp him into oblivion.

The Tuch-Dah lunged at Defoe with his left. This time Defoe ducked under the blow, grabbing the Thal's left hand with both of his, ignoring the injured right. Lacking the strength to go the distance, Defoe held grimly to the Tuch-Dah's good hand. He sent the bellowing ogre cartwheeling over his shoulder, letting the Thal's own weight and momentum bend the left wrist until it snapped.

The Neanderthal lay dazed, one wrist badly sprained, the other broken. A firm believer in kicking a fellow when he was down, Defoe brought his boot heel sharply on the Thal's tattooed instep, to discourage the brute from getting up. Mean and Ugly moaned.

Dusting himself off, Defoe glanced over at Willungha. The Tuch-Dah chieftain gave a congratulatory grunt. Defoe was free to search the yurt. He hoped to hell he'd find something.

As soon as he lifted the bison hide, Defoe knew that whatever was in the yurt stank all the way to Spindle. Urine, sweat, and burning dung mixed with moldy leather. Worming his way in, he startled a gaggle of Thal children playing beside the central fire. They piled out past him, terrified by a *Homo sapiens* bogeyman turned real.

The yurt was dank and smoky, walled with soot and skins; aside from body paint and tattoos, Thals did not bother with decoration. What he was looking for sat in the back, amazingly alive. Alert brown eyes ringed with fatigue stared back at him, hardly believing what they were seeing. "Lila Battle, I presume?"

She managed a nod. Tuch-Dah methods were crude and pitiless. To keep Lila in place, a long yoke was fitted around her neck, made from two heavy lengths of wood lashed together with leather. Her hands were free, but the ends of the yoke were out of reach, anchored to the bed of the yurt. She could move enough to feed herself and attend to body functions, but could not reach the knots holding the yoke in place.

As he cut Lila loose, Ellenor Battle came crawling in, dragging her wings. She hurriedly strapped her medikit around Lila's forearm. Mother and daughter were reunited in the fetid interior of a Tuch-Dah yurt, a touching moment lasting about a nanosecond. Lila was clearly Ellenor's daughter, and neither was given to excess sentiment. Before they had finished hugging, Ellenor wanted to know what had happened, and Lila was telling them.

"Helio did it. The bastard flagged us down for a face-to-face. The next thing I knew, I was being bundled up and given to the Tuch-Dahs."

Defoe had suspected something of the sort—it wasn't in Willungha's nature to mix with *Homo sapiens*, either as friends or as enemies. Full-fledged humans had to be behind this. But he was sorry to find out it was Helio. He had liked the arrogant asshole.

Hauling out the recorder, he gave Lila a look at her "last stand." She shook her head. "I wish I had put up that fight, but I never saw it coming." She knew nothing about the fate of her ship and team.

"Dead and burned," Ellenor told her daughter bluntly. Everything else had been digitally programmed straight into the dimwitted recorder's memory. A decent scheme, but not foolproof. The chance selection of Lila's recorder had made her mother suspicious, while Defoe was always willing to believe the worst.

"Why didn't he just kill me?" Lila wondered. Having spent the last few days bound in the back of a Tuch-Dah yurt, she was in many ways the most amazed.

"You are his insurance shot." Defoe set the recorder next to his knee. "A good hunter always has an extra charge handy, to insure his prey is nailed. The crash and fake recording were not enough to thoroughly implicate the Tuch-Dahs. But by the time your body turned up, it would be obvious who had you." Willungha's people probably had no idea why Helio wanted one of his females carted about against her will. But the Thal he had made the deal with fought to keep up his end. Touching in a terrible way.

"But why do this at all?" For once Ellenor looked at a loss. "Why wipe out our team? Why blame it on the Tuch-Dahs?"

"Because Azur is dying." Lila spoke softly. "The sea is overloaded. The steppe is salting up." From the way Ellenor scowled, Defoe guessed this was an old argument.

Lila matched her mother's stubbornness, insisting, "Sea and grass aren't returning water to the air as fast as the canals are draining it away. The thin layer of soil atop this cinder and bedrock cannot absorb new arrivals. We saw it. Helio sees it. Willungha must know as well. Helio wants the Azur closed off to settlement. So do I. But he apparently thinks it will take a war to do it."

Ellenor gave Lila a sour to-think-I-suckled-you look. But as far as Defoe could see, Helio might be right, even AID wouldn't dump settlers into a war zone. With the colonists diverted and the Tuch-Dah pushed back, Helio would have the Azur to himself.

Hearing hoots outside, Defoe lifted the bison hide for a peek. Thals were looking up. From over the steppe came the beat of paired propellers, announcing more unwanted company. The *Joie de Vivre* was approaching.

Ellenor swore. Her daughter began to gather her strength for a getaway. No one was burning to confront the guilty culprit. Defoe had pictured them sending a signal to Spindle, then lying low until AID organized a rescue operation. Armed and reckless felons should be cared for by the pros.

While Ellenor hustled her daughter out, Defoe scooped up the recorder. Telling his navmatrix to turn the recorder on, he pointed the business end at the yurt fire, getting a long shot of the flames.

By the time Defoe tumbled out, the *Joie de Vivre* was poking her nose over the nearest rise, looming larger as she descended. Mother and daughter were disappearing into the long grass beyond the yurt circle. When he caught up with them, Ellenor had her wings on and communicator out, preparing to punch through a call to Spindle. He grabbed her hand, stopping her from opening the channel. "Wait."

"Why?" Ellenor looked angry, annoyed, and scared. Her recoilless pistol was out and armed.

"Helio will be listening," he reminded her. Ellenor might be absolutely ready to sacrifice everything just to see justice done, but Defoe was not near as determined to die for the law. "Give us a chance to get away first."

"How?" she demanded. Running was ridiculous. Helio would swiftly spot them. Nor was there any reason for Willungha to take their side.

"Start by lying down," Defoe insisted, "so we don't disturb the grass tops. Right now we can see him, but Helio can't see us." He had to make the most of that.

The *Joie* settled down on a hillock near camp, close enough to cover the exits, but not so close as to disturb the Tuch-Dahs. SuperChimps swarmed down the ground lines and anchored the airship to the hilltop. Helio and his gunmen trooped down the control-car gangway, sporting rifles tucked under their arms, fanning out as they approached the yurts.

"Get ready to run." Defoe aimed the recorder at the airship. "I'm going to create a diversion."

Lila nodded gamely. Ellenor remained unconvinced. "What sort of a diversion?"

"Fire and panic." Defoe told his navmatrix to set the recorder on playback, projecting a continuously expanding loop using the most recent image in memory. "No matter what you see, run straight for the *Joie de Vivre*, and up that gangway. Got it?" Both women nodded. "Then go," he hissed, triggering the recorder.

They broke cover as a red glow appeared on the hull of the airship—the image of the yurt fire magnified by the recorder—growing into a terrible circle of fire. SuperChimps hooted in terror, scattering away from the ship. In seconds the image covered half the hull, looking for all the world like a trillion cubic centimeters of hydrogen bursting into flame. The control-car crew dived out the gondola windows.

Defoe topped the hill. Shoving Ellenor and Lila toward the gangway, he began releasing ground lines. Lightened by the loss of men and chimps, the airship strained at her anchors, heaving about above him like a whale in labor.

Someone yelled stop. Without bothering to answer, Defoe leaped on the last line, pulling the anchor pin, letting the line hoist him up and away. The airship tore off downwind, wallowing drunkenly, her control gondola empty. Dangling cables rattled through the stand of acacias.

Seeing he could not clear the trees, Defoe had his navmatrix send a frantic call to the *Joie's* emergency system, releasing the landing ballast. Tons of water cascaded past. The ship shot upward, out of Helio's range and reach.

His navmatrix ticked off altitude increases. One thousand, two thousand, three thousand meters. Savanna spun below him. Time he hauled himself aboard. Holding on with his left hand, Defoe reached up with his right, grasping the taut line. Getting a good grip, he let go with his left.

He fell, steel line sliding through his fingers. His right hand would not hold. Making a frantic grab with his left, he managed to catch the line.

Dangling left-handed, Defoe realized his right arm was useless. It would no longer support him. The medikit strapped to his leg had masked his pain, and the damage done by the Thal. Betraying him into trying too much.

Swinging silently, several kilometers in the air beneath a bucking airship, he pondered his next move. Unable to climb one-handed, Defoe kicked at the end of the line with his boot. If he could snag the anchor loop, he could hang safely until someone hauled him up.

Too far. His foot would not reach. Grass tops whirled dizzily below him. The *Joie de Vivre* topped four kilometers, still rising.

Loosening his left hand, he slid down the line, feeling with his boot for the loop. His toe went in. He gave a silent cheer. He had made it.

Just as his boot settled in, the line jerked—the *Joie* had reached her pressure height, automatically venting hydrogen. Nosing down, she took a drunken dip, porpoising out of control.

Defoe fought to regain his grip. Fatigued fingers weren't quick enough. The line snapped away. Two sleepless nights, the fight with the Thal, the struggle on the line, had all taken too much out of him.

Arms flailing, he fell slowly backward, his booted foot twisting in the loop. Two-thirds g gave him enough time to make a last lunge at the line. And miss.

Dangling upside down, holding on by his boot, he could feel his foot slipping. Doubling up, Defoe made a grab at the boot with his good hand. He got it. Fingers gripped the boot as his foot slipped free and the line bounded away.

He was falling. Holding tight to the useless boot, Defoe shrieked in fright and exasperation. He could see the snaking line above him and the shadowy form of the airship starting to dwindle. Five kilometers away, ground rushed silently up to greet him.

Defoe felt none of the dreamy complacency the dying were supposed to enjoy. Even in two-thirds g, onto soft grass, he knew he would hit hard, bounce badly, and not get up. Ever. His navmatrix ticked off the fall. Slow at first. A few meters per second—but ever faster. Numbers began to blur.

The horrible silence was broken by the rush of wings. Hands seized him. Primaries beat frantically. He could feel flaps straining against the sky.

Ellenor Battle had him. Pulling out of her stoop, she was trying to brake, wings beating against better than twice her weight. Good shot, thought Defoe. But the wing loading was way too high. He could feel her stalling, about to tumble into a spin—unless she let go.

But she dug in instead, spreading her wings, defiant to the end, her contorted face centimeters from his.

Then came a miraculous jerk, and the impossible happened. Defoe bounded to a dead stop in midair.

A line stood taut between Ellenor's shoulders. She had clipped a cable to her harness before diving after him. Staring up at the skyline, Defoe tried to cheer, getting out a grateful croak. The woman was a pigheaded genius, and he wanted to kiss her. But then Ellenor might really drop him.

Meter by meter he felt himself being hauled to safety. The AID woman was grinning.

As they were drawn aboard the galloping airship, Defoe saw Rigger Ray working the winch. Lila lay full out on the deck, reaching down to help her mother. Catwalk Charlie was holding tight to a girder, eyes shut, still waiting for the flaming crash. Defoe could hear him mumbling:

Our Satan that art in Hell,
Damned be thy name.
Lead us into temptation,
And encourage our trespasses . . .

Defoe was shocked. Charlie had never *looked* religious. But a brush with death will bring out the Devil in anyone.

Gingerly sliding his boot on, Defoe told his navmatrix to take control of the airship. The *Joie* righted herself, turning back toward Shacktown.

Hearing Ellenor put in her call to Spindle, Defoe wondered how Helio was doing with Willungha. After murdering two AID workers, trying to frame the Tuch-Dahs, then bungling the cover-up, Helio had serious problems ahead. But so did everyone on Glory. And the first ten thousand colonists were already on their way, leaving Epsilon Eridani at near light speed.

Defoe for one did not want to be there when trouble arrived. Right now he was headed back for Spindle, to spend long lazy hours of enjoying himself and looking for a ship headed out-system. AID could deal with the mess they had made. More people meant more traffic, and one day dirtside and all its dangers would be a batch of not-too-pleasant recollections. The sort of memories you were free to file and forget.

A DRY, QUIET WAR

One of the fastest-rising new stars of the nineties, Tony Daniel grew up in Alabama, lived for a while on Vashon Island, in Washington state, and in recent years, in the best tradition of the young bohemian artist, has been restlessly on the move, from Vashon Island to Europe, from Europe to New York City, from New York City to Alabama, and, most recently, back to New York City again. He attended the Clarion West Writers Workshop in 1989, and since then has become a frequent contributor to *Asimov's Science Fiction,* as well as to markets such as *The Magazine of Fantasy & Science Fiction, Amazing, SF Age, Universe, Full Spectrum,* and elsewhere.

Like many writers of his generation, Tony Daniel first made an impression on the field with his short fiction. He made his first sale, to *Asimov's,* in 1990, "The Passage of Night Trains," and followed it up with a long string of well-received stories both there and elsewhere throughout the first few years of the nineties, stories such as "The Careful Man Goes West," "Sun So Hot I Froze to Death," "Prism Tree," "Death of Reason," "Lost in Transmission," "God's Foot," "Candle," "Aconguaca," and others. His first novel, *Warpath,* a lush, baroque Planetary Romance full of deliberately over-the-top tropes such as superpowered Indians "paddling" birch-bark canoes across the gulfs of interstellar space, was released simultaneously in America and England in 1993, and he subsequently won two thousand dollars and the T. Morris Hackney Award for his unpublished mountain-climbing novel *Ascension,* based on his story "Aconcagua."

Daniel's career seemed to be well launched at this point, with his short stories receiving a lot of attention and *Warpath* getting largely positive reviews, but then he was unable to find a publisher for *Ascension* (it remains unpublished to this day), he stalled on his second novel, and his career abruptly seemed to run out of steam. Little would be heard from him during the middle years of the decade, while he moved restlessly around the world, from one minor job to another. In 1995, though, he returned suddenly to the field with a string of new stories, work even stronger and at a higher level of literary accomplishment than his previous stuff, including "Life on the Moon," which was a finalist for the Hugo Award in 1996, "No Love in All of Dwingeloo," "The Joy of the Sidereal Long-Distance Runner," "A Dry, Quiet War," and a highly impressive novella called "The Robot's Twilight Companion." In 1997, he published a major new novel, *Earthling,* which has gotten enthusiastic reviews everywhere from *Interzone* to the *New York Times.* His career seems to be firmly back on track again, knock wood, and I have a feeling he'll be one of the major players in SF in the opening decades of the new century.

Like George R.R. Martin, Daniel is a lushly romantic writer, and his characters also tend toward Byronism, although Daniel's brooding Byronic heroes tend to be darker, more cynical, and more violent than Martin's are, and also tend to possess Zelaznyesque superpowers and abilities of a sort that Martin's usually do not. One of the major influences on Daniel's work, of course, is clearly that of his one-time mentor, Lucius Shepard, although the impact of Zelazny, van Vogt, Walter M. Miller, Jr., and, oddly, Ray Bradbury can also be demonstrated fairly clearly. Like some of his other young colleagues, though, Daniel's other influences spread far beyond the boundaries of the genre, and even beyond the print world itself; the influence of Japanese samurai movies and spaghetti Westerns on the vivid, violent story that follows are pretty clear, for instance, and Daniel himself has specifically said that one of his direct inspirations for the story was the movies of John Ford.

In "A Dry, Quiet War," he spins a colorful and exotic story of a battle-weary veteran who returns from a bewilderingly strange high-tech future war only to face his greatest and most sinister challenge right at *home.* . . .

I cannot tell you what it meant to me to see the two suns of Ferro set behind the dry mountain east of my home. I had been away twelve billion years. I passed my cabin to the pump well, and taking a metal cup from where it hung from a set-pin, I worked the handle three times. At first it creaked, and I believed it was rusted tight, but then it loosened, and within fifteen pulls, I had a cup of water.

Someone had kept the pump up. Someone had seen to the house and the land while I was away at the war. For me, it had been fifteen years; I wasn't sure how long it had been for Ferro. The water was tinged red and tasted of iron. Good. I drank it down in a long draft, then put the cup back onto its hangar. When the big sun, Hemingway, set, a slight breeze kicked up. Then Fitzgerald went down and a cold, cloudless night spanked down onto the plateau. I shivered a little, adjusted my internals, and stood motionless, waiting for the last of twilight to pass, and the stars—my stars—to come out. Steiner, the planet that is Ferro's evening star, was the first to emerge, low in the west, methane blue. Then the constellations. Ngal. Gilgamesh. The Big Snake, half-coiled over the southwestern horizon. There was no moon tonight. There was never a moon on Ferro, and that was right.

After a time, I walked to the house, climbed up the porch, and the house recognized me and turned on the lights. I went inside. The place was dusty, the furniture covered with sheets, but there were no signs of rats or jinjas, and all seemed in repair. I sighed, blinked, tried to feel something. Too early, probably. I started to take a covering from a chair, then let it be. I went to the kitchen and checked the cupboard. An old malt-whiskey bottle, some dry cereal, some spices. The spices had been my mother's, and I seldom used them before I left for the end of time. I considered that the whiskey might be perfectly aged by now. But, as the saying goes on Ferro, we like a bit of food with our drink, so I left the house and took the road to town, to Heidel.

It was a five-mile walk, and though I could have enhanced and covered the ground in ten minutes or so, I walked at a regular pace under my home-world stars. The road was dirt, of course, and my pant legs were dusted red when I stopped under the outside light of Thredmartin's Pub. I took a last breath of cold air, then went inside to the warm.

It was a good night at Thredmartin's. There were men and women gathered around the fire hearth, usas and splices in the cold corners. The regulars were at the bar, a couple of whom I recognized—so old now, wizened like stored apples in a barrel. I looked around for a particular face, but she was not there. A jukebox sputtered some core-cloud deak, and the air was thick with smoke and conversation. Or was, until I walked in. Nobody turned to face me. Most of them couldn't have seen me. But a signal passed and conversation fell to a quiet murmur. Somebody quickly killed the jukebox.

I blinked up an internals menu into my peripheral vision and adjusted to the room's temperature. Then I went to the edge of the bar. The room got even quieter. . . .

The bartender, old Thredmartin himself, reluctantly came over to me.

"What can I do for you, sir?" he asked me.

I looked over him, to the selection of bottles, tubes, and cans on display behind him. "I don't see it," I said.

"Eh?" He glanced back over his shoulder, then quickly returned to peering at me.

"Bone's Barley," I said.

"We don't have any more of that," Thredmartin said, with a suspicious tone.

"Why not?"

"The man who made it died."

"How long ago?"

"Twenty years, more or less. I don't see what business of—"

"What about his son?"

Thredmartin backed up a step. Then another. "Henry," he whispered. "Henry Bone."

"Just give me the best that you do have, Peter Thredmartin," I said. "In fact, I'd like to buy everybody a round on me."

"Henry Bone! Why, you looked to me like a bad 'un indeed when you walked in here. I took you for one of them glims, I did," Thredmartin said. I did not know what he was talking about. Then he smiled an old devil's crooked smile. "Your money's no good here, Henry Bone. I do happen to have a couple of bottles of your old dad's whiskey stowed away in back. Drinks are on the house."

And so I returned to my world, and for most of those I'd left behind it seemed as if I'd never really gone. My neighbors hadn't changed much in the twenty years local that had passed, and of course, they had no conception of what had happened to me. They knew only that I'd been to the war—the Big War at the End of Time—and evidently everything turned out okay, for here I was, back in my own time and my own place. I planted Ferro's desert barley, brought in peat from the mountain bogs, bred the biomass that would extract the minerals from my hard ground water, and got ready for making whiskey once again. Most of the inhabitants of Ferro were divided between whiskey families and beer families. Bones were distillers, never brewers, since the Settlement, ten generations before.

It wasn't until she called upon me that I heard the first hints of the troubles that had come. Her name was Alinda Bexter, but since we played together under the floorplanks of her father's hotel, I had always called her Bex. When I left for the war, she was twenty, and I twenty-one. I still recognized her at forty, five years older than I was now, as she came walking down the road to my house, a week after I'd returned. She was taller than most women on Ferro, and she might be mistaken for a usa-human splice anywhere else. She was rangy, and she wore a khaki dress that whipped in the dry wind as she came toward me. I stood on the porch, waiting for her, wondering what she would say.

"Well, this is a load off of me," she said. She was wearing a brimmed hat. It had a ribbon to tie under her chin, but Bex had not done that. She held her hand on it to keep it from blowing from her head. "This damn ranch has been one big thankless task."

"So it was you who kept it up," I said.

"Just kept it from falling apart as fast as it would have otherwise," she replied. We stood and looked at one another for a moment. Her eyes were green. Now that I had seen an ocean, I could understand the kind of green they were.

"Well then," I finally said. "Come on in."

I offered her some sweetcake I'd fried up, and some beer that my neighbor, Shin, had brought by, both of which she declined. We sat in the living room, on furniture covered with the white sheets I had yet to remove. Bex and I took it slow, getting to know each other again. She ran her father's place now. For years, the only way to get to Heidel was by freighter, but we had finally gotten a node on the Flash, and even though Ferro was still a backwater planet, there were more strangers passing through than there ever had been—usually en route to other places. But they sometimes stayed a night or two in the Bexter Hotel. Its reputation was spreading, Bex claimed, and I believed her. Even when she was young, she had been shrewd but honest, a combination you don't often find in an innkeeper. She was a quiet woman—that is, until she got to know you well—and some most likely thought her conceited. I got the feeling that she hadn't let down her reserve for a long time. When I knew her before, Bex did not have many close friends, but for the ones she had, such as me, she poured out her thoughts, and her heart. I found that she hadn't changed much in that way.

"Did you marry?" I asked her, after hearing about the hotel and her father's bad health.

"No," she said. "No, I very nearly did, but then I did not. Did you?"

"No. Who was it?"

"Rall Kenton."

"Rall Kenton? Rall Kenton whose parents run the hops market?" He was a quarter-splice, a tall man on a world of tall men. Yet, when I knew him, his long shadow had been deceptive. There was no spark or force in him. "I can't see that, Bex."

"Tom Kenton died ten years ago," she said. "Marjorie retired, and Rall owned the business until just last year. Rall did all right; you'd be surprised. Something about his father's passing gave him a backbone. Too much of one, maybe."

"What happened?"

"He died," she said. "He died too, just as I thought you had." Now she told me she would like a beer after all, and I went to get her a bottle of Shin's ale. When I returned, I could tell that she'd been crying a little.

"The glims killed Rall," said Bex, before I could ask her about him. "That's their name for themselves, anyway. Humans, repons, kaliwaks, and I don't know what else. They passed through last year and stayed for a week in Heidel. Very bad. They made my father give over the whole hotel to them, and then they had a . . . trial, they called it. Every house was called and made to pay a tithe. The glims decided how much. Rall refused to pay. He brought along a pistol—Lord knows where he got it—and tried to shoot one of them. They just laughed and took it from him." Now the tears started again.

"And then they hauled him out into the street in front of the hotel." Bex took a moment and got control of herself. "They burnt him up with a p-gun. Burned his legs off first, then his arms, then the rest of him after they'd let him lie there a while. There wasn't a trace of him after that; we couldn't even bury him."

I couldn't take her to me, hold her, not after she'd told me about Rall. Needing something to do, I took some tangled banwood from the tinder box and struggled to get a fire going from the burnt-down coals in my hearth. I blew into the fireplace and only got a nose full of ashes for my trouble. "Didn't anybody fight?" I asked.

"Not after that. We just waited them out. Or they got bored. I don't know. It was bad for everybody, not just Rall." Bex shook her head, sighed, then saw the trouble I was having and bent down to help me. She was much better at it than I, and the fire was soon ablaze. We sat back down and watched it flicker.

"Sounds like war-ghosts," I said.

"The glims?"

"Soldiers who don't go home after the war. The fighting gets into them and they don't want to give it up, or can't. Sometimes they have . . . modifications that won't let them give it up. They wander the timeways—and since they don't belong to the time they show up in, they're hard to kill. In the early times, where people don't know about the war, or have only heard rumors of it, they had lots of names. Vampires. Hagamonsters. Zombies."

"What can you do?"

I put my arm around her. It had been so long. She tensed up, then breathed deeply, serenely.

"Hope they don't come back," I said. "They are bad ones. Not the worst, but bad."

We were quiet for a while, and the wind, blowing over the chimney's top, made the flue moan as if it were a big stone flute.

"Did you love him, Bex?" I asked. "Rall?"

She didn't even hesitate in her answer this time. "Of course not, Henry Bone. How could you ever think such a thing? I was waiting to catch up with you. Now tell me about the future."

And so I drew away from her for a while, and told her—part of it at least. About how there is not enough dark matter to pull the cosmos back together again, not enough mass to undulate in an eternal cycle. Instead, there *is* an end, and all the stars are either dead or dying, and all that there is is nothing but dim night. I told her about the twilight armies gathered there, culled from all times, all places. Creatures, presences, machines, weapons fighting galaxy-to-galaxy, system-to-system, fighting until the critical point is reached, when entropy flows no more, but pools, pools in endless, stagnant pools of nothing. No light. No heat. No effect. And the universe is dead, and so those who remain . . . inherit the dark field. They win.

"And did you win?" she asked me. "If that's the word for it."

The suns were going down. Instead of answering, I went outside to the woodpile and brought in enough banwood to fuel the fire for the night. I thought maybe she would forget what she'd asked me—but not Bex.

"How does the war end, Henry?"

"You must never ask me that." I spoke the words carefully, making sure I was giving away nothing in my reply. "Every time a returning soldier tells that answer, he changes everything. Then he has two choices. He can either go away, leave his own time, and go back to fight again. Or he can stay, and it will all mean nothing, what he did. Not just who won and who lost, but all the things he did in the war spin off into nothing."

Bex thought about this for a while. "What could it matter? What in God's name could be worth fighting *for?*" she finally asked. "Time ends. Nothing matters after that. What could it possibly matter who won . . . who wins?"

"It means you can go back home," I said. "After it's over."

"I don't understand."

I shook my head and was silent. I had said enough. There was no way to tell her more, in any case—not without changing things. And no way to *say* what it was that had brought those forces together at the end of everything.

And what the hell do *I* know, even now? All I know is what I was told, and what I was trained to do. If we don't fight at the end, there won't be a beginning. For there to be people, there has to be a war to fight at the end of things. We live in that kind of universe, and not another, they told me. They told me, and then I told myself. And I did what I had to do so that it would be over and I could go home, come back.

"Bex, I never forgot you," I said. She came to sit with me by the fire. We didn't touch at first, but I felt her next to me, breathed the flush of her skin as the fire warmed her. Then she ran her hand along my arm, felt the bumps from the operational enhancements.

"What have they done to you?" she whispered.

Unbidden the old words of the skyfallers' scream, the words that were yet to be, surfaced in my mind.

They sucked down my heart
to a little black hole.
You cannot stab me.

They wrote down my brain
on a hard knot of space.
You cannot turn me.

Icicle spike
from the eye of a star.
I've come to kill you.

I almost spoke them, from sheer habit. But I did not. The war was over. Bex was here, and I knew it was over. I was going to *feel* something, once again, something besides guile, hate, and rage. I didn't yet, that was true, but I *could* feel the possibility.

"I don't really breathe anymore, Bex; I pretend to so I won't put people off," I told her. "It's been so long, I can't even remember what it was like to *have* to."

Bex kissed me then. At first, I didn't remember how to do that either. And then I did. I added wood to the fire, then ran my hand along Bex's neck and shoulder. Her skin had the health of youth still, but years in the sun and wind had made a supple leather of it, tanned and grained fine. We took the sheet from the couch and pulled it near to the warmth, and she drew me down to her on it, to her neck and breasts.

"Did they leave enough of you for me?" she whispered.

I had not known until now. "Yes," I answered, "there's enough." I found my way inside her, and we made love slowly, in a way that might seem sad to any others but us, for there were memories and years of longing that flowed from us, around us, like amber just at the melting point, and we were inside and there was nothing but this present with all of what was, and

what would be, already passed. No time. Finally, only Bex and no time between us.

We fell asleep on the old couch, and it was dim half-morning when we
awoke, with Fitzgerald yet to rise in the west and the fire a bed of coals as
red as the sky.

Two months later, I was in Thredmartin's when Bex came in with an evil
look on her face. We had taken getting back together slow and easy up till
then, but the more time we spent around each other, the more we understood that nothing basic had changed. Bex kept coming to the ranch and I
took to spending a couple of nights a week in a room her father made up for
me at the hotel. Furly Bexter was an old-style McKinnonite. Men and
women were to live separately and only meet for business and copulation.
But he liked me well enough, and when I insisted on paying for my room,
he found a loophole somewhere in the Tracts of McKinnon about cohabi-
tation being all right in hotels and hostels.

"The glims are back," Bex said, sitting down at my table. I was in a dark
corner of the pub. I left the fire for those who could not adjust their own
internals to keep them warm. "They've taken over the top floor of the hotel.
What should we do?"

I took a draw of beer—Thredmartin's own thick porter—and looked at
her. She was visibly shivering, probably more from agitation than fright.

"How many of them are there?" I asked.

"Six. And something else, some splice I've never seen, however many that
makes."

I took another sip of beer. "Let it be," I said. "They'll get tired, and
they'll move on."

"What?" Bex's voice was full of astonishment. "What are you saying?"

"You don't want a war here, Bex," I replied. "You have no idea how bad
it can get."

"They killed Rall. They took our *money.*"

"Money." My voice sounded many years away, even to me.

"It's muscle and worry and care. You know how hard people work on
Ferro. And for those . . . *things* . . . to come in and take it! We cannot let
them—"

"—Bex," I said. "I am not going to do anything."

She said nothing; she put a hand on her forehead as if she had a sickening fever, stared at me for a moment, then looked away.

One of the glims chose that moment to come into Thredmartin's. It was
a halandana, a splice—human and jan—from up-time and a couple of possible universes over. It was nearly seven feet tall, with a two-foot-long neck,
and it stooped to enter Thredmartin's. Without stopping, it went to the bar
and demanded morphine.

Thredmartin was at the bar. He pulled out a dusty rubber, little used, and
before he could get out an injector, the halandana reached over, took the en-

tire rubber and put it in the pocket of the long gray coat it wore. Thredmartin started to speak, then shook his head, and found a spray shooter. He slapped it on the bar, and started to walk away. The halandana's hand shot out and pushed the old man. Thredmartin stumbled to his knees.

I felt the fingers of my hands clawing, clenching. Let them loosen; let them go.

Thredmartin rose slowly to one knee. Bex was up, around the bar, and over to him, steadying his shoulder. The glim watched this for a moment, then took its drug and shooter to a table, where it got itself ready for an injection.

I looked at it closely now. It was female, but that did not mean much in halandana splices. I could see it phase around the edges with dead, gray flames. I clicked in wideband overspace, and I could see through the halandana to the chair it was sitting in and the unpainted wood of the wall behind it. And I saw more, in the spaces between spaces. The halandana was keyed in to a websquad; it wasn't really an individual anymore. Its fate was tied to that of its unit commander. So the war-ghosts—the glims—were a renegade squad, most likely, with a single leader calling the shots. For a moment, the halandana glanced in my direction, maybe feeling my gaze somewhere outside of local time, and I banded down to human normal. It quickly went back to what it was doing. Bex made sure Thredmartin was all right, then came back over to my table.

"We're not even in its timeline," I said. "It doesn't think of us as really being alive."

"Oh God," Bex said. "This is just like before."

I got up and walked out. It was the only solution. I could not say anything to Bex. She would not understand. I understood—not acting was the rational, the *only*, way, but not *my* way. Not until now.

I enhanced my legs and loped along the road to my house. But when I got there, I kept running, running off into the red sands of Ferro's outback. The night came down, and as the planet turned, I ran along the length of the Big Snake, bright and hard to the southwest, and then under the blue glow of Steiner, when she rose in the moonless, trackless night. I ran for miles and miles, as fast as a jaguar, but never tiring. How could I tire when parts of me stretched off into dimensions of utter stillness, utter rest? Could Bex see me for what I *was*, she would not see a man, but a kind of colonial creature, a mash of life pressed into the niches and fault lines of existence like so much grit and lichen. A human is anchored with only his heart and his mind; sever those, and he floats away. Floats away. What was I? A medusa fish in an ocean of time? A tight clump of nothing, disguised as a man? Something else?

Something damned hard to kill, that was certain. And so were the glims. When I returned to my house in the star-bright night, I half expected to find Bex, but she was not there. And so I rattled about for a while, powered down for an hour at dawn and rested on a living-room chair, dreaming in one part of my mind, completely alert in another. The next day, Bex still did not come, and I began to fear something had happened to her. I walked partway into Heidel, then cut off the road and stole around the outskirts, to a mound of shattered, volcanic rocks—the tailings of some early prospector's pit—not far from the town's edge. There I stepped up my vision and hearing, and made a long sweep of Main Street. Nothing. Far, far too quiet, even for Heidel.

I worked out the parabolic to the Bexter Hotel, and after a small adjustment, heard Bex's voice, then her father's. I was too far away to make out the words, but my quantitatives gave it a positive ID. So Bex was all right, at least for the moment. I made my way back home, and put in a good day's work making whiskey.

The next morning—it was the quarteryear's double dawn, with both suns rising in the east nearly together—Bex came to me. I brought her inside, and in the moted sunlight of my family's living room, where I now took my rest, when I rested, Bex told me that the glims had taken her father.

"He held back some old Midnight Livet down in the cellar, and didn't deliver it when they called for room service." Bex rubbed her left fist with her right fingers, expertly, almost mechanically, as she'd kneaded a thousand balls of bread dough. "How do they know these things? How do they know, Henry?"

"They can see *around* things," I said. "Some of them can, anyway."

"So they read our thoughts? What do we have left?"

"No, no. They can't see in *there*, at least I'm sure they can't see in your old man's McKinnonite nut lump of a brain. But they probably saw the whiskey down in the cellar, all right. A door isn't a very solid thing for a warghost out of its own time and place."

Bex gave her hand a final squeeze, spread it out upon her lap. She stared down at the lines of her palm, then looked up at me. "If you won't fight, then you have to tell *me* how to fight them," she said. "I won't let them kill my father."

"Maybe they won't."

"I can't take that chance."

Her eyes were blazing green, as the suns came full through the window. Her face was bright-lit and shadowed, as if by the steady coals of a fire. You have loved this woman a long time, I thought. You have to tell her something that will be of use. But what could possibly be of use against a creature that had survived—*will* survive—that great and final war—and so must survive *now?* You can't kill the future. That's how the old sergeants would explain battle fate to the recruits. If you are meant to be there, they'd say, then nothing can hurt you. And if you're not, then you'll just fade, so you might as well go out fighting.

"You can only irritate them," I finally said to Bex. "There's a way to do it with the Flash. Talk to that technician, what's his name—"

"Jurven Dvorak."

"Tell Dvorak to strobe the local interrupt, fifty, sixty tetracycles. It'll cut off all traffic, but it will be like a wasp nest to them, and they won't want to get close enough to turn it off. Maybe they'll leave. Dvorak better stay near the node after that too."

"All right," Bex said. "Is that all?"

"Yes," I said. I rubbed my temples, felt the vague pain of a headache, which quickly receded as my internals rushed more blood to my scalp. "Yes, that's it."

Later that day, I heard the crackle of random quantum-tunnel spray, as split, unsieved particles decided their spin, charm, and color without guidance from the world of gravity and cause. It was an angry buzz, like the hum of an insect caught between screen and windowpane, tremendously irritating to listen to for hours on end, if you were unlucky enough to be sensitive to the effect. I put up with it, hoping against hope that it would be enough to drive off the glims.

Bex arrived in the early evening, leading her father, who was ragged and half-crazed from two days without light or water. The glims had locked him in a cleaning closet, in the hotel, where he'd sat cramped and doubled over. After the buzz started, Bex opened the lock and dragged the old man out. It was as if the glims had forgotten the whole affair.

"Maybe," I said. "We can hope."

She wanted me to put the old man up at my house, in case the glims suddenly remembered. Old Furly Bexter didn't like the idea. He rattled on about something in McKinnon's "Letter to the Canadians," but I said yes, he could stay. Bex left me with her father in the shrouds of my living room.

Some time that night, the quantum buzz stopped. And in the early morning, I saw them—five of them—stalking along the road, kicking before them the cowering, stumbling form of Jurven Dvorak. I waited for them on the porch. Furly Bexter was asleep in my parents' bedroom. He was exhausted from his ordeal, and I expected him to stay that way for a while.

When they came into the yard, Dvorak ran to the pump and held to the handle, as if it were a branch suspending him over a bottomless chasm. And for him it was. They'd broken his mind and given him a dream of dying. Soon to be replaced by reality, I suspected, and no pump-handle hope of salvation.

Their leader—or the one who did the talking—was human-looking. I'd have to band out to make a full ID, and I didn't want to give anything away for the moment. He saved me the trouble by telling me himself.

"My name's Marek," he said. "Come from a D-line, not far down-time from here."

I nodded, squinting into the red brightness reflected off my hardpan yard.

"We're just here for a good time," the human continued. "What you want to spoil that for?"

I didn't say anything for a moment. One of Marek's gang spat into the dryness of my dirt.

"Go ahead and have it," I said.

"All right," Marek said. He turned to Dvorak, then pulled out a weapon—not really a weapon, though, for it is the tool of behind-the-lines enforcers, prison interrogators, confession extractors. It's called an algorithmic truncheon, a *trunch*, in the parlance. A trunch, used at full load, will strip the myelin sheath from axons and dendrites; it will burn up a man's nerves as if they were fuses. It is a way to kill with horrible pain. Marek walked over and touched the trunch to the leg of Dvorak, as if he were lighting a bonfire.

The Flash technician began to shiver, and then to seethe, like a teapot coming to boil. The motion traveled up his legs, into his chest, out his arms. His neck began to writhe, as if the corded muscles were so many snakes. Then Dvorak's brain burned, as a teapot will when all the water has run out and there is nothing but flame against hot metal. And then Dvorak screamed. He screamed for a long, long time. And then he died, crumpled and spent, on the ground in front of my house.

"I don't know you," Marek said, standing over Dvorak's body and looking up at me. "I know *what* you are, but I can't get a read on *who* you are, and that worries me," he said. He kicked at one of the Flash tech's twisted arms. "But now you know *me.*"

"Get off my land," I said. I looked at him without heat. Maybe I felt nothing inside, either. That uncertainty had been my companion for a long time, my grim companion. Marek studied me for a moment. If I kept his attention, he might not look around me, look inside the house, to find his other fun, Furly Bexter, half-dead from Marek's amusements. Marek turned to the others.

"We're going," he said to them. "We've done what we came for." They turned around and left by the road on which they'd come, the only road there was. After a while, I took Dvorak's body to a low hill and dug him a grave there. I set up a sandstone marker, and since I knew Dvorak came from Catholic people, I scratched into the stone the sign of the cross. Jesus, from the Milky Way. Another glim. Hard to kill.

It took old-man Bexter only a week or so to fully recover; I should have known by knowing Bex that he was made of a tougher grit. He began to putter around the house, helping me out where he could, although I ran a tidy one-man operation, and he was more in the way than anything. Bex risked a trip out once that week. Her father again insisted he was going back into town, but Bex told him the glims were looking for him. So far, she'd managed to convince them that she had no idea where he'd gotten to.

I was running low on food and supplies, and had to go into town the following Firstday. I picked up a good backpack load at the mercantile and some chemicals for treating the peat at the druggist, then risked a quick look-in on Bex. A sign on the desk told all that they could find her at Thredmartin's, taking her lunch, should they want her. I walked across the street, set my load down just inside Thredmartin's door, in the cloakroom, then passed through the entrance into the afternoon dank of the pub.

I immediately sensed glims all around, and hunched myself in, both mentally and physically. I saw Bex in her usual corner, and walked toward her across the room. As I stepped beside a table in the pub's middle, a glim—it was the halandana—stuck out a long, hairy leg. Almost, I tripped—and in that instant, I almost did the natural thing and cast about for some hold that was not present in the three-dimensional world—but I did not. I caught myself, came to a dead stop, then carefully walked around the glim's outstretched leg.

"Mind if I sit down?" I said as I reached Bex's table. She nodded toward a free chair. She was finishing a beer, and an empty glass stood beside it. Thredmartin usually had the tables clear as soon as the last drop left a mug. Bex was drinking fast. Why? Working up her courage, perhaps.

I lowered myself into the chair, and for a long time, neither of us said anything to the other. Bex finished her beer. Thredmartin appeared, looked curiously at the two empty mugs. Bex signaled for another, and I ordered my own whiskey.

"How's the ranch," she finally asked me. Her face was flush and her lips trembled slightly. She was angry, I decided. At me, at the situation. It was understandable. Completely understandable.

"Fine," I said. "The ranch is fine."

"Good."

Again a long silence. Thredmartin returned with our drinks. Bex sighed, and for a moment, I thought she would speak, but she did not. Instead, she reached under the table and touched my hand. I opened my palm, and she put her hand into mine. I felt the tension in her, the bonework of her hand as she squeezed tightly. I felt her fear and worry. I felt her love.

And then Marek came into the pub looking for her. He stalked across the room and stood in front of our table. He looked hard at me, then at Bex, and then he swept an arm across the table and sent Bex's beer and my whiskey flying toward the wall. The beer mug broke, but I quickly reached out and caught my tumbler of scotch in midair without spilling a drop. Of course, no ordinary human could have done it.

Bex noticed Marek looking at me strangely and spoke with a loud voice that got his attention. "What do you want? You were looking for me at the hotel?"

"Your sign says you're open," Marek said in a reasonable, ugly voice. "I rang for room service. Repeatedly."

"Sorry," Bex said. "Just let me settle up and I'll be right there."

"Be right there *now*," Marek said, pushing the table from in front of her. Again, I caught my drink, held it on a knee while I remained sitting. Bex started up from her chair and stood facing Marek. She looked him in the eyes. "I'll *be* there directly," she said.

Without warning, Marek reached out and grabbed her by the chin. He didn't seem to be pressing hard, but I knew he must have her in a painful grip. He pulled Bex toward him. Still, she stared him in the eyes. Slowly, I rose from my chair, setting my tumbler of whiskey down on the warm seat where I had been.

Marek glanced over at me. Our eyes met, and at that close distance, he could plainly see the enhancements under my corneas. I could see his.

"Let go of her," I said.

He did not let go of Bex.

"Who the hell are you?" he asked. "That you tell *me* what to do?"

"I'm just a grunt, same as you," I said. "Let go of her."

The halandana had risen from its chair and was soon standing behind Marek. It-she growled mean and low. A combat schematic of how to handle the situation iconed up into the corner of my vision. The halandana was a green figure, Marek was red, Bex was a faded rose. I blinked once to enlarge it. Studied it in a fractional second. Blinked again to close it down. Marek let go of Bex.

She stumbled back, hurt and mad, rubbing her chin.

"I don't think we've got a grunt here," Marek said, perhaps to the halandana, or to himself, but looking at me. "I think we've got us a genuine skyfalling space marine."

The halandana's growl grew deeper and louder, filling ultra and subsonic frequencies.

"How many systems'd you take out, skyfaller?" Marek asked. "A couple of galaxies worth?" The halandana made to advance on me, but Marek put out his hand to stop it. "Where do you get off? This ain't nothing but small potatoes next to what *you've* done."

In that moment, I spread out, stretched a bit in ways that Bex could not see, but that Marek could—to some extent at least. I encompassed him, all of him, and did a thorough ID on both him and the halandana. I ran the data through some trans-d personnel files tucked into a swirl in n-space I'd never expected to access again. Marek Lambrois. Corporal of a back-line military-police platoon assigned to the local cluster in a couple of possible worlds, deserters all in a couple of others. He was aggression enhanced by trans-weblink anti-alg coding. The squad's fighting profile was notched to the top level at all times. They were bastards who were now *preprogrammed* bastards. Marek was right about them being small potatoes. He and his gang were nothing but mean-ass grunts, small-time goons for some of the nonaligned contingency troops.

"What the hell?" Marek said. He noticed my analytics, although it was too fast for him to get a good glimpse of me. But he did understand something in that moment, something it didn't take enhancement to figure out. And in that moment, everything was changed, had I but seen. Had I but seen.

"You're some bigwig, ain't you, skyfaller? Somebody that *matters* to the outcome," Marek said. "This is your actual, and you don't want to fuck yourself up-time, so you won't fight." He smiled crookedly. A diagonal of teeth, straight and narrow, showed whitely.

"Don't count on it," I said.

"You won't," he said, this time with more confidence. "I don't know what I was worrying about! I can do anything I want here."

"Well," I said. "Well." And then I said nothing.

"Get on over there and round me up some grub," Marek said to Bex. "I'll be waiting for it in room forty-five, little lady."

"I'd rather—"

"Do it," I said. The words were harsh and did not sound like my voice. But they were my words, and after a moment, I remembered the voice. It was mine. From far, far in the future. Bex gasped at their hardness, but took a step forward, moved to obey.

"Bex," I said, more softly. "Just get the man some food." I turned to Marek. "If you hurt her, I don't care about anything. Do you understand? Nothing will matter to me."

Marek's smile widened into a grin. He reached over, slowly, so that I could think about it, and patted my cheek. Then he deliberately slapped me, hard. Hard enough to turn my head. Hard enough to draw a trickle of blood from my lip. It didn't hurt very much, of course. Of course it didn't hurt.

"Don't you worry, skyfaller," he said. "I know exactly where I stand now." He turned and left, and the halandana, its drugs unfinished on the table where it had sat, trailed out after him.

Bex looked at me. I tried to meet her gaze, but did not. I did not look down, but stared off into Thredmartin's darkness. She reached over and wiped the blood from my chin with her little finger.

"I guess I'd better go," she said.

I did not reply. She shook her head sadly, and walked in front of me. I kept my eyes fixed, far away from this place, this time, and her passing was a swirl of air, a red-brown swish of hair, and Bex was gone. Gone.

They sucked down my heart
to a little black hole.
You cannot stab me.

"Colonel Bone, we've done the prelims on sector eleven sixty-eight, and there are fifty-six class-one civilizations along with two-hundred seventy rationals in stage-one or -two development."

"Fifty-six. Two hundred seventy. Ah. Me."

"Colonel, sir, we can evac over half of them within thirty-six hours local."

"And have to defend them in the transcendent. Chaos neutral. Guaranteed forty percent casualties for us."

"Yes, sir. But what about the civs at least. We can save a few."

They wrote down my brain
on a hard knot of space.
You cannot turn me.

"Unacceptable, soldier."

"Sir?"

"Unacceptable."

"Yes, sir."

All dead. All those millions of dead people. But it was the end of time, and they had to die, so that they—so that we *all*, all in time—could live. But they didn't know, those civilizations. Those people. It was the end of time, but you loved life all the same, and you died the same hard way as always. For nothing. It would be for nothing. Outside, the wind had kicked up. The sky was red with Ferro's dust, and a storm was brewing for the evening. I coated my sclera with a hard and glassy membrane, and unblinking, I stalked home with my supplies through a fierce and growing wind.

That night, on the curtains of dust and thin rain, on the heave of the storm, Bex came to my house. Her clothes were torn and her face was bruised. She said nothing, as I closed the door behind her, led her into the kitchen, and began to treat her wounds. She said nothing as her worried father sat at my kitchen table and watched, and wrung his hands, and watched because there wasn't anything he could do.

"Did that man . . ." her father said. The old man's voice broke. "Did he?"

"I tried to take the thing, the trunch, from him. He'd left it lying on the table by the door." Bex spoke in a hollow voice. "I thought that nobody was going to do anything, not even Henry, so I had to. I had to." Her facial bruises were superficial. But she held her legs stiffly together, and clasped her hands to her stomach. There was vomit on her dress. "The trunch had some kind of alarm set on it," Bex said. "So he caught me."

"Bex, are you hurting?" I said to her. She looked down, then carefully spread her legs. "He caught me and then he used the trunch on me. Not full strength. Said he didn't want to do permanent damage. Said he wanted to save me for later." Her voice sounded far away. She covered her face with her hands. "He put it in me," she said.

Then she breathed deeply, raggedly, and made herself look at me. "Well," she said. "So."

I put her into my bed, and he sat in the chair beside it, standing watch for who knew what? He could not defend his daughter, but he must try, as surely as the suns rose, now growing farther apart, over the hard pack of my homeworld desert.

Everything was changed.

"Bex," I said to her, and touched her forehead. Touched her fine, brown skin. "Bex, in the future, we won. I won, my command won it. Really, really big. That's why we're here. That's why we're all here."

Bex's eyes were closed. I could not tell if she'd already fallen asleep. I hoped she had.

"I have to take care of some business, and then I'll do it again," I said in a whisper. "I'll just have to go back up-time and do it again."

Between the first and second rising, I'd reached Heidel, and as Hemingway burned red through the storm's dusty leavings, I stood in the shadows of the entrance foyer of the Bexter Hotel. There I waited.

The halandana was the first up—like me, they never really slept—and it came down from its room looking, no doubt, to go out and get another rubber of its drug. Instead, it found me. I didn't waste time with the creature. With a quick twist in n-space, I pulled it down to the present, down to a local concentration of hate and lust and stupidity that I could kill with a quick thrust into its throat. But I let it live; I showed it myself, all of me spread out and huge, and I let it fear.

"Go and get Marek Lambrois," I told it. "Tell him Colonel Bone wants to see him. Colonel Henry Bone of the Eighth Sky and Light."

"Bone," said the halandana. "I thought—"

I reached out and grabbed the creature's long neck. This was the halandana weak point, and this halandana had a ceramic implant as protection. I clicked up the power in my forearm a level and crushed the collar as I might a tea cup. The halandana's neck carapace shattered to platelets and shards, outlined in fine cracks under its skin.

"Don't think," I said. "Tell Marek Lambrois to come into the street and I will let him live."

This was untrue, of course, but hope never dies, I'd discovered, even in the hardest of soldiers. But perhaps I'd underestimated Marek. Sometimes I still wonder.

He stumbled out, still partly asleep, onto the street. Last night had evidently been a hard and long one. His eyes were a red no detox nano could fully clean up. His skin was the color of paste.

"You have something on me," I said. "I cannot abide that."

"Colonel Bone," he began. "If I'd knowed it was *you*—"

"Too late for that."

"It's never too late, that's what you taught us all when you turned that offensive around out on the Husk and gave the Chaos the what-for. I'll just be going. I'll take the gang with me. It's to no purpose, our staying now."

"You knew enough *yesterday*—enough to leave." I felt the rage, the old rage that was to be, once again. "Why did you do that to her?" I asked. "Why did you—"

And then I looked into his eyes and saw it there. The quiet desire—beaten down by synthesized emotions, but now triumphant, sadly triumphant. The desire to finally, finally *die*. Marek was not the unthinking brute I'd taken him for after all. Too bad for him.

I took a step toward Marek. His instincts made him reach down, go for the trunch. But it was a useless weapon on me. I don't have myelin sheaths on my nerves. I don't have nerves anymore; I have *wiring*. Marek realized this was so almost instantly. He dropped the trunch, then turned and ran. I caught him. He tried to fight, but there was never any question of him beating me. That would be absurd. I'm Colonel Bone of the Skyfalling 8th. I kill so that there might be life. *Nobody* beats me. It is my fate, and yours too.

I caught him by the shoulder, and I looped my other arm around his neck and reined him to me—not enough to snap anything. Just enough to calm him down. He was strong, but had no finesse.

Like I said, glims are hard to kill. They're the same as snails in shells in a way, and the trick is to draw them out—way out. Which is what I did with Marek. As I held him physically, I caught hold of him, all of him, *over there*, in the place I can't tell you about, can't describe. The way you do this is by holding a glim still and causing him great suffering, so that they can't withdraw into the deep places. That's what vampire stakes and Roman crosses are all about.

And, like I told Bex, glims are bad ones, all right. Bad, but not the worst. *I* am the worst.

Icicle spike
from the eye of a star.
I've come to kill you.

I sharpened my nails. Then I plunged them into Marek's stomach, through the skin, into the twist of his guts. I reached around there and caught hold of something, a piece of intestine. I pulled it out. This I tied to the porch of the Bexter Hotel.

Marek tried to untie himself and pull away. He was staring at his insides, rolled out, raw and exposed, and thinking—I don't know what. I haven't died. I don't know what it is like to die. He moaned sickly. His hands fumbled uselessly in the grease and phlegm that coated his very own self. There was no undoing the knots I'd tied, no pushing himself back in.

I picked him up, and as he whimpered, I walked down the street with him. His guts trailed out behind us, like a pink ribbon. After I'd gotten about twenty feet, I figured this was all he had in him. I dropped him into the street.

Hemingway was in the northeast and Fitzgerald directly east. They both shone at different angles on Marek's crumple, and cast crazy, mazy shadows down the length of the street.

"Colonel Bone," he said. I was tired of his talking. "Colonel—"

I reached into his mouth, past his gnashing teeth, and pulled out his tongue. He reached for it as I extracted it, so I handed it to him. Blood and drool flowed from his mouth and colored the red ground even redder about him. Then, one by one, I broke his arms and legs, then I broke each of the vertebrae in his backbone, moving up his spinal column with quick pinches. It didn't take long.

This is what I did in the world that people can see. In the twists of other times and spaces, I did similar things, horrible, irrevocable things, to the man. I killed him. I killed him in such a way that he would never come to life again, not in any possible place, not in any possible time. I wiped Marek Lambrois from existence. Thoroughly. And with his death the other glims died, like lights going out, lights ceasing to exist, bulb, filament and all. Or like the quick loss of all sensation after a brain is snuffed out.

Irrevocably gone from this timeline, and that was what mattered. Keeping this possible future uncertain, balanced on the fulcrum of chaos and necessity. Keeping it *free*, so that I could go back and do my work.

I left Marek lying there, in the main street of Heidel. Others could do the mopping up; that wasn't my job. As I left town, on the way back to my house and my life there, I saw that I wasn't alone in the dawn-lit town. Some had business out at this hour, and they had watched. Others had heard the commotion and come to windows and porches to see what it was. Now they knew. They knew what I was, what I was to be. I walked alone down the road, and found Bex and her father both sound asleep in my room.

I stroked her fine hair. She groaned, turned in her sleep. I pulled my covers up to her chin. Forty years old, and as beautiful as a child. Safe in my bed. Bex. Bex. I will miss you. Always, always, Bex.

I went to the living room, to the shroud-covered furniture. I sat down in what had been my father's chair. I sipped a cup of my father's best barley-malt whiskey. I sat, and as the suns of Ferro rose in the hard-iron sky, I faded into the distant, dying future.

Paul J. McAuley

ALL TOMORROW'S PARTIES

Born in Stroud, England, in 1955, Paul J. McAuley now makes his home in London. A professional biologist for many years, he sold his first story in 1984, and has gone on to be a frequent contributor to *Interzone,* as well as to markets such as *Amazing, The Magazine of Fantasy & Science Fiction, Asimov's Science Fiction, When the Music's Over,* and elsewhere.

Like his friend and colleague Stephen Baxter, McAuley has a foot in several different camps of science fiction writing, being considered to be one of the best of the new breed of British writers (although a few Australian writers could be fit in under this heading as well) who are producing that brand of rigorous hard science fiction with updated modern and stylistic sensibilities that is sometimes referred to as "radical hard science fiction," but he also writes Dystopian sociological speculations about the very near future, and he *also* is one of the major young writers who are producing that revamped and retooled widescreen Space Opera that has sometimes been called the New Baroque Space Opera, reminiscent of the Superscience stories of the thirties taken to an even higher level of intensity and scale (wait a minute! how many feet does he *have,* anyway?). His first novel, *Four Hundred Billion Stars,* one of the earliest examples of the New Space Opera, was published in 1988, and won the Philip K. Dick Award. It was followed by sequels, *Secret Harmonies* and *Eternal Light,* and by one of the most vivid of the recent spate of Martian novels, *Red Dust.* With his next novel, *Pasquale's Angel,* he put yet another foot down in yet another camp, producing an ingenious and gorgeously colored Alternate History where Leonardo di Vinci brings modern technology to Europe centuries before its time. His next novel, 1996's *Fairyland,* perhaps his best-known novel and perhaps also his best performance to date at novel length, took us to a troubled future Europe thrown into chaos by fractional politics and out-of-control biotechnology, only a few years into the next century; it won the Arthur C. Clarke Award and the John W. Campbell Award. With his next novel project, though, he is plunging back into Space Opera territory, on an even more ambitious scale, with a major new trilogy, *Confluence,* set ten million years in the future, the first volume of which, *Child of the River,* has just been published.

McAuley is not as prolific at shorter lengths as Baxter, having built most of his reputation to date on his novels, but has produced some memorable short work over the last fourteen years, with stories such as "The Temporary King," "Jacob's Rock," "Exiles," "Inheritance," "Karl and the Ogre," "Gene Wars," and others. In the last couple of years, his stories seem to have increased in impact and complexity, and recent stories such as "Slaves," "Children of the Revolution," "Prison

Dreams," "Recording Angel," "Second Skin," "17," and "Sea Change, With Monsters" strike me as being even better than his already distinguished previous work, and I look forward with anticipation to see what he produces in the years to come.

A wide range of influences can be seen in McAuley's work, from Cordwainer Smith and Brian Aldiss to Roger Zelazny and Larry Niven, topped off with a dash of Samuel R. Delany, with perhaps some H. G. Wells to give a bottom to the mixture. All of which and more are evident in the evocative, supercharged, and intense little story that follows, packed with enough new ideas to fuel many another author's six hundred-page novel, that takes us far into the future and thousands of light-years from home for a very odd sort of family reunion. . . .

McAuley's other books include two collections of his short work, *The King of the Hill and Other Stories* and *The Invisible Country,* and an original anthology coedited with Kim Newman, *In Dreams.*

And with exactly a year left before the end of the century-long gathering of her clade, she went to Paris with her current lover, racing ahead of midnight and the beginning of the New Year. Paris! The Premier Quartier: the early Twentieth Century. Fireworks bursting in great flowers above the night-black Seine, and a brawling carnival which under a multicolored rain of confetti filled every street from the Quai du Louvre to the Arc de Triomphe.

Escorted by her lover (they had been hunting big game in the Pleistocene–era taiga of Siberia; he still wore his safari suit, and a Springfield rifle was slung over his shoulder), she crossed to the Paleolithic oak woods of the Ile de la Cité. In the middle of the great stone circle naked druids with blue-stained skins beat huge drums under flaring torches, while holographic ghosts swung above the electric lights of the Twentieth Century shore, a fleet of luminous clouds dancing in the sky. Her attentive lover identified them for her, leaning against her shoulder so she could sight along his arm. He was exactly her height, with piercing blue eyes and a salt-and-pepper beard.

An astronaut. A gene pirate. Emperor Victoria. Mickey Mouse.

"What is a mouse?"

He pointed. "That one, the black-skinned creature with the circular ears."

She leaned against his solid human warmth. "For an animal, it seems very much like a person. Was it a product of the gene wars?"

"It is a famous icon of the country where I was born. My countrymen preferred creatures of the imagination to those of the real world. It is why they produced so few good authors."

"But you were a good author."

"I was not bad, except at the end. Something bad always happened to all good writers from my country. Sometimes slowly, sometimes quickly, but without exception."

"What is it carrying?"

"A light saber. It is an imaginary weapon that is authentic for the period. They were obsessed with weapons and divisions. They saw the world as a struggle of good against evil. That was how wars could be called good, except by those who fought in them."

She didn't argue. Her lover, a partial, had been modelled on a particular Twentieth Century writer, and had direct access to the appropriate records in the Library. Although she had been born just at the end of the Twentieth Century, she had long ago forgotten everything about it.

Behind them, the drums reached a frenzied climax and fell silent. The sacrificial victim writhed on the heel stone and the chief druid lifted the still beating heart above his head in triumph. Blood that looked black in the torchlight ran down his arms.

The spectators beyond the circle clapped or toasted each other. One man was trying to persuade his companion to fuck on the altar. They were invisible to the druids, who were merely puppets lending local color to the scene.

"I'm getting tired of this," she said.

"Of course. We could go to Cuba. The ocean fishing there is good. Or to Afrique, to hunt lions. I think I liked that best, but after a while I could no longer do it. That was one of the things that destroyed my writing."

"I'm getting tired of you," she said, and her lover bowed and walked away.

She was getting tired of everything.

She had been getting tired of everything for longer than she could remember. What was the point of living forever if you did nothing new? Despite all her hopes, this *faux* Earth, populated by two billion puppets and partials, and ten million of her clade, had failed to revive her.

In one more year, the fleet of spaceships would disperse; the sun, an ordinary G2 star she had moved by the pressure of its own light upon gravity tethered reflective sails, would go supernova; nothing would be saved but the store of information which the Library had collected and collated. She had not yet accessed any of that. Perhaps that would save her.

She returned to the carnival, stayed there three days. But despite use of various intoxicants she could not quite lose herself in it, could not escape the feeling that she had failed after all. This was supposed to be a great congress of her own selves, a place to share and exchange memories that spanned five million years and the entire Galaxy. But it seemed to her that the millions of her selves simply wanted to forget what they were, to lose themselves in the pleasures of the flesh. Of course, many had assumed bodies for the first time to attend the gathering; one could perhaps excuse them, for this carnival was to them a genuine farewell to flesh they would abandon at the end of the year.

On the third day she was sitting in cold dawn light at a green café table in the Jardin des Tuileries, by the great fountain. Someone was sculpting the clouds through which the sun was rising. The café was crowded with guests, partials and puppets, androids and animals—even a silver gynoid, its face a smooth oval mirror. The air buzzed with the tiny machines which attended the guests; in one case, a swirling cloud of gnat-sized beads *was* a guest. After almost a century in costume, the guests were reverting to type.

She sipped a *citron pressé*, listened to the idle chatter. The party in Paris would break up soon. The revelers would disperse to other parts of the Earth. Except for a clean-up crew, the puppets, partials and all the rest would be returned to store. At another table, a youthful version of her erstwhile lover was talking to an older man with brown hair brushed back from his high forehead and pale blue eyes magnified by the thick lenses of his spectacles.

"The lions, Jim. Go to Afrique and listen to the lions roar at night. There is no sound like it."

"Ah, and I would love that, but Nora would not stand it. She needs the comforts of civilization. Besides, the thing we must not forget is that I would not be able to see the lions. Instead I think we will drink some more of this fine white wine and you will tell me about them."

"Aw hell, I could bring you a living lion if you like," the younger man said. "I could describe him to you and you could touch him and smell him until you got the idea." He was quite unaware that there were two lions right there in the park, accompanying a naked girl child whose feet, with pigeon's wings at the ankles, did not quite touch the ground.

Did these puppets come here every day, and recreate a conversation millions of years dead for the delectation of the guests? Was each day to them the same day? Suddenly, she felt as if a cold wind was blowing through her, as if she was raised up high and naked upon the pinnacle of the mountain of her millions of years.

"You confuse the true and the real," someone said. A man's voice, soft, lisping. She looked around but could not see who amongst the amazing people and creatures might have said such a thing, the truest realest thing she had heard for . . . how long? She could not remember how long.

She left, and went to New Orleans.

Where it was night, and raining, a soft warm rain falling in the lamplit streets. It was the Twentieth Century here, too. They were cooking crawfish under the mimosa trees at every intersection of the brick-paved streets, and burning the Maid of New Orleans over Lake Pontchartrain. The Maid hung up there in the black night sky—wrapped in oiled silks and shining like a star, with the blue-white wheel of the Galaxy a backdrop that spanned the horizon—then flamed like a comet and plunged into the black water while cornet bands played *"Laissez le Bon Temps Rouler."*

She fell in with a trio of guests whose originals were all less than a thousand years old. They were students of the Rediscovery, they said, although it was not quite clear what the Rediscovery was. They wore green ("For Earth," one said, although she thought that odd because most of the Earth was blue), and drank a mild psychotropic called absinthe, bitter white stuff poured into water over a sugar cube held in silver tongs. They were interested in the origins of the clade, which amused her greatly, because of course she was its origin, going amongst the copies and clones disguised as her own self. But even if they made her feel every one of her five million years, she liked their innocence, their energy, their openness.

She strolled with her new friends through the great orrery at the waterfront. Its display of the lost natural wonders of the Galaxy was derived from records and memories guests had deposited in the Library, and changed every day. She was listening to the three students discuss the possibility that humans had not originally come from the Earth when someone went past and said loudly, looking right at her, "None of them look like you, but they are just like you all the same. All obsessed with the past because they are trapped in it."

A tall man with a black, spade-shaped beard and black eyes that looked at her with infinite amusement. The same soft, lisping voice she had heard in the café in Paris. He winked and plunged into the heart of the white-hot whirlpool of the accretion disc of the black hole of Sigma Draconis 2, which drew matter from the photosphere of its companion blue-white giant—before the reconstruction, it had been one of the wonders of the Galaxy. She followed, but he was gone.

She looked for him everywhere in New Orleans, and fell in with a woman who before the gathering had lived in the water vapor zone of a gas giant, running a tourist business for those who could afford to download themselves into the ganglia of living blimps a kilometer across. The woman's name was Rapha; she had ruled the worlds of a hundred stars once, but had given that up long before she had answered the call for the gathering.

"I was a man when I had my empire," Rapha said, "but I gave that up too. When you've done everything, what's left but to party?"

She had always been a woman, she thought. And for two million years she had ruled an empire of a million worlds—for all she knew, the copy she had left behind ruled there still. But she didn't tell Rapha that. No one knew who she was, on all the Earth. She said, "Then let's party until the end of the world."

She knew that it wouldn't work—she had already tried everything, in every combination—but because she didn't care if it worked or not, perhaps this time it would.

They raised hell in New Orleans, and went to Antarctica.

It was raining in Antarctica, too.

It had been raining for a century, ever since the world had been made.

Statite sails hung in stationary orbit, reflecting sunlight so that the swamps and cycad forests and volcanic mountain ranges of the South Pole were in perpetual day. The hunting lodge was on a floating island a hundred meters above the tops of the giant ferns, close to the edge of a shallow viri-descent lake. A flock of delicate, dappled *Dromiceiomimus* squealed and splashed in the shallows; great dragonflies flitted through the rainy middle air; at the misty horizon the perfect cones of three volcanoes sent up threads of smoke into the sagging clouds.

She and Rapha rode bubbles in wild loops above the forests, chasing di-nosaurs or goading dinosaurs to chase them. Then they plunged into one of the volcanoes and caused it to erupt, and one of the hunters overrode the bubbles and brought them back and politely asked them to stop.

The lake and the forest were covered in a mantle of volcanic ash. The sky was milky with ash.

"The guests are amused, but they will not be amused forever. It is the hunting that is important here. If I may suggest other areas where you might find enjoyment . . ."

He was a slightly younger version of her last lover. A little less salt in his beard; a little more spring in his step.

She said, "How many of you have I made?"

But he didn't understand the question.

They went to Thebes (and some of the hunting party went with them), where they ran naked and screaming through the streets, toppling the stat-ues of the gods. They went to Greenland, and broke the rainbow bridge of Valhalla and fought the trolls and ran again, laughing, with Odin's thunder about their ears. Went to Troy, and set fire to the wooden horse before the Greeks could climb inside it.

None of it mattered. The machines would repair everything; the puppets would resume their roles. Troy would fall again the next night, on schedule.

"Let's go to Golgotha," Rapha said, wild-eyed, very drunk.

This was in a bar of some Christian–era American town. Outside, a cou-ple of the men were roaring up and down the main street on motorcycles, weaving in and out of the slow-moving, candy-colored cars. Two cops watched indulgently.

"Or Afrique," Rapha said. "We could hunt man-apes."

"I've done it before," someone said. He didn't have a name, but some kind of number. He was part of a clone. His shaved head was horribly scarred; one of his eyes was mechanical. He said, "You hunt them with spears or slings. They're pretty smart, for man-apes. I got killed twice."

Someone came into the bar. Tall, saturnine, black eyes, a spade-shaped beard. At once, she asked her machines if he was a partial or a guest, but the question confused them. She asked them if there were any strangers in the world, and at once they told her that there were the servants and those of her clade, but no strangers.

He said softly, "Are you having a good time?"

"Who are you?"

"Perhaps I'm the one who whispers in your ear, 'Remember that you are mortal.' Are you mortal, Angel?"

No one in the world should know her name. Her true name.

Danger, danger, someone sang in the background of the song that was playing on the jukebox. *Danger,* burbled the coffee pot on the heater behind the counter of the bar.

She said, "I made you, then."

"Oh no. Not me. You made all of this. Even all of the guests, in one way or another. But not me. We can't talk here. Try the one place which has any use in this *faux* world. There's something there I'm going to take, and when I've done that I'll wait for you."

"Who are you? What do you want?"

"Perhaps I want to kill you." He smiled. "And perhaps you want to die. It's one thing you have not tried yet."

He walked away, and when she started after him Rapha got in the way. Rapha hadn't seen the man. She said the others wanted to go to Hy Brasil.

"The gene wars," Rapha said. "That's where we started to become what we are. And then—I don't know, but it doesn't matter. We're going to party to the end of the world. When the sun explodes, I'm going to ride the shock wave as far as I can. I'm not going back. There's a lot of us who aren't going back. Why should we? We went to get copied and woke up here, thousands of years later, thousands of light-years away. What's to go back for? Wait! Where are you going?"

"I don't know," she said, and walked out.

The man had scared her. He had touched the doubt which had made her organize the gathering. She wanted a place to hide so that she could think about that before she confronted him.

Most of the North American continent was, in one form or another, modeled after the Third Millennium of the Christian Era. She took a car (a red Dodge as big as a boat, with fins and chrome trim) and drove to Dallas, where she was attacked by tribes of horsemen near the glittering slag of the wrecked city. She took up with a warlord for a while, poisoned all his wives, grew bored and seduced his son, who murdered his father and began a civil war. She went south on horseback through the alien flower jungles which had conquered Earth after humanity had more or less abandoned it, then caught a *pneumatique* all the way down the spine of Florida to Key West.

A version of her last lover lived there, too. She saw him in a bar by the beach two weeks later. There were three main drugs in Key West: cigarettes, heroin, and alcohol. She had tried them all, decided she liked alcohol best. It helped you forget yourself in an odd, dissociative way that was both pleasant and disturbing. Perhaps she should have spent more of her long life drunk.

This version of her lover liked alcohol, too. He was both lumbering but shy, pretending not to notice the people who looked at him while he drank several complicated cocktails. He had thickened at the waist; his beard was white and full. His eyes, webbed by wrinkles, were still piercingly blue, but his gaze was vague and troubled. She eavesdropped while he talked with the barkeep. She wanted to find out how the brash man who had to constantly prove himself against the world had turned out.

Badly, it seemed. The world was unforgiving, and his powers were fading.

"I lost her, Carlos," he told the barkeep. He meant his muse. "She's run out on me, the bitch."

"Now, Papa, you know that is not true," the young barkeep said. "I read your article in *Life* just last week."

"It was shit, Carlos. I can fake it well enough, but I can't do the good stuff any more. I need some quiet, and all day I get tourists trying to take my picture and spooking the cats. When I was younger I could work all day in a café, but now I need . . . hell, I don't know what I need. She's a bitch, Carlos. She only loves the young." Later, he said, "I keep dreaming of lions. One of the long white beaches in Afrique where the lions come down at dusk. They play there like cats, and I want to get to them, but I can't."

But Carlos was attending to another customer. Only she heard the old man. Later, after he had gone, she talked with Carlos herself. He was a puppet, and couldn't understand, but it didn't matter.

"All this was a bad idea," she said. She meant the bar, Key West, the Pacific Ocean, the world. "Do you want to know how it started?"

"Of course, ma'am. And may I bring you another drink?"

"I think I have had enough. You stay there and listen. Millions of years ago, while all of what would become humanity lived on the nine worlds and thousand worldlets around a single star in the Sky Hunter arm of the Galaxy, there was a religion which taught that individuals need never die. It was this religion which first drove humanity from star to star in the Galaxy. Individuals copied their personalities into computers, or cloned themselves, or spread their personalities through flocks of birds, or fish, or amongst hive insects. But there was one flaw in this religion. After millions of years, many of its followers were no longer human in form or in thought, except that they could trace back, generation upon generation, their descent from a single human ancestor. They had become transcendents, and each individual transcendent had become a clade, or an alliance, of millions of different minds. Mine is merely one of many, but it is one of the oldest, and one of the largest.

"I brought us here to unite us all in shared experiences. It isn't possible that one of us could have seen every wonder in the Galaxy, visit every world. There are a hundred billion stars in the Galaxy. It takes a year or two to explore the worlds of each star, and then there is the travel between the stars. But there are ten million of us here. Clones, copies, descendants of clones and copies. Many of us have done nothing but explore. We have not seen everything, but we have seen most of it. I thought that we could pool all our information, that it would result in . . . something. A new religion, godhead. Something new, something *different*. But it seems that most just want to party, and I wonder how much I have changed, for they are so little like me. Many of them say that they will not return, that they will stay here until the sun ends it all. Some have joined in the war in China—a few even refuse regeneration. Mostly, though, they want to party."

"There are parties every night, ma'am," the barkeep said. "That's Key West for you."

"Someone was following me, but I lost him. I think he was tracing me through the travel net, but I used contemporary transport to get here. He frightened me and I ran away, but perhaps he is what I need. I think I will find him. What month is this?"

"June, ma'am. Very hot, even for June. It means a bad hurricane season."

"It will get hotter," she said, thinking of the machine ticking away in the core of the sun.

And went to Tibet, where the Library was.

For some reason, the high plateau had been constructed as a replica of part of Mars. She had given her servants a lot of discretion when building the Earth; it pleased her to be surprised, although it did not happen very often.

She had arrived at the top of one of the rugged massifs that defined the edge of the vast basin. There was a shrine here, a mani eye painted on a stone pillar, a heap of stones swamped with skeins of red and blue and white and yellow prayer flags raveling in the cold wind. The scarp dropped away steeply to talus slopes and the flood lava of the basin's floor, a smooth, lightly cratered red plain mantled with fleets of barchan dunes. Directly below, nestling amongst birches at the foot of the scarp's sheer cliff, was the bone-white Library.

She took a day to descend the winding path. Now and then pilgrims climbed past her. Many shuffled on their knees, eyes lifted to the sky; a few fell face-forward at each step, standing up and starting again at the point where their hands touched the ground. All whirled prayer wheels and muttered their personal mantra as they climbed, and few spared her more than a glance, although at noon while she sat under a gnarled juniper one old man came to her and shared his heel of dry black bread and stringy dried yak meat. She learned from him that the pilgrims were not puppets, as she had thought, but were guests searching for enlightenment. That was so funny and so sad she did not know what to think about it.

The Library was a replica of the White Palace of the Potala. It had been a place of quiet order and contemplation, where all the stories that the clade had told each other, all the memories that they had downloaded or exchanged, had been collected and collated.

Now it was a battleground.

Saffron-robed monks armed with weaponry from a thousand different eras were fighting against man-shaped black androids. Bodies of men and machines were sprawled on the great steps; smoke billowed from the topmost ranks of the narrow windows; red and green energy beams flickered against the pink sky.

She walked through the carnage untouched. Nothing in this world could touch her. Only perhaps the man who was waiting for her, sitting cross-legged beneath the great golden Buddha, which a stray shot from some energy weapon had decapitated and half-melted to slag. On either side, hundreds of candles floated in great bowls filled with water; their lights shivered and flickered from the vibration of heavy weaponry.

The man did not open his eyes as she approached, but he said softly, "I already have what I need. These foolish monks are defending a lost cause. You should stop them."

"It is what they have to do. They can't destroy us, of course, but I could destroy you."

"Guests can't harm other guests," he said calmly. "It is one of the rules."

"I am not a guest. Nor, I think, are you."

She told her machines to remove him. Nothing happened.

He opened his eyes. He said, "Your machines are invisible to the puppets and partials you created to populate this fantasy world. I am invisible to the machines. I do not draw my energy from the world grid, but from elsewhere."

And then he leaped at her, striking with formal moves millions of years old. The Angry Grasshopper, the Rearing Horse, the Snapping Mantis. Each move, magnified by convergent energies, could have killed her, evaporated her body, melted her machines.

But she allowed her body to respond, countering his attacks. She had thought that she might welcome death; instead, she was amused and exhilarated by the fury of her response. The habit of living was deeply ingrained; now it had found a focus.

Striking attitudes, tangling in a flurry of blows and counterblows, they moved through the battleground of the Library, through its gardens, moved down the long talus slope at the foot of the massif in a storm of dust and shattered stones.

At the edge of a lake which filled a small, perfectly circular crater, she finally tired of defensive moves and went on the attack. The Striking Eagle, the Plunging Dragon, the Springing Tiger Who Defends Her Cubs. He countered in turn. Stray energies boiled the lake dry. The dry ground shook, split open in a mosaic of plates. Gradually, a curtain of dust was raised above the land, obscuring the setting sun and the green face of the Moon, which was rising above the mountains.

They broke apart at last. They stood in the center of a vast crater of vitrified rock. Their clothes hung in tatters about their bodies. It was night, now. Halfway up the scarp of the massif, small lightnings flashed where the monks still defended the Library.

"Who are you?" she said again. "Did I create you?"

"I'm closer to you than anyone else in this strange mad world," he said.

That gave her pause. All the guests, clones or copies or replicants, were of her direct genetic lineage.

She said, "Are you my death?"

As if in answer, he attacked again. But she fought back as forcefully as before, and when he broke off, she saw that he was sweating.

"I am stronger than you thought," she said.

He took out a small black cube from his tattered tunic. He said, "I have what I need. I have the memory core of the Library. Everything anyone who came here placed on record is here."

"Then why do you want to kill me?"

"Because you are the original. I thought it would be fitting, after I stole this."

She laughed. "You foolish man! Do you think we rely on a single physical location, a single master copy? It is the right of everyone in the clade to carry away the memories of everyone else. Why else are we gathered here?"

"I am not of your clade." He tossed the cube into the air, caught it, tucked it away. "I will use this knowledge against you. Against all of you. I have all your secrets."

"You say you are closer to me than a brother, yet you do not belong to the clade. You want to use our memories to destroy us." She had a sudden insight. "Is this war, then?"

He bowed. He was nearly naked, lit by the green light of the Moon and the dimming glow of the slag that stretched away in every direction. "Bravo," he said. "But it has already begun. Perhaps it is even over by now; after all, we are twenty thousand light-years above the plane of the Galactic disc, thirty-five thousand light-years from the hub of your Empire. It will take you that long to return. And if the war is not over, then this will finish it."

She was astonished. Then she laughed. "What an imagination I have!"

He bowed again, and said softly, "You made this world from your imagination, but you did not imagine me."

And he went somewhere else.

Her machines could not tell her where he had gone; she called upon all the machines in the world, but he was no longer on the Earth. Nor was he amongst the fleet of ships which had carried the guests—in suspended animation, as frozen embryos, as codes triply engraved in gold—to the world she had created for the gathering.

There were only two other places he could be, and she did not think he could have gone to the sun. If he had, then he would have triggered the machine at the core, and destroyed her and everyone else in the subsequent supernova.

So she went to the Moon.

She arrived on the farside. The energies he had used against her suggested that he had his own machines, and she did not think that he would have hidden them in full view of the Earth.

The machines which she had instructed to recreate the Earth for the one hundred years of the gathering had recreated the Moon, too, so that the oceans of the Earth would have the necessary tides; it had been easier than tangling gravithic resonances to produce the same effect. It had taken little extra effort to recreate the forests which had cloaked the Moon for a million years, between the first faltering footsteps and the abandonment of the Earth.

It was towards the end of the long Lunar night. All around, blue firs soared up for hundreds of meters, cloaked in wide fans of needles that in the cold and the dark had drooped down to protect the scaly trunks. The gray rocks were coated in thin snow, and frozen lichens crunched underfoot. Her machines scattered in every direction, quick as thought. She sat down on top of a big rough boulder and waited.

It was very quiet. The sky was dominated by the triple-armed pinwheel of the Galaxy. It was so big that when she looked at one edge she could not see the other. The Arm of the Warrior rose high above the arch of the Arm of the Hunter; the Arm of the Archer curved in the opposite direction, below the close horizon. Star clusters made long chains of concentrated light through the milky haze of the galactic arms. There were lines and threads and globes and clouds of stars, all fading into a general misty radiance dissected by dark lanes which barred the arms at regular intervals. The core was knitted from thin shells of stars in tidy orbits concentrically packed around the great globular clusters of the heart stars, like layers of glittering tissue wrapped around a heap of jewels.

Every star had been touched by humankind. Existing stars had been moved or destroyed; millions of new stars and planetary systems had been created by collapsing dust clouds. A garden of stars, regulated, ordered, tidied. The Library held memories of every star, every planet, every wonder of the old untamed Galaxy. She was beginning to realize that the gathering was not the start of something new, but the end of five million years of Galactic colonization.

After a long time, the machines came back, and she went where they told her.

It was hidden within a steep-sided crater, a castle or maze of crystal vanes that rose in serried ranks from deep roots within the crust, where they collected and focused tidal energy. He was at its heart, busily folding together a small spacecraft. The energy of the vanes had been greatly depleted by the fight, and he was trying to concentrate the remainder in the motor of the spacecraft. He was preparing to leave.

Her machines rose up and began to spin, locking in resonance with the vanes and bleeding off their store of energy. The machines began to glow as she bounded down the steep smooth slope towards the floor of the crater, red-hot, white-hot, as hot as the core of the sun, for that was where they were diverting the energy stored in the vanes.

Violet threads flicked up, but the machines simply absorbed that energy too. Their stark white light flooded the crater, bleaching the ranks of crystal vanes.

She walked through the traps and tricks of the defenses, pulled him from his fragile craft and took him up in a bubble of air to the neutral point between the Moon and the Earth.

"Tell me," she said. "Tell me why you came here. Tell me about the war."

He was surprisingly calm. He said, "I am a first generation clone, but I am on the side of humanity, not the transcendents. Transcendent clades are a danger to all of the variety within and between the civilizations in the Galaxy. At last the merely human races have risen against them. I am just one weapon in the greatest war ever fought."

"You are my flesh. You are of my clade."

"I am a secret agent. I was made from a single cell stolen from you several hundred years before you set off for this fake Earth and the gathering of your clade. I arrived only two years ago, grew my power source, came down to steal the memory core and kill you. Although I failed to kill you before, we are no longer in the place where you draw your power. Now—"

After a moment in which nothing happened, he screamed in frustration and despair. She pitied him. Pitied all those who had bent their lives to produce this poor vessel, this failed moment, although all the power, the intrigues and desperate schemes his presence implied were as remote from her as the politics of a termite nest.

She said, "Your power source is not destroyed, but my machines take all its energy. Why did your masters think us dangerous?"

"Because you would fill the Galaxy with your own kind. Because you would end human evolution. Because you will not accept that the Universe is greater than you can ever be. Because you refuse to die, and death is a necessary part of evolution."

She laughed. "Silly little man! Why would we accept limits? We are only doing what humanity has always done. We use science to master nature just as man-apes changed their way of thinking by making tools and using fire. Humanity has always striven to become more than it is, to grow spiritually and morally and intellectually, to go up to the edge and step over it."

For the first time in a million years, those sentiments did not taste of ashes. By trying to destroy her, he had shown her what her life was worth.

He said, "But you do not change. That is why you are so dangerous. You and the other clades of transhumans have stopped humanity evolving. You would fill the Galaxy with copies of a dozen individuals who are so scared of physical death that they will do any strange and terrible thing to themselves to survive."

He gestured at the blue-white globe that hung beneath their feet, small and vulnerable against the vast blackness between galaxies.

"Look at your Earth! Humanity left it four million years ago, yet you chose to recreate it for this gathering. You had a million years of human history on Earth to choose from, and four and a half billion years of the history of the planet itself, and yet almost half of your creation is given over to a single century."

"It is the century where we became what we are," she said, remembering Rapha. "It is the century when it became possible to become transhuman, when humanity made the first steps beyond the surface of a single planet."

"It is the century you were born in. You would freeze all history if you could, an eternity of the same thoughts thought by the same people. You deny all possibilities but your own self."

He drew himself up, defiant to the last. He said, "My ship will carry the memory core home without me. You take all, and give nothing. I give my life, and I give you this."

He held up something as complex and infolded as the throat of an orchid. It was a vacuum fluctuation, a hole in reality that when inflated would remove them from the Universe. She looked away at once—the image was already burned in her brain—and threw him into the core of the sun. He did not even have a chance to scream.

Alone in her bubble of air, she studied the wheel of the Galaxy, the ordered pattern of braids and clusters. Light was so slow. It took a hundred thousand years to cross from one edge of the Galaxy to the other. Had the war against her empire, and the empires of all the other transcendents, already ended? Had it already changed the Galaxy, stirred the stars into new patterns? She would not know until she returned, and that would take thirty-five thousand years.

But she did not have to return. In the other direction was the limitless Universe, a hundred billion galaxies. She hung there a long time, watching little smudges of ancient light resolve out of the darkness. Empires of stars wherever she looked, wonders without end.

We will fight the war, she thought, and we shall win, and we will go on forever and ever.

And went down, found the bar near the beach. She would wait until the old man came in, and buy him a drink, and talk to him about his dream of the lions.

Peter F. Hamilton

ESCAPE ROUTE

Prolific new British writer Peter F. Hamilton has sold to *Interzone*, *In Dreams*, *New Worlds*, *Fears*, and elsewhere. He sold his first novel, *Mindstar Rising*, in 1993, and quickly followed it up with two sequels, *A Quantum Murder* and *The Nano Flower*. Hamilton's first three books managed to slip into print without attracting a great deal of attention, on this side of the Atlantic, at least, but that changed dramatically with the publication of his next novel, *The Reality Dysfunction*, a huge modern Space Opera (it needed to be divided into two volumes for publication in the United States) that is itself only the start of a projected trilogy of staggering size and scope. *The Reality Dysfunction* has been attracting the reviews and the acclaim that his prior novels did not and has suddenly put Hamilton on the map as a writer to watch, perhaps a potential rival for writers such as Dan Simmons, Iain M. Banks, Paul J. McAuley, Gregory Benford, C. J. Cherryh, Stephen R. Donaldson, Colin Greenland, and other major players in the expanding subgenre of Modern Baroque Space Opera, an increasingly popular area these days. The second novel in the trilogy, *The Neutronium Alchemist*, is just out and generating the same kind of excited critical buzz. Upcoming is the third novel in the trilogy, *The Naked God*, and Hamilton's first collection, *A Second Chance at Eden*.

In the pyrotechnic novella that follows, one as packed with intriguing new ideas and fast-paced action and suspense as many another author's four-hundred-page novel, he unravels the mystery of an enigmatic object found in deep space, one that may prove to be harder—and considerably more dangerous—to get *out* of than it was to get *in*. . . .

Marcus Calvert had never seen an asteroid cavern quite like Sonora's before; it was disorientating even for someone who had spent 30 years captaining a starship. The center of the gigantic rock had been hollowed out by mining machines, producing a cylindrical cavity twelve kilometers long, five in diameter. Usually, the floor would be covered in soil and planted with fruit trees and grass. In Sonora's case, the environmental engineers had simply flooded it. The result was a small freshwater sea that no matter where you were on it, you appeared to be at the bottom of a valley of water.

Floating around the gray surface were innumerable rafts, occupied by hotels, bars, and restaurants. Taxi boats whizzed between them and the wharfs at the base of the two flat cavern walls.

Marcus and two of his crew had taken a boat out to the Lomaz bar, a raft which resembled a Chinese dragon trying to mate with a Mississippi paddle steamer.

"Any idea what our charter is, Captain? asked Katherine Maddox, the *Lady Macbeth*'s node specialist.

"The agent didn't say," Marcus admitted. "Apart from confirming it's private, not corporate."

"They don't want us for combat, do they?" Katherine asked. There was a hint of rebellion in her voice. She was in her late forties, and like the Calverts her family had geneered their offspring to withstand both freefall and high acceleration. The dominant modifications had given her thicker skin, tougher bones, and harder internal membranes; she was never sick or giddy in freefall, nor did her face bloat up. Such changes were a formula for blunt features, and Katherine was no exception.

"If they do, we're not taking it," Marcus assured her.

Katherine exchanged an unsettled glance with Roman Zucker, the ship's fusion engineer, and slumped back in her chair.

The combat option was one Marcus had considered possible. *Lady Macbeth* was combat-capable, and Sonora asteroid belonged to a Lagrange-point cluster with a strong autonomy movement. An unfortunate combination. But having passed his sixty-seventh birthday two months ago he sincerely hoped those kind of flights were behind him.

"This could be them," Roman said, glancing over the rail. One of Sonora's little taxi boats was approaching their big resort raft.

The trim cutter curving around towards the Lomaz had two people sitting on its red leather seats.

Marcus watched with interest as they left the taxi. He ordered his neural nanonics to open a fresh memory cell, and stored the pair of them in a visual file. The first to alight was a man in his mid-thirties, dressed in expensive casual clothes; a long face and a very broad nose gave him a kind of imposing dignity.

His partner was less flamboyant. She was in her late twenties, obviously geneered; Oriental features matched with white hair that had been drawn together in wide dreadlocks and folded back aerodynamically.

They walked straight over to Marcus's table, and introduced themselves as Antonio Ribeiro and Victoria Keef. Antonio clicked his fingers at the waitress, and told her to fetch a bottle of Norfolk Tears.

"Hopefully to celebrate the success of our business venture, my friends," he said. "And if not, it is a pleasant time of day to imbibe such a magical potion. No?"

Marcus found himself immediately distrustful. It wasn't just Antonio's phony attitude; his intuition was scratching away at the back of his skull. Some friends called it his paranoia program, but it was rarely wrong. A family trait, like the wanderlust which no geneering treatment had ever eradicated.

"The cargo agent said you had a charter for us," Marcus said. "He never mentioned any sort of business deal."

"If I may ask your indulgence for a moment, Captain Calvert. You arrived here without a cargo. You must be a very rich man to afford that."

"There were . . . circumstances requiring us to leave Ayachcho ahead of schedule."

"Yeah," Katherine muttered darkly. "Her husband."

Marcus was expecting it, and smiled serenely. He'd heard very little else from the crew for the whole flight.

Antonio received the tray and its precious pear-shaped bottle from the waitress, and waved away the change.

"If I may be indelicate, Captain, your financial resources are not optimal at this moment," Antonio suggested.

"They've been better."

Antonio sipped his Norfolk Tears, and grinned in appreciation. "For myself, I was born with the wrong amount of money. Enough to know I needed more."

"Mr Ribeiro, I've heard all the get-rich-quick schemes in existence. They all have one thing in common, they don't work. If they did, I wouldn't be sitting here with you."

"You are wise to be cautious, Captain. I was, too, when I first heard this proposal. However, if you would humor me a moment longer, I can assure you this requires no capital outlay on your part. At the worst you will have another mad scheme to laugh about with your fellow captains."

"No money at all?"

"None at all, simply the use of your ship. We would be equal partners sharing whatever reward we find."

"Jesus. All right, I can spare you five minutes. Your drink has bought you that much attention span."

"Thank you, Captain. My colleagues and I want to fly the *Lady Macbeth* on a prospecting mission."

"For planets?" Roman asked curiously.

"No. Sadly, the discovery of a terracompatible planet does not guarantee wealth. Settlement rights will not bring more than a couple of million fuseodollars, and even that is dependant on a favorable biospectrum assessment, which would take many years. We have something more immediate in mind. You have just come from the Dorados?"

"That's right," Marcus said. The system had been discovered six years earlier, comprising a red dwarf sun surrounded by a vast disc of rocky particles. Several of the larger chunks had turned out to be nearly pure metal. Dorados was an obvious name; whoever managed to develop them would gain a colossal economic resource. So much so that the governments of Omuta and Garissa had gone to war over who had that development right. It was the Garissan survivors who had ultimately been awarded settlement by the Confederation Assembly. There weren't many of them. Omuta had deployed twelve antimatter planetbusters against their homeworld. "Is that what you're hoping to find, another flock of solid metal asteroids?"

"Not quite," Antonio said. "Companies have been searching similar disc systems ever since the Dorados were discovered, to no avail. Victoria, my dear, if you would care to explain."

She nodded curtly and put her glass down on the table. "I'm an astrophysicist by training," she said. "I used to work for Forrester-Courtney; it's a company based in the O'Neill Halo that manufactures starship sensors, although their speciality is survey probes. It's been a very healthy business recently. Consortiums have been flying survey missions through every catalogued disc system in the Confederation. As Antonio said, none of our clients found anything remotely like the Dorados. That didn't surprise me, I never expected any of Forrester-Courtney's probes to be of much use. All our sensors did was run broad spectrographic sweeps. If anyone was going to find another Dorados cluster it would be the Edenists. Their voidhawks have a big advantage; those ships generate an enormous distortion field which can literally see mass. A lump of metal 50 kilometers across would have a very distinct density signature; they'd be aware of it from at least half a million kilometers away. If we were going to compete against that, we'd need a sensor which gave us the same level of results, if not better."

"And you produced one?" Marcus inquired.

"Not quite. I proposed expanding our magnetic anomaly detector array. It's a very ancient technology; Earth's old nations pioneered it during the twentieth century. Their military maritime aircraft were equipped with crude arrays to track enemy submarines. Forrester-Courtney builds its array into low-orbit resource-mapping satellites; they produce quite valuable survey data. Unfortunately, the company turned down my proposal. They said an expanded magnetic array wouldn't produce better results than a spectrographic sweep, not on the scale required. And a spectrographic scan would be quicker."

"Unfortunate for Forrester-Courtney," Antonio said wolfishly. "Not for us. Dear Victoria came to me with her suggestion, and a simple observation."

"A spectrographic sweep will only locate relatively large pieces of mass," she said. "Fly a starship 50 million kilometers above a disc, and it can spot a fifty-kilometer lump of solid metal easily. But the smaller the lump, the higher the resolution you need or the closer you have to fly, a fairly obvious equation. My magnetic anomaly detector can pick out much smaller lumps of metal than a Dorado."

"So? If they're smaller, they're worth less," Katherine said. "The whole point of the Dorados is that they're huge. I've seen the operation those ex-Garissans are building up. They've got enough metal to supply their industrial stations with specialist microgee alloys for the next 2,000 years. Small is no good."

"Not necessarily," Marcus said carefully. Maybe it was his intuition again, or just plain logical extrapolation, but he could see the way Victoria Keef's thoughts were flowing. "It depends on what kind of small, doesn't it?"

Antonio applauded. "Excellent, Captain. I knew you were the right man for us."

"What makes you think they're there?" Marcus asked.

"The Dorados are the ultimate proof of concept," Victoria said. "There are two possible origins for disc material around stars. The first is accretion; matter left over from the star's formation. That's no use to us, it's mostly the light elements, carbonaceous chondritic particles with some silica aluminum thrown in if you're lucky. The second type of disc is made up out of collision debris. We believe that's what the Dorados are, fragments of planetoids that were large enough to form molten metal cores. When they broke apart the metal cooled and congealed into those hugely valuable chunks."

"But nickel iron wouldn't be the only metal," Marcus reasoned, pleased by the way he was following through. "There will be other chunks floating about in the disc."

"Exactly, Captain," Antonio said eagerly. "Theoretically, the whole periodic table will be available to us, we can fly above the disc and pick out whatever element we require. There will be no tedious and expensive refining process to extract it from ore. It's there waiting for us in its purest form; gold, silver, platinum, iridium. Whatever takes your fancy."

Lady Macbeth sat on a docking cradle in Sonora's spaceport, a simple dull-gray sphere 57 meters in diameter. All Adamist starships shared the same geometry, dictated by the operating parameters of the ZTT jump, which required perfect symmetry. At her heart were four separate life-support capsules, arranged in a pyramid formation; there was also a cylindrical hangar for her spaceplane, a smaller one for her Multiple Service Vehicle, and five main cargo holds. The rest of her bulk was a solid intestinal tangle of machinery and tanks. Her main drive system was three fusion rockets capable of accelerating her at eleven gees, clustered around an antimatter intermix tube which could multiply that figure by an unspecified amount; a sure sign of her combat-capable-status. (By a legislative quirk it wasn't actually illegal to have an antimatter drive, though possession of antimatter itself was a capital crime throughout the Confederation.)

Spaceport umbilical hoses were jacked into sockets on her lower hull, supplying basic utility functions. Another expense Marcus wished he could avoid; it was inflicting further pain on his already ailing cash-flow situation. They were going to have to fly soon, and fate seemed to have decided what flight it would be. That hadn't stopped his intuition from maintaining its subliminal assault on Antonio Ribeiro's scheme. If he could just find a single practical or logical argument against it . . .

He waited patiently while the crew drifted into the main lounge in life-support capsule A. Wai Choi, the spaceplane pilot, came down through the ceiling hatch and used a stikpad to anchor her shoes to the decking. She gave Marcus a sly smile that bordered on teasing. There had been times in the last five years when she'd joined him in his cabin, nothing serious, but they'd certainly had their moments. Which, he supposed, made her more tolerant of him than the others.

At the opposite end of the spectrum was Karl Jordan, the *Lady Mac*'s systems specialist, with the shortest temper, the greatest enthusiasm, and certainly the most serious of the crew. His age was the reason, only twenty-five; the *Lady Mac* was his second starship duty.

As for Schutz, who knew what emotions were at play in the cosmonik's mind; there was no visible outlet for them. Unlike Marcus, he hadn't been geneered for freefall; decades of working on ships and spaceport docks had seen his bones lose calcium, his muscles waste away, and his cardiovascular system atrophy. There were hundreds like him in every asteroid, slowly replacing their body parts with mechanical substitutes. Some even divested themselves of their human shape altogether. At sixty-three, Schutz was still humanoid, though only twenty per cent of him was biological. His body supplements made him an excellent engineer.

"We've been offered a joint-prize flight," Marcus told them. He explained Victoria's theory about disc systems and the magnetic anomaly array. "Ribeiro will provide us with consumables and a full cryogenics load. All we have to do is take *Lady Mac* to a disc system and scoop up the gold."

"There has to be a catch," Wai said. "I don't believe in mountains of gold just drifting through space waiting for us to come along and find them."

"Believe it," Roman said. "You've seen the Dorados. Why can't the elements exist in the same way?"

"I don't know. I just don't think anything comes that easy."

"Always the pessimist."

"What do you think, Marcus?" she asked. "What does your intuition tell you?"

"About the mission, nothing. I'm more worried about Antonio Ribeiro."

"Definitely suspect," Katherine agreed.

"Being a total prat is socially unfortunate," Roman said. "But it's not a crime. Besides, Victoria Keef seemed levelheaded enough."

"An odd combination," Marcus mused. "A wannabe playboy and an astrophysicist. I wonder how they ever got together."

"They're both Sonora nationals," Katherine said. "I ran a check through the public data cores, they were born here. It's not that remarkable."

"Any criminal record?" Wai asked.

"None listed. Antonio has been in court three times in the last seven years; each case was over disputed taxes. He paid every time."

"So he doesn't like the tax man," Roman said. "That makes him one of the good guys."

"Run-ins with the tax office are standard for the rich," Wai said.

"Except he's not actually all that rich," Katherine said. "I also queried the local Collins Media library; they keep tabs on Sonora's principal citizens. Mr Ribeiro senior made his money out of fish breeding; he won the franchise from the asteroid development corporation to keep the biosphere sea stocked. Antonio was given a 15 per cent stake in the breeding company when he was twenty-one, which he promptly sold for an estimated 800,000 fuseodollars. Daddy didn't approve, there are several news files on the quarrel; it became very public."

"So he is what he claims to be," Roman said. "A not-very rich boy with expensive tastes."

"How can he pay for the magnetic detectors we have to deploy, then?" Wai asked. "Or is he going to hit us with the bill and suddenly vanish?"

"The detector arrays are already waiting to be loaded on board," Marcus said. "Antonio has several partners; people in the same leaky boat as himself, and willing to take a gamble."

Wai shook her head, still dubious. "I don't buy it. It's a free lunch."

"They're willing to invest their own money in the array hardware. What other guarantees do you want?"

"What kind of money are we talking about, exactly?" Karl asked. "I mean, if we do fill the ship up, what's it going to be worth?"

"Given its density, *Lady Mac* can carry roughly 5,000 tons of gold in her cargo holds," Marcus said. "That'll make maneuvering very sluggish, but I can handle her."

Roman grinned at Karl. "And today's price for gold is three and a half thousand fuseodollars per kilogram."

Karl's eyes went blank for a second as his neural nanonics ran the conversion. "Seventeen billion fuseodollars worth!"

He laughed. "Per trip."

"How is this Ribeiro character proposing to divide the proceeds?" Schutz asked.

"We get one third," Marcus said. "Roughly five point eight billion fuseodollars. Of which I take 30 per cent. The rest is split equally between you, as per the bounty flight clause in your contracts."

"Shit," Karl whispered. "When do we leave, Captain?"

"Does anybody have any objections?" Marcus asked. He gave Wai a quizzical look.

"Okay," she said. "But just because you can't see surface cracks, it doesn't mean there isn't any metal fatigue."

The docking cradle lifted *Lady Macbeth* cleanly out of the spaceport's crater-shaped bay. As soon as she cleared the rim her thermo-dump panels unfolded, sensor clusters rose up out of their recesses on long booms. Visual and radar information was collated by the flight computer, which datavised it directly into Marcus's neural nanonics. He lay on the acceleration couch at the center of the bridge with his eyes closed as the external starfield blossomed in his mind. Delicate icons unfurled across the visualization, ship status schematics and navigational plots sketched in primary colors.

Chemical verniers fired, lifting *Lady Mac* off the cradle amid spumes of hot saffron vapor. A tube of orange circles appeared ahead of him, the course vector formatted to take them in towards the gas giant. Marcus switched to the more powerful ion thrusters, and the orange circles began to stream past the hull.

The gas giant, Zacateca, and its moon, Lazaro, had the same apparent size as *Lady Mac* accelerated away from the spaceport. Sonora was one of fifteen asteroids captured by their Lagrange point, a zone where their respective gravity fields were in equilibrium. Behind the starship, Lazaro was a grubby gray crescent splattered with white craters. Given that Zacateca was small for a gas giant, barely 40,000 kilometers in diameter, Lazaro was an unusual companion. A moon 9,000 kilometers in diameter, with an outer crust of ice 50 kilometers deep. It was that ice which had originally attracted the interest of the banks and multistellar finance consortia. Stony iron asteroids were an ideal source of metal and minerals for industrial stations, but they were also notoriously short of the light elements essential to sustain life. To have abundant supplies of both so close together was a strong investment incentive.

Lady Mac's radar showed Marcus a serpentine line of one-ton ice cubes flung out from Lazaro's equatorial mass-driver, gliding inertly up to the Lagrange point for collection. The same inexhaustible source which allowed Sonora to have its unique sea.

All the asteroids in the cluster had benefited from the plentiful ice, their economic growth racing ahead of equivalent settlements. Such success always bred resentment among the indigenous population, who inevitably became eager for freedom from the founding companies. In this case, having so many settlements so close together gave their population a strong sense of identity and shared anger. The cluster's demands for autonomy had become increasingly strident over the last few years. A situation agitated by numerous violent incidents and acts of sabotage against the company administration staff.

Ahead of the *Lady Mac*, Marcus could see the tidal hurricane Lazaro stirred up amid the wan amber and emerald stormbands of Zacateca's upper atmosphere. An ocean-sized hypervelocity maelstrom which followed the moon's orbit faithfully around the equator. Lightning crackled around its fringes, 500-kilometer-long forks stabbing out into the surrounding cyclones of ammonia cirrus and methane sleet.

The starship was accelerating at two gees now, her triple fusion drives sending out a vast streamer of arc-bright plasma as she curved around the bulk of the huge planet. Her course vector was slowly bending to align on the star which Antonio intended to prospect, 38 light-years distant. There was very little information contained in the almanac file other than confirming it was a K-class star with a disc.

Marcus cut the fusion drives when the *Lady Mac* was 7,000 kilometers past perigee and climbing steadily. The thermo-dump panels and sensor clusters sank down into their jump recesses below the fuselage, returning the ship to a perfect sphere. Fusion generators began charging the energy-patterning nodes. Orange circles flashing through Marcus's mind were illustrating the slingshot parabola she'd flown, straightening up the farther the gas giant was left behind. A faint star slid into the last circle.

An event horizon swallowed the starship. Five milliseconds later it had shrunk to nothing.

"Okay, try this one," Katherine said. "Why should the gold or anything else congeal into lumps as big as the ones they say it will? Just because you've got a planetoid with a hot core doesn't mean it's producing the metallic equivalent of fractional distillation. You're not going to get an onion-layer effect with strata of different metals. It doesn't happen on planets, it won't happen here. If there is gold, and platinum and all the rest of this fantasy junk, it's going to be hidden away in ores just like it always is."

"So Antonio exaggerated when he said it would be pure," Karl retorted. "We just hunt down the highest-grade ore particles in the disc. Even if it's only 50 per cent, who cares? We're never going to be able to spend it all anyway."

Marcus let the discussion grumble on. It had been virtually the only topic for the crew since they'd departed Sonora five days ago. Katherine was playing the part of chief skeptic, with occasional support from Schutz and Wai; while the others tried to shoot her down. The trouble was, he acknowledged, that none of them knew enough to comment with real authority. At least they weren't talking about the sudden departure from Ayachcho any more.

"If the planetoids did produce ore, then it would fragment badly during the collision which formed the disc," Katherine said. "There won't even be any mountain-sized chunks left, only pebbles."

"Have you taken a look outside recently?" Roman asked. "The disc doesn't exactly have a shortage of large particles."

Marcus smiled to himself at that. The disc material had worried him when they arrived at the star two days ago. *Lady Mac* had jumped deep into the system, emerging three million kilometers above the ecliptic. It was a superb vantage point. The small orange star burned at the center of a disc 160 million kilometers in diameter. There were no distinct bands like those found in a gas giant's rings; this was a continuous grainy copper mist veiling half of the universe. Only around the star itself did it fade away; whatever particles were there to start with had long since evaporated to leave a clear band three million kilometers wide above the turbulent photosphere.

Lady Mac was accelerating away from the star at a twentieth of a gee, and curving around into a retrograde orbit. It was the vector which would give the magnetic arrays the best possible coverage of the disc. Unfortunately, it increased the probability of collision by an order of magnitude. So far, the radar had only detected standard motes of interplanetary dust, but Marcus insisted there were always two crew on duty monitoring the local environment.

"Time for another launch," he announced.

Wai datavised the flight computer to run a final systems diagnostic through the array satellite. "I notice Jorge isn't here again," she said sardonically. "I wonder why that is?"

Jorge Leon was the second companion Antonio Ribeiro had brought with him on the flight. He'd been introduced to the crew as a first-class hardware technician who had supervised the construction of the magnetic array satellites. As introverted as Antonio was outgoing, he'd shown remarkably little interest in the arrays so far. It was Victoria Keef who'd familiarized the crew with the systems they were deploying.

"We should bung him in our medical scanner," Karl suggested cheerfully. "Be interesting to see what's inside him. Bet you'd find a whole load of weapon implants."

"Great idea," Roman said. "You ask him. He gives me the creeps."

"Yeah, Katherine, explain that away," Karl said. "If there's no gold in the disc, how come they brought a contract killer along to make sure we don't fly off with their share?"

"Karl!" Marcus warned. "That's enough." He gave the open floor hatch a pointed look. "Now let's get the array launched, please."

Karl's face reddened as he began establishing a tracking link between the starship's communication system and the array satellite's transponder.

"Satellite systems on line," Wai reported. "Launch when ready."

Marcus datavised the flight computer to retract the satellite's hold-down latches. An induction rail shot it clear of the ship. Ion thrusters flared, refining its trajectory as it headed down towards the squally apricot surface of the disc.

Victoria had designed the satellites to skim 5,000 kilometers above the nomadic particles. When their operational altitude was established they would spin up and start to reel out 25 gossamer-thin optical fibers. Rotation insured the fibers remained straight, forming a spoke array parallel to the disc. Each fiber was 150 kilometers long, and coated in a reflective, magnetically-sensitive film.

As the disc particles were still within the star's magnetosphere, every one of them generated a tiny wake as it traversed the flux lines. It was that wake which resonated the magnetically-sensitive film, producing fluctuations in the reflectivity. By bouncing a laser pulse down the fiber and measuring the distortions inflicted by the film, it was possible to build up an image of the magnetic waves writhing chaotically through the disc. With the correct discrimination programs, the origin of each wave could be determined.

The amount of data streaming back into the *Lady Macbeth* from the array satellites was colossal. One satellite array could cover an area of 250,000 square kilometers, and Antonio Ribeiro had persuaded the Sonora Autonomy Crusade to pay for 15. It was a huge gamble, and the responsibility was his alone. Forty hours after the first satellite was deployed, the strain of that responsibility was beginning to show. He hadn't slept since then, choosing to stay in the cabin which Marcus Calvert had assigned to them, and where they'd set up their network of analysis processors. Forty hours of his mind being flooded with near-incomprehensible neuroiconic displays. Forty hours spent fingering his silver crucifix and praying.

The medical monitor program running in his neural nanonics was flashing up fatigue toxin cautions, and warning him of impending dehydration. So far he'd ignored them, telling himself discovery would occur any minute now. In his heart, Antonio had been hoping they would find what they wanted in the first five hours.

His neural nanonics informed him the analysis network was focusing on the mass-density ratio of a three-kilometer particle exposed by satellite seven. The processors began a more detailed interrogation of the raw data.

"What is it?" Antonio demanded. His eyes fluttered open to glance at Victoria, who was resting lightly on one of the cabin's flatchairs.

"Interesting," she murmured. "It appears to be a cassiterite ore. The planetoids definitely had tin."

"Shit!" He thumped his fist into the chair's padding, only to feel the restraint straps tighten against his chest, preventing him from sailing free. "I don't care about tin. That's not what we're here for."

"I am aware of that." Her eyes were open, staring at him with a mixture of contempt and anger.

"Sure, sure," he mumbled. "Holy Mother, you'd expect us to find some by now."

"Careful," she datavised. "Remember this damn ship has internal sensors."

"I know how to follow elementary security procedures," he datavised back.

"Yes. But you're tired. That's when errors creep in."

"I'm not that tired. Shit, I expected results by now; some progress."

"We have had some very positive results, Antonio. The arrays have found three separate deposits of pitchblende."

"Yeah, in hundred-kilogram lumps. We need more than that, a lot more."

"You're missing the point. We've proved it exists here; that's a stupendous discovery. Finding it in quantity is just a matter of time."

"This isn't some astrological experiment you're running for that university which threw you out. We're on an assignment for the cause. And we cannot go back empty handed. Got that? Cannot."

"Astrophysics."

"What?"

"You said astrological, that's fortune-telling."

"Yeah? You want I should take a guess at how much future you're going to have if we don't find what we need out here?"

"For Christ's sake, Antonio," she said out loud. "Go and get some sleep."

"Maybe." He scratched the side of his head, unhappy with how limp and oily his hair had become. A vapor shower was something else he hadn't had for a while. "I'll get Jorge in here to help you monitor the results."

"Great." Her eyes closed again.

Antonio deactivated his flatchair's restraint straps. He hadn't seen much of Jorge on the flight. Nobody had. The man kept strictly to himself in his small cabin. The Crusade's council wanted him on board to ensure the crew's continuing cooperation once they realized there was no gold. It was Antonio who had suggested the arrangement; what bothered him was the orders Jorge had received concerning himself should things go wrong.

"Hold it." Victoria raised her hand. "This is a really weird one."

Antonio tapped his feet on a stikpad to steady himself. His neural nanonics accessed the analysis network again. Satellite eleven had located a particle with an impossible mass-density ratio; it also had its own magnetic field, a very complex one. "Holy Mother, what is that? Is there another ship here?"

"No, it's too big for a ship. Some kind of station, I suppose. But what's it doing in the disc?"

"Refining ore?" he said with a strong twist of irony.

"I doubt it."

"Okay. So forget it."

"You are joking."

"No. If it doesn't affect us, it doesn't concern us."

"Jesus, Antonio; if I didn't know you were born rich I'd be frightened by how stupid you were."

"Be careful, Victoria my dear. Very careful."

"Listen, there's two options. One, it's some kind of commercial operation; which must be illegal because nobody has filed for industrial development rights." She gave him a significant look.

"You think they're mining pitchblende?" he datavised.

"What else? We thought of the concept, why not one of the black syndicates as well? They just didn't come up with my magnetic array idea, so they're having to do it the hard way."

"Secondly," she continued aloud, "it's some kind of covert military station; in which case they've tracked us from the moment we emerged. Either way, we're under observation. We have to know who they are before we proceed any further."

"A station?" Marcus asked. "Here?"

"It would appear so," Antonio said glumly.

"And you want us to find out who they are?"

"I think that would be prudent," Victoria said, "given what we're doing here."

"All right," Marcus said. "Karl, lock a communication dish on them. Give them our CAB identification code, let's see if we can get a response."

"Aye, sir," Karl said. He settled back on his acceleration couch.

"While we're waiting," Katherine said. "I have a question for you, Antonio."

She ignored the warning glare Marcus directed at her.

Antonio's bogus smile blinked on. "If it is one I can answer, then I will do so gladly, dear lady."

"Gold is expensive because of its rarity value, right?"

"Of course."

"So here we are, about to fill *Lady Mac*'s cargo holds with 5,000 tons of the stuff. On top of that you've developed a method which means people can scoop up millions of tons any time they want. If we try and sell it to a dealer or a bank, how long do you think we're going to be billionaires for, a fortnight?"

Antonio laughed. "Gold has never been that rare. Its value is completely artificial. The Edenists have the largest stockpile. We don't know exactly how much they possess because the Jovian Bank will not declare the exact figure. But they dominate the commodity market, and sustain the price by controlling how much is released. We shall simply play the same game. Our gold will have to be sold discreetly, in small batches, in different star systems, and over the course of several years. And knowledge of the magnetic array system should be kept to ourselves."

"Nice try, Katherine," Roman chuckled. "You'll just have to settle for an income of a hundred million a year."

She showed him a stiff finger, backed by a shark's smile.

"No response," Karl said. "Not even a transponder."

"Keep trying," Marcus told him. "Okay, Antonio, what do you want to do about it?"

"We have to know who they are," Victoria said. "As Antonio has just explained so eloquently, we can't have other people seeing what we're doing here."

"It's what *they're* doing here that worries me," Marcus said; although, curiously, his intuition wasn't causing him any grief on the subject.

"I see no alternative but a rendezvous," Antonio said.

"We're in a retrograde orbit, 32 million kilometers away and receding. That's going to use up an awful lot of fuel."

"Which I believe I have already paid for."

"Okay, we rendezvous."

"What if they don't want us there?" Schutz asked.

"If we detect any combat wasp launch, then we jump outsystem immediately," Marcus said. "The disc's gravity field isn't strong enough to affect *Lady Mac*'s patterning node symmetry. We can leave any time we want."

For the last quarter of a million kilometers of the approach, Marcus put the ship on combat status. The nodes were fully charged, ready to jump. Thermo-dump panels were retracted. Sensors maintained a vigilant watch for approaching combat wasps.

"They must know we're here," Wai said when they were 8,000 kilometers away. "Why don't they acknowledge us?"

"Ask them," Marcus said sourly. *Lady Mac* was decelerating at a nominal one gee, which he was varying at random. It made their exact approach vector impossible to predict, which meant their course couldn't be seeded with proximity mines. The maneuver took a lot of concentration.

"Still no electromagnetic emission in any spectrum," Karl reported. "They're certainly not scanning us with active sensors."

"Sensors are picking up their thermal signature," Schutz said. "The structure is being maintained at 36 degrees Celsius."

"That's on the warm side," Katherine observed. "Perhaps their environmental system is malfunctioning."

"Shouldn't affect the transponder," Karl said.

"Captain, I think you'd better access the radar return," Schutz said.

Marcus boosted the fusion drives up to one and a half gees, and ordered the flight computer to datavise him the radar feed. The image which rose into his mind was of a fine scarlet mesh suspended in the darkness, its gentle ocean-swell pattern outlining the surface of the station and the disc particle it was attached to. Except Marcus had never seen any station like this before. It was a gently curved wedge-shape structure, 400 meters long, 300 wide, and 150 meters at its blunt end. The accompanying disc particle was a flattened ellipsoid of stony iron rock, measuring eight kilometers along its axis. The tip had been sheared off, leaving a flat cliff half a kilometer in diameter, to which the structure was clinging. That was the smallest of the particle's modifications. A crater four kilometers across, with perfectly smooth walls, had been cut into one side of the rock. An elaborate unicorn-horn tower rose 900 meters from its center, ending in a clump of jagged spikes.

"Oh Jesus," Marcus whispered. Elation mingled with fear, producing a deviant adrenaline high. He smiled thinly. "How about that?"

"This was one option I didn't consider," Victoria said weakly.

Antonio looked round the bridge, a frown cheapening his handsome face. The crew seemed dazed, while Victoria was grinning with delight. "Is it some kind of radio astronomy station?" he asked.

"Yes," Marcus said. "But not one of ours. We don't build like that. It's xenoc."

Lady Mac locked attitude a kilometer above the xenoc structure. It was a position which made the disc appear uncomfortably malevolent. The smallest particle beyond the fuselage must have massed over a million tons; and all of them were moving, a slow, random three-dimensional cruise of lethal inertia. Amber sunlight stained those near the disc's surface a baleful ginger, while deeper in there were only phantom silhouettes drifting over total blackness, flowing in and out of visibility. No stars were evident through the dark, tightly packed nebula.

"That's not a station," Roman declared. "It's a shipwreck."

Now that *Lady Mac*'s visual-spectrum sensors were providing them with excellent images of the xenoc structure, Marcus had to agree. The upper and lower surfaces of the wedge was some kind of silver-white material, a fuselage shell which was fraying away at the edges. Both of the side surfaces were dull brown, obviously interior bulkhead walls, with the black geometrical outline of decking printed across them. The whole structure was a cross-section torn out of a much larger craft. Marcus tried to fill in the missing bulk in his mind; it must have been vast, a streamlined delta fuselage like a hypersonic aircraft. Which didn't make sense for a starship. Rather, he corrected himself, for a starship built with current human technology. He wondered what it would be like to fly through interstellar space the way a plane flew through an atmosphere, swooping around stars at a hundred times the speed of light. Quite something.

"This doesn't make a lot of sense," Katherine said. "If they were visiting the telescope dish when they had the accident, why did they bother to anchor themselves to the asteroid? Surely they'd just take refuge in the operations center."

"Only if there is one," Schutz said. "Most of our deep space science facilities are automated, and by the look of it their technology is considerably more advanced."

"If they are so advanced, why would they build a radio telescope on this scale anyway?" Victoria asked. "It's very impractical. Humans have been using linked baseline arrays for centuries. Five small dishes orbiting a million kilometers apart would provide a reception which is orders of magnitude greater than this. And why build it here? Firstly, the particles are hazardous, certainly to something that size. You can see it's been pocked by small impacts, and that horn looks broken to me. Secondly, the disc itself blocks half of the universe from observation. No, if you're going to do major radio astronomy, you don't do it from a star system like this one."

"Perhaps they were only here to build the dish," Wai said. "They intended it to be a remote research station in this part of the galaxy. Once they had it up and running, they'd boost it into a high-inclination orbit. They had their accident before the project was finished."

"That still doesn't explain why they chose this system. Any other star would be better that this one."

"I think Wai's right about them being long-range visitors," Marcus said. "If a xenoc race like that existed close to the Confederation we would have found them by now. Or they would have contacted us."

"The Kiint," Karl said quickly.

"Possibly," Marcus conceded. The Kiint were an enigmatic xenoc race, with a technology far in advance of anything the Confederation had mastered. However, they were reclusive, and cryptic to the point of obscurity. They also claimed to have abandoned starflight a long time ago. "If it is one of their ships, then it's very old."

"And it's still functional," Roman said eagerly. "Hell, think of the technology inside. We'll wind up a lot richer than the gold could ever make us." He grinned over at Antonio, whose humor had blackened considerably.

"So what were the Kiint doing building a radio telescope here?" Victoria asked.

"Who the hell cares?" Karl said. "I volunteer to go over, Captain."

Marcus almost didn't hear him. He'd accessed the *Lady Mac*'s sensor suite again, sweeping the focus over the tip of the dish's tower, then the sheer cliff which the wreckage was attached to. Intuition was making a lot of junctions in his head. "I don't think it is a radio telescope," he said. "I think it's a distress beacon."

"It's four kilometers across!" Katherine said.

"If they came from the other side of the galaxy, it would need to be. We can't even see the galactic core from here there's so much gas and dust in the way. You'd need something this big to punch a message through."

"That's valid," Victoria said. "You believe they were signaling their homeworld for help?"

"Yes. Assume their world is a long way off, three-four thousand light-years away if not more. They were flying a research or survey mission in this area and they have an accident. Three quarters of their ship is lost, including the drive section. Their technology isn't good enough to build the survivors a working stardrive out of what's left, but they can enlarge an existing crater on the disc particle. So they do that; they build the dish and a transmitter powerful enough to give God an alarm call, point it at their homeworld, and scream for help. The ship can sustain them until the rescue team arrives. Even our own zero-tau technology is up to that."

"Gets my vote," Wai said, she gave Marcus a wink.

"No way," said Katherine. "If they were in trouble they'd use a supralight communicator to call for help. Look at that ship, we're centuries away from building anything like it."

"Edenist voidhawks are pretty sophisticated," Marcus countered. "We just scale things differently. These xenocs might have a more advanced technology, but physics is still the same the universe over. Our understanding of quantum relativity is good enough to build faster than light starships, yet after 450 years of theoretical research we still haven't come up with a method of supralight communication. It doesn't exist."

"If they didn't return on time, then surely their homeworld would send out a search and recovery craft," Schutz said.

"They'd have to know the original ship's course exactly," Wai said. "And if a search ship did manage to locate them, why did they build the dish?"

Marcus didn't say anything. He knew he was right. The others would accept his scenario eventually, they always did.

"All right, let's stop arguing about what happened to them, and why they built the dish," Karl said. "When do we go over there, Captain?"

"Have you forgotten the gold?" Antonio asked. "That is why we came to this disc system. We should resume our search for it. This piece of wreckage can wait."

"Don't be crazy. This is worth a hundred times as much as any gold."

"I fail to see how. An ancient, derelict, starship with a few heating circuits operational. Come along. I've been reasonable indulging you, but we must return to the original mission."

Marcus regarded the man cautiously, a real bad feeling starting to develop. Anyone with the slightest knowledge of finance and the markets would know the value of salvaging a xenoc starship. And Antonio had been born rich. "Victoria," he said, not shifting his gaze. "Is the data from the magnetic array satellites still coming through?"

"Yes." She touched Antonio's arm. "The captain is right. We can continue to monitor the satellite results from here, and investigate the xenoc ship simultaneously."

"Double your money time," Katherine said with apparent innocence.

Antonio's face hardened. "Very well," he said curtly. "If that's your expert opinion, Victoria, my dear. Carry on by all means, Captain."

In its inert state the SII spacesuit was a broad sensor collar with a protruding respirator tube and a black football-sized globe of programmable silicon hanging from it. Marcus slipped the collar around his neck, bit on the tube nozzle, and datavised an activation code into the suit's control processor. The silicon ball began to change shape, flattening out against his chest, then flowing over his body like a tenacious oil slick. It enveloped his head completely, and the collar sensors replaced his eyes, datavising their vision directly into his neural nanonics. Three others were in the preparation compartment with him; Schutz, who didn't need a spacesuit to EVA, Antonio, and Jorge Leon. Marcus had managed to control his surprise when they'd volunteered. At the same time, with Wai flying the MSV he was glad they weren't going to be left behind in the ship.

Once his body was sealed by the silicon, he climbed into an armored exoskeleton with an integral cold-gas maneuvering pack. The SII silicon would never puncture, but if he was struck by a rogue particle the armor would absorb the impact.

When the airlock's outer hatch opened, the MSV was floating 15 meters away. Marcus datavised an order into his maneuvering pack processor, and the gas jets behind his shoulder fired, pushing him towards the small egg-shaped vehicle. Wai extended two of the MSV's three waldo arms in greeting. Each of them ended in a simple metal grid, with a pair of boot clamps on both sides.

Once all four of her passengers were locked into place, Wai piloted the MSV in towards the disc. The rock particle had a slow, erratic tumble, taking 120 hours to complete its cycle. As she approached, the flattish surface with the dish was just turning into the sunlight. It was a strange kind of dawn, the rock's crumpled gray-brown crust speckled by the sharp black shadows of its own rolling prominences, while the dish was a lake of infinite black, broken only by the jagged spire of the horn rising from its center. The xenoc ship was already exposed to the amber light, casting its bloated sundial shadow across the featureless glassy cliff. She could see the ripple of different ores and mineral strata frozen below the glazed surface, deluding her for a moment that she was flying towards a mountain of cut and polished onyx.

Then again, if Victoria's theory was right, she could well be.

"Take us in towards the top of the wedge," Marcus datavised. "There's a series of darker rectangles there."

"Will do," she responded. The MSV's chemical thrusters pulsed in compliance.

"Do you see the color difference near the frayed edges of the shell?" Schutz asked. "The stuff's turning gray. It's as if the decay is creeping inwards."

"They must be using something like our molecular binding force generators to resist vacuum ablation," Marcus datavised. "That's why the main section is still intact."

"It could have been here for a long time, then."

"Yeah. We'll know better once Wai collects some samples from the tower."

There were five of the rectangles, arranged in parallel, one and a half meters long and one meter wide. The shell material below the shorter edge of each one had a set of ten grooves leading away down the curve.

"They looks like ladders to me," Antonio datavised. "Would that mean these are airlocks?"

"It can't be that easy," Schutz replied.

"Why not?" Marcus datavised. "A ship this size is bound to have more than one airlock."

"Yeah, but five together?"

"Multiple redundancy."

"With technology this good?"

"That's human hubris. The ship still blew up, didn't it?"

Wai locked the MSV's attitude 50 meters above the shell section. "The micropulse radar is bouncing right back at me," she informed them. "I can't tell what's below the shell, it's a perfect electromagnetic reflector. We're going to have communication difficulties once you're inside."

Marcus disengaged his boots from the grid and fired his pack's gas jets. The shell was as slippery as ice; neither stikpads nor magnetic soles would hold them to it.

"Definitely enhanced-valency bonds," Schutz datavised. He was floating parallel to the surface, holding a sensor block against it. "It's a much stronger field than *Lady Mac*'s. The shell composition is a real mix; the resonance scan is picking up titanium, silicon, boron, nickel, silver, and a whole load of polymers."

"Silver's weird," Marcus commented. "But if there's nickel in it our magnetic soles should've worked." He maneuvered himself over one of the rectangles. It was recessed about five centimeters, though it blended seamlessly into the main shell. His sensor collar couldn't detect any seal lining. Half way along one side were two circular dimples, ten centimeters across. Logically, if the rectangle was an airlock, then these should be the controls. Human back-ups were kept simple. This shouldn't be any different.

Marcus stuck his fingers in one. It turned bright blue.

"Power surge," Schutz datavised. "The block's picking up several high-voltage circuits activating under the shell. What did you do, Marcus?"

"Tried to open one."

The rectangle dilated smoothly, material flowing back to the edges. Brilliant white light flooded out.

"Clever," Schutz datavised.

"No more than our programmable silicon," Antonio retorted.

"We don't use programmable silicon for external applications."

"It settles one thing," Marcus datavised. "They weren't Kiint, not with an airlock this size."

"Quite. What now?"

"We try to establish control over the cycling mechanism. I'll go in and see if I can operate the hatch from inside. If it doesn't open after ten minutes, try the dimple again. If that doesn't work, cut through it with the MSV's fission blade."

The chamber inside was thankfully bigger than the hatch: a pentagonal tube two meters wide and 15 long. Four of the walls shone brightly, while the fifth was a strip of dark-maroon composite. He drifted in, then flipped himself over so he was facing the hatch, floating in the center of the chamber. There were four dimples just beside the hatch. "First one," he datavised. Nothing happened when he put his fingers in. "Second." It turned blue. The hatch flowed shut.

Marcus crashed down onto the strip of dark composite, landing on his left shoulder. The force of the impact was almost enough to jar the respirator tube out of his mouth. He grunted in shock. Neural nanonics blocked the burst of pain from his bruised shoulder.

Jesus! They've got artificial gravity.

He was flat on his back, the exoskeleton and maneuvering pack weighing far too much. Whatever planet the xenocs came from, it had a gravity field about one and a half times that of Earth. He released the catches down the side of his exoskeleton, and wriggled his way out. Standing was an effort, but he was used to higher gees on *Lady Mac*; admittedly not for prolonged periods, though.

He stuck his fingers in the first dimple. The gravity faded fast, and the hatch flowed apart.

"We just became billionaires," he datavised.

The third dimple pressurized the airlock chamber; while the fourth depressurized it.

The xenoc atmosphere was mostly a nitrogen-oxygen blend, with one per cent argon and six per cent carbon dioxide. The humidity was appalling, pressure was lower than standard, and the temperature was 42 degrees Celsius.

"We'd have to keep our SII suits on anyway, because of the heat," Marcus datavised. "But the carbon dioxide would kill us. And we'll have to go through biological decontamination when we go back to *Lady Mac*."

The four of them stood together at the far end of the airlock chamber, their exoskeleton armor lying on the floor behind them. Marcus had told Wai and the rest of the crew their first foray would be an hour.

"Are you proposing we go in without a weapon?" Jorge asked.

Marcus focused his collar sensors on the man who alleged he was a hardware technician. "That's carrying paranoia too far. No, we do not engage in first contact either deploying or displaying weapons of any kind. That's the law, and the Assembly regulations are very specific about it. In any case, don't you think that if there are any xenocs left after all this time they're going to be glad to see someone? Especially a space-faring species."

"That is, I'm afraid, a rather naive attitude, Captain. You keep saying how advanced this starship is, and yet it suffered catastrophic damage. Frankly, an unbelievable amount of damage for an accident. Isn't it more likely this ship was engaged in some kind of battle?"

Which was a background worry Marcus had suffered right from the start. That this starship could ever fail was unnerving. But like physical constants, Murphy's Law would be the same the universe over. He'd entered the airlock because intuition told him the wreck was safe for him personally. Somehow he doubted a man like Jorge would be convinced by that argument.

"If it's a warship, then it will be rigged to alert any surviving crew or flight computer of our arrival. Had they wanted to annihilate us, they would have done so by now. *Lady Mac* is a superb ship, but hardly in this class. So if they're waiting for us on the other side of this airlock, I don't think any weapon you or I can carry is going to make the slightest difference."

"Very well, proceed."

Marcus postponed the answer which came straight to mind, and put his fingers in one of the two dimples by the inner hatchway. It turned blue.

The xenoc ship wasn't disappointing, exactly, but Marcus couldn't help a growing sense of anticlimax. The artificial gravity was a fabulous piece of equipment, the atmosphere strange, the layout exotic. Yet for all that, it was just a ship; built from the universal rules of logical engineering. Had the xenocs themselves been there, it would have been so different. A whole new species with its history and culture. But they'd gone, so he was an archaeologist rather than an explorer.

They surveyed the first deck, which was made up from large compartments and broad hallways. The interior was made out of a pale-jade composite, slightly ruffled to a snake-skin texture. Surfaces always curved together, there were no real corners. Every ceiling emitted the same intense white glare, which their collar sensors compensated for. Arching doorways were all open, though they could still dilate if you used the dimples. The only oddity were 50-centimeter hemispherical blisters on the floor and walls, scattered completely at random.

There was an ongoing argument about the shape of the xenocs. They were undoubtedly shorter than humans, and they probably had legs, because there were spiral stair-wells, although the steps were very broad, difficult for bipeds. Lounges had long tables with large, rounded stool-chairs inset with four deep ridges.

After the first 15 minutes it was clear that all loose equipment had been removed. Lockers, with the standard dilating door, were empty. Every compartment had its fitted furnishings and nothing more. Some were completely bare.

On the second deck there were no large compartments, only long corridors lined with gray circles along the center of the walls. Antonio used a dimple at the side of one, and it dilated to reveal a spherical cell three meters wide. Its walls were translucent, with short lines of color slithering around behind them like photonic fish.

"Beds?" Schutz suggested. "There's an awful lot of them."

Marcus shrugged. "Could be." He moved on, eager to get down to the next deck. Then he slowed, switching his collar focus. Three of the hemispherical blisters were following him, two gliding along the wall, one on the floor. They stopped when he did. He walked over to the closest, and waved his sensor block over it. "There's a lot of electronic activity inside it," he reported.

The others gathered around.

"Are they extruded by the wall, or are they a separate device?" Schutz asked.

Marcus switched on the block's resonance scan. "I'm not sure, I can't find any break in the composite around its base, not even a hairline fracture; but with their materials technology that doesn't mean much."

"Five more approaching," Jorge datavised. The blisters were approaching from ahead, three of them on the walls, two on the floor. They stopped just short of the group.

"Something knows we're here," Antonio datavised.

Marcus retrieved the CAB xenoc interface communication protocol from a neural nanonics memory cell. He'd stored it decades ago, all qualified starship crew were obliged to carry it along with a million and one other bureaucratic lunacies. His communication block transmitted the protocol using a multispectrum sweep. If the blister could sense them, it had to have some kind of electromagnetic reception facility. The communication block switched to laser-light, then a magnetic pulse.

"Nothing," Marcus datavised.

"Maybe the central computer needs time to interpret the protocol," Schutz datavised.

"A desktop block should be able to work that out."

"Perhaps the computer hasn't got anything to say to us."

"Then why send the blisters after us?"

"They could be autonomous, whatever they are."

Marcus ran his sensor block over the blister again, but there was no change to its electronic pattern. He straightened up, wincing at the creak of complaint his spine made at the heavy gravity. "Okay, our hour is almost up anyway. We'll get back to *Lady Mac* and decide what stage two is going to be."

The blisters followed them all the way back to the stairwell they'd used. As soon as they started walking down the broad central hallway of the upper deck, more blisters started sliding in from compartments and other halls to stalk them.

The airlock hatch was still open when they got back, but the exoskeletons were missing.

"Shit," Antonio datavised. "They're still here, the bloody xenocs are here."

Marcus shoved his fingers into the dimple. His heartbeat calmed considerably when the hatch congealed behind them. The lock cycled obediently, and the outer rectangle opened.

"Wai," he datavised. "We need a lift. Quickly, please."

"On my way, Marcus."

"Strange way for xenocs to communicate," Schutz datavised. "What did they do that for? If they wanted to make sure we stayed, they could have disabled the airlock."

The MSV swooped over the edge of the shell, jets of twinkling flame shooting from its thrusters.

"Beats me," Marcus datavised. "But we'll find out."

Opinion on the ship was a straight split; the crew wanted to continue investigating the xenoc ship, Antonio and his colleagues wanted to leave. For once Jorge had joined them, which Marcus considered significant. He was beginning to think young Karl might have been closer to the truth than was strictly comfortable.

"The dish is just rock with a coating of aluminium sprayed on," Katherine said. "There's very little aluminium left now, most of it has boiled away in the vacuum. The tower is a pretty ordinary silicon-boron composite wrapped around a titanium load structure. The samples Wai cut off were very brittle."

"Did you carbon-date them?" Victoria asked.

"Yeah." She gave her audience a labored glance. "Give or take a decade, it's 13,000 years old."

Breath whistled out of Marcus's mouth. "Jesus."

"Then they must have been rescued, or died," Roman said. "There's nobody left over there. Not after that time."

"They're there," Antonio growled. "They stole our exoskeletons."

"I don't understand what happened to the exoskeletons. Not yet. But any entity who can build a ship like that isn't going to go creeping around stealing bits of space armor. There has to be a rational explanation."

"Yes! They wanted to keep us over there."

"What for? What possible reason would they have for that?"

"It's a warship, it's been in battle. The survivors don't know who we are, if we're their old enemies. If they kept us there, they could study us and find out."

"After 13,000 years, I imagine the war will be over. And where did you get this battleship idea from anyway?"

"It's a logical assumption," Jorge said quietly.

Roman turned to Marcus. "My guess is that some kind of mechanoid picked them up. If you look in one of the lockers you'll probably find them neatly stored away."

"Some automated systems are definitely still working," Schutz said. "We saw the blisters. There could be others."

"That seems the most remarkable part of it," Marcus said. "Especially now we know the age of the thing. The inside of that ship was brand new. There wasn't any dust, any scuff marks. The lighting worked perfectly, so did the gravity, the humidity hasn't corroded anything. It's extraordinary. As if the whole structure has been in zero-tau. And yet only the shell is protected by the molecular bonding force generators. They're not used inside, not in the decks we examined."

"However they preserve it, they'll need a lot of power for the job, and that's on top of gravity generation and environmental maintenance. Where's that been coming from uninterrupted for 13,000 years?"

"Direct mass to energy conversion," Katherine speculated. "Or they could be tapping straight into the sun's fusion. Whatever, bang goes the Edenist He3 monopoly."

"We have to go back," Marcus said.

"NO!" Antonio yelled. "We must find the gold first. When that has been achieved, you can come back by yourselves. I won't allow anything to interfere with our priorities."

"Look, I'm sorry you had a fright while you were over there. But a power supply that works for 13,000 years is a lot more valuable than a whole load of gold which we have to sell furtively," Katherine said levelly.

"I hired this ship. You do as I say. We go after the gold."

"We're partners, actually. I'm not being paid for this flight unless we strike lucky. And now we have. We've got the xenoc ship, we haven't got any gold. What does it matter to you how we get rich, as long as we do? I thought money was the whole point of this flight."

Antonio snarled at her, and flung himself at the floor hatch, kicking off hard with his legs. His elbow caught the rim a nasty crack as he flashed through it.

"Victoria?" Marcus asked as the silence became strained. "Have the satellite arrays found any heavy metal particles yet?"

"There are definitely traces of gold and platinum, but nothing to justify a rendezvous."

"In that case, I say we start to research the xenoc wreck properly." He looked straight at Jorge. "How about you?"

"I think it would be prudent. You're sure we can continue to monitor the array satellites from here?"

"Yes."

"Good. Count me in."

"Thanks. Victoria?"

She seemed troubled by Jorge's response, even a little bewildered, but she said: "Sure."

"Karl, you're the nearest thing we've got to a computer expert. I want you over there trying to make contact with whatever control network is still operating."

"You got it."

"From now on we go over in teams of four. I want sensors put up to watch the airlocks when we're not around, and start thinking about how we communicate with people inside. Wai, you and I are going to secure *Lady Mac* to the side of the shell. Okay, let's get active, people."

Unsurprisingly, none of the standard astronautics industry vacuum epoxies worked on the shell. Marcus and Wai wound up using tether cables wrapped around the whole of the xenoc ship to hold *Lady Mac* in place.

Three hours after Karl went over, he asked Marcus to join him.

Lady Mac's main airlock tube had telescoped out of the hull to rest against the shell. There was no way it could ever be mated to the xenoc airlock rectangle, but it did allow the crew to transfer over directly without having to use exoskeleton armor and the MSV. They'd also run an optical fiber through the xenoc airlock to the interior of the ship. The hatch material closed around it forming a perfect seal, rather than cutting through it.

Marcus found Karl just inside the airlock, sitting on the floor with several processor blocks in his lap. Eight blisters were slowly circling around him; two on the wall were stationary.

"Roman was almost right," he datavised as soon as Marcus stepped out of the airlock. "Your exoskeletons were cleared away. But not by any butler mechanoid. Watch." He lobbed an empty recording flek case onto the floor behind the blisters. One of them slid over to it. The green composite became soft, then liquid. The little plastic case sank through it into the blister.

"I call them cybermice," Karl datavised. "They just scurry around keeping the place clean. You won't see the exoskeletons again, they ate them, along with anything else they don't recognize as part of the ship's structure. I imagine they haven't tried digesting us yet because we're large and active; maybe they think we're friends of the xenocs. But I wouldn't want to try sleeping over here."

"Does this mean we won't be able to put sensors up?"

"Not for a while. I've managed to stop them digesting the communication block which the optical fiber is connected to."

"How?"

He pointed to the two on the wall. "I shut them down."

"Jesus, have you accessed a control network?"

"No. Schutz and I used a micro SQUID on one of the cybermice to get a more detailed scan of its electronics. Once we'd tapped the databus traffic it was just a question of running standard decryption programs. I can't tell you how these things work, but I have found some basic command routines. There's a deactivation code which you can datavise to them. I've also got a reactivation code, and some directional codes. The good news is that the xenoc program language is standardized." He stood and held a communication block up to the ceiling. "This is the deactivation code." A small circle of the ceiling around the block turned dark. "It's only localized, I haven't worked out how to control entire sections yet. We need to trace the circuitry to find an access port."

"Can you turn it back on again?"

"Oh yes." The dark section flared white again. "The codes work for the doors as well; just hold your block over the dimples."

"Be quicker to use the dimples."

"For now, yes."

"I wasn't complaining, Karl. This is an excellent start. What's your next step?"

"I want to access the next level of the cybermice program architecture. That way I should be able to load recognition patterns in their memory. Once I can do that I'll enter our equipment, and they should leave it alone. But that's going to take a long time; *Lady Mac* isn't exactly heavily stocked with equipment for this kind of work. Of course, once I do get deeper into their management routines we should be able to learn a lot about their internal systems. From what I can make out the cybermice are built around a molecular synthesizer." He switched on a fission knife, its ten-centimeter blade glowing a pale yellow under the ceiling's glare. It scored a dark smoldering scar in the floor composite.

A cybermouse immediately slipped towards the blemish. This time when the composite softened the charred granules were sucked down, and the small valley closed up.

"Exactly the same thickness and molecular structure as before," Karl datavised. "That's why the ship's interior looks brand new, and everything's still working flawlessly after 13,000 years. The cybermice keep regenerating it. Just keep giving them energy and a supply of mass and there's no reason this ship won't last for eternity."

"It's almost a Von Neumann machine, isn't it?"

"Close. I expect a synthesizer this small has limits. After all, if it could reproduce anything, they would have built themselves another starship. But the principle's here, Captain. We can learn and expand on it. Think of the effect a unit like this will have on our manufacturing industry."

Marcus was glad he was in an SII suit; it blocked any give-away facial expressions. Replicator technology would be a true revolution, restructuring every aspect of human society, Adamist and Edenist alike. And revolutions never favored the old.

I just came here for the money, not to destroy a way of life for 800 star systems.

"That's good, Karl. Where did the others go?"

"Down to the third deck. Once we solved the puzzle of the disappearing exoskeletons, they decided it was safe to start exploring again."

"Fair enough, I'll go down and join them."

"I cannot believe you agreed to help them," Antonio stormed. "You of all people. You know how much the cause is depending on us."

Jorge gave him a hollow smile. They were together in his sleeping cubicle, which made it very cramped. But it was one place on the starship he knew for certain no sensors were operational; a block he'd brought with him had made sure of that. "The cause has become dependent on your project. There's a difference."

"What are you talking about?"

"Those detector satellites cost us a million and a half fuseodollars each; and most of that money came from sources who will require repayment no matter what the outcome of our struggle."

"The satellites are a hell of a lot cheaper than antimatter."

"Indeed so. But they are worthless to us unless they find pitchblende."

"We'll find it. Victoria says there are plenty of traces. It's only a question of time before we get a big one."

"Maybe. It was a good idea, Antonio, I'm not criticizing. Fusion bomb components are not easily obtainable to a novice political organization with limited resources. One mistake, and the intelligence agencies would wipe us out. No, old-fashioned fission was a viable alternative. Even if we couldn't process the uranium up to weapons-quality, we can still use it as a lethal large-scale contaminate. As you say, we couldn't lose. Sonora would gain independence, and we would form the first government, with full access to the Treasury. Everyone would be reimbursed for their individual contribution to the liberation."

"So why are we mucking about in a pile of xenoc junk? Just back me up, Jorge, please. Calvert will leave it alone if we both pressure him."

"Because, Antonio, this piece of so-called xenoc junk has changed the rules of the game. In fact we're not even playing the same game any more. Gravity generation, an inexhaustible power supply, molecular synthesis, and if Karl can access the control network he might even find the blueprints to build whatever stardrive they used. Are you aware of the impact such a spectrum of radical technologies will have upon the Confederation when released all together? Entire industries will collapse from overnight obsolescence. There will be an economic depression the like of which we haven't seen since before the invention of the ZTT drive. It will take decades for the human race to return to the kind of stability we enjoy today. We will be richer and stronger because of it; but the transition years, ah . . . I would not like to be a citizen in an asteroid settlement that has just blackmailed the founding company into premature independence. Who is going to loan an asteroid such as that the funds to re-equip our industrial stations, eh?"

"I . . . I hadn't thought of that."

"Neither has the crew. Except for Calvert. Look at his face next time you talk to him, Antonio. He knows, he has reasoned it out, and he's seen the end of his captaincy and freedom. The rest of them are lost amid their dreams of exorbitant wealth."

"So what do we do?"

Jorge clamped a hand on Antonio's shoulder. "Fate has smiled on us, Antonio. This was registered as a joint-venture flight. No matter we were looking for something different. By law, we are entitled to an equal share of the xenoc technology. We are already trillionaires, my friend. When we get home we can *buy* Sonora asteroid; Holy Mother, we can buy the entire Lagrange cluster."

Antonio managed a smile, which didn't quite correspond with the dew of sweat on his forehead. "Okay, Jorge. Hell, you're right. We don't have to worry about anything any more. But . . ."

"Now what?"

"I know we can pay off the loan on the satellites, but what about the Crusade council? They won't like this. They might—"

"There's no cause for alarm. The council will never trouble us again. I maintain that I am right about the disaster which destroyed the xenoc ship. It didn't have an accident. That is a warship, Antonio. And you know what that means, don't you? Somewhere on board there will be weapons just as advanced and as powerful as the rest of its technology."

It was Wai's third trip over to the xenoc ship. None of them spent more than two hours at a time inside. The gravity field made every muscle ache; walking around was like being put on a crash exercise regimen.

Schutz and Karl were still busy by the airlock, probing the circuitry of the cybermice, and decrypting more of their programming. It was probably the most promising line of research; once they could use the xenoc program language they should be able to extract any answer they wanted from the ship's controlling network. Assuming there was one. Wai was convinced there would be. The number of systems operating—life-support, power, gravity—had to mean some basic management integration system was functional.

In the meantime there was the rest of the structure to explore. She had a layout file stored in her neural nanonics, updated by the others every time they came back from an excursion. At the blunt end of the wedge there could be anything up to 40 decks, if the spacing was standard. Nobody had gone down to the bottom yet. There were some areas which had no obvious entrance; presumably engineering compartments, or storage tanks. Marcus had the teams tracing the main power lines with magnetic sensors, trying to locate the generator.

Wai plodded after Roman as he followed a cable running down the center of a corridor on the eighth deck.

"It's got so many secondary feeds it looks like a fishbone," he complained. They paused at a junction with five branches, and he swept the block around. "This way." He started off down one of the new corridors.

"We're heading towards stairwell five," she told him, as the layout file scrolled through her skull.

There were more cybermice than usual on deck eight; over 30 were currently pursuing her and Roman, creating strong ripples in the composite floor and walls. Wai had noticed that the deeper she went into the ship the more of them there seemed to be. Although after her second trip she'd completely ignored them. She wasn't paying a lot of attention to the compartments leading off from the corridors, either. It wasn't that they were all the same, rather that they were all similarly empty.

They reached the stairwell, and Roman stepped inside. "It's going down," he datavised.

"Great, that means we've got another level to climb up when we're finished."

Not that going down these stairs was easy, she acknowledged charily. If only they could find some kind of variable gravity chute. Perhaps they'd all been positioned in the part of the ship that was destroyed.

"You know, I think Marcus might have been right about the dish being an emergency beacon," she datavised. "I can't think of any other reason for it being built. Believe me, I've tried."

"He always is right. It's bloody annoying, but that's why I fly with him."

"I was against it because of the faith gap."

"Say what?"

"The amount of faith these xenocs must have had in themselves. It's awesome. So different from humans. Think about it. Even if their homeworld is only 2,000 light-years away, that's how long the message is going to take to reach there. Yet they sent it believing someone would still be around to receive it, and more, act on it. Suppose that was us; suppose the *Lady Mac* had an accident a thousand light-years away. Would you think there was any point in sending a lightspeed message to the Confederation, then going into zero-tau to wait for a rescue ship?"

"If their technology can last that long, then I guess their civilization can, too."

"No, our hardware can last for a long time. It's our culture that's fragile, at least compared to theirs. I don't think the Confederation will last a thousand years."

"The Edenists will be here, I expect. So will all the planets, physically if nothing else. Some of their societies will advance, possibly even to a state similar to the Kiint; some will revert to barbarism. But there will be somebody left to hear the message and help."

"You're a terrible optimist."

They arrived at the ninth deck, only to find the doorway was sealed over with composite.

"Odd," Roman datavised. "If there's no corridor or compartment beyond, why put a doorway here at all?"

"Because this was a change made after the accident."

"Could be. But why would they block off an interior section?"

"I've no idea. You want to keep going down?"

"Sure. I'm optimistic enough not to believe in ghosts lurking in the basement."

"I really wish you hadn't said that."

The tenth deck had been sealed off as well.

"My legs can take one more level," Wai datavised. "Then I'm going back."

There was a door on deck 11. It was the first one in the ship to be closed.

Wai stuck her fingers in the dimple, and the door dilated. She edged over cautiously, and swept the focus of her collar sensors around. "Holy shit. We'd better fetch Marcus."

Decks nine and ten had simply been removed to make the chamber. Standing on the floor and looking up, Marcus could actually see the outline of the stairwell doorways in the wall above him. By xenoc standards it was a cathedral. There was only one altar, right in the center. A doughnut of some dull metallic substance, eight meters in diameter with a central aperture five meters across; the air around it was emitting a faint violet glow. It stood on five sableblack arching buttresses, four meters tall.

"The positioning must be significant," Wai datavised. "They built it almost at the center of the wreck. They wanted to give it as much protection as possible."

"Agreed," Katherine replied. "They obviously considered it important. After a ship has suffered this much damage, you don't expend resources on anything other than critical survival requirements."

"Whatever it is," Schutz reported. "It's using up an awful lot of power." He was walking around it, keeping a respectful distance, wiping a sensor block over the floor as he went. "There's a power cable feeding each of those legs."

"Is it radiating in any spectrum?" Marcus asked.

"Only that light you can see, which spills over into ultraviolet, too. Apart from that, it's inert. But the energy must be going somewhere."

"Okay." Marcus walked up to a buttress, and switched his collar focus to scan the aperture. It was veiled by a gray haze, as if a sheet of fog had solidified across it. When he took another tentative step forward the fluid in his semicircular canals was suddenly affected by a very strange tidal force. His foot began to slip forwards and upwards. He threw himself backwards, and almost stumbled. Jorge and Karl just caught him in time.

"There's no artificial gravity underneath it," he datavised. "But there's some kind of gravity field wrapped around it." He paused. "No, that's not right. It pushed me."

"Pushed?" Katherine hurried to his side. "Are you sure?"

"Yes."

"My God."

"What? Do you know what it is?"

"Possibly. Schutz, hang on to my arm, please."

The cosmonik came forward and took her left arm. Katherine edged forward until she was almost under the lambent doughnut. She stretched up her right arm, holding out a sensor block, and tried to press it against the doughnut. It was as if she was trying to make two identical magnetic poles touch. The block couldn't get to within 20 centimeters of the surface; it kept slithering and sliding through the air. She held it as steady as she could, and datavised it to run an analysis of the doughnut's molecular structure.

The results made her back away.

"So?" Marcus asked.

"I'm not entirely sure it's solid in any reference frame we understand. That surface could just be a boundary effect. There's no spectroscopic data at all; the sensor couldn't even detect an atomic structure in there, let alone valency bonds."

"You mean it's a ring of energy?"

"Don't hold me to it, but I think that thing could be some kind of exotic matter."

"Exotic in what sense, exactly?" Jorge asked.

"It has a negative energy density. And before you ask, that doesn't mean antigravity. Exotic matter only has one known use, to keep a wormhole open."

"Jesus, that's a wormhole portal?" Marcus asked.

"It must be."

"Any way of telling where it leads?"

"I can't give you an exact stellar coordinate; but I know where the other end has to emerge. The xenocs never called for a rescue ship, Marcus. They threaded a wormhole with exotic matter to stop it collapsing, and escaped down it. That is the entrance to a tunnel which leads right back to their homeworld."

Schutz found Marcus in the passenger lounge in capsule C. He was floating centimeters above one of the flatchairs, with the lights down low.

The cosmonik touched his heels to a stikpad on the decking beside the lower hatch. "You really don't like being wrong, do you?"

"No, but I'm not sulking about it, either." Marcus molded a jaded grin. "I still think I'm right about the dish, but I don't know how the hell to prove it."

"The wormhole portal is rather conclusive evidence."

"Very tactful. It doesn't solve anything, actually. If they could open a wormhole straight back home, why did they build the dish? Like Katherine said, if you have an accident of that magnitude then you devote yourself completely to survival. Either they called for help, or they went home through the wormhole. They wouldn't do both."

"Possibly it wasn't their dish, they were just here to investigate it."

"Two ancient unknown xenoc races with FTL starship technology is pushing credibility. It also takes us back to the original problem: if the dish isn't a distress beacon, then what the hell was it built for?"

"I'm sure there will be an answer at some time."

"I know, we're only a commercial trader's crew, with a very limited research capability. But we can still ask fundamental questions, like why have they kept the wormhole open for 13,000 years?"

"Because that's the way their technology works. They probably wouldn't consider it odd."

"I'm not saying it shouldn't work for that long, I'm asking why their homeworld would bother maintaining a link to a chunk of derelict wreckage?"

"That is harder for logic to explain. The answer must lie in their psychology."

"That's a cop out; you can't simply cry alien at everything you don't understand. But it does bring us to my final query, if you can open a wormhole with such accuracy across God knows how many light-years, why would you need a starship in the first place? What sort of psychology accounts for that?"

"All right, Marcus, you got me. Why?"

"I haven't got a clue. I've been reviewing all the file texts we have on wormholes, trying to find a solution which pulls all this together. And I can't do it. It's a complete paradox."

"There's only one thing left then, isn't there?"

Marcus turned to look at the hulking figure of the cosmonik. "What?"

"Go down the wormhole and ask them."

"Yeah, maybe I will. Somebody has to go eventually. What does our dear Katherine have to say on that subject? Can we go inside it in our S11 suits?"

"She's rigging up some sensors that she can shove through the interface. That gray sheet isn't a physical barrier. She's already pushed a length of conduit tubing through. It's some kind of pressure membrane, apparently, stops the ship's atmosphere from flooding into the wormhole."

"Another billion-fuseodollar gadget. Jesus, this is getting too big for us, we're going to have to prioritize." He datavised the flight computer, and issued a general order for everyone to assemble in capsule A's main lounge.

Karl was the last to arrive. The young systems engineer looked exhausted. He frowned when he caught sight of Marcus.

"I thought you were over in the xenoc ship."

"No."

"But you . . ." He rubbed his fingers against his temples. "Skip it."

"Any progress?" Marcus asked.

"A little. From what I can make out, the molecular synthesizer and its governing circuitry are combined within the same crystal lattice. To give you a biological analogy, it's as though a muscle is also a brain."

"Don't follow that one through too far," Roman called.

Karl didn't even smile. He took a chocolate sac from the dispenser, and sucked on the nipple.

"Katherine?" Marcus said.

"I've managed to place a visual-spectrum sensor in the wormhole. There's not much light in there, only what soaks through the pressure membrane. From what we can see it's a straight tunnel. I assume the xenocs cut off the artificial gravity under the portal so they could egress it easily. What I'd like to do next is dismount a laser radar from the MSV and use that."

"If the wormhole's threaded with exotic matter, will you get a return from it?"

"Probably not. But we should get a return from whatever is at the other end."

"What's the point?"

Three of them began to talk at once, Katherine loudest of all. Marcus held his hand up for silence. "Listen, everybody, according to Confederation law if the appointed commander or designated controlling mechanism of a spaceship or free-flying space structure discontinues that control for one year and a day then any ownership title becomes null and void. Legally, this xenoc ship is an abandoned structure which we are entitled to file a salvage claim on."

"There is a controlling network," Karl said.

"It's a sub-system," Marcus said. "The law is very clear on that point. If a starship's flight computer fails, but, say, the fusion generators keep working, their governing processors do not constitute the designated controlling mechanism. Nobody will be able to challenge our claim."

"The xenocs might," Wai said.

"Let's not make extra problems for ourselves. As the situation stands right now, we have title. We can't not claim the ship because the xenocs may return at some time."

Katherine rocked her head in understanding. "If we start examining the wormhole they might come back, sooner rather than later. Is that what you're worried about?"

"It's a consideration, yes. Personally, I'd rather like to meet them. But, Katherine, are you really going to learn how to build exotic matter and open a wormhole with the kind of sensor blocks we've got?"

"You know I'm not, Marcus."

"Right. Nor are we going to find the principle behind the artificial gravity generator, or any of the other miracles on board. What we have to do is catalogue as much as we can, and identify the areas that need researching. Once we've done that we can bring back the appropriate specialists, pay them a huge salary, and let them get on with it. Don't any of you understand yet? When we found this ship, we stopped being starship crew, and turned into the highest-flying corporate executives in the galaxy. We don't pioneer any more, we designate. So, we map out the last remaining decks. We track the power cables and note what they power. Then we leave."

"I know I can crack their program language, Marcus," Karl said. "I can get us into the command network."

Marcus smiled at the weary pride in his voice. "Nobody is going to be more pleased about that than me, Karl. One thing I do intend to take with us is a cybermouse, preferably more than one. That molecular synthesizer is the hard evidence we need to convince the banks of what we've got."

Karl blushed. "Uh, Marcus, I don't know what'll happen if we try and cut one out of the composite. So far we've been left alone; but if the network thinks we're endangering the ship. Well . . ."

"I'd like to think we're capable of something more sophisticated than ripping a cybermouse out of the composite. Hopefully, you'll be able to access the network, and we can simply ask it to replicate a molecular synthesizer unit for us. They have to be manufactured somewhere on board."

"Yeah, I suppose they do. Unless the cybermice duplicate themselves."

"Now that'd be a sight," Roman said happily. "One of them humping away on top of the other."

His neural nanonics time function told Karl he'd slept for nine hours. After he wriggled out of his sleep pouch he airswam into the crew lounge and helped himself to a pile of food sachets from the galley. There wasn't much activity in the ship, so he didn't even bother to access the flight computer until he'd almost finished eating.

Katherine was on watch when he dived into the bridge through the floor hatch.

"Who's here?" he asked breathlessly. "Who else is on board right now?"

"Just Roman. The rest of them are all over on the wreck. Why?"

"Shit."

"Why, what's the matter?"

"Have you accessed the flight computer?"

"I'm on watch, of course I'm accessing."

"No, not the ship's functions. The satellite analysis network Victoria set up."

Her flat features twisted into a surprised grin. "You mean they've found some gold?"

"No way. The network was reporting that satellite seven had located a target deposit three hours ago. When I accessed the network direct to follow it up I found out what the search parameters really are. They're not looking for gold, those bastards are here to get pitchblende."

"Pitchblende?" Katherine had to run a search program through her neural nanonics encyclopedia to find out what it was. "Oh Christ, uranium. They want uranium."

"Exactly. You could never mine it from a planet without the local government knowing; that kind of operation would be easily spotted by the observation satellites. Asteroids don't have deposits of pitchblende. But planetoids do, and out here nobody is going to know that they're scooping it up."

"I knew it! I bloody knew that fable about gold mountains was a load of balls."

"They must be terrorists, or Sonora independence freaks, or black syndicate members. We have to warn the others, we can't let them back on board *Lady Mac.*"

"Wait a minute, Karl. Yes, they're shits, but if we leave them over on the wreck they'll die. Even if you're prepared to do that, it's the captain's decision."

"No, it isn't, not any more. If they come back then neither you, me, nor the captain is going to be in any position to make decisions about anything. They knew we'd find out about the pitchblende eventually when *Lady Mac* rendezvoused with the ore particle. They knew we wouldn't take it on board voluntarily. That means they came fully prepared to force us. They've got guns, or weapons implants. Jorge is exactly what I said he was, a mercenary killer. We can't let them back on the ship, Katherine. We can't."

"Oh Christ." She was gripping the side of her acceleration couch in reflex. Command decision. And it was all hers.

"Can we datavise the captain?" he asked.

"I don't know. We've got relay blocks in the stairwells now the cybermice have been deactivated, but they're not very reliable; the structure plays hell with our signals."

"Who's he with?"

"He was partnering Victoria. Wai and Schutz are together; Antonio and Jorge made up the last team."

"Datavise Wai and Schutz, get them out first. Then try for the captain."

"Okay. Get Roman, and go down to the airlock chamber; I'll authorize the weapons cabinet to release some maser carbines . . . Shit!"

"What?"

"I can't. Marcus has the flight computer command codes. We can't even fire the thrusters without him."

Deck 14 appeared no different to any other as Marcus and Victoria wandered through it. The corridors were broad, and there were few doorways.

"About 60 per cent is sealed off," Marcus datavised. "This must be a major engineering level."

"Yeah. There's so many cables around here I'm having trouble cataloguing the grid." She was wiping a magnetic sensor block slowly from side to side as they walked.

His communication block reported it was receiving an encrypted signal from the *Lady Mac*. Sheer surprise made him halt. He retrieved the appropriate code file from a neural nanonics memory cell.

"Captain?"

"What's the problem, Katherine?"

"You've got to get back to the ship. Now, Captain, and make sure Victoria doesn't come with you."

"Why?"

"Captain, this is Karl. The array satellites are looking for pitchblende, not gold or platinum. Antonio's people are terrorists, they want to build fission bombs."

Marcus focused his collar sensors on Victoria, who was waiting a couple of meters down the corridor. "Where's Schutz and Wai?"

"On their way back," Katherine datavised. "They should be here in another five minutes."

"Okay, it's going to take me at least half an hour to get back." He didn't like to think about climbing 14 flights of stairs fast, not in this gravity. "Start prepping the ship."

"Captain, Karl thinks they're probably armed."

Marcus's communication block reported another signal coming on line.

"Karl is quite right," Jorge datavised. "We are indeed armed; and we also have excellent processor blocks and decryption programs. Really, Captain, this code of yours is at least three years out of date."

Marcus saw Victoria turn towards him. "Care to comment on the pitchblende?" he asked.

"I admit, the material would have been of some considerable use to us," Jorge replied. "But of course, this wreck has changed the Confederation beyond recognition, has it not, Captain?"

"Possibly."

"Definitely. And so we no longer require the pitchblende."

"That's a very drastic switch of allegiance."

"Please, Captain, do not be facetious. The satellites were left on purely for your benefit; we didn't wish to alarm you."

"Thank you for your consideration."

"Captain," Katherine datavised. "Schutz and Wai are in the airlock."

"I do hope you're not proposing to leave without us," Jorge datavised. "That would be most unwise."

"You were going to kill us," Karl datavised.

"That is a hysterical claim. You would not have been hurt."

"As long as we obeyed, and helped you slaughter thousands of people."

Marcus wished Karl would stop being quite so blunt. He had few enough options as it was.

"Come now, Captain," Jorge said. "The *Lady Macbeth* is combat-capable; are you telling me you have never killed people in political disputes?"

"We've fought. But only against other ships."

"Don't try and claim the moral high ground, Captain. War is war, no matter how it is fought."

"Only when it's between soldiers; anything else is terrorism."

"I assure you, we have put our old allegiance behind us. I ask you to do the same. This quarrel is foolish in the extreme. We both have so much to gain."

And you're armed, Marcus filled in silently. Jorge and Antonio were supposed to be inspecting decks 12 and 13. It would be tough if not impossible getting back to the airlock before them. But I can't trust them on *Lady Mac*.

"Captain, they're moving," Katherine datavised. "The communication block in stairwell three has acquired them, strength one. They must be coming up."

"Victoria," Jorge datavised. "Restrain the captain and bring him to the airlock. I advise all of you on the ship to remain calm, we can still find a peaceful solution to this situation."

Unarmed combat programs went primary in Marcus's neural nanonics. The black, featureless figure opposite him didn't move.

"Your call," he datavised. According to his tactical analysis program she had few choices. Jorge's order implied she was armed, though a scan of her utility belt didn't reveal anything obvious other than a standard fission blade. If she went for a gun he would have an attack window. If she didn't, then he could probably stay ahead of her. She was a lot younger, but his geneered physique should be able to match her in this gravity field.

Victoria dropped the sensor block she was carrying, and moved her hand to her belt. She grabbed the multipurpose power tool and started to bring it up.

Marcus slammed into her, using his greater mass to throw her off balance. She was hampered by trying to keep her grip on the tool. His impact made her sway sideways, then the fierce xenoc gravity took over. She toppled helplessly, falling *fast*. The power tool was swinging around to point at him. Marcus kicked her hand, and the unit skittered away. It didn't slide far, the gravity saw to that.

Victoria landed with a terrible thud. Her neural nanonics medical monitor program flashed up an alert that the impact had broken her collar bone. Axon blocks came on line, muting all but the briefest pulse of pain. It was her program again which made her twist around to avoid any follow-on blow; her conscious mind was almost unaware of the fact she was still moving. A hand scrabbled for the power tool. She snatched it and sat up. Marcus was disappearing down a side corridor. She fired at him before the targeting program even gave her an overlay grid.

"Jorge," she datavised. "I've lost him."

"Then get after him."

Marcus's collar sensors showed him a spray of incendiary droplets fizzing out of the wall barely a meter behind him. The multipurpose tool must be some kind of laser pistol. "Katherine," he datavised. "Retract *Lady Mac*'s airlock tube. Now. Close the outer hatch and codelock it. They are not to come on board."

"Acknowledged. How do we get you back?"

"Yes, Captain," Jorge datavised. "Do tell."

Marcus dodged down a junction. "Have Wai stand by. When I need her, I'll need her fast."

"You think you can cut your way out of the shell, Captain? You have a fission blade, and that shell is held together by a molecular bonding generator."

"You touch him, shithead, and we'll fry that wreck," Karl datavised. "*Lady Mac*'s got maser cannons."

"But do you have the command codes, I wonder. Captain?"

"Communication silence," Marcus ordered. "When I want you, I'll call."

Jorge's boosted muscles allowed him to ascend stairwell three at a speed which Antonio could never match. He was soon left struggling along behind. The airlock was the tactical high ground; once he had secured that, Jorge knew he'd won. As he climbed his hands moved automatically, assembling the weapon from various innocuous-looking pieces of equipment he was carrying on his utility belt.

"Victoria?" he datavised. "Have you got him?"

"No. He broke my shoulder, the bastard. I've lost him."

"Go to the nearest stairwell, I expect that's what he's done. Antonio, go back and meet her. Then start searching for him."

"Is that a joke?" Antonio asked. "He could be anywhere."

"No, he's not. He has to come up. Up is where the airlock is."

"Yes, but—"

"Don't argue. And when you find him, don't kill him. We have to have him alive. He's our ticket out. Our only ticket, understand?"

"Yes, Jorge."

When he reached the airlock, Jorge closed the inner hatch and cycled the chamber. The outer hatch dilated to show him the *Lady Macbeth*'s fuselage 15 meters away. Her airlock tube had retracted, and the fuselage shield was in place.

"This is a no-win stand-off," he datavised. "Captain, please come up to the airlock. You have to deal with me, you have no choice. The three of us will leave our weapons over here, and then we can all go back on board together. And when we return to a port none of us will mention this unfortunate incident again. That is reasonable, surely?"

Schutz had just reached the bridge when they received Jorge's datavise.

"Damn! He's disconnected our cable from the communication block," Karl said. "We can't call the captain now even if we wanted to."

Schutz rolled in mid air above his acceleration couch and landed gently on the cushioning. Restraint webbing slithered over him.

"What the hell do we do now?" Roman asked. "Without the command codes we're bloody helpless."

"It wouldn't take that long for us to break open the weapons cabinet," Schutz said. "They haven't got the captain. We can go over there and hunt them down with the carbines."

"I can't sanction that," Katherine said. "God knows what sort of weapons they have."

"Sanction it? We put it to the vote."

"It's my duty watch. Nobody votes on anything. The last order the captain gave us was to wait. We wait." She datavised the flight computer for a channel to the MSV. Wai, status please?"

"Powering up. I'll be ready for a flight in two minutes."

"Thank you."

"We have to do something!" Karl said.

"For a start you can calm down," Katherine told him. "We're not going to help Marcus by doing anything rash. He obviously had something in mind when he told Wai to get ready."

The hatchway to the captain's cabin slid open. Marcus air-swam out and grinned around at their stupefied expressions. "Actually, I didn't have any idea what to do when I said that. I was stalling."

"How the hell did you get back on board?" Roman yelped.

Marcus looked at Katherine and gave her a lopsided smile. "By being right, I'm afraid. The dish is a distress beacon."

"So what?" she whispered numbly.

He drifted over to his acceleration couch and activated the webbing. "It means the wormhole doesn't go back to the xenoc homeworld."

"You found out how to use it!" Karl exclaimed. "You opened its other end inside the *Lady Mac*."

"No. There is no other end. Yes, they built it as part of their survival operation. It was their escape route, you were right about that. But it doesn't go somewhere; it goes some*when*."

Instinct had brought Marcus to the portal chamber. It was as good as any other part of the ship. Besides, the xenocs had escaped their predicament from here. In a remote part of his mind he assumed that ending up on their homeworld was preferable to capture here by Jorge. It wasn't the kind of choice he wanted to make.

He walked slowly around the portal. The pale violet emanation in the air around it remained constant, hazing the dull surface from perfect observation. That and a faint hum were the only evidence of the massive quantity of power it consumed. Its eternal stability a mocking enigma.

Despite all the logic of argument he knew Katherine was wrong. Why build the dish if you had this ability? And why keep it operational?

That factor must have been important to them. It had been built in the center of the ship, and built to last. They'd even reconfigured the wreck to ensure it lasted. Fine, they needed reliability, and they were masters of material science. But a one-off piece of emergency equipment lasting 13,000 years? There must be a reason, and the only logical one was that they knew they would need it to remain functional so they could come back one day.

The SII suit prevented him from smiling as realization dawned. But it did reveal a shiver ripple along his limbs as the cold wonder of the knowledge struck home.

• • •

On the *Lady Mac*'s bridge, Marcus said: "We originally assumed that the xenocs would just go into zero-tau and wait for a rescue ship; because that's what we would do. But their technology allows them to take a much different approach to engineering problems."

"The wormhole leads into the future," Roman said in astonishment.

"Almost. It doesn't lead anywhere but back to itself, so the length inside it represents time not space. As long as the portal exists you can travel through it. The xenocs went in just after they built the dish and came out again when their rescue ship arrived. That's why they built the portal to survive so long. It had to carry them through a great deal of time."

"How does that help you get here?" Katherine asked. "You're trapped over in the xenoc wreckage right now, not in the past."

"The wormhole exists as long as the portal does. It's an open tube to every second of that entire period of existence; you're not restricted which way you travel through it."

In the portal chamber Marcus approached one of the curving black buttress legs. The artificial gravity was off directly underneath the doughnut so the xenocs could rise into it. But they had been intent on traveling into the future.

He started to climb the buttress. The first section was the steepest; he had to clamp his hands behind it, and haul himself up. Not easy in that gravity field. It gradually curved over, flattening out at the top, leaving him standing above the doughnut. He balanced there precariously, very aware of the potentially lethal fall down onto the floor.

The doughnut didn't look any different from this position, a glowing ring surrounding the gray pressure membrane. Marcus put one foot over the edge of the exotic matter, and jumped.

He fell clean through the pressure membrane. There was no gravity field in the wormhole, although every movement suddenly became very sluggish. To his waving limbs it felt as if he was immersed in some kind of fluid, though his sensor block reported a perfect vacuum.

The wormhole wall was insubstantial, difficult to see in the meager backscatter of light from the pressure membrane. Five narrow lines of yellow light materialized, spaced equidistantly around the wall. They stretched from the rim of the pressure membrane up to a vanishing point some indefinable distance away.

Nothing else happened. Marcus drifted until he reached the wall, which his hand adhered to as though the entire surface was one giant stikpad. He crawled his way back to the pressure membrane. When he stuck his hand through, there was no resistance. He pushed his head out.

There was no visible difference to the chamber outside. He datavised his communication block to search for a signal. It told him there was only the band from one of the relay blocks in the stairwells. No time had passed.

He withdrew back into the wormhole. Surely the xenocs hadn't expected to crawl along the entire length? In any case, the other end would be 13,000 years ago. Marcus retrieved the xenoc activation code from his neural nanonics, and datavised it.

The lines of light turned blue.

He quickly datavised the deactivation code, and the lines reverted to yellow. This time when he emerged out into the portal chamber there was no signal at all.

"That was ten hours ago," Marcus told his crew. "I climbed out and walked back to the ship. I passed you on the way, Karl."

"Holy shit," Roman muttered. "A time machine."

"How long was the wormhole active for?" Katherine asked.

"A couple of seconds, that's all."

"Ten hours in two seconds." She paused, loading sums into her neural nanonics. "That's a year in 30 minutes. Actually, that's not so fast. Not if they were intending to travel a couple of thousand years into the future."

"You're complaining about it?" Roman asked.

"Maybe it speeds up the further you go through it," Schutz suggested. "Or more likely we need the correct access codes to vary its speed."

"Whatever," Marcus said. He datavised the flight computer and blew the tether bolts which were holding *Lady Mac* to the wreckage. "I want flight-readiness status, people, please."

"What about Jorge and the others?" Karl asked.

"They only come back on board under our terms," Marcus said. "No weapons, and they go straight into zero-tau. We can hand them over to Tranquillity's serjeants as soon as we get home." Purple course vectors were rising into his mind. He fired the maneuvering thrusters, easing *Lady Mac* clear of the xenoc shell.

Jorge saw the sparkle of bright dust as the explosive bolts fired. He scanned his sensor collar around until he found the tethers, narrow gray serpents flexing against the speckled backdrop of drab orange particles. It didn't bother him unduly. Then the small thrusters ringing the starship's equator fired, pouring out translucent amber plumes of gas.

"Katherine, what do you think you're doing?" he datavised.

"Following my orders," Marcus replied. "She's helping to prep the ship for a jump. Is that a problem for you?"

Jorge watched the starship receding, an absurdly stately movement for an artifact that big. His respirator tube seemed to have stopped supplying fresh oxygen, paralyzing every muscle. "Calvert. How?" he managed to datavise.

"I might tell you some time. Right now, there are a lot of conditions you have to agree to before I allow you back on board."

Pure fury at being so completely outmaneuvered by Calvert made him reach automatically for his weapon. "You will come back now," he datavised.

"You're not in any position to dictate terms."

Lady Macbeth was a good 200 meters away. Jorge lined the stubby barrel up on the rear of the starship. A green targeting grid flipped up over the image, and he zeroed on the nozzle of a fusion drive tube. He datavised the X-ray laser to fire. Pale white vapor spewed out of the nozzle.

"Depressurization in fusion drive three," Roman shouted.

"The lower deflector coil casing is breached. He shot us, Marcus, Jesus Christ, he shot us with an X-ray."

"What the hell kind of weapon has he got back there?" Karl demanded.

"Whatever it is, he can't have the power capacity for many more shots," Schutz said.

"Give me fire control for the maser cannons," Roman said. "I'll blast the little shit."

"Marcus!" Katherine cried. "He just hit a patterning node. Stop him."

Neuroiconic displays zipped through Marcus's mind. Ship's systems coming on line as they shifted over to full operational status, each with its own schematic. He knew just about every performance parameter by heart. Combat sensor clusters were already sliding out of their recesses. Maser cannons powering up. It would be another seven seconds before they could be aimed and fired.

There was one system with a faster response time.

"Hang on," he yelled.

Designed for combat avoidance maneuvers, the fusion drive tubes exploded into life two seconds after he triggered their ignition sequence. Twin spears of solar-bright plasma transfixed the xenoc shell, burning through deck after deck. They didn't even strike anywhere near the airlock which Jorge was cloistered in. They didn't have to. At that range, their infrared emission alone was enough to break down his SII suit's integrity.

Superenergized ions hammered into the wreck, smashing the internal structure apart, heating the atmosphere to an intolerable pressure. Xenoc machinery detonated in tremendous energy bursts all through the structure, the units expending themselves in spherical clouds of solid light which clashed and merged into a single wavefront of destruction. The giant rock particle lurched wildly from the explosion. Drenched in a cascade of hard radiation and subatomic particles, the unicorn tower at the center of the dish snapped off at its base to tumble away into the darkness.

Then the process seemed to reverse. The spume of light blossoming from the cliff curved in on itself, growing in brightness as it was compressed back to its point of origin.

Lady Mac's crew were straining under the five-gee acceleration of the starship's flight. The inertial guidance systems started to flash priority warnings into Marcus's neural nanonics.

"We're going back," he datavised. Five gees made talking too difficult. "Jesus, five gees and it's still pulling us in." The external sensor suite showed him the contracting fireball, its luminosity surging towards violet. Large sections of the cliff were flaking free and plummeting into the conflagration. Fissures like black lightning bolts split open right across the rock.

He ordered the flight computer to power up the nodes and retract the last sensor clusters.

"Marcus, we can't jump," Katherine datavised, her face pummelled into frantic creases by the acceleration. "It's a gravitonic emission. Don't."

"Have some faith in the old girl." He initiated the jump.

An event horizon eclipsed the *Lady Macbeth*'s fuselage.

Behind her, the wormhole at the heart of the newborn micro-star gradually collapsed, pulling in its gravitational field as it went. Soon there was nothing left but an expanding cloud of dark snowdust embers.

They were three jumps away from Tranquillity when Katherine ventured into Marcus's cabin. *Lady Mac* was accelerating at a tenth of a gee towards her next jump coordinate, holding him lightly in one of the large blackfoam sculpture chairs. It was the first time she'd ever really noticed his age.

"I came to say sorry," she said. "I shouldn't have doubted."

He waved limply. "*Lady Mac* was built for combat, her nodes are powerful enough to jump us out of some gravity fields. Not that I had a lot of choice. Still, we only reduced three nodes to slag, plus the one dear old Jorge damaged."

"She's a hell of ship, and you're the perfect captain for her. I'll keep flying with you, Marcus."

"Thanks. But I'm not sure what I'm going to do after we dock. Replacing three nodes will cost a fortune. I'll be in debt to the banks again."

She pointed at the row of transparent bubbles which all held identical antique electronic circuit boards. "You can always sell some more Apollo command module guidance computers."

"I think that scam's just about run its course. Don't worry, when we get back to Tranquillity I know a captain who'll buy them from me. At least that way I'll be able to settle the flight pay I owe all of you."

"For Heaven's sake, Marcus, the whole astronautics industry is in debt to the banks. I swear I never could understand the economics behind starflight."

He closed his eyes, a wry smile quirking his lips. "We very nearly solved human economics for good, didn't we?"

"Yeah. Very nearly."

"The wormhole would have let me change the past. Their technology was going to change the future. We could have rebuilt our entire history."

"I don't think that's a very good idea. What about the grandfather paradox for a start? How come you didn't warn us about Jorge as soon as you emerged from the wormhole?"

"Scared, I guess. I don't know nearly enough about quantum temporal displacement theory to start risking paradoxes. I'm not even sure I'm the Marcus Calvert that brought this particular *Lady Macbeth* to the xenoc wreck. Suppose you really can't travel between times, only parallel realities? That would mean I didn't escape into the past, I just shifted sideways."

"You look and sound pretty familiar to me."

"So do you. But is my crew still stuck back at their version of the wreck waiting for me to deal with Jorge?"

"Stop it," she said softly. "You're Marcus Calvert, and you're back where you belong, flying *Lady Mac.*"

"Yeah, sure."

"The xenocs wouldn't have built the wormhole unless they were sure it would help them get home, their true home. They were smart people."

"And no mistake."

"I wonder where they did come from?"

"We'll never know, now." Marcus lifted his head, some of the old humor emerging through his melancholia. "But I hope they got back safe."

Mary Rosenblum

THE EYE OF GOD

One of the most popular and prolific of the new writers of the nineties, Mary Rosenblum made her first sale, to *Asimov's Science Fiction,* in 1990, and has since become a mainstay of that magazine, and one of its most frequent contributors, with more than twenty-five sales there to her credit. She has also sold to *The Magazine of Fantasy & Science Fiction, Science Fiction Age, Pulphouse, New Legends,* and elsewhere.

Rosenblum has produced some of the most colorful, exciting, and emotionally powerful stories of the nineties, earning her a large and devoted following of readers. Her linked series of "Drylands" stories have proved to be one of *Asimov's* most popular series, but she has also published memorable stories such as "The Stone Garden," "Synthesis," "Flight," "California Dreamer," "Casting at Pegasus," "Entrada," "Rat," "The Centaur Garden," and many, many others. Her novella "Gas Fish" won the *Asimov's* Readers Award Poll in 1996, and was a finalist for that year's Nebula Award. Her first novel, *The Drylands,* appeared in 1993 to wide critical acclaim, winning the prestigious Compton Crook Award for Best First Novel of the year; it was followed in short order by her second novel, *Chimera,* and her third, *The Stone Garden.* Her most recent book was her first short-story collection, *Synthesis and Other Stories,* widely hailed by critics as one of the best collections of 1996. She recently sold a trilogy of mystery novels under a pseudonym, and has just finished the first book in the series, *The Devil's Trumpet.*

Most of Rosenblum's work has a strong adventure element, but only recently has she started taking us away from future Earths of one sort or another and out among the stars, in stories such as "Gas Fish" and the exciting and exotic adventure that follows, "The Eye of God." In it she takes us to a remote and hostile planet where human and alien antagonists must fight a battle of wits and will and nerve with the lives of the contestants literally hanging by a thread (over a thousand-foot drop!), with the destiny of the human race and the redemption of an individual's soul at stake. . . .

Rosenblum is another young and prolific writer who works very hard and with great discipline, and if she doesn't vanish into the mystery world completely to become the new Agatha Christie, it will be very interesting to see what directions she moves in and what she produces in the years to come; whatever it is, I'm sure it will be as vivid and compulsively readable as the rest of her work has been. A graduate of Clarion West, Mary Rosenblum lives with her family in Portland, Oregon.

The coral-reeds' agitation alerted her. Etienne came out onto the porch of her cottage to watch three Rethe wade through the thick blue-green stems. From this distance, they could have been three tall women, as human as herself. The coral-reeds stirred at their passage, the anxious rasp of their stems like distant whispering—words at the bare edge of comprehension.

She had never expected to see Rethe here. Etienne swallowed, fighting back memories that she had banished years ago. For a moment she entertained the hope that this visit was a mistake, or some kind of minor bureaucratic ritual.

She knew better.

Abruptly, she turned on her heel, and went inside to make tea. The Rethe would drink tea. That much at least humanity knew about them.

Etienne filled the teapot and arranged fruit-flavored gels on a plate. She had bought them in the shabby squatter village that had grown up around the Gate. Vat-grown in someone's back yard as masses of amorphous cells, the orange and ruby cubes bore no resemblance to apricot or cherries except taste. The plants on this world—or sessile animals that photosynthesized—did not bear fruit. She missed apples the most—crisp and tart after a frost. Vilya had bought her a miniature apple tree in a pot. For their balcony. It was a winesap—a true genetic antique. She had never gone back for it.

Etienne realized that she was arranging and rearranging the gels on their plate, and took her hand away. Outside, the reeds rustled softly. The squatters ate them—cracked their silicaceous stems and sucked out the flesh inside. They turned your urine orange, but they didn't make you sick.

She had never eaten one. Sometimes Etienne entertained the fantasy that that was the reason for the whispering meadow of the creatures that had formed around her cottage. Anthropomorphism, she thought. A seductive danger, in her profession as interpreter of aliens.

Her former profession.

Angry at herself for this lapse into yesterday, Etienne picked up the tray of tea, gels, and utensils. The Rethe were waiting for her on the shaded porch. Politely. Patiently. They nodded in unison as she came through the door, and Etienne froze. Memory was optional. Life went on for a long time, and yesterdays gathered like dust in the cramped vault of the human skull. You could go to a reputable body shop and have a well-trained tech in sterile greens sweep it all away. Or, for more money, you could have them sweep out only selected bits. Memory could be tucked, tightened, and tailored, as easily as any other part of the body.

She had never chosen to excise Vilya from her memory. Etienne set the tray down on the small table so hard that tea slopped over beneath the pot's lid. Staring at the smallest of the Rethe—the one who stood at the rear, right on the boundary between shade and searing sun—Etienne wished suddenly that she had done so.

First real contact with an alien species, the Rethe disturbed humanity. Not because they were creepy nightmares or incomprehensible monsters. That might have been easier to take. But they looked utterly human. And utterly female, although each individual possessed three X and three Y chromosomes. Gender was one of the many things about themselves that the Rethe refused to discuss. All humans and Rethe were referred to as "it" in translated conversation.

The small Rethe whose wide face was slashed by sun and shadow looked utterly like Vilya.

Etienne looked down at the amber puddle soaking into the napkins she had laid out on the tray. "Would you care for tea?"

The oldest of the Rethe—at least her . . . his? . . . face looked oldest—extended a hand, palm up. A small iridescent vial lay on her . . . his? . . . palm.

She, Etienne decided as she scowled at the vial. They were all *she*, and to hell with their chromosomal makeup. The vial contained a fungus that would infiltrate her ear canal, growing mycocelia through her skull within minutes to interface directly with her brain. A translator, it was a bit of Rethe bio-tech, and as yet incomprehensible. But necessary. Because the Rethe weren't about to share their language, or waste their time learning humanity's dialects. The Rethe was waiting silently, *her* eyes on Etienne's face, smiling.

Impatient behind that smile. "No need." Etienne arched an eyebrow. "I was infected nearly two decades ago. As you must surely know, if you checked me out at all."

The eldest Rethe bowed, still smiling. Dropped the vial into a pocket in her loose robe. "I hope you will pardon our intrusion."

"You're pardoned." Etienne began to fill mugs. "So why are you here?"

"Retirement from public service must provide many benefits." The Rethe lifted her steaming mug in a small salute. "Not the least of which is the privilege to be rude."

"I didn't retire. I quit. Yes, I'm rude." Etienne sat down in the only chair and smiled up at the Rethe. Waiting.

For several minutes the Rethe sipped their tea, their expressions relaxed and appreciative, as if they had come all this way in the hot sun to savor her cheap tea, bought from the squatters. But their impatience hummed in the air and made the nearest coral-reeds shiver.

At last, the eldest Rethe sank gracefully to the fabbed-wood planks of the porch and folded her legs into lotus position. "I am Grik." She nodded at the two Rethe behind her. "Rnn and Zynth."

Zynth was the one who might have been Vilya's twin. Etienne turned her eyes away as that one sat down. The loose garments that the Rethe wore hinted at solid bone and sleek, thickly muscled bodies. Peasant body, Vilya used to say of her stocky form. Etienne clenched her teeth and made a show of arranging her caftan. "Since I am entitled to be rude, why *are* you here?"

"To hire you." Grik reached for a cherry gel. "It is a matter of rescue."

"I . . . am no longer a registered empath. As you obviously know. And I retired from Search and Rescue last year." Etienne offered the plate of gels to the other two Rethe. The one called Rynn declined with a smile and nod. Zynth gave her boss a quick apprehensive look and took an orange cube.

"And I'm not for hire in any case." Etienne put the plate down on the table with a decisive thump. The girl's diffident air annoyed her. "I'm sorry you wasted your time coming here."

Grik lifted her left hand, palm up, tilted it in a pouring gesture.

Etienne interpreted a shrug from the emotional context. As she reached for her mug of tea, she noticed that Zynth had closed her hand into a fist. Orange gel leaked between her white-knuckled fingers, and the reeds rustled at her anguish.

Basic emotion seemed to be such a universal language, Etienne thought bitterly. Pleasure, anger, pain, and fear. Reeds, and humans, and Rethe. Etienne looked at Grik, who was smiling gently.

"Your superior at the Interface Center referred us to you," she said. "It told us that you were the best empath it had worked with."

"That was long ago." It jolted her that he would remember. He had been angry when she had quit to work for Search and Rescue.

"It said that it was time someone reminded you." She shrugged. "I do not understand what it meant."

Anton. Colonel Xyrus Anton, chief of the Interface Team—the euphemism for the human negotiators with the aloof Rethe. Etienne looked out at the reeds bathing and feeding in the planet's young hot sun. *We need you,* he had yelled at her when she had turned in her resignation. *We need every edge we can get against the Rethe. We never really believed that we'd meet a species more advanced than us. Not in our gut. Look what it's doing to us. Our morale as a race is eroding all over the planet. This is a war, and we need to win.*

"I don't understand either," she murmured. "But it doesn't matter."

"One of your . . . creators of art became a friend to one of our people." Grik went on as if Etienne hadn't spoken. "Its sincerity was apparently impressive. So that one offered it access to a world we have not opened to your species."

"You haven't opened many worlds to us."

The Rethe did the pouring-gesture again. "The art-creator was lost there in a tragic accident."

"There are several registered empaths working for Search and Rescue." Etienne watched the Rethe narrowly. "Why *me*? We are back to that question."

"According to your datafile, you are a very intelligent human." Grik placed her hands palm up on her thighs, her eyes shifting very slightly toward the young Zynth. "Do I truly need to answer this question for you?"

Zynth sat with her head bowed, pale, her anguish an almost palpable mist. The reeds had inched away from her, leaving a semicircle of clear soil beyond her. Etienne knew suddenly who had invited the artist onto a forbidden world.

"You closely control the Gates—allow us onto only a few poor planets. Like this one. Only the culls for us humans, eh? And you won't transport extraction technology for us—in the name of environmental concern." Etienne turned back to Grik, teeth bared. "We accept that limitation because you awed us. And because we can't operate the Gates without you." She smiled. "If you go to a registered empath, the media will surely find out about this . . . art-creator. And interview him or her. The grass is always greener in someone else's pasture, and now you've let one of us through the fence. We're quite an envious bunch, and we don't stay awed very long." She grinned and reached for a cherry gel. "A species trait, I'm afraid. People will begin to clamor for admittance to these wonderful forbidden worlds and there will be friction. Since our treaty with you is up for renewal this year, friction could be . . . a problem. Thus, you come to an unregistered empath, hoping to keep the media out of it."

The Rethe turned her hands palm down. "We will pay you well," she said. "Ending a life—even accidentally—is no trivial matter to us."

Etienne stole a glance at Zynth. She was looking at Etienne now, fear and desperate hope like a violin note humming on the hot, dusty air. The reeds quivered to its song, and Etienne sighed. "I will not take any money," she said, and wondered how much she was going to regret this.

A synskin habitat had been anchored to a wide terrace cut into a cliff. Below, dark water lapped at the roots of worn ancient mountains. They were capped and streaked with a white deposit that looked more like guano than snow. But it wasn't the severely beautiful landscape that held Etienne's attention. It was the moon. Huge, bloated, haloed by a pink mist, it floated above the horizon. An irregular brown blotch in the center of the blue and white orb gave it the appearance of a giant, unwinking eye. Beautiful, she thought. Unforgiving. And she shivered, although her light thermal suit kept her warm enough. The habitat shivered too, straining against its anchors.

Behind her, invisible and undetectable to any human tech, lay a Rethe Gateway. Zynth had brought them through. A dozen steps could take Etienne back to summer heat and whispering coral-reeds. But only if Zynth escorted her. The bio-engineering of the Gates didn't work for humans.

This was humanity's humiliation. That the Rethe could walk across the galaxy unhindered and in moments. Human technology didn't so much lag behind—it was as extinct as the dinosaurs. And it left humanity obedient to the Rethe—for the price of the Gateways that the Rethe opened for them. Once, she had been one of the negotiators. They had staffed the Interface Team with empaths, hoping for an edge, a clue as to how the Rethe could be met as equals. It hadn't yet happened. With each renewed Treaty, humanity lost a little more ground, granted a few more concessions. Eventually, they'll own us, Etienne thought cynically. For the price of a few mediocre planets.

Vilya had been fascinated by the Rethe. She had understood them far better than Etienne ever would.

A sudden gust of wind shoved Etienne so that she staggered. That invisible doorway behind her seemed less than real beneath the inhuman scrutiny of that planetary eye. I do not want to be here, she thought.

"The Eye of God." Zynth's voice was clear and high.

She would sing mezzo. Like Vilya. "I wish it would close." Etienne tensed as Zynth laid a gentle hand on her arm. "Please don't touch me." She shook her off.

"Are you well?" Zynth's dark eyes were full of concern.

"Yes, yes, I'm fine." Etienne let her breath out in a rush. "Why couldn't we have come here at the beginning of the day?" She glowered at the girl, needing to be angry at her, because no emotion except anger was safe. "It's too dark to search. Why spend the night here?"

"I . . . am required to be here." Zynth's eyes evaded hers. "Until the artist is found. All life is sacred, and I permitted it to be put at risk. This is a place of truth. Beneath the Eye of God, I must face my failure. Can you understand?" She spread her fingers wide. "But I can open the Gateway for you. You may go back to your home and return in fifteen hours. It will be dawn then. I am thoughtless." She raised her face to the bloated moon. "There is no need for you to be here."

"I'll stay." Etienne turned her back on that unsettling orb, realizing that she had offered to stay because Zynth was afraid. "Who named that thing, anyway? I'd call it the Dead Eye, myself." Etienne stomped over to their habitat, ignoring Zynth's shocked silence. "Why don't you tell me how this person got lost—and where?" She knelt and shoved her way into the sphinctered opening. The transparent smart-plastic squeezed her body gently as she crawled through, blocking out the wind, but not the judgmental stare of the Eye. It's a *moon*, she told herself. A planetoid with weird coloring. But she couldn't deny her relief as she touched the light strip and warm yellow light subdued its glare. "We need to plan our search for the morning," she said as Zynth crawled through the sphincter after her.

As the Rethe began to take off her thermal suit, Etienne pulled a sleeping bag over against the wall and wrapped it around her. Like armor. The sculpted curves of Zynth's muscled arms and shoulders showed through her undershirt. It was warm in here. Thermal fibers were woven into the shell, and Etienne was sweating in her own suit. But she was damned if she'd strip, too.

"I will tell you," Zynth said in a low voice. "It is my shame." She flung herself onto her own bag with a grace so much like Vilya's that Etienne's throat closed.

"So I guessed," she managed, felt immediately guilty as Zynth flinched.

"I met him at our embassy in New Amsterdam." Propped on her elbows, she kept her eyes on the floor. "He had been hired to create several visual environments for the conference center there. The environments . . . moved me. We talked a lot. And one evening I told him about the Eye of Truth, and the song of this place. He . . . asked me to bring him here. The seeing mattered to his soul, so I did." She clenched one fist slowly. "I returned to find this camp empty. Duran was gone. I do not know. . . ."

"Shit!" Etienne slammed her fist down on the synskin floor.

Zynth's eyes widened. "I . . . I am sorry," she stammered, her cheeks flaming. "Grik said that you were . . . friends."

This was *Duran's* bloody camp! He had slept here, breathed the air in here. Etienne got abruptly to her feet, afraid she might catch his scent, some trace of his physical presence. I hope he fell over the damn cliff! she thought savagely. She lifted her head to face the bloated eye staring at her through the shuddering walls of the habitat. That's the truth, she told it silently.

"Etienne, please. I apologize." The anguish in Zynth's voice pierced her.

"Apologize?" Etienne laughed, winced at the cracked sound, and stared down at the kneeling Rethe. "What for?"

Tears streaked Zynth's face and she looked frightened. "For referring to its . . . status," she whispered. "He . . . it . . . told me that it had been the *giver* for a child. And I thought that because you were its friend, you must know." She bowed from the waist until her forehead rested on the floor at Etienne's feet. "I was wrong to be so familiar."

"Sit up. I knew *he* . . . fathered a child." Tight-lipped, Etienne turned away, met the Eye's stare. "I knew very well, thank you. You can call *him* he, or it, or whatever you want. It was his name that startled me. That's all."

"But he is a friend?" Zynth asked eagerly. "That will make it easier for you to find him, perhaps?"

The Eye's stare prodded her and Etienne licked her lips. "I didn't expect to run into him again," she said shortly. Not if she could help it anyway. Interesting that Grik hadn't mentioned his name, since she obviously knew of Etienne's connection to Duran. "So Duran talked you into bringing him here, and you got in trouble for it. That sounds like Duran. Always the opportunist."

"It wasn't . . . like that." Zynth stared at the floor between her knees, her face stricken.

Almost without volition, Etienne reached across the space between them to brush wisps of dark hair from her face. "I'm not angry at you." She let her breath out in a slow sigh. "Really."

"I should never have told it about . . . the Eye."

"Him." Etienne's lips were tight. "Say *him.*"

"Him." Head bowed, Zynth spoke so softly that Etienne could barely make out her words. "He . . . said that he would translate the Eye into sound and vision . . . so that you might know it, too. And . . . I could see the light of the Eye shining in his face as he spoke. So I . . . opened the door for him, even though it is forbidden. And then I came back for him and . . . he was no longer here." She raised her head at last, and her face was composed now. "He could not have passed the Gateway, so he must have fallen. I told Grik."

"Because the Eye was watching?"

"Because life is sacred." Zynth drew herself up straight, then hesitated. "And yes." She bowed her head. "Because the Eye watches."

Etienne sighed. "Will you be punished?"

"This *is* my punishment."

She was afraid. Fear was such a universal. Even the coral-reeds felt fear. "It's just a moon." Etienne put her arm around Zynth's shoulders. "Duran is careless." Careless enough to have cost Vilya her life. "If he fell, it's his own fault."

Zynth flinched at her tone. "I just . . . I have never been . . . in danger." She began to tremble. "That is one of the things I like most about your race. There are so *many* of you," she said in a nearly inaudible voice. "Is that why you can all walk down the street, have jobs, *do* things? It . . . he . . . Duran told me how he climbed up the sides of mountains. He *risked* himself!"

"Huh?" I should have a recorder, Etienne thought dizzily. We don't know any of this. "I don't understand," she said.

"He is a . . . giver." She blushed. "A breeder? Is that your word? Grik said that because so many of you can create life, none of you really matter to each other." She eyed Etienne apprehensively. "But you can go with anyone you wish, do anything you want, even risk yourself—just like any it of our people. True?"

"We matter to each other. Some of us matter a lot." Was love a universal, like fear? Etienne touched Zynth's cheek lightly. "Can't your people go with anyone they wish?"

"The ones who are *it* can." She hunched her shoulders. "The . . . few who are *he* or *she* . . ." She blushed. ". . . We love. But we can love only one of the cooperative expression. It can be no other way. We . . . are the jewels of our people, treasured by all. We are tomorrow."

We. Etienne was beginning to understand. "What you're saying is that very few of you can breed?" Secretive as they were about their culture, the Rethe were more than open about their physical attributes. They seemed to be potentially hermaphroditic for all their feminine form. Which troubled humanity even more than their female appearance, Etienne thought cynically. Etienne's blush had deepened. Obviously, reproduction was not a topic of casual conversation.

"I'm sorry. I don't mean to embarrass you." Etienne ruffled her hair lightly, then took her hand quickly away. That was how she had touched Vilya when she needed to be teased from one of her dark moods. Beyond the flimsy wall, the Eye glared, reminding her that Duran was here and that this was not Vilya. Did *she* know that he was lost? Etienne wondered suddenly. Duran's daughter?

Vilya's daughter, too.

As if that thought had conjured Duran, she felt him. Or someone. The jagged note of human pain and despair pierced her briefly, then faded, dissipating like smoke in a breeze. Etienne turned, automatically groping to pinpoint the source, responding with years of search and rescue practice. But it had been too brief, too weak, for her to be sure of more than a vague direction.

"What is it? Do you sense him?" Zynth's hands came up, fingers stiffly together. "He is alive? Oh please, he is still alive?"

"Yes." Etienne looked up to meet the Eye's stark gaze. "He's alive. And injured. I don't know how badly."

"He must live." Zynth leaned forward to clutch Etienne's hand. "Your biotechnology is quite good, really. We will find him, and your people will heal him. Where is he?"

"Out there." Etienne nodded at the cliff edge. "I couldn't get an accurate position," she said stiffly. Zynth smelled of cinnamon, with a musky undertone that was unfamiliar, but not repulsive. Not like Vilya at all.

"We will climb down, and then you can hear him better." Zynth began to rummage urgently in the pack she had brought through the Gateway. "Here." She handed Etienne a tangle of neon blue webbing. "You know how to put this on, yes?"

A climbing harness. "You've pried into my entire damn life, haven't you?" Etienne clenched her fingers around the supple webbing, wanting to throw it across the chamber. "I don't climb any more," she said between clenched teeth.

"Grik did the research." Zynth put on her thermal suit, and began to don a second harness. She moved clumsily. "You know *how.* I do not. We cannot use a floater because of the wind."

"If you don't know how to climb, then no way you go over that edge." Etienne crossed her arms.

"It will be safe." Zynth reached for the pack. "We will anchor the line to the top of the cliff. And you will be with me. So I am not afraid at all." Her smile filled her face with beauty. Vilya's face had been filled with the same beauty on that long ago morning when she had propped herself on one elbow in Etienne's bed and whispered *I think I love you.* They had both been so young. So sure.

"No." Etienne swallowed, fighting the images. "Open the Gate for me. I'm leaving. I won't be responsible for your death. Life is sacred to me, too, damn it!"

For a moment, Zynth faced her, head thrown back, face burning with defiance and Vilya's beauty. Then her shoulders slumped, and she turned away. "All right, I'll stay," she whispered, and her hands quivered with defeat. "I am afraid to go without you. Will you go down?"

Etienne nodded and crawled out of the habitat, with Zynth on her heels. Bending into the gusty wind, she snapped the clasps on her harness. Her fingers were trembling. I will get you for this night, she promised Grik silently. Somehow, some day, I will pay you back for doing this to me. Lips tight, she took the anchor drill that Zynth handed her.

"Can you hear him?" Zynth peered over her shoulder as Etienne drilled the anchor into the gray stone well back from the cliff edge.

The rock wanted to fracture. Bad stone for an anchor point, but there wasn't anything better. "I'll listen when I can concentrate." Satisfied at last that the anchor would hold, she threaded the tough thin rope through it and tied it off to her harness.

It moved in her hands and she almost dropped it. Bio-fibers, she realized. Another bit of Rethe biotechnology. The rope was woven of thousands of living fibers that could heal minor injuries and responded to direct stimuli such as stress. She tugged once on the rope, then stepped deliberately to the lip of the chasm. For a heartbeat she hesitated, reluctant to trust herself to this alien rope. Then the wind gusted fiercely, and she swayed with it, leaning outward, with her feet planted firmly on the lip of stone. The rope tensed in her fingers. And held her.

Your small-act-of-defiance ritual, Vilya had dubbed this preliminary testing. Couldn't she have found a better climbing partner? Etienne asked the staring orb of the Eye. Why *Duran?* Just because he had provided chromosomes for her daughter? Or had she been trying to wound Etienne—replacing the expert partner with the novice?

It had cost her her life.

There are a hundred labs that can put a kid together for you, she had yelled during their last fight. They could recombine your own gametes. They could use my DNA and . . . fix what's wrong. Her voice hadn't given her away when she had said that. *Wrong,* because that was how Vilya thought of her empathic talent. As a burden—too much for a child to have to bear.

Vilya had refused to get angry. If we create her, she had said implacably, if some technician snips out sections of your code and replaces them, then what is she? Not you—not me—but our *construct.* I don't want that. I want her to be her own person—not our creation.

You're in love with this Duran, aren't you? Etienne's angry words had scalded her throat. Don't give me that artificial insemination song again either. Maybe I'm a failure, a genetic mutation, but that's not really the issue, is it? You just want to fuck him!

Vilya had walked out of their condo and closed the door gently behind her. That had hurt the worst—that she hadn't even slammed the damn door. Etienne had packed and left that afternoon. She didn't know if Vilya had ever come back to the apartment.

Far below, still water filled the fjord-like channel between this cliff and the rounded mountains beyond. Their blue-white images reflected in water that gleamed purple beneath the baleful glare of the Eye. No wind down there? Maybe the Eye was just trying to blow them off the cliff, she thought bitterly.

She turned around in time to see Zynth lift her face to the Eye, hands weaving a graceful pattern in the air.

Acceptance? Reverence? Worship?

A human empath could read only a few universal emotions. Beyond that, you guessed what the Rethe were really feeling. Zynth's head was bowed now, and Etienne caught the gleam of tears on her face, within the shadow of her thermal suit's hood. Her grief she could be sure of. Without another word, Etienne began to rappel cautiously down the cliff. When you trust your rope, your life seeps into it and it becomes part of you. You feel the solid mass of the anchoring stone, feel the quivering strain in the rope as if it is your own tendon and ligament straining, your fingers wrapped around that ring of steel far above. The biofiber rope tensed like muscle in her gloved hands.

The wind snatched at her, trying to smash her against the wall. Teeth clenched, Etienne fought it. The cliff face was sheer, polished to a smoothness that was eerie. It made her wonder if the damned wind blew forever up here. Grit stung her face and she regretted that she hadn't asked for goggles. The only holds were tiny cracks and uneven protrusions. It would be a bad climb back up.

And he was down there. Duran. She had picked the wrong place to go over—he was off to the right. She wondered if he had tried to climb down—if he was that stupid. From above, Zynth's flash beam probed the darkness, a weak finger of light that didn't penetrate much below Etienne's position.

An eye for an eye. The words shivered through her and Etienne paused for a moment, looked up to meet the Eye's stare. She remembered those words most clearly from her childhood brush with religion: An eye for an eye. A life for a life.

Duran's consciousness was like a whisper in the darkness. His lack of skill had cost Vilya her life. It had cost Vilya's infant daughter a mother. Etienne's groping foot came down hard on a ledge and the shock jarred up through the top of her skull. Standing on the bare meter of polished stone, Etienne listened to the wind and the faint murmur of Duran's dying. Maybe Zynth's flash beam would find him. Maybe not. He wouldn't live much longer. Until daylight?

"Zynth?" She raised her voice. "I hear only wind." Only truth beneath the Eye's stare. She met it, cold inside, maybe cold forever—but everything has a price. "I'm coming back up."

"No." The determination in Zynth's voice pierced Etienne with memory.

You can't quit the team, Vilya had said, again and again, when Etienne got tired of the endless meetings, the familiar boring dance of diplomat circling diplomat. We need to understand the Rethe, we need to learn that we are their equals. If we don't, our spirit will die.

Throat tight, she threaded the loose end of the rope through the autobrake, and searched the rock face in front of her for a toehold. The living rope quivered and she looked upward. "Stop!" she cried as the dark shape of Zynth backed out over the cliff edge. "Zynth, go back up!"

"I cannot." Zynth's voice was calm. "This is my punishment—that I should risk my life."

"That anchor won't hold us both!" Etienne's fingers clenched uselessly around her own rope. "Zynth! Stop!"

Zynth's foot slipped on the polished stone face. Etienne sucked in a gasping breath as the Rethe skidded downward, but the rope jerked her to a bouncing stop before she had fallen more than three meters. Either she had managed to use the auto-brake but not properly, or this living rope had the ability to stop a fall. "Climb back up," she croaked. "Before the anchor goes. If you have to come down here, I'll put in another anchor. Do it *now.*"

Too late. A gust of wind slammed along the cliff face, striking Etienne like a giant fist. Staggering, gasping for breath, Etienne skidded across the narrow ledge. The rope was stretching, thinning as it took up the strain. Then stone crumbled beneath her, and she dangled briefly over the void. The rope gave. Etienne threw her weight forward, clawing her way onto the ledge.

The anchor was breaking loose. "Climb up!" she screamed into the howling wind. "Damn it, Zynth, climb *up.*"

Another hammering fist struck them. A vague shape flapped along the edge of the cliff, stooping like an alien bird of prey. The habitat had torn loose from its anchors. For a moment Zynth was obscured by the twisting folds of plastic. Then the rope convulsed in Etienne's hands and went slack. Zynth's scream echoed from the walls as Etienne flung herself against the face of the cliff. Zynth's falling body was directly above her—seeming to drift downward in slow motion. In another moment, she would hit, would smash her downward and outward, and they would both fall into that dark void beneath the Eye's mocking stare.

Because I lied, Etienne thought.

Zynth's wide eyes met hers for a second, sharing fear, sharing death. Then her body twisted convulsively, and she hit the wall, rebounding as she clawed for a hold.

She missed Etienne, hit the widest part of the narrow ledge. Etienne threw herself on top of her, knowing that it was a stupid thing to do, that they would both go over. Her toes dug into the slippery stone as Zynth's momentum torqued them both toward the lip of darkness.

They stopped, poised on the brink, still alive. Etienne inched her way backward, arms around Zynth, pulling her away from that dark drop. "Zynth?" she breathed, her heart pounding in her chest. "Are you hurt?"

Zynth sobbed once deep in her throat, burrowed her face against Etienne's shoulder. "Yes," the whisper was a breath of terror. "It hurts so bad. Inside." Her body tensed convulsively within Etienne's arms. "What if I'm damaged? Etienne? I . . . I can't be damaged."

She was so young—perhaps too young yet to have learned she was mortal. It could come as such a shock to you to realize that you could really die. "It's all right. It's going to be all right." She stroked Zynth's hair, holding her close, smothering her own fear. "I'm going to climb up," she murmured. "I'll get Grik. She'll bring help." Oh God. The Gateway. The Rethe could come and go, but not humans. Not without a Rethe.

"I'm afraid," Zynth whispered. "Don't leave me?"

Don't leave me. The words echoed through the black tunnel of the past, and Etienne raised her face to the Eye, remembering the image of Vilya's pale face on her e-mail screen. Don't leave me, Etienne. I love you. Why can't you understand? When Etienne hadn't answered, she had sent no more mail. "I may not be able to leave you." The words caught in her throat, choking her. "The Gate . . ."

"It's all right." Zynth drew back a little, her face clearing, pain lines smoothing into an expression of peace. "Etienne . . . I need to tell you . . ." She lifted her hand, fingers opening like the petals of a flower. Gently she touched Etienne's face. "I wish . . . you could have been . . . other than what you are." She closed her eyes, her fingers exploring the planes of Etienne's face as if to commit it to memory. "You can go and I won't be afraid." She opened her eyes, her smile making her beautiful. "You will need to take the key. It's just below my collarbone. On the left."

"Key?"

"To the Gate. You will have to take it out." She shuddered. "But it is just beneath the skin, so it should not hurt much."

So, the Rethe's ability to manipulate the Gateways was *not* an inborn psychic ability, as they had claimed! They used tech after all! Even as these thoughts were running through her head, Etienne had clicked on her flesh and was opening the neck of Zynth's suit, feeling beneath her shirt. Her flesh was clammy and her skin had gone pale. Shock? Internal bleeding? Her pain was seeping shrilly into Etienne's head, as she found a tiny sub-dermal lump just below the knob of Zynth's left collarbone. She looked into Zynth's wide eyes, brushed sweaty hair back from her forehead. "I'll be quick," she said softly.

"Thank you." Zynth swallowed. Her eyes followed Etienne's hand as it slid into the pocket of her suit to retrieve her laser blade. As Etienne thumbed it on, Zynth shuddered and closed her eyes.

Etienne placed a restraining hand on her shoulder, but Zynth lay utterly still as the tiny beam of energy sliced neatly through the skin just above the sphere. She caught her breath as Etienne pinched the embedded sphere free of the surrounding tissue, but made no other sound. "Press." Etienne placed Zynth's fingers over the gash. "It's not bleeding much." Fingers red with Zynth's blood, she studied the sphere. It was made of a matte black material, was about the size of a garden pea. Carefully, Etienne slipped it into an inside pocket on her suit, sealed the pocket closed. "I'm going to climb up. It shouldn't take me too long. We'll be back soon." She leaned down to kiss Zynth gently on the forehead. "I promise."

Zynth's eyes opened and she reached up to cup Etienne's face between her palms. "I know you'll come back." She kissed Etienne slowly, sensuously, on the lips. "Be careful."

"I will." Etienne got stiffly to her feet. The damned wind had died, as if the Eye had accomplished what it had wanted to accomplish. Or maybe it thought that they were trapped. You've never watched me climb, Etienne told it silently. When I come back, I will come back for them both. She bowed slowly, formally to the Eye, then turned and searched for the first holds.

You never look down. You look up, to the sides, focus on that next crevice or ledge where you might jam fingers or toes. You don't think about wind or the seconds ticking by as a girl dies.

And a man, too. She caught a whisper of Duran's delirium, pressed her lips together, and eased her weight upward.

You don't look at the top, either. Not after your muscles start to shake and your fingers are numb and you know that you can't do this a whole lot longer. So when she reached up, groping blindly, and her hand slapped down on level ground, she almost lost her grip and fell. With a final spasm of exhausted muscles, she shoved herself upward, lunging over the edge to flop belly-down onto the blessed stone. For awhile she simply lay there, panting and shaking. Then she forced herself to her feet.

It was still dark—didn't dawn ever come here?—and the habitat was gone, of course. Etienne staggered to her feet and stumbled away from the cliff edge. Clutching the tiny key, she headed for the place where the Gate had been. For a moment she thought that it wasn't going to work—there was still nothing to see. Then, in an eyeblink of time, she stepped through into the dusty square near the squatter village. The shacks and pre-fab cottages drowsed in the hot afternoon sun, and Grik sat beneath a tower of branching turquoise silicate that housed a native hive creature.

Asleep, her head leaning back against the stem of the structure, Grik's face was carved into gaunt lines of worry, or exhaustion. She jerked awake as Etienne approached.

"Where is . . . it." She bolted to her feet.

"Hurt." Etienne took a single step toward her, fists clenching. "Are you satisfied? Has she been punished enough, or does she have to die there?"

"You mean . . . injured?" Grik's face had gone pinched and white. "She needed to risk herself, yes . . . but to be *injured* . . ." Outrage filled her voice. "How could you let that happen? Impossible!"

"I was right," Etienne said coldly. "About why you hired me."

"Enough." Grik was already striding toward the gate. "How badly is she injured?"

"I don't know." Etienne had to trot to keep pace with her. "She said it hurt inside."

Grik made a short ugly chopping gesture with both hands. "Remain here."

She took a single long stride into the air and vanished.

How the hell did they know where the damn Gates *were?* Etienne wondered. More buried hardware? She wasn't buying the "higher evolution" explanation any more. She looked toward the cottages. A girl peeped at her from the sparse reed bed that grew along the south side of the square. She ducked out of sight when she saw Etienne looking. Her excited curiosity came to Etienne like the bright smell of rain on summer dust. Etienne smiled at her, closed her fist around the black sphere, and stepped through the Gateway.

A dozen Rethe clustered at the top of the cliff. Light globes mounted on long poles flooded the area with blue-white radiance and four of the Rethe lowered a stretcher. Another Rethe was just clipping herself to an anchor. Fast response time, Etienne thought cynically. They must have been waiting at another Gate for just such an emergency. This whole escapade felt more and more orchestrated. She didn't see Grik, but another anchor and rope suggested that she might be below. Etienne walked over to the small red-haired Rethe who was about to climb over the edge and put a hand on her shoulder. The Rethe recoiled with a sharp clap of her cupped palms, but Etienne ignored her as she unclipped the rope from her harness.

They had researched her well enough to give Zynth a rope without a clip, knowing that Etienne always tied off. With an angry snap, she secured the clip to the harness she still wore. The Rethe was saying something, but Etienne ignored her. Grabbing the ropes, she stepped over the edge. No time for small defiances now. She was going for a big one. The Eye stared down impassively as she bounced fast down the wall, ignoring caution, eyes fixed on the single figure crouched beside Zynth's curled body.

"What are you doing here?" Grik barely looked up as Etienne knelt beside her.

Zynth's eyes were closed. Fine blue veins webbed the pale skin of her eyelids, and for a terrible instant, Etienne thought she wasn't breathing. She touched her throat, felt the reassuring twitch of a pulse before Grik shoved her hand away.

"Don't touch me again," Etienne said carefully. "Or I will throw you off this ledge." Only truth beneath the Eye of God. She smiled thinly as Grik recoiled. "You have used me very thoroughly." She kept her eyes on Grik's face. "What did you do? Review the personal profiles of every empath on the planet? Until you found someone who would be highly motivated to keep your breeder safe? She *is* fertile, isn't she? One of your national treasures?" Her lips drew back from her teeth. "And you needed to punish her properly so as to satisfy your evolved sense of *ethics*." She spat the word. "But you didn't really want to *risk* her, eh? An eye for an eye? You haven't really evolved beyond us, have you? You've just learned how to cheat." She looked down at Zynth. "Well, I took care of her—for her own sake," she said softly.

"I thank you for the risk you assumed." Grik's nostrils flared slightly, but whatever her emotions were, they were too complex for Etienne to read. "That is a difficult climb." She inclined her head at the sheer cliff face behind her.

"Why did you make her do this?" Etienne asked softly.

"Your race is sated with fertility. The creation of new life has little value to you." Her face looked as smooth and hard as marble in the Eye's cold glare. "For us . . . there are very few who can rightfully claim the pronouns you so casually toss around. We have avoided the internal strife that has weakened you as a race, but everything has its price. Continuation of our species is a privilege and an obligation that involves the species—above and beyond the individual. You cannot comprehend." She made a chopping gesture. "The rule that Zynth broke was not a minor infraction. In our society, the failure of the individual is the failure of us all. The punishment— the risk of her loss—was inflicted upon us all." She stood and looked beyond Etienne. Two more Rethe were descending, guiding the stretcher downward. In a moment, it was going to get very crowded on the ledge.

"The creation of new life isn't always a casual thing for us, either." Etienne looked down at Zynth, remembering the trust in her voice. She didn't look so much like Vilya now. "I care about her," she said softly. "For herself, not for her face."

"Do not fantasize, Empath." Grik's tone was icy. "Love is only possible with another . . . appropriate Rethe. That is the way it is."

Etienne smiled at her. "What is the penalty for lying beneath the Eye?"

Grik turned abruptly away to speak to the descending Rethe. Etienne moved back as far as she could along the diminishing ledge. Duran's dying whispered in her mind. It strengthened suddenly, and a murky image formed in her head—a girl with dark hair, pale, with a spare, elegant face. Etienne felt a piercing grief. Duran's vision, Duran's grief. For a rending moment, she thought he was remembering Vilya, but he hadn't known Vilya when she was that young. And then she realized . . .

His daughter. Terane.

His daughter. That was how she had thought of the child. She had been a baby when Vilya had died, and Duran had laid legal claim to her. So Etienne had never seen her. Not because Duran had forbidden it. She herself had forbidden it. *His* daughter. She closed her eyes, but his love and grief beat in her head, filling her brain with the merciless image of the girl who was Vilya's daughter, too.

Grik believed that Zynth could not love anyone who couldn't father a child for her. Etienne looked up into the Eye, met its cold stare. "So did I," she murmured. "Grik!" She raised her voice and the Rethe paused as she was about to begin her climb to the top of the cliff. "Send the stretcher back down," she called.

"Why?"

"For Duran," she said shortly. "You sent me here to find him, didn't you?"

The two Rethe with the stretcher paused and looked down, too, and for a moment there was only the sound of wind across the ledge. "You are correct." Grik sounded reluctant. "I will . . . send the stretcher down."

"How is she doing?" Etienne forced out the question. Brown and green blobs like fat slugs clung to Zynth's forehead, chest, arms, and belly. More Rethe biotech? "Grik?"

"She may live." Grik shrugged and began to climb. After a second, the two other Rethe continued to ease the stretcher up the cliff face.

Go to hell, Etienne thought, but she was too weary to say it aloud. Taking a deep breath, she leaned out over the void. One more small defiance. The living rope quivered in her hands as she turned around, found a toe hold, and began to follow Duran's grief for his daughter, crevice by crevice, across the face of polished stone.

He lay on another ledge, similar to the one Zynth had landed on. It occurred to Etienne, as she pulled some slack into the rope and knelt beside his huddled body, that they were remarkably regular. Perhaps too regular to be natural, but she was too exhausted to worry about it. In the light of her flash, she saw that Duran's hair was beginning to go gray, and his face had thinned a bit in twenty years. He was no youth any more, but he looked pretty much as she remembered him. Blood stained the fabric of his thermal suit, red and fresh in one place. That arm was crooked, and a touch confirmed her diagnosis. Compound fracture, and he had bled a lot. Broken leg, too, and probably more damage that wasn't so obvious. There was no sign of a climbing harness.

His eyelids fluttered as she started to get up. "Wh . . . who?" he mumbled, squinting up at her. "E . . . tienne?" Dried blood crusted his lips, and one side of his face was scraped and bruised from the fall. "*You?*"

She was surprised that he recognized her. She had been older than Duran, when he and Vilya had first been friends. Older, verging on old. Twenty years of search and rescue work had changed her a lot. "It's me, Duran. Help is on the way." Maybe. She looked up at the cliff top, yanked on the rope. A part of her half expected it to come loose and fall around her in writhing living coils. Who would know if the Rethe left both of them to die here?

"Hang on," she said to him. Conscious, his pain beat at her, bad enough to get in past her barriers. She fumbled in her belt pack, took out a couple of pain patches. Two would put him out, or nearly so. She peeled the protective backing from the first patch, smoothed it onto his throat.

She didn't want any more of his grieving images. But he fumbled a hand up to stop her before she could apply the second patch. "Etienne?"

"Yes, it's me. Help is on the way."

"Can you hear it?" His eyes were ringed with white, mundane gray turned to a clear blue by the Eye's glare. "The voice of God, of *their* God. It shaped them, hear it? The wind is its breath. It sings to them, Etienne. This is their soul. Zynth told me, and it's true. This is where they . . . were born."

Their soul? Their God? Etienne remembered Zynth, her hands weaving worship on the lip of the cliff. *The* Eye of God. Not just a casual name dubbed onto an alien landmark then. Their God. Their . . . homeworld. She looked out into the purple darkness and shivered. No wonder Grik had spoken of Zynth's transgression as a sin. And it occurred to her suddenly that perhaps Grik *hadn't* been searching for an empath who would protect a precious breeder.

Perhaps she had been searching for an empath who would kill.

"I wanted . . . to tell you . . . how she died." Duran was losing consciousness as the drugs hit him. "It was my fault. I . . . tried to stop her fall, but she . . . had too much rope. She . . . cut it. So I wouldn't fall, too. I . . . tried to tell you. I'm . . . so sorry, Etienne. I should have stopped her fall. So . . . sorry . . ." His eyes closed and his hand fell away from her wrist.

So Vilya had fallen, not he. And she had relinquished her last chance of life, in order to save Duran. So that her daughter would have a parent?

And if *you* had been there, Etienne? To be a parent? That was what Vilya wanted.

The whisper in her head was in her own voice, but she looked up at the Eye. Slowly, she got to her feet. The accident report was public record. She could have looked it up any time in the last twenty years. If she had wanted to know.

Only truth beneath the Eye of God?

Something scraped loudly behind her and she started. It was the stretcher bumping down the face, followed closely by the two Rethe. "He has a broken arm and leg," she called up to them. "Maybe internal injuries. I'll help you move him."

She wasn't sure how flexible Rethe ethics might be, after all.

But the team was efficient and careful. They helped her strap Duran into the stretcher, and guided him silently up the face of the cliff. The wind eased off again, as if this god was willing to let them depart in peace now. At the top of the cliff, the remaining two Rethe unhooked the stretcher from the ropes, and carried it silently through the Gateway. Grik and Zynth had disappeared. Etienne trudged after them, exhaustion dragging at her. The two Rethe who had climbed with her flanked her. Oh yeah. Operating the Gateway, because she was a mere human. They didn't realize yet that she had a key. Etienne blinked as they emerged from night into bright day. The same girl was still at the edge of the plaza, playing some game with a ball and bits of empty reed shell.

The girl leaped to her feet as the Rethe set the stretcher down in the dust and went running barefoot across the dusty ground, her shift flapping around her thighs. She was heading for the small medical clinic.

Etienne sighed as her Rethe escort made identical wiping motions with their left hands. Good riddance? Farewell? Still silent, they walked back through the Gateway and vanished. Wanting only to drag herself home and climb into bed, Etienne squatted beside the stretcher. She was already sweating in her thermal suit, and she unsealed it. Duran was still alive. She held his wrist, his pulse faltering beneath her fingertips. "I don't like you," she said softly. "I don't think I can change that." Three of the squatters came running toward her, dust rising from their feet. "But I don't blame you anymore," Etienne said. And she looked up automatically, as if the Eye would be there in the off-blue sky.

It wasn't, of course. The squatters—two men and a woman in cut-offs and grimy shirts—arrived. "I'm the med-tech," said the woman. "Pick up an end and give us a hand," she snapped at Etienne. "Then you can tell me what's going on here."

The reeds swayed and rattled, happy in the morning sun. Etienne kneaded bread dough in her small hands-on kitchen, listening to the familiar susurration. The reed-song soothed her as the dough stretched and flattened beneath her palms. But as she shaped a round loaf, the reeds' song changed to a scattered rattle. A visitor? Etienne wiped her hands on a towel, scrubbing briefly and vainly at the drying dough on her fingers.

She hoped it wasn't Duran, come to thank her for saving his life. But it had only been three days since the accident. The med-tech at the squatters' clinic had told her it would be at least a week before Duran could be released. Medical technology was less than cutting-edge out here.

Tossing the towel onto the counter, she crossed the small living room in three strides and flung the door open. She had tried to hide it from herself—how much she wanted it to be Zynth waiting on the porch. The sight of her actually standing there took Etienne's breath away, and made her blush, because she felt about as transparent as a teenager in the throes of true love.

"May I come in?" Zynth sounded as uncertain as Etienne felt. Her hand lifted in the direction of her shoulder, and Etienne followed its movement. Ah yes. Grik was hovering. Of course.

"Please do." Etienne was impressed with the cool graciousness of her tone. What a lie! She backed, held the door open as Zynth walked through, then closed it firmly, before Grik could follow. "Would you care for tea?"

"We began here." Zynth stood in the middle of the floor, her arms at her sides. "It seems like a long time ago, but it was not."

"You're all right," Etienne said softly.

"Yes." Zynth's smile faltered. "If you had not climbed . . ." She shook her head, her hair sliding forward to hide her expression. "I don't think Grik believed that . . . I would climb down. I think it believed that I would be too afraid, that I would humiliate myself in sight of the Eye."

The Eye. Etienne heard all the nuance now. Maybe you could begin to understand another race once you caught a glimpse of their soul. "Your homeworld," she said softly.

"Is it such a sin, for you to know?" Her hands lifted in a fragile, pleading gesture. "We hide so much from you. Why?"

"Because I think we are too much alike," Etienne said softly.

Zynth smiled. "On that ledge, I was not afraid. I knew that you would not let me die."

The words made her shiver, and Etienne clenched her fists at her sides. She averted her head as Zynth stepped close.

"I will remember you forever." Her breath tickled Etienne's throat, warm as summer. "Please realize how much I . . . care."

"You're saying goodbye." Etienne's voice was harsh.

"I do not think that we will meet again." Zynth's voice trembled. "It is . . . a tremendous sorrow."

"Grik won't let it happen, you mean. Grik is afraid of me." Etienne clasped her hands behind her back, resisting the urge to grab Zynth by the shoulders and kiss her, or shake her. "I . . . love you." And she bit her lip because she hadn't meant to say those words out loud. Not ever.

"No," Zynth whispered. She was trembling. "It is *my* choice, not Grik's. *I* am afraid of you. Because I can forget that you are . . . other."

"That's right." Etienne didn't try to soften the bitterness in her voice. "You can only love another breeder. I forgot."

"You do not understand," Zynth said softly. "Grik says you would not, and I think now, that it is right." Her fingers were gentle on Etienne's face.

"I wish you a wonderful life," Etienne said through clenched teeth. "I hope you find a nice fertile *he*."

Zynth's sigh touched her like the last warm wind of fall. "I am a giver, not the one who nurtures the life within." She laughed softly, sadly. "A *he*, as you say."

Anthropomorphism, Etienne thought dizzily. Look at a child with the face of a girl you once loved, and what do you see? Not a man. The irony was so wonderful. She laughed.

"I am sorry." Zynth stepped back, affront in the stiff posture of her body.

"I'm laughing at *me*, not you." Etienne held out her hand, didn't let herself flinch as Zynth took it. "Don't mind me. I'm old and bitter, and I see ghosts. I really do wish you . . . love. And children."

"Thank you." Zynth's smile was beautiful, but still tinged with sadness. He paused with his hand on the door, looked back over his shoulder. "I love you, too," he said. "For all that it is wrong."

Then the door closed behind him and he was gone. Etienne sat down on a floor cushion and listened to the reeds whisper their contentment to the summer heat. Love was another universal. Like pain, and fear. And grief. She rested her forehead on her knees and didn't cry. After a time—when the Rethe had had plenty of time to leave—she got up. Her joints still ached from her climb, and she felt suddenly old—as old as she really was.

Outside, the sun was high. The reeds brushed her thighs as she waded through them, touching her like a lover's fingers. The girl wasn't at the plaza today. Etienne strode across the open space and stepped onto the unmarked patch of ground that should be a Gate.

Her foot landed on gray stone, and the Eye stared dispassionately down. Slowly, Etienne walked over the broken remains of the habitat's anchor, and stopped on the lip of the chasm. Far below, blue-white mountains reflected in still water like purple ink. Duran had heard the soul of a people in the song of this world. Is that what you loved about him, Vilya? Braced against the gusts, Etienne lifted her face to the Eye. Duran's ability to *hear*— like her empathic sense, but different? Safer?

Truth only, beneath the Eye of God. She bent her head and the first tears spotted the cracked stone where her anchor had pulled loose. Tears for Vilya, because she had never cried for her—no—she had never let herself cry. And for herself, because Terane could have been her daughter, as well as Duran's and Vilya's.

And for Zynth who would find someone to love who was as fertile as she . . . he . . . was. Because he had to.

Etienne wondered if Terane had inherited Duran's ability to image a soul in light and music. She turned her back on the cliff and the Eye, trudged slowly back across the gray stone. At the edge of the Gateway, she paused, her fingers curling around the sphere that was the key to this technology. "You want truth?" Etienne looked up at the Eye. "Our awe is wearing thin. It's time for us to look you in the eye." Courtesy of Duran. "We're good at unraveling tech." As she stepped forward, she wondered if her old boss Anton would be surprised to hear from her. Maybe not.

Her foot landed in sun and dust, and her ears filled with the whisper of reeds. She didn't turn toward home. Instead, she began to trudge past the squatters' shacks toward the clinic. She didn't want to know how much Duran might have loved Vilya, but she needed to talk to him. She needed to ask about . . . their daughter. She needed an address. Too late to be a mother, maybe she could be a friend, offer another version of Vilya. Maybe not, but she could try.

The reeds sang contentment, and the dust puffed up from beneath her feet to blow away on the wind.